Blackout

Also by Chris Ryan

The One That Got Away
Stand By, Stand By
Zero Option
The Kremlin Device
Tenth Man Down
The Hit List
The Watchman
Land of Fire
Greed
The Increment

Chris Ryan's SAS Fitness Book
Chris Ryan's Ultimate Survival Guide

In the Alpha Force Series

Survival
Rat-Catcher
Desert Pursuit
Hostage
Red Centre

CHRIS RYAN
Blackout

CENTURY · LONDON

Published by Century in 2005

1 3 5 7 9 10 8 6 4 2

First published in the United Kingdom in 2005 by Century
The Random House Group Limited
20 Vauxhall Bridge Road, London SW1V 2SA

Random House Australia (Pty) Limited
20 Alfred Street, Milsons Point, Sydney,
New South Wales 2061, Australia

Random House New Zealand Limited
18 Poland Road, Glenfield
Auckland 10, New Zealand

Random House South Africa (Pty) Limited
Endulini, 5a Jubilee Road, Parktown 2193, South Africa

The Random House Group Limited Reg. No. 954009

www.randomhouse.co.uk

A CIP catalogue record for this book is available
from the British Library

Papers used by Random House are
natural, recyclable products made from wood grown in
sustainable forests. The manufacturing processes conform to
the environmental regulations of the country of origin

ISBN 1 8441 3438 5

Typeset by Palimpsest Book Production Limited
Polmont, Stirlingshire

Printed and bound in Great Britain by Mackays of Chatham Ltd, Chatham, Kent

ACKNOWLEDGEMENTS

To my agent Barbara Levy, editor Mark Booth, Kate Watkins, Charlotte Bush and all the rest of the team at Century.

PROLOGUE

April 20th. Night.

The air was warm and humid, with the faint smell of the wild irises that dotted the hillside drifting through the night air. Josh Harding paused. He lifted the Russian-built AN-30 rifle to his shoulder, the butt nestling into the thin linen shawl wrapped across his shoulder. His eyes narrowed, the skin of his face creasing as he focused all his concentration into the thin cross-hairs of the gunsight.

The man in those sights was about thirty, with a black, wispy beard and the slow, ponderous movements of someone preparing for bed after a long hard day. The flickering embers of a fire were illuminating the darkness, sending pale shafts of light out across the tiny encampment. Josh could see various people moving in and out of the shadows. Ignore them, he told himself. He narrowed his gaze still further. Stay focused. Wait until the weapon and the target are perfectly aligned. Then squeeze the trigger.

One bullet, thought Josh. That's all it takes to shatter a man's skull.

There were only a tiny handful of people in the world whom you could assassinate with total peace of mind. With no doubts, no regrets. And Khalid Azim − one of the top five al-Qaeda leaders in the world, and the man charged with delivering a terrorist atrocity in Britain − was one of them.

A movement. A woman slipped across the camp, blocking

Josh's line of fire. Josh hesitated. The bullet he had loaded into the AN-30 was made of hardened tungsten, a lethal alloy designed for the battlefield: it was said that it could kill one person, move straight through a body, and still have enough strength to kill the next person it hit. That was in the manufacturer's manual, thought Josh. Every soldier knew that the kit never did what it said on the box. There was a *chance* that the bullet *could* slice straight through the woman, and then take out Azim. But it was risky. A bone or even a thick artery could deflect it from its path, sending it harmlessly into the ground. And once Josh fired, the whole camp would know he was up here in the hills.

If I ever set up an assassination school, Josh told himself, I know what my first lesson will be. *You only get one shot. Make sure it's the right one.*

Azim moved away. The woman was still in front of him, blocking Josh's line of fire. Two other men stepped forward, both heavily armed, shadowing Azim's steps as he went back inside the tent. 'Fuck it,' muttered Josh to himself. 'I've lost him.'

He rested his forearm, letting the gun drop to his side and looked down towards the camp with disappointment. Ashfaq Dasmunshi moved across to where Josh was standing. 'We'll still get him,' he said.

Josh nodded. For three months he had been tracking both Azim and Osama bin Laden through the border region where al-Qaeda still had its most loyal supporters, and where its leaders still returned to retrain and re-equip them-selves while they planned their next atrocity. Since joining the Regiment five years ago, he had been on some tough assignments: first in Bosnia, then in the Afghan invasion, then in Gulf Two. But this was the toughest of the lot. Placed on secondment to The Firm's specialist anti-terrorist unit, he had been sent out here to the Afghanistan-Pakistan borders with a mission that was as simple to define as it was difficult to accomplish: to track down and execute any al-Qaeda leaders he could find, spending whatever money it took, running whatever risks he had to.

'We need help,' said Josh. 'I'll speak to base.'

Ashfaq nodded. The pair of them had been together for three months now. They worked their way through the region on foot and by motorbike, bribing and cajoling local villages into giving them any information that might lead them towards their target.

Josh knew that Ashfaq was a mercenary: he was only doing this for the five hundred dollars a day he was being paid, and he would go back to his village and live like a king on the money he had made in the past few weeks.

Still, a decade of soldiering had taught Josh that mercenaries were as good as any other men on the battlefield. It didn't matter whether a man was fighting for the security of his country or the security of his wallet – as long as he knew how to hold his weapon, and how to play for the team, Josh was never going to question his motives.

'We'll have to be quick,' said Ashfaq. 'They won't be at that camp for more than three hours. Four hours maximum.'

Josh glanced back down at the camp. He had counted a dozen people, at least two of them women. A squadron of about thirty-six men would be enough for an assault, so long as they were properly armed and properly led. He picked up the satellite phone, checked the area to make sure that they were still hidden from view, then punched through the call.

'What do you want, Harding?' said Mark Bruton.

The base camp was at Khost, about eighty miles back along the border. It served as the headquarters for the British and American soldiers who had been in the country since it had been invaded two years ago. Although it was three months now since Josh had been back there, it was the place he reported back to for orders.

'We've found Azim,' said Josh. 'I need back-up to take him out.'

'What's your position?' barked Bruton.

Over the satellite phone, the voice was transmitted as clearly as if the man was sitting right next to him. It doesn't matter where the Rupert is, reflected Josh as the tone of the commanding office grated on his nerves. Smug, self-satisfied, and dead wrong – they all sound the same.

Josh read out the GPS coordinates. They were nestling high in the mountains, just on the Afghan side of the border, among tribesmen and warlords who recognised no law or government other than their own. Borders didn't mean anything out here: every tribe was a government all to itself.

'Stay where you are, Harding,' said Bruton. 'I'll send in a cruise to blow the camp. I'll put a couple of drones into the mix to clear up any stragglers, then send along a Black Hawk to pick you up. Got that?'

Josh gripped the side of the Motorola 9500 sat phone. It was hooked up to an Iridium satellite a couple of miles up in the sky and he could feel the slim black plastic casing of the machine vibrating in his tight grip. 'I've spent three months tracking this man,' snapped Josh. 'I can't wait for a missile strike. All I need are some guys in a chopper and we can go in and get him.'

There was a pause. Even at a distance of three thousand miles, Josh could feel Bruton's annoyance. 'Nobody's going to win a bloody medal on this one, Harding. We're using missiles. Now hold your sodding ground, and wait for the big boys.'

'But . . .'

The single word struggled from Josh's lips, but the rest of the sentence was never born.

'That's a bloody order, Harding. Got it?'

'I'll guide the fireworks home, sir,' he replied stiffly.

He put the phone down, flicking off its power. Ten years

in the Army, five in the Parachute Regiment before he moved up to Hereford, had taught Josh about anger management. A girl he had knocked around with once had even given him a book on it: take deep breaths, find a still spot somewhere inside yourself, accentuate the positive, and some other rubbish he couldn't remember. The girl had chucked him after he'd lost his rag once too often, and he'd never finished the book.

Whoever wrote it had never had to deal with a quarter-brained Rupert like Mark Bruton. He'd get a whole chapter all to himself.

'The tosser,' said Josh contemptuously, looking towards Ashfaq. 'He's sending some cruises in, then a chopper to bring us out.'

'That could take hours,' said Ashfaq.

Josh nodded.

A look of disappointment flashed across Ashfaq's face. Josh knew that the other man was as anxious as he was to get the fighting over and done with. There was a thousand-dollar bonus for every al-Qaeda operative they captured and killed.

'Azim never sleeps in the same place two nights running, and he never sleeps for more than a few hours. He's constantly on the move, that's how he stays alive,' said Ashfaq. He swatted away a mosquito that had landed on his thick, trimmed beard. 'Maybe we'll be lucky, maybe not. We'll see.'

Josh glanced at his watch. It was just after eleven at night. Dawn would start breaking about five tomorrow morning. The chances were that Azim would be gone by three. That gave them less than four hours.

Josh fed the coordinates of the position back to base, then lay down on the pebbled ground. In the past three months, he had grown used to sleeping on the open ground, his body hardened to the roughness of the surface. The dusty perfume of the mountain flowers even made sleeping easy. You woke after an hour or two as alive and fresh as if you'd just come out of the gym.

Josh glanced up at the stars. Missile strikes weren't the answer to this war, he reflected to himself. That was just robot wars, not proper soldiering. You had to be willing to take the same risks the enemy were. *That meant putting your life on the line.*

Josh started to close his eyes. The Motorola phone strapped to his belt was switched to vibrate: a call a few minutes before the missile strike would wake him. Take the sleep when you can get it, he told himself. You never know when the chance will come again.

Waking, he turned over, looking at his watch. It was one-fifteen in the morning. Josh sat bolt upright. He placed the AN-30 to his shoulder, using its telescopic sights to scan the camp. Apart from a single guard patrolling the perimeter, there was no sign of movement.

Where the hell are they? Josh thought.

He scanned the night sky, looking for a vapour trail among the twinkling stars. He'd seen enough cruise missiles to be able to spot them: they flew gently through the sky, like ducks skimming the surface of the water. A low, throaty hum was the only sound they made. They are a familiar enough sight in Afghanistan, he told himself. *Even the kids recognise them.*

He picked up the Motorola and punched out the number. 'What's happening?' he said into the phone.

'Hold your position, Harding,' said Bruton. 'The missiles are being got ready.'

Josh glanced down at the camp. 'It won't wait much longer.'

'Just sit tight, man,' snapped Bruton. 'The fireworks will start soon enough.'

Josh snapped the phone shut. He lay back down on the

ground. Cruise missiles are no way to fight a war, he said to himself. *We'd be better off with swords and sabres.*

Josh checked his watch. Two-fifteen. He felt certain that he could see a man moving in the camp. Were they preparing to leave? he wondered. Or were they just changing the night guard?

He punched the same number into the Motorola. 'Where are they?' he demanded.

'Couple of glitches on the cruises,' said Bruton. 'For two million dollars a pop, you'd think they'd give you a bugger with a proper starter motor on it. We're having to send one in from one of the American subs in the Indian Ocean. Might be a bit of a delay.'

Josh lay back down on the ground and tried to sleep some more. His eyes closed, but sleep wouldn't come. He was burning with anger. Three months I've spent tracking these bastards through this wilderness. Three months of crap food, no washing, and only a sodding cave to sleep in. *And now that I've finally tracked one of the bastards down, they're going to let him slip from my grasp.*

Another hour. It was three twenty-five now. More movement in the camp. The guard was drawing some water from the barrels strapped onto one of the trucks. For washing, thought Josh. That meant they would be leaving soon.

'There isn't much longer left,' he snapped into the phone.

'Relax,' said Bruton. 'The missiles are airborne, and the chopper is on its way. Get ready to evacuate. You're coming home for a shower.'

Josh stood on the hillside. He could see the guard preparing a basin and boiling a kettle, taking them towards the tent. Leaving, he thought. A quick wash and a cup of tea, and they'll be on their way.

He looked up to the sky. If it was coming from one of the American subs, they'd be sending a Raytheon Tomahawk cruise missile. They were subsonic, travelling at around five hundred miles an hour, about the same speed as a commercial passenger aircraft. If it was being fired from a sub in the Indian Ocean it could still be another ten minutes or so before the strike.

Josh started pacing, walking around in smaller and smaller circles. A breeze was starting to blow across the mountain, rustling through the white robes that hung loosely on his body. After three months without anything except a stream to wash in, or a cave to sleep in, he could feel the dirt clinging to his body. Good to get back to base, he told himself. *But I don't want to go back without a notch or two on my belt.*

He fingered the trigger on the AN-30. There was a just a chance he could take them himself. To risk Ashfaq's life would be unfair. The other guy was just a hired hand. Yet one man with a machine gun could do a lot of damage against a camp that was waking up. Take the guard with a single shot from here. Put down some grenades to distract them. Then go in quick, dressed like a local, and hope to get them all before they realise what's hit them.

No, he told himself. You can't bank on that kind of luck. It's suicide. And there's no glory in that.

'Did you hear something?' he whispered towards Ashfaq.

The Afghan nodded. 'A starter motor,' he replied. 'The white truck. It's leaving.'

Josh strained his eyes. He could see a man climbing into the passenger side, another climbing into the driver's seat, firing up the engine. It started to pull away, moving down the mountainside.

The bastard is escaping.

He peered through the AN-30's telescopic sights again. One bullet, he told himself. Blow a tyre out, and hope that sends the car crashing down the mountain. Behind him, he could hear the distant drone of the Tomahawk, like an aeroplane, except quieter, and lower in the sky. He squeezed the trigger.

The bullet smashed into empty scrubland. The truck kept on moving.

In the next instant, a blinding flash lit up the sky. A BGM 109, the Tomahawk could either be equipped with a thousand-pound high-explosive bomb, for destroying big targets or penetrating deep bunkers, or it could be equipped with a thousand pounds of cluster bomblets, which showered a camp with dozens of tiny, lethal explosives. Now Josh saw that this one had a deadly pack of cluster bombs built into its nose. The bombs were spinning out of the missile like confetti. A rain of fire drenched the camp, sucking up everything within it as the fireball gathered force. Josh could hear the pop, pop, pop of the charges exploding down in the valley, the echoes bouncing off the sides of the mountains to build a murderous wave of noise.

Josh turned his gaze back to the white truck. It was disappearing along the single-track road that led away from the valley. It's him, thought Josh grimly. *They can send across as many clouds of fire as they want. It's useless unless the target is standing right beneath them.*

Now Josh could hear the roar from the helicopter blades slicing through the air above him. A smell of avgas filled the air as the machine dropped out of the sky. The Black Hawk hovered a few feet above the ground. A soldier was leaning out, waving him on board.

Josh looked towards the truck. A trail of dust had been kicked up as it turned the corner and vanished from view. *Just as I thought. The bastard has escaped.*

Dawn was starting to break as the helicopter dropped down at the centre of the compound. Josh hopped from its side hatch, walking out across the thin strip of tarmac that led away from the landing circle. Three months, he thought to himself, looking across to the low, prefabricated row of huts that made up the mess room, the barracks, and the debriefing centres. A long time to be out in the wilderness, with only your own wits to live on.

Some beer, some food, a shower and then some sleep. In that order, Josh thought.

'Harding?' said a young soldier, standing by the side of the road.

Josh nodded. The man was maybe nineteen or twenty, a signaller on his first proper tour of duty by the looks of him. I'm only thirty myself, reflected Josh. But already the raw recruits are starting to seem like boys to me.

'That's me,' he replied.

He could see the signaller running his gaze over him. Dressed in a long white robe, with sandals on his feet, a black beard, and with his rifle slung across his back, Josh knew that he was starting to look more like an Afghan tribesman than a British soldier. His face was tanned to a dark shade of brown, and the sweat and dirt had seeped into his skin, giving it the appearance of raw leather.

'Bruton will see you in an hour,' said the soldier. 'Room C.' He paused. 'You might want to have a bit of a wash before you go in.'

'Too much of a pong for you?' said Josh.

'*Diabolical.*'

Josh grinned. 'There's worse smells than me in the field. You'll find that out soon enough.'

He smiled as he walked towards the mess. Khost had been an Allied base since soon after the invasion of Afghanistan. Of all the bases established by the Allied forces, this was the roughest: up closer to Kabul, the invaders had been welcomed, or at least tolerated, but down here the American and British soldiers were hated with an intensity that only religion could inspire. They weren't just the invader. They were the infidel.

Step outside, and the chances were that you'd find one of the local kids lobbing a petrol bomb at you. It was, Josh told himself, like Ulster. *But with snakes and curry.*

'Hey, it's Osama,' shouted a man from across the room.

Josh smiled again. He recognised Peter Boshell at once. Same age, and one of five Regiment men stationed at Khost. But he could well be the only other British soldier on the base right now, because Khost was mainly an American set-up and the Regiment guys were spending most of the time out on patrol. That was the way it had to be. You weren't going to catch any terrorists sitting around the base playing computer games – whatever the Americans thought.

'Nab him, boys,' continued Boshell. 'We let the fucker get away at Tora Bora. Don't want to do that again.'

Josh walked across to the bar. Boshell was sitting with a group of tough-looking American marines, their heads shaved and the tattoos bright on the huge muscles of their biceps. 'What's happening?' asked Josh.

'World War Three, by the looks of it,' said Boshell.

Josh grabbed himself a Coke and a packet of crisps and sat down. The television was tuned to Fox News, and the dozen soldiers sitting around the mess were gripped by what they were watching.

Josh turned his gaze towards the screen. 'The most dramatic day in the War on Terror since 9–11,' said the newsreader.

Josh took a swig of the Coke, and threw some of the crisps into his mouth: it was three months now since he'd had anything apart from the local curries.

'In a day of mayhem that has already been dubbed the Three Cities Attack, power supplies were today switched off in three of the world's major cities: London, Paris and New York,' continued the newsreader.

Christ, thought Josh. *What's happened now?*

Up on the screen, Josh could see a familiar backdrop: Trafalgar Square at twilight, the road turned into a mess of snarling traffic, and the square thronging with more people than on New Year's Eve. 'The day's events started in Paris, at noon local time precisely. Power systems throughout the city shut down, leaving millions of people stranded in subways and on roads, and shutting schools and offices. One hour later, at noon local time, the power went out in London, closing the city completely. The police reported widespread incidents of panic, looting and total confusion as the transport networks ground to a halt. Troops were deployed around Whitehall and Parliament Square as speculation grew of a major terrorist incident. London Mayor Ken Livingstone and Prime Minister Tony Blair appealed for calm, but to little avail. Then, in the most dramatic development of the day, precisely five hours later, again at noon local time, the power shut down in New York. Mayor Bloomberg was appealing for calm as panic-stricken New Yorkers feared another devastating strike on their city. Police had to try to restore order at several skyscrapers as workers emptied buildings that could become targets.'

Josh looked at the faces of the other men in the mess. They were watching the screen intently, talking among themselves. Their tone was hushed, whispering to one another, as if they were both exhilarated and appalled by the events being played out in front of them. Just as I am, Josh thought.

'Already people are speculating that the Three Cities Attack must be the work of al-Qaeda terrorists,' continued the newsreader. 'If so, it would be the most audacious coup by the organisation since 9–11.' Josh watched as the screen switched to a reporter standing outside the Pentagon, his hair disturbed in the strong gusts of wind blowing past the building. 'Military sources are denying that this is necessarily a co-ordinated terrorist attack,' said the reporter. 'They are insisting that it is possible for the power to fail accidentally in all three cities at precisely the same time. But so far, no information is available on what caused the power failures, or how it can be prevented from happening again.' The reporter paused to deliver the emphasis on the final sentence. 'Outside the government, some experts are saying this is likely to be the work of al-Qaeda.'

'So is it a terrorist attack, or isn't it?' said the newsreader, looking towards the reporter.

'Right now, we just don't have enough information to say,' answered the reporter. 'The world may now have to get used to the terrifying possibility that somebody, some-where, can get control of the world's power systems. And can turn off the electricity at will.'

Josh put down his Coke. Now there was silence in the room. An ad break had interrupted the news, and nobody was saying anything. 'Think it's al-Qaeda?' said Josh finally, looking towards Boshell.

Boshell shrugged. 'Who else?'

'Has to be,' said one of the Americans. 'Nobody else could pull a stunt like that.'

'The Pentagon is saying that it doesn't think so,' said Josh.

The soldier smiled, revealing a huge set of white teeth. 'Hell, I've been on missions myself that those sons of bitches were denying before we got back to base.'

'Al-Qaeda taking control of power systems for cities around the world?' said Boshell. 'Of course they're not going to own up to something like that. There'd be panic.'

'Looks like we've got work to do, then,' said Josh.

He could see himself being summoned across the room by the young signaller. Josh finished his Coke and started walking towards the corridor. The walk was a short one, but he suddenly felt the energy drain out of him. It was months since he'd slept in a proper bed, or eaten a decent meal. Soldiering was like that sometimes. Your nerves held up fine while the battle was still on. But once it was all over, the exhaustion hit you: the adrenalin drained away, and every wound, knock and bruise suddenly started screaming out in pain.

'Back to your cave, Osama,' shouted Boshell.

Josh looked back and grinned. During the last three months he had missed the camaraderie of the Regiment.

'I'll get you a razor,' said Bruton as soon as Josh stepped into the room. 'You look like crap.'

'The whole country looks like crap, sir,' said Josh. 'I blend in.'

Bruton was a tall man, with dark hair cropped close to his skull, a thick, round nose, and ears that stuck out from the side of his head like the handles on a jug. In the six months that he'd been under his command, Josh had not warmed to him: there were plenty of Ruperts who made stupid decisions, but few of them could do it as consistently as Bruton.

'Well, good to see you again,' continued Bruton. 'And congratulations.'

Josh looked around the room. There was a detailed map of the Afghanistan-Pakistan border on the wall, and next to it a series of thirty pictures: the most wanted al-Qaeda terrorists believed to be operating in the area. Azim, the man The Firm reckoned was charged with delivering a major attack on Britain, was among them.

There was a water cooler in the corner. Josh helped himself to a plastic beaker, then sat down on the single chair facing the desk. Bruton sat opposite him, a pad of paper spread out in front of him. He was swivelling a biro between his fingers, tapping its end against his mouth.

'We'll do a full debrief in the morning,' he said. 'But the good news is that the strike was a success. Azim is dead. The boys in Vauxhall are going to be pleased with that one.'

Josh looked at him, scrutinising his face. He could see no trace of hesitation or doubt there. 'Azim's not dead.' He paused, his eyes flicking upwards. 'Sir.'

Bruton leant forward. 'The Tomahawk went into the precise location you gave us,' he said firmly. 'A drone flew overhead and took some pictures. Everything in that camp was burned to a cinder.'

'There was a truck,' said Josh. 'A white one. It left the camp a few minutes before the missile came in. Azim was in it. He escaped.'

Bruton shook his head. 'The mission was a success, Harding. That's what it's going to say in the files.'

Josh took a deep breath. Anger management, he told himself. 'It took too long,' he said, his voice steely. 'If we'd got the missile in sooner, we'd have got him. But I'm telling you, he escaped.'

'Listen to me, Harding,' said Bruton. He stood up and walked across the room, standing in front of Azim's picture and tearing it from the wall. 'When I say a man's dead, he's dead. And he stays dead. Got it?'

Josh stood up. 'Then we'll just have to wait until the bugger comes back with a different name. And then kill him again.'

ONE

Monday, June 1st. Morning.
The smell drifted past Josh's nostrils. His senses twitched, coming slowly back to life as he struggled to regain consciousness. A faint musty smell mixing lavender with some kind of spice. I know it, thought Josh. I know that perfume. It's on the tip of my tongue.

If only I could remember the name.

For a moment, Josh struggled, annoyed with himself for not being able to dredge up the name from his memory. Sod it, he told himself finally. I never was any good at remembering perfumes.

Slowly, Josh tried to open his eyes. But the skin on his lids felt heavy and unyielding. He was starting to become aware of a pain, throbbing slowly yet still intense, starting at the side of his neck and running down deep into his spine. Another pain was rippling up from his calf. Then his left eye sprang open first, a flash of light flooding his senses as a fierce sun shone into his face. He closed the eye quickly, succumbed to another wave of pain, then opened it again.

A woman. A bright lock of red hair.

Josh closed the eye.

Where the hell am I? *What the fuck has happened to me?*

He tried the right eye this time. The same heavy sensation as the lids were reluctantly prised open, and the same blinding effect as sunlight overwhelmed the retina. He shut it hard, let a fresh wave of pain roll down from his neck into his back, then opened both eyes.

The woman was leaning over him.

She was in her late twenties, maybe just thirty, but no older. Her skin was tanned and freckly, and still moist and clear. Her eyes were bright blue, shaped like almonds, set above her nose and full red lips. But it was the hair that held Josh's attention. A thick red wave of curls, it tumbled playfully across him, growing away from the woman's face like a lion's mane.

He started to speak. The words started somewhere in his brain, then travelled down towards his throat. 'I . . . I . . .' he started.

Suddenly Josh was aware of another terrible pain shooting through his neck. He stopped, choking on the rest of the sentence, unable to deliver it.

A finger came to rest on his lips, thin and elegant, and without any ring on it. 'Don't speak,' she said. 'You're hurt.'

'I . . . I . . .' Josh started again.

'You're hurt,' she repeated, her tone firmer this time. 'I'll put you in the truck.'

It was too painful for Josh to speak. The jabbing in his neck was growing worse, and his leg was feeling numb: it was a pain that he knew he had felt before, although he couldn't now remember where. He started to turn on his shoulders. He was lying in a ditch of baked, cracked earth. Ahead of him he could see a thin strip of tarmac: a one-lane road, nothing more. Behind it, a giant rock loomed, its pitted surface made of red and yellow stone, and beneath the rock flaked and chipped slices of the mountain lay in a jumbled heap. The air was dry and dusty, without even the murmur of a breeze to soften the fierce heat of the sun beating down on them.

Josh looked out across the bleak landscape. Somewhere in the distance, he could see some dust rising up from a ridge. The place was completely empty.

Where am I? he wondered.

He swivelled quickly, staring at the ditch into which he had fallen. A crimson stain had spread out into the sand.

Blood. My blood, Josh thought.

He started to run a hand across his body, making a rough reckoning of the extent of his wounds. He had been shot in the neck, he guessed: there was a gaping flesh wound, and the bullet must have missed his windpipe only narrowly. He was lucky to be alive. The calf of his left leg had taken a hit as well. A chuck of flesh the size of his index finger had been blown away: he could still see pulpy, messy fragments of the torn tissue lying in the dirt. At least a pint of blood, maybe two, had been spilled already.

What in the name of Christ happened to me here?

'Quick,' said the woman. 'You need treatment.'

Her hand was wrapping itself around Josh's wrist, taking his pulse. He could just see her lips moving as she silently counted out the beating of his heart. 'We need to get some drugs into you,' she said. 'Right away.'

Josh let her arms slip around his waist. She didn't have the strength to lift a man of his size but she could help him balance himself as he used the strength left in his legs to push himself upwards. He felt dizzy, and his vision was clouding up as he started to move his feet. The left leg, where the bullet had struck, was screaming with pain: every nerve seemed to have been set on fire, sending burning jabs of pain up through his body. His breathing was ragged and the loss of blood had sapped his energy, making it hard for him to hold onto consciousness for more than a few minutes straight. He was already suffering from palpitations and his lips were sweaty, enough to suggest that he'd maybe lost more than a couple of pints.

'Hold me,' he muttered, some blood spitting from his mouth as he pronounced the words.

The woman was strong, he could tell that. She was five-nine, maybe five-ten. She couldn't have weighed more than a hundred and ten pounds: she was thin, not in an anorexic fashion-model way, but thin as in wiry, muscly, and tough. She was dressed in blue denim shorts, with a pale pink T-shirt: a deeper pink heart was stencilled on the cotton, just below the delicate curve of her small breasts. A country girl, thought Josh suddenly. Good with horses and dogs, and she probably knows how to handle herself in a fight pretty well.

That perfume, thought Josh, as he leaned into her, using the strength of her shoulders to help keep his balance. What's its name again? *I just can't remember.*

He stepped forward. His left leg was in the worst pain, so he was using his right one to carry his weight. About ten yards ahead of him he could see the pick-up truck: a black Ford Ranger, at least five years old, with a thick layer of mud and dust coating its wheels and some thick scratches to its bodywork. Not far to walk, he told himself. Even on a shot-up leg, I should be able to manage ten yards.

'Careful,' said the woman, steering him to the left.

Josh looked down. He was fighting to straighten out his vision, taking deep gulps of air to try to calm the spinning in his head that was clouding up his eyes. Suddenly he was able to focus. At his feet there lay a body.

A corpse.

Josh stopped. He had moved sideways to avoid stepping on it. It was a boy, no more than fifteen. He had thick black hair, down to the back of his neck, and he was wearing black jeans and a huge pair of Nike trainers. Josh couldn't see his face: he was lying face down in the dirt. But he could see the wounds. One bullet had torn into the centre of his neck, taking out his throat. Another had ripped into the centre of his skull, entering from the back and blowing his brains out through his forehead. A pool of blood was still seeping from both the wounds.

'Wh—' Josh started to say.

'No, quiet,' hissed the woman, her tone turning sterner now. 'You want to end up like him?'

Josh hobbled forwards. No time to think, he told himself. Don't worry now about who you are, what you are doing here, or why there is a corpse lying in front of you. In a fight you don't look for explanations. You just try to survive.

Another three yards. The pain in his left leg was terrible, and he could feel the pressure of hobbling forward crunching the nerve endings, the tendons and the muscles. Every step, he knew, was only making the injury worse. He had to find somewhere where he could lie up for a few days, assess the extent of his injuries, and start to recover his strength.

Not here. *Not surrounded by corpses.*

The door of the pick-up was open. Josh threw himself inside, using his forearms to lever himself up onto the battered cloth seats. There the glass had magnified the fierce sunlight, and if it was thirty degrees outside, here in the scrublands, it must have been closer to forty inside the truck. Sweat started to pour from Josh's skin, mixing with the blood already caked to the surface of his body. His breath stabbed against his chest as the hot, humid air filled his lungs.

The woman handed him a bottle of water. 'Try to drink something.'

Josh took the plastic container in his hand. It could have been thirty degrees as well. I could use it to brew up a nice cup of tea, he reflected sourly. Wrenching the top free with his teeth, he slung the neck of the bottle into his mouth, pouring the water down his throat, then letting it splash across his face. One tooth was missing, he figured: maybe he'd lost it when the bullets had slammed him onto the ground. There was a dull throbbing pain at the base of his jaw, spreading out from the gums, and the water was making it worse, a sure sign of a broken tooth. Sod it, he told himself. I have to drink. *And right now a trip to the dentist is the least of my worries.*

The Ranger roared into life as the woman slotted the key into its ignition. The Ford had a big, powerful engine, and even though it had overheated in the midday sun it still kicked to life with a snarl. The smell of petrol started to flood through the air, making Josh's stomach churn. He lifted his foot into position, relieved to finally be taking the pressure off it, and looked closely at the woman as she gripped the steering wheel and turned the truck onto the road.

She's afraid, he noted. A trickle of sweat was running down her back, staining the fabric of her T-shirt.

Josh closed his eyes. His brain was still fuzzy, and the blurring in front of his eyes was still severe. Unconsciousness, he knew, was just a breath away. He could feel the truck vibrating as it kicked past the stones on the single-track road and started to pick up speed.

Just try and stay alive until you get there, he told himself. *Wherever 'there' might be.*

Then there was a new sound. It was vicious and sharp, the noise of metal digging into metal. Josh opened his eyes with a start, instantly recognising what he had just heard. A bullet. The truck had been hit by a bullet.

He looked across at the woman. She was gripping the wheel, swerving the truck as the shot winged its side. Her grip was tight and her expression grim. The truck was swaying violently. Another bullet. Amid the deafening noise Josh couldn't be certain where it had come from. Maybe one of the high rocks? A sniper. Maybe another vehicle, already in hot pursuit. He looked across at the woman. 'Evade,' he snapped. 'You have to evade.'

His throat had strained to produce the words, the muscles in his neck screaming with pain as he flexed them.

'Keep still,' she screamed. 'Otherwise you'll die.'

Sod it, thought Josh. I'll die anyway, the way you're driving.

He turned round. He could feel some blood starting to seep down his neck as the scab that had formed across the open wound cracked. A bike was on their trail. A Honda, he judged. Big and powerful, with chrome handlebars that glistened in the sun. He could see nothing of its rider. The man was wrapped in black leather, with shades pulled down over his eyes and a helmet covering the top half of his face. His left hand was gripping the handlebars, and in his right there was a pistol. Josh couldn't tell the make from where he sprawled in the truck. But it was a heavy piece of kit, he could tell that much. The biker was straining to hold the gun steady.

Josh looked straight back. For a moment, he had the sensation that he was looking straight down the barrel of the gun.

Another shot. The biker jerked back slightly as the recoil from the pistol forced him to lose his balance. The bullet winged the side of the truck, opening up a gash in the metal along the driver's side. The vehicle swayed again under the impact, then gripped the road once more.

'You got a gun?' hissed Josh.

The woman shook her head.

'Then I'm driving,' snapped Josh.

She shook her head again, more fiercely this time.

'I said I'm driving.'

The woman turned to face him, her eyes bright with anger. 'No,' she said, her tone harsh. A bead of sweat was rolling down from her forehead onto her face. 'You don't even have the strength to stand up. Don't even think about driving.'

'When I need the strength, I'll find it,' answered Josh.

The truck swerved. Another bullet had hit it, this time smashing into its back. Its frame vibrated under the force of the impact. Josh moved swiftly across the front seat, pushing the woman with his open palm and taking hold of the wheel. He left some traces of blood smeared across the front of her T-shirt.

'Okay,' she said angrily. 'You drive if you have to.'

They'd have to switch places while they were driving: a tricky move at the best of times, but even harder when you were under fire. 'Just take your foot off the accelerator,' said Josh.

The woman shifted sideways, her foot easing off the pedal. She kept one hand on the wheel. Josh now grabbed it with his left hand. The truck was starting to wobble and swerve. He pushed himself up and over the woman's lap, blood dripping down onto her jeans. The truck started to drift seriously off to the left. Josh gripped the wheel harder as he slipped into the driver's seat. His foot jammed down onto the accelerator, taking the speed back up again.

'I need your help,' he muttered.

She looked across at him.

'I'm losing too much damned blood,' he snapped. 'I have to stop it.'

With his left hand still on the wheel, Josh ripped a strip of cloth from his shirt, handing it across to the woman Leaning down, she gripped it between her hands. Her fingers dug into Josh's thigh. She was searching for the femoral artery he knew. Dig into that hard enough, and it would staunch the bleeding. Next, she took the cloth, and wrapped it tight around his thigh. Josh could feel the bleeding starting to slow immediately. But the amount of blood loss was still worrying him. More than four pints and he'd pass out.

The truck swerved violently as Josh struggled to keep control of the wheel as another bullet flew past them. Get a grip, man, Josh told himself. *Or else we'll both be dead in the next few minutes.*

The road stretched out in front of him. Dazzling sunlight was searing through the high windscreen of the Ranger. Josh flipped the sunshield down, protecting his eyes. He was struggling to focus. From a glance in the mirror, he could see the bike tracking him ten yards to his rear, the rider steadying himself on the machine again, his hand raised high in the air as he tried to line up the next shot.

One of those is going to hit its target, Josh realised. *That's just the law of averages.*

He started to swing the truck from side to side, jerking the wheel to produce an unpredictable, irregular motion. That was the first rule of any kind of evasive action: make yourself a hard target.

I might be a hard target, but I'm still a big one. This truck weighs a ton and half. Hard to miss.

Now the swaying of the truck was starting to make Josh feel sick. Blood loss had already weakened him and, with the violence of the vehicle's motion, he could feel his concentration draining away and his vision starting to blur again. Keep your grip, man, he told himself. *You can do this.*

The bike was holding a steady distance, ten yards to his rear. Another shot. This time the bullet smashed through the window at the back of the Ranger, shattering the glass into a thousand pieces, sending it cascading forward across Josh and the woman like hard confetti. Tiny splinters of glass flicked across Josh's back, peppering the skin of his neck and getting into his hair. He could also feel a pair of wounds opening up, fresh blood streaming from the scabs.

Makes no difference, thought Josh with grim resolve. *I couldn't be in much worse shape than I am already.*

He heard the woman screaming: a long agonised howl of fear. Had the glass shattering broken her nerve? Josh reached across to her with his right hand, while his left held the steering wheel. There was one cut at the top of her neck, and a splinter of glass seemed to have lodged itself underneath the skin. That would be painful to get out. But otherwise she was okay. 'We're all right,' hissed Josh, gasping for air.

The bullet had travelled though the cab of the truck and drilled through the windscreen, one foot to the left of the driver's seat. A fissure had opened up down the centre of the glass, but although it had cracked it hadn't yet broken. Close, realised Josh. The rear window had deflected its path, steering the bullet slightly to the left. Without that deflection, the bullet would have landed a foot to the right. In the centre of my skull, Josh mused.

He glanced in the mirror. The biker was still there, the pistol still raised in his right hand. You're not a bad shot, pal, Josh thought grudgingly.

The rider's tactics weren't hard to figure out. The bike had plenty of power, more than enough to accelerate past the Ranger if he wanted to. He was just holding his position a steady ten yards behind, firing shot after shot after shot. Sooner or later, he was going to land one right into Josh's brain. *And the way he was shooting, it was going to be sooner rather than later.*

Josh jammed his foot hard on the accelerator. The Ranger might have a few years and many more miles on the clock, but there was still plenty of power in its 3.2 litre engine. Now that engine roared and revved, and Josh could feel the truck surging forward. He was up to a hundred miles an hour, skidding across the hot surface of the tarmac. Another glance in the mirror. The bike was still there, a steady ten yards behind him, the pistol already lined up for the next shot.

I haven't the strength for a long chase, realised Josh. If I was fit and healthy, I might be able to out-drive and outwit this opponent. Not in my current state. I stand and fight. *That's my only chance.*

Josh tapped the brake. The truck started to slow. He

bunched all his strength into his shoulders, took a second to compose himself, then threw himself into action. I'm getting one chance at this, he told himself. *Screw it up, and it's an early supper for the vultures.*

With his right hand, Josh wrenched hard at the steering wheel, spinning it around. With his left hand, he pulled savagely on the handbrake as his foot jabbed viciously against the footbrake. The combined impact of the sudden deceleration and the violent turning of the wheel yanked the vehicle into a classic bootlegger's turn. The heat of the day had already made the truck's tyres soft and slippery, loosening their grip on the road. The Ranger skidded, hurtling off the track and out onto the scrubland. A huge cloud of dust kicked up, briefly blocking Josh's vision. Beneath him, he could hear the engine roar and the suspension creak under the pressure put upon it by the sudden manoeuvre.

'Hold steady,' Josh rasped to the woman at his side.

She looked back at him, clutching the side of the door as the suddenness of the movement threw her sideways. 'I'm trying.'

Josh swivelled his gaze right, looking up the road. It had worked. The speed of the turn had caught the biker by surprise. In the seconds that it had taken him to assess what was happening and react, he had sped past and was now fifty yards up the road. Already Josh could see that he was slowing, preparing to turn around. Just as I thought you would, Josh exulted inwardly.

My plan owes nothing to brains or cunning, he told himself. *Just guts and adrenalin.*

The trick was to get behind your assailant. In any battle between a pick-up truck and a motorbike, the bike was always going to win on speed and agility. But the truck, like a tank, could win on size and strength. From the right position it could attack.

And that position was from behind.

Josh started driving into the scrub. The wheels of the Ranger kicked up sand in every direction, but its grip was steady. Summoning his strength into his shoulders again, he spun the wheel hard to the left, and yanked again on the handbrake. The truck stopped, its metal frame shuddering, then started to turn. The wheels struggled to get a grip on the sandy surface of the ground and for a moment Josh could sense the vehicle skidding. He was losing control – he could feel the truck starting to slide backwards. Then the tyres found some pebbles they could grip onto. Slowly, the Ranger started to move around, facing directly back at the road.

Turn, Josh told himself. Then drive straight into the bastard. He'll get one shot, straight at me, through the windscreen. And if he doesn't kill me with that shot, then I'll crush him like an insect.

Josh tapped his foot on the accelerator, waiting for the surge of power to carry him forward.

The engine stalled.

Christ, thought Josh. *Prayer time.*

'Duck,' he hissed to the woman. 'Get your bloody head down and keep it down.'

Up ahead he could see the biker turning, could hear the wheels of the Honda screeching. Josh pushed his head down low, taking himself below the level of the windscreen. The truck was still moving forwards, carried by its momentum even after the engine had died, but it was slowing fast. Josh's leg was squeezed up against the pedals, sending terrible pains jabbing upwards through his spine.

Count to five, he told himself. The engine might just be flooded. Give it a moment to cool down, then try it again. *One, two . . .*

A bullet smashed into the windscreen, this time shattering the glass. The shards tumbled downwards, falling on them like solid, sharp-edged rain. The woman gasped, her hand shooting upward to try and protect her head and her face. 'No, no,' she screamed.

Three, four . . .

Josh jabbed the Ranger's key back into the ignition, twisting it viciously. For a brief moment, his action was greeted only by silence. Sod it, Josh muttered to himself. Then the engine spluttered. Josh jammed his foot on the accelerator, twisting his body to reach it while still taking cover beneath the dashboard and now the engine revved into action, roaring into life, a sudden surge of power shaking the truck's frame. Josh levered himself upwards as the Ranger leaped forwards, skidding across the rough surface of the scrubland. The left tyre collided with a rock, jerking the truck upwards. The force of the impact briefly jolted Josh sideways, making him loosen his grip on the wheel. The truck swerved violently to the right, bouncing a foot into the air.

The pain searing though his body was making it tough for Josh to hold himself at the wheel. He was sweating and shaking from loss of blood. Concentrate, he told himself. Concentrate or die.

He could see the biker sixty yards ahead. The man had completed his turn with military precision and was now riding the bike hard out into the open scrubland. Josh could see nothing of his expression through the shades and helmet that masked the whole of his face, but he could tell from the way he was opening up the throttle and firing up the gas that there was not a flicker of fear or doubt running through the man. He was riding with total confidence, his gun held high in his right fist, certain that his opponent could be eliminated before he could retaliate.

That's your mistake, pal. *Always be a little bit afraid.*

Josh levered himself higher up into the driving seat, pressing hard on the accelerator, then slamming the steering wheel hard right. The bike lay directly in his path – sixty yards of open sand was all that separated the two vehicles.

Still not a flicker of fear from the biker. Nor any sign of him changing direction. You're a brave man, pal, Josh repeated to himself. *Brave, but stupid.*

'You're going to hit him,' said the woman at his side, the words delivered as if she was trying to warn Josh of some terrible, impending catastrophe.

'You bloody bet I am.'

'You're fucking crazy,' she screamed.

'You got a better idea, you've got three seconds to tell me.'

Josh looked back into the open scrubland. The biker had raised his gun again. He was steadying himself, struggling to hold the bike level so that he could aim the pistol accurately. One factor is on my side, reckoned Josh. It's always hard to fire a gun from a moving vehicle and even harder when that vehicle is racing across rough terrain.

He ducked instinctively as the gun was fired: above the noise of the Ranger's engine, it was impossible to hear the gunshot. But he could tell from the way the man's hand jerked backwards that the bullet had already left the chamber giving him time to duck.

Prayer time.

The shot struck the metal frame of the truck. Where it had hit, Josh couldn't tell.

Not me, that's all that counts.

Using all the remaining strength in his leg, Josh pressed even harder on the accelerator, urging every last ounce of power out of the machine. The Ranger sped forward, spitting huge clouds of dust up from its heavy wheels. Thirty yards left. The biker could see that his shot had missed. Decision time, mate, thought Josh. See if you've got time for another shot. Or just turn and try to run.

For just a fraction of a second, he could see the biker struggling with the decision. *Half a second is too long.*

The biker started to turn, swinging the handlebars to the

left. There was a downward slope on that side of him, enough to give him some extra speed.

Twenty yards, and closing.

The biker was turning, his engine spluttering and his boots dragging on the ground. Josh adjusted his steering and powered forwards.

Ten yards.

The biker reared back, putting pressure on his machine's back wheel to try to complete the turn.

Five yards.

'Hold on!' Josh shouted at the woman.

Three yards.

He had lost sight of the biker as the man and the machine disappeared from view. Suddenly he could feel the force of the blow. It started with the front wheels. The Ranger was thrust up several feet into the air, Josh's head banging against the roof of the vehicle as the collision threw him up from the driver's seat. The engine stalled, and Josh slammed his feet hard on the brakes. The impact of the front wheels would kill any normal man. *After the back wheels had chewed him up, even the rattlesnakes would think twice about having him for their lunch.*

The truck landed hard on the ground. Josh could feel it swerve sideways as the rear wheels kicked in hard against the fallen bike. He gripped the steering wheel to try to bring the machine back under control. Slowly, the Ranger juddered to a halt. The sand kicked up by its wheels was still falling through the air, making the atmosphere thick and dusty: Josh's lungs were already filling up with the tiny particles that were choking off his breath and clogging up his vision.

Suddenly he could feel the energy draining out of him. In the midst of the battle, the adrenalin had kept his pain under control. Now it was flooding back through him. His leg was numb with agony, and blood was still seeping from the open wound in his neck. He looked behind him. Ten yards to the right, the bike was lying broken and mangled on the ground. The handlebars had been crushed into the front wheel, leaving a messy spaghetti of tubes, tyres, piping and wires. The petrol tank had broken open, but had not burst into flame: instead, the liquid had spilled out over the wreckage, covering it with a thin oily film. Josh looked harder, peering out beyond the bike.

He saw the leg first. The separation must have been relatively clean, he decided. If the boot had caught on the underside of the Ranger while the torso had stayed with the mangled bike, then the leg could have been pulled clean from its socket, the muscles, veins and tendons snapping like a pod being popped open to expose its peas. Six yards further on, the rest of the body lay face down in the dirt. Blood was still pulsing from the socket where the leg had been attached.

No man could have survived that kind of pain. *It would have been unendurable.*

The biker was dead.

Turning the key in the ignition, Josh fired the truck back into life. Wearily he started to reverse, using the rear-view mirror to help him to steer the Ranger back over the broken torso of his opponent. 'Broken into a thousand pieces, pal,' muttered Josh as the debris kicked up by the Ranger's wheels spread a sprinkling of dirt over the bleeding body of the biker.

Josh pulled the truck back up towards the road, then slumped back, leaving the engine still idling. The pain was starting to win now. Josh could feel himself starting to lose concentration. Nothing else mattered except trying to fight back the terrible agony assailing every inch of his body. He could feel himself starting to become afraid.

'I'll drive,' said the woman, leaning across him and starting to pull him away from the driving seat. With difficulty, they swapped seats again. 'I'll get you home. You need treatment.'

Josh had no intention of resisting. He moved back across to the passenger seat, trying to rest his head in the space between it and the driver's place. He could feel the woman brushing her hand across his forehead, gauging his temperature. For the touch alone he was grateful.

There was nothing worse than the thought of dying alone. And right now I feel as if I really might die, Josh thought.

'Who am I?' asked Josh, looking up into the woman's eyes.

She shrugged, tossing back a lock of her red hair that had fallen down over her forehead. 'How the hell should I know? I just found you at the side of the road.'

Josh struggled to keep his eyes open, fighting to hold on to consciousness. Suddenly, he had a sense that if he closed his eyes he might never open them again. Even in the humid, sweaty cabin of the Ranger, he could feel himself growing colder. 'No, I'm serious,' he said, gripping the woman's hand hard. 'I don't know who I am.'

TWO

Tuesday, June 2nd. Afternoon.

The sweat lay thick on Josh's forehead. He opened his eyes reluctantly. The light flooded over him as he glanced towards the window. Through the doorway he could see a yard with two pick-up trucks parked on the gravel, and a barn that looked as if it had been empty for years. Somewhere in the distance he could hear a dog barking, but otherwise it was completely silent. The heat was still stifling.

The woman was leaning across him, a swab of cotton wool in one hand and a bottle of disinfectant in the other. That perfume again, thought Josh, as the fragrance drifted over him. *What was its bloody name?*

The woman dabbed some disinfectant on the cotton wool, then started rubbing it onto Josh's arm.

A jolt of pain shot through his system, running deep into his spine. He pushed her aside. 'No,' he said firmly.

'Let me,' she replied. 'I'm a doctor.'

Josh looked up into her eyes. She was wearing a blue denim skirt, and a white blouse through which Josh could just see the outline of a white lace bra. There was some make-up on her face — a dab of face powder and some pale red lipstick — but she still looked fresh and natural. Her hair was tied up behind her neck and a pair of sunglasses was pushed up over her forehead.

'A doctor?' said Josh, the surprise evident in the tone of his voice.

The woman nodded. 'And you're sick. Very sick. So just lie back and let me treat you.'

Josh's gaze roamed around the room. Wherever it was, it certainly wasn't a hospital. Or a doctor's surgery. The room was about ten foot by five, with a pair of French windows at one end that led out into the yard. It was painted a pale grey-cream, but Josh reckoned that it was at least five years since anyone had run a paintbrush over it. There was nothing on the walls, and the bed he was lying on was a single, with a wooden frame and with only one sheet covering his body. Next to the bed was a jug of iced water and a face flannel. Apart from that, the room was empty.

Josh lay with his head back against the pillow. A thick bandage was strapped to the side of his neck, and beneath it his skin felt burning hot. His head was throbbing with pain, as if someone was chipping away at the inside of his skull with a chisel. The beat of the pain was a dull, steady rhythm that kept time like a jazz drummer. Every three seconds came another beat, making it almost impossible for Josh to hold a straight thought.

First things first, he told himself. Figure out where you are, what's wrong with you. Who attacked you yesterday? *And who the hell are you?*

The woman dabbed some more disinfectant onto his arm, sending another bolt of jabbing pain through him. She paused, as if she was wondering where to start. 'You were shot,' she replied. 'Twice.'

Josh nodded. 'How bad?'

'Once in the neck — that was the worst one,' the woman replied. 'It went in just to the left of the windpipe, nicking the skin and blowing out a chunk of flesh. Another centimetre and you'd be dead. I've cleaned it up and cut away all the infected skin. That bandage stays on your neck for at least two weeks, and I'll need to change it every three days. Keep it clean, though, and you should be okay. You were lucky.'

She *sounded* like a doctor, thought Josh. She could discuss his injuries with a cool, professional detachment, as if she was explaining how to fix a machine.

'The second bullet went into your left calf. Nasty and painful, but not as dangerous. It took out a chunk of flesh but didn't sever any of the main arteries. The bullet was lodged in there but I took it out, and I think the wound's pretty clean. You lost at least two pints of blood, and you're going to have a nasty scar there, but it will heal okay. I'll keep the bandage on for a few days, then go in and take another look.'

The woman looked closely at Josh. 'You're strong,' she said softly. 'A lot of men would have died from these wounds. You know how to take a bullet.'

Josh sighed. The throbbing in his head was still intense. He leaned across the bed, pouring himself a glass of water and raising it to his lips. From the heat of his body, he suspected that he was suffering from a fever as well as from his wounds. 'What am I on?' he asked.

'I've patched up and cleaned your wounds, and given you some painkillers,' the woman replied. 'Trust me, you'd be feeling a lot worse without them. I haven't got any blood here, but if I had, I'd have given you some. What you lost is making you feel a lot weaker. It's going to take a few days in bed, lots of rest, and plenty to eat before you start getting your strength back. And that's before we start worrying about the wounds healing.'

Josh examined her closely, watching how she held herself when she spoke. She certainly seemed to know what she was talking about.

'Who are you?' he asked.

The woman took the sunglasses from her forehead, holding them in her right hand. 'I'm sorry, we haven't been introduced,' she answered, an easy smile playing across her lips. 'My name is Kate. Kate Benessia.'

'How long have I been sleeping?' said Josh.

'Just over a day,' said Kate, putting her shades back on. 'We got here just after one yesterday. It's now three o'clock on Tuesday afternoon. You slept for twenty-six hours, and, believe me, you needed it. That's partly the painkillers. But I gave you some sleeping tablets as well. A man in your state needs a lot of rest.'

Josh paused and drank some more of the water. His throat felt as if it was made of rock, and the throbbing in his head was making it hard to concentrate. Nothing makes any sense, he told himself. Who is she? *What am I doing here?*

'Where are we?' he asked.

'Near Fernwood, in Coconino County,' Kate answered. 'Although it's just a tiny town with a gas station, a diner and a general store, and even that's two miles away. Boisdale is bigger but that's ten miles away. So you might say we're in the middle of nowhere.'

Josh looked out into the yard. The ground was bone dry, the soil caked and cracked. A few weeds had sprouted through the earth, but even they seemed to have dried up and died. 'I'm sorry, I don't even know which country I'm in.'

Kate laughed. 'You really don't know?' She looked towards the window. 'Coconino is in Arizona. That's part of a country called the United States. Big place, just between the Atlantic and Pacific oceans. You've probably heard of it.'

Josh had heard of it. It seemed that the general knowledge was still there. He knew what the capital of France was and how many inches made up a foot. He just didn't know anything about himself or his own history.

If only I could stop my head from hurting, thought Josh. I need to concentrate on who I am, and how I got here. *I need to start remembering things.*

Kate took the shades off, her eyes looking down at him

intently. 'What were you doing lying in a ditch with two bullet holes in you?'

'I don't know,' said Josh.

'Okay, we'll worry later about how the wounds got there. Now, who are you?'

A cold sense of fear started in Josh's mind, then began to creep down his spine, slowly spreading through every nerve in his body. 'I told you, I don't know.'

Kate smiled, but her lips tightened as she did so, and her expression was angry. It was the kind of forced smile that doctors use on difficult patients. 'Take a deep breath, relax, then tell me who you are.'

Josh could feel his hand starting to shake.

I don't know, he repeated to himself. *I don't even know my own name.*

'Just try taking it slowly,' said Kate. 'Say it out loud. My name is . . .'

Josh hesitated. 'My name is . . .'

Nothing.

A wound was one thing. A lump of steel could bury itself in your leg, and after a few weeks there would be nothing to remind you that it had ever happened apart from a scar. A soldier could lose his money, even a lot of his blood, and still recover. But without his name he was nothing.

Get a grip, man. Remember. *It's there somewhere, you just have to find it.*

'I . . . I can't remember,' Josh said, looking up at Kate.

Her expression told him that she was suspicious. Her eyes were narrowing, and a frown had started to crease her brow. 'Think,' she said. 'Just relax and think.'

Josh shook his head. 'I can't,' he stammered nervously. 'I don't know.'

'Your age, then,' said Kate.

My age, thought Josh. I feel about a hundred and three right now, but that's not it. He attempted to think, taking a moment to try and bring the throbbing in his head under control. Nothing. The memories just weren't there.

'I don't know,' he replied.

'Okay,' said Kate. 'Your mother's name?'

'Nothing,' answered Josh, shaking his head. 'Is that sort of memory loss possible?' he asked, looking back up at Kate. 'Medically?'

'It's rare, except when it is drug-induced,' she said. 'But it *can* be a consequence of severe injuries. Maybe the bullet wound to your neck has done something to your nervous system.'

Josh closed his eyes for a second. He tried again, stretching the muscles of his mind to see if he could recover anything, but it was like pushing your foot on the accelerator of a car that had an empty petrol tank.

'Can it be fixed?' He looked up at her, scrutinising her reaction.

Kate lowered her eyes, then looked back into his. 'Depends,' she said slowly. 'Usually it's just a short-term thing. A few days' rest and recuperation, then it will all start to come flooding back.' A smile suddenly curled her lips. 'A month, and you'll be remembering your second cousin's birthday.'

'And *un*usually?' asked Josh. 'What then?'

'I'm not an expert, so I can't really say,' answered Kate. 'Memory is a very delicate thing. Nobody really understands what memories are, or where they are stored. People forget things all the time, then remember them, then start remembering them slightly differently. Who can say how all of that works?'

'Which means that I might not be okay?'

'Which means that if the memories don't come back naturally in a week or two, then you're into a strange place which doctors don't understand very well.'

Josh lay back on his pillow. He was fighting a desperate urge to rip the bandage from his neck, and start scratching his wound: it was itching, as if pepper had just been rubbed into the raw skin. His leg was aching too, and his eyes were starting to water from the constant throbbing in his head. A fly had come through the window. It flicked past Josh, then landed on the side of his cheek, but he lacked the strength to swat it away. Kate brushed it off for him.

'I know nothing about myself,' he said, speaking as much to himself as to the woman at the side of his bed. 'I don't even know what I do.'

'He's a soldier,' said a man standing in the doorway.

Josh glanced upwards. The man was about sixty, with grey hair combed back over his head, grown long so that it reached the top of his shoulders. He was wearing black jeans and a pale blue linen shirt. His skin was tanned and heavily lined, carved like an old piece of granite. And his nose was long and prominent.

'This is my father,' said Kate. 'Marshall.'

Marshall walked forward, standing next to the bed and examining Josh as though he were a piece of livestock at a cattle market: he was probing Josh's character and worth, without any detectable trace of sympathy.

'You said I was a soldier?' Josh asked.

Marshall nodded. 'Yes,' he replied. 'You have the build and physique of a military man. Seen some action as well, I reckon.' The words were delivered slowly and carefully.

Josh tried to sit up, but the pain in his body was too great: he could command his muscles to move, but right now he could not make them obey. 'What makes you say that?'

'I was a soldier myself, once,' said Marshall. 'Vietnam. Two tours. 1968 to '69. Then 1971 to '72. The worst of it. Saw a lot of men get wounded. So I like to think I can recognise the scars.'

He leaned over, gently removing the cotton sheet that was covering Josh. He pointed towards a scar running across his abdomen. 'See this?' he continued, his voice dropping down to a whisper. 'Knife wound. Whoever gave it to you was clearly aiming for your heart, but you rolled sideways, took it in the stomach instead. That's military training. If the blade is going to cut you, try to make sure it's somewhere it can't do too much damage.'

Marshall moved sideways. 'Then here,' he said, pointing to the top of Josh's leg. 'That's a scar from where a dumdum bullet has gone in. Only on a battlefield are you going to find that kind of ammunition in use.'

Marshall shrugged. 'There has to be some explanation for those scars on your body. You could just be some small-time drug dealer who's got caught up in one too many street fights, but I don't think so. Look, a series of small wounds up the side of your rib cage. Those are frag wounds, the kind you get from a hand grenade. That tells me you're a soldier.'

'What kind of soldier?' asked Josh.

Marshall shrugged. 'A lucky one, I'd say, and that's the best kind. You took a lot of damage yesterday, and you've taken some big hits before. But you're still alive. Be grateful for that. There are plenty who aren't.' He ran his right hand through his long, greying strands of hair. 'Those tattoos. They're military as well.'

At the top of Josh's arm a pair of wings was etched in thick black ink, the design fluttering every time he moved his shoulder muscle. Beneath the wings was the letter 'O', then the word 'Pos'.

'Do you know what that means?' asked Marshall.

Josh shook his head. Wings, he was wondering to himself. *What the hell have I got that for?*

'British Parachute Regiment,' said Marshall. 'An O-pos will be your blood group. A lot of soldiers get that info tattooed onto themselves so that the doctors know what to pump into them if they get dragged off the battlefield and need a lot of blood in a hurry.'

'He needs sleep, dad,' Kate interrupted.

Josh looked up towards Marshall. 'Someone came after us on a bike,' he said. 'He was trying to kill us.'

'Seems like you're an unpopular man,' said Marshall drily.

'Who the hell was it?' snapped Josh.

Kate looked at him fiercely. 'You need to sleep,' she repeated.

'I need to know who was on the bike,' Josh shot back.

'Later. Sleep first,' said Kate quickly.

Josh could see the hypodermic needle in her hand. A shaft of sunlight had caught its tip. He winced as the device approached his leg, inhaling sharply as he felt it pierce his skin. He could feel the liquid starting to flow into his bloodstream.

'What is it?' he snapped, looking up at Kate.

'Easy, boy,' said Marshall. 'She's just trying to help.'

'This will help you sleep,' said Kate softly. 'You need it. You're very weak.'

Josh could feel his eyes starting to close. For a moment he resisted. A sense of dread overcame him. He could feel the sweat trickling off his forehead. Get a grip, he commanded himself, for the second time that afternoon. You'll be okay. You just need to get some sleep, and start getting your strength back. *Then you can figure out who you are and what happened to you.*

His mind emptied. Except for a single image that now flashed through his mind. It was briefly as clear and vivid as a picture on a cinema screen. A boy running. And a man falling to the ground.

THREE

Wednesday, June 3rd. Morning.
Josh reached up to feel his forehead. The sweat was still there, but there was less of it than he remembered from yesterday. A light breeze was wafting in from the two open doors: the air was hot but dry, and somehow its movement cooled his face.

Sleep, he told himself. *You must restore your strength.*

Slowly he opened his eyes. The light was fierce, but he couldn't see enough of the sun from his bed to get any fix on the time. Morning, that was all he could tell. He reached across for the water, taking the full glass and throwing its contents down his throat. The skin inside his mouth was parched and dry, the way it would get after a hard drinking session, and even a second glass did nothing to help.

His head was still throbbing but now it was only as if someone was chipping at the inside of his skull with a screwdriver, not a chisel.

Welcome to another day, Josh told himself, a grim smile twisting his lips. *Mr Nobody.*

He tried to lift himself. His bandaged neck was still itching, and the wound in his leg was jabbing at his nerve endings. But his torso was beginning to feel better: the strength was starting to come back to his upper body. He could feel more blood filling up his veins. Using his elbows, he levered himself upwards, taking a deep breath as he did so. He sat on the edge of the bed. Next to the single chair there was an old crutch, made from aluminium and plastic. About a foot away.

I can make it.

Josh started to stand. He winced as his leg rebelled against the movement. Then a blinding flash of pain burst through him. He sat down, closing his eyes, trying to bring it under control. Count, he told himself. Do anything to take your mind off it.

At the count of fifty, he tried again. More carefully this time. He stood on his right leg only, using his arms to balance himself, then took one hop. He could feel himself wobbling, and for a moment he was terrified that he might fall onto the wounded leg. But, steadying himself, he grabbed for the crutch, holding on to it as if it was the last lifeboat leaving a sinking ship.

Steady yourself, man. You can do this.

Holding on to the crutch, Josh started to hobble forwards painfully. He grabbed a blue dressing gown that was hung on a hook on the door, then stepped outside. It felt good to feel sunlight on his face again, and to smell the air. The yard measured twenty feet by fifteen. There was nothing there but scrub, and one slow-dripping tap in the corner. To his right he could see two pick-up trucks: the Ranger, which looked shot to pieces, and a three-year-old Chevy Avalanche which aside from a layer of dust covering its bodywork and one dent above the rear left wheel looked in reasonable shape. Josh looked up. In the distance, he could see a mountain: a thick slab of reddish rock that looked as if it had dropped straight into the desert from space. About a mile or so down the flat road, he could see another building, but whether it was a barn or a house he couldn't tell from this distance. Aside from that, the landscape was empty: just sand, dust and scrub stretching out as far as the eye could see.

Why the hell would anyone want to live here? he asked himself.

For a moment, Josh lent against the window, trying to compose himself. My memories, he asked himself. *Where are my memories?*

He started searching around in his mind again but it was like walking through a pitch-black maze. There was nothing there to guide him. He ran through the same questions he had tried yesterday – what's my name, how old am I, who was my mother – but no matter how hard he concentrated, there was nothing there.

The main building was ten yards in front of him. A low bungalow, probably prefabricated, it was just one step up the housing ladder from a mobile home. The house was a rectangle, about sixty yards long, divided into different rooms. Next to it was a satellite dish, but otherwise nobody had done any work on its appearance. Not for years.

Josh stepped forward, biting his lip to control the pain in his leg as he did so. He could hear voices from a television. 'Anyone up?' he called, leaning against the aluminium frame of the French windows that led from the kitchen into the yard.

Kate looked up, startled. 'You,' she said. 'You should be in bed.'

Josh hobbled towards her, using the crutch to steady himself. The kitchen looked as though it had been put together from a flat-pack at Wal-Mart a decade ago: a slab of Formica ran around its perimeter, interrupted only by a sink, a cooker and a pair of cupboards. Kate was sitting at the small wooden table – cheap pine – eating a bowl of cereal. The television in the corner was tuned to Fox News.

'If I can walk, I'll walk,' said Josh. 'The first thing I need to get back is my will-power.'

Kate nodded. She was wearing pale blue slacks, and a loose blouse with the top two buttons undone, displaying an inch of freckled cleavage. Some powder and lipstick had brightened up her face. 'Sit down,' she commanded, pointing to the spare seat. 'You don't need any weight on that leg.'

Josh placed himself beside the table, relieved to take the weight off his feet. Naturally he couldn't remember whether he'd ever had to walk with a crutch before. But it took practice. And it was more tiring than it looked: all the weight had to be carried in his shoulders and arms. Even travelling a few yards strained the wound in his neck.

He took a sip of the coffee that Kate had placed in front of him. The caffeine hit him like a gale blowing into a tree: he could feel his head swaying as it shot into his bloodstream. It had been at least two days now since he'd had anything to drink but water, and he could feel the coffee-jolt rushing through him, delivering a sudden and unexpected burst of energy.

Josh glanced towards the television. The newsreader was discussing a power cut in Memphis last night: the lights had gone off for a few brief minutes, causing a tremor of panic and alarm throughout the city. 'Could it be a repeat of the Three Cities attack of earlier this year?' asked the newsreader. 'We'll have more after this break.'

Kate looked at Josh. 'So how're you feeling?' she asked.

He paused. It was a difficult question to answer. He was in bad shape, yet, in truth, not as bad as he had been twenty-four hours earlier. Physically, I'm probably starting to get better, although it's still a long road back to full health, he mused. *Mentally, I'm feeling worse.*

'Like a field mouse that's just been dragged backwards through a combine harvester.' Josh smiled. 'But I'm getting better – slowly. I think.'

'We'll need to do a proper check soon,' said Kate. 'Blood pressure, temperature, the works. I'm going to keep those bandages on today because I don't want to disturb the wounds. We'll change them tomorrow.' She stood up, taking down a bowl of cornflakes from the cupboard. 'Now, you need to eat. Get some calories back into the system. You like cereal?'

'Can't remember,' answered Josh, glancing back at her. 'I'll try.'

Kate put the food on the table. Josh dipped his spoon into the cereal, raising it to his lips. His throat was still dry and sore, and it was difficult for him to swallow. The food tasted okay: bland, but he could feel the energy starting to sink into him, restoring his strength. I have my hunger back, he thought, and that's a start.

'Even if I don't know who I am,' said Josh, pushing aside the cereal bowl and taking another sip on the coffee, '*somebody* knows — because they tried to kill me.'

'And they sure came close,' said Marshall.

The older man had just walked into the room. He poured himself a coffee and looked across at Josh. 'What do you think happened?'

'Someone tried to kill me,' Josh repeated. 'That's all I know.'

'Or you tried to kill someone?' Marshall asked.

Josh paused. The thought that he might have killed someone had been lying there somewhere, beneath the conscious surface of his mind. *When you couldn't remember who you were, there was no way of knowing what you were capable of.*

Marshall smiled, the lines on his weather-beaten face creasing up. 'Even out here in Arizona, a man has a couple of bullet holes in him, we reckon he ran into someone who knew who he was and wasn't too well disposed to him. The trouble is, boy, we don't know who the hell you are.'

'What was I wearing?' asked Josh.

'Pair of jeans, and a black T-shirt,' replied Kate. 'They're covered in blood, and the jeans have a hole in them where the bullet went into your leg. I threw them away. Marshall has some spare pairs — you can wear one of 'em when you feel able to walk properly.'

Josh leaned forward on the table. 'Nothing on me?' he asked. 'No wallet, driving licence, credit card?'

Kate shook her head. 'We found three thousand dollars in cash in your back pocket. It's up there on the shelf, in an envelope. Take it when you need it. Apart from that, nothing. No clue to who you might be.' She paused. 'You are clearly a man who travels light.'

'Three thousand dollars,' said Marshall. 'What kind of man carries that amount of money around with him?'

Josh stayed silent.

'A gangster?' persisted Marshall.

Josh started to squeeze his knuckles together. 'We'll find that out when we know who I am,' he said, the statement delivered more to himself than to anyone else. 'Right now I need to know who was trying to kill me and why? What the hell was I doing there?' He looked down at the floor. 'If I can figure that out, I can start to figure out who I am.'

The sandwich tasted good. A thick slice of turkey breast, with some salad on top and a hefty dollop of mayonnaise, wrapped between two hunks of chewy white bread. Josh bit down on it, tearing off big mouthfuls with his teeth. He sipped on the Coke that he had poured into the tall, thin glass, and looked out onto the surrounding scrubland. It had a harsh beauty to it. The terrain rolled into the distance, dipping towards the far horizon, scarcely disturbed by any living thing, whether animal or human. *If you wanted to hide, this would be a good place.*

I've been here before, he told himself. Mountains. Rugged landscape. Sand and dust. I don't know when or where but I've seen this or something very like it.

My memory is there somewhere.

Kate stepped out onto the porch and sat down next to him. She was holding a hypodermic syringe in her hand. Josh looked down at its needle and winced. There was only one man's skin that needle was going to puncture, he thought. And I'm living in it.

'You're eating,' she said softly. 'Another day or two and you'll be surprised at how strong you are feeling.'

Josh nodded. 'My body will be okay, I can feel it. It's my mind.'

'Any memories yet?'

Josh shook his head. 'Nothing.'

'You're a soldier – we've figured that out.'

Josh nodded. 'If you say so.'

'I reckon you're British as well,' continued Kate. 'From the accent.'

'You recognise it?'

'From films, that kind of stuff. I've never been there.' Kate took her shades from her face and started fidgeting with them. 'You may not sound much like Hugh Grant. But I still reckon you're a Brit.'

'Then what was I doing here?'

'In Arizona?'

Josh nodded. 'A British soldier. Serving or not serving. Lying in a ditch with a bullet through him. That's some puzzle.'

'I'll try some associations,' said Kate. 'I'll say a word. You tell me what it makes you think of. Okay?'

Josh took another bite of his sandwich, chewing vigorously. He felt that if he could just eat enough to get his strength back, maybe he would start to drag some memories out of the back of his brain.

'Army,' said Kate.

Josh stopped eating. 'Nothing,' he said.

'War?'

Josh shook his head again.

'Okay, I'll try another track,' said Kate. 'Family.'

'Nothing.'

'Parents?'

Josh shook his head once more.

'Home town?'

The look of sadness was visible on Josh's face as he shook his head yet again.

'Conspiracy,' said Kate.

Josh hesitated. 'Me,' he replied slowly. 'You said conspiracy, and I thought of myself.'

'Maybe we're getting somewhere,' said Kate, a hint of excitement in her tone. 'Mystery?' she went on.

'TV, films,' said Josh, his tone hopeful.

Kate stopped him. 'No, we need real memories. Not just stuff you've seen on TV.'

'Then, nothing,' said Josh.

'If you're British, you must come from somewhere over there. Maybe Liverpool?'

'I don't know.'

'London?'

'I don't know,' Josh repeated.

'How about Manchester?'

Josh shook his head – it was getting to be a habit, he thought.

'Birmingham?'

'Not a sodding Brummie. Maybe it's better not to get my memory back if that's all there is to look forward to.'

'How old do you reckon you are?' said Kate.

Josh shrugged.

'You look about thirty.'

'I could be. I don't know.'

'Married?' she asked.

Josh shrugged again. 'I can't remember.'

Kate laughed, raising her hand to her lips. 'I bet you use that line on all the girls.'

FOUR

Thursday, June 4th. Afternoon.
Josh lifted his head from the pillow. He kept his eyes closed, trying to cling on to the image that had been playing through his mind as he awoke. A man falling. A boy running. A shot. Then a shout.

The shout. What was he saying?

Josh squeezed his eyes tight shut, trying to hold himself in a state where he was half awake, half asleep. The shout, he repeated to himself. *What the hell did it say?*

No good.

The image had gone now, consigned to the dustbin, along with all the rest of his memories.

Josh opened his eyes. He took a long drink of water, looking at the clock. It was just after four in the afternoon. He must have slept for at least twenty-four, maybe twenty-five hours. His body felt lazy and tired still, but the aching in his head was starting to ease, and the itch on his neck underneath the thick layer of bandages was getting weaker.

If there was a shot, was it my finger on the trigger?

Twenty-five hours, thought Josh. Whatever Kate jabbed into me must have been the strongest stuff in her locker.

A fly landed on the sheet. Josh slammed down his fist, squashing it against the white linen. Getting my strength back, reflected Josh. *And my reflexes.*

He levered himself from the bed, using all the strength in his elbows. Carefully, he put his left foot on the floor, pressing it against the cold tiles. The pain was still there, but it didn't scream up through his leg the way it had yesterday. His eyes were still bloodshot, but the red streaks running through his pupils were not quite so thick. And the fever heat on his brow seemed to be lessening. Gently, he reached out for the crutch and started to walk.

A gunshot rang out from the yard.

Instinctively, Josh ducked, his shoulders turning sideways, his hunched posture protecting both his head and his torso from any bullets that might come flying through the window. Looking around, he started searching through the room for something that could be improvised as a weapon. Nothing. The crutch might make a staff, but against a man with a gun it would be useless.

Another shot echoed across the empty landscape. Josh looked through the window. Marshall was standing in the yard, a pistol in his hand. Fifty yards away he had lined up a row of tin cans and was firing at them one by one.

A soldier, Josh thought to himself. They said they thought I was a soldier. And those were a soldier's instinctive reactions to the sound of gunfire. Shield yourself. Stay alive. *And look for a way to fight back.*

He watched Marshall from the window, noticing the ease with which the older man carried the weapon in his hand. A Browning, Josh noticed. A Browning Buck Mark field pistol, with its distinctive black metal barrel and polished walnut grips. Who are these people? he wondered to himself. Why have they taken me into this house? Why are they looking after me?

What do they want from me?

A tin can had fallen to the ground as one of Marshall's bullets tore through it.

'Nice shot,' said Josh, stepping out from the porch.

The heat of the midday sun was still beating down on the parched ground. It must be at least forty degrees, reckoned

Josh. As soon as he stepped outside, he could feel the sun burning into the back of his neck, but the air was so dry and arid that it hardly raised a bead of perspiration on his skin.

'I'm not really any good,' said Marshall. 'I can fire a gun if I have to, but I was never really blessed with a natural aim. Only a few men are.' He looked hard at Josh, his eyes narrowing. 'How about you?'

Josh shrugged. 'I wouldn't know.'

Marshall smiled, walking across the dusty yard towards the back of the main building. Josh hobbled at his side, using the crutch to hold his weight as he moved forwards. He was dressed in just his gown, and the ground felt hot on the soles of his feet. 'Take a shot,' suggested Marshall. 'I think it might be good exercise for you. Get your senses working again.'

Josh just nodded. So far, he was uncertain what he should make of Marshall. Kate was a doctor, although even her motives were hard to figure out. But the old guy, thought Josh – he was a puzzle without any clues.

The door swung open to reveal a storeroom full of guns and ammunition. There must have been a dozen hunting rifles stacked in rows. Josh ran his gaze over them, recognising a Saiga, a Kalashnikov, a Winchester, a Marlin and a Browning. They were all sporty, heavy-duty models with polished wooden stocks, designed to fell a deer or a stag at two hundred yards in the woods. Next to them was a range of pistols.

'Pick one,' said Marshall.

Josh looked at the weapons and let his instincts guide him. He took a Sig-Sauer P228 pistol, cocked it, then uncocked it and activated the firing-pin safety.

'I keep these loaded all the time,' said Marshall. 'Give it a go.'

Marshall held the gun for him while Josh hobbled outside.

He walked across to the side of the porch, leaned his crutch against the wall and used the frame of the door to support some of his weight.

'Think you can hit one of those cans?'

'I have no idea,' answered Josh.

He released the safety, lifted the pistol and gripped the weapon in both hands, his feet positioned slightly apart like a boxer's. He raised the gun so that it was level with his eye.

'The weaver position,' said Marshall.

'What?' asked Josh.

Marshall smiled. 'Never mind. It's a police term.'

Josh squinted, concentrating on the tiny sight at the tip of the barrel. The tin can was fifty yards distant, and only just visible. He lined up the pistol's barrel, then took a deep breath to steady the muscles in his shoulders and his forearms.

Is this instinct? he wondered. Like a dog chewing on a bone. *Or have I been trained to do this?*

He squeezed the trigger gently, exerting only as much pressure as was needed to release the bullet. The barrel of the gun slammed backwards with the recoil but Josh had enough strength to control the kickback. Without thinking, he fired again. A double tap: two bullets in quick succession.

The tin can spun into the air, then shot forward as the second bullet punched through it.

'A shot,' said Marshall, standing two yards behind him. 'I thought so.' He paused. 'Try again.'

Josh steadied the pistol, took aim and fired. One shot, then two. The can clattered to the ground.

'Again,' said Marshall.

Josh paused, took a breath, then squeezed the trigger – once, then twice. Another can bit the dust.

Marshall stepped in front of him. He took a swig of the beer bottle gripped in his right hand, emptying its contents down his throat. He glanced across towards Josh. 'Let's see if you can hit a moving target.'

With a swing of his hand, Marshall slung the bottle high up into the air. Josh followed it with his stare, tracking the arc of its movement. Wait until it peaks and starts to fall, he told himself. That is when it will slow down. *That is when it will be easier to hit.*

He squeezed the trigger. The bullet streaked high into the sky, hitting nothing. Almost instantaneously, Josh released the second round. This time he could hear the satisfying crunch of steel smashing into glass, sending a shower of tiny fragments of the bottle down from the sky.

'Like I said, a marksman,' said Marshall, stepping towards him. 'A soldier always fires twice. It's drilled into him.'

'You already said I was a soldier.'

Marshall nodded, his expression turning serious. 'Plenty of soldiers can't shoot straight,' he replied. 'Look at the way you always fire twice. Assault troops do that – it's part of their training. If you want to kill a man, two bullets are always twice as good as one. Squeeze once, then twice, then drop your weapon.'

'Assault troops?' asked Josh.

Marshall shrugged. 'Special forces, maybe.'

Josh looked down at the ground. The shot. The memory he had woken up with. It was still there, struggling to emerge, like a worm trying to wriggle its way out of a hard piece of ground. The noise of it was vivid in his ears now: he could hear the echo of the bullet spreading out across the empty scrubland.

Did I shoot someone?

'A beer,' said Marshall, reaching down into the icebox propped up on the front of the porch. 'You like beer?'

'Maybe. I can't remember,' replied Josh with an easygoing smile.

Marshall handed across a beer, snapping off its cap

between his right thumb and forefinger. 'I never met a soldier who didn't like beer,' he said.

Josh put the bottle to his lips. The taste was familiar. The alcohol hit his bloodstream, sending a sudden rush of energy surging through him. He felt light-headed, giddy. But he could also feel the aching in his head starting to ease. 'I like beer, that's for sure,' he said, looking back towards Marshall.

The older man nodded, looking down at the ground, the beer bottle still in his hand. 'What do you want to do?'

Josh turned to look at him. 'I'll stay, if you'll let me.' He took another hit of the beer. 'Just for a few days, until I get myself straightened out. I can pay you from the cash that was in my pocket.'

'The money doesn't matter,' said Marshall. 'You're not costing us anything apart from a few scraps of food.'

'I could go to a hospital,' continued Josh. 'I've thought about it. But I don't know who I am, or what happened to me back there. Like you said, a man doesn't get shot for no reason. Maybe I was mixed up in something illegal.'

'You're worried that if you check into a hospital the cops are going to be looking out for you?'

Josh gripped the beer bottle tightly between his hands. 'I just don't know, do I?'

'You got no idea what you were doing?'

Josh shook his head. 'None.'

'Rest, that's what you need,' said Marshall. 'Give it a few days. A memory is like a woman. You have to let them come to you.'

'No.' Josh smiled, more to himself than to Marshall. 'I need to chase.'

'Meaning?'

'I'm a hunter. I like to track things down. Women, memories, whatever. That's who I am.'

'You don't know who the hell you are, boy,' answered Marshall.

'But I do know that much about myself,' said Josh quickly. 'Like you said, I'm a soldier. We don't wait for things to come to us.'

Marshall laughed. 'The clever ones do.'

Josh stood up, using the crutch for support. It still hurt, but he needed to push himself: he knew that until he started exercising his muscles again his strength was never going to return. 'Maybe I'm not a good one,' he said, looking back towards Marshall. Josh stretched his arms to relieve the pain in his shoulders. 'Take me back to where you found me.'

'What for?'

'It might trigger something,' said Josh. 'If I could see the place, then maybe I'll get a sense of what happened. Maybe I can find some evidence about who attacked me.'

He sat down again. The pain in his leg was growing worse, making it hard for him to stand for any length of time. 'Now,' he said. 'I want to go back now.'

Marshall shook his head. 'Too hot,' he answered. 'Maybe we'll take you in the morning. When it's cooler. And when Kate says you're strong enough.'

Josh caught the words on the lips, just as he was about to speak. An instinct was burning within him: to tell the older man that he wanted to be taken to the place where they'd found him, and he wanted to be taken there now. No, he reminded himself. Until I have my strength back, I have to depend on these people. I'm an invalid. *I can do nothing for myself.*

'Tomorrow, then,' said Josh stiffly.

Marshall grinned. 'At dawn, before the bull snakes are awake.'

Josh looked out across the scrub. A truck was moving along the road, doing about forty miles an hour. Apart from that the landscape was as bleak and empty as it always was. 'What are you doing out here?' he asked.

'Keeping myself to myself,' said Marshall. 'Soldiering does

that to a man sometimes. You might find that out one day for yourself.'

'Not too quiet?'

'Not for me, no. I like quiet.'

'What do you do?' asked Josh, looking across at the older man. 'It doesn't look as if there are any jobs out here.'

Marshall took another sip of his beer. 'Veterans from the war,' he replied. 'I run a website that helps keep vets in touch with one another. Gives them help and advice on their benefit payments, medical treatment, the rest of it. There are still a lot of men out there who are in pretty bad shape, both mentally and physically, and for many of them it gets worse as they get older. A lot of them live out in remote places like this because they don't like the noise and the sweat of the cities. So the site helps them stay in touch. Lets them talk. They pay a small subscription, so it doesn't make a lot of money, but it makes a bit. We get by.'

'And Kate?' said Josh, nodding back towards the main building. 'She's a young woman, full of life. What's she doing out here?'

Marshall paused, and Josh could sense the older man growing tense: his hand was tightening its grip on his beer bottle, and his brow was starting to furrow. 'That's her business,' he said.

'Okay,' said Josh, backing away. 'I was just curious.'

'Listen,' continued Marshall. 'I don't mind you being here. You're a soldier, and I like soldiers. But just make sure you keep your hands off my daughter. That way you and I are going to get along just fine.'

The pizza felt sticky and heavy in Josh's hand. It had a thick layer of cheese on top, plus some wedges of ham and pineapple. I can't remember whether I like pizza or not, Josh said to himself. *But I certainly don't like it with sodding pineapple on it.*

He took another bite, flicking one of the pineapple chunks onto the ground, then chewing the slice quickly. Get it inside you, he told himself. Every bite you take will get you a bite closer to being stronger again. *And strength is what you need.*

'I had a memory,' said Josh.

Kate looked surprised. She turned to face him, a smile flashing across her lips. 'Just now?'

'Earlier,' answered Josh. 'As I was waking up this afternoon.'

It was a little after nine at night, and the final rays of sunlight had just dipped below the horizon. The fierce redness of the sunset against the reddish-browns of the desert landscape had held Josh's attention for more than an hour: he had been happy just to sit and watch the gradual fading of the light, and the smears of colour it left behind. By the time Kate had come out of the kitchen with a giant pizza and a pitcher of iced tea he had been feeling better than at any time since he'd been shot. The pain from his wounds was ebbing, and the headache was tuning down to just a mild, irregular drumbeat.

Now a moon was starting to rise in the sky, arcing across the distant mountain and bathing the flat land in a silver light. Ahead of him, Josh could see a huge inch-and-a-half-long bug crawling across the scrub, its eyes glinting through the darkness. The creature had a thick black skin, and was moving at speed across the ground.

Is that dangerous? wondered Josh as he watched the spider's progress. That's the real risk from losing your memory: a lifetime's experience of knowing how to look after yourself is lost in a split second.

'Morning is the time when you're most likely to find some memories stirring within you,' said Kate, looking up towards Josh. 'Whenever you feel yourself waking up, try and keep your mind empty and relaxed. Eventually some memories will sneak back in there.'

'There was a shot,' said Josh, looking towards Kate. 'A gunshot.'

'Aimed at you?' she asked. 'Was it someone shooting at you?'

Josh shook his head. 'No, I don't think so,' he answered. 'I hear a shot. And then I see a boy running. Across some kind of dark landscape. Then that's it. The memory goes.'

'It's a start,' said Kate. 'It's locked up in there somewhere. We just have to find a key that opens the box.'

Josh took a further bite of his pizza, flicking another piece of pineapple on the ground and watching the spider crawl towards the discarded fruit. 'The key's pretty well locked up right now.'

'Try some of the stuff you were watching on TV,' said Kate. 'Maybe that will trigger something.'

'Hasn't yet,' said Josh, taking a sip of the iced tea.

'Iraq,' said Kate. 'What does that mean to you personally? Have you been there?'

Josh paused. Something. He could feel it in his brain, a slight flickering of recognition. But nothing more came. 'No,' he replied. 'Nothing.'

'Okay,' said Kate. 'Let's try something else.' She hesitated. 'What's my name?'

Josh looked at her and grinned. 'Kate.'

'My father's name?'

'Marshall.'

'What did I give you for breakfast yesterday?'

'Cereal.'

Kate nodded. 'And how was the weather?'

'Hot,' answered Josh. 'Bloody hot.'

Kate poured herself a glass of iced tea. She was wearing a pale blue linen skirt and a white blouse, the most dressy clothes Josh had seen her in. He noticed the smooth outline of her legs beneath the fabric. Her skin was tanned a rich, light brown from constant exposure to the sun. The bright locks of red hair against the tanned skin gave her an exotic appearance that was all the more captivating for being so unusual. Most redheads had pale skins, reflected Josh. She was an unusual woman. In a thousand different ways, no doubt.

'There are two different types of memory loss,' said Kate. 'Anterograde, which means the patient can't learn anything new. And retrograde, which means they can't remember anything that happened before a certain point. They can remember general stuff, but nothing personal. We've just tested you on the past couple of days and you're doing fine. You remember everything that happened since you came here. So what you are suffering from is retrograde memory loss. That tells us there isn't any brain damage. Rest. You'll get it back.'

'And if I don't?'

Kate shrugged. 'You'll just have to learn again. Everything. From scratch, like a kid.'

Josh glanced towards Kate. For the first time since he had woken up here two days ago he could feel himself starting to relax. The itching in his neck was subsiding, and his leg was almost strong enough to stand on without him having to use a crutch. He could move without his whole body rebelling in pain.

Everything's going to be okay, he said to himself. I don't know how or when. But I can sense it. *I'm going to pull through this.*

'What are *you* doing out here?'

He sipped on his iced tea and looked at Kate, at the same time gesturing towards the desolate landscape.

'Don't you like it?' she asked.

He could detect the hint of defiance in her voice. 'It's a wilderness,' he replied.

'I like it. It's natural. Unspoilt. The way the world should be.'

Josh looked out onto the scrubland. Some of the pizza

was still sitting at his side, but he had eaten as much as he could manage this evening. 'I don't mean that,' he said. 'You're a doctor, but you don't practise. You're an attractive young woman, but you live out here, a hundred miles from the nearest decent-sized town. I'm sorry, I don't get it.'

He looked at Kate. 'What are you hiding from?'

Kate stood up briskly. Her manner had grown cold and distant: her shoulders were hunched up into her neck, and her gaze flicked past Josh as if she were searching for something in the distance. 'You need some rest,' she said. 'That's an order from your doctor.'

Josh woke up with a start. His head was spinning and his breathing was ragged. He was about to speak, but he could feel Kate's hand covering his lips.

'Quiet,' she whispered fiercely in his ear. 'There are men approaching the house. Police.'

Josh struggled to wrap the sheet around his naked body. He could feel the tension flooding through him. Glancing outside, he could see that it was night: the yard was in shadow, with only some moonlight throwing a few pale beams across the pathway.

'What shall I do?'

'Hide, quick,' said Kate. 'There's a place under the floorboards.'

Josh got to his feet, using his crutch to walk across the yard to the kitchen. He could see two police cars turning the corner, driving along the narrow strip of road that led up to the house. 'Quick,' said Kate at his side.

Marshall was waiting in the kitchen. He was holding up a layer of lino, pointing to a patch of exposed floor. 'Down there,' he snapped, pushing aside two planks to reveal a trapdoor. 'There's a space just big enough to hold a man.'

Josh looked into the darkness. He could see almost nothing. Next to him, Marshall switched on a flashlight. The beam illuminated a set of six steps that led down to a curved space. Josh started to step downwards, leaving his crutch behind. His leg still throbbed painfully as his weight rested upon it. Using his hands, he levered himself into position.

The rectangular trench measured ten feet by ten. It was five feet deep. The space had been cut into the earth below the foundations of the bungalow, with strips of wood used to prop up its sides. Josh lay down on his back. 'I'm going to switch the flashlight off now,' said Marshall. 'I'll get you out when they've gone.'

The flashlight flicked off, and suddenly Josh was plunged into blackness. He could see nothing, only hear footsteps moving above him. The air down in the trench was hot – at least forty degrees – and stale. Josh could feel the sweat starting to form on his skin. He could sense the cracked earth all around him, and a few feet away he could smell the pipe that led down from the bathroom towards the septic tank.

Why do they have a one-man hiding place beneath their house? thought Josh. *Who the hell are these people?*

He heard a knock on the door. One set of footsteps, then another. Two men. Josh was certain they were men. The steps were heavy and deliberate, walking slowly through the house as if they were searching for something.

Voices. They were too muffled for him to make out at first. He strained his ears, struggling to catch the words being spoken just a few yards above him.

'An Englishman,' he heard a voice saying. 'We're looking for a man with a British accent. He's in the area somewhere.'

Josh could hear Kate speaking, but he couldn't catch what she was saying. A whisper was all that filtered down, the words indistinct.

'He might be dangerous,' he heard the man saying. 'Only might be, mind. We just want to bring him in for questioning.'

They think I did it. They think I shot somebody. And – who knows? – maybe I did, thought Josh to himself. *What kind of man am I? What might I be capable of?*

Another pause. Kate was speaking again but still Josh couldn't catch the words.

'You haven't seen anything suspicious in the area?' asked the man. 'We think he might be pretty badly hurt too, so he couldn't have gone far.'

Josh could hear Kate now. 'We haven't seen anybody,' she said. 'And, as you know, it's pretty isolated up here. If there was anyone, we'd've seen them.'

'Mind if we look around?'

Now Josh could hear Marshall walking across the floor. 'Feel free,' the older man said.

Josh lay completely still. He could hear the footsteps tramping across the floor above him. And he could hear the sounds of cupboards being opened and beds being moved.

Suddenly he felt something moving across his skin. The thing's touch felt dry and coarse, with the texture of an old belt. A snake. Josh could feel his flesh starting to creep. Goose bumps were rising on every inch of his skin, and a shiver of cold fear started to run down his spine. His hand was trembling, and he had to focus his mind to try and steady it.

I'm learning new things about myself all the time. I have a fear of snakes.

Stay still, he told himself. Stay perfectly still and you'll be okay.

The snake moved further across his torso. Josh caught a glimpse of its eyes, glinting back at him. His own eyes had become more accustomed to the darkness and he could make out that the reptile had wide bands of red and black skin interspersed with narrow ones of white and yellow. Its head was completely black, with a snubbed snout, and its long tongue flicked lazily across Josh's chest to lick some of the sweat from his body. Was its bite venomous?

Hold steady, man, thought Josh, tracking the snake's movements. Just keep your nerve.

He could hear footsteps moving towards the door. 'Nothing in the other building?' he heard the policeman say.

'Just a guest room,' Marshall replied.

More movement. Then Kate said something that Josh couldn't catch. The snake started to move up along Josh's body towards his neck. Its tail was flicking against his buttocks.

'Sure?' Josh heard the policeman say suspiciously.

'Sure,' said Marshall. 'Go take a look.'

Another pause. Josh felt a desperate need to scratch the bandage on his neck. The snake was pushing up against the wound.

Another inch, thought Josh, and I'll have to move.

'You can contact us in Fernwood,' he heard the man say. 'You see or hear anything strange, then you let us know. And don't attempt to approach this guy. He might be dangerous.'

Josh took a deep breath. The snake was pushing its head against his bandage, nuzzling it open with the hard bone of its snout. It can smell the blood in there, he realised. And it wants a taste.

Above him he could hear the sound of a starter motor turning, then of an engine running. The police car was starting to pull out onto the roadway. Slowly he counted to five, making sure that the car was safely away from the house before risking betraying himself with any sudden movements.

Now I know I'm a wanted man, Josh reflected sourly. And Kate and Marshall are protecting me. *I should be grateful, but why are they doing it?*

With a swift, violent movement, Josh flicked his hand upwards. He grabbed the snake by the throat, squeezing as hard as he could on the thin tube of flesh, skin and bone until the breath emptied out of its body, its tail flapping against Josh's legs, lashing at the skin.

He cast the corpse to one side.

Already, Marshall was beaming his flashlight down into the trench. 'You okay?' he shouted.

FIVE

Friday, June 5th. Dawn.
The Chevy Avalanche pick-up truck bounced along the pitted surface of the road. Josh wound down the window, letting the morning air rush over his face. Traces of red were splattered across the sky. His mind was fresh from another five hours of sleep after the police had left and the caffeine from the coffee he had drunk for breakfast was still flowing through his veins.

'Much further?' he said, looking across at Marshall.

The older man was gripping the wheel of the pick-up truck. 'About two miles,' he said, his voice tired. 'I'll tell you when we're there.'

The drive had taken just under an hour, and they had left the house at six. The route had taken them through a rough, mountainous landscape, the surface of the ground pitted with boulders and dried-out trenches. The first town, Fernwood, was just over a mile away, but that was a just a gas station with a diner and general store attached, and a collection of a dozen houses. Since then, they had passed through two more towns, both of them just as small. A pair of ranches had been signposted off the road. Otherwise, nothing. Cococino County was as empty of people as Josh's mind was of memories.

Cowboy country, thought Josh as he gazed out of the window.

The truck started to slow down. The Ford Ranger had been left back at their house – Marshall was still fixing some of the damage it had taken in the fight at the start of the week. As they turned the corner, Marshall jabbed his foot on the brakes, and the tyres made a screeching sound as they gripped the surface of the road.

'Here,' said Marshall.

Kate was sitting between Josh and her father. She looked at Josh, scrutinising his expression as he looked out over the valley. To the right, behind them, there was a high ridge of red-rock hills. The road twisted along their side. To the left, the land was flat, rolling out several miles into the distance, its smooth, sandy surface punctuated only by cacti and the occasional boulder.

Nothing, thought Josh, a pang of disappointment stabbing at his chest. *It is as if I never saw the place before in my life.*

Marshall pushed open the driver's door and hopped down onto the ground. Kate offered Josh her hand to help him down, but he shook his head. The crutch would do just fine. The pain in his leg was still there, but he was getting used to hobbling, and he knew that the more he exercised it the better.

He was wearing an old pair of Gap jeans that Marshall had lent him: they were a size too big, and he'd had to put an extra notch in the belt to pull them tight enough around his waist. On top, he wore a blue denim shirt that he'd found in a cupboard. Doesn't matter what I look like, he told himself. In this gear, I'll just blend into the landscape. *Another cowboy without much money to spend on his wardrobe.*

'Somewhere around here,' said Kate, stepping away from the side of the road. 'This is where I found you.'

Josh followed a yard behind her until she stopped beside a ridge. He paused, smelling the air: the dust, the rock and the heat combined to create a hazy, earthy odour that reminded him of somewhere. A camp, maybe. On a hillside. With men, and noise. And screaming.

Josh tried to get a grip on the memory, but it had already slipped from his grasp. Lost, he thought. *Down into the pit where the rest of my memories are.*

He stepped forward. Kate was pointing to a ditch that measured thirty feet across and ten feet deep. 'Here,' she said. 'I found you right here.'

Josh knelt down on the ground. He closed his eyes, hoping that the darkness would stir something inside his mind. Empty. He looked down, running his fingers into the dust. A few yards to the right, there was a patch of rusty brown. Even after five days' exposure to the baking sun, it was clear what had made that stain. Blood. Human blood.

My blood, thought Josh.

'Remember anything?' asked Kate.

Josh shook his head. 'Blank,' he replied.

He stood up, looking out across the horizon. Two hundred, maybe three hundred yards distant, he could see a cordoned-off strip of the road, with a taped barrier. A car was drawing up to it, moving at no more than ten miles an hour. As it stopped, a man in uniform and wearing sunglasses climbed out.

'Police,' said Josh. 'I'm going to see what they know.'

Kate grabbed his arm, tugging back at the sleeve of his shirt. Her strength surprised Josh, and he could feel himself losing his grip on the crutch. 'No,' she snapped. 'The police are looking for you.'

Josh brushed her hand away. 'I just need to find out what happened here.'

'It's too risky,' said Kate.

'I'll be the judge of what risks I run.'

Marshall glanced at both of them, as if he was assessing the respective strengths of two boxers in the ring. 'I'll come with you,' he said. 'Kate, you follow us in the car.'

Josh started to hobble down the road. He was becoming more practised with his crutch, swinging forward with long, confident strides. Every third step he was putting some weight on the wounded leg, tolerating the pain that rippled through him every time it touched the ground. He knew that if you were fit, your muscles would rebuild themselves more quickly.

A couple more days and I might be able to walk normally again. So long as I keep the nerves and muscles exercised.

Marshall was walking at Josh's side, his arms folded across his chest. 'You let me do the talking, boy,' he whispered. 'They hear your accent, they're going to be suspicious right away.'

The policeman was standing by himself. About three hundred pounds, with a belly that was bursting out of his khaki Sheriff's Department shirt, the man was leaning against the hood of his Ford Taurus Estate. There was a big polystyrene cup of coffee on the bonnet of the machine, and next to it a box of six doughnuts. Three of them were already eaten. Obviously a man who liked his breakfast.

'What happened here?' said Marshall, nodding gently towards the policeman.

Josh glanced up at the cop and smiled.

'Kid got shot, back on Monday,' said the policeman. 'Didn't you see it on TV?'

Marshall laughed. 'Been out of the county a few days. Who was he?'

The policeman reached behind him for a doughnut, keeping his gaze fixed on Marshall all the time. 'Kid named Ben Lippard,' he replied, starting to chew on his food. 'You know him?'

Marshall shook his head slowly from side to side. 'No. Was he mixed up in something? Drugs?'

The policeman looked across to Josh, his stare locking onto his crutch and the thick white bandage wrapped around his neck. He finished his doughnut, then wiped some saliva away from his chin with the back of his hand.

'What do I look like? A fucking newspaper? You want to find out what happened, you go buy one.'

Marshall backed away a step, raising his hand. 'Hey, steady, pal,' he said. 'I just wanted to find out. That's all.'

The policeman took a step forward from the car. 'Who's your friend?' he asked angrily, jabbing his thumb towards Josh. 'How'd he get so badly hurt?'

'Mountain climbing,' said Marshall quickly. 'We were up at the Grand Canyon for a few days. Had a bit of a fall.'

'I lost something near here,' Josh interrupted. 'A wallet. Some ID. You find anything like that?'

As soon as he spoke, Josh noticed Marshall shooting him a deadly glance: Doesn't matter, Josh decided. I'll take some risks with the police if I have to. Maybe I shot this boy, and maybe I didn't. *If I don't start asking questions, I'll never find out.*

'Are you the man?' asked the policeman.

'What man?' said Josh.

The policeman took another step forward. Now Josh could smell the jam and sugar of the doughnut on his breath. 'What man?' repeated Josh, a ragged edge of anger creeping into his tone.

'There was a third man, guy who got injured on the murder scene,' said the policeman. 'He left some traces of blood in the sand. We got his DNA, so we know who he is.' He looked more closely at Josh. 'I'm wondering if it might be you.' He paused. 'That accent. Is that Australian, or British, or what?'

Josh was about to speak again but Marshall stepped swiftly in front of him. 'He's a veteran. First Iraq war. He . . .' Marshall paused. 'He has some problems.'

The policeman looked past Marshall, still staring at Josh. 'I'm taking you down to the sheriff's office. We need to check out who you are.'

Josh started backing away.

'No need to run,' said the policeman, his tone rising. 'I'm not saying we'll keep you. Just check you out, ask you a few questions, then send you on your way.'

Marshall's fist landed hard in the policeman's stomach. Josh was surprised by the power of the blow that the older man struck, followed through with all the force of his shoulder. The kind of blow that a professional boxer would deliver, thought Josh. *That man knows how to fight.*

The policeman doubled up in pain. He was too fat for his job, and his belly was full of sugar and air. The punch winded him, knocking him sideways and loosening his balance. His right hand slipped down to the leather holster flapping at his belt and his fingers grasped the weapon. He started to pull it free but Marshall had already swung his leg up towards the man's crotch. His boot landed hard in the man's groin, and a scream rose from the cop's lips as the pain shot up through his body.

His hand was still on his gun, a Sig-Sauer P226, a neat, compact black metal handgun that was used by the US Navy Seals and FBI as well as by hundreds of local sheriffs' departments.

Josh stepped forward, swung his crutch in the air, then smashed it hard into the policeman's hand. It struck his knuckles with the force of a metal cane and the gun fell to the ground.

Marshall bent down swiftly, grabbed the gun and jabbed it up against the policeman's head. The man was sweating with fear: a thin film of liquid was streaming down his red, blotched face. He looked wildly towards Marshall, then at Josh. 'Don't hurt me,' he whimpered. 'I got a wife, kids. Please don't hurt me.'

Josh picked up his crutch from the ground, using it to steady himself, then leaned towards the man.

'Whose blood was found at this crime scene?' he said, his tone harsh and determined. 'What's his name?'

'I don't know.'

Marshall rammed the gun harder against the side of the cop's head. 'Tell us,' he said slowly. 'Tell us now, or your brains are cactus fertilizer.'

The man's nose was starting to bleed. 'I don't know, I tell you – I don't know. The name is classified. I'm just guarding the crime scene.'

'Maybe you want me to make it simpler for you to understand,' growled Marshall. 'Tell us before I count to three, or you're a fucking dead man.'

'No, no,' pleaded the policeman.

'One,' said Marshall.

The cop was starting to shake with fear. 'No, *please*.'

'Two,' said Marshall, his tone even harsher.

'I don't know anything.'

Marshall cocked the P226. 'Three,' he said. He pronounced the word with an air of finality.

'I don't know,' said the policeman again.

Marshall's finger was taking first pressure on the trigger. He glanced towards Josh.

'Christ, no,' said Josh. 'He doesn't know anything.'

'Then we finish him,' said Marshall.

'That's murder,' said Josh angrily. 'Bloody leave him. He doesn't know anything.'

'No, we finish him now,' snarled Marshall.

His face was red, and his stare was locked onto Josh who could see the violence building up inside the older man. The gun was squeezed tight in Marshall's hand, as if he was on the brink of shooting.

Josh leaned down, gripped Marshall's hand tight, and pulled the gun away. 'Leave it,' he snapped. 'We kill a cop, we're in real trouble.'

Kate had put a hamburger down on the table, followed by a bottle of beer. Josh took the food, picked out the fried onions from it and started eating.

'Why are you helping me?' he said, looking up at the woman.

After getting back to the house, Kate had given Josh another injection that had put him back to sleep for eight hours. She insisted that he needed the sleep, and Josh hadn't felt like resisting. He knew from what they had learned out in the scrubland that morning that a boy had been killed at the same time as he had been shot, and the police were searching the area for a man with an English accent.

And now he also knew that Marshall could be violent. Maybe Kate as well.

Maybe I killed the boy? *Maybe they did?*

'Why shouldn't I help you?' said Kate, her tone cool. 'I'm a helpful person.'

She was wearing black jeans that clung tight to her curves, and a white T-shirt with a black diamond printed on its back. When Josh had woken up later that afternoon she had dressed the wounds on his neck and his leg, clearing away the old bandages and replacing them with new ones. Without her and Marshall he'd probably be dead by now. Or languishing in an Arizona jail.

Josh took another bite of the hamburger, then looked back up at Kate. 'You could have just pulled me out of the ditch, patched me up, then sent me on my way – that would've been helpful. Nobody goes to this amount of trouble unless they have an angle.'

'I'm a doctor, remember?' said Kate, a flash of anger in her eyes. 'I'm *meant* to look after sick people.' She sat down opposite him, reaching across the tiny Formica table and taking a bite of the hamburger for herself. Anger makes her hungry, Josh noted. She devours her food the same way she devours arguments: with a ravenous appetite.

'No,' he replied, shaking his head. 'A doctor would just take me to a hospital, patching me up on the way if they had to.' He paused, letting the silence hang between them. 'A regular doctor, that is.' His gaze flicked towards her. For a moment, Josh wondered if he'd gone too far. I hardly know this woman, he reminded himself. I have no idea where the boundaries are.

Then her face sagged, her spirit deflating like a tyre that has just been punctured. She sniffed, and wiped away a small tear that had started to form in the corner of her left eye.

'It's painful for me to talk about,' said Kate.

'What's painful?'

'The reason.'

'What reason?'

'The reason I'm here,' she said. 'The reason I'm helping you.'

Josh pushed away the hamburger, leaning forward on the table. He reached forward, brushing the edge of her palm with the tips of his fingers. Briefly, she looked as if she were about to pull her hand away, but then she let it stay in place. 'Look at me, Kate,' he said. 'I'm all shot to pieces. I don't even know who I am. I'm no threat to anyone. You can talk to me.' He paused. 'Hell, I probably won't even remember anything you say to me.'

Kate laughed, throwing back her red hair as she did so, although Josh noticed that there was not much happiness in her expression. She looked down at the floor. 'I was married,' she said. 'To a man called Danny.'

'Who was he?'

'A soldier, like you.'

Josh nodded, but remained silent.

'A Navy Seal. We grew up together, down in New Mexico. Small town. High school sweethearts, the whole thing. He joined the Navy straight after graduation, while I went off to medical school. But we always stayed together, no matter how far apart we were. Nobody else ever mattered.'

'Where is he now?'

'He's dead.'

Again, Josh reached out for her hand to comfort her, but this time she took it away.

'He was killed in Afghanistan. Just over two years ago. He was stationed at a place called Khost, along the Afghanistan–Pakistan border. He was part of a special-forces unit. Men sent out alone into the small villages, working under cover, looking for al-Qaeda leaders.'

'One of them killed him?'

'I don't know who killed him. He was shot in a struggle, that's all I know. Three times through the chest. Nobody knows who did it. He was left for dead beside some road somewhere. He was there for thirty-six hours in a ditch, without anything to eat or drink or any kind of treatment. A woman from one of the local villages took him in, and started nursing him. She gave him food and water, and tried to put some bandages on his wounds.' She paused, wiping away another tear. 'But it was already too late for Danny. A hospital might have been able to help him, but this woman had no antibiotics, not even any proper disinfectants. He died after three days and the US Army picked his body up a week later when word finally got back to them about where he was.'

'But she helped him, didn't she?' said Josh. 'That's what this is all about.'

Kate looked up at him, her gaze locking with his. 'She saw a soldier in a ditch, and she did what she could to help him, even though he might be the enemy.'

'As I might be.'

Kate looked away again. 'I don't think so,' she replied. 'But that's what I'm doing out here. Taking some time to myself to get over losing Danny. He was the only man who ever meant anything to me, and now he's gone.'

She stood up, walking towards the sink to pour herself a glass of water. 'And that's why I had to help you. Who knows? Maybe there's a wife out there somewhere, worrying about where you are and what's happened to you. I'll do what I can because I know how she'll feel if you die.'

SIX

Saturday, June 6th. Morning.
Josh put the crutch to one side and started walking. He pressed his wounded foot against the dusty ground, testing the nerves to see how much pain he could bear. The leg stung, as though it was being bitten, and the pain rippled up through it into his groin. Josh gritted his teeth and hobbled towards the kitchen.

I've got to lose the crutch. It draws too much attention to a man.

The sun had already climbed high in the sky and the air was getting hot. Josh hadn't checked what time it was, but he guessed that it was between ten and eleven. Another twelve hours' sleep, he figured: Kate had given him his regular cocktail of sleeping juice and painkillers the night before. *Another half-day closer to getting my strength back.*

He had tried to hold on to his thoughts as he woke up, but there had been nothing there this morning: the only thing he remembered was Kate sobbing about her lost husband just before he went to bed, and his attempts to comfort her.

But what use is it? he asked himself. *How can you comfort a woman who has lost her husband?*

Josh pushed open the kitchen door. Kate was already at the table, the remains of some cereal in front of her. She looked up at Josh and smiled. 'You feeling better?' she asked.

Josh nodded. 'Some,' he replied.

'The crutch,' said Kate. 'Where is it?'

'Back in the room,' answered Josh. 'I wanted to walk without it.'

Kate stood up, looking down at the leg. 'How does it feel?'

'Hurts a bit,' said Josh. 'When I put pressure on it.'

'Don't push it too far. You'll end up with a permanent limp if you don't let it heal properly.'

Josh poured some coffee from the pot next to the sink. He stirred in just a dash of milk and took a sip of the resultant strong liquid. The headache had subsided this morning for the first time in the past week. Now his head felt surprisingly clear, settled and relaxed.

I can think again.

He glanced towards the television playing in the corner and punched up the volume. The weather girl was just wrapping up her forecast. A forty-degree high, and no hint of rain. Not even a cloud. Why do they bother with a forecast? wondered Josh. It's a desert. *Of course it's bloody hot.*

'Returning to our main story of the week, the Ben Lippard murder in Coconino County,' said the newsreader.

A picture had come up on the screen. A boy. About sixteen, and a thrash-metal fan, Josh guessed, judging by the long black hair that fell down past his shoulders. His face was long, and thin, but with eyes that were sparkling with curiosity and boyish life.

So young, thought Josh, looking at the face staring back at him.

'And there is still no sign of his friend Luke Marsden who went missing on the same day,' continued the newsreader.

Another picture flashed onto the screen. Another boy, also about sixteen. He had a rounder face than the Lippard kid with sandy hair cut away from his face. He was wearing a pale blue shirt with a couple of buttons open at the neck, revealing a strong chest

'Nobody has heard from Luke Marsden since the day of

Ben Lippard's murder last Monday,' continued the newsreader. 'The sheriff's office say they are urgently looking for Luke, but have so far failed to make contact with him.'

Josh looked at the picture again. The boy's face had the innocence that nearly all teenagers have, but there was an edge to the half-smile that was playing on his lips. A smart kid, thought Josh. A kid who knows more than he lets on.

'The sheriff's office has told this station that if anyone sees Luke they should contact them immediately,' continued the newsreader.

Something was happening in Josh's mind. An image had started to play out in front of him. He could see a flat landscape, with rocks in the distance. He could see the sun burning down from the sky. He could see scrub, and a cloud of dust. He squeezed his eyes tight shut, blocking out all the light, and concentrated his mind, closing out the sound of the television. A boy. He could see a boy.

A gunshot.

Another boy was falling.

Ben.

Then a voice. Josh redoubled his concentration, trying to relax his mind so that nothing would soften or blur the moving picture that was playing out in his mind. One of the boys, Luke, was shouting something. He was looking towards Josh and his lips were forming words but although Josh could see he could not hear.

Try, he told himself.

What did he say to you?

'And now, with the latest sports round-up,' said the newsreader, 'here's Dan Smotten.'

Josh cursed and opened his eyes, noticing that Kate was looking at him. The picture had gone, blown right out of his mind. He took a breath, concentrating, struggling to bring it back.

Nothing.

'A memory?' asked Kate, her tone hopeful.

Josh nodded.

Kate stood up from her chair, walked across the room and gripped Josh's arm. He could feel her nails digging into his skin. 'What?' she said quickly. 'What was the memory?'

Josh nodded towards the TV screen. 'Him,' he replied slowly. 'I was there. I saw Ben murdered. And I saw Luke. He was running away from me and he was shouting at the same time.'

Kate's nails dug harder into the skin of Josh's forearm. 'What?' she insisted. 'What did he say?'

Josh shook his head from side to side. 'I don't know. The memory is blurred. I can see, but I can't hear. I can feel him looking at me, and see his lips move, but I don't know what it is he is saying.'

'Try, Josh, try.'

Josh broke free of Kate's grip. He took another hit of the coffee, letting the caffeine flood into his veins, hoping that the energy would put him back in touch with the memory. Nothing. His mind was still a blank.

'I can't see anything else,' he replied. 'It's gone.'

'It's a start,' she said. 'Once your memory starts recovering, it should all start coming back to you.'

'So long as you stay safe,' said Marshall as he stepped into the room.

'I know something about that murder,' said Josh. 'I don't know what it is exactly, but I know *something*. I was there.'

'Maybe it *was* you,' said Marshall. 'The Sheriff's office certainly seems pretty damned keen to talk to you.'

The question had been rattling through his mind for the past few days. Am I a murderer? he kept asking himself. *Could I shoot a boy in cold blood?*

'Do the letters S–A–S mean anything to you?' asked Marshall.

Josh paused. His mind was jumping all over the place,

making associations, but he couldn't pin anything down. The headache was coming back: the chisel was starting to tap away insistently at the inside of his skull again. 'No, nothing,' he answered blankly.

'The Regiment,' said Marshall. 'Hereford.'

Josh shook his head. 'Nothing. Why?'

Marshall took a step closer. There was still a bruise on his arm from the fight with the policeman yesterday, and his eyes had the rough appearance of a man who had slept badly. 'Couple of days back, when we were shooting together,' he said, 'you chose a Sig-Sauer P228 like it came natural to you. Like you already knew that gun. So I checked around with some of the veterans who use my website. I wanted to know which British regiments might have trained with that handgun. One guy had the answer.' He paused, looking towards the light beaming in through the window. 'The SAS. British special forces. They used to use Browning High Powers but then they moved on to Sig-Sauers, both the P226 and the P228 models.'

Josh let the words settle in his mind, rubbing his hand against the thick stubble that was growing fast on his face. He repeated the three letters a couple of times to himself. He closed his eyes and tried to relax his mind, intoning the letters silently in his head. No, nothing. No triggers, no flashes of recognition, no pictures. *I don't even know what the sodding letters stand for.*

'Mean anything to you, boy?'

Josh shook his head. 'I already had one memory today. I think that's my lot.' He attempted a smile but could tell it was not likely to be reciprocated.

'You're SAS,' persisted Marshall. 'The guns you know. The way you handle yourself when you shoot. I'm sure of it.' He took another step towards Josh, so close that he could smell the shaving foam that had just been washed off the older man's cheeks. In Marshall's eyes, Josh could suddenly see a flash of the same anger and violence that he had seen yesterday: in that second Josh was certain that Marshall was a killer.

Maybe it was *you* that shot the boy? thought Josh. *Maybe that's why your daughter happened to be in the area.*

'What I want to know is this,' continued Marshall. 'What the hell is a British special forces man doing in the back-waters of Arizona tracking a pair of runaway teenagers?'

Josh could feel his own anger starting to build. The chisel was getting worse, slamming into the side of his skull, and his neck wound was playing up, sending tiny jabs of pain running down from his neck into his spine. 'I don't bloody know, do I?' shouted Josh. 'I've lost my fucking memory.'

'What are you, boy?' snapped Marshall. 'What the hell are you?'

Kate stood up. 'Easy, Dad – he's not well.'

Josh held his hand against his brow. 'I can't handle this any more,' he said. 'I'm going into that police station tonight to find out who I am, and what the hell I've done.'

'You're not going, man!' shouted Marshall.

Josh stood up straight. 'Nobody gives me orders,' he snapped. He brushed past Marshall, heading towards the door.

'You're going to walk the whole way,' shouted Marshall. 'It's ten miles.'

Josh and Kate had been watching crap TV for hours. Marshall had gone to bed. Josh looked at Kate. 'I need a smoke,' he said. 'You got any cigarettes?'

Kate shook her head. 'I'm a doctor, remember?'

Josh stood up. 'I'm bloody gagging for one now. Maybe I could borrow the car and drive into town to get some. There should be a gas station open, even at this time of night.'

Kate turned to look at him. 'You've been okay without them until now.'

'Well, now I need one.'

'Good time to give up,' said Kate. 'If you made it through three days, you're over the worst. Take some advice. Quit.'

Josh grinned. He reached down into his pocket. The car keys he'd picked up from the table earlier were right there. Doesn't matter what she says, he told himself. I need to get into town.

'I'm going,' he said.

Turning around, Josh walked swiftly from the kitchen and out into the back yard. The night was quiet and still. He walked across to where the Avalanche pick-up truck was parked, pressed the key button, and watched the doors unlock. He sat himself down in the driver's seat, glancing around for the ignition, and checking out where the other controls were. He fired up the engine. Suddenly, the door burst open. Kate was staring at him, her eyes burning with anger. 'Where the hell are you going?'

'I told you, I need a smoke.'

'Then I'm coming with you.'

Kate sat down in the Avalanche's passenger seat, slamming the door behind her. Josh pulled the car out onto the road, heading in the direction of the small town. 'Just on your way in,' said Kate coldly, 'there's a Texaco gas station. You'll get some cigarettes there. Since you seem to need them so badly.'

Christ, thought Josh. With this woman on my case, I really *will* need to start smoking.

They both remained silent for the twenty minutes that it took to drive into town. When he saw the Texaco sign, Josh pulled up. 'I'll be just two minutes,' he said.

'Don't be any longer,' said Kate. 'And you can't smoke in the car. Marshall doesn't like it.'

Josh walked towards the counter. He had no intention of buying any cigarettes. So far as he knew he didn't smoke, and he certainly didn't plan to start now. It was just an excuse to get away from Kate. He stopped at the counter, picked up two packets of gum, and looked up at the boy behind the desk. 'Where's the gents'?' he said as he handed over a dollar bill.

The boy nodded towards a back door. Josh walked up to it and went through. There was one door that led to the toilets, and another that led outside. He stepped quickly through it. The gas station backed onto some scrubland, leading down to the town. Despite the aching in his leg, Josh started running into the darkness.

By the time Kate realised he'd slipped out of sight, it would be too late.

The rocks provided some cover. Josh hobbled between the boulders, leaning against one, then another to support himself as he moved forward. Keep going, he told himself.

High above him, the moon was casting a silvery light down on the plain. The town of Boisdale had a population of ten or fifteen thousand people judged Josh, thinking back to the map he had studied at Kate's house. It had a Wal-Mart, a Motel 6, and a carpet factory that was the main local employer. If you want quiet, Boisdale was the place to find it, reckoned Josh as he looked down towards the neat row of suburban dwellings that led down towards the centre of the town.

Nobody comes here? *So why the hell did I?*

The Sheriff's office was on the edge of town, on Roosevelt Avenue. It was a big, square concrete block, set fifty yards back from the road. About a hundred metres long and thirty deep, its front was protected by a wall. At the back was a fifty-square-metre courtyard. Josh raised a pair of binoculars he had brought with him to his eyes and peered down into the yard: he could see a shooting range, a pound for keeping the dogs, and a row of motorcycles.

If I can keep out of the way of the dogs, that's how I'm going in.

He edged forward. The boulders were littered along a patch of scrubland that led up to the start of the town. From here it was thirty yards to the sheriff's office. He had equipped himself with a grappling rope taken from Marshall's garage, plus the Sig-Sauer P228. *It's just a small-town sheriff's office*, he told himself. *It's already two in the morning. At most there's going to be one fat old night guard on duty, and he's probably fallen asleep in front of the TV. I shouldn't have any trouble breaking in here.*

Somewhere in there they may have my blood sample. If they've tested the DNA, they will know who I am. In a few minutes I'll know as well.

Josh moved down next to the back wall, walking as quickly as he could on his wounded leg, and as he did so he could feel the adrenalin starting to surge through his veins. Then he paused. A snake was crawling across the ground. Josh remained perfectly still, letting the animal pass, but he realised that he was sweating with fear. He looked up at the wall. It was seven feet high, made from concrete breeze-blocks. About fifteen, maybe twenty years old, he judged. Old enough for the mortar between the blocks to be crumbling. He dug his nails into the space between the blocks. There was some give there. Enough for a man to get a grip.

Whoever I am, this comes naturally to me.

Josh cast aside the rope and started to scale the wall. He used the strength in his shoulders, trying to avoid using his wounded leg as anything more than a dead weight. He stuck his fingers into the mortar, pulled, then rested his legs, balanced himself, and started again. In three swift movements, his fingers were gripping the top of the wall. He hauled himself upwards, lying flat on its one-foot-wide top, looking down into the courtyard below. A seven-foot drop. *So long as I don't land on the wounded leg, or on my neck, I'll be fine.*

But suddenly Josh could hear the sounds of a siren wailing: his eardrums were starting to rattle as the screeching noise seeped into his brain.

His gaze darted forward. A searchlight had flicked on at the back of the courtyard, bathing the building in a harsh, brilliant light. Josh could feel it dazzling his eyes. A shot rang out. Then another. Josh tried to look into the courtyard, but the light was too harsh.

Run, man, he told himself. *Run like every dog from hell was on your trail.*

Using his arms, Josh started to lower himself down from the wall. He pressed his feet and knees together, the same position he'd adopt for a parachute drop. His feet deflected the blow, then he rolled to the left to lessen the impact.

He turned to look back in the direction he'd come from, back up through the boulders, two, maybe three hundred yards, to where Kate had parked the Avalanche.

If she's still there, maybe I can make it.

Another volley of fire rang out from inside the station. Josh could see dust flicking down from the wall where the bullets were raking the concrete, sending flakes of it puffing into the air.

Christ, he thought to himself. They're not looking to make an arrest. *They're shooting to kill.*

He started to move forwards, dodging between the boulders that lined the route. His wounded leg felt dead, the pressure it had taken from the fall numbing all feeling in it. He paused, sheltering behind a boulder, glancing up towards the road. He could see the lights from the Texaco gas station. Kate was there, parked in a lay-by along the road, about fifty yards from the forecourt.

Another shot broke through the silence of the night air. Josh could hear it ricocheting off one of the rocks. Snipers must already be in position, he guessed. Ready and willing to shoot anything that moved.

It was fifty yards up a moderate ridge to the road. There were three boulders between here and there, Josh counted: enough to give him some cover if he could move quickly enough.

Another shot. Another ricochet from the boulder. Christ, thought Josh. *I haven't much time.* He started running. A man running for his life can handle a lot of pain, he reflected as he ducked behind the second boulder. He looked up. Thirty yards.

With luck, I can make it. Trouble is, I've used up most of my luck this week.

Josh pushed himself forwards with all the strength he could muster. The ground felt dusty beneath his feet, and he was taking care not to lose his grip. One stumble would certainly cost him his life. Behind him, he could see more searchlights starting to flood the night sky with their harsh artificial light.

One more boulder.

Josh ducked behind it, looking up to the road. He could hear the starter ignition turning in the Avalanche.

Then something else. Another engine. The sound of rotor blades. And the smell of avgas wafting down from the sky: a thick, nauseous smell that always made Josh's stomach churn.

Josh looked up, his heart already filled with dread.

A helicopter.

A searchlight was beaming out from its front turret, scouring the empty landscape.

'Come out with your hands up,' boomed a voice from a loudspeaker mounted on the chopper.

The beam of light swung out across the ridge, narrowly missing Josh as he ducked behind the boulder. Move, he told himself. Bloody move now, before that chopper completes its circuit.

He threw himself forwards again, ignoring the pain raging through him, burning up the few yards that separated him from the pick-up truck like a hare unleashed from its trap. The roar of the helicopter just forty yards from the ground was filling the sky with a deafening noise, splitting his eardrums. Its racket was only interrupted by the sound of gunfire behind him.

Five yards, he told himself.

A bullet kicked up a tiny cloud of dust to his left. He swerved, then lunged forward, grabbing the door of the Avalanche and hauling himself inside.

'What the hell have you started?' said Kate, looking up at him, a flash of anger in her eyes. 'World War Three?'

'Just bloody drive,' snapped Josh.

The motor was already running. It revved into life with a roar, and Kate steered the truck out on the highway.

'Not the road,' snapped Josh. 'And switch off the lights.'

'Oh, right,' said Kate. 'And how the hell am I meant to drive?'

Josh leaned across, flicking the light switch off with his hand. The lights died and the Avalanche was suddenly surrounded by darkness. He grabbed the steering wheel and yanked it hard to the right, pulling the truck off the tarmac and into the scrubland. From scouting the area earlier that day, Josh knew that the land stretching away from Boisdale was flat: there were a dozen miles until you hit a range of mountains that rose up sharply from the wilderness. It was pitted with craters and boulders. You would drive through it only with extreme caution.

Not at night, and not without lights on, thought Josh. *Unless it was your only chance of survival.*

The Avalanche started to bounce across the scrubland, the suspension rolling with each blow to the undercarriage. Pain shot through Josh as each thump lashed into him with the force of a leather whip. Kate was gripping the steering wheel, hanging onto it as if it were a rope from which she was dangling from a precipice.

He looked across at her. 'Out on the road, the chopper can pick us off. We might as well be waving a big flag saying "Shoot me". But a single truck in the darkness, in scrubland, with no lights on. That has a chance.'

'Yeah, but they'll find a wrecked truck in the morning,' said Kate. 'With a couple of corpses in it.'

'That's one possibility,' said Josh roughly. 'But we stay on the road, we're corpses for sure. They're not looking to take us in for questioning. They want us dead.'

The Avalanche swerved sideways as its front left tyre crashed over a boulder, then sank into a small crater. The truck shook as if it was about to break up, then found its grip again and jerked forwards.

Josh looked behind him. The light of the moon was starting to dim as a cloud drifted across it, and suddenly the plain was plunged into total darkness. Josh could hear the chopper: the noise of its blades cutting through the air filled the sky. Behind them the chopper's searchlight was sending out a narrow beam of light, flashing onto the ground, seeking its target. Looking forwards, he could only see a wall of blackness, into which they were driving at an ungodly speed.

Prayer time.

'You're doing great,' said Josh, glancing across at Kate. 'Just keep the wheel straight, and try to ride with all the knocks. We'll be okay.'

They drove for what seemed like an hour but which, when Josh checked his watch later, turned out to be just twenty minutes. The chopper's lights could only illuminate a narrow stretch of land at a time: by keeping an eye on that they could tell they were moving further and further away from it. Josh reckoned that they were about a mile away. They both remained silent, Kate clutching onto the steering wheel, Josh listening to the sky, monitoring the sound of the chopper.

'Here,' said Josh eventually. 'Stop here.'

In twenty minutes they had covered several miles of open scrubland. The sight and sounds of the chopper were no more. They had seen and heard nothing for at least five minutes. If the police had no fix on which direction they had been driving in, then they could be anywhere within a thirty mile radius of the road. They had vanished. For now.

They'll come looking for us in the morning, thought Josh. *We'll be okay until then.*

He stepped down out of the Avalanche. The temperature had dropped from the scorching heat of the day to a mild ten degrees centigrade at night, and there was a slight breeze, making it feel still cooler. The moon was still shaded by a cloud. It was impossible to see more than a few yards ahead, and he wasn't going to risk switching on the vehicle's head-lamps. Darkness I can handle, he told himself. *So long as no one is shooting at me.*

'What the fuck happened back there?' asked Kate angrily. 'You fucking tricked me. You were trying to break into the police station to find your file, weren't you? You must be fucking nuts.'

She was standing in front of him. Sweat soaked her blouse: through the damp material Josh could see the outline of her breasts. 'I triggered an alarm when I went over the wall,' he said. 'That place was wired up like the Pentagon. It's not just some sheriff's office in Hicksville. The place must be crawling with Feds.' He paused. 'What do they have in Boisdale to protect it with that kind of firepower?'

'Nothing,' said Kate. 'It's just a factory town. Fifteen thousand people. Used to be twenty-five thousand, but times haven't been so good in the carpet business.'

Josh took a swig of water from the bottle on the passenger seat of the Avalanche. 'Something,' he said firmly. 'There's something there, and I'm betting it's to do with those boys.'

'They're just teenagers,' said Kate. 'At least that's what it said in the news. Hoodlums.'

Josh passed the water bottle across to Kate. 'Bollocks,' he said. 'Unless I've lost my mind as well as my memory, there's something going on in this town. And I reckon those two boys were at the centre of it.'

'What?' said Kate. 'What do you think it is?'

Josh shook his head. 'I don't know.'

'Think,' Kate ordered him.

'First we rest,' said Josh.

He looked around the area where the Avalanche had come to a halt. There was a ridge in the ground, leading down to what looked in the murky light like the dried-out remains of a river bed. Across from that were some large boulders where Josh reckoned they might find some shelter in the grooves in the rock carved out by water. 'Over there,' he said. 'It's just after two in the morning now. Sun rises about six. We sleep for two hours, then start walking. Once the sun is up, they're going to be able to follow the tracks of that truck into the scrub. We don't want to be anywhere near it when they find it.'

Josh looked at Kate. 'You should go home. It's too dangerous for you out here.'

'I'm staying,' she said.

SEVEN

Sunday, June 7th. Morning.

In the distance, Josh could see the police cordon blocking off the main road. Two patrol cars were slewed across the highway, stopping and checking everyone entering the town. Me, thought Josh. It's me they are looking for.

A dangerous time to start scouting around. But I don't have any other choice.

'Where do we start?' asked Kate.

'Let's pick up the trail at the motel,' said Josh. 'Place like this, any strangers in town are going to be passing through the motel.'

Josh looked down from the hill. They were a mile outside the town, to the east, on one of the hillsides that rose up towards the canyons in the far distance. Josh had woken at four a.m., using the alarm on his wristwatch, surprised to find Kate curled into his chest and sleeping soundly. The rocks were a reddish sandstone, not a hard granite: you could sleep on them in moderate comfort. His wounds ached, but no worse than usual. He woke Kate with a gentle shake, then started walking. The chopper would find the Avalanche within a couple of hours once the sun had risen. They had to be at least four or five miles away by then: that meant two hours of solid walking.

Josh's first decision had been to hide the Avalanche. As soon as dawn broke, there would be police helicopters out, scouring the scrubland. Leave it in the open and the truck would lead them straight back to Kate. They had to hide it somewhere that would be invisible from the air; it could take weeks to track it on foot.

He'd scoured the area in the dark. There was a dried-out creek, but he rejected that because it didn't provide enough cover. Then he found a small stand of trees, but that wasn't going to work either, he decided. The Avalanche was a big truck, and a helicopter was going to spot it underneath any tree if it was flying low enough. Eventually he found a group of tall boulders arranged in a haphazard circle, which formed a natural shelter. He drove the Avalanche inside. It was a tight squeeze, and he tore a big gash in the side panel of the machine as he tried to ram it into the limited space.

'I'll pay you for the damage,' he joked to Kate. 'If the insurance doesn't cover it.'

After hiding the Avalanche, they started the long walk to town. Josh stepped carefully across the rough ground, telling Kate, a couple of yards ahead of him, to do the same. It was hard walking in the darkness, weaving a path through the boulders, brambles, and cactus. Josh dragged a stick behind him to brush away any traces of the trail. That was slow work. Even so, they made good progress, following an arc that Josh had calculated would take them back towards the town.

After two miles they had found a creek, with some water in a pool surrounded by thick evergreens. There was nobody around and Josh stripped down to his boxer shorts, washing himself in the cool water. Kate slipped into the pool in her pale blue cotton bra and pants, then dried herself with her T-shirt before slipping it back on. In the half-light Josh could see that her body was slim and lithe as he watched her splash the water through her hair and face: her figure was toned and tanned, the physique of an athlete rather than a model, but supple and sexy all the same.

She might be a doctor, thought Josh, but she isn't a city girl. *She knows how to survive in the wild.*

'How do you want to get there?' asked Kate, pointing to the town.

'On foot,' replied Josh with a rough grin. 'But if you see a cab, hail it.'

Kate smiled back and started walking. A track led down the hillside away from the patrol cars, then the first section of paved road led up to a truck depot, closed this morning, with just a pair of chrome monsters sitting on its forecourt. Ahead, a mile distant, Josh could see the Motel 6 sign rising thirty feet into the air. They kept walking, pacing their way slowly through the first of the suburban streets that led to the centre of town. It was still only eight in the morning, and although the sun was starting to rise through the sky the temperature was still only around fifteen degrees, and a gentle breeze was blowing.

Kate suggested that they should stop at the diner, on the corner of Coral Street and Roosevelt Avenue, and grab some coffee. 'I'll wait outside,' said Josh. 'You go in and get them.'

When Kate returned, she handed him an extra-large cup of foamy, milky coffee, and two honey waffles, wrapped in white tissue paper. Josh hunched down against the fence of the parking lot and started eating. The waffles tasted thick and doughy, and Josh didn't care for the taste. Still, he told himself, it doesn't matter: I need all the calories I can get.

'Did you see the man in the blue sweatshirt?' said Josh, glancing towards the window of the diner.

Kate nodded.

'What do you make of him?'

Kate shrugged. 'Bald guy reading the sports section of the newspaper,' she replied. 'I didn't make anything of him.'

'He's a Fed.'

Kate took a long sip of her coffee, looking thoughtful. 'An FBI agent? Is that what you mean?'

Josh nodded. 'There's something about the way he's sitting, just minding his own business. It looks artificial, practised – like he learned it on a training course.' He turned towards Kate. 'He's surveillance.'

'For you?'

Josh shook his head. 'I don't know. But I bet this town is crawling with agents – it has to be if they've got a helicopter stationed here. They're looking for somebody.'

And if it's not me, then who the hell is it?

Josh slung the rest of his coffee down his throat, finished off the waffles and started walking. The limp from his wounded leg was starting to heal: he could just about conceal the fact that he'd taken a bullet in the past few days. He hadn't shaved since he was wounded and the hair on his face had started to grow into a thick black beard. A trim, and it would look like he had worn it for years. That, plus civilian clothes, should make him different enough from any pictures of him that might be on file.

Just so long as I don't draw any attention to myself.

They know who I am, thought Josh as he walked on steadily. But do they know what I look like?

It was half a mile to the Motel 6, a distance covered in ten minutes at a steady pace. The building was at the end of the long commercial strip: a couple of car dealerships, a hairdresser, a hardware store, and then the motel. As he glanced up at it, Josh wondered if he had been there before. There was no flash of recognition but if he'd been staying in the town he must have visited the motel.

And even if I don't recognise *it*, somebody might recognise *me*.

Josh nodded towards the entrance. 'We go in together.'

'They might think we want a room.' She smiled. 'For an hour or so.'

Josh stepped inside. The clerk was watching some baseball on the TV. A boy of nineteen or twenty, Josh judged, he had floppy back hair, and two prominent spots on his left cheek. 'You looking for a room?' he said, looking up at Josh.

Josh scanned the boy's face for some sign that he recognised him, but there was not a flicker. The reception was flat-pack standard, the same yellow and black furniture found in every Motel 6 lobby in the country. It looked out onto the main road, and behind the desk was a set of photos of the main local tourist attractions: the Grand Canyon, Death Valley, Phoenix, then Las Vegas. Those were all a hundred miles away or more, Josh noted. The only guests that this Motel had were travelling salesmen.

'We're looking for some information,' said Josh.

The boy glanced first at Josh, then at Kate. His name was Darren, Josh noted from the name tag pinned to his regulation yellow shirt. There was a look of suspicion in his eyes, but also a spark of curiosity. Life was slow on the desk of this Motel 6, Josh figured. Darren was desperate for anything that might liven the morning up.

'What kind of information?' he said.

'Information about guests, Darren,' continued Josh.

Darren turned down the sound on the television.

'We're freelance journalists,' continued Josh. 'We're researching a programme for the BBC. We're interested in the Lippard story. We're just wondering if there are any other reporters in town covering the case who we might be able to hook up with?'

He talked slowly, keeping his tone relaxed. Only liars talk quickly, Josh reminded himself.

Darren's expression was that of a man who knew that he probably shouldn't help but couldn't fight the temptation. 'The BBC?' he said. 'What's your name?'

Josh hesitated. 'Ben,' he said. 'Ben Webster, and this is Kate. We're researchers.'

'Yeah, there *have* been some reporters checking in,' said Darren.

'Who?' said Josh.

Darren looked down at his desk book. 'A TV crew from Phoenix were here for a couple of night. News Five. They parked their van right there in the lot. But they left this morning.'

'Who else?'

Darren looked down at his book again. 'That was it. I guess the Lippard killing isn't such a big deal outside this town. There's a woman from the local paper who's been writing stories for the *Phoenix Republic* and the *Las Vegas Sun*. She has an office just a few blocks down this strip. She might be able to help you out.'

'What's her name?' asked Kate.

'Elaine,' replied Darren. 'Elaine Johnston. Paper comes out Monday, so she might even be in the office this morning.'

'Can I look at the registration book?' asked Josh.

If I stayed here, I must have given a name, he reasoned to himself. If I see it, then maybe I'll recognise it.

Darren looked uneasy. 'Company rules,' he said. 'I'm not allowed.'

'Just a quick look,' said Josh, attempting a smile.

'No way, man,' snapped Darren.

Josh reached down for the roll of dollar bills in his pocket. He took them out. 'Maybe I could buy you a drink.'

'Like I said, company policy,' said Darren quickly.

Kate glanced up at him. 'We'd be really grateful,' she said.

'This is the only job I got,' said Darren angrily. 'If you don't drop it, I'm calling the cops.'

'Okay, okay,' said Josh quickly. He took Kate by the arm. 'Come on, we're going.'

Outside, the sun was higher in the sky and there was more traffic on the road. Josh hesitated as he left the Motel 6, glancing back towards the two-storey row of rooms stretching back a hundred yards from the lobby. I have been here before, he realised.

I might even have stayed at this motel before I was shot.

'Some more coffee,' Josh said to Kate. He was thirsty again: the same dry, burning thirst in his throat that he'd had ever since he'd been shot. 'Then we go see if this Elaine woman works on Sunday mornings.'

Another man sitting alone and sipping a coffee. This guy had a baseball cap pulled down tight onto his forehead. Josh looked at him once, through the window of the restaurant, then averted his gaze. More surveillance, he judged. He couldn't be sure how he knew. Maybe I've had that training myself, he mused. Maybe that's why I can recognise them.

Kate came out of the restaurant with two cups of coffee and two turkey-breast sandwiches, and walked across to where Josh was waiting. Ten yards away, a couple were getting their kids out of their car, and a group of bikers had just pulled up in the parking lot of the diner. There were six of them: big men, with long hair, muscles that bulged out of their T-shirts, and fat guts that hung out of their jeans. Half past ten. Boisdale was starting to wake up.

'Let's go,' said Kate. 'We can eat while we walk. If we're going to be sure of catching this reporter we need to get to her office now.'

Josh started to walk down the street, taking bites from his sandwich as he did so.

'Josh,' cried a woman's voice from the parking lot.

He ignored her and carried on walking. Who the hell is Josh? he wondered.

'Josh,' she shouted again.

Is that me she's calling?

Quiet, woman, he thought. Too much commotion and you're going to alert that spotter sitting at the back of the diner.

'Hell, Josh, aren't you even going to say hello to me?'

Suddenly the voice's owner was tugging at the sleeve of

his shirt. Up ahead, Josh could see Kate spinning around to see what was happening.

Josh looked down. The woman was maybe twenty, twenty-one. She had long blonde hair tied up behind her head, and a thick chubby face. She could have been a size twelve, borderline fourteen. She was wearing tight blue jeans, and a yellow Madonna T-shirt that exposed a roll of tanned flesh around her midriff. A pair of studs pierced her belly button. Around her neck there was a gold cross, and a pair of silver earrings dangled from her lobes.

'What did you call me?'

Suddenly frightened, the woman backed away, letting go of Josh's sleeve. It was his turn to grab hold of her arm.

'What did you call me?' said Josh, his voice angrier this time.

'Josh.' She hesitated, her expression hurt and confused. 'Josh, I . . . I . . .'

'Josh – you called me Josh?'

The woman pulled her arm away. 'Let go of me, you asshole.'

She turned, walking quickly across the tarmac of the parking lot. Josh started to hurry after her. 'Stop,' he snapped.

To his left, he could see one of the bikers stepping away from the Harley Touring bikes – some of them bastardised, with different handlebars stuck onto the original frames. The man was wearing leather trousers, a white linen shirt, and a thick pair of studded leather gloves.

'This guy bothering you, lady?' he asked the woman.

'Get him away from me,' she said.

A tear was already running down the side of her face.

'I just need to—' But then Josh saw that the biker was stepping towards him and further back two more bikers were climbing down from their Harleys, watching closely.

'The lady doesn't want to talk,' said the first one. 'Take a hike, bud.'

Josh knew that he was in no shape for a fight: certainly not for a brawl with three two-hundred-and-fifty-pound bikers.

Now Kate was behind him and was tugging at his sleeve. 'Leave it,' she snapped.

'Yeah, leave it, man,' said the biker, leering in the direction of Kate. 'You already got a girlfriend.'

'We're going,' said Kate, taking Josh's arm and steering him towards the road. A truck went by, belching a thick cloud of dirty exhaust fumes into the air. Josh choked. Behind him, he could see the young woman going into the diner, talking to the biker who had come to her rescue. Sir Galahad, thought Josh to himself. *In her dreams.*

'What are you doing, you idiot?' snapped Kate. 'You get into a fight, the police are going to come and arrest you.'

'That woman,' said Josh. 'She knew my name.'

'Your name?'

'Josh. She called me Josh.'

Kate smiled, her expression brightening.

'Josh,' repeated Kate, rolling the sound on her tongue. 'I like it. Kind of suits you. I would have had you down as a Sam or an Ed. But Josh will do just fine.'

'How did she know who I was?' said Josh.

'Don't you have any memories?' asked Kate hopefully.

Josh shook his head. 'I must have spent time here,' he said. 'Maybe before I was shot?'

But why? he asked himself. *What was I doing here?*

Josh looked back towards the diner. The spotter, the man he had seen earlier, had finished his coffee and folded away his newspaper. He was staring straight at them.

Josh tugged Kate by the arm. 'Quick,' he said. 'I think he's moving in on us.'

Kate glanced towards the restaurant window.

'Don't look,' hissed Josh.

He started walking along the street. From the corner of

his eye he could see the spotter walking out of the restaurant, then glancing up and down the street. Josh tried to assess him. *My best guess is that he doesn't know who I am. I'm just someone who's acting suspiciously around town, and he wants to find out more.*

'The newspaper office,' said Josh.

From the directions that Darren had given them, the office should only be a couple of hundred yards up this street.

'You sure?' Kate asked nervously.

'No,' snapped Josh. 'But it's the best option we have. And don't walk too fast or that guy's going to call down half the FBI on our trail.'

Elaine Johnston cast a professional eye over Kate and Josh as they sat in the chairs opposite her. *Advertisers or stories,* thought Josh. *We have to fall into one category or the other. Otherwise, she's not interested.*

'What do you want to know about?' she asked.

'The Lippard murder,' answered Josh.

The office of the *Boisdale Ledger* occupied two rooms, on the third floor of a modern concrete office building that also housed an accounting firm, a travel agency and a couple of farm-machinery distributors. Johnston's desk was a mass of paper. Five empty coffee cups perched on top of a few old files, and there were two packets of nicotine patches, both opened. Today she was the only person home.

'Everyone wants to know about that,' she said.

Johnston was a woman in her fifties, wearing grey slacks and a black sweater. He hair was greying, cut short, but her face was fresh and inquisitive. She was, Josh noted, possibly the only person in Arizona without any kind of a tan.

'We're researching a TV documentary for the BBC,' continued Josh. 'Looking at small-town murder cases. My name is Ben Webster, and this is my assistant Kate. We were hoping that you might be able to tell us a bit more about the case.' He paused. 'Perhaps you could be on the programme.'

'On the BBC?' Johnston laughed. 'Like the Queen, maybe.'

'Maybe,' said Josh, with a smile. 'And there would be a fee, of course.'

'What do you want to know?'

Kate leaned forwards. 'Just whatever *you* know. Take it from the beginning.'

Johnston shot Kate a look that suggested she didn't like her much, then glanced back at Josh. She played with her pencil as if it was a cigarette. 'Ben and Luke were just a couple of computer nerds,' she said. 'We got lots of them around here. Nothing different about these two. They were fifteen, at the local high school They were friends with each other, but not with many other kids. The girls weren't interested. Too many spots and not enough money. Not a combination to get the cheerleaders hot.' Johnston laughed. 'Not even here in Boisdale.'

'What kind of families?' asked Josh.

Johnston shrugged. 'They weren't millionaires, that's for sure. Ben's father was a car mechanic. Ben lived with both parents, about six miles out of town. Nothing grand, but a nice home, with an acre of land and a small pool.'

'And Luke? How about Luke?'

'He lived with his mom, Emily, 'bout ten miles from town, off the Havertree Road. Ask around, people will tell you about Emily. She used to be the town drunk. Always falling out of bars at two in the morning. Town slut as well, from what people say. Nobody knows who Luke's daddy is. Maybe Emily doesn't even know herself. If she does, she never told anyone.'

Josh looked across the room to the water cooler. 'Mind if I get a drink?' he asked.

Johnston nodded. Josh stepped across the room, filled a paper cup and gulped down the cold water. His throat still felt bone dry. He held the bandage tight against his neck:

some air had seeped into the wound, irritating the raw skin underneath.

'What happened to you?' asked Johnston.

'Fell off my bike,' said Josh. 'Emily? She still drinking?'

Johnston shook her head. 'No. Cleaned up her act about five, six years ago. Got religion, although I think that only lasted a couple of years. Anyway, it helped her straighten her head out. She lives outside of town, in what we locals call the empty country, in an old mining house. Just her and Luke. She's devoted to him.'

'The boys into anything?'

'As I said, computers,' said Johnston. 'They were both obsessed with their computers, the way young boys are these days. They both got into trouble at school for hacking into the school computer and changing everyone's grades. We wrote a story about it in the paper. I don't think they meant any harm. They were nice enough boys in their own way. It's a real shame about Ben.'

'They do any drugs?' asked Kate.

Johnston nodded. Her pencil was dangling from the side of her mouth now. 'Some, I reckon. Just some dope.' She laughed, and the pencil dropped to the floor. 'It's not the most exciting town in the world. Quite a few of the grown-ups do a bit of weed from time to time as well. It helps to pass the time, I believe. Emily grows some out on her land. That and some part-time waitressing are her only income.'

'How about crime?' asked Josh. 'Were the boys mixed up in anything like that?'

'Apart from hacking and dope?' replied Johnston. 'No, not as far as I know. They were okay boys. I spoke to the sheriff, Jim Kelly, yesterday. You spoken with him yet?'

Josh shook his head.

'Well, you'll need to.' She looked at Josh, giving him a smile that he found impossible to read. 'I could introduce you if you like.'

'Thanks,' answered Josh neutrally. 'Go on.'

Johnston sat back in her chair. The window was open, and the mid-morning sunlight was starting to stream into the untidy room. 'Right now, they don't have any significant leads. The best theory they have is that the boys were bored at school and decided to take off for a couple of days. Maybe they ran short of money, and tried to rip off one of the local dealers. That's a good enough reason to get shot. They reckon Luke will turn up in a few days, scared out of his wits. He'll tell them what happened, and then this case will be closed.'

Josh stood up, already glancing towards the door. 'Thanks,' he said. 'That was helpful.'

'I haven't told you anything that you couldn't have figured out for yourself by reading tomorrow's paper.'

Josh smiled. 'Still good to hear it in person,' he said. 'From someone who knows.'

'You going to make that programme?'

'We'll have to see.'

'Because I'd be happy to take part.'

Something about the smile with which Johnston delivered the offer told Josh that she didn't expect it to ever be taken up. 'We'll be in touch,' he said.

Then he took Kate's arm and started guiding her towards the door.

'So who are you really?' said Johnston.

'Like I said, researchers,' said Josh. 'For British TV.'

Johnston was following them towards the door. 'I'm a reporter,' she said. 'I have instincts, and I've learned to rely on them. I know when people are shilling me.' She reached across her desk, taking a card from a box perched next to her computer. 'You're involved,' she said, handing Josh the card. 'I don't know how. But when you feel like saying, call me. I'm sure it's going to make a good story.'

EIGHT

Sunday, June 7th. Evening/night.
Josh scanned the street as he stepped out of the newspaper office. There was no sign of the spotter. Whether he was still looking for them or whether he had called in reinforcements or just moved on, Josh had no way of knowing.

The bikes had disappeared too. The street was empty. 'I think it's okay,' he said to Kate, moving swiftly out onto the pavement.

She followed him out of the building. Josh started walking, keeping alert. Anyone sitting in a car, or just hanging around on a corner, would trigger his suspicion. So far, he could see nothing. *Maybe we're in the clear.*

'I don't think those kids were dopeheads,' said Josh.

'That seems to be the local theory,' said Kate.

Josh shook his head. 'Doesn't make any sense to me. There's something bigger than that happening in this town. A couple of runaway teenagers don't cause this much excitement.'

'Look,' said Kate.

She was nodding towards a car across the road.

Josh looked up. Two men were sitting in the front seat of a car parked twenty yards down from the restaurant. One of them was drinking from a plastic bottle of water, the other was unwrapping a stick of gum. Josh recognised both of them. The two spotters he'd seen earlier.

And if I recognise them, maybe they will recognise me.

'Stay cool,' he said. 'Just keep walking like nothing is happening.'

Josh picked up his pace. The leg was hurting, and it was tough to move at more than a fast walking pace.

Kate was steering him along. A hundred yards, then two hundred, then three hundred. Josh glanced back once. The two men were still sitting in their car. Neither of them had moved. It's okay, he decided. They aren't looking for us specifically. But they are looking for someone.

'We need to get out of town,' said Kate.

'Where?' said Josh.

'Marshall knows people,' said Kate. 'Out in the wilderness. They'll know where to hide us.'

They kept on walking. Up ahead, Josh could see the bright yellow sign of the Motel 6. He glanced towards Kate, but she seemed lost in her own thoughts. Up beyond the motel was a set of dusty hills rising high into the distance. We're walking right into them, he realised. Good hiding country.

Josh tried to concentrate. A new memory was constantly fading in and out like a badly tuned radio signal. But there was no mistaking it. The girl he had seen earlier, the one who had spoken to him outside the restaurant. Her name was Madge. A big Madonna fan: her iPod had every Madonna track ever recorded stored on it, and was constantly plugged into her ear. She was naked. And she was lying in bed in the motel. With me.

Christ, I'm not surprised she was angry. *I slept with her and now I don't even remember her name.*

Josh stopped and turned to face Kate. 'I have to go back to the motel,' he said.

They were almost a mile out of town now, on a dirt track that led away from the main road up into the hills. 'What?' snapped Kate.

'That girl in the parking lot,' said Josh. 'She works at the motel. The evening shift. She . . .' He paused. 'I've met her before.'

Kate laughed angrily. 'Met her?'

'Right.'

'You mean you fucked her.'

Josh nodded. 'She knows who I am,' he said. 'I need to go and speak to her.'

He could feel Kate gripping his wrist, holding tight onto it. 'No,' she said firmly.

'She knows who I am,' repeated Josh. 'I have to speak to her.'

He could feel Kate's hand squeezing his wrist tighter as she struggled to control her temper. 'Okay,' she said, releasing him. 'If you have to.'

'I have to,' Josh said again.

'I'm going to find Marshall's friends,' said Kate. 'They'll be out looking for us. Keep going along this track for two miles. When you see an abandoned mine, take the track heading due north for one mile. You'll see a rock formation to the right. We'll be there for the night.'

Josh turned around, and started walking back into town.

Josh paused outside the motel, scanning the building. The town was crawling with policemen and agents, he reminded himself. There could easily be one here.

As he stepped into the lobby of the Motel 6, Madge's expression changed from a pout to a scowl. She was by herself, dressed in the regulation yellow tunic of the chain: underneath the nylon of the shirt, Josh could make out the blue fabric of her bra. He noticed the plump swelling of her breasts inside it. 'What do you want?' she said.

Josh stepped forward, leaning against the edge of the counter.

'This motel is full,' she said, her face reddening with anger.

'Madge, I'm really sorry.'

'We're full,' she repeated.

Josh held his position. 'You don't understand, Madge,' he continued. 'I was hurt. I've been shot twice, and it's affected my memory. I didn't know my own name, who I was or where I came from. I just didn't realise who you were this morning.' He hesitated, making sure that she could detect the lump in his throat. 'Or how much you meant to me.'

Madge's expression softened. She pushed away the hair that had fallen in front of her face. 'What happened?' she said.

'I don't know,' Josh replied. 'Monday, I was involved in some kind of accident. Or worse.'

Suddenly, Madge threw her arms around him and kissed his cheeks with her wet lips. 'I was lying,' she whispered in his ear. 'We've got lots of room. And I'm closing the desk five minutes early.'

Twenty minutes later, they were lying in bed together, their bodies naked, stretched out on the crumpled white sheets.

Josh hugged Madge close to him. Their bodies were hot and sticky, her arms still cradling his chest. She reached up and kissed him on the lips, resting her hands against the bandage wrapped around his neck.

'I was so angry when I thought you'd forgotten who I was,' she said. 'I wanted to kill you.'

Josh smiled, removing her hand from the bandage. 'If you want to kill me. you'll have to join the queue.'

Madge turned on to her side, her cheek against the pillow. Room 19 was a compact, pre-designed box, with a double bed, a pair of side lights, and a picture of the Californian coast on the wall. There was a TV, a shower room, and not much else. Grabbing a room whenever she wanted to sleep with a guy was one of the perks of Madge's job, decided Josh.

'They came to question me,' she said.

Josh suddenly jerked out of the post-coital slumber into which he had drifted. 'Who?'

'Federal agents, Josh,' she said. 'They showed me their

cards and everything. They said I should talk to them. They said that you were a witness to the shooting of Ben Lippard.'

Her worried stare met Josh's. 'Is that true?'

'I think so,' answered Josh. 'I can't say for certain because I can't remember anything.'

Madge pulled up the white cotton sheet so that it covered her breasts. 'I told them I didn't know anything. I just said Josh is a fine man. He wouldn't hurt anyone.'

I hope that's true, thought Josh to himself. *Right now I wouldn't be so certain.*

'They accepted that?'

'They looked pretty pissed off. But eventually they went away.'

'How long was I here for?'

'You?'

Josh nodded. 'How long was I at the motel?'

'Nine days,' said Madge. 'I noticed you as soon as you checked in. You had a nice smile.'

'And what was I doing?'

'You don't know what you were doing?'

Josh shook his head. 'I told you, I don't remember anything.'

'Scouting tourist sites,' said Madge, sounding bored by the question. 'You said you worked for a tour company in England. You were planning routes, finding hotels, checking places to eat.'

I lied to her, thought Josh. *Whatever the hell I was doing here, that sure wasn't it.*

Josh squeezed her tight, caressing her shoulders. 'And who else was staying at the hotel at the same time as me?'

Madge looked thoughtful. 'Usual people,' she replied. 'Salesmen. A couple of stray tourists. People who were moving house. Husbands who'd been thrown out by their wives. I don't pay much attention to the guests at the Motel 6.' She snuggled up close to Josh. 'I certainly don't do *this* with them.'

'Anyone unusual?'

Madge's nose tilted disdainfully. 'One guy.'

'Who?'

'An Italian,' said Madge. 'Carrying an Italian passport when he checked in. I noticed it because I've never seen one of those before, and we don't get many foreigners in Boisdale. Heck, we don't even get that many people who aren't from Arizona. First, an Englishman, then this Italian. I couldn't help but notice.'

'You said there was something suspicious about him?'

Madge nodded. 'Just the way he acted. I didn't like it.'

'In what way?'

'I don't know.'

Josh looked at her intently. 'Describe him to me.'

'I can show you a picture.'

Josh picked himself up from the bed, and started walking towards the shower. He had to be careful when he washed not to disturb the bandage on his neck. He dried himself off, put the towel on the rack, and slipped on his jeans and shirt.

'Show me the picture, Madge, and I'll love you for ever,' he said. He could tell that she was enjoying the drama and mystery of all this.

She followed him outside. It was after eleven at night, but the air was still hot and the breeze had dropped, making the night sticky and sweaty. Josh could see one car pulling up down in the parking lot but the middle-aged man getting out looked harmless enough: the town might be crawling with spotters but he wasn't one of them. Madge took the metal staircase, then used her staff key to let herself into the lobby: the reception was closed at this time of night.

'Here,' she said, reaching into a grey metal filing cabinet in the small office behind the desk. 'We keep the guest records in here. We photocopy the passports of foreigners, and keep the details on file for three months.'

'Can I see mine?' said Josh.

She took the file and placed it in front of him. For a second, Josh could feel his blood surging through his veins. I'm about to find out who I am.

Josh looked down at the photocopy of his passport. Josh Bellamy, born in Sunderland.

That's not it, I'm not a Geordie. I was travelling under a false name, and a false passport. *My name might not even be Josh.*

Why would I be travelling under a false name?

Madge started rifling through the drawer, then pulled out a single sheet of white photostatted paper. On it was imprinted the image of a man. Josh looked down. Like all passport photos, it was small, with a white backdrop, and the person was wearing their most sombre expression.

The man in this photocopy had dark, smooth skin, just the way Madge had described him. His hair was black, brushed away from his face, and his dark eyes were set far apart from each other. The jaw looked as though it had been chiselled from stone, but the nose was crooked, as if it had been broken. It was a distinguished face, Josh decided: the mask of a man who knew both what he wanted, and how to hide it.

I've seen him before, thought Josh. I don't know where or how, but I know this man.

And I feel certain that I'll see him again.

'How long was he here?'

'Just the Sunday and Monday nights,' said Madge.

He arrives just before I get shot, thought Josh. *And he leaves straight afterwards.*

It was a four-mile walk back from the motel, taking three quarters of an hour: a mile to get out of town, two miles along the track, then, as the light faded, another mile up into the hills where Kate had told him they would be camping out for the night. Along the way, Josh had been thinking through all the things he had learned from Madge. A hundred different possibilities were running through his head: he needed time to sort them out and start making sense of what had happened to him.

What do I know? he asked himself. My name was Josh – maybe. I was staying in Boisdale. I lied about what I was doing, and I may have travelled under a false name. A man I recognise from somewhere came to stay at the hotel. Then I got shot.

The more he thought about it, the less sense it made.

His legs were aching from the effort of walking so many miles in one day. The wounds needed rest but that wasn't possible, not yet. There was still too much to be done.

He took the dirt track, letting the moonlight light up the path for him, until he hit the abandoned mine. Then he took the turning that Kate had described to him. Another mile dragged wearily by. As he drew closer, he wasn't sure how much longer he could keep going. He must have travelled at least twenty miles on foot in the last twenty-four hours: a punishing walk, even for a man who hadn't recently taken some lead.

Eventually, he saw the boulder formation. Sniffing the air, he could smell a fire, although he couldn't yet see it. Whoever was hiding there was clearly experienced enough to know how to build a fire, yet at the same time shield its light from the main track. Josh stepped forwards, pushing into the collection of boulders, letting his nose lead him.

Then, in front of him, he made out two men who blended into the landscape the same way a boulder blends into a rockfall. Their skin was tanned, leathery and lined. Both of them had grey hair and grey beards, although they looked no more than forty. A fire was burning in front of a cave, sending tiny plumes of smoke climbing upwards into the clear night sky: on top of the flames, its body pierced by a crooked stick, was some kind of small animal. A bird of some sort, figured Josh, as he smelled the charred flesh. Christ, maybe even a snake. *These guys look like they'll eat anything.*

'You okay?' Kate asked, a trace of anxiety in her voice as she emerged from the shadows.

Josh nodded. 'Who are they?'

One of the two men looked up at Josh, then stabbed the tiny creature. The fat from its body spluttered, falling into the fire, sending a sheet of sparks flying upwards.

Kate took Josh by the arm. 'This is Danny O'Brien,' she said, 'and this is Richie Morant.' She looked up at Josh. 'Marshall sent them out to look for us when we disappeared,' she said. 'They're here to help.'

'What the hell is this place?' said Josh, looking around the tiny, rough camp.

'It's a survivalist base,' said Kate. 'Many people believe that the UN is going to invade the United States one day. They've got all the kit here that they need to organise the local resistance. Food, fuel, explosives, some ammunition. The works.'

Great, thought Josh. Nutters.

He looked up. O'Brien was the shorter of the pair. His eyes were a pale grey, and you could see the Irish ancestry in him still: his head was broad and square, like a concrete block, and his shoulders were massive, but his manner was relaxed and genial. Morant, a bigger man, had a thick scar running down his left cheek, and the build of a brickie: he too had huge shoulders and biceps, a beefy torso tapering to a thin waist, then a pair of legs like tree trunks. Both men looked strong and healthy, and there was something wild about their appearance. Their hair was thick with grease. And they carried with them the dry, dusty smell of the desert.

'Is it you?' said O'Brien.

'Is it me, what?' asked Josh, looking towards him.

'Who's set the Feds crawling all over the place,' O'Brien said.

'You can't move for the motherfuckers,' said Morant. 'Nice quiet bit of the desert we had out here. Now it's crawling with agents. United Nations. Foreigners.'

Christ, thought Josh. *Where the hell did Kate find these two?*

'I'm hiding from them myself,' said Josh.

O'Brien nodded, and a smile suddenly flashed across his face. 'Marshall says you're okay, a soldier.'

'I think so,' said Josh. 'He told you about me?'

'Said you might need some help,' said Morant.

He reached out for the animal roasting on the home-made spit, and took it from the fire. It was long and thin, but it had legs: that ruled out a snake. Its flesh was singed from the flames, but the smell was good: a succulent, fatty odour somewhere between chicken and pork. Josh was famished.

'Want some?' said Morant, offering him a chunk of meat. 'It's crane.'

Josh nodded. He took a bite from the greasy lump of flesh now sitting in his hands. It was stringy, with the texture of rabbit.

'I need help,' he said. 'Marshall was right about that.'

'What kind of help?' asked O'Brien.

Josh was sitting next to the fire now. The temperature had dropped, making the warmth a welcome respite from the chilled air. In the light of the fire, he could see the faces of both men more clearly. There was a determination in both of them: an inner core of strength. But also a light-ness of spirit.

Josh tapped the side of his head. 'I lost my memory when I got shot,' he said. 'Over in the Sheriff's office, they know who I am. I want to get in there and see my files.'

'Fucking government,' said O'Brien. 'Got no right keep-ing files on any man.'

'When the fucking UN takes over the country,' said

Morant, 'they're going to take down anyone who tries to oppose them. This damned country's going to be finished.'

'Assholes,' said O'Brien. A thick wedge of cooked meat was dangling from his teeth. 'They got no fucking files on us, that's for sure. So far as the law is concerned, we don't exist. And we're keeping it that way.'

'You'll help me?'

'You're a fucking foreigner,' spat O'Brien. 'We only deal with Americans.'

'We don't trust you,' said Morant.

'We only trust our own kind,' added O'Brien.

'Even if I'm against the Feds?' said Josh.

There was a silence while both men paused for thought.

'Marshall told you—' began Kate.

'Marshall's pretty pissed with you for disappearing in the middle of the night,' said O'Brien.

NINE

Monday, June 8th. Night.

Madge gave Josh a long, lingering kiss on the lips. He took her in his arms, holding her tight to his chest.

'My shift doesn't end for another two hours,' she said. 'But I needed to see you.'

'Why?' asked Josh.

Madge looked around the drab foyer of the Motel 6. Her uniform was looking tighter today, as if it had shrunk in the wash or she had put on a couple of extra pounds. 'Because some men were snooping around the hotel last night.'

Josh and Kate had stayed the night in the mountains, hiding out with O'Brien and Morant. They had spent an uneasy night at the survivalist base. Josh wasn't at all sure how much he trusted the other men and he didn't think that they trusted him either.

In the morning, he'd said that he'd go back into town to draw up a plan of attack on the sheriff's office while O'Brien and Morant would put together some kit.

O'Brien had a red Mustang that he assured them was clean and couldn't be traced by the police. He'd let Kate drive it to drop Josh on the outskirts of town.

Then, as Josh was walking past the motel, Madge had run out to speak to him.

'What kind of men?' asked Josh.

'Bikers,' replied Madge, steering him back into the motel. 'Here, I'll show you.'

The back office of the Motel 6 was painted battleship grey, and had just one desk, two telephones and a computer screen. On one side of the desk there was a bank of four CCTV screens, each one just twelve inches square, displaying different views of the hotel: they monitored the car park, the foyer, and both of the two corridors along which the rooms were arranged. Only one flaw, Josh realised. There was nobody watching. The cameras would record a crime, but there would be no one there to stop it.

'This happened last night,' said Madge. She sat down at the desk, spooling back the tape until she reached the section she wanted. 23.19 was the time recorded on the screen in tiny white lettering. 'Look,' she said, her finger jabbing against the screen. 'Here.'

Josh leaned forwards, resting his hands on the table and peering into the screen. He could see three men pulling up their bikes in the parking lot, then walking around to the back of the hotel. They clambered up the fire escape, methodically looking through the back windows built into the rooms. Each man weighed at least two hundred and fifty pounds and had a long beard, but they were surprisingly agile, moving swiftly and silently around the building. They looked different from the bikers who had stood up for Madge in the restaurant parking lot: meaner, and fiercer, moving with an almost military precision. Next, the man who appeared to be the leader of the group walked up to the lobby, breaking its flimsy lock with his bare hands. Once inside, he started rummaging through the registration book, then spent ten minutes sitting in front of the hotel's computer in the reception. At one point he looked up, and the CCTV camera froze, capturing a perfect image of his face. Even obscured by the crash helmet still strapped securely to his head, it was easy to make out his main features. He had the thick, strapping skull of a pirate, with deep, dark eyes, bored like pits into the front of his face. His hair was long, wrapped up behind his head in a ponytail, while his beard was a foot long, jet black, and neatly combed. His skin, from what little Josh could see of it between the helmet and the beard, looked as if he had been suffering from acute acne for at least four decades. The moon has a smoother surface than your cheeks, pal, Josh decided.

I've seen him before, thought Josh. *I don't know where but I've seen that animal somewhere before.*

'What do you think they were looking for?' asked Madge.

'Me,' answered Josh. 'And they'll be back.'

On the motel computer, he printed out two still frames from the CCTV footage, sliding the pictures into the inside of his shirt. 'Motel 6 aren't going to miss one shot, are they?'

Madge shook her head.

Josh planted a resounding kiss on her lips. 'I love you,' he said.

O'Brien and Morant were already cooking on the fire. The flames were licking around the body of another small animal, and the smell of singed fat and charcoal was already filling the air. 'More crane?' said Josh, looking down.

'Not crane,' said O'Brien. 'No crane around this evening. At least none that we could catch.'

'We don't mind fighting the law, but we do so on a full stomach,' said Morant.

Both men laughed.

Kate was sitting just behind them, her hair tied up behind her neck. She looked across at Josh and smiled. It was just after eight in the evening, and it was already dark.

Josh took the leg of meat that O'Brien had just offered him and sank his teeth into the hot flesh. A dribble of fat ran down the side of his chin, and he brushed it away with a handkerchief. It tasted more like wild boar than anything else, but had a sharper, tangier flavour. Don't ask, he reminded himself. *If you ask what it is, you'll lose your appetite.*

'You guys ready?' he asked, looking across at the two men.

O'Brien and Morant nodded in turn. 'For fighting the cops, there's no time like the present.'

'Let's go through the plan once more,' said Josh. 'We go into town. But first we knock out the FBI agent so that we can use his pass to get us into the Sheriff's office. Once we're inside we look up all the details they have on me, then get the hell out of there.'

O'Brien nodded. 'The bit I like is at the start,' he said. 'Where we knock out the fucking Fed.'

The plan was that Kate would drop them off on the outskirts of town, then drive back to Marshall's to wait for them.

O'Brien made it his business to monitor the movements of every law-enforcement official in the region and prided himself on keeping tabs on all their routines. A Federal agent stopped at the Texaco station two miles outside Boisdale every night not long after midnight, pulling up for coffee and a doughnut. When they'd disposed of the agent they'd proceed into town, using his car.

Now the three men walked in silence: the track was too rough to use a car or a bike. Josh was using a stick to relieve some of the pressure on his leg, but he could move with freedom. I'm not going to let it slow me down, he kept telling himself every time he felt a bolt of pain shooting up his spine.

He sensed excitement in O'Brien and Morant as they reached the gas station. They were just waiting, he realised, for the right moment to teach the Feds a lesson about who controlled this land.

'He'll be here in a moment,' said O'Brien, as they circled

round the patch of scrubland at the back of the Texaco station. 'He usually stops between 12.30 and 1.00.'

'And he usually takes a leak,' said Morant. 'Weak bladder, I guess. We'll take him there.' He chuckled to himself. 'Always wanted to smash up a Fed bastard with his trousers down.'

Josh stayed silent. Now he could see a Ford Taurus pulling up at the station, the driver climbing out and starting to fill his tank. The man was around thirty-five, with sandy brown hair, and a dull, undistinguished face, already starting to run to fat around the cheeks. He was wearing grey slacks and a beige short-sleeved shirt.

'Motherfucker,' muttered Morant under his breath. 'Thinks he can come down from Washington and start snooping around our town.'

The man put the gas pump's nozzle back into its holder, then walked towards the gents'. Josh was sitting behind two huge plastic rubbish bins, filled to overflowing with the debris from the station: half-filled cups of coffee, and the remains of the micro-waved burgers sold inside. The smell was mixing with the fumes of gas and diesel and the odours drifting across from the toilet to make Josh feel queasy. Get this over with, he told himself. *I can't stand the stink much longer.*

The door slammed shut on the toilet.

The three men moved out onto the forecourt and stepped into the gents'. It was painted grey, with white tiles running halfway up the wall and Texaco logos above the sinks. The man was standing with his back to them, pissing into the urinal. Josh took a quick glance at him, making a rough mental calculation of his size, weight and strength, then worked out the force of the blow that would be needed to take him down. The man glanced back, nodded, then looked back at the urinal. Josh curled his fist into a ball and drew his arm back, coiling the pressure in his shoulder muscles. Then he released his punch.

The blow landed on the side of the man's neck. The muscles there were loose and relaxed: the man had had no warning of the attack and so had done nothing to prepare himself. The breath was forced out of his windpipe, making him choke. At his side, O'Brien had prepared another blow, delivering his punch straight to the gut. Next, Morant's boot smashed upwards, colliding with the agent's groin, sending a vicious bolt of pain searing up through his body at the same moment that all the oxygen emptied out of his lungs.

Still gripping his penis, some urine still trickling from it, the man crumpled to the floor.

Josh reached down, grabbing the man's throat and squeezing the air out of him. He could see the agent's eyes closing as shortage of oxygen to his brain made him lose consciousness.

But suddenly his eyes were open, staring straight up at Josh, and his hand was clutching at Josh's leg, tearing away at the bandage underneath his jeans, jamming the cotton into the raw wound. Josh bit his tongue to stifle a scream as the pain ripped through him. 'Fucker,' he gasped. He drove his fist hard into the side of the man's face. The agent slumped backward and his hand fell away as his head slammed against the floor.

A slow trickle of blood had started to seep down the side of Josh's leg.

'Not much fight in the fucker, is there?' snarled Morant. 'Let's cut his balls off, and hang them on the door. A warning to the others.'

Christ, thought Josh. I know the enemy of my enemy is my friend, and all that. *But these guys are bloody nutters.*

Josh took a tissue from his pocket and stuffed it inside the man's mouth. Next he took a roll of duct tape and started to bind up the man's mouth and hands. 'We'll stuff him in the can,' he said. 'This time of night, it should be a couple of hours at least before anyone finds him. That gives us enough time.'

Gratuitously, O'Brien smashed his fist into the man's gut again, making his unconscious body jerk. 'Why aren't we killing him?'

'Because if you kill a Fed, you'll get the whole bloody FBI coming down to the town, that's why,' snapped Josh. The pain in his leg was terrible, his head was starting to ache again and his temper was about to fly out of the room.

'Bring 'em on,' muttered Morant. 'Bring 'em on.'

'Fucking liberal,' said O'Brien, glancing towards Josh.

'Christ, let's just get out of here,' said Josh angrily. He grabbed the agent by the shoulders, heaving his body up. 'Hold his legs,' he snapped at O'Brien. He watched while O'Brien took the man by the legs, then they bundled him towards the toilet cubicle. 'Let's go,' said Josh.

O'Brien and Morant followed him out. Josh paused on the step, checking that no one had seen them. It was 12.45 a.m. now, and the forecourt was empty. The clerk sitting at the desk was the only person there, and he was watching the TV next to his desk. There were CCTV cameras, but they were trained on the cash desk. Nothing was recording people coming in and out of the toilet.

'You get in the car,' hissed Josh. 'I'll pay the bill.'

He had taken the jacket off the agent and put it on himself.

'We're not paying for the fucking Fed's gas,' snarled Morant. 'We should have just killed him.'

'Right,' said Josh. 'And you think we can drive out of the gas station without paying the bill and nobody will notice? Get in the car.'

Christ, thought Josh. *It's a miracle these morons have stayed out of jail this long.*

He walked swiftly towards the cash desk, checking that O'Brien and Morant had made it to the car. I'm taking a risk, he told himself, but a manageable one. Chances were the kid on the cash desk hadn't bothered to look at the man as he stepped out of the car and headed to the loos after filling up. And I'm wearing the guy's jacket. So long as the petrol is paid for he'll be happy enough.

They drove in silence from the gas station to the Sheriff's office. All three of them were recovering their breath after the fight. And they were focusing on the battle that lay ahead.

A battery of spotlights was shining down from the front of the Sheriff's office. Josh pulled the Taurus up on the street outside, switching off its lights.

He could feel the nerves in his stomach starting to get jumpy. Of course this was risky, but he had to find out who he was. Morant had assured him that the police station was lightly manned at night: one patrol car and one duty officer. Even so, this town was crawling with agents. It was impossible to know for sure how many people might be in there.

And he was worried that the officer Marshall had beaten up might be there. If so, he would certainly recognise Josh.

I'm taking my life in my hands.

Josh took the wallet from the Fed's jacket he was wearing and looked down at the ID. The name on the badge was Arnie Canestra, FBI Agent Number 2234B. There was a picture, but it was tiny. The memory of the heavy security around the building that he had encountered the other night was still fresh in his mind: they were going to have to make this act convincing if they hoped to get away with it. Let's just hope that O'Brien and Morant don't get any smart ideas.

'You stay in the car,' Josh said, looking at Morant. 'Keep the engine switched off, or it will attract attention. But keep it ready to move. We might need to get out of here in a hurry.'

An Italian–American, thought Josh as he stepped towards the entrance to the Sheriff's office. Agent Canestra. *Maybe I should talk like Al Pacino.*

'Walk quickly,' whispered Josh to O'Brien as he stepped through the doorway. 'A man walks quickly through any building, people assume he's doing something important. They are going to be nervous about stopping him.'

The corridor was painted pale cream. There was a duty desk, empty at this time of night. The corridor was lined with pictures of men on the wanted list: rough-looking characters, Josh noted, with pinched, violent faces, full of malevolence and anger. *I wouldn't be surprised to see either O'Brien or Morant up there along with the rest of the losers and psychopaths.*

'This way,' he said softly. Josh walked briskly towards the back office. He could feel his pulse racing. Last time he'd been here, he'd been chased away by a helicopter. So far as he could see, the place looked a lot quieter this evening. Or maybe it just appeared that way.

The corridor led into a large open-plan room. A lingering smell of sugar and coffee filled the air. About twenty desks were arranged opposite each other, all made from the same cheap wood, each with a regulation grey bin at the side. One cop who looked like a local guy was sitting alone at a desk close to the entrance. Another pair were checking their revolvers before heading out on a night patrol. It looked like there were only three of them.

In my jeans and T-shirt I don't look much like an FBI agent, thought Josh. *But in the middle of the night, I'll pass.*

'Agent Canestra,' he said, showing his badge, his tone clipped and purposeful as he nodded towards the one cop sitting at a desk. The man, nearing fifty and with a balding head, was looking down at a pile of papers, ticking boxes one by one.

'Need to check the computers,' continued Josh. 'That okay?'

The man glanced up, grunted something that Josh didn't catch, then went back to his work. Us Feds aren't very popular around here, Josh figured. *Treading on their turf, and nobody likes that.* He noticed the other two cops clock him as they left to go out on patrol.

He chose a desk in the far right hand corner of the office. So far, so good, he told himself with quiet satisfaction. There's a chance I might get away with this.

O'Brien followed him as he sat down, bringing up the opening page on the computer. His eyes started scanning down the rows of files. It took a few minutes to start navigating his way around the system. There were files on local laws, state laws, and federal laws. Procedural files and training files. Budgets and duty rosters. All of it operated from the same central database. Josh couldn't be certain, but it made sense that the local police would keep files on every murder case in the county. And the most likely place to keep those files would be on the computer.

'Open files,' said an icon on the screen.

Josh clicked on it. A list of names scrolled up onto the screen. Josh started scrolling through them alphabetically until he found what he was looking for. Lippard. 'Open,' he commanded the computer with a click of the mouse.

Josh started reading. The main report told him little that he didn't already know. Ben had been shot between eleven and twelve on the morning of Monday, June the first. Four bullets had been found in his body, fired from a Smith & Wesson Mountain Lite revolver. No trace had been made on the gun, nor had the weapon been found. There were no witnesses to the shooting, and the police had so far identified no leads and had no suspects.

Just like I thought. They are groping around in the dark.

Tiny jabs of pain were starting to hammer the inside of Josh's leg. He glanced down and saw that blood was dripping from the side of his thigh. It had seeped into the cloth of his jeans and was trickling down onto the tiled surface of the floor. A tiny trail of red droplets was leading from the doorway to this desk. He glanced anxiously at the cop in the corner.

He was standing up. He can't miss it, the bastard, thought Josh. Even the drowsiest cop has to see a trail of blood leading through his own office.

I haven't got much time.

He scrolled further through the files, his fingers moving swiftly across the keyboard. Against the back of his neck, he could feel O'Brien breathing heavily. 'Quick,' O'Brien muttered. 'All these cops are making me uncomfortable.'

Three words flashed up: 'The Third Man.' Josh clicked on the file, bringing the Word document up onto the screen. He glanced anxiously towards the door. No sign of the cop.

Josh started reading. 'Crime Scene Report, 6/1/05: Report File No: 34521DF. Reporting officer: Dick McNamara. Traces of blood were also found at the scene of the crime, just a few yards away from Lippard's body. Initially that was assumed to be Lippard's blood, but a test showed that it belonged to another person. The blood sample was sent to the National Crime Laboratories in Washington for DNA analysis. The NCL replied three days later. They had identified the person, and were awaiting security clearance before releasing the name and details of the person to the Boisdale sheriff's office.'

The third man? thought Josh, sitting back in his chair and staring intently at the screen. Security clearance? *Christ, what the hell am I doing in this country?*

'What did you say your name was again?' said a voice behind him.

Josh spun around.

The cop was looking straight down at him.

His face was puffy and tired, but the message in his eyes was clear enough. He had decided that Josh was not who he said he was. Now he was weighing up what to do about it.

'Agent Canestra,' snapped Josh. 'This is my colleague Dave Freemantle. We're busy, if you don't mind.'

'You don't look like Feds,' said the cop, delivering his words slowly. 'You've got a weird accent. And there's a trail of blood leading from the doorway to your desk.'

I've got two choices, figured Josh, his mind tabbing quickly through the available options. I can bluff my way out of this. Or run.

He's probably already called in reinforcements. Maybe that's why he disappeared for so long. That patrol car has probably turned round and is on its way back now. He just wants to keep me talking until they show up. There's nothing to gain by trying to talk my way out. *Run, man, while you still have the chance.*

'Like I said, we're busy,' snapped Josh, his tone rising.

'Then what about the blood?' asked the cop.

Josh's elbow snapped backwards, crashing into the side of the cop's jaw. Josh could feel his bone striking against the other man's, the point of his elbow joint digging deep into the soft flesh of the policeman's cheek. At the same moment, O'Brien drove his fist into the man's neck.

The cop reeled, then regained his balance. There was more strength in him than Josh had expected: he was a big man and his rolls of flesh turned out to contain as much muscle as fat. His hand slammed down on the desk, steadying himself, then his knee jerked upwards, smashing into Josh's chest. He could feel his ribcage vibrating with the impact, a bolt of pain shooting out into his body. Josh stepped backwards, steadying himself, then swung his leg forward, driving it hard into the cop's side. Then O'Brien gripped his neck between his forearms, jerking it backwards, and Josh could see the man's face turn red.

Josh heard a snapping sound. *Christ, is that his neck breaking?*

'Punch him out,' hissed O'Brien. 'Punch him out.'

Josh drew back his fist. He could see a look of fear flash across the cop's face. He was wriggling like a fish on a hook, but O'Brien's lock on his neck was strong.

I'll make it quick, pal, thought Josh. *You're better off with me punching you out than you'd be with either of these other head cases.*

Josh punched first with his right hand, then with his left, delivering a swift uppercut straight below the cop's jaw. A trickle of blood started to seep from the man's mouth and nose, and his eyes closed.

'He's out,' snapped O'Brien.

'Then let's get the hell out of here,' said Josh.

He started moving swiftly towards the street door. It was ten yards away, and some blood was flowing more freely now from the opened wound on his leg, spattering the floor with more red droplets. *They've got my DNA already, even if they don't know who I am. They will know that the third man has been here. And they'll turn over every last grain of sand in the desert to find me.*

The sound of a siren ripped through the quiet of the night sky. Josh lunged towards the doorway, looking out along the road. He could see Morant waiting in the Taurus. The car swung out into the road to meet him. But up on the main street, maybe three hundred yards away, Josh could now make out the patrol car accelerating towards them, its siren wailing and its warning strobe sending arcs of blue light spinning out into the night sky.

'They're bloody onto us,' Josh shouted, throwing himself into the passenger seat of the Taurus. Behind him, O'Brien was slamming his own door shut.

'Just bloody drive,' yelled Josh.

Morant was gripping the steering wheel of the Taurus hard. His foot slammed down on the accelerator as the car sped out onto the road leading out of town. Josh glanced behind him. The patrol car was already ramped up to full speed. It was travelling at a hundred, maybe a hundred and ten an hour, gaining on them with every second.

'Faster,' he muttered under his breath.

I've assaulted their office, and punched out one of their own men. *They're not going to be in a mood to take any prisoners.*

'I'm going blindfold,' Morant warned. He switched off the headlamps, plunging the road ahead into darkness. The patrol car was throwing off some light, but that was still two hundred yards behind them. This far from the town there were no more street lamps. Josh could see nothing ahead, not even the curve of the road.

He gripped the side of the seat. This was going to be a rough ride.

Looking across at the speedometer, he could see the Taurus gaining pace. It was hitting a hundred and twenty an hour, and Josh could hear the engine straining as it struggled to gets the revs it needed for that kind of speed. Another glance back. The patrol car was still gaining. A hundred yards behind, figured Josh. A hundred and fifty if we're lucky.

'The fuckers, they're fast,' shouted Morant, a gleeful wild edge to his voice.

'Cross-country,' shouted O'Brien from the back seat.

Josh couldn't be sure whether it was a question or a command.

'Hell, yes,' shouted Morant, struggling to make himself heard above the roar of the car's engine.

The Taurus swerved viciously to the right, its suspension shuddering as the tyres collided with the rough surface of the scrubland. This is just a suburban cruiser, realised Josh. Not an SUV or a 4x4, and it wasn't designed for driving off-road. *Every crevice, curve and rock is going to hit me straight in the spine.*

'The river,' shouted O'Brien from the back seat. 'Head for the river.'

Josh searched the ground ahead. He was peering through the windscreen, trying to figure out where they were going, but it was impossible to make out anything apart from a few murky shapes. They could be boulders, they could be plants. It was impossible to tell. The car was skidding across the dusty ground like a stone skimming across the surface of a lake, hardly touching its surface.

The river? What the hell do they mean, the river?

He checked the mirror. The patrol car had been thrown as they turned off the road. It had taken the driver a few seconds to react. But now powerful headlamps were beaming out across the open countryside, picking up the trail of the Taurus.

He might be four, five hundred yards behind us, realised Josh. *But he's still got us in his sights.*

'Left, left,' shouted O'Brien.

Josh could feel himself being pressed against the door as the car swerved viciously to the left. Something collided with the car's side with a terrifying thump, crashing into the metal. He could hear screeching and tearing as the Taurus's frame started to buckle. 'Harder left,' shouted O'Brien.

Josh drew a breath. At his side, Morant flashed him a smile. 'Hold on to your seat, boy,' he snapped.

'Why?'

Morant laughed. 'Trust me, you don't want to know.'

Josh gripped the black cloth seat of the car. He wondered whether he should put his safety belt on but decided against it. Whatever the health-and-safety monkeys said, seat belts killed as many people as they saved because they stopped you getting out of the car quickly.

And I may well want to get out of this one in a real hurry.

Josh looked ahead. All he could see was darkness. What Morant was driving by, he couldn't tell. Instinct, or an encyclopaedic knowledge of the terrain. Either way it was working. *So far.*

Suddenly he could hear nothing. The sound of the tyres rubbing protestingly against the surface of the rough ground disappeared. Christ, Josh said disbelievingly to himself. *We're flying.*

The idiot's driven off the edge of a cliff.

Prayer time.

Next, there was a deafening crash as the car hit the ground. Every bolt in the Taurus shook loose, a huge cloud of steam rose up from the engine, and the lights started flashing on and off. Water was gushing all around them, spitting up against the windscreen and seeping through the door until the carpet at Josh's feet was a sodden mess.

This is what he meant by the river.

The engine coughed, then roared. Josh could see Morant stabbing at the brakes, but to little effect. Broken, Josh realised. The steering was erratic, and the suspension had broken in at least two places, making every turn and twist a strain on the car. *One thing's certain. This machine's not passing its MOT.*

'Swing right,' shouted O'Brien.

Morant was twisting on the wheel but the power steering was gone, and Josh could see that the wheels were submerged in two feet of fast-running water. The car was sliding as much as it was being driven. Morant tugged harder on the wheel, and the car started drifting right, skimming across stones and pebbles, then picking up speed as it started to drive along a narrow tributary that – in the direction they were going – led away from the river.

Josh looked behind him. He could see nothing, only darkness.

No sign of the patrol car. *Maybe we lost them.*

The brakes still weren't working, so Morant killed the engine and let the car drift slowly to a halt. 'Shit, that was fun,' he said, climbing out of the car.

Josh stood up, slamming the door behind him. About six inches of water were running beneath his feet. He bent down, scooped up a handful and started to drink. The liquid slowly calmed his nerves, and he paused to examine his injuries. Blood was still dripping from his leg, and the cloth of his jeans was stained red on that side. There was some bruising to his calf and his chest where he'd been rammed against the door of the car and hit by the policeman. Otherwise I'm okay, he told himself. *Not much worse than usual.*

'There's a dried-out creek, right to the left of here,' said O'Brien, pointing to a turn in the stream about a hundred yards ahead of where they were standing. 'Just follow that. It will take you back to Ferndale. From there you can make you way back to Marshall's house.'

'Where are *you* going?' asked Josh.

'Into the wilderness,' said O'Brien. 'We have bases all over this county. They'll never find us because they don't know the ground anything like as well as we do.'

'Well, thanks for the help.'

Morant laughed roughly. 'Hell, we don't need any encouragement to go up against the Feds. I'm just pissed we didn't finish off that guy in the gas station.'

It takes all sorts, decided Josh as he started walking. Even out here.

It was just past two in the morning. It was dark but from the sliver of moon in the sky he could just make out the dried-up bed of the stream that O'Brien had told him about. I can follow that trail, he told himself. It could be twenty miles back to Marshall's house, a four-or five-hour walk depending on how his leg held out against the pain.

There aren't any choices but to walk my way out of trouble, Josh reminded himself through gritted teeth. *I don't want to be around here when the sun rises.*

Dawn was not far away now, Josh realised. He couldn't see any signs of light breaking over the horizon yet, nor could he see any streaks of orange piercing through the dark sky.

But he could smell it. There is a freshness to the air just before the sun rises, he thought. You can sense it in the dew hanging in the air, and in the stillness of the air just before the birds wake for the day.

He had checked his trail a dozen times since he'd been walking, and felt certain that the Sheriff's car that had been chasing them last night had been lost.

They will still be out there looking for me. But for now they've lost the scent.

Josh began to recognise the outline of the land. The house was just a mile away. The creek had led Josh back to Ferndale, just as O'Brien had said it would.

Josh paused. He scanned the empty landscape, looking for any signs of patrol cars, helicopters or any other kind of surveillance. There was nothing. Only a light breeze was blowing across the empty plain.

The sheriff's office don't know about Kate and Marshall, he realised. *They don't know that they are helping me.*

The house looked dead as Josh approached it. No lights, no sounds. He leaned on the frame of the door leading out from the kitchen. The flimsy lock gave way surprisingly quickly. Josh stood alone in the kitchen. He was out of breath and his tongue was parched dry from the walk. Beads of sweat were rolling down his back. He leaned over the sink, splashing his face with water. It felt good against his skin. He reached out for a slice of bread from the packet lying open on the side.

Bread and water, Josh reminded himself. *The basics of keeping yourself alive.*

The light flashed on. Kate was standing in the doorway. A towel was wrapped tightly around her body, tied into a knot just above her breasts. It stopped just an inch below her hips. 'What the hell happened to you?'

'National security,' said Josh. 'I got as far as finding my file. The Feds know who I am, but they haven't told the local cops yet.' He looked hard at Kate. 'Who the hell am I?'

'I don't know, Josh.'

She walked closer towards him, her eyes flashing towards the dark crimson patch on his jeans. 'You're hurt.'

Josh nodded. 'Bit of a scrap.'

A look of anxiety crossed her face. 'You've been shot?'

'No,' said Josh. 'The old wound started bleeding.' He looked down into her eyes. 'It gave us away in the police station, leaking out all over the floor.'

'Come here,' said Kate. 'I'll clean it up for you.'

She led him towards her bedroom. Josh hadn't been to the back of the house before. The room was small, no more than ten feet by fifteen, with a single bed at one side of it. It was painted pale yellow: the only room in the house that looked as if it had seen a paintbrush at any time in the past decade.

This can't be the place where she lives all the time, thought Josh as he glanced around.

It's not a woman's room. There are no cushions delicately arranged. No attempt to match the sheets with the curtains. No cuddly toys or framed photographs. Just a bed, and a dressing table, and a suitcase that has only been half opened.

'Take off your jeans,' said Kate.

'Yes, doctor,' said Josh, flashing a grin at her.

He unbuckled his belt and looked towards the bed. With a look, she ordered him to lie down. Josh lay back against the white sheet: he could smell Kate's perfume on the pillow where she had been sleeping just a few minutes before. The mattress was hard and springy, and Josh could feel the bruises and cuts along his body suddenly start to ache and quiver with pain. His feet were blistered and tired from the long walk, and the sweat was clinging to every inch of his skin.

Give me a can of Special Brew and I'll fit right in underneath any set of arches in London.

The flannel felt wet and cool against the side of his leg.

Josh glanced up. Kate had already unpeeled the torn bandage, exposing the wound. The flesh was twisted and charred, the hole that the bullet had made in its surface still clearly visible. The blood had dribbled down his leg, drying into the hairs to make a thin, crimson crust. Kate poured some disinfectant onto her cloth, rubbing it into the skin. As she did so, the nerve endings rebelled in pain, jabs of agony rolling up through his body. Then the pain subsided throughout him, to be replaced by a tingling sensation as if a mild current of electricity had just passed through him.

'That hurts, doesn't it?' said Kate.

Josh wasn't sure if she was worried or amused. 'I can handle it,' he answered.

She was leaning across him, applying more disinfectant to his leg. He could feel her red hair brushing across his chest, tickling him. With only the towel covering her body, her legs were naked and he could feel her skin brushing against his.

He looked up, their gazes making contact.

He paused, allowing his gaze to linger on her for a fraction longer, then reached up with his hand to run his fingers through her hair. It was soft, and immaculately combed. He could hear the small murmur of pleasure escape from her mouth as his hands started to caress her scalp.

His head jerked upwards and he kissed her on the lips.

For a fraction of a second, it was as if nothing had happened. Kate's lips were motionless next to his, and her breathing was calm. Then, like a car with the accelerator jammed down hard, she started to react. Her tongue flicked out to meet his, and her arms slid down across his chest. Her body was smothering him now, her hips grinding into his groin. Josh reached up, untying the simple knot that held her towel in place, releasing her breasts. He held them between his hands, flicking at her nipples with the tip of his tongue, then running his hands down her arched back.

'I think there's something in the medical guidelines about fucking the patients,' she said, a giggle playing in her voice.

'What does it say?'

Her tongue ran down the side of his chest. 'Only if they're cute.'

Josh rolled Kate over on her back. The sex that followed was tender, yet satisfying. She responded to each touch and caress, guiding him towards the zones of her body that would deliver the fastest pleasure: Josh was surprised by how quickly their bodies locked together, as if they had been preparing for this for weeks.

Afterwards, she lay on his chest. Josh could feel her heart thumping against his skin. 'You don't live here, do you?' he said. 'Not all the time.'

'For now, I'm here,' said Kate.

Her voice was tired, uninterested.

'This is not for you, Kate,' said Josh. 'It's a wilderness out here. Your husband's dead, you have to move on.'

She smiled at him. 'Maybe that's what I've just done.'

'Then move out.'

Kate closed his lips with the fingers of her right hand. 'You're not well,' she said. 'You need to sleep.'

At the side of the bed, Josh could see Kate holding a syringe between her fingers. Dawn was breaking through the window: a shaft of orange light was streaming into the room. The needle glistened. 'I don't need it,' said Josh. 'I'll be fine.'

Before he could even finish the sentence, the needle had pierced the skin of his arm and the pale liquid inside the syringe had already shot into his bloodstream. Josh could feel himself starting to grow drowsier.

'I'm your doctor,' said Kate softly. 'If I say you need it, then you need it.'

Josh struggled to keep his eyes open, but sleep was catching up on him fast, forcing him down. As his eyes shut, he could see something. A desert. A rock. A boy shouting, then another one speaking. At him.

Luke. And Ben.

He struggled to hold on to the image. But sleep had already overwhelmed him.

TEN

Tuesday, June 9th. Morning.

Even though his eyes were still closed, Josh could feel the first rays of dawn pressing against them. He squeezed his eyelids shut, maintaining the darkness for a few more moments. An image was playing through his head. A man in some kind of uniform, shouting something. A concrete room. He closed his eyes tighter, trying to empty his mind of every other sensation, pouring all his energy into focusing on the memory. The man was tearing a picture from a wall, shouting at Josh as he did so. But the words were impossible to make out, nor could Josh even be certain that it was him that was being shouted at.

What the hell does that mean?

A noise.

Josh woke up with a start. He looked around anxiously. The room was unfamiliar. It was only when he smelled Kate's perfume on the crumpled sheets that he remembered where he was and what had happened. That scent? *What was its name?*

Josh yawned, stretched, and pulled himself up. The morning air was cool and fresh. At his side, Kate was still asleep: her red hair had fallen across her face. From the slow movement of her lips, he could tell that it would be a while before she woke. He dipped his head and brushed his lips against her forehead, planting a small kiss on her cool skin.

If it weren't for you, I'd be dead, he reminded himself.

Walking through to the kitchen, he started boiling some water. There was no sign of Marshall in the house.

Kate had dressed his neck wound last night, using some pure alcohol that Marshall had stored in the house: whether it was for drinking or medical emergencies, Josh couldn't be sure. Probably both. It stung like hell as she rubbed it into the thick scab running across the side of his neck. But by the time she covered it again with a smaller bandage it felt better: the skin didn't itch so much, and he could move his neck without pain running down into his spine.

The leg is strong enough to walk on, if not run. And the neck is starting to heal, Josh thought.

But still no more than the occasional flicker of a memory.

Josh took another sip of his coffee, watching the sun rise over the horizon: the reddish landscape of the rocks and the earth blended into the dawn's rays to turn the world orange. Like I've landed on another planet, thought Josh.

I wonder what kind of family I have? A wife? Children, maybe. I must have a mum and dad, everyone's got one of those. A home town. Places that I recognise, and people that I know. But am I ever going to see them again? *And if I do, will I even know them?*

No mind games, Josh told himself. Pull yourself together, man. *There's work to be done.*

Josh poured an extra cup of coffee, and walked across to the bedroom. Kate had rolled over, her hand resting across her face, and he could see her breasts gently rising and falling as she breathed. He put his hand on her shoulder, giving it a shake.

'Coffee in bed,' he said with a bright smile. 'And there's beans for breakfast.'

Kate rose gently, sitting forward. Her eyes were still sleepy. 'What's the plan? she asked.

Josh hesitated. He'd been turning the same question over

in his mind. 'Luke's mother,' he said. 'That's the only lead we've got.'

Music was blasting from the house, the volume turned way up high. Josh leaned forwards in the car, trying to get a closer look. One car in the driveway. No lights on. The chances were that Emily Marsden was alone.

'Shall we go inside?' asked Kate.

Josh nodded, climbing out of the red Ford Mustang. It was getting close to lunchtime, and the sun was already scorching. The building was just one storey, made from rough stone and with a roof that was a mixture of tin and slate. At the back was a yard, a hundred feet long and fifty feet wide. One section of the wall had broken down, and some shrubs were growing between the stones. If you couldn't hear the music, thought Josh to himself, you might think the place was a deserted ruin.

The volume of the music increased as they walked together down the pebbled path that led towards the main drive.

'Dogs begin to bark and hounds begin to howl/Watch out, strange cat people/Little red rooster's on the prowl,' went the song.

Josh paused. I know that song, he thought.

Suddenly he could see a picture in his mind. A house. Somewhere in England, he felt sure of that. A woman, with dark hair and a shapely figure. A girl. Aged two, maybe three, a dummy in her mouth.

'If you see my little red rooster/Please drive him home/Ain't had no peace in the farmyard/Since my little red rooster's been gone,' continued the song, the growing voice delivering the words over a solid drum and guitar backbeat.

The woman was saying something to Josh. The girl was crying. She was looking for her dummy. Josh was trying to comfort her.

A silence. The song had ended, and the next track on the album hadn't started yet. As the music faded, so did the memory, disappearing back into the recesses of Josh's mind.

That girl, wondered Josh. Was she mine?

'The singer?' asked Josh. 'You recognise it?

Kate laughed. 'You really *have* lost your memory, haven't you?'

'Who is it?' asked Josh angrily.

'The Rolling Stones,' said Kate. '"Little Red Rooster." From the *Rolling Stones Now* album, which came out in 1965, I think. Before either of us was born, anyway.'

Josh nodded. I'll buy it if I can find a copy, he decided. It's sparking memories. Maybe I used to be a Stones fan? There are worse things. Elton John sounded familiar, but not in a good way.

He rang the doorbell, waited for a moment to see if there was a reply, then rang again. The next track – 'Surprise, Surprise' – had already started up, the strumming guitars blasting out of the speakers so loud, that the mortar between the bricks seemed to be shaking. Josh rang again then knocked. Nothing. No good, he told himself. You can't hear yourself thinking above this music. *You certainly can't hear the doorbell.*

The door swung open as Josh pushed against it. The hallway was high and dark, with a sofa along one side and two bikes propped up against a wall. Kate followed as Josh stepped inside. Two rooms led off the hallway, and there was a staircase at the back of the building. The music was coming from behind the door on the left-hand side. He pushed it open and stepped forwards.

A woman was standing in the centre of the room. Approaching fifty, she had streaked blonde hair, a thin, wiry frame, and a face that had once been pretty but which had succumbed to the ravages of time and exhaustion. Too much drinking had left thick creases embedded in the skin of her face. Light was streaming down from the two high windows, filling the room which was furnished with two old sofas, both with oriental drapes thrown across them. There was a huge tapestry on one wall, and a mural on another. At the back of the room there was an expensive-looking NAD hi-fi system, the only bit of kit in the room that looked as if it had cost more than a few dollars in a junk store.

The woman turned slowly around, her hips still swaying to the music. Josh saw that she was holding a shotgun, pointed straight at his chest. 'Get the fuck out of my goddam house,' she said.

Josh raised his hands in the air. He sensed that he'd looked down plenty of gun barrels in his life.

You developed an instinct for who was going to pull the trigger and who wasn't. This woman wasn't. *There's a certain look in their eye that people get just before they are about to shoot you, and she didn't have it.*

'You must be Emily,' he said, trying to make his tone as relaxed and friendly as possible.

She stayed silent.

Did she hear me? wondered Josh. He walked slowly towards the back of the room, keeping his hands in the air. Then he flicked down the volume dial on the NAD until the music was just a murmur. Suddenly he could hear himself think again.

'You must be Emily,' he repeated.

Emily laughed. 'In this country, you can shoot a man for turning down your music.'

'Shoot him twice if it's the Stones?' said Josh with a grin. He walked slowly towards her until the gun barrel was only inches from his chest. 'My name's Josh. This is Kate.'

The gun held steady. 'What do you want?'

'Some dope,' said Josh. 'Heard from some friends of ours that this was the best place to get some.'

Emily Marsden lowered the gun, tossing it back on the sofa. Josh flinched. She didn't appear to have any idea how easy it was to fire a shotgun accidentally. 'What kind of accent is that? English?'

'English.'

'Long way to come for some weed.'

'I heard that you grow the best.'

Emily smiled. 'Ain't that the truth. You and your honey take the weight off your feet and I'll go get you some.'

As she left the room, Josh sat down on one of the sofas. Now he noticed that there was a smell of bourbon, dope and perfume in the air: a pleasant enough mixture of scents, but one that made you feel drowsy. He looked towards Kate, noting the suspicion in her eyes. 'Let me do the talking,' he said. 'Just pretend to be my girlfriend.'

Emily walked back into the room, carrying a pouch with a few leaves in it. She took out a pack of tobacco and some Rizla papers, and started rolling a joint. Her fingers worked quickly, Josh noted. She didn't even need to look down. 'Here,' she said, handing across a thick spliff after she'd lit it. 'Try before you buy, that's my policy.'

Josh took a hit of the smoke, letting it fill his lungs. He had a vague memory that it worked pretty well as a painkiller as well as whatever else it was supposed to do. *I could use some of that.*

'Good stuff,' he said.

Emily smiled. 'It's good country for growing any kind of hot-weather plant up here. Just so long as you water it enough. Never rains around here. Hasn't rained for five years now.'

Josh took another drag on the joint, then passed it across to Kate. Not too much, he warned himself. *You don't want to lose your concentration.*

'Here, you try it, honey,' he said.

He looked back at Emily. 'Put whatever fifty dollars will buy me into a bag.'

On the next sofa, he could see Kate sitting back, taking three long hits on the joint in a row before passing it back to Emily. The room was suddenly filled with smoke. 'I heard about your boy Luke,' said Josh, still looking at Emily. 'I'm sorry.'

She started rubbing an eye, and Josh could suddenly see how bloodshot it was. She held the joint between her left index finger and her thumb but her hand was starting to tremble and the tip of the ash tumbled onto the floor. She looked first at Kate, then at Josh. 'It's been nine days now since I heard from him, nine whole days,' she said, her voice fragile and shaky. 'Luke's not like that. He was wild some-times, the way young boys are. Difficult. But hell, we're close, real close. He'd never go that long without contacting me. He'd know how much I was worrying about him.' She paused, sucking at the joint like it was an oxygen tank and she'd just emerged from being held underwater. 'Not unless something happened to him.'

'We might be able to help,' said Josh.

A look of fear suddenly passed across Emily's face. 'You're not the Feds, are you?' she said, her voice quivering with anxiety. 'I don't grow a lot of dope, you know. Just a bit for myself. And to give to my friends.'

'We're not police,' said Kate.

'Then who the hell are you?'

Josh could see that she was eyeing the shotgun again. 'I saw something,' he said.

There was a silence. Josh could see Emily taking another drag on the joint, her lips trembling. 'You saw Luke?' she said. 'Tell me you saw Luke. Tell me he's okay.'

'I don't know what I saw, not exactly,' said Josh. 'I can't even tell you who I am. But I saw *something*.'

'What the hell are you talking about?' said Emily angrily. 'Either you saw something or you didn't.'

Kate leaned forward in her chair. 'Josh has lost his memory, but he was there when Ben got shot. He got shot at the same time, that's why he's injured.'

'I saw Ben, and I think I saw Luke running away. I don't know what I was doing there, but I think I was involved in some way.'

Emily waved her spliff in the air, spilling more ash onto the carpet. 'Christ, you've been smoking even more of this stuff than I have.'

Kate reached out, trying to hold on to her hand, but Emily snatched it away suspiciously. Luke's in some kind of danger, that's obvious,' Kate said. 'The police are going to lose interest in a couple of days. Teenage boy runs away, there's nothing to interest them there. We're the only people who are going to help you.'

'How do I know you didn't kill him?' said Emily. 'How do I know you didn't kill Ben as well?' She paused. 'You both look pretty fucking weird to me.'

Maybe she's right, thought Josh. Christ, I don't even know myself. *Maybe I did kill Ben.*

'Listen, I'll tell you what I know, then you can make up your own mind whether to help us or not,' said Josh. 'I'm British. Some kind of soldier or agent, I think. I figure I was on a mission, and that led me to track Ben and Luke. Then Ben got shot, and so did I. Luke escaped, I'm sure of it. I saw him running.'

'An agent,' said Emily, laughing bitterly. 'Like James damned Bond or something?' She waved her spliff at him. 'I'm not growing this any more.'

'No, think, Emily,' said Josh, his tone turning even more serious. 'Your son's life could be at stake here.'

'I know that – and I'm supposed to waste my time listening to some dope-head who walks into my house and starts talking this kind of shit?'

'You got a better explanation, let's hear it,' said Josh. 'Listen, Ben and Luke disappeared nine days ago. Seven days ago Ben got shot. They'd already gone two days by the time that happened and they were ninety miles away. What do you think happened?'

Now a tear was rolling down Emily's face. 'You said you were there?'

Josh nodded.

'Bullshit.'

Josh closed his eyes, and rolled his head back. 'Limp Bizkit,' he said. 'Does Luke like that band?'

'Thrash-metal crap.'

'His T-shirt,' said Josh. 'He was wearing a Limp Bizkit '02 tour T-shirt. And I reckon it was an extra-large because it was way too big for him.'

'You saw that on TV,' said Emily.

'It hasn't been on TV,' said Kate. 'They've been showing an old high-school picture of Luke.'

'What was he wearing the day he left?' asked Josh.

'The T-shirt,' said Emily. 'The Limp Bizkit T-shirt. Christ, you really *were* there.' She looked hard at Josh. 'Is he okay? Tell me he's okay.'

'He ran, I know that much,' said Josh. 'I can't tell you where he is now, or whether he's still alive, because I just don't know.' He looked hard at Emily. 'But I don't think Luke was just some teenager who went on the run for a few days with his mate because he was a bit bored. I think he was mixed up with something. And I think I was mixed up in it as well.'

'The trouble is, we don't know what the hell it was,' said Kate.

'That's why we'd like you to help us,' said Josh. 'We need to know what Luke was involved with.'

Emily remained silent.

'What was it?' persisted Josh. 'What was Luke involved with?'

Emily still remained silent, her stare fixed on the floor.

'We're the only people who are going to help you, Emily,' interrupted Kate. 'The *only* people.'

Emily walked across to the window, looking out as if she was searching for something in the empty, scorched landscape that lay around the house. The sunlight streamed though her hair, making it look almost white. Her lips started to move, but no sound emerged.

'Luke might still be in danger,' said Josh.

Emily nodded. She turned around so that the sun was now behind her. Josh noticed how pale she looked, as if all the blood had suddenly been emptied from her veins. 'Hacking,' she said. 'Luke was into hacking.'

She walked back across the room. 'He and Ben, they used to go up to his room and play around on their computers for hours and hours. I didn't know much about what they were doing. Myself, I can't even turn the damned things on. But they got into trouble for it at school, after they changed everyone's grades on the school computer. I told them to stop.' She shrugged. 'But how are you to stop a boy playing around on his computer? And anyway, it seems pretty harmless. Better than running wild, shooting guns and riding bikes. That's what all the other boys around here do.'

'So you think the hacking might have been what got him into trouble?'

Emily sat down on the sofa. She folded her arms on her lap. For the first time since Kate and Josh had come into the room, she seemed to be unwinding: it was as if she had decided to trust them, and that was relaxing her.

'About three months ago, Luke started talking about how we wouldn't have to live in this old shack any more,' she started. 'It's always been tough for us financially. I do some waitressing and I grow some dope. Neither of those professions pays very well, as you probably know. We get by, that's the best you can say. Luke started telling me that soon we wouldn't have to worry about money any more, that everything was going to be okay. We could buy a big car, a house in California, maybe another one down in Jamaica. He was getting into reggae.'

Emily reached across the sofa and rolled herself a cigarette, one with just tobacco in it this time. A thin stream of smoke blew out of her nostrils. 'I just humoured him. Yes, yes, Luke, I used to say. I'm looking forward to it. Buy me an SUV as well. One of those big Mercedes ones, or maybe a Lexus. Something fancy. Then he used to get cross, and start telling me that he really *was* going to make a lot of money, that he was doing something on his computer that was going to make him a fortune.'

Emily jabbed the cigarette in the air, her tone turning darker. 'Then he disappeared. And I can't help thinking that maybe he was doing something on his computer. Something that got him into trouble.'

'Have you told the police about this?' asked Josh.

Emily shook her head. 'I don't want to get him into even worse trouble. I mean, if he was doing something on his computer, it probably wasn't legal. But they knew he was into hacking because of what happened at school. And they took his computer away for examination.'

'And you have no idea what he might be doing?' asked Josh.

'Like I said, I didn't take much notice of it at the time. Just boy's talk. Bravado. It was only after he disappeared that I started to think there might be something to it.'

'He never mentioned any websites he was visiting, nothing like that?'

Emily stubbed out her cigarette. Her expression was thoughtful, as if she was weighing different options. 'No,' she said finally. 'But he had *two* computers. The police took his desktop, the one up in his room. But Luke had a laptop, the one he used to take around to Ben's house. That's the one he mainly worked on, I think. The desktop was just for playing games and stuff.'

'And the police didn't take that one?'

'I didn't tell them about it.'

There was a silence. Some cigarette smoke was drifting through the air. Josh knew what question he wanted to ask next, but decided to pause before pressing it. Better to wait, he told himself. She knows the question. *She just doesn't know the answer yet.*

'You said you were a soldier?' she asked. 'That you might have been looking for Luke?'

Josh nodded. 'I'm not going to kid around – I don't know who I am. But I think I was involved with Luke. I think he's out there somewhere. And I'm going to try and find him.'

'You want his laptop?' said Emily. 'You think that might help?'

'If there's something on it, we'll find it,' said Josh.

'Follow me,' said Emily.

She stood up and walked out of the room. Josh followed closely behind, with Kate beside him. He could feel his heart thumping inside his chest. This was the first real break-through: if they could find out what Luke had been hacking into, they would have unlocked a door.

Slowly, the jigsaw of who I am is about to be reassembled.

The midday sun was frying the scrubland outside the house. At least forty, Josh judged as he stepped out of the building. Emily's house was on an open stretch of plain, at least twenty miles from any hills, in a dip in the land: the heat gathered up each last atom of moisture, sweating it out of every grain of dust.

Boiling hot scrub. *After the Gobi Desert this must be the cheapest real estate in the world.*

The barn was just a shack, with some farm equipment that looked as if it dated from the 1930s rusting inside. A trailer was slung onto the back of a tractor, with a tarpaulin sheet stretched across it. Emily pulled it aside, taking out a sleek black Dell Inspiron. 'Here,' she said. 'This is what he used.'

Josh took the laptop under his arm. 'We'll bring it back,' he said.

'I don't care if you bring it back or not,' Emily snapped. 'Bring *Luke* back – that's what I want.'

'I'll try,' said Josh.

Emily turned around and started to walk back towards the house.

'One other question,' said Josh. 'Who's Luke's dad?'

Emily looked startled. 'His dad?'

Josh nodded. Sometimes you asked a question without being quite sure why, or what the answer might be. When you are stuck in the middle of a mystery, you have to examine every angle. Otherwise, you'll never find the way out. 'If something has happened to Luke, maybe his father was involved somewhere along the line,' said Josh. 'Who was he?'

Emily looked at him contemptuously. 'It doesn't matter,' she snapped. 'That's private.'

Josh turned around. No point pressing, he realised. He was clearly stepping into dangerous territory. 'Well, if you ever think it might be relevant, get in touch.'

'Just bring him back,' said Emily. 'I just want him back with me, that's all.'

ELEVEN

Tuesday, June 9th. Midday.
The coffee was steaming in a pot in the centre of the table.
Josh took a long drink of the thick black liquid, refilling
the cup as soon as he had drained it. The coffee washed
down his throat, gradually sweeping away the tiredness that
the dope he'd smoked at Emily's house had left in his system.
He glanced out at the sweeping, empty scrubland. The sun
was beating down, scorching the life out of everything
beneath it, but a stronger wind was blowing today, sending
vicious swirls of dust spinning up through the boulders,
and clump of weeds rolling along the ground.

'We are the pilgrims, master/We shall go always a little
further.'

Josh spun around. Marshall was standing in the doorway,
a bottle of beer in his hand.

'Recognise it?' he asked, stepping forward into the room.

Josh shook his head. 'No,' he replied.

That wasn't quite true, he told himself. As he'd heard the
words recited *something* had stirred within his mind. A
shadowy memory of a long, concrete room. A barracks. Some
men standing around. Another man shouting. A rainstorm.

They were just fleeting, disjointed images. You couldn't
piece them together. *They didn't make any sense.*

'What is it?' Josh asked.

'The SAS,' answered Marshall. 'The Regiment's poem.
You sure it didn't stir anything?'

'Maybe something,' said Josh.

'Then that's who you are,' said Marshall. 'British special forces – I was right.' He walked up to the front door, opened it and stepped outside. 'Heard you had quite an adventure with my two friends.'

Josh nodded.

'You know how to handle yourself.'

'I'm still alive.'

'You can't stay here,' said Marshall. 'There's going to be deputies crawling all over the county by the end of the day.'

'Don't worry, daddy, we're going,' Kate interrupted.

Marshall looked at Kate and nodded. She looked different this afternoon, Josh noted. Calmer, more relaxed. Her skin was shining, and although she was trying to disguise it, there was the hint of a smile in her eyes. Josh wasn't sure what was behind it, but he hoped that Marshall wouldn't notice.

'Where?' said Marshall.

Kate placed a laptop down on the kitchen table. 'To find out what's on this. It belonged to Luke, that boy.'

'You got anyone who can help us with this?' asked Josh, the question directed at Marshall.

The older man nodded, raking a finger through his grey hair. 'I know the guy you need. Lives up in Utah. About two .hundred miles north of here. Goes by the name of Kessler.' He paused, as if searching around for something in his memory. 'Sam Kessler.'

'You think he will help us?' Kate asked.

'If I tell him he has to he will,' snapped Marshall.

'Then I'll pack a bag,' said Kate. 'We're leaving.'

Josh dug deep into the pocket at the back of his jeans. The previous pair was still stained with his blood, but he had borrowed another pair of Marshall's: at this rate, Josh noted, the older guy wasn't going to have much left in his wardrobe. He pulled out two pictures. They were creased and smudged, but still recognisable. They were stills from the video clips that Madge had given him yesterday, showing the leader of the group of men who had broken into the Motel 6. Josh felt sure that the men had been looking for him.

'This guy,' said Josh, his finger jabbing down at the table as he pointed at the man. 'Any chance that you or one of your friends might know who he is?'

Marshall picked up the photograph, scrutinising the man portrayed there. 'Ugly-looking mother.'

'It would be better if I could find him before he finds me,' said Josh.

'And what makes you think that I might know him?' There was a dangerous look on Marshall's face, Josh realised. His stare was boring into him like a drill. For a moment, he wondered whether Marshall had heard him slipping into Kate's bedroom last night.

'I didn't say that – I only asked if you might know who he was – but you seem pretty well connected around here,' Josh replied.

A smile broke out on Marshall's face, as if Josh was the funniest guy he'd ever met. 'You catch on quick.' He picked up the pictures, folded them, and tucked them into the breast pocket of his denim shirt. 'I'll see what I can do,' he said. 'Call me. I'll let you know if I discover anything.'

The road twisted down to the ranch house through a steep valley. It was no more than a dirt track, pitted with holes, and the suspension of the Mustang clattered as it bounced down the hill. 'Think he'll be pleased to see us?' said Josh.

'No,' replied Kate, with a curt shake of her head.

Josh looked out from the car. On one side the hills rose up towards the sky, but on the other side a flat plain stretched out for several miles. A river trickled along near the horizon: at this stage of the summer, it had dried to just a few inches of water. He could just make out some trees growing in a thicket about a mile away. A pack of semi-wild horses were watering themselves by the river. Otherwise, it was just grass-land and scrub. There was not another building anywhere in sight.

This is about as remote as you can get within a civilised country. A good place to hide.

The house was just one storey, made from wood. A porch ran along its entire front. To the right there was a giant set of solar panels and to the left a fifteen-foot satellite dish pointed up to the sky. Electricity and TV, noted Josh. All a man needs to survive.

He hopped out of the car and walked towards the door. It was just after five in the evening, and the heat of the day was starting to ebb. From Ferndale, it had taken them four hours straight to drive here, heading due north up through Arizona, crossing over the state line into Utah, and turning due east, crossing another fifty miles until they hit Kanab, the closest town to the ranch house.

'Are you Sam Kessler?' said Josh to the man who opened the door.

The man nodded. To Josh, he looked at least fifty, with a face that bore the scars of a difficult life. His hair was black but had thick streaks of grey running through it. He wore it long, tumbling down over his neck, and he had a thick moustache that almost hid his mouth. His eyes were round, set close to his nose, and his jaw was thick with folds of fat.

'You're Marshall's friend?' said Kessler.

Josh nodded.

'Then you better come in.'

Marshall had only given Josh the sketchiest outline of Kessler, and of how he'd come to know him. He'd been in Vietnam, but had then made a career for himself in computers, working for the big companies in Silicon Valley across in California, until a decade ago he'd moved out to

this decaying horse ranch in Utah. He lived by himself –
his wife hadn't thought much of the wilderness and had
moved back to California after a couple of years – and
supported himself by freelancing as a computer-security
consultant. If local companies wanted someone to make
their systems secure, Kessler was the man they turned to.
'If anyone can find anything on that computer, Kessler can,'
Marshall had said to them just before they'd left.

'I'm grateful for your time,' said Josh, stepping into the
hallway.

Inside, the hall had stone flooring and wooden walls. It
was decorated with riding ornaments: saddles, stirrups,
horseshoes and whips. Kessler led them through into the
kitchen. There was no offer of coffee or even a glass of
water: Josh decided that asking would be a mistake.

'Where's the kit?' said Kessler.

Kate took the laptop from its bag, putting it down on
the table. Kessler glanced down, then raised an eyebrow.
'What's the problem?'

'It's empty,' said Josh. 'All the files have been erased.'

Kessler sat down at the table. He flipped open the laptop,
switched it on and looked at the screen. 'Maybe there's
nothing there,' he said. 'Maybe somebody just bought it.'

Josh sat down at the other side of the table. 'No, there
was definitely something there,' he said firmly. 'I think they
deleted the files.'

'Who did it belong to?'

Kessler's stare shot up to meet Josh's as he posed the
question.

'That doesn't matter,' said Kate quickly.

'It matters to me,' said Kessler. 'In my experience,
computers are kind of personal. People don't like other
people fishing around in their kit, the same way they don't
like them breaking into their houses – or screwing their
wives.'

Josh glanced at Kate then back towards Kessler. 'That doesn't matter,' he snapped. 'The guy this machine belonged to won't mind you looking at it. We're trying to help him.' Josh paused. 'Trust me.'

'Trust you?' Kessler laughed. 'I've only just met you – how the hell am I going to trust you?'

Josh reached out for the laptop, snapping its cover shut. 'If you don't want to help us, that's fine. We're sorry to have wasted your time.' He started to lift himself from the seat.

'I'll tell Marshall that you weren't able to do anything for us.'

Kessler raised his hand. 'I'll look at it,' he said wearily. 'Give me a couple of days. I'll tell you if I can find anything.'

Josh placed the laptop back down on the table. 'Two days is too long,' he said. 'I need it done now. We can wait here while you take a look at it.'

'I work on my own terms or not at all,' said Kessler. 'I'll get to you as fast as I can. But this isn't Hackers-While-U-Wait. Take it or leave it.'

'I'll take it,' said Josh. 'Thanks.'

Kessler took back the laptop and put it on the side of the table. 'I'm going to give you a cellphone,' he said. 'It's a secure line. All traces of who it belonged to have been erased, and I'm the only person who has the number. Any message transmitted through it can't be traced. I'll call you on that when I'm ready.'

Josh nodded. Kessler was clearly a man who had plenty of clients who liked to keep their business very secret. 'Just make it as fast as possible,' he said. 'We'll be waiting to hear from you.'

Josh handed over two twenty-dollar bills to the clerk at the gas station, and waited for his change. He glanced out towards Kate who was sitting waiting for him in the

Mustang. The sun was setting but the air was still hot and dry, and Josh added a couple of bottles of cold Coke and some biscuits to his purchases.

We're getting closer, he told himself. I can smell it. I may not know who I am yet but I know about endgames. *And this one is starting to come together.*

'You got a phone?' he asked the clerk.

'Out back, by the toilets,' said the clerk, handing across the change.

Josh started walking to the back of the gas station. An image was flashing through his mind. O'Brien, Morant and himself attacking an FBI agent as he stood at a urinal. Step carefully, he told himself. You don't want to get coshed while you're making a call of nature.

He fed fifty cents into the phone's coin box, checking the surrounding area as he did so. So far as he could see, it was empty. They had taken a back road through Utah back into Arizona, keeping clear of the Interstate in case there were any police checks at the state or county boundaries. The road was empty. Even at the gas stations there were only a few customers.

Marshall picked up the phone after a couple of rings. 'Kate with you?' he said as soon as Josh said hello.

'Yup, she's fine,' said Josh.

'Kessler helping you?'

'Reluctantly,' said Josh. 'What do you have on him?'

'Doesn't matter,' said Marshall. 'He helped, didn't he? That's all that counts.'

True enough, Josh reckoned. 'Any leads on the man in the picture?'

Josh felt certain that if Marshall could identify the man in the picture that he'd given him, then that would be another lead.

Something in the drawn-out silence that followed his question suggested to Josh that he was going to be told something, but not everything. With Marshall, he never felt he was getting more than half the story.

'I reckon it's a guy called Jim Flatner,' said Marshall eventually.

'Who's he?'

Another pause, while Marshall seemed to weigh up how much to say. 'He's a biker.'

'I figured that from his clothes,' said Josh. 'Either that or he's some old queen who likes to dress up in leather.'

Marshall chuckled. 'He hangs out in the empty country, about twenty miles east of Scottsdale. There's about thirty of them living out in the mountains. Mostly men, but there are a few girls there as well. A few kids, too. It's kind of an alternative community.'

'What do they do?'

'Anything that pays,' said Marshall. 'Some drug dealing. Fencing stolen goods. That kind of thing. They try not to bother the local community, and the locals stay out of their way.'

'They were looking for me,' said Josh. 'I'm sure of it.'

'I think you can be twice as sure now.'

Josh gripped the phone tighter in his hands. He looked out across the forecourt of the station. Kate had climbed out of the car, and was walking up and down impatiently. A truck had pulled up, filling up its tank with diesel. 'Why?'

'Your friend Madge,' said Marshall. 'She's dead.'

Josh paused. An image of the girl lying in his arms was playing out in his mind: the way she was just a few days ago, when she was full of passion and life. 'What the hell happened?'

'There was a story on the local news,' said Marshall. 'Said she killed herself. Threw herself off a bridge in Boisdale.'

'That's a lie.'

Marshall chuckled again. 'Probably the oldest lie the police ever heard.'

'I was with her just couple of days ago,' continued Josh, glancing at Kate. 'She wasn't the kind of girl who kills herself. She had no reason to, and even if she had she wouldn't do it. She just wasn't the type.' Josh paused. 'Somebody killed her. And if they killed her, they'll want to kill me as well.'

Josh started walking back towards the car. Why the hell would anyone want to kill Madge? he wondered to himself. Christ, it must have been because she was in touch with me. I told her that if she found out anything more, then she should get in touch with me at Marshall's house.

He could feel his stomach churning with guilt. Just that tiny sliver of information cost the girl her life.

Could those bikers be working for the Feds? No, that doesn't make any sense. Then who? Who the hell are they and what do they want? What can I possibly have known that was worth all this?

Josh made a decision. He didn't want to just hang around and wait for Kessler to come up with something. Find those bikers – and find out who they are working for, he told himself.

A fire was burning down in the camp. Josh held the binoculars to his eyes, scanning the tiny community. From his vantage point high up in the hills, he could count about fifteen homes. They were made from wood, canvas and corrugated iron: rough, shanty-town shelters that could be taken down as quickly as they had been thrown up.

He turned towards Kate. 'You reckon he's down there somewhere?'

She nodded. 'This is his territory,' she said. 'It's only a few square miles of desert, but Marshall says Flatner rules it like some medieval warlord.'

After hearing of Madge's death, they had driven straight into the mountains where Marshall said the bikers had their camp, stopping only once at a gas station to grab a pair of microwaved burgers. Josh sensed that there was little time for delay. The conspiracy was closing in on them fast. If they'd found Madge, soon they would find both him and Kate. And it might be sooner than they knew.

Take the fight to the enemy. I don't know where the hell I remember that from, but it was good advice.

They'd parked the Mustang three miles away, and had covered the rest of the distance on foot. It was too dangerous to approach the camp in a car. There was only one dirt track leading up through the mountains, and Josh had to assume that it was watched. The bikers could have posted lookouts. Or they could have rigged it up with electronic sensors. It didn't matter which. Either way, Josh had to assume that it was under surveillance. They would certainly detect a car.

The trek had been a long and hard one. The first mile was fine, but after that the country had started to rise sharply upwards, and Josh had found the ground heavy going. They had stopped on the way to pick up some supplies from a gas station: four litres of water, some tinned beans, bacon and biscuits, and some matches, plus a couple of cheap plastic rucksacks to sling their kit over their backs. The weight of the gear was making the going tougher. Josh could tell that his leg was still far from healed: there was nothing he could do about the damage inflicted on his muscles, however. *Recuperation will have to wait,* he told himself. *Right now, the best I can hope for is to stay alive.*

Josh folded away his binoculars and put them back in his pocket. He'd seen a fire at the centre of the camp, and he could see some men sitting around, smoking joints and drinking beer. But at this distance, and in this darkness, it was impossible to get a clear line on any of their faces. 'We won't see anything tonight,' he said. 'Too late and too dark.'

'And what are you hoping to find exactly, Josh?' said Kate.

He turned to face her. Not for the first time in the few days that they had spent together, he found himself wondering what was driving her on. At times she was considerate, at others angry, sometimes helpful, and sometimes just difficult. Maybe I've forgotten what women are like, he wondered to himself. *Maybe I never knew.*

'The key,' he said. 'My memory is there somewhere, I know it. I get glimpses. All I need is something to unlock it all.'

'And you think that it might be here?'

Josh shook his head. 'I won't know it until I find it,' he replied.

Kate had started unfurling the cloth that they had picked up along with the rest of their supplies. It looked like a picnic rug, with a plastic sheet on one side. The mountainside was rising above them, with the valley and the camp stretched out down below. They were about halfway up on a steep incline, with a set of boulders shielding their position from anyone looking up from the camp. Josh broke out some biscuits and a bottle of water, and went to lie next to Kate on the rug.

'I'm frightened, Josh.'

He put his arm around her, grateful for the warmth of her skin next to his. The exhaustion of the day had seeped into every bruised limb: the wound on his leg was weeping with pain and his brain was spinning as he tried to make sense of everything that had happened in the past few days.

The same question played itself, over and over, like a tape stuck in a loop. *What can I have done that this many people want me dead?*

Kate was running her lips down the side of his neck. He pulled her tighter against him, aware of her breath on his skin. He started to roll her over onto her back, but she pushed him away playfully, pinning his arms down and slowly unbuttoning his shirt with her teeth. He reached out, glancing towards the stars, then at the magnificent mane of red hair streaming above him. Taking each button of her blouse in turn, he undressed her with the same care and attention with which he would field-strip a treasured gun. As he did so, he listened to her whimpers and moans of pleasure as they disturbed the silence of the desert night.

Josh closed his eyes. Suddenly, he was startled to find another image playing in front of his eyes. Another woman was making love to him. A brunette. With long dark hair and deep brown eyes, she had skin that was smooth, supple and tanned to perfection. There was a metal stud in her belly button. And her face was sculpted as if from marble, with delicate eyes, a straight nose, high, narrow cheekbones, and a wicked, mischievous mouth.

Who is she? Josh wondered. A girlfriend. *A wife?*

'You okay, baby?' Kate whispered in his ear, as she rode him towards her own climax.

Josh shuddered, then nodded. Memory can be a dark and dangerous place, he thought. There is so little I know about myself.

Kate rolled away from him, her passion exhausted, and for a few minutes they lay still and silent, their bodies bathed by the starlight shining down on the mountains. Kate reached down for her shirt, pulling it back up over her breasts. Then she squeezed herself tight against Josh, as if looking for shelter from the cold of the night.

'You don't have to be with me,' said Josh. 'This is my fight. I can handle it on my own.'

Kate swung her head from side to side, her lips reaching up to peck at Josh's mouth. 'Now that I've found you, I'm not letting you out of my sight.'

TWELVE

Wednesday, June 10th. Dawn.

Josh struggled to shake the sleep from his eyes. He could tell that it was set to be another baking-hot day, but the night had been cold and there was still a chill in the air. His bones felt stiff from the rough ground on which Kate and he had slept, and the wound in his leg was teasing his nerves: a vicious tingling sensation was running down the main artery, shooting into his knee. It feels like a cheese grater rubbing against my skin, he reflected. *From the inside.*

'Any memories, Josh?' said Kate.

She opened a bottle of Coke and passed a plastic cup across to Josh, and he took it between his hands, letting the cola drink's caffeine sink slowly into his veins. A coffee would have been good, but it was too dangerous to light a fire up here: the smoke would reveal their position. Down below, the camp was starting to stir to life. He could see some men walking through the rows of tin and canvas shacks: big, bearlike creatures, with beards, and tattoos on their bulging forearms. A few yards from the shacks, a group of children were playing on some old tyres attached by ropes between a pair of up ended cars to make a simple swing. In the centre, he could see some women starting a fire. At least they're probably women, thought Josh. *They had longer hair, bleached blonde, and not so many tattoos.*

'Nothing,' he replied. 'It's going to be a long hard slog to get them back.'

He sat down on a boulder, using the binoculars to continue his search. 'There,' said Josh. 'That's him.'

He passed the binoculars across to Kate. Whilst she peered down at the camp, he tracked the man walking across the rough scrubland. It was Flatner, Josh felt certain of it. He was flipping open a mobile phone, and pacing around while he talked.

'Yeah, definitely,' said Kate.

'What the hell are they all doing down there?' asked Josh.

She shrugged. 'Bikers — who knows what the hell they do?' she answered. 'Most of them aren't as weird as they look. Lots of them have jobs and families and houses and stuff. They come up here for a few days, mess around with their Hondas and Yamahas, do some drugs, and trade some stolen goods.'

'Bloody funny place to do it.'

'Look to your left.'

Josh glanced to the left of the camp. He could just about see some long rows of cacti, their ground-hugging green compact bulbs broken up by strings of light purple flowers. There were different kinds of cacti growing all over the wilderness, but these looked fresher. They were arranged in straight lines. Someone was cultivating them.

'Peyote,' continued Kate. 'It grows wild along this valley. It's one of the oldest and most effective psychedelic drugs known. The desert tribes of the South-West used it. So did the Aztecs. And now the bikers as well. You get good prices for that stuff in California.'

Josh looked across at Kate. 'Do think there might be a good electronics shop anywhere nearby?'

Now that he'd seen that they were carrying mobiles, he knew what he needed: an interceptor that would allow him to eavesdrop on their calls.

'There's a mall outside Scottsdale,' she replied. 'They've probably got one there. Why?'

'Flatner's conversations. I want to listen to them,' replied Josh. 'I want to know who he is and what he's doing.'

The journey was a long and arduous one. From Kate and Josh's base in the mountains, it was a three-mile walk back down to the car. At least no one had nicked the Mustang, thought Josh as he put the keys into the ignition. Next, there was a twenty-mile drive to The Village, a mall just outside Scottsdale. Josh had been wary on the road, keeping a close eye out for police patrols, and now he watched the security guards closely as they stepped inside. As soon as they arrived, he picked up some cheap plain-glass spectacles from a drugstore: they would change the shape of his face and make him harder to recognise. Then he found a public toilet and gave himself a wash. Next he made for a barber's shop to get the beard that he had been growing trimmed and his hair cut, telling the girl to give it a left parting — so that it would help him look different to any picture of him that might exist. A man who stinks of the desert, and who looks like he hasn't washed or shaved in a week stands out, he figured. Just the smell would be enough to mark you out.

'I don't know about cleanliness being next to godliness, but I do know that it helps you stay in the shadows,' he pointed out to Kate as he directed her towards the hairdresser to get her own hair shampooed and blow-dried.

The electronics shop was a huge barn, filled with sockets, connections, wires and plugs. When Josh explained that he wanted an LAN receiver, the clerk sitting at the information desk had looked puzzled. 'Check your stocklist,' Josh told him sharply. Sure enough, they had a Yellowjacket in the storeroom. Eight hundred dollars, explained the clerk. Josh whistled, then started counting out the cash. The three thousand dollars in cash that he'd had on him when he was shot had already been whittled down to just a thousand bucks.

I'd better find out who I am soon, he thought to himself. *And I hope I have some sodding money in my account.*

'How does that work?' asked Kate. They were back up the mountains.

The three-mile trek from where they had concealed the Mustang had put the dust and grime back into her freshly done hair, but she still looked magnificent, thought Josh. Her eyes were burning with curiosity, and the spirit of adventure was warming her blood, bringing a glow to her cheeks.

Josh held the Yellowjacket Wireless Receiver in his hand. The device measured eighteen inches long, by ten across, and weighed just one pound. It was encased in a frame of thick black plastic, with a tiny liquid-crystal screen displaying the radio frequencies as you scrolled through them.

I know how to use this, thought Josh to himself, looking down at the receiver. I don't know where or when, but somebody taught me how to spy on people. 'A cellphone transmits over a local area network to its closest base station,' he said. 'Most phones and networks are digital these days, so that makes them pretty hard to hack into unless you have access to the encryption software run by the phone company. That's enough security for the average user, although if you are really worried about it you can scramble your own calls. These guys aren't doing that.'

'So what does *this* thing do?'

'This device is a high-powered radio receiver,' said Josh, 'with a built-in digital decoder. The encryption doesn't kick in until the call reaches the base station and gets processed by the computers of the phone company. But if you can intercept the call between the cellphone and its base station, you can tune into it as if you were tuning into your local radio station. All we have to do is sit back and listen.'

Josh hunkered down behind a boulder. The Yellowjacket

was lying in the sand next to him, along with a bottle of water. It was three in the afternoon now, and the sun was still hanging high above him in the sky. Even at altitude the heat was punishing. Beads of sweat were running down his back, soaking his shirt, and the air was so dry and over-heated that it was scorching the back of his throat. A snake was winding its way through the boulders: a nasty-looking yellow and black creature. Josh watched it slither its way across the boulders. He held a sharp rock in his hand, ready to smash the reptile to death if it came any closer.

A man could fry to death out here. If the snakes didn't poison him first.

Using his thumb, Josh was scanning through the frequencies on the Yellowjacket. Most mobile systems transmitted at between 2,300 and 2,600 megahertz, a narrow range of radio bands. Which one any particular phone was using depended on the network operator, and the amount of voice traffic that they were carrying.

The receiver locked on to a signal. Josh plugged in the earphone and started listening.

'I need an FA135,' said a voice.

'We haven't got any.'

'Where can I get some?'

'No idea, man. Try the Honda dealer in Phoenix.'

Brake pads, realised Josh. One of the bikers down in the camp was looking for some new brake pads for his Honda. He swivelled the dial, locking out that call and looking for another one.

'I can deliver you the stuff Tuesday, man. That okay?'

Josh listened intently. What stuff?

'I can handle three. Think you can get that many?'

'No way, man. Three Mercedes by this week, no way. There aren't that many Mercs to steal in the whole of fucking Arizona. I can get you a couple of Mercs, maybe a Beamer and a Ford. A nice pick-up, a Ranger, whatever.'

'Forget it. I'll take a Merc and a Beamer if you can get them, but no Fords. We can't even sell the new ones, so forget the hot mothers.'

Josh leaned back against the boulder. He took a bottle of water, putting it to his lips, letting the liquid pour down his throat, taking a couple of degrees off his body heat. Got to be careful with the water, he thought. The bikers are doing a lot of business up here in the hills. They talk a lot. *It could be a long wait.*

Josh pushed the earphone into his anticle, pressing the tiny lump of black plastic tight against his flesh, making sure that he caught every word. Dusk had started to fall across the valley, and there was a fire burning down in the centre of the camp. Even high up in the hills, Josh could smell the charred flesh of the animal roasting on the spit: the odours of the juices of the cooked meat were making him hungry as he nibbled his way to the bottom of the day's second packet of biscuits.

Then he sat bolt upright. The rest of the bikers, he reckoned, were just dope-heads and small-time crooks. If there was anything important happening down there, it was going to be channelled through Flatner. He was their leader.

And suddenly there was a new voice on the line. 'I want him dead Flatner,' said the voice. 'Do you understand me? Dead, as of today. And that Luke boy as well.'

'Do you hear me?' repeated the voice, its tone rising into a nasal, bullying whine. 'Dead.'

He wants who dead? Josh asked himself.

Me?

Josh fiddled with the scanner on the Yellowjacket, making sure that it stayed locked on to the call.

'We've got men roaming the area,' answered Flatner. 'We're going to nail him.'

'And the boy?' said the man.

'We're still hunting.'

'Redouble your efforts,' said the voice. 'Spend whatever money you have to. Hire whoever you have to. The expense doesn't matter.' He paused on the line. As Josh looked down on the valley, he could see Flatner standing just outside the camp, his huge shoulders hunched upwards and his brow furrowed. 'I need both of them.'

'Understood, sir,' said Flatner. 'We're already measuring up the coffins,' he chuckled as he snapped the phone shut.

It's not often that a man gets to listen to his own death sentence, reflected Josh as he pulled the plug from his ear.

Looking down at the Yellowjacket, he started punching the dials on the device. He was working purely from instinct – he had no memory of when or where he might have received the training to do this – but he knew that it was possible to access the incoming call number. The numbers were digitally encoded, but the device slowly unpicked the code until the incoming call data was clearly described in soft green lettering on the instrument's LCD screen.

Josh looked down at the eleven digits displayed in front of him. 08732 611544.

That's the number of the man who wants to kill me. All I need to know now is his name.

He looked up at Kate. She was stretched out on the rug, dozing gently. He had been sitting there for hours waiting for the one call that would give him the breakthrough he needed.

Inside Kate's rucksack a cellphone rang.

Josh jumped, worried that even the quiet ring tone might give away their position.

'Yes?' he said.

'That Josh?'

Josh recognised the voice: the same gruff, unhelpful tone that he had listened to yesterday. Kessler. 'You found something?'

A pause. Even over a mobile line, Josh could see the man's face, the skin around his beard twitching as he calculated how much information he wanted to reveal. 'You bet.'

'What is it?' said Josh. 'What's on the computer?'

Another pause. *Can't you just get to the point, man?*

'We can't speak on the phone.'

'I thought you said this was a secure line.'

Kessler laughed drily. 'I'm not telling you on any kind of phone.'

'I'll come to your house, then,' said Josh. 'Tonight.'

'No way,' said Kessler quickly. 'I don't want you coming anywhere near my house.'

Christ, what's he found?

'Where, then?'

'About a mile west of Kanab, just after you cross into Utah from Arizona on Interstate 89, there's a mall called The Waterfall. In there, you'll see a Taco Bell. It's open twenty-four-hours. When can you get there?'

Josh thought for a moment, running the calculations in his head. An hour to walk back to where the car was hidden, then at least a two or three hours' drive. 'Three hours, maybe four,' he replied.

'Then I'll see you there at midnight,' said Kessler. 'Don't go inside. I'll meet you in the parking lot. Look for a yellow VW Beetle.'

'Fine, we'll be there.'

'And listen – I'm doing this as a favour for Marshall,' continued Kessler. 'I'll talk to you for half an hour. After that I never want to see you again.'

THIRTEEN

Wednesday, June 10th. Midnight.

There were only two other cars in the parking lot as Josh steered the Mustang through the entrance to the Taco Bell. A pick-up truck and a new Audi. Josh killed the Mustang's engine, and leaned back in his seat. No sign of a yellow Beetle. He'd made sure they'd arrived a few minutes early so he could check that the parking lot was safe before they went in. He'd seen two cars at Kessler's ranch: a Ford and a Land Rover. *No sign of a Beetle. Maybe he's fixed himself up with a different car just for this trip. To make sure that no one can trace him.*

He's scared. *And he doesn't look like a man who scares easily.*

'Can you see him?' Josh said, glancing across to Kate.

She shook her head. 'We've still got ten minutes,' she replied. 'A computer nerd. I've got a feeling he's going to be punctual.'

'Want something to eat?'

'Hell, why not? When you drive two hundred miles to a Taco Bell you might as well treat yourself. Make it a half-pound burrito combo, with some cheesy fiesta potatoes on the side.'

She looks thin enough, thought Josh as he walked towards the counter inside the restaurant. *Not like most of the customers at Taco Bell.*

It was now ten to midnight, he noted, checking the clock

on the wall. They had walked quickly down the mountainside, back to the curve of the road where they had hidden the Mustang behind a heap of boulders. The drive had been a fast one. There was little traffic at this time of night. And Josh's adrenalin was pumping furiously, pushing him forwards. *If we can crack what was on that computer, maybe I'll know what I was out here looking for.*

Returning to the car, he handed Kate her burrito and took a bite from his own Double Decker Taco. The combination of beef, flour, cheese and lettuce tasted good. Fast food is what you need on the run, he reflected. *Constant hits of sugary, over-flavoured food to keep your energy levels up.*

Just then, the Beetle drove into the parking lot. Josh and Kate climbed out of the Mustang.

Kessler stepped from his car and walked the few yards across the parking lot to where Josh and Kate were standing. His eyes swivelled from side to side, checking the space for surveillance. One man was sitting inside the restaurant, eating a Tostada and listening to some music on his iPod. Otherwise the place was empty. As Kessler reassured himself that no one could see him his manner slowly unwound.

'Cheesy potato?' asked Josh, offering him one of the outsized chips.

'I'm not hungry,' snapped Kessler.

'Golden potatoes topped with warm nacho-cheese sauce,' continued Josh, reading from the side of the carton. 'They're delicious.'

'Let's make this quick,' said Kessler.

'Suits me,' answered Josh, putting down his food on the car. 'What did you find?'

Kessler put a black leather computer case down on the bonnet, unzipped it, and took out the Dell Inspiron. The machine lay silent and inert, a harmless-looking lump of plastic, wire, and silicon. 'Take it,' said Kessler, a rasp in his voice. 'I never want to see it again.'

Josh put his hand down on the computer. 'I will,' he said softly. 'But first I want to know what's on it.'

Kessler wiped his brow. Even though there was a cool breeze blowing through the night air, a few beads of sweat had formed on his forehead. 'The hard drive had been wiped,' he said. 'Done it pretty well, too. Whoever owned this machine clearly knew a bit about computers. They knew how to get right inside the operating system and carefully erase all traces of what programs it had been running, and what websites it had visited.'

'But it wasn't all wiped clean?' Josh asked.

'Just about. But Windows is a hell of a program. There are layers and layers of code in there, with different bits plugged into the thing as they update it every year. I reckon even Bill Gates doesn't really understand it any more.' Kessler paused to smile at his own joke. 'Eventually I found a few traces. Took me all day but there were bits of code wrapped inside other bits of code. Once you unpeeled those you had a few keys. And I didn't like what I found.'

Josh reached down to pick up his taco. 'What?' he said quickly.

'Ever heard of a company called Porter–Bell?' said Kessler, his eyes flicking upwards nervously.

'Vaguely,' interrupted Kate. 'Software, right? Run by a billionaire called Edward Porter.'

Kessler nodded. 'A vicious company,' he said. 'Among the hackers and phreakers and the rest of the alternative software community, they are nick-named Hanging-Bell. That's because if you touch one of their patents, or stray onto any of the bits of commercial territory they control, they come after you like a posse on speed. They make Microsoft look like a bunch of Boy Scouts. Nobody messes with them. Not if they've got any sense.'

'What do they make?' asked Josh.

'Industrial software,' said Kessler. 'The really big pieces of kit that are used to control complex urban systems. The chances are that if you stop at a red light, or ride the subway to work, then you'll be relying on some Porter-Bell software. They are global, and in that space they are the best there is.'

As he listened to the explanation, Josh could sense himself growing more and more uneasy. 'Let me guess,' he said. 'Luke was hacking into it.'

'Big time,' said Kessler, his gaze sweeping across the sparse parking lot. 'What I found on his computer was a shadow. That's traces of a different operating system that has a different basic programming language to Windows. It's a proprietary system, one that belongs to just one company. I looked it up. It was designed by Porter-Bell. The kid must have been good, because that company has more security than the Pentagon. But I reckon there's only one explanation for what I found in that Dell. He'd been into their systems and stolen some of their codes.'

Josh whistled. He already had a sense of what he was about to hear, but asked the question anyway. 'What kinds of codes?'

'Security codes, of course,' replies Kessler. 'In particular, the codes for power-grid systems. You know about those?'

Josh shook his head. *Maybe I don't want to know, either.*

'Porter-Bell installs and operates power-grid software, the kit that gets the juice from the power station to the kettle in your kitchen,' said Kessler. 'It's like the holy grail of hackers. Get access to that software, and you could switch the power on and off at will. Gradually, Porter-Bell has been installing new software around the world, with upgraded systems that were meant to make the software invulnerable to attack.'

'Where were the upgrades?' said Kate. 'Where did they start?'

'Three different cities,' said Kessler. 'London, Paris and New York.'

'Christ,' said Josh. 'You think Luke was responsible for the Three Cities attack earlier this year?'

Kessler nodded. 'And that's why I don't want anything more to do with you.' He finally took a cheesy potato. 'I'm talking to you now, and after that I hope that I never have to see you again.' A slow smile crossed his lips. 'Heck, maybe *nobody* will.'

With his right hand, Kessler pushed the computer further across the bonnet of the car: he touched it only with the tips of his fingers, as if it might be contaminated. 'Here's what I think happened,' he continued. 'I think this kid managed to hack into the codes, and then turned off the lights in those three cities to see if the program he had written worked. Maybe he's a great hacker, or maybe he's just some punk who happened to get lucky. That happens from time to time – you get some bright kid who gets a few breaks and cracks into the Pentagon computers. But however he did it, your kid didn't know what he was messing with.'

'Meaning what?' says Kate.

'Meaning, crack open that code, and Porter–Bell wants to kill you, the Government wants to arrest you, and every nut, psychopath and terrorist is going to try and steal it off you.'

A malevolent smile was playing on Kessler's face and Josh was sure that he could detect just a hint of jealously in his voice. 'Think about it. The ability to turn off the power anywhere in the world at will. Everyone wants it, and you've got it. There ain't no safe place in the world for you to hide.'

Kessler turned around, walking back in the direction of the parked Beetle. 'Next time my lights go off, I'll be thinking of you.'

Josh watched as the car pulled out of the parking lot, disappearing along the slip road that led back out to the highway. He took the last bite out of his taco, and threw the remains of the food in the bin.

'Come on,' he said to Kate. 'Let's get out of here.'

'To where?' Kate asked. 'Where the hell are we going?'

'To find Luke,' replied Josh. 'Before they do.'

FOURTEEN

Thursday, June 11th. Dawn.

Kate lay at Josh's side, her eyes still closed, her red hair draped across her face. Josh stood up, and walked gingerly towards the Mustang. Reaching for a bottle of water, he threw some down his throat, drinking a quarter of a litre in one gulp. Slowly, he could feel himself starting to wake up.

The ground beneath them was dusty and harsh. Josh could feel a wind blowing across his face: grating, violent gusts of air, filled with grit, that seemed to smash into his skin.

As he looked around, he briefly wondered where he was. Behind him he could see a gently sloping hill dotted with pine trees. Below him he could see the narrow road twisting into the distance. Further away he could see a river meandering its way towards the horizon.

Neither of them had had enough energy to drive far last night. After Kessler left, they took the Mustang out into the back roads along the state border. It was too dangerous to risk checking into a motel, and neither Josh nor Kate knew enough about this countryside to find adequate shelter for the night. So after driving through the darkness for twenty minutes, Josh turned off the road, ploughing along a dirt track that twisted its way through some fields. They might as well stay there, he had decided. They weren't going to find anywhere better.

As they lay down together, pulling the one blanket they had in their kitbags over their heads, Kate suddenly grabbed hold of Josh, pulling his body close against her: her fingers clawed him as if she were clinging onto him in fear that he might escape from her.

Josh had fallen immediately into a deep sleep, blocking out all his senses. As he drifted off, an image suddenly drifted through his mind. The brunette. The one he had seen a few days ago. Her lips were moving. She was shouting. But he couldn't hear anything she was saying.

Now Josh paced around to try and warm himself up. They had learned so much in the last twenty-four hours. Flatner was looking for Josh, as well as for Luke. Someone was paying him to do it. And he wanted Josh dead. It was a fair conclusion that whoever that was, he'd also had something to do with Josh's shooting.

Then again, Luke had been hacking into the software systems of Porter-Bell. His mother had told them that he'd been talking about how he was going to make a lot of money sometime soon. That wasn't hard to figure out. He and Ben had cracked some lucrative code, and had thought that they could make some money out of it.

Edward Porter, Josh had concluded as they completed the long drive. That's the link. *We need to know a lot more about him.*

He walked across to Kate. 'Wake up,' he said gently, passing her a bottle of water.

Her eyes opened, drowsy at first, then fiercely alert. She snapped out of her sleep, looking around her. 'Where the hell are we?' she said, glancing up at Josh.

'Nowhere.'

Kate took the water, drinking a few mouthfuls, then using the rest of the bottle's contents to wash her face and hands. Some of the dust and grime from the field was sticking to her shirt and jeans, and some earth had lodged itself in her hair.

'What's the plan?' said Kate. 'Where do you want to start?'

'Your house,' said Josh.

There was a pause. 'You think he's there?'

Josh shook his head. 'No,' he answered. 'But Marshall has a fine collection of guns. I'm going to see if I can borrow some. For the next stage of this battle, I think we need to be armed.' He chuckled harshly. 'To the teeth.'

'It's two hundred miles back there,' said Kate.

'Then we'd better get started.'

Josh walked carefully towards the house. His eyes were scanning first left, then right, and his ears were tuned for the slightest noise: a whisper of wind, the wings of a bird, or the movement of a snake through the sand, any of them would have alerted him instantly. But there was nothing. The place was as still as a graveyard.

If anyone is there waiting, then I'm done for, thought Josh. It's at least two hundred yards to the house. *They will see me long before I can see them.*

He picked up his pace. There was no cover, and no way of approaching the building without being seen. Checking that Kate was still behind him, he started to run towards the front door.

'I don't like it,' said Kate suddenly. 'Something's wrong.'

The hinge of the door was hanging loose. Josh stood next to the entrance to the house, holding on to a fragment of wood that had once been part of the door.

'My God,' said Kate. 'What the hell happened?'

It was only as they approached the porch that they could see the extent of the damage that had been done to the house. They stepped inside together, noticing at once that the television was still on. The door had been smashed in. An axe, Josh guessed, given the way in which the wood had splintered and split. The hall had been left untouched, but both the bedrooms had been turned upside down, every drawer flung open, the contents tossed onto the floor. The mattresses had been ripped open with knives – the stuffing was bulging out of them. Across the floor the scattered debris was lying in a heap.

And Josh noticed something else as well. *There was no sign of Marshall.*

Josh moved through to the kitchen. Every cupboard door had been ripped from its hinges, the food tipped out, and every box and jar thrown open. Flies had started to invade the house, settling thickly on the food spread out everywhere: a couple flew away as Josh stepped into the room, but the rest just carried on eating. Looking down, Josh could see that the intruders had discovered the hiding place beneath the floor: the boards had been ripped apart and the staircase smashed up.

'Where the hell is my dad?' said Kate, her voice ragged.

Josh took a moment to survey the damage. Professionals, he concluded. They knew how to search a building quickly and efficiently, and they didn't care how much damage they did. 'They were looking for me,' said Josh.

Kate shook her head from side to side. Her expression was concentrated, intense. 'No,' she said. 'They were looking for something smaller than a man, something that might be hidden here. They've ripped open mattresses. They've opened up all the food jars. A man can't hide in one of those.'

'Then it's the computer,' said Josh. 'Luke's computer – that's what they want.'

'Or a disk,' said Kate.

'Christ, I hope they haven't attacked Luke's mother,' said Josh.

Josh walked quickly through to the room where he had slept. The bed had been knifed to shreds. Next, he strode to the back of the house, to the small room where Marshall kept his guns. Nothing. The rack was still there: a thick, solid slab of finely polished wood, with a dozen oblong slots in it. But the weapons were all gone.

'The guns,' shouted Josh to Kate. 'All taken. And there's still no sign of Marshall.'

Josh walked back to the kitchen. Kate was standing by herself, next to the sink. The glasses were all broken, but she'd found a plastic beaker and was taking a sip of water. Josh could see her eyes flickering toward the TV. Whoever had ransacked this place must have left it on. Probably checking the TV actually worked, figured Josh. Not just an empty box with something hidden inside it. *Like I thought, professionals.*

The newsreader was the kind of highlighted blonde who dominated every news channel in America. 'In a terrifying reprise of the Three Cities Attack earlier this year, the power was dramatically switched off in four different cities for precisely one hour this morning,' she was saying.

Josh put his arm around Kate's shoulder, watching the news intently. He could feel the tension rippling through her as he held her body next to his.

'At precisely nine o'clock this morning the power got switched off in Orlando, Seattle, in the historic holiday town of Jamestown in New York State, and in Harrison in Tennessee. In each incident, the power shutdown caused widespread panic and confusion. Road systems stopped working, factories, office buildings and schools had to be closed and hospitals had to shut their doors since even their emergency back-up generators couldn't cope with the demand for electricity. Although the power has now been restored in each city, reports are coming in of several injuries in both Seattle and Orlando, mainly caused by traffic accidents as the street lights went down. Air traffic control was suspended in the cities, and all flights in and out have had to be diverted. There are also reports of widespread looting in Orlando as local police failed to stop panic spreading through the streets.'

'So what caused this latest blackout? There is plenty of

speculation about a terrorist assault, just as there was with the Three Cities Attack earlier this year. Some people are saying that it could have been a blow against Microsoft because Seattle was one of the cities where the power was shut down and that is where the software giant is based. Other people are saying it could be an attack on the Kennedy Space Centre, based near Orlando, although no rocket launches were scheduled for this morning.'

'A spokesman for the White House said that they were at this stage ruling out the possibility of a terrorist attack, and that a full investigation was now under way into how the power failed in four cities across the United States at precisely the same moment. The White House is due to make a fuller statement later today. After this break, we go over live to our correspondent in Orlando to find out how local people are coping with the aftermath of the blackout.'

Josh looked towards Kate. 'Luke,' he said simply. 'He's still out there.'

'Or his software,' said Kate. 'Maybe somebody else has got hold of it by now.'

'You think they took Marshall?'

'Maybe they killed him?'

Josh shook his head. 'You see any sign of a struggle?' he replied. 'Blood on the floor? Gunshot holes in the wall? No. I reckon if they had taken Marshall there would have been a fight. He left before they got here.'

She's brave, thought Josh. Her father has disappeared, and yet she appears confident that he's okay. *Maybe she just has a lot of faith in the old guy.*

'But they've linked the two of us,' said Josh. 'I reckon they got Marshall's name from Madge before they killed her. That's why they came out here. Whoever did this, they now know that you and Marshall have been helping me.'

Kate walked to the back of the hallway. A computer was plugged into the wall, and although the cable linking the screen to the keyboard and the power box had been ripped apart it looked to have been undamaged. Kate spent a few seconds checking the machine, then fired it up. 'That number you took, the man who called Flatner telling him to find you,' she said. 'Have you still got it?'

'We haven't got enough time,' snapped Josh. 'How the hell do we know when they'll be back?'

'We have to know for certain,' said Kate. 'Without that, we have nothing.'

Josh sat down next to her. There was a stillness to the house. The sun was beating down outside, its rays spilling across the broken and scattered furniture. There was not even a hint of a breeze and the insects that populated the yard had fallen quiet. Josh read out the number that he had already committed to memory. '08732 611544.'

I may not remember much, but I can remember that.

Josh watched as Kate fired up the Internet connection. She was searching through a succession of different websites, then sent out some e-mail from her Hotmail address. Her expression was one of total concentration: her stage was fixed on the screen and her fingers were moving swiftly across the keyboard. In her left hand, she was playing with a pencil, toying with it in her mouth as if it was a cigarette. *She looks just the way she was when I first opened my eyes.*

Standing up from the desk, Josh started to walk back through the shattered house. Sometimes it was best to give people a few moments to themselves, he decided. He started sorting through some of the rubbish, trying to figure out what kinds of weapons had been used. Some sharp knives, he figured. An axe. Maybe a hammer and a wrench. *The bastards brought a whole branch of B&O with them.*

The yard was empty. Josh stood outside, shielding his eyes from the burning sun. He looked out across the dusty plain, his eyes scanning the horizon for any kind of movement.

Nothing. The landscape looked lifeless. Whoever had come here, they had left no trace of themselves.

I won't be sorry to see the back of this godforsaken country.

He took a sip of water, trying to clear the headache that was scratching against the inside of his skull. What the hell am I doing? he wondered to himself. Why don't I just hand myself in to the police?

'Found it,' shouted Kate from the back of the corridor.

Josh walked swiftly back to where she was sitting. She was leaning into the computer. He looked down. On the screen, he could see an e-mail, but it seemed to have been sent from an anonymous account. The words were printed in small bold lettering. 'The number 08732 611544 is a private cellphone number operated by Verizon Wireless. The account is registered in the name of a Mr Edward Porter.'

'So it's him,' breathed Josh. 'That's the fucker who sent Flatner to kill me.'

Kate nodded, her expression impassive.

'It's starting to make sense,' said Josh. 'Luke and Ben hacked into their software. So they want to kill him. That figures. Unless the software is invulnerable to attack, no city anywhere is going to want to install it to manage their power system. Those two boys could end up costing that company billions of dollars.'

Josh turned away, looking towards the kitchen. 'But why do they want to kill me?' he said. 'I don't get it. I *just* don't get it.'

'Maybe they don't want to kill you, Josh.'

He looked at Kate, puzzled.

'Maybe they want to find you,' she continued.

'What for?' snapped Josh. 'What the hell for?'

'Maybe you know something, Josh – don't you see?' said Kate.

Josh turned to face her. Her voice sounded raw and

ragged. 'But what?' he said coldly. '*What* do I know?'

'Think, Josh,' she said, her voice sounding choked. 'Can't you remember *anything*? Anything at all?'

Josh slammed his fist down on the sideboard, the wood, already splintered and broken, shaking under the force of the blow. Some dust fell to the floor. 'I can't bloody remember, I tell you,' he shouted. 'This is useless. I need a hospital, I need the police.'

'No, Josh, no,' said Kate.

Her voice sounded suddenly scared, desperately anxious. She rushed to him, putting her arms around his body and hugging him to her chest. 'It's going to be okay, baby.'

Josh shook his head. 'I need help.'

'*I'm* here to help you,' she said.

'You go to the police, a hospital, Porter will know about it, then kill you,' said Kate. 'Hell, if they think you had anything to do with shutting down the power system, they might not even bother to question you first. We need to fix this together. We need to find Luke.'

Josh took a sip of his water. A single sentence was drumming through his mind. She's right. *She's right.*

'I need to know more about Porter,' said Josh. 'You have to know what sort of man your enemy is.'

Josh sat down at the computer. In the next twenty minutes, he started to compile a brief biography of Edward Porter, culled from the archives of a dozen different business magazines. Porter had been born in California in 1950, and had graduated from Berkeley in physics and computing. He'd spent two years in the 5th Marine Regiment, fighting in Vietnam, but had left the armed forces after being wounded in the leg. Next, he'd spent five years working first for IBM, then for Cray Supercomputers. He'd founded Porter-Bell in 1977 with a partner, Sam Bell, but Bell had left the company in 1980. It had grown rapidly in the 1980s, first with a series of military contracts, then expanding into building city and industrial systems. As factories and power systems became automated during that decade, Porter-Bell developed and built the software that controlled them. It made a fortune.

In 1992, the company listed on the NASDAQ technology exchange, making Porter an instant billionaire. He was now estimated to be worth at least ten billion dollars, and Porter-Bell dominated its sector of the market. Twice divorced, with a string of mistresses, Porter had a reputation as a mean, combative entrepreneur, who ran his company with ruthless discipline and crushed the competition with relentless ferocity. Scouring the web, Josh found that there were countless articles testifying to the ferocity with which rivals who tried to muscle in on Porter-Bell's territory were flattened. For the last two years, the US Justice Department had been trying to prosecute the company for a series of anti-trust violations, but its lawyers had fought the actions all the way.

'We have to find Morant and O'Brien,' said Josh. 'Maybe they will know where Marshall is. And if they don't, they'll be able to get us guns and ammunition, and maybe even reinforcements.'

'We don't need weapons, Josh.'

'What the hell *do* we need, then?'

'We need your memory back. That's the only way we can get to Luke before Porter and Flatner get to them. That's what this is all about. We have to get to Luke before they do.'

'But where is he?'

Kate stood closer to him. 'You know where he is, Josh,' she said softly. 'You just need to remember, that's all.'

The road twisted ahead of them. Kate was driving the Mustang, steering it along the road that led away from the house and out into the mountains. A truck passed, then a car, but there was no sign of any patrol cars, nor of any of Flatner's bikers.

The road is safe, thought Josh. *For now.*

'How far?' he asked.

'A couple of miles,' said Kate.

She was driving them to one of their mountain hideouts. This one was thirty miles to the east of Boisdale, in a dusty mountain range that had once been home to a couple of tin mines but had long since been abandoned by everything except a few snakes and the occasional flock of wild cranes. Kate knew that Morant and O'Brien moved from camp to camp and she had a good hunch that this was where they would find them. For five hundred dollars, they could equip Kate and Josh with a pair of mules and enough food to last them for a month: they could collect water from creeks and wells out in the scrub. Morant would give them a map of the water sources that the survivalists used and the caves they slept in at night. They knew this terrain better than anyone else alive. *It won't be comfortable, thought Josh when Kate explained it to him, but we'll survive.*

The plan, thought Josh, running it afresh through his mind, was to get out into open country. His sense was that if Luke was hiding, it would be out there somewhere. He didn't have the resources or the knowledge to travel far, not without being detected. And if anyone can find him, we can. *Then, maybe, he can tell me what happened.*

Dusk was just starting to fall. The sun was dipping down towards the horizon and the light was fading. Shadows from the mountains far to the east were lying across the road, spiked and threatening, like snakes lying in wait for their victims. Josh kept his eyes focused on the road, aware that if their enemies knew Kate was helping him, then they could trace this easily enough.

The next few miles will be the most dangerous. Until we get out into the empty country.

A hitch-hiker was thumbing a lift on the side of the road: a boy of eighteen or nineteen, noticed Josh, with a rucksack at his side. For a brief moment, Josh wondered if it might be Luke. 'Keep going,' he muttered to Kate.

Josh checked the rear-view mirror, expecting to see the boy shaking his fist or giving them the finger: cars were rare enough on this empty stretch of road for a hitch-hiker to be angry with anyone who didn't stop.

But he wasn't doing anything, Josh noticed. He looked hard into the mirror, straining to make out the shape disappearing into the distance. Then he twisted round to get a better look. The boy had turned around, walking a couple of yards off the road. His shoulders were hunched, and he was holding something in his hand. Christ, thought Josh. A mobile. He's making a call.

'Slow down,' he barked.

'What?'

'Slow the bloody car,' repeated Josh.

Kate turned to look at him, fear flashing through her eyes.

'He's a spotter – that bloody kid's a spotter,' said Josh.

Kate slipped down the gears on the Mustang, putting it into second, letting the car crawl along the road at a nervous twenty miles an hour. Behind them the boy was moving swiftly across the scrubland, his phone still in his hand. He didn't look back. It was impossible to tell whether he knew they'd seen him.

Josh scanned the area, his stare swivelling across the flat empty desert to the west and the mountain range rising up to the east. He tried to block out the noise of the car, straining to detect any other sounds. We'll hear it soon enough, he said to himself grimly. The sound of attack.

'You going after him?' asked Kate.

Josh shook his head. 'No point,' he snapped. 'He's already told them we're on the road.'

'Any turnings?'

Josh scanned the road. The tarmac stretched out onto the horizon, as straight as a ruler, with no sign of any crossroads. 'Nothing,' he said bitterly.

'Want to go cross-country?'

Josh looked both right and left. The mountains half a mile distant on the right would provide some cover. Maybe they could even find somewhere to hide there. But there was no way they could drive through them. They would have to take their chances on foot. On the left, the scrub was stretching into the far distance, its flat surface punctuated only by cacti and jagged, dangerous-looking boulders. There was nowhere to hide out there, realised Josh. They would be picked up within a few minutes.

'No,' he said briskly. 'Too risky.'

Now he could hear the rumble of motors, growling out across the flat scrubland like the first warning of a distant storm. They were somewhere to his right, about a mile distant, sneaking through the mountains. I know that sound, he told himself. The oily roar of an engine revving into life. A motorbike. *Maybe a whole bloody army of them.*

'All right, I reckon it's Plan B,' said Josh.

Kate looked at him, and even though he could see the tension rippling through her, there was a hint of amusement in her eyes. 'Okay,' she said softly. 'What's Plan B?'

'Run like a rat on roller skates — and start praying.'

Kate's foot jammed down on the accelerator. The Mustang roared, its engine howling as it started to pick up power and speed. Josh cursed himself for not taking the wheel for this stretch of the journey, but it was too late now.

He checked behind. Three motorbikes were powering down the side of the mountain, driving in a tight V-formation. They were eight or nine hundred yards away but doing at least eighty or ninety miles an hour, and closing fast. A furious cloud of dust was being kicked up into the air as their back wheels bit into the caked mud of the desert. They spun out onto the tarmac, hurtling towards the Mustang at well over a hundred miles a hour now.

'Faster, faster,' snapped Josh.

He could see the sweat trickling down Kate's face as she hammered the accelerator. The Mustang's two-litre engine was roaring as she struggled to extract some more power from the machine. By now they had climbed past a hundred, and were touching a hundred and ten miles an hour. The tyres were screeching against the hot tarmac. There's not much acceleration left in this tin can, realised Josh. And the bikers are still gaining on us.

He looked in front. About half a mile ahead, more bikes, four this time, were shrieking out from behind a boulder, their engines already revved up to maximum speed. Two were in front, with two more flanking them as outriders. Definitely Flatner's men, decided Josh. As they sped towards the Mustang, he could see the men riding them: burly, leather-clad creatures, with tattoos on their arms and helmets slung down low across their faces. Except for the leader: he was wearing a Nazi helmet, with a pair of cattle horns drilled into the sides. Not much use if you had a crash, decided Josh. *But good for scaring people.*

'Which way?' shouted Kate, her eyes swivelling desperately towards Josh.

The bikes five hundred yards ahead were bearing down on them, and the bikes behind were gaining speed. Trapped, thought Josh.

I outwitted these fuckers right after I was shot, he decided. *Maybe I can do it again.*

'Keep going,' he barked. 'Drive straight into them, then swerve at the last minute and try to get past them.'

Kate's hands were vibrating on the wheel. Josh's stare was locked on the road ahead, tracking the four bikes flanking the road as they sped towards each other.

Four hundred yards, he calculated. Three hundred . . .

'Turn,' he shouted.

Kate hauled the wheel hand over. Too much pressure, Josh realised the instant she had made her move. The Mustang skidded, its wheels losing contact with the ground. It had gone into a backspin as the momentum from the rear wheels overwhelmed the vehicle, turning it through ninety degrees within a fraction of a second.

'Hold the wheel, hold the wheel,' shouted Josh.

Reaching down, he grabbed the handbrake, yanking it up to try and control the spin. The brake discs howled as they clamped against the wheels and Josh released his grip. No good, he told himself. *We'll have to take our chances in the scrub.*

A cloud of dust rose up from the side of the road as the Mustang slewed off it. He'd counted seven bikes in total, closing in fast, but now he could see nothing except for the swirling dirt all around them. The smell of burnt rubber filled the air. 'Go forward,' he shouted. 'Just go forward.'

A shot. Josh recognised the sound instantly: the thud of a cartridge fired from a sawn-off shotgun.

The back window of the Mustang crashed inwards, splinters of glass flying into their backs like a hailstorm. Josh felt two shards pricking his skin: one on his neck, the other in his back, and a hot trickle of blood ran down the edge of his spine.

Another shot, then another. Josh heard a ripping sound. A tyre. The Mustang skidded again as first one tyre blew out, then another. The power in the engine was starting to fade as the lead pellets from the shotguns ripped through the car's bodywork, smashing into the suspension, brakes and engine.

Josh looked up. Kate was still clinging to the wheel, frantically trying to bring the machine under control. The dust clouds were still obscuring their vision. Josh could just make out some boulders. A ditch that might be a dried-out creek. Then the mountains behind.

And now, looming through the dust clouds like shadows in the night, the outlines of two bikers.

Death on wheels.

Another shot. This time the bonnet flipped open, the sheet of metal catching in the wind and shooting straight upwards. The engine snarled, then stalled. To his right, Josh could smell petrol leaking onto the ground. 'Get out, get out,' he shouted. 'They're going to kill us if we stay in here.'

The Mustang was slowing fast, down to fifteen or twenty miles an hour, losing power, its steering gone. It was skidding across the surface of the ground, out of control. Josh flipped the door open. He could see moving scrub, the ground pitted with gravel and rock. Just roll out, he told himself. And pray you don't crack open your skull on one of those stones.

'Just jump,' he shouted to Kate. 'It's your only chance. Just jump and run like hell.'

'I'm not leaving you,' she shouted, straining to make her voice heard over the sound of the engine and the gunfire.

'We'll rendezvous with O'Brien and Morant,' shouted Josh.

Josh tightened his shoulder muscles. The trick to hitting the ground at speed was to wrap yourself into a ball so that the force of the impact was deflected throughout your body. You used your arms to protect your face and your head: that was where the worst injuries would be sustained. Go, man, go, he told himself. *This is your only shot at saving yourself.*

He kicked back from the car with his legs, tumbling out onto the ground. At his side, he could see Kate doing the same as the Mustang ploughed onwards under its own momentum, heading straight for the jagged edges of a massive boulder formation.

The ground impacted against his ribcage first. Josh could feel his bones rattling. None broken, he hoped, although it was impossible to tell through the pain of the fall. He rolled one yard, two, then three. The ground felt rough and harsh, grating into his skin. His jeans snagged on something. A rip opened up, then something cut into his skin. He could feel his wound throbbing, the worst it had been for days. Slamming his hands down, he gripped into the dirt, breaking a nail as he dug his fingers into the ground, bringing himself to a halt.

Josh looked up. Kate was already on her feet, running. He could not see where she was heading.

Next, he looked ahead. The Mustang was moving straight for the boulders. As it struck, a horrific noise erupted: the sound of metal being shredded by rock. The vehicle shuddered, then a storm of sparks flew up where the metal was scraping along the boulders. Josh closed his eyes, already aware of what was going to happen next. He heard the air being sucked forwards, then felt the first waves of the explosion brush against the skin of his face. The heat was scorching: a wave of hot air, blowing round him with gale-force strength. The fireball rose straight up into the sky, scattering parts of the car in every direction and sending a huge, oily cloud of thick black smoke boiling up. The sun was briefly blocked out, and the air smelled of petrol, scorched metal and fried dust.

Slowly, the force of the explosion subsided. As the clouds of black smoke cleared, Josh could see two bikes driving straight towards him. The riders were each holding one end of a rope in their hands, sweeping it across the scrubland like a fishing net. Josh stood to his feet, swallowing the pain, and then he started to run. One of his shoes had come loose and was catching on his foot, threatening to trip him. No time to stop, he told himself, willing himself forwards. *Another second, and they've got me.*

In the next moment, he felt the rope smash into the centre of his back. It started dragging him down, pushing him hard onto the ground. Josh tried desperately to pick himself up, but it was too late. The two bikes had screeched to a halt, kicking up a wall of dust, and the rope was pinning him to the dirt, cutting into the skin of his arms, and digging deep welts into his back. The pain jabbed through him.

I'm done for. *Dead in a miserable desert, where only the wolves and the vultures will pick over my bones.*

The bikers came to a halt, stepping quickly towards him, both men holding an end of the rope tightly in their fists. The leader stood over Josh, peering into his eyes. The horns on the Nazi helmet were glistening in the sunlight. 'Make it easy for yourself,' he muttered, spitting a mouthful of stale breath into Josh's face. 'Try to sleep.'

Josh could feel a fist smashing into the side of his neck – once, then twice. His eyes began to cloud over, a dazzling mist drifting across his line of vision. He could feel the pain rippling through him. It started in his neck, then ran down his spine, settling in his gut.

Another fist, this time on the other side of his neck. The blow glanced upwards, the fist colliding with his ear. Josh could feel consciousness starting to abandon him. His mind was shutting down. Before his eyes, he could see a picture. The brunette, the woman he had seen twice now. The little girl with blonde hair, three or maybe four, opening a present, then holding out a Barbie doll. She was saying something. Her lips were moving. *But what? If only I could hear as well as see her.*

Josh willed himself to stay awake, to hold on to the image. It faded, clouding before his eyes. He went under, blackness overwhelming him. Then, briefly, he was awake again. Someone was lifting him up, one man taking his legs, another his shoulders. The bikers. *Where the hell are they taking me?*

As his body swayed from side to side, consciousness started to fade and Josh could feel himself going under again. Another image flashed in front of his eyes. This time it was

Luke. Running. Then the boy was turning around, shouting something. What was it? 'Touch,' realised Josh. He was shouting 'Touch,' plus some other words that were indistinct. Touch, thought Josh, the word rattling through his mind. What the hell did he want me to touch?

The image faded as quickly as it had arisen, and suddenly Josh could see nothing. He opened his eyes, but the vision had gone. He could see only the darkness. Is this what it's like when you die? he wondered. *If I've been captured, that might be the best I can hope for.*

FIFTEEN

Thursday, June 11th. Noon.
Where's the cyanide pill? thought Josh.

Where's the sodding cyanide pill?

He closed his eyes, then opened them again, hoping against hope that maybe it was just a dream. As he pulled his eyelids slowly open, it took him a few minutes to adjust to the darkness of his surroundings. He was lying on a rough dirt floor, his hands bound tightly behind his back and his feet strapped together. A stake had been driven into the ground and the ropes wrapped around his legs had been tied to it, making it impossible for him to wriggle forward more than a yard. The room measured ten feet square, and looked to have been dug out of some kind of dried mud: a hole, driven straight down into the ground. Looking up, he could see that it was covered by some thick sheets of metal. Not a glimmer of light was breaking through. Josh could hardly even see his own body in the darkness.

It was impossible to tell what time of day it was. His watch had been taken from his wrist.

It could by any time of day, any day of the week.

What happened yesterday? Josh asked himself. What the hell happened?

A sudden jolt of cold fear ran down his spine. *Christ, not more memory loss.*

But slowly, in his mind, he started to reassemble the events of the last twenty hours. He had been with Kate, he remembered that. They had been driving, on their way to meet O'Brien and Morant. They had been attacked. The bikers had been there in force: at least seven of them, maybe more in reserve. It had been impossible to run, and they'd had no weapons with which to fight. The last thing he remembered was Kate running for her life across the open scrubland, while the bikers punched him unconscious.

I don't even know if she is alive or dead. I don't even know if I'm going to live much longer.

Josh tried to stretch his limbs. Assess the state of the damage you've taken, he decided. His neck hurt badly. The bandage on his gunshot wound had been pulled off, and the punches he'd taken to the side of his head had broken the skin open again. It had been bleeding, he could tell, and some dirt might have got in there, but the flow of blood had staunched itself while he'd been unconscious, and some fresh scabs had started to form. The nerves in his leg wound were throbbing with agony, as if his leg was being drilled open. And his ribs were aching from the fall from the car and the beating he'd taken from the bikers: none of them seemed to be broken, but the muscles were strained and they ached every time he moved.

So far they haven't roughed me up much at all. Just brought me back and tossed me in this hole. Concentrate, he told himself. Don't give in to despair. *So long as you are alive you can pull through this.*

His bladder was aching. Josh was desperate for a piss, but it was impossible to stand or even squat. 'Hey,' he shouted, looking up. 'Who's there?'

His voice was hoarse, and rasping. Something was hurting the back of his throat as he tried to speak but he couldn't identify what: so many different types of pain were already assaulting him that it was hard to tell them apart.

'Who's bloody there?' he shouted again, louder this time.

A chink of light opened in the space above him. Josh's

stare shot up to track the movement. A ray of fierce sunshine burst through, sending a narrow shaft of light down into Josh's face. He tracked the movement of the covering as it slid open. A rope ladder dropped down into the hole, then Josh could see a man starting to climb down into the pit. His boots came into view first, then his black jeans, then his leather jacket, his black beard and his thick ponytail. Josh recognised him at once. Flatner.

'How you doing today, pretty boy?' Flatner said, looking down.

Josh struggled to sit up, but the tight leash made it impossible: the best he could manage was to raise his face a few feet from the ground.

'I need a piss,' said Josh.

'And so do I,' said Flatner.

With deliberate slowness, Flatner unzipped his flies and pulled out his penis. Holding it in his hands, he sprayed Josh with his urine. The liquid felt warm as it splashed against the cloth of Josh's jeans and T-shirt. The smell made Josh cough in disgust. His own bladder could contain itself no longer: his own urine started running down the side of his leg, forming a noxious puddle on the ground.

'Talk to me, man, talk to me,' said Flatner roughly. 'You'll save yourself a lot of pain.'

'Fuck off,' Josh spat.

Josh rested his head back on the ground. The air inside the hole was already thirty or thirty-five degrees, and the sunlight now beaming in was making it even hotter. I'm going to take a beating, he told himself. *I just have to try and survive it as best I can.*

'You can make this easy for yourself, or you can make it hard,' said Flatner.

Josh looked up, making eye contact with Flatner for the first time. His expression was as hard as rock: solid and unyielding. 'What do you want?' he asked.

'The kid, Josh,' said Flatner. 'I want to know where the kid is.'

'Which kid?'

Flatner knelt down, leaning close into Josh's face, so close that Josh could smell his sour breath. 'A word of advice, man,' he said. 'Don't try to be funny and don't try to be clever. You know which fucking kid.'

'Luke?'

Flatner nodded just once.

'I don't know.'

The punch was delivered to his ribcage. Flatner's fist collided with the side of Josh's chest, sending a dull pain though his body. That was just a friendly warning, Josh warned himself. *The man can deliver a far more violent blow than that.*

'I'll ask you again,' said Flatner. 'Where's the fucking kid?'

'I don't know,' Josh repeated.

The punch was harder this time, delivered to the same point on his ribcage. The wind emptied out of his gut, and he could feel his skin turning numb. 'I don't know,' he said again.

He could see Flatner starting to draw his fist back, readying the next blow. 'No, listen,' said Josh, a ragged edge creeping into his voice. 'I really don't know.'

Flat's fist was poised to crash down against Josh's ribcage. 'Don't know?'

'I lost my memory,' said Josh.

Flatner smiled, revealing a huge set of jagged teeth. His eyes looked down at Josh, dark and morose. 'Don't try to get smart with me, pretty boy.'

'It's true,' snapped Josh. 'I was shot in the neck, and the leg. My memory's gone to pieces. Even if I did know where the hell Luke was once, I sure as hell don't know any more.'

From his back pocket, Flatner pulled out a page torn from a newspaper. 'Recognise this?'

Josh shook his head.

'It's the *New York* fucking *Times*, man. Paper of record, right?'

Josh remained silent.

'And it has a report here about what it calls The Four Cities Attack. Couple of days ago the power gets turned off in four different cities around the United States. Just like The Three Cities Attack a couple of months ago. Want me to read you what it says?'

Flatner paused for breath, not looking to Josh for a response.

'It says this: "The timing of the attacks has been described as simultaneous, but according to power-industry experts the blackouts started in different cities at slightly different local times. In Jamestown, the power went down at 9.01.00; in Orlando at 9.01.15; in Seattle at 9.01.30; and in Harrison at 9.01.45. Each blackout started at precisely fifteen seconds after the last one. But according to power-industry sources that may have just been the result of differences in local systems, and in the length of time it takes for the systems to shut themselves down."' Flatner put the paper down on the ground at his side. 'What do you think that means?'

'No bloody idea,' said Josh. 'Like it says, differences in local power systems.'

'You think so? Then maybe you're as fucking dumb as you look. Four cities. Jamestown, Orlando, Seattle and Harrison. That mean anything to you?'

Josh shook his head.

'You're a dumb son of a bitch. J-O-S-H. It spells fucking Josh. The kid shut down the power in those four cities deliberately, and he spaced out the attacks because he knew you were so fucking stupid you might have trouble figuring it out for yourself. J-O-S-H. Spells Josh.'

Flatner raised his fist as if he was about to launch another punch. Instinctively, Josh could feel himself flinching. 'Now are you still going to tell me you don't know where he is?'

The letters were spinning through Josh's mind. J-O-S-H,

he repeated to himself. Luke is sending me a message, he has to be. *But what the hell is he trying to say?*

'I don't know,' mumbled Josh.

The punch landed on his ribcage again, sending vibrations of pain rippling up into his chest. Josh clamped his teeth together, trying not to scream out in pain. The side of his chest was numb, and even though he couldn't see it he could sense the flesh and muscle swelling under the impact of the blows.

'Now tell me where the fuck he is,' roared Flatner.

'I don't know.'

'Tell me, you son of a bitch.'

'I don't know.'

Flatner's arm was raised high, ready to strike again. 'Tell me.'

'I don't bloody know.'

'Tell me!'

'I don't know.'

Flatner struck once, then again, both times hitting Josh in the same section of his ribcage. Josh screamed with pain. Each blow was worse than the last one: the flesh was softened, already wounded, and every nerve was set alight each time Flatner thumped him.

'I don't even know who I bloody am,' screamed Josh.

Flatner reached for his shoulder, yanking Josh forwards so that he was lying with his face at Flatner's feet. 'Your name is Josh Harding,' he said. 'You are a British soldier, working undercover in the United States. You were sent here just after the juice got turned off in London. Your mission was to find out what happened and to stop it happening again.'

Flatner drew himself up, standing above Josh, his thick muscles bulging as he crossed his forearms. 'But you know what, pretty boy? Right now, you don't belong to the British fucking army. You don't belong to that bitch you've been going around with. You don't even belong to yourself. And unless you start thinking about how to get your mouth working again, you're just going to be fertiliser for a fucking cactus.'

He turned around, starting to climb the rope ladder up out of the hole. Josh watched as he slowly slid the metal covers back into place. Just as he was finishing, Flatner stuck his head down, blocking out what remained of the light. 'I want you to lie here in the dirt, and I want you to think of the worst thing that can possibly happen to a man,' he growled. 'And I want you to know that it's going to happen to you soon if you don't tell me where the fucking kid is.'

Josh lay silently. He turned onto his side, trying to take the pressure off his bruised ribs. Harding, he thought to himself. Flatner said that my name is Josh Harding. Josh racked his brains, trying to see if the surname could summon up any more memories.

If I can't think of anything to tell him, I'm going to take a terrible beating.

And now, in the darkness, Josh could at last feel a memory stirring within him. He was sitting in a concrete room. A man was standing in front of a group of soldiers, lecturing them, his expression serious. Josh couldn't remember the names of any of the men who sat there alongside him, but he could hear the words as clearly as if they were playing on a radio right next to him. The man in front was telling them how any member of the special forces had to expect to be captured at least once in his career. And if he was taken prisoner, he had to expect to be tortured. 'We don't do the nice Geneva Convention wars,' he was saying. 'We go into the places where we aren't meant to be and we do the rough stuff. We get captured, we expect to get slapped around a little. Goes with the territory. You want to dish it out, you have to learn how to take it as well. That's what I'm here for. To teach you how to take it.'

The man went on to outline a few simple techniques for

surviving torture. Josh struggled to keep the memory intact, trying to make sure that he remembered each word exactly as it was spoken. *This could mean the difference between life and death.*

You have to be physically fit, the man was telling them. That goes without saying. But you have to be mentally fit as well. You have to know how to stay on level terms with your tormentor.

There were five lessons that had been drilled into them. You have to have a 'mental home base': a mental safe house, into which you could retreat to protect yourself against the inevitable fits of depression and despair. You need a 'Focus Word', either a prayer or a poem that you can latch on to, to help get you through the day. You need to use visualisation to help you cope with the pain, turning the pain into an object such as a football that you can kick away. You have to use all your imagination and powers of imagery to try and construct fantasy worlds into which you can escape. And you have to create a 'magic box': a place outside yourself into which you can pour all your fears, anxieties, and pain.

At the time, me and the rest of the blokes thought it was just a load of psycho-bollocks. Now I'm not so sure. Now I might need it.

'You have to want to survive,' their lecturer had concluded, writing the words up on a blackboard. 'You have to know what you are living for and why. That's the only way you can make it through the pain.'

Josh repeated the words to himself, running his own private tape loop in his mind.

You have to want to survive

You have to want to survive.

But how can you want to survive, how can you know what you are living for, when you don't even know who you are?

SIXTEEN

Thursday, June 11th. Night.
The cover slid open, letting a chink of moonlight shine down into the hole. Josh turned onto his side, ignoring the pain still jabbing upwards from his ribs. He could see the ladder being tossed into the pit, and he could see a pair of thick leather boots starting their descent towards him.

'It's night-time, Josh,' said Flatner, laughing. 'Your nightmare is just starting.'

Josh kept silent. He had no clear idea what time it was. He knew that torture victims were supposed to try to keep track of the hours and the days as a way of keeping themselves sane, but it had proved impossible: with neither light nor sounds, there had been nothing to mark the passage of the hours. *It could be Thursday, Friday, any day.*

'Feeling good?' Flatner asked.

Josh glanced up. Another pair of boots was clambering down the ladder. Within a few short seconds, another of the bikers was standing at Flatner's side. Josh looked at the man's face, but in the murky light it was hard to make out any distinguishing features. His hair was matted and black, and his beard grew down more than a foot. He wore shades pulled down over his eyes, and his head was wrapped in a Confederate bandanna. Otherwise, he looked the same as all the other bikers Josh had seen walking through the camp.

Another monster. They have their own species developing

here, thought Josh. *The missing link between the great apes and the morons.*

'Not in the mood to talk, pretty boy?' said Flatner. 'Then we'll just have to juice you up a little bit.'

Anticipation was the worst part of the process, Josh realised. For the last few hours, he had been lying in the dark imagining the different types of torture that might be inflicted upon him. The bones in his fingers could be broken one by one. His skin could be burnt. A limb could be amputated every day until he agreed to speak. There could be sexual abuse, or a hundred different forms of mental torture: they might use white noise, water drips, drugs. It was hard to believe there was any cruelty that they would regard as too extreme.

The same question repeated itself in his head again and again. *How much pain do I have to suffer before they believe that I don't know where Luke is?*

'Strap him, Mark,' snapped Flatner.

The second biker moved across to where Josh was lying and knelt down. Close up, Josh could get a better view of him. Mark was thin, with the build of an athlete, and looked no more than twenty-five, Josh judged. In his eyes, he had the cold professional glare of a man who took pride in his work. He's done this before, sensed Josh. And he enjoys it.

If the Waffen-SS was still recruiting, he'd be first in the queue.

Mark was holding what looked like a thick leather belt in his hand. It was ten inches wide, with thick Velcro straps to help secure it to the body, and with a grey battery case clipped to its back. Mark opened up the belt, threading it around Josh's waist. Using his hands, he tugged at the Velcro, squeezing it into position.

'Too tight for you?' Mark asked, leering down at Josh. 'Well, hell. I don't give a fuck. A few minutes' time, that's going to be the least of your worries.'

'What is it?' snapped Josh.

'A stun belt,' said Flatner. 'The cops use them on prisoners. Put one of these babies around them, then if they complain about anything you just press a button from up to a hundred yards away and the belt delivers an electric shock. 50,000 volts frying up your body from all sides. Well, that's usually the maximum dose used by the law enforcement boys, but you know what, I think they're just a bunch of pussies looking after another bunch of pussies. So I tweaked this one. Took it up to 100,000 volts. Makes things a bit more interesting. At the same time it's giving you a shock, it makes a noise like one of those car alarms. A hundred and ten decibels.' Flatner laughed. 'Your guts are going to be frying and your ears bleeding,' he chuckled. 'And you know what the best thing is? You won't even know when it's coming because you won't be able to see me press the button. That doubles the shock.'

Magic box, Josh told himself. Take yourself away to the magic box. *That's the only way you'll get through this.*

'Get the blanket, Mark,' Flatner ordered.

Josh watched as Mark unfurled a blanket that was already dripping with water.

Electricity, realised Josh. They're going to electrocute me. And they're going to put me on a wet blanket while they are doing it so that the shock is administered evenly throughout my body. Hold yourself together, man. *This is going to be rough.*

'Move your ugly butt, man,' said Mark. 'I need to get this underneath you.'

'Fuck off,' spat Josh.

Mark's boot slammed into Josh's shoulder, the leather top colliding hard with the collarbone, sending a harsh pulse of pain surging out across his upper body. Instinctively, he rolled away at the impact. As he did so, Mark laid the wet blanket on the ground.

'You're a dumb fuck,' shouted Flatner. 'You're going to have to learn to cooperate.'

The blanket was spread out on the ground now, and two cables had already been chucked down the hole. Mark had attached the end of one to the underside of the blanket, putting the other cable to the top side. Josh lay on the ground next to the blanket, unable to move any further away. 'Lie on it,' said Mark softly.

Josh remained silent.

'I said lie on it,' repeated Mark.

Josh tightened his muscles, preparing himself for the inevitable blow. Soak up as much pain as you can, he reminded himself. Never cooperate until you have to. *Only total strength, total conviction, and total self-belief are going to get you through this.*

The boot landed in the centre of his back this time. His spine shuddered under the force of the kick. And although he resisted, it was impossible to stop himself rolling forwards onto the blanket. Immediately, Mark strapped a rope across him, using what looked like a tent peg to stake it into the ground. Trapped, realised Josh. The juice is going to start flowing any minute.

'Give it five,' shouted Flatner, looking up towards the edge of the hole.

Josh braced himself. The first jolts of electricity started jabbing at his feet, followed by an assault on his shoulders. Within seconds his whole body was being tossed around. The senses had shut down along his spine, and it was the nerves at the end of his body that were taking the worst beating: each of his toes and fingers felt as if it were being set alight in turn.

Somewhere he could smell burning. *My shirt? My skin? I can't tell.*

A scream rose up, starting in Josh's gut, tearing through his lungs, and exploding from his lips. It's okay to show pain, he told himself. It's okay to show fear. *This is about survival, not about proving yourself.*

'Cut it,' shouted Flatner.

A last surge of power tore through Josh's body, then faded away. He lay limp and breathless. The dampness of the blanket was seeping up into his skin, making his body itch all over. Small puffs of steam were rising up from the fabric, mixing with the already fetid air of the hole. Josh could feel some vomit rising in the back of his throat, but he struggled to keep it back.

'That was just a taster, pretty boy,' said Flatner. 'Just like a minor accident. The kind of thing that might happen when you change a light bulb.' He leaned down, the end of his beard brushing against Josh's skin. 'Now talk to me.'

You can beg, bargain, and plead, thought Josh. *But unless you can give them what they want, they aren't going to let you go.*

'I don't know anything.'

Josh was surprised by how weak his voice was already sounding: it was as if all the character and grit had already been shaken out of it. His throat was parched dry, and he could feel his body starting to dehydrate – one of the most common side effects of electric shocks.

'I didn't want to hear that, Josh,' said Flatner. 'I didn't want to hear that.'

A pause. Josh tried to count the silence. Six, maybe seven seconds. *A brief respite to prepare yourself for the next assault.*

'Frying time,' shouted Flatner.

Josh could feel his body convulsing violently as the wave of electricity rushed through him. It was impossible to say any more where the pain started and stopped: it was as if every nerve in his body was being attacked simultaneously. 'No,' he shouted. 'Please, no.'

Voice the pain, he told himself. You have to voice the pain. *Let it all flow straight out of you.*

'Cut it,' shouted Flatner.

The power dropped again, leaving Josh limp and lifeless. He felt as if all the blood was draining out of him. 'Now, pretty boy, let's have it,' said Flatner. 'Where's the kid?'

'Listen, you have to believe me,' said Josh, his voice raw. 'I don't know. I might have been in contact with him, but I don't know anything anymore. Take me through it step by step, I'll tell you everything that I know. I just don't know *where* he is.'

'Don't play for fucking time, pretty boy. I'm not that stupid.'

'I'm not playing for bloody time. I just don't *know*.'

Josh's hands were shaking like a pair of leaves being tossed around in a gale. Not fear, he noted. Part of the involuntary muscle movements you could expect after a long series of electric shocks.

This is going to get a lot worse, he thought grimly.

'Fry him,' shouted Flatner.

Another surge. Josh felt as if he'd been hit from the inside, as the pain exploded throughout his body. He closed his eyes, trying to think about the last time he'd been lying alone with Kate, imagining her hands running across his skin and her lips soothing away the pain. Anything, he told himself. *Anything to take your mind to a better place.*

'You ready to squeal yet, pretty boy?' said Flatner. 'Or you want me to soften you up a bit more? Get that tongue nice and loose.'

'I don't know, I tell you.'

Flatner turned around and started to climb the rope ladder. His massive body stretched it down, and he rose slowly as he slung one arm over the other. 'You're not a weak man, Josh Harding, I'll give you that. You're a tough stupid fuck. But you'll break, hear me? You'll fucking break. Because no man can survive the hell you're about to go through.'

The cover of the hole slid shut. Josh was plunged into darkness again. His body felt wet from the moisture on the electrocution blanket and from the sweat that had poured off him.

Stay still, he ordered himself. Let your body relax. Try to unwind, get some sleep. *Only by resting can you hope to pull through.*

Josh closed his eyes. All the time, he was worrying about the damage that was being done to his body. Even if he lived, it was impossible to tell whether he would ever recover properly: the electric shocks would leave burn marks on his skin, but those would heal. It was the long-term damage to his nervous system that worried him.

Then his mind was drifting. He thought about Madge, then Kate, but found that did nothing for him. Madge was dead, probably killed by Flatner, and Kate could well be dead as well.

Who the hell am I? What kind of life will I have out there if I get through this?

A jab of pain. Instinctively, Josh's body jerked upwards. His bones felt brittle and strained. The pain subsided, and he fell back onto the wet blanket. Tears of misery and stress were starting to roll down his face. A vicious noise was rattling through the hole, making Josh's ears bleed with pain. The stun belt, he realised. They're going to keep me here in the dark, delivering occasional random bolts of pain and noise from the belt.

He started to remember some of the other things he been warned about during his torture survival classes. The human mind is rarely so ingenious as when it is devising new forms of cruelty. The torturer's training manual ran to a hundred volumes. But the most effective techniques were all psychological, not physical. Sleep deprivation, sexual abuse, random beatings, all were parts of the armoury. A trained soldier could be expected to withstand a heavy load of physical pain. Yet mental anguish killed even the bravest of spirits eventually.

There was no better form of mental torture than surprise. Sometimes a man would be blindfolded and then pushed downstairs, so that he couldn't see himself falling. Other times the torturer would strap his victim to a chair before assaulting him from behind. The stun belt was just a refinement of some age-old techniques.

While I've got this belt on, I can't sleep, can't relax, can't lower my guard even for an instant.

Josh rolled over on the blanket, looking at the shaft of light shining downwards as the covers were taken off the hole. He could see a rope ladder being chucked down and a pair of heavy black boots starting their ominous descent.

Another day in hell.

'Breakfast time, pretty boy,' shouted Flatner.

Josh could feel himself coughing. Whether he had slept at all during the night he couldn't say. There might have been a few minutes when a kind of nervous exhaustion had overtaken him. But rest? No. That wouldn't be the word for it.

Because the stun belt had been triggered at least a dozen times during the last twelve hours. Short sharp attacks that left Josh feeling like he'd just taken a hundred thunderous blows to different parts of his body. There wasn't a vein left within him that didn't feel as if it was swollen and puffy. His eyes were bloodshot and streaming with pale liquid. Hunger was hollowing out his stomach. And the growing stench of urine within the hole was making his stomach heave.

'How you feeling today, pretty boy?' Flatner asked. 'Feel like talking?'

'I need some food,' said Josh.

'You need some food?' Flatner laughed, the roar echoing

up the narrow sides of the hole. 'Shit, man. Should have called for room service.'

'I need food, and water,' repeated Josh. 'I'll bloody die if I don't get something soon.'

His throat burnt as he spoke. His tonsils seemed to be engorged, and his tongue had swollen. Every word was delivered through the pain.

'Well, shit, man, you're tugging at my heartstrings.'

'You're a fucking idiot,' snapped Josh. 'I'm no bloody good to you dead, am I?'

'You're no fucking good to me *silent*, pretty boy,' said Flatner. 'If you're not saying anything, you might as well be a corpse for all I care. Least I wouldn't have to listen to your fucking whining all day.'

'Listen,' said Josh. 'I'm telling you, I can't remember anything. I need treatment. I need help. Give me that, get my memory back, and I swear I'll help you.'

Flatner chuckled. 'You're a twisty little fuck, Harding,' he said. 'I'm not so dumb I'm falling for a line like that.'

'I'm telling you I need help. When I know where Luke is I'll tell you. What do I care about some stupid kid?'

'You'll tell me?'

'Of course,' said Josh. 'Just give me some food and water. Some rest. Get my memories back, and I'll tell you everything you need to know.'

A punch landed hard in Josh's stomach. The skin was already so numb that he hardly felt it. But he coughed violently, some bile rising up in his parched throat and landing on the back of his tongue.

'You need some more fucking pain, that's what you need, pretty boy. I'm going to fry you to within an inch of your life. Then you'll talk to me.'

Change tack, Josh told himself. Keep pushing every button you can until you find something that works. 'I know who you work for.'

Flatner paused. 'I work for myself, pretty boy. That understood?'

'You work for Edward Porter, the boss of Porter-Bell. He's the guy who's paying you to torture me.'

'So?' replied Flatner, his tone amused. 'There's always somebody paying for everything,'

'There are several people who know about that. Anything happens to me, it's going to be traced back to Porter, then to you.'

Flatner laughed, then landed a heavy slap across the side of Josh's cheek. He could feel his jaw ache under the impact. 'Nobody's going to give a fuck about what happens to you, pretty boy. For one, you don't exist. And for two, by the time I'm finished with you even the vultures won't recognise you as a human being.'

Josh rolled back. He tried to think of some words, tried to summon up some memories, anything at all that he might be able to cling on to to get him through the next dozen or so hours. Most dying men cried for their mothers. He'd heard them on the battlefield, weeping for them as the bullets tore the life out of them. I don't even know who my mother is – or was. Whether she is alive or dead.

I'm living for two things only. Finding out who is responsible for all that has happened to me in the last few weeks – *and then ripping their stupid brains out of their miserable heads.*

Josh tried to bury his face into the hardened mud, desperate to find some way to keep the noise out of his ears. The decibels were screaming around him, making it impossible to think. Every few seconds, the belt sent a new shot of electricity up through his body. He jerked, then shook, as shock surged along his spine, shooting off along the main arteries within his body until they felt as if they were about to explode.

Then it stopped. Josh slumped forwards, catching his

breath. The atmosphere within the hole was fetid and stale. Not a breath of air was circulating, and he'd been here for at least two nights now, filling the cramped space with the stench of his own urine and sweat.

Fear, realised Josh. *That's the main thing you can smell in here.*

Flatner had been down here twice more, taking a malicious pleasure in attaching the electrodes to the blanket. Each time, Josh had been subjected to a half-hour or more of brutal physical and mental pain: huge doses of electricity were mixed with beatings and abuse. Every round of abuse had been matched by another round of furious denials from Josh.

He doesn't believe me. I'll be dead before he realises the truth.

Josh started poking his fingers into the dried mud. It was impossible to say when the hole had been dug. Given that it hadn't rained for at least five years in this patch of desert, it could have been there at least that long. His fingernails scratched into the hardened earth. Maybe something has been left down here, Josh mused. A tool that I might be able to use as a weapon. Maybe a scrap of some old plant that I can eat. Or just a trace of moisture that I can rub against my parched lips.

A fingernail broke but Josh ignored the pain. Compared with what he'd just been through, it was nothing. He burrowed further, getting down one inch, then two. Nothing. It was useless, he realised, rolling over onto the blanket. The ropes tagging him down chafed against his skin.

The stun belt will start up again in a minute, just when I least expect it, he told himself grimly. Flatner will be back down, with more threats, more shots of electricity, more beatings. There's nothing left for me. Just the darkness and the pain.

I'm broken. That bastard just doesn't realise it yet.

Somewhere up above him, Josh could hear a scratching

sound. One of the covers was moving. His heart sank within him. What was left of his spirit deserted him. Flatner, he guessed and another round of beatings.

A rope this time, without a ladder, Josh noticed as his stare turned upwards. A figure was sliding downwards. Thin and dark. Not Flatner, realised Josh. Not Mark either. Maybe they're tired. *Maybe they're sending in the B team to rough me up a bit.*

The man landed softly, alighting on the ground with the silent agility of a cat. His gaze focused on Josh with a mixture of pity and curiosity. Now Josh could see him clearly. He was dressed in black jeans, a black T-shirt, and around the lower half of his face he had wrapped a black cloth. Whether it was to hide his face or to protect himself, Josh couldn't tell. Only his eyes were visible: brown, and gleaming out of the darkness.

Not a biker, thought Josh. *Whoever the hell he is, he isn't a biker.*

'Who are you?' said Josh hoarsely.

The man remained silent. He moved across to where Josh was lying. In his left hand, Josh could see the curved outline of a steel blade, its handle crafted in wood and ivory. The blade flashed forwards. Instinctively, Josh flinched, trying to prepare himself for the knife penetrating his flesh. Not butchery, he said inwardly. He'd heard of torturers cutting men open. *Please, God, not that.*

The rope sprang loose. Josh held his breath as the man cut one rope, then another. The blade on the knife was as sharp as a razor, slicing through the bindings with ease. One by one, Josh could feel his limbs released from their captivity. 'Who are you?' he repeated, his voice louder this time.

'Stay completely quiet,' said the man, his voice barely a breath above a whisper. 'I'm here to help you.'

For a brief moment, Josh wondered if he might be dreaming. An hallucination, maybe. He knew that happened to torture victims sometimes. The pain and the despair overwhelmed their minds and the victims slipped into trance-like states where they genuinely believed that they were being rescued. Josh closed his eyes, struggling to concentrate. He could feel the ropes snapping loose, and the man's hands on his chest rolling him across the dirt floor.

It's not a trance, he told himself. *It's bloody real.*

His eyes snapped open. The ropes were all cut now. Slowly Josh sat up. His body felt limp, weaker than it had ever felt before. The muscles were slow to respond to his commands, and Josh immediately started to wonder if he'd suffered some long-term nerve damage from the massive quantities of electricity that had surged through his body in the last two days.

'Can you stand?' whispered the man.

Josh struggled to his feet. His knees felt soft and flabby, as if the bone had been taken out of them, and his feet were having trouble keeping a grip on the ground. The man slung an arm around his shoulder, hauling him upwards. Josh clung on to him, as if he was hanging on to a lifebelt in a stormy sea. Slowly, they inched their way across the hole's floor to where the rope was dangling.

Who the hell are you? wondered Josh. *What are you doing here?*

'Think you can climb?'

I can hardly bloody stand up, pal, thought Josh. *But I could climb the sodding Eiffel Tower if it meant escaping from this hell.*

'I don't know,' he said. 'I'll try.'

'I'll stand behind you, and help push you up.'

Josh gripped the rope. He reckoned he'd scaled a million different ropes in his life, and this one was only twelve feet long, lying against a dried-mud wall with plenty of grip in it. It shouldn't be any harder than climbing a staircase. *Unless your body had been shot to pieces by two days of torture.*

He clamped his right hand around the rope, followed by his left. His grip was limp and feeble. Summoning up all his powers of concentration, he squeezed hard on the rope and started to drag himself upwards. His shoulders were buckling under the strain, and his bones felt as if they'd been stretched on a rack. You can do this, he told himself silently. One burst of effort and then you'll be free.

Josh could feel the man beneath him using his back to help support Josh's weight. He gripped harder on the rope, hauling himself upwards foot by foot. He could see the lip of the hole, just two feet away. Kicking down, he rested his feet on the other man's back, using his support to help lever himself another few inches upwards.

Maybe Kate sent him, thought Josh. Maybe he's one of Marshall's survivalist friends.

His fingers grabbed up towards the edge. Below him, the other man was now climbing up the rope himself, still using the strength in his back to help propel Josh upwards. For a thin man, he had the toughness of a person twice his size. Josh's nails dug into the hardened mud at the surface. Above him, he could see the night sky. He levered himself up another few inches, bringing his eyes level with the ground. One more heave, he told himself. *And I'll be free.*

Josh had no idea what might be waiting for him once he got out of the hole. He didn't even know where he had been imprisoned: he assumed it was in the biker's camp, but he had no way of telling for sure. If there was anyone guarding the site, he had to assume that he'd be shot on sight.

I'll take my chances. *Right now, a bullet is a fate I'd gladly settle for.*

His gaze swivelled first right, then left. A grunt escaped from his lips as, with one last effort from his tortured muscles, he dragged himself over the edge. The hole had been dug about fifty yards from the main camp. He could see the tents and the shacks, and the parked rows of gleaming, chrome-laden motorbikes, but little sign of life. Judging by the position of the moon, it was three or four in the morning: the dead of night. About ten yards from the hole a man was lying face down in the dust. A knife was sticking out of his back. And a trickle of blood was seeping down into the ground.

The night guard, reckoned Josh. At his side lay the controller used to trigger the stun belt.

'Go,' whispered the man below him. 'We haven't got much time.'

That accent, thought Josh. Not quite English, and not quite American either. I can't place it.

Josh scrambled onto the surface. Within an instant, the man was lying at his side. 'There,' he said. 'There's a horse behind that boulder. Think you can make it?'

Josh nodded. *I'd run right across a bed of razor blades in my bare feet to get out of this place.*

His feet kicked back against the ground. The strength is always there when you need it, he reflected as he started running the two hundred metres towards the boulder. Sometimes it's buried so deep that you don't even know it is there. But if you can dig it out, you can survive.

Josh didn't look back as he ran. He just sped forwards, ignoring the pain in his legs. The breath came hard and heavy in his lungs but he kept going. The other man was running at his side. A little over fifty yards, he told himself. *Then you'll have escaped.*

The horse was an elegant grey stallion, the side of its neck dotted with brown freckles. Josh didn't know much about horses, but he could tell at a glance that this one was built for speed. A leather rein tethered the animal to the stump of a tree, and the horse was idly chewing some of the weeds sprouting through the rocky ground.

On this terrain, there could be no better getaway vehicle.

'Get on its back,' said the man. 'This isn't going to be comfortable, but it *is* going to be quick.'

The man got up on the horse first, pulling himself up in one swift, well-practised movement. I've seen him, thought Josh. Somewhere. There was no saddle, just a cloth slung over its back. Nor were there any stirrups, just a leather bridle and rein.

The man grabbed Josh's hand, yanking him upwards. Again, Josh was impressed by the power he packed into his slight frame. Josh landed on the horse's back and sat astride the animal, clinging on to his rescuer's shoulders.

'Hold on tight,' whispered the man. Then he delivered a swift kick to the stallion's side and suddenly they were in motion. Josh gripped hard, adjusting to the rhythm of the gallop. He could feel the adrenalin surging through him as he looked backwards and saw the biker's camp receding into the background.

I'll be back, he vowed. *And when I return my hands will drip with your blood.*

The stallion sped over the open countryside. Josh had little idea where he was going. He clung on tight, grateful to be breathing free air again. His body had taken a terrible beating. Hunger and thirst were eating away at him, but he sensed that if he could just get clear of this place then he might survive. Right now, that's all that counts, he thought. Survival.

The horse was sure-footed and the man was an expert enough rider to steer it through the rough terrain. They were heading north, Josh noted, up towards the heartlands of Arizona. He glanced back a couple of times, but the getaway had been clean enough. If the bikers had found their murdered guard by now, then they hadn't sent out a search party yet. Even if they did, it should be too late by now. The stallion was putting good distance between them and the camp, and taking them across terrain that couldn't be covered on a bike.

My rescuer can ride fast, noted Josh. Without stirrups.

Something sparked in Josh's mind. Without stirrups?

The animal whinnied beneath them, then halted as the man tugged on its reins. 'Here,' he said, pointing down towards a dark pool of water between some rocks. 'He needs to drink. So do you.'

The horse had already stuck his muzzle into the pool, and was taking huge draughts of the water. Josh climbed down uneasily, careful not to hit the ground too hard. He walked unsteadily towards the pool. His legs were shaking beneath him. Keeping to a straight line required all his concentration. Slowly, he knelt down. The thirst was burning within him, but he knew that after two days without water he had to be careful. Too much, too quickly would be damaging. *Just a few sips.*

The man was standing at his side. 'Drink, drink,' he said. 'It'll do you good.'

Josh dipped his hand into the water. It felt cool and refreshing. He lifted his hand and let the water trickle across his face. Next, he used his fingers to rub some of the liquid into his lips. The skin was cracked and parched, and stung at the touch of the fluid. Gradually he started to lick some of the water out of his hands, letting just a few drops at a time into his mouth.

He felt dizzy and disorientated. I haven't slept for two days, he reminded himself.

The horse was finishing its drink, raising its head from the pool and chewing on a clump of weeds. No stirrups, thought Josh again. *Why does that keep bothering me?*

Josh looked again at the man. He was holding on to the reins of the horse, the leather held tight in his grip. The black bandanna was still strapped tight around the lower half of his face, masking him from view.

Josh took another sip of water, letting the cool liquid settle inside him. He could feel it affecting his ragged, electrocuted nerve endings, making his body tingle. Arabia, he thought to himself. That's where men learn to ride horses without stirrups. Arabia. Josh looked down into the pool. In a shaft of moonlight, he caught a glimpse of his own reflection. He scarcely recognised the man looking back at him. There was several more days' growth of beard and his hair was matted with sweat and streaks of blood. His skin was pallid, and there were scratches all down the side of his cheek. But it was the eyes that shocked Josh the most. They had a hunted, scared look.

Suddenly, Josh could see the face of his rescuer reflected next to his own in the pool. I've seen you before, he repeated to himself. The man who'd been staying in the Motel 6, the one who had said he was an Italian, the one who Madge gave me a picture of.

You're not an Italian. You're al-Qaeda.

Josh turned around, looking up into the man's face. He tried to smile, but his lips were still too cracked. 'Thank you for rescuing me.'

The man raised his hand. 'You won't be thanking me soon,' he replied.

The hand slammed into the side of Josh's face. He could feel himself growing dizzy. His body wobbled and in the next instant he crashed face down into the cold water.

SEVENTEEN

Saturday, June 13th. Afternoon.
The light hit Josh's face. He struggled to open his eyes, adjusting his vision to the sunshine streaming in through the open window. Blinking hard, he looked around. A white room. A white bed. With white sheets. And a white towelling bath robe wrapped around him.

Where the hell am I now? A hospital, maybe.

He sat bolt upright, feeling his body ache as he stretched himself forwards. It took him a moment to collect his thoughts. My name is Josh Harding, he told himself. I am a British soldier. *And, right now, I'm in some serious shit.*

His memories came flooding back, filling his mind with a hundred different bits of information at the same time. He had been captured by the bikers. He'd been rescued. But his rescuer was, he felt certain, an al-Qaeda agent.

I haven't been rescued at all. *I've just swapped one prison for another.*

Josh paused, taking a moment to asses the damage that had been inflicted upon him in the last two days. There were plenty of cuts and bruises where he had been punched by Flatner, but probably no permanent damage there. It was the electricity that had taken the heaviest toll. Any damage that might have done would be internal. It might be days before his nervous system was working properly. Maybe never.

But it doesn't look like a prison, decided Josh, glancing round the room. It was clean. It was light. There was a glass of water by the bed. A television sat on a simple wooden stand in one corner. Nothing was holding him down. No chains. No handcuffs. No bars. *But it still doesn't mean you're a free man. The worst jails don't look like jails.*

'Are you feeling better this afternoon?'

Josh looked up. It was the man who had rescued him last night. He was dressed in cream chinos and a dark blue polo shirt. There were touches of grey in his hair. His face, without the bandanna to mask it, had a harder edge to it. It was tough and craggy, and the cheeks bore the marks of old wounds. It was the face of a man who had spent much of his life in combat.

I've seen you before, Josh realised. *And not just in the picture that Madge showed me.*

'I don't know,' said Josh. 'It'll take a few days to learn how badly I'm hurt.'

A woman stepped into the room. She was dressed all in white: white tunic, white tights, white gloves, white shoes. And she wore a white linen veil across her face. Her dark brown eyes and black hair were the only part of her body that Josh could see. In one hand, she was carrying a bowl of water, in the other some cotton wool and a bottle of disinfectant.

'We need to dress those wounds,' said the man.

The woman remained silent. She leaned over the side of the belt, removing the sheet. Apart from a new pair of boxer shorts, Josh was naked. The woman dabbed the cotton wool into the water, then pressed the bottle of disinfectant to it. Starting with the neck, she started washing the wounds, bruises and scratches on Josh's body. His skin stung as she did so, but her touch was delicate and gentle.

'What am I doing here?' asked Josh.

The man raised a finger to his lips. 'Quiet,' he said. 'You need to recover your strength.'

'I need to know where I am.'

'No, quiet,' said the man. He smiled, flicking on the television. 'Here, watch some television. Try to relax. Get your strength back.'

Josh lay back on the bed. There was nothing obvious to keep him in place. The man didn't appear to be armed. He couldn't hear any guards outside. Still, he knew that there was no way he could just get up and walk out of here. Sometimes you didn't need to see your jailers. *The strongest chains were the invisible ones.*

There was a weather forecast on the television. It was tuned to CNN. Another bright sunny day for Arizona, Josh noticed. *At least they haven't taken me out of the country.*

'Our top story this hour,' started the newsreader as soon as the weather forecast had finished. 'Another terrifying Cities Attack. We'll be back with all the details after this break.'

Josh stared at the television. His chest was stinging where the woman was dabbing disinfectant into the raw flesh of a wound. Maybe one of the places Flatner had kicked him.

A dog-food advert faded away, then the news started up again. Three o'clock, Josh noted. He'd been asleep for a long time. 'Our top story this hour: another terrifying series of blackouts, this time in the United Kingdom,' started the newsreader. 'At precisely nine this morning, local time, the power was switched off in four British cities. Liverpool, Harrogate, Peterborough and Exeter. In each city, the power went off at just after nine in the morning, and the blackout lasted for precisely one hour. In scenes that have become distressingly familiar across the world, there was widespread chaos in each city as the power shut down. Schools and hospitals were closed, traffic ground to a halt, and factories and offices emptied for the day. In Liverpool there was an outbreak of looting as a shopping mall came under attack from an angry mob. Now, almost ten hours later, police are still struggling to bring the city under control.'

Luke, thought Josh instantly. *He's still out there. He's still operating.*

'There is now heightened speculation that the blackouts that started several months ago with the Three Cities Attack are the work of a terrorist network, suspected to be al-Qaeda,' continued the newsreader. 'Power industry experts are saying it is impossible that the simultaneous shutdowns of so many networks in so many different cities could be a coincidence. The fact that Britain, America's closest ally in the War on Terror, has been targeted has only fuelled speculation that the blackouts are part of the terrorist campaign waged against the West.'

'Prime Minister Tony Blair issued a statement this afternoon, saying that the nation would not flinch in the face of these attacks, and saying the outrage justified his decision to support the US in the invasion of Iraq. However, Liberal Democrat leader Charles Kennedy said he believed that Britain should now withdraw its troops from Iraq. We'll be back with more reactions to today's events right after this break.'

The television suddenly went dead. The man put down the remote at the foot of Josh's bed and turned to him, a half-smile playing on his lips. 'So you see, Josh Harding, there is much for us to speak of.'

The woman had finished with Josh for the time being, dressing the last of his wounds and applying a final plaster to a cut in his skin. She bowed, staying silent, then withdrew from the room. Josh shut his eyes. Something was happening. An image was sliding behind his closed eyelids, hazy at first, like an out-of-focus picture, but gradually sharpening. *A memory.*

Josh struggled to concentrate as the picture hovered in front of him. A concrete room. He was standing in front of someone. Josh was dressed in white robes, and was dirty and unshaven. The other man was older, dressed in a uniform. He was shouting at him. Josh was shouting back. Bugger it, thought Josh. I can't hear anything. What the hell were we arguing about?

He kept his eyes closed. He could see himself shouting at the man, then standing up. He was moving across to the wall. A picture was in his hands. He was tearing the picture, throwing the torn strips of paper onto the floor.

But even though the picture was shredded by his own hands, Josh could see the face clearly enough. The same face that was standing right next to him now. Khalid Azim. *One of the most wanted al-Qaeda terrorists in the world.*

'I know who you are,' said Josh, his stare meeting Azim's.

'I am your rescuer,' said Azim.

'Your name is Khalid Azim.'

Azim nodded. 'I'm glad to see that your memory is coming back to you,' he said. 'It should make the next few hours so much easier.' He paused. 'For both of us.'

'I've tried to kill you once,' snapped Josh. 'Next time, I will bloody succeed.'

Azim laughed. 'You don't have much in the way of small talk, do you?' he said. 'Still, never mind. For what we have to discuss, only a few words will be needed.'

He walked slowly the length of the small room to stand right next to Josh. 'I have been tracking you for some weeks, following you from place to place. Even after you were shot, I stuck to you, watching you from afar. It was only after those idiots on bikes took you captive that I realised I had to intervene. They were going to kill you, either on purpose or just through sheer bloody carelessness. And that I couldn't allow. Why? Because I knew that if I followed you, you would eventually lead me to what you know I want.' Azim paused, rubbing his left hand reflectively over his jowls. 'Luke. I want to know where Luke is.'

Turning around, he gestured towards the television set. 'They are talking as if these attacks on power stations around the world were organised by al-Qaeda. If only they were, I keep saying to myself. If only they were.' He paused. 'Think of the power that would put into our hands, Josh. Anywhere in the world, at will, with the flick of a few switches, we could plunge whole nations into darkness. Chaos, confusions, riots and anarchy – they would all be ours, at the mere touch of a few buttons. And so they will soon be, Josh. So they will soon be.'

Azim clapped his hands together. The woman walked back into the room. She was carrying a tray on which were a jug of orange juice, a bowl of mixed fruits and a plate of sandwiches. Carefully, she placed it down at the side of the bed. Josh eyed the food hungrily. It was two days since he had eaten anything, but he kept his hands still.

How the hell do I know they are not about to drug me?

'Luke has the software, doesn't he, Josh?' continued Azim. 'And we want it. As soon as we have it, these blackouts really will be the work of al-Qaeda, just as they are describing it on the news.'

'I don't know where he is,' snapped Josh. 'Even if I did, I wouldn't tell you.'

Azim took an apple from the fruit bowl, rolling it between his hands like a cricket ball. 'I don't think you've been paying attention, Josh. Maybe you've taken too many blows to the head. It might have made it hard for you to concentrate. We saw the first attack. Jamestown, Orlando, Seattle, and Harrison. It spells Josh. Now we see there is another attack. What did they say on the news? Liverpool, Peterborough, Exeter, and Harrogate. But I bet when we get all the details tomorrow, we'll find that there was a delay in the sequence of the blackouts. I imagine it went Harrogate, Exeter, Liverpool and then Peterborough.'

Azim took a bite from the apple, a sly smile playing on his face. 'J-O-S-H H-E-L-P,' he said, spelling out each letter carefully. 'I think he's trying to tell you something. Don't you?'

'I don't know what he's bloody trying to do,' said Josh, the anger rising within him. 'And anyway, it doesn't bloody matter. You can kill me if you want to. You'll get nothing from me.'

Azim laughed. 'That SAS bravado – I like it,' he said. 'The bulldog spirit. It is one of the things we can all admire about the British. But let me tell you this. You'll break. They all break. Within a day or two you'll be begging me to kill you. And at some stage I'll put you out of your misery. But only when you've told me where the boy is.'

'Then you might as well kill me now,' spat Josh. 'Get it over with, and save us all a lot of trouble.'

Azim passed across another apple. 'Eat something.'

'Fuck off.'

Azim placed the apple down on the white cotton sheet. 'Eat something,' he repeated. 'We need to build you up again, get your strength back. Why? Because a strong man will feel the pain more acutely than a weak one. And I want you to feel the pain, Josh. I want you to feel every second of it.'

Before leaving, Azim put a gun to Josh's head, holding it tightly against his temple while the nurse snapped a handcuff onto the side of the bed, securing Josh's left hand. Another cuff chained his left foot to the bed's frame, and the bed itself was fixed to the floor. It didn't matter how violently Josh shook himself, he couldn't make it move an inch. Next the woman returned with a syringe, jabbing the needle hard into his thigh, injecting the pale-coloured liquid straight into his bloodstream. Whether it was a truth serum, a poison, or just a tranquiliser Josh didn't know but within minutes he'd fallen into a deep sleep.

When Josh awoke he had no idea how long he had slept. A few hours or a whole day, it was impossible to tell. He was alone in the room, with just a single pale light shining down from the centre of the ceiling. The TV was switched off. The door was closed, and Josh couldn't hear a single sound from the corridor outside.

I don't even know what kind of building I'm in.

He reached across to the side of the table, taking an apple with his right hand. His left was still chained to the bed. Azim was right, realised Josh as he took a big bite of the fruit. *If my strength returns, I will feel the pain more acutely. But I'll also be able to withstand it for longer.*

The food tasted good. It was two, maybe three days since he had eaten. His stomach was empty and, as with the water, he knew that he had to pace himself. Too much food, eaten too quickly, would only make him feel sick. His body wouldn't be able to take it.

Stomach ache, he thought with a rueful smile to himself. *Somehow, I've got a feeling that's going to be the least of my worries.*

The door opened. Azim walked slowly into the room, his gaze running over Josh. *They must know I'm awake*, he realised. He scanned the room, looking for cameras, but could see nothing. *That doesn't mean anything. Azim knows I'm awake. He's watching me somehow.*

'You slept well, I hope,' said Azim.

Josh remained silent. In the few minutes that he had been alone, the lessons on torture and how to survive it had been swirling through his mind. This was going to be different from the beatings he'd taken from Flatner and his thugs. Now he knew that he'd need to withstand the greatest subtleties of mental torture.

'We gave you an injection,' said Azim. 'It should have helped to clear your mind.'

The jab, thought Josh. *They've put something into me to try and bring my memory back. They want me to remember everything – so they can squeeze the information out of me.*

And the worst of it was this: it was working.

Since he'd been awake, Josh's mind had been working with new clarity. He knew that his name was Josh Harding. He knew that he was a serving soldier in the Regiment. He couldn't say for certain, but he thought he was about thirty. He knew he'd been in the Army for twelve years, and in the special forces for five. And he knew that he'd seen Azim before – and tried to kill him.

I am a long way from a full recovery. But it's starting. My memories are coming back. And that's going to make this a hundred times worse. Flatner couldn't break me because there was nothing to break. Now I'm going to have to use will-power to make sure that I don't tell them anything.

I have to learn how to take my secrets to my grave.

Azim reached out for a pear from the fruit bowl. He took a knife and started peeling it, offering the fruit in cubes to Josh. 'The Prophet teaches us when to be merciful and when to be cruel,' he said. 'First we take care of you, then we bleed you for the information that we need. That is our way.'

Josh took a slice of the pear. He could feel the fear eating away at his gut: nothing had happened yet, but he could be certain that it would. 'I know nothing,' he said. 'You saw the beating I took from those bikers. If I didn't tell them anything, I certainly won't tell *you* anything.' He looked up towards Azim, his expression hardening. 'I'm a British soldier. I know when I'm done for, and I'm enough of a man not to complain about it. So if your fucking Prophet is so merciful, just kill me now and get it over with.'

'Brave words, Josh,' said Azim. 'And soon we'll set about our gruesome business. Then we'll see if the strength of your spirit matches the strength of your language. But first, I should make you an offer. You should understand that I am not a cruel man. I take no pleasure in what is about to happen. Talk now. Save yourself the pain that is about to come.'

'Piss off.'

Azim clasped his hands together, as if in prayer. 'The torturer abandons his humanity as much as his victim does. Spare us both the indignity. Talk to me now. Tell me where Luke is.'

'I don't know,' spat Josh. 'And if I *did* know, what's the bloody point of telling you? You'll kill me anyway. You're not going to release me. Not now that I know you're here.'

Azim nodded. 'Of course,' he replied. 'Your demise is inevitable now – we both know that. And let me assure you, in a few hours' time you'll welcome it more eagerly than you ever welcomed a woman into your bed. Death is not so frightening to men such as us. An honourable death – what more could a warrior ask for?'

Azim paused, turning away from the bed and walking to the back of the room. He reached around the half-open door, collecting a small wicker box, then turned back towards Josh. 'But there are many different ways to die. A death with honour on the battlefield. A death in your own bed, with your wife and children around you to say goodbye. None of those are so bad. But this isn't going to be like that. It will be a nasty, squalid, vicious death, filled with fear, despair, defeat and the stench of self-loathing. That's what awaits you, Josh.'

Azim walked closer to the bed, the wicker basket swinging in his hand. Josh watched it closely, trying to see what it contained. It measured ten inches by twenty. Enough room for a whole array of instruments of torture, noted Josh grimly. Knives, manacles, thumbscrews. It could be anything.

'Once more, Josh,' said Azim. 'Just tell me where Luke is.'

'I don't bloody know,' shouted Josh.

He gritted his teeth. Close your eyes, he told himself. *Let your imagination take you away to a better place.*

But his eyes wouldn't shut. Josh watched with mounting dread as Azim opened the small basket. His hand slipped inside, then emerged. Sticking up from his tightly clenched fist was the head of a snake. 'You don't like these, do you, Josh?' said Azim, a soft smile breaking out on his lips.

The reptile had been sleeping. Its neck was held tightly within Azim's fist, and its long thin body drooped down into the basket. Slowly it was starting to wake up. One bright green eye opened, then another. The snake's skin was black, mottled with greens and blues, with ridges running down the side of its thick, leathery skin. Its tongue darted from its mouth, then shot back inside as it closed one eye.

'What the fuck is that?' snapped Josh.

'An Arizona Black Rattlesnake, also known as a *Crotalus cerberus*,' said Azim.

'Keep it away from me!'

Azim smiled. 'Talk to me, Josh. Then I'll get rid of the beast.'

'I told you — I don't bloody know anything.'

Azim put the snake back in the basket and clapped his hands together. The woman re-entered the room. She was still wearing the veil wrapped across her mouth, yet Josh could look straight into her cold brown eyes. He could feel himself recoiling from her presence.

'Handcuff him,' commanded Azim.

Josh's left hand was already manacled to the bed, as was his left foot. The woman approached him, a set of steel handcuffs held before her. She sat down next to Josh. Slowly she reached out for his right hand.

'Leave me alone,' shouted Josh.

Within a second, Azim had whipped a pistol from inside his tunic: an American-made Mauser M2. The snubbed steel nose of the weapon was now nestling against Josh's ear, cool and hard against his skin. 'Do as she says, Josh.'

'Kill me now, you bastard,' shouted Josh, a note of hysteria in his voice. 'Get the bloody thing over with.' The gun was pressing tighter against his skin. He could feel it pressing into the bone of his skull. 'Hold still, man,' whispered Azim. 'Let her cuff you.'

Josh rolled sideways, snatching his hand away from the woman. She pushed herself on top of him, straddling him with a thick and powerful pair of thighs. He could feel her weight, hot and sticky against his body, making it impossible for him to move any further. The gun was still pressing against his head and Azim's finger was twitching on its trigger. The woman spat in his face. A warm ball of saliva landed hard against his cheek. As Josh brushed it aside, she grabbed his right hand, snapping one cuff into place. Her movement was swift and practised. In a fraction of a second she had placed the other cuff round the bedpost and snapped it shut. Josh was trapped. Both hands were secured and so was one foot.

I can't move, he told himself grimly. *I can't escape.*

'Infidel pig,' sneered the woman. She spat again, this time landing a ball of saliva just next to Josh's eye. Her breath smelled of onions and sugar, and so did her spit. But with both hands cuffed, it was impossible for Josh to wipe it away.

Now the woman climbed away from his chest, straightening out her white skirt as she stood back on the floor. Azim picked up the wicker case, lifting out the snake again. The reptile opened an eye, looking around the room lazily. Gripping it by the head, Azim put it down at the foot of the bed.

'Want to tell me where Luke is?'

'Piss off.'

Azim pulled a dead mouse from his pocket. He held the small corpse up by its tail, then placed it down on Josh's chest. Dead for a day or two, reckoned Josh from the look of the animal. It was already starting to smell like the sewers it had probably come from. He could see the snake focusing its beady green eyes on it.

'He's hungry,' said Azim. 'And when he starts eating, he doesn't stop.'

Azim looked down at Josh, his expression sympathetic. 'Talk to me.'

'Fuck off.'

Azim leaned across him. In his right hand he was holding a black wooden cane with which he tapped the snake on its back. Suddenly, its eyes, filled with anger, fixed on Josh.

Azim turned around and walked towards the door. 'When you're ready, call for me. I'll be listening.'

Josh could hear the door shutting. His stare was riveted on the snake. The reptile's head had reared up, and it was sniffing the air. Slowly it started to advance. Its head moved across Josh's leg, then the rest of its three-foot-long body started sliding over him.

He could feel himself starting to tremble. Get a bloody grip, man, he ordered himself. *You show any fear, this animal's going to bite you for sure.*

The snake was moving closer. It stopped at Josh's groin, sniffing the skin for several minutes, its tongue flashing in and out of its mouth. Then it moved on upwards. Its skin felt like a rubber tyre: thick and fleshy, yet also tepid. Its eyes looked up towards Josh. At first it seemed to be afraid, but then it grew in confidence as it noticed that Josh wasn't making any move to protect himself.

The snake knows, thought Josh. It knows that I can't move. *It's laughing at me.*

It paused, sniffing the mouse. Its tongue darted across the animal's skin, licking the gradually decomposing flesh. Then its teeth sank into the mouse's body, tearing at it ferociously. Small bits of fur dropped onto Josh's chest, mixing with the saliva drooling from the snake's open mouth.

Josh could feel his hands shaking. The fear was taking control of him. Don't bite me, he muttered to himself, repeating the phrase over and over. Please God, don't bite me.

The beast paused, looking up towards Josh. Then it sniffed the hairs on his chest. Its tongue flicked against them.

Stay still, man. Stay as still as a rock and maybe it won't bite you.

Shall I call Azim? No, Josh told himself, gripping onto the side of the bed. You can't tell Azim *anything*.

Just kill me with one bite, thought Josh, looking towards the snake. Get it over with.

The movement was so sudden that its swiftness bewildered Josh. One second the snake was eyeing him idly, as if calmly assessing his strength, then he could see its tongue flicking out and its head dipping downwards, like a seagull swooping on a fish in the sea.

The teeth felt icy cold as they sank into Josh's chest. The snake's sharp fangs easily pierced his skin. He could feel his flesh being punctured. Next he felt the reptile's tongue flash forwards. A stinging sensation burned through him.

The venom.

The snake has bitten me.

Josh could feel blood starting to seep out across his chest. The snake whipped around and started slithering back down his body.

Already Josh was starting to feel dizzy. His vision was clouding. He could feel his limbs beginning to stiffen as his skin turned numb. His body felt chilled, as if the air-conditioning had been turned on.

Blackness. Josh tried to open his eyes, but the eyelids refused to move. An image was floating through his mind. The brunette. And, next to her, the little girl. Paula, realised Josh. The brunette's name was Paula. And the little girl was called Emily. He could hear her laughter as he played with her, and the sound of her breathing gently in his arms as he cradled her to sleep.

My daughter. *I have a daughter.*

Who I might never see again.

The venom had him in its grip now. Josh couldn't open his eyes, nor could he move. His breathing was slow. A terrible pounding was beating against the side of his head.

Stay awake, Josh ordered himself.

But he could feel his consciousness departing. As the darkness overwhelmed him Josh wondered if he was dying.

EIGHTEEN

Sunday, June 14th. Morning.
Josh's head was splitting as he gradually emerged from a deep sleep. He opened one eye first, adjusting it to the bright light shining over him. Then the other. I should be dead, he thought. That sodding snake's poison should have killed me. But then bloody Azim would never get any info out of me, about Luke or anything else. He and that bitch nurse or whatever she is must have shot me full of anti-venom serum as soon as I'd passed out.

He could see Azim peering down at him, a smile playing on his lips. 'Good morning, Josh,' he said, his tone ingratiating and insincere. 'Welcome to another day in hell.'

Josh rattled his handcuffs. The metal frame of the bed creaked and groaned as he shook it angrily but all he was doing was hurting himself, he realised. The two sets of cuffs holding his arms in place were still locked tight, as was the single set securing his left foot. The metal rings around his wrists and ankle cut into his skin as he struggled to pull himself free.

'Stop fighting, Josh,' said Azim. 'And talk to me.'

Josh stayed silent. He was still trying to collect his thoughts, to remember where he was, who he was, and what he had to do.

My name is Josh Harding. I'm a British soldier. *And I'm about to die for my country.*

'The Americans are amateurs when it comes to torture,'

said Azim. 'Flatner and his idiots, they knew nothing. Just like those idiots in Abu Ghraib back in Iraq. Brute force, that's all they understand.'

He was toying with a thin glass tube, turning it over and over in his hands. 'But torture is a subtle art, as subtle in its own way as the arts of love. Your victim is like a woman. You must coax him to give up his secrets, just as you would coax a woman into giving up her innocence.'

'And what if your victim doesn't know anything?'

'But he will, Josh, he will,' said Azim. 'You see, a man's memory is a delicate thing. The Arab world has its own traditions of medicine. The greatest doctors of medieval times were all Arab. Much of their wisdom might have been lost, but there are still lessons that have been passed down through the ages. And one of them is about memory.'

Christ, thought Josh. *This guy's trying to bore me to death.*

Azim held up the glass tube between his fingers. Inside Josh could see a pale red liquid. 'A memory can be restored through care, treatment and rest,' Azim continued. 'But it can also be restored through pain and suffering. The careful application of pain can sharpen and sensitise the nerves until the mind yields up its secrets. Trust me, when you want to die enough, then your memory will come back.'

'What the hell is that?' said Josh, nodding towards the tube.

'Blood, Josh. Your blood.'

Josh could feel his stomach muscles tightening.

'We took a pint while you slept,' continued Azim. 'And we're going to keep taking pints from you. Our blood is our strength. You're a soldier, you know the truth of that. Without our blood, we are nothing, we are weak. And that's how I want you, Josh. Weak.'

Azim flung the tube down. Josh could hear the glass cracking and splintering. He could see the liquid spill out, spreading a thick crimson stain across the floor. My own blood, he thought in appalled fascination.

'Talk to me,' barked Azim.

'Piss off.'

'Talk to me,' shouted Azim again, his voice louder this time.

Josh struggled to stay silent. A rage was burning within him. His head was spinning, and his vision weak. With mental fingertips, he was clinging desperately to the memories that he'd recovered last night. Paula. My wife, or maybe ex-wife. And Emily. My daughter. Suddenly he could see her smile and hear her laugh as vividly as if she was cuddling up to him in his arms. That's something to survive for – and something worth dying for, too, he thought.

'You're a fool, Josh. You're going to tell me, and then you're going to die. Make it easy for yourself.'

'Piss off,' yelled Josh again, summoning as much strength as possible into his voice.

Josh tried to lash out with his hand, trying desperately to strike Azim, but the chain binding him to the bed cut into his skin. He could see Azim pulling a white handkerchief from his jacket pocket. He slowly unfolded it, revealing three white pills. 'Here,' he said, leaning down in front of Josh. 'Take them.'

'What the hell are they?'

'Two aspirin, and one warfarin,' said Azim.

Josh hesitated. Aspirin was a painkiller, and warfarin was a drug given to heart patients and anyone else who needed their blood thinning. Christ, realised Josh, aspirin thins the blood as well, that's why it too is recommended to heart patients. If you get a cut after taking those three pills it will be impossible for the body to form a clot to stop the bleeding. The blood is going to pour out of you like a tap.

'Fuck off,' spat Josh. 'If you want me to bleed to death, then just cut me open, you bastard.'

He glanced up. The woman had walked into the room and was standing at the foot of the bed, with a syringe in her hand. She stood close to the bed, looking down at Josh.

'Take the pills, Josh,' said Azim. 'It will hurt less than the injection, and the end result will be the same. Any antico-agulant can be taken as a pill or a jab, as I'm sure you know.'

'Just get her away from me,' shouted Josh.

'Talk to me, then,' snapped Azim.

Josh stayed silent.

'Jab him,' Azim said, glancing towards the woman.

The needle stabbed into the flesh of his thigh. Josh tried to struggle, but against the cuffs on his hands and leg it was useless. The woman stirred the syringe around, searching for a vein, then squeezed hard. The liquid disappeared. Josh yelped as the needle was pulled roughly out of his body.

'I'll give you another chance,' said Azim coldly. 'Tell me where Luke is.'

'Do your worst, you bastard.'

Azim drew a knife from his pocket. Nothing fancy. Just a plain steel kitchen knife, four inches long, the sort of thing for chopping onions. Doesn't matter, thought Josh grimly. It'll do the job.

'Spare us both the misery, Josh,' said Azim.

Josh bit his tongue, preparing himself for the pain that he now accepted was inevitable. Azim leaned over the side of Josh's body, examining him the way a butcher might examine a steak that he was about to carve. He held the knife steady in his hand, then jabbed it into the top of Josh's shoulder. Josh cried out in pain as blood started to seep from the wound. He could feel himself getting drowsier as the drugs took effect. Blood was gushing from the wound, turning the sheets bright crimson.

Josh closed his eyes. The strength was draining out of him, as if he was about to die.

The sound of the television roused Josh from his slumber. He opened his eyes, blinking hard at the screen. The news.

A blonde woman was mouthing the words, but Josh was struggling to concentrate.

More blood, he realised. They took more blood out of me while I was sleeping. The strength is literally draining out of me.

'Another terrifying Three Cities Attack,' said the news-reader on the TV screen.

Josh tried to calm his mind as he focused on what she was saying. A harsh neon light was filling the room, and the television was turned up loud. His throat was parched, and his limbs felt numb and lifeless. Hunger was gnawing away at his gut.

'In a pattern that is now terrifyingly familiar, there were blackouts today in Little Rock, Arkansas, in Birmingham, Alabama, and in Jersey City. In each city, the power was switched off at nine a.m. local time precisely, and remained switched off for one hour. Local law-enforcement authorities reported widespread panic, confusion and chaos as traffic systems, airports, schools and hospitals were all shut down. But after this fourth attack – the third in just a few days – the emergency services already have in place a well rehearsed plan for dealing with them. Within minutes of the attack, National Guard personnel were patrolling the streets, preventing the outbreaks of looting and rioting seen in earlier incidents. Still, two people in Birmingham died when a truck rammed into a hairdressing salon after failing to spot an emergency traffic signal. And one person died in Little Rock when the power was turned off during heart surgery and the hospital's back-up generators failed to switch on in time.'

Josh squinted at the screen, trying to shake off the pounding headache beating at the inside of his forehead and the terrible waves of fear that were assaulting his nervous system. Another attack, he told himself. Luke's still out there. But where the hell is he? *And why the hell does he keep doing this?*

'After yet another attack, more and more people are becoming convinced this must be the work of terrorists, possibly al-Qaeda,' continued the newsreader. 'A spokesman for the Pentagon said earlier today that, despite earlier denials, the possibility that terrorists may have worked out a way to hijack power systems is now being taken seriously. We are going to go over live now to our correspondent at the Pentagon, Ken Flagstaff. Ken, what's the latest you're hearing?'

Azim flicked off the television. He stood over the bed, looking down at Josh, his expression a mixture of pity and contempt. 'We don't need to listen to some prattling reporter outside the Pentagon, do we, Josh? We know who's responsible for these blackouts. All we need to know now is where to find him.'

Josh looked first at the blank TV screen, then up at Azim. He could feel himself starting to become afraid, and the emotion disgusted him. He had felt many different emotions in his life: despair, anger, confusion, rage – they were all part of what a soldier expected to experience on the field of battle.

But abject, cowardly fear? I hoped I could always resist that.

'So where is he, Josh? Where is he?'

Josh shook his head. 'I've told you that I don't know.'

Azim clapped his hands together. The woman walked into the room. She was still dressed all in white, and she still had a veil wrapped around her mouth, as if she refused to breathe the air of a room that Josh had slept in. Her brown eyes turned icily towards where he was lying, and Josh sensed that she was enjoying herself: there was a hint of amusement in her expression as she advanced towards him at a snail's pace.

She had a wicker basket in her hands. Through the silence, Josh could hear the sound of something rustling.

Please God, not another snake.

'First we get J-O-S-H. Then we get H-E-L-P.' Azim paused. 'And now we get L-B-J. What does that mean, Josh?'

He shrugged. 'Lyndon B. Johnson. An American President during the Vietnam War.'

Azim shook his head. 'I don't think so. Unless it's some kind of clue. I think it's a message. He asks you for help, then he tells you where to find him. I think the letters L, B and J mean something. Either in that order, or in some other sequence. But that's the signal. So where is he, Josh?'

'I don't know, I've told you that.'

The woman stepped closer. Josh thought that he could smell the snake inside her basket.

'Tell me, Josh,' said Azim, his voice growing louder. 'Tell me, and I'll let you die like a man.'

'I don't know,' shouted Josh. 'I've bloody told you that.'

Azim clapped his hands together. Silently, the woman unfastened the basket. The head of a snake slipped out. Its pale green-eyed stare darted hungrily around the room. About three feet long, with banded black, red, and ivory skin, the muscles in its neck were straining as it looked across at Josh. From its manic writhing Josh could tell that the animal was starving. Probably not been fed for a couple of days, he realised with mounting dread. *The bastard is going to bite everything in sight.*

Azim tapped Josh's chest with his cane. 'We're going to keep doing this until you tell me,' he said flatly.

'I'd tell you if I knew,' Josh yelled. 'Just keep it bloody off me.'

'The pain will stir your memories, Josh. When you genuinely want to die, then you'll tell me.'

'Just keep the snake off me, please. Please.'

Josh could hear his own whimpering and hated himself. He was willing himself to be strong, but the strength was ebbing out of him. Another day, another two days, maybe three at most. *I'm starting to break. I can feel it.*

'Just one bullet, Josh, and this can all be over,' said Azim. 'Just tell me what I want to know.'

Josh remained silent, clenching his fists. Another place, he told himself angrily. *Take yourself to another place.*

'Let it out,' said Azim angrily, turning on his heels and walking out of the room.

The woman placed the open basket at the foot of the bed. The snake slithered out, its long thin body sliding up across the sheets and rubbing against Josh's body. It moved roughly across him.

Josh screamed, a curling howl that seemed to fill the tiny room.

The snake paused and looked at Josh, first in surprise, then with curiosity. It flicked its tail angrily against the skin of Josh's thigh. Then it started sniffing his chest.

I know, thought Josh, suddenly terrified by the knowledge sweeping over him. I know what L, B and J means. *And I know where I can find Luke.*

Josh rolled over onto his side. There was a terrible pain in his chest where the snake had bitten him. Looking down, he could see the marks where its fangs had dugs deep into his skin, and he could see where his own blood had dripped onto the white sheets.

He tried to see if the snake was lying somewhere in the room, satiated and sleeping. But he could see no sign of it.

He had been lying awake for an hour now. The ceiling's fluorescent lights were shining down on him. He no longer had any idea what time it was. Nor what day it was. The fruit had been taken away, and so had the water. His body felt weak and exhausted. Josh had no idea what it was like to die, but he wouldn't have been surprised if it felt something very much like this.

He could remember the snake sinking its teeth into his chest. He could remember losing consciousness as the waves of fear, pain and disgust had washed through him. And he could remember something else as well: a set of memories that had come flooding back into his mind just before he'd gone under. Josh couldn't be sure if it was the blood loss or the snakes' venom that was making him remember.

But he ordered himself to hold on to them. *Those memories may be the thread on which your life is hanging.*

Josh struggled to concentrate, slowly reassembling the elements of the story. The initials meant something. L, B, and J were a code, a set of letters that he and Luke had agreed with each other. He couldn't recall the precise time or place, but he could see the picture as clearly as if it were playing on the TV in front of him. He and Luke were sitting in the mountains somewhere. There were rocks and boulders behind them, and scrubland stretching below them. A small campfire was burning next to them, providing the only illumination apart from the stars and the moon in the sky. Luke had a laptop open on his knees. The machine was plugged into a car battery placed next to them in the dust. They were discussing something, although not all the words were clear to Josh. He could see Luke's lips moving, but he couldn't hear all the words. Word by word, Josh started to piece together what had been agreed between them. If they were separated in the next twenty-four hours, then Luke would contact Josh by switching off the power in three different cities. The first letters of those cities would be a code: use the code and it would give you the GPS coordinates of where the other person had hidden themself. L, B, and J, were the letters. All Josh would need was a GPS machine that could be picked up for a few dollars in any electronics store and that would tell him where Luke was.

I know, he realised. *I know where Luke is.*

Josh, help. L, B and J.

But what possible help can I be to him now?

The best I can hope for is to die quickly without revealing where he is.

Josh lay silently in the bed. The handcuffs were still

holding his hands and one foot in place, and he had stopped trying to move. The next few hours and days were going to be the hardest of his life, he told himself. As long as his memory had been shot to pieces, it had been possible to take the torture. That's why commanders send out their men with only the minimum of information. That's why terrorists organise themselves in cells, with no contact between different groups even in the same town. You can't reveal any secrets you don't know, no matter what they do to you.

But now I know. And at some point they're going to squeeze the information out of me. The will-power of even the strongest man will snap eventually. *It's just a matter of finding his breaking point.*

Josh steeled himself. At some point Azim would be back. So would the woman. They would have snakes with them. Maybe something worse. My best hope is to provoke them, he told himself grimly. I need to rile them. I need to get their blood up so high they make a mistake.

I need to push them over the edge. So that they kill me.

Josh could feel the silence all around him. He didn't want to die, he knew that. Enough memories had come back to him in the past few days for him to know that there was a life back home waiting for him. There was Paula. He thought they had split up, but she was still the most beautiful woman he'd ever seen. Maybe they'd all get back together some day. There was Kate too. He still had no way of knowing whether she'd escaped Flatner and his thugs. If she was okay, if he escaped, maybe there would be something between them. And most of all there was Emily. A little girl with the looks of an angel. Emily. My daughter. Whatever happens, I must act in a way that would at least make her proud of my memory.

I don't mind dying if I have to. So long as it's dignified.

The door slid open. There was a creak where the hinge needed oiling, and Josh had learned to fear the sound. He glanced upwards. The woman was slipping silently into the room. In the past day, Josh had also started to recognise her scent: a mixture of onions, cheap perfume and disinfectants. His stomach was already churning as he took in the vile smell. He could see a long syringe in her hands, its metal tip sparkling under the neon light. My blood, realised Josh. They're coming to drain more blood from me.

He lay perfectly still. Azim had a cold intelligence that Josh could only respect. The woman was more hot-blooded. Her eyes were full of anger and contempt. The rage within her was always going to make her vulnerable. If she was provoked, she might lash out.

Of the two of them, she's more likely to make a mistake. She's the one who might kill me.

She was leaning over him now, looking at his skin. Josh kept his eyes closed, tracking her movements by the stale smell of her breath. She thinks I'm asleep, he told himself. He felt the needle jab his shoulder. The metal tip was thick, and he could feel his nerves stinging as it pierced the skin and started probing its way towards the vein. Now, he told himself. *Strike.*

Using all the strength he had left, Josh bucked upwards with a sharp jerking motion. 'Get the fuck off me, you bitch,' he roared.

The woman looked petrified, as if Josh had just risen from the grave. The hypodermic fell out of her hand and onto the floor. For a moment she froze, unable to move. Josh was heaving himself up, ignoring the pain of the hand-cuffs cutting into his wrists. 'Untie me, you bloody bitch,' he shouted. 'Untie me before I bloody kill you.'

The woman slapped him hard on his cheek.

'Kanith, kanith,' shouted Josh.

I may not have learned much Arabic in my time as a soldier. *But I know the word for 'Fucker'.*

He could feel her solid palm hitting his skin, and the

flesh underneath started to swell. 'Get back to your bloody camel, bitch,' shouted Josh.

He spat up into her face, putting a gob of saliva directly into her eye.

She hit him again and again, the fury rising within her. The blows rained down on Josh's body and he could feel his strength ebbing away under the punishment. The veil had fallen away from the woman's mouth, and he could see her full face for the first time: an ugly, sour set of features – a pinched, thin mouth and a heavy, brutal jaw.

This is it, thought Josh. I'm going to die. But at least I'll take my secret with me . . .

Azim ran into the room. He yanked the woman hard by the shoulders. 'Stop it, Nadia, in the name of all that is sacred, stop it,' he yelled. 'You'll kill the man. You'll kill him.'

The woman resisted Azim, still trying to strike Josh with her fists. She hit his face again, then his ribs. The pain raged through Josh's body. I haven't eaten, I haven't drunk, I've been tortured for four days, I've got no strength, no endurance left. Lose consciousness now, and I'll never wake up.

'Stop it *now*,' roared Azim, throwing both his arms around the woman in an effort to control her.

'He insulted me,' she spat. 'He dies.'

Azim slapped her hard across the face. A trickle of blood started to seep from her nose. 'Calm,' said Azim. 'Calm down.'

Her breathing started to slow, and her fists dropped to her side. A tear was running down the side of her face.

Josh lay still on his back. Every inch of his body was screaming out in pain. The bruises and swellings on the front of his chest were turning purple, and he could still see the punctures where the snakes had bitten him. Still alive, he told himself grimly. I can't even get myself killed.

And I can't do another round with the snakes.

Azim turned to him and smiled. 'Clever, Josh, clever,' he said. 'You want us to kill you. And we will, don't worry. A nice clean bullet to the head. Right after you tell us where Luke is.'

Another day, another two days, that's how long I have to hold out. Luke has sent me a message, but if I don't respond in two or three days he must realise that something has gone wrong. He must realise it's time for him to move on. He won't keep waiting for me.

Take the punishment for another forty-eight hours. Then tell them. *And let it all end with a simple bullet to the head.*

'Get the snake,' snapped Azim.

The woman stooped to collect her veil from the floor. She rearranged it over her face, then stalked from the room.

'The snakes aren't bloody working,' said Josh. 'Haven't you got anything else?'

Azim rubbed his hands together. 'Torture is not a pick 'n'mix buffet,' he said. 'That is the trouble with the infidels. They have no attention-span any more. If they don't get instant results they lose interest. That is not the way a real torturer works. He picks his point of weakness and he scratches away at it until the stress and the pain become unbearable.'

He leaned down close to Josh's face. 'You see, I've heard the screams, Josh. I've heard the moans and the howls as the reptiles sink their teeth into your flesh. And I know that snakes are *your* weakness.'

The woman had walked back into the room, the wicker basket in her hand.

'Please, no,' said Josh, the anxiety already building inside him. 'I've told you, I don't know anything.'

The woman unfastened the basket's lid and the snake inside shot out: this time it was one with yellow eyes and a skin that was jet black. Josh could feel himself recoiling: every muscle and nerve in his body screamed with pain, begging him to snap, to reveal where Luke was.

Josh closed his eyes, but despair was starting to overwhelm him.

'Luke, Luke . . .' he started.

Azim turned to look at him, his stare burning with curiosity.

'Yes, Josh? What about Luke?'

'Luke, Luke . . .'

The words had taken Josh himself by surprise, tumbling out of his mouth as if he could no longer control his own tongue. The snake was edging along the side of the bed, its eyes darting from side to side. A dead mouse was already dangling from Azim's hand, ready to be placed on Josh's chest.

'What about Luke? Where is he?'

'L, B and J,' stuttered Josh. 'It means . . . you need . . . I . . .'

No, he screamed silently to himself. No, hold on, man. If al-Qaeda gets hold of that software they'll wreak havoc on the whole world.

You mustn't break for at least another forty-eight hours.

Just take the punishment. You're a bloody soldier.

'What does it mean?' shouted Azim.

'Fuck off,' spat Josh. He felt relief flooding through him as he regained control of his tongue. 'Fuck off,' he spat again.

'The snakes will chew you to ribbons, Josh,' shouted Azim. 'Just tell me.'

Josh pressed his lips together.

Azim turned around and strode from the room. 'You're breaking, Josh,' he said coldly as he left. 'I can smell it. You're breaking. And in a few minutes you'll be mine.'

The snake was slithering up the side of Josh's leg, its tongue darting out of its mouth. Josh could feel sweat pouring off his body as he steeled himself for the reptilian attack that was inevitable.

Somewhere in the distance, Josh heard an explosion. And gunfire.

NINETEEN

Sunday, June 14th. Evening.
The explosion had come from fifty, maybe a hundred yards away, Josh judged.

The snake was advancing up towards his neck, its dry skin scratching against his chest. Josh could ignore it because he was listening out for more explosions, more gunfire. He could hear feet running along the corridor.

A rescue. Please God, let it be a rescue.

Then Azim burst into the room, the woman at his side. 'Unchain him,' he shouted. 'Get him to the car. I'll fight them off.'

The woman leaned over Josh, unlocking the two pairs of handcuffs. With a sweeping movement of her hand, she struck the snake on the side of its head, knocking the startled reptile to the floor. She had a .45 Colt automatic in her grip. Then Josh was dragged to his feet. The gun was pressed against his head, and he had only a pair of boxer shorts for protection.

'One wrong move, and I'll shoot you,' she hissed.

Josh could feel the adrenalin surging through his veins. A few minutes ago he'd been ready to die. Now there was the possibility of survival.

Stay calm, he told himself. Think clearly. *You've got a chance.*

Azim had left the room again. From somewhere in the distance, Josh could hear another burst of gunfire. A machine gun, he reckoned, from the sound. He got unsteadily to his feet. It had been two days since he'd been allowed to walk, and his body had taken a terrible beating. His balance was unsteady, and he needed the woman's hands on him to help him hold himself up.

'Move,' she shouted, pointing to the door. 'Move.'

Josh edged his way to the corridor.

'Faster,' she shouted. 'Move, *kwanii*, move.'

Josh picked up on the Arabic expression. *She's calling me a faggot.*

Another man was standing in the corridor. A guard, guessed Josh. He pointed a Colt pistol like the woman's at Josh, and nodded him towards the doorway. Suddenly Josh was starting to get some bearings. The building was a cheaply built bungalow. One central corridor ran through it and Josh's room had been at the end. He could see a living area and kitchen at the front, and through a doorway lay a dark patch of lawn fronting the road.

The gunshots seemed to be coming from the front of the building, but amid the noise of shooting it was impossible for Josh to get a precise fix on their location.

Josh could see another guard running with Azim to the front of the bungalow. Both guards were young Arab men, stocky, dressed in jeans and black T-shirts with bulging muscles and trim black beards.

'This way, this way,' hissed the first guard, urging Josh on along the corridor towards the back.

I'll make my move any moment now, Josh decided. *If I die trying, then that's what I wanted all along.*

Josh reckoned he'd already figured out Azim's plan. The terrorist wanted to hold off his opponents for a few minutes to buy himself enough time to hustle Josh into a van and get him out of the area. To another safe house.

They passed a window and Josh glanced out. In the gloom of the evening he thought he could make out at least three men crouched behind boulders in the scrubland outside. They were at least thirty yards away. Their faces were obscured but he could see the muzzles of their rifles. At the end of the corridor, Azim and his guard were stationed behind the metal door frame, using it to protect themselves, their own weapons ready.

Azim began to lay down a deadly barrage of fire that would make it impossible for the attackers to advance.

A stand-off, thought Josh.

'Faster, faster,' shouted the woman, her voice breathless.

Both the guard and the woman had pistols rammed hard into Josh's flesh. A terrible thought struck him, slowing him down. *Maybe I'm not being rescued? Maybe it's just Flatner and his thugs come to take me back?*

Maybe I'm better off making a run for it and letting them shoot me now.

The woman shoved him through the back door. Immediately, Josh could feel the blast of warm air hitting him in the face. His vision was blurred. He paused, taking two deep breaths.

The back of the building gave onto a square compound, marked by a boundary of rocks but no fence. The tarmac driveway circled the building and ended up there, in a parking space ten yards from the back door.

A white van was sitting on the tarmac. The woman pointed to it. 'There,' she hissed. 'Get in.'

Josh started to move. The woman was gripping his arm, and ahead of them the guard had already unlocked the van's door and was gesturing to Josh to get inside. A thin mattress was laid out on the floor, and chains, ropes and manacles were attached to the inside of the van. Great, thought Josh. *A bloody travelling torture chamber.*

'Get in now, man,' hissed the guard, in an accent that was part American, part Saudi Arabian.

No, decided Josh. I'm not bloody getting in there, pal.

You can shoot me if you want to, but I'm not bloody going.

He swung his elbow sharply upwards, smashing it into the woman's jaw. It was a move he'd first learned as a defender for the school football team, and he'd found it as effective as anything he'd ever learned. The woman spun around, shocked by the sudden pain shooting through her face, her gun loose in her hand.

A deafening roar rolled out across the yard which was instantly filled with the smoke of the explosion. A stun grenade, reckoned Josh. Or some kind of home-made mortar shell. He closed his eyes and mouth to protect himself. He could feel the heat of something burning, and he started to run to get away from the blaze.

'Stop or I shoot,' shouted the guard, his voice ragged and tense.

Feel free, pal. My funeral can't start soon enough.

Josh kept running, his eyes still tight shut, stumbling forwards. He wanted to get round to the front of the house where the attackers were.

He heard a shot, then another one.

Somewhere nearby he could hear a bullet slamming into the ground.

'Quick, this way, man,' snapped a voice. 'Fucking run, man.'

Josh recognised the coarse croak. O'Brien.

Josh swivelled to the left. He heard another shot. The guard was shooting blind.

Josh pushed forwards, picking up speed. He was holding back the pain as best he could.

Death or freedom, pal, he yelled inwardly as he willed himself forward. *Either is better than going back to that hell.*

'Here, over here,' shouted O'Brien, somewhere off to Josh's left.

Another explosion. Someone was laying down a heavy barrage of stun grenades and smoke bombs. Rescue tactics, Josh realised. Put down enough fire and confusion to get your man out without killing him in the process. *These guys know what they are doing.*

The air was thick with sulphurous smoke. Josh swerved further to the left, avoiding the explosions letting himself be guided by the lethal heat behind him and the noise ahead.

'Jump, man, jump,' shouted O'Brien. 'Over the ridge.'

Josh glanced up. The ridge to the right of the compound that surrounded the bungalow was just ten yards away. The ground rose up steadily until it reached its full height. He would just have to take a run and jump at it. There was no other way.

Ten yards, then five. Despite the waves of pain crashing through him, Josh did his best to pick up all the speed he could. Then he jumped, pushing back with his legs to gain as much height as he could. For a brief instant he was flying through the air. Then he landed hard on the ground. It took another second to find his balance again. He opened his eyes. O'Brien was kneeling in a ditch in the classic firing position, an XM8 assault rifle – a weapon issued only to American troops and still in extremely restricted circulation even among criminals – tucked against his shoulder. With a distinctive brown plastic casing and a black metal barrel, the weapon was capable of laying down a ferocious 750 rounds of deadly fire a minute.

A hand reached up, dragging Josh down behind the bank of earth that O'Brien was using for cover. 'You okay, man?' shouted O'Brien, starting to stand up.

A shot rang out. A splatter of blood hit Josh on the chest, smearing his bruised skin. For a second he thought that he'd been hit. He was waiting for the pain to kick in. Then he saw O'Brien drop to his knees. Blood was pouring from a head wound and there was a pitiful whimpering sound coming from his lips. Dying, realised Josh. Only seconds left. No point in even putting him out of his misery.

Josh's eyes swivelled desperately around. Where the hell

did that shot come from? he wondered. He was positioned behind a ridge of earth overlooking the bungalow. The van the guard had been trying to put him in was already engulfed in flames, filling the area with thick, ugly clouds of black smoke, and the guard was lying bleeding on the ground. There was no sign of the woman.

From the noise of the gunfire, Josh reckoned that there were three, maybe four men attacking the house. About as many defending it.

Josh reached down and grabbed the XM8. The barrel of the weapon was wet and slippery with O'Brien's blood. Another shot whistled over the ridge. It glanced against the casing of the gun, knocking it from his grip. Josh stumbled backwards, his balance thrown by the force of the impact. He noticed that the noise of the gun battle and the grenades had stopped. For a moment there was silence. Then . . .

'Hold it right there, Josh.'

Josh recognised the voice immediately: it was cold and precise. Azim.

You can take me if you want to, Josh told himself, but not alive.

The XM8 was lying in the dirt. Josh glanced up. He could see Azim standing ten yards away, walking slowly towards him. The terrorist was holding a Swiss-made Sig-Sauer P220 handgun, the American version with a stainless-steel casing, a weapon noted for its reliability and accuracy. It was pointed straight at Josh's head. And Azim didn't look like a man who would miss a shot like that. Not at ten yards.

I'm not going back, Josh told himself. *I'll take a soldier's death if it's offered to me.*

He reached down quickly for the XM8, planning to grab it in one movement and then turn it on Azim. The chances of survival were poor, but Josh no longer cared. His heart was thumping furiously as he began the move, but his mind was suddenly calm. You make a decision, he told himself. And once it's made, that's it.

Another shot. The XM8 jumped off the ground and into the air, striking Josh's hand. By the time it landed again, the trigger mechanism had been bent out of shape by the impact of the Sig's bullet. 'Hold it, Josh,' Azim shouted again. 'Stay still, and put your hands in the air.'

Josh pulled himself upright. The XM8 was useless now, he realised bitterly. He looked up at Azim. There was a smile on the man's lips. 'Morant is dead. O'Brien is dead. There is no one to help you,' he said coldly. 'Now, do as I told you and put your hands in the air.'

Josh remained perfectly still. Whether he was the only man left standing it was impossible to say. He couldn't hear or see anyone. Right now it was just him against Azim. One against one.

You're not taking me, Josh repeated to himself, the phrase hammering inside his head. You're not taking me alive.

Azim was walking slowly towards him, taking tiny cautious steps. The Sig was aimed straight at Josh's head. My only hope is to rush him, Josh thought. Throw my body against him, and hope that his reaction times are too slow for him to shoot me first. My chances of survival? *Above zero − but only just.*

'Give me the bullet now,' snarled Josh. 'Just bloody give it to me now.'

Azim wiped a bead of sweat away from his brow with the back of his left hand, while using the right to keep the Sig aimed straight at Josh. 'A nice, clean soldier's death here on a battlefield of your own choosing? We've already had this discussion, Josh. It's not going to happen.' There was a mocking, lilting tone to his voice as he spoke: the sound of a man charmed by his own rhetoric.

'Just give me the fucking bullet,' shouted Josh.

'Your friends have tried to rescue you and they've failed.

You're mine now, and you'll break. I know it, you know it.'

The throbbing inside Josh's head was getting worse. L, B, J, he repeated to himself. That was the code from Luke. *I know where he is.*

'Give me the bullet,' he shouted.

'Start moving sideways, very slowly, Josh,' Azim ordered. 'Do exactly as I say.'

'Hold your ground, Josh.'

Josh spun around. Marshall was standing ten yards behind him, holding an American-made M1 Garand sniper rifle. Its long narrow barrel was pointed straight at Azim. Josh judged that Marshall must have crept round the back of the ridge. Josh looked up at him. In the older man's eyes he could see the calm, implacable expression of an old soldier. *A man who would be happy to kill you if he needed to.*

'Hold your ground,' Marshall repeated, his voice firm and clear.

Josh stood steady, every muscle in his body tense but rock solid. He could see Azim's finger twitching on the trigger of his Sig. The gun was still trained on Josh, but his stare was fixed on Marshall.

'Back away,' Azim hissed. 'Or I'll kill him.'

'You need him alive,' snapped Marshall. 'Wounded, crippled, mutilated, whatever. But his brain needs to be alive. You need what's inside it.'

'I need nothing from you,' hissed Azim. 'Back away now, old man. He means nothing to you. Don't throw away your own life.'

Marshall kept the rifle trained on the terrorist. One bullet, thought Josh. He knew that the older man was, at best, only an average shot. *If that aim isn't true, we're all corpses. Or worse.*

The Garand fired. Azim rocked backwards. The bullet had hit him in the shoulder.

'Run, Josh, run,' shouted a voice.

A woman. Kate.

She was standing next to the Mustang, twenty yards away. A single thought ran through Josh's mind. *Escape.*

Azim was stymied by Marshall's gun. Josh started running, surprised at his own speed and agility. His feet pounded against the ground.

Behind him, Josh could hear a shot, then another. He raced towards the car. 'Drive, drive, drive,' he shouted, his lungs burning as he yelled the world.

As he reached Kate he could see her expression changing. A look of horror flashed into her eyes. Her shoulders sagged, and her face creased up. Josh looked behind him. Marshall had fallen to the ground.

The bullet hole in the centre of his forehead was clearly visible.

Dead.

'Into the car,' shouted Josh.

Kate remained motionless, frozen like a statue.

'Into the car,' shouted Josh again, louder this time.

Using the back of his hand, he slapped her across the cheek. She stays like this, he told himself, we all die. 'You can't help him now,' he shouted. 'Drive the bloody car.'

She opened the door of the Mustang. Josh threw himself into the passenger seat, instinctively diving for cover. At his side, Kate had turned on the ignition. The engine roared to life, revving furiously as she jammed her foot on the accelerator and turned the car hard along the dusty track.

'Drive like hell,' he shouted.

The car spun away on a surge of power. Josh looked briefly behind him. Azim was struggling to his feet. With his left hand, he was clutching his shoulder, trying to staunch the flow of blood that was weeping from the bullet would. With his right hand, he was holding the Sig-Sauer P220. And pointing it straight at the Mustang.

TWENTY

Monday, June 15th. Afternoon.
It was the smell that brought Josh back to consciousness. He lay with his eyes closed, inhaling the aroma of fresh coffee that was wafting across to where he lay. I don't want to open my eyes, he told himself. I just want to lie here. *Smelling freedom.*

'You need to drink something,' said Kate. 'It will make you feel better.'

Josh opened his eyes. Kate was kneeling beside him, her red hair tied back behind her head. She looked tired and drawn, her face smudged with tears, but after the trauma of the last few days it was a relief for Josh just to see a friendly face.

He looked up, noticing the shimmering brightness of the sky above him. As he glanced around, he could see the high boulders and deep crevices of the mountain range.

'Where are we?'

'In the mountains,' answered Kate. 'We're safe — we're in another of the survivalist camps.'

Josh took the coffee that she'd made him. They were sitting behind a rock formation on a patch of ground with a small cave at one side. Kate had dressed him in some blue chinos and a black sweatshirt: anonymous, easy-wearing gear, just right for a man on the run.

Looking down, Josh could see the plain stretching out below them. There was one road, maybe three or four miles distant, and a dirt track, along which Kate had driven the Mustang. The car was parked about twenty yards away: there were some scratches and dents, but it still looked to be intact.

Safe, thought Josh, savouring the word. *Safe.*

He took a first sip of coffee. There were bandages around his chest, and the wounds on his neck and legs had been freshly treated. His body was clean, and his beard had been trimmed. He could feel swellings in his chest where he had been bitten by the snakes, and there was a numbness in his shoulder where his flesh had been cut open by Azim. The extent of the damage would take a few days to become clear. He couldn't quite be sure how long he had been sleeping. At least twenty hours.

'I'm sorry about Marshall,' he said.

Kate's expression remained stoical. 'So am I,' she replied.

Josh fell silent. It was a terrible thing to lose a father. Once the fog of amnesia had started to clear, the memories had come flooding back to him. Now he had a clear recollection of comrades who had fallen during his time in the Regiment. He knew that he had broken the news to wives who had lost husbands, and to parents who had lost sons. And he knew that there were no words of consolation, no explanations, and no justifications that would ever make even the tiniest dent in the grief they faced.

There was nothing you could say to dim the intensity of the pain. Nothing.

'You okay?'

Kate looked away. 'It was his choice,' she said softly. 'He knew the risks he was running.'

'You shouldn't have done it,' said Josh. 'I'm not worth it. You should have left me in the ditch. This isn't your fight.'

'When I start something I finish it – I told you that.'

Josh shook his head. 'No,' he said softly. 'Trust me, sometimes you have to know which battles to fight, and which to skip.'

'Well, this one I fight.'

'Why?' snapped Josh. 'I'm just some guy you found in a ditch. I know your husband died, but you have to stop torturing yourself about that. You have to move on.'

'Move on? They've killed my father,' said Kate. 'Now it's my fight too.' She was cradling her own cup of coffee in her hand. How long she'd been awake, Josh couldn't say. He knew that she'd escaped with him last night, but how long the drive up here had been he couldn't say: he'd lost consciousness soon after they'd made their getaway in the Mustang. She must have driven them up here, then treated his wounds and given him something to help him sleep. She was a brave woman, he reflected: she had lost weight in the past few days, emphasising her elegant chiselled features, but there was iron in her heart.

'That software is important. If it falls into the wrong hands then it would be incredibly dangerous,' said Kate. Her eyes flashed. 'Marshall cared about that. I care about that. So we'll do what we have to do to stop that happening.'

Something's not right, thought Josh. *Something still doesn't make sense.*

'We need help,' he said. 'We can't fight this on our own any more.'

'What kind of help?'

Kate's tone was nervous, as if she was frightened of something.

'My memory,' said Josh. 'It's back. Not all of it. Lots of things are still fuzzy. But enough.'

Kate leaned across, taking his hand. 'You know where Luke is?'

Josh nodded. He took another gulp of the coffee, his eyes scanning the empty horizon. In his other hand he held a thick biscuit from the camp supplies and started chewing on it. The food was doing him good, he reflected: he was still weak, and his nerves were still in a poor state, but he was still alive, and so long as he ate and rested there was no reason why he shouldn't recover.

Rest, he thought grimly, and maybe one day I'll feel fit and healthy again.

'There was a code,' Josh said.

'I saw it, the third attack in a few days,' Kate said. 'J, B, L, or B, J, L, or something.'

Josh smiled. 'I know what it means. Luke told me, shortly before I got shot. He's waiting for me. I just have to go and find him. The code tells me where he is.'

Kate reached out to touch Josh's shoulders with her outstretched palm. Her skin felt good against his. The fleeting caress was soft, feminine, caring: the kind of touch that he had thought he would never feel again. 'Where, Josh?' she said softly. 'Where?'

'Like I said, we need help. We can't fight this on our own. It's too big.'

'But Luke is waiting for *you*.'

Josh wondered if he could hear a hint of irritation in her voice. 'My memory is back. I know who I am, and what I have to do,' he said.

Kate took her hand away from his shoulder. 'And that is?'

'My name is Josh Harding. I'm a British soldier, serving in the SAS, but on secondment to anti-terrorist operations. I was sent out here on a mission to find Luke. And I found him.' Josh hesitated. The pieces of the jigsaw were reassembling in his head, but he knew that the picture was still some way from being complete. 'Now I know where he is, my duty is clear.' He paused, looking down to the wilderness below. 'I report back for duty.'

'For duty?'

Josh nodded. 'I'm a soldier, like I said. That's what we do.'

Kate shook her head. 'You told me that you've been tortured, Josh,' she said. 'You said that first they electrocuted you to within an inch of your life. Next you had snakes biting you almost to death. You're weak, Josh. Your nerves are shot to pieces. You're not thinking straight.'

Josh could see the intensity in her expression: her stare was focused completely upon him, as if he were a patient on her examining table. 'Trust me, Josh. I'm a doctor. I know about these things.'

'I have to check back in. I know where Luke is, but I can't handle this on my own any more. I've already been captured twice. I can't expect you to help me again. I need to go and get reinforcements, go and get Luke, bring him in, and get this thing over with.'

'You're missing something.'

Josh said nothing.

'Why were you shot, Josh?' Kate persisted. 'Why is Luke just sending messages to you? Why isn't *he* calling for the reinforcements?'

She paused, lowering her gaze to the ground. 'There's something else going on. What happened between you and Luke?'

Josh shook his head. 'I can't remember.'

'Try, Josh, try.'

Josh concentrated. The memories were swimming in and out of his head. Catching them was like trying to catch fish in the river with your bare hands. As soon as you grabbed for them, they were already gone. What was I talking to Luke about, he asked himself?

His head was throbbing with pain and frustration. Nothing was clear. 'I have to check back in with my unit,' he said flatly. 'It's my duty.'

'Just tell me where Luke is,' said Kate. 'We'll go find him together.'

'No,' snapped Josh. 'I have to go back in.'

'You're an idiot.'

'No – I have to get back to the Regiment.'

'That's a dumb choice.'

'I'm a soldier,' said Josh angrily. 'We don't have choices. We just have our duty. Without that, we're nothing.'

Josh held the phone in his hand. From their hiding place, it had been an hour's walk down into the valley and across the plain before he'd found the road. Then it had been another half-mile before he'd found one of the payphones dotted along the highway for stranded motorists. The pain had been intense, stumbling his way through the scrub and boulders. The swelling in his chest from the snakebites was getting worse: two thick purple bruises were spreading out across his chest. And his legs were still weak from the electric shocks.

My body is weak, but my nerves are even weaker, he told himself. Kate is wrong. I have to get back to base. *I can't do this by myself.*

'My name is Josh Harding,' he said, as soon as the call was answered. 'I need to speak to the Administrative Vice-Consul.' He was ringing through to the British consulate in Los Angeles, the British government office nearest to Arizona. Every British embassy and major consulate in the world has an administrative vice-consul: supposedly a person in charge of the running of the office, but in reality the representative of The Firm, Regiment slang for the security services. The vice-consul would know who he was. And he would know what to do. If a Regiment operative was in trouble anywhere in the world, that was who they called.

'He's in a meeting,' said a secretary when Josh was put through.

Josh checked his watch. It was six-fifteen. Dusk was starting to settle over the wilderness. It was quiet. There was the low murmur of a breeze, but nothing else.

It was the quiet space between day and night, reflected Josh. A good time for a man to disappear.

'Tell him it's Josh Harding,' he snapped. 'From Hereford.'

'I'll put you through,' said the secretary. 'Right away.'

'Kenneth Adams here,' said a voice on the line. 'Who's this?'

The accent was pure Oxbridge, noted Josh. It probably belonged to a man in his mid-thirties, who'd drifted between the Foreign Office and The Firm. Maybe sandy-coloured hair, maybe dark. *Either way he'd be a Rupert.*

'Josh Harding.'

There was a pause. Josh could imagine the surprise on the man's face.

'Bugger it, man, where the hell have you been?' said Adams. 'We've been looking for you everywhere.'

I bet you have, thought Josh. *Could have tried a bit bloody harder as well while I was getting my balls fried for Queen and Country.*

'I got held up,' said Josh. 'But I'm coming in.'

'Where are you?'

Josh rolled his eyes up towards the sky. Thick streaks of red were smudged across the horizon as the sunlight ebbed away. The moon was already making its ascent. Bloody nowhere, he thought sourly.

'Arizona,' he replied. 'Keeping a low profile.' He paused, checking his watch. It was getting late, and he needed a few hours' rest before he attempted another journey. 'I've got access to a vehicle. I could be in LA by the morning.'

'Stay right where you are,' said Adams fiercely. 'Give us the coordinates, and we'll pick you up right now.'

'I can come in under my own steam,' said Josh. 'I'll see you in the morning.'

'No,' snapped Adams. 'Just tell us where you are and we'll get our American friends to lend us a Black Hawk for the night. We want you back on dry land.'

'I need to rest,' said Josh. 'It can wait until morning.'

'You're coming in tonight, Harding,' said Adams. 'And that's an order.'

Welcome back to the world of the Ruperts, Josh told himself. *Maybe I was better off without my memory.*

The thunderous roar of the Sikorsky Black Hawk UH 60 shattered the silence of the scrublands. Dust and clumps of twisted grass were swept up, caught in the whirlwind of swirling air beneath the machine's rotor blades.

Josh stepped forward from behind the boulder where he had taken shelter. It was just after ten at night. It had taken him an hour to walk back to their hiding place, then there had been a brief but furious exchange with Kate when he'd told her that a chopper would be picking him up within a couple of hours.

'Come with me,' Josh said again as he heard the first rumble of the chopper echoing out across the mountains.

'No way,' she snapped back.

'I still need help,' said Josh. 'We'll find Luke together.'

'You're a fucking idiot, Josh,' she shouted. 'There's something wrong, I tell you. Something else that you haven't remembered. This is a trap.'

'This is the British Army,' said Josh, 'Don't be ridiculous.'

'It's your neck on the block,' Kate said coldly, turning away and disappearing among the boulders. 'But if you need me, if anything goes wrong, I'll be waiting by that phone booth you used on the road.'

Her words were still echoing in his ears. *If anything goes wrong, I'll be waiting.*

Nothing's going to go wrong, Josh told himself as he stepped forward towards the waiting Black Hawk. A man he assumed was Adams was beckoning him forwards with impatient movements of his arms. He wasn't quite as Josh had expected: he was shorter and stouter, with greying hair, and with a thick layer of fat bulging over the waistband of the trousers of his black suit.

But I'm back with my own tribe, reckoned Josh. Within

the hour, I'll be part of the Regiment again.

'Are you Josh Harding?' said Adams.

Josh climbed on board the Black Hawk. The moment his feet left the ground, the machine soared upwards. The roar of the rotor blades through the open doors felt like it was splitting open his eardrums, and the swirling dust clogged his lungs and hurt his eyes.

He could feel his spirits lifting as the huge blades of the chopper lifted it high into the sky. Support. Back-up.

'That's me,' shouted Josh.

'Then get to the back of the bloody chopper,' Adams shouted back.

Josh started to walk to the back of the helicopter. The machine swayed noticeably in flight and he had to hold on to its metal walls to steady himself.

He looked down the length of the chopper. At the back were two military policemen, sitting with their weapons held ready. Like Adams, they were wearing headphones so that they could talk to each other over the roar of the Black Hawk's engine. Their expressions were sombre. Glancing back towards Adams, Josh could see the signature breast pocket bulge of a man carrying a handgun in a shoulder holster.

'Why the policemen?' said Josh, looking at Adams.

'Because you're under bloody arrest.'

Josh blinked. No, he told himself. I must have misheard. It must have been the noise of the Black Hawk. *He must have said something else.*

'I don't . . . *What?*'

'You're under arrest,' snarled Adams. 'Now sit bloody still.'

'What the fuck for?' shouted Josh.

'Insubordination,' said Adams. 'Disobeying orders. Then desertion. They'll court-martial you. And from what I hear about you, I hope they bring back the sodding firing squad.'

Josh's gaze roamed through the Black Hawk. The pilot was sitting at the controls, taking the machine up above the desert.

Both of the MPs were gripping their standard-issue Heckler Koch MP5 sub-machine guns. They'll shoot me if they're told to, and won't even think twice about it, Josh thought.

Adams was still to the back of him, now hunched down on one of the metal seats that lined the interior of the Black Hawk.

'It's not bloody true,' Josh snarled.

'Save your whingeing for the court martial, Harding,' snapped Adams.

'The power failures, the blackouts, the attacks — there's going to be more of them,' said Josh. 'I'm the only man who can stop them.'

'I've told you to shut it.'

'I'm the only man who can stop it,' shouted Josh, his voice raw with anger. 'Can't you bloody understand that?'

Adams looked towards the MPs. One of them looked at Josh, his finger poised on the trigger of his MP5. 'You're under arrest,' he barked. 'You'll have your chance to defend yourself.'

'There's going to be a catastrophe.'

'I don't care,' shouted Adams. 'You're a British soldier. Just follow the bloody orders.'

'The orders are fucking stupid.'

'Doesn't make any difference,' snapped Adams. 'You follow them all the same. You break them, you deserve whatever shit gets thrown at you.'

Josh looked out of the chopper's door. The air was rushing past at three hundred miles an hour. Darkness had already fallen, but the Black Hawk was equipped with electronic guidance. It could probably find its way back to LA without a pilot, never mind without any light.

A river: Gazing down, Josh could just make out its twisting contours. He started racking his brains, trying to dredge up whatever memories he could. A river from Arizona, running west. The Colorado. It had to be. If the pilot was tracking that, at some point they were going to hit the Hoover Dam. A dam meant a lake.

Josh smiled inwardly. A lake. That meant a man could jump from a helicopter and have a chance of surviving.

Maybe only a one in ten chance. *But it was still something*.

I have to escape, he told himself. I *have* to. Not to save myself. But if I don't get to Luke soon, then Azim or one of his thugs will get to him first. Then the whole world will be in trouble.

Josh started to make his calculations. The helicopter door was open. The Black Hawk was designed for close-quarter military contacts, designed to put down fresh troops and pick up casualties in a hurry, which was why it was usually flown with a side door open. They were flying at about two thousand feet, snaking their way across the open countryside. Josh was sitting on one of the bucket seats, across from the doorway, not far from where the MPs were sitting.

Josh stood up and walked towards Adams. He could feel the two MPs tracking him with their stares. 'You're making a bloody mistake,' he said.

'What?' shouted Adams, straining to hear him above the noise of the Black Hawk's engine.

'I said you're making a bloody mistake,' said Josh, not bothering to raise his voice.

'What?'

Adams leaned forward, trying to catch Josh's softly spoken words.

You're mine.

With a sudden swift movement, Josh thumped him in the chest with his left hand. In the same instant, his right hand whipped down and grabbed the gun from beneath Adams's jacket. It was a simple Glock 19, a gun that Josh was familiar with. He gripped it tight, jabbing the barrel against Adams's right ear.

'Hold bloody still,' he shouted at the two MPs. 'Hold bloody still or I shoot.'

Both men froze, staring hard at Josh.

'Hold your fire,' said Adams, speaking into his mouthpiece so that the two MPs could hear him on their headphones.

Glancing from the side of the chopper, Josh could see that they were now flying over Lake Mead. I just have to get to Luke, he repeated to himself. *I just have to get to Luke before Azim does.*

He grabbed Adams by the scalp, yanking hard on his greying hair. With the Glock still pressed against the man's ear, Josh dragged him down to the front of the Black Hawk. The pilot was staring back at him. A man of twenty-four, twenty-five, Josh couldn't help admiring the way he was holding the Black Hawk on a rock-steady course despite the fracas. 'Take her down,' snapped Josh. 'Take the bloody thing down.'

'You're making it worse for yourself, man,' Adams shouted.

'I'll be the judge of that,' roared Josh, tugging harder on the man's hair.

'Just put the gun down, Harding. I'll make sure you get a fair hearing.'

Josh ignored him, looking back towards the pilot. 'Just bring the fucking thing down,' he growled.

'Don't,' barked Adams.

The pilot held the Black Hawk steady on its progress across the lake.

They're trying to outsmart me, thought Josh. They know I can't bring this bird down while I'm holding a gun on Adams. *I'm buggered.*

Unless . . .

Josh fired once, then twice. The bullets smashed into the Black Hawk's control panel. A shower of sparks flew out of it, spitting up into the pilot's face. Now Josh jammed the pistol back against Adams's head. Already he could feel the chopper starting to sway and swerve through the air as the controls jammed, then died.

Josh glanced at the altimeter.

Now we're going down.

Fast.

Sixteen hundred yards. *At one hundred, I jump.*

Josh could feel the Black Hawk start to plummet. It was as if his legs had collapsed beneath him. His heart was jumping up into his throat. The pilot was wrestling desperately with the controls, trying to regain control of the machine.

'You're a fucking madman, Harding,' shrieked Adams. 'You're going to die.'

'At least we'll all go together,' shouted Josh.

One thousand one hundred yards.

The lake was so close that Josh could almost smell it.

The two MPs tried to stand up, but as the Black Hawk lurched through its descent they were thrown back down again.

'Finish him,' yelled Adams. 'Finish the fucker.'

Five hundred and fifty yards.

One of the guards was holding his MP5 straight in front of him, trying to point it straight at Josh, but the Black Hawk was swaying violently as its descent gathered speed. The nose was starting to turn down as the aircraft hurtled faster towards the black, icy waters of the lake.

Two hundred and ten yards.

A burst of gunfire rattled against the metal walls of the machine. Amid the violent motion, it was impossible for the guard to maintain his aim.

Josh glanced towards the open door.

A hundred and sixty yards.

He let go of Adams and kicked back, compressing all his strength into his calf muscles to give himself maximum lift.

His body started to arc through the air towards the open doorway. A churning vortex of air was swirling just outside.

The air hit Josh hard, first in the face, then in the chest, thumping the wind from him and making it almost impossible to breathe. For a second it seemed as if he was hurtling horizontally, flying level with the Black Hawk. He could hear the sound of gunfire behind him. One bullet, then two, then three.

Nothing hit.

Suddenly he could feel himself falling at a terrifying velocity. The Black Hawk was high above him. The swirling wind started to spin him around. His head was dizzy, and it was hard to keep his eyes open against the rush of oncoming air.

He flung his arms and legs wide, maximising the surface area of his body. Slowly he could feel himself starting to get control. His body was stable, his spreadeagled state buffering him from the full impact of the rushing air. Up above, he could see the Black Hawk starting to bank, turning hard as it continued to descend rapidly.

Josh put all his strength into trying to hold himself steady. But there was nothing he could do about the accelerating speed of his fall. And in a few seconds he was going to hit the water.

Below him he could see its icy blackness.

TWENTY-ONE

Monday, June 15th. Night.

In the last seconds of the fall, Josh had arched his body into a smooth diving position, his arms stretched out in front of him and his hands clasped together. His head had been tucked just behind the arms, slightly bowed so that the first impact from the water would come on the crown: the skull there was the thickest lump of bone in the body, designed that way by evolution to protect the brain, and if you had to take a hard blow that was the best place to take it. He had held his legs together behind him, as straight as poles.

The perfect diving position.

It had made no difference. The impact had been a moment of shattering terror. As first his hands, then his head and his shoulders had sliced into the water, he'd felt as if every bone in his body had suddenly been pulverised.

The pain hit him first, rippling up through him in wave after wave. He lost control of his muscles. Then the icy cold of the water numbed his body, freezing the blood in his veins. His breathing stopped, and it felt as if his heart had stopped beating.

For a moment, Josh was convinced that he was dead. It seemed unimaginable that he could survive any more punishment.

Then the motion stopped. A splitting headache was throbbing inside his skull. Josh could feel that he was no longer moving. The water was still swirling around him, and a strong underwater current had started to catch hold of him, dragging him forwards.

He was probably thirty feet below water, he reckoned. Slowly, he started to kick his legs. They responded lazily at first. There was little strength left in his muscles to fight against the current. He tried again, harder this time. Both legs started to move and Josh could feel his body start to move.

It had been impossible to take a proper mouthful while he'd been in free fall. Now he was desperately short of air.

I just hope I've landed close to the shore. Even if I get to the surface in time, I haven't the strength to swim very far.

Josh kicked hard, using his arms to help drag himself back up to the surface. He opened his eyes. The water was fresh and clean, but it still took a moment to adjust his vision. He looked straight up. He could see something moving. A shallow wave. The surface.

Then his head broke through. Josh opened his mouth, taking great lungfuls of air. The oxygen filled his chest, hitting his bloodstream and instantly clearing his splitting headache.

Alive.

The word sent a jolt of exhilaration through him. He looked quickly around the dark, choppy waters of Lake Mead. About three hundreds yards ahead of him he could see the massive wall of the dam that had created the lake. The current was dragging the water slowly towards it, allowing the Colorado River to continue its journey towards the coast. To the north, reckoned Josh, was Nevada. To the west, California. And safety? he wondered bitterly to himself. *That probably wasn't in any direction at all.*

Now, straight ahead of him, he could see the Black Hawk crash into the water. A huge wave rolled out as the machine was sucked down. It was at least a mile away, but through the dark night air Josh could still hear the shouts as the crew jumped out. And then he could see a dinghy starting to move away from the crash site.

It's a massive lake, he told himself. *They've little chance of finding me.*

Josh started swimming. He reckoned it was a good two hundred, two hundred and fifty yards to the closest shoreline. A pebbled beach and some conifer trees were all he could make out.

The shoreline was a national park, and it must be close to midnight by now. There shouldn't be anyone around. Just the occasional bear.

But I've got to move, Josh told himself, because in a few minutes Adams will have half the American army out here looking for me.

He swam furiously, dipping his head below the surface of the water and surfacing only when he had to for air.

If I can keep my strength, I can do this, Josh told himself. I just have to believe.

After ten minutes he reached the shore, his teeth chattering from the cold. The beach was made up of tiny pebbles. Josh lay still for a moment, recovering his breath. He cupped some water in his hands, drinking as much as he could get inside himself, then crawled forwards. The trees were ten yards away. He curled up behind one of the massive pine trunks. The shoreline was completely empty.

I need a few minutes to rest, he told himself. *Then I make my escape.*

His clothes were sodden. Every inch of his skin felt damp and chilled. He struggled to pick himself up, standing uneasily. Got to get away, he told himself, staggering forwards. Got to get away.

If they find me, they're going to kill me.

Josh walked for two hours through the forest that ran down to the lakeside. He knew there would already be hunting parties out looking for him, but the national park surrounding the lake covered a hundred and fifty square miles. Locating a single man would take a team of hundreds. *For a few hours at least he should be safe.*

He still had money on him. Two hundred dollars in cash, and a pocketful of loose change: the notes were dripping wet but would dry out in time. Eventually he found a small road and, after walking along it for an hour and a half, a payphone placed there for anyone who broke down in their car. He called Kate on the payphone that she'd said she'd be waiting by and told her what had happened. 'Stay right where you are,' she told him. 'Hide in the woods. I can drive down there in a couple of hours.'

After speaking with Kate and giving her his position, Josh retreated fifty yards back from the road, into a thicket of tall pine trees. He pushed some leaves together to form a bed, then lay down, his eyes closing almost instantly. He breathed deeply, drawing in the rich restorative oxygen of the woodlands. For the first time in weeks, his mind was clear. He knew who he was. *And he knew what he had to do.*

He rested for two hours, catching enough sleep to get some strength back into his system: the ability to sleep on demand was one of the first lessons he'd learned in the army. Then he trudged back up to the road, settling behind a group of trees close to the spot where he'd told Kate to meet him. It was past two in the morning, and the narrow strip of tarmac running through the forest was empty. His heart pounded inside his chest in the twenty minutes he had to wait until he saw the Mustang pull around the corner. Kate was the only person he could think of who could help him now. *And if they didn't get to Luke soon, then Azim would find him.*

After the Mustang pulled up to the side of the road, Josh waited a couple of minutes, making sure it hadn't been followed, then ran out to meet Kate. They drove the car fifty yards into the woods so that it wouldn't be visible from the air, then went back towards Josh's hiding place. The air was damp and cold, and a light breeze was whistling through the trees. But it felt good to have her back at his side.

'How much damage have I taken?' said Josh as Kate started to examine his wounds.

'Too much,' she replied. She bathed the wound in his neck with a swab of disinfectant, then replaced the bandage.

'Normally, I'd recommend at least a week or two of complete relaxation and recuperation,' she said with a gentle smile.

'Doctor's orders?' said Josh.

Kate nodded. 'But you're a bad patient,' she said. 'The kind that doesn't listen to their doctor.'

He reached up to kiss her. Her lips felt warm and soft and moist, and as her tongue stabbed against his skin he could feel some of his wounds starting to heal. When a man feels certain that he is about to die, Josh reflected, there are many things that he thinks about. There are a hundred different regrets that flash through his mind: places he never visited; people he never met; the daughter he wouldn't see again. But foremost among them is the realisation that he'll never hold a woman in his arms again, never feel her yield under his touch, nor hear her whisper in his ear.

Over the last few days, there had been many moments when he'd felt he was about to die. There'd been times when he would have welcomed death as warmly as if it were a long-lost brother. But now that he'd escaped death's clutches, he was grateful to be alive. Every moment, he resolved, was there to be savoured as if it were a succulent piece of fruit hanging from a tree.

So Josh held Kate tight, drawing strength from the warmth of her body. She lay down next to him, resting on the strip of ground surrounded by the tall pine trees that filled this bank of the lake. For a few minutes, Josh was content just to feel her embrace. It was only after a while that he started to unbutton her blouse, and slowly and gently make love to her.

'You told me something wasn't right,' he said, lying next to her when they had finished.

Her lips caressed his forehead, soothing him more effectively than any tranquilliser could. 'Don't worry, baby. It doesn't matter. We'll go find Luke now.'

The first shafts of daylight were breaking through the trees. 'Christ, it's morning,' said Josh. 'We've wasted time.'

Kate looked behind her. The sun was rising above the horizon. Through the trees they could see the still waters of the lake, the orange light of early morning playing across its surface. 'It would be nice just to enjoy this place for a few days,' she said. 'It's so beautiful.'

Josh hugged her closer to him. 'After we've completed the mission,' he said. 'We'll go somewhere together.'

Kate nodded: 'Here?'

'Maybe. But next time I'm not jumping out of a bloody helicopter.'

There was a silence between them. It was foolish to talk of the future. There was too much to do. 'You know where Luke is?' said Kate.

Josh nodded.

They drove due north from the lake, tracking the minor roads. When they reached a small town, Josh waited in the car while Kate went into the mall to run her errands. His eyes scanned the horizon carefully. He could see a security guard patrolling the outer perimeter of the car park. He could see a man ambling though the parked cars, checking each one. Just some guy who's looking for his own vehicle? wondered Josh. Or a Fed? Josh ducked, shielding his face so that no one could see him.

You watch everyone like a hawk, Josh told himself. That what it's like to be a hunted man.

Kate slammed the Mustang's door shut. 'Here,' she said, handing across a large Burger King paper bag.

Josh glanced down at the food. A Bacon Double Cheeseburger, a Whopper with cheese, two extra-large portions of fries, and a big carton of Coke. The first meat he'd have eaten in days, he suddenly realised. *I need it.*

He pulled the Mustang out of the parking lot and started heading due north, away from the town. There was a sheriff's office by the side of the road, and as they went past it Josh instinctively felt himself gunning the accelerator. Take it easy, he warned himself. This is a big country, men get lost for years. So long as you stay calm you can buy yourself the day or two you need to find Luke.

His head had been spinning ever since his arrest. That was the last thing he'd expected. For the first few hours he'd been driven just by the adrenalin of his escape, then by finding Kate again. But he still didn't know what he could have done to make the Army turn on him so viciously.

My memory, he reflected grimly. It's still shot full of holes. Something happened between me and Luke. Something that is still unfinished. Something that the Army didn't like.

I just don't know what it is.

I have to find him. I have to find out what happened in those few hours and minutes before I was shot.

He pulled the car into a lay-by at the side of the road. The forests that surrounded the narrow stretch of irrigated land bordering Lake Mead had long since faded from view, and they were now driving through the harsh wilderness that separated the lake from Las Vegas. There were signs on the road offering land for sale at a dollar an acre. But no takers, decided Josh: it was a brutal landscape, untouched by rain for years at a stretch, where even the toughest, hardiest of animals would struggle to survive.

Josh took a bite of the Whopper, gobbling down the

food. He needed protein, carbohydrates, and sugar, and he needed them fast.

The main battle still lay ahead. He would need whatever strength he could summon up.

'Did you get all the stuff?' he asked Kate.

She nodded. 'A GPS locator. And a copy of *London Calling* by the Clash.' She hesitated, holding up the slim black machine that could locate any spot in the world from a single set of coordinates, and then a copy of the CD, with its iconic cover of Paul Simenon smashing his bass guitar against the stage of a concert hall. 'The GPS device I understand. It'll tell us where Luke is, so long as we have the right numbers to feed into it.' She held up the CD, glancing at its cover. 'And this. Well, I don't know.'

Josh grinned. '*London Calling*, right?'

'He's in London?'

Josh shook his head. 'Three letters, that was the signal. L, B, and J.'

Kate looked confused. 'Okay, tell me.'

'The first three tracks of *London Calling*. The title track, that's an L.'

Kate flipped the CD over, looking down the track listing. '"Brand New Cadillac". Followed by "Jimmy Jazz".'

'Right. L, B, and J.'

'So where is Luke?'

Josh reached across for the CD. He ripped off the plastic covering and pulled out the inner sleeve. 'Take the times of those three tracks, then feed the number of seconds into our GPS locator. So if the track lasts three minutes, twenty-eight seconds, put in twenty-eight.' He handed the CD back to Kate. 'Whatever comes out, then that's where Luke is.'

Her fingers worked feverishly. Josh sat patiently, chewing his way through the rest of the Whopper, then attacking the Bacon Double Cheeseburger. He took a handful of the fries and slipped them into his mouth. At his side, Kate was holding the GPS device in one hand and the CD in the other. Her fingers were hitting the tiny plastic keyboard with the force of a carpenter banging a nail into a wall.

'Swansea,' she said, her tone excited. 'He's in Swansea.'

Josh felt a couple of fries lodge themselves in his throat. He started coughing violently. 'What's he doing there? With the bloody Taffies?'

'What?'

Josh looked at her expression. Blank. She's never heard of Swansea, he thought.

'Where is it?' he asked.

'Swansea, Arizona,' said Kate. 'About a hundred miles north-east of here. In the middle of just about nowhere.'

'Then that's where we're going,' said Josh.

Josh slipped the CD in the Mustang's audio system, then fired up the engine and pulled the car out into the road. The first sweeping, howling chords that opened the album boomed up through the Mustang's speakers.

'London calling,' yelped Joe Strummer's rasping, hoarse voice as the song cranked up.

Josh tapped his fingers against the dashboard, allowing the beat of the music to surge through his veins. Instinctively, he started to mouth the familiar words. For an apocalypse, there was no better soundtrack.

TWENTY-TWO

Tuesday, June 16th. Noon.

The road twisted up the side of the mountain, its surface pitted with holes and strewn with dust and boulders. Josh was gripping onto the wheel of the Mustang, letting it roll with the bumps. His body had taken so many knocks in the past two weeks that he could no longer locate the pain precisely: there was just a dull, insistent ache that seemed to be burning up every nerve in his body.

It had taken three hours to drive here, longer than Josh had expected. They had stopped once at a gas station to shower and get some coffee. Then they had stopped at an all-day store to pick up some fresh supplies for the day ahead: water, matches, some tinned food and biscuits, plus as much spare petrol as they could get into a selection of jerrycans and fit onto the back seat of the Mustang.

The route had been a long and hard one, taking Kate and Josh through the empty back roads of western Arizona. They drove up through high mountains, coloured a mixture of reds, bronzes and yellows, and twisted their way through steep valleys filled only with boulders and a few stray cacti barely managing to stay alive in the miserable soil. The heat of the morning was baking, and as Josh looked up at crystal-blue skies uninterrupted by even a whisper of cloud he could feel himself growing wary of the sunshine. They were only a few dozen miles from Death Valley, the hottest place in North America, where the heat still claimed a few careless tourists every year.

Swansea was a mining town, started by the Clara Consolidated Gold and Copper Company in 1909. It had remained inhabited until the mine finally shut down in 1924. At its peak, it had had a population of 750 people and a railway that connected it to the main Arizona transport arteries. As well as the mine, there had been a smelter, a barber's, a hotel and a sheriff. Now nothing remained. Unlike many of the Arizona ghost towns, it wasn't on any of the tourist maps: it was too new for anyone interested in the history of the Old West, and it had been home to none of the famous gunfighters of an earlier era. Year by year, it was turning back into the dust from which it had been built.

Josh's gaze flickered up to the horizon. The ground levelled off at an altitude of around a thousand metres. There were deep gullies and crevices etched into the side of the mountain where the rain had washed off its sides, but as they climbed higher the ground became smoother, its surface covered with fine dust. 'There,' said Josh, spotting the small collection of tumbledown buildings emerging in the distance. 'That's it.'

The road broke out onto a plateau, and suddenly widened. The layout of the town was clearer now. A main street, with a collection of ruined buildings. A flat mountain top. And just beyond that a huge ditch, hundreds of metres long and at least fifty metres deep, sitting like a giant scar on the side of the town: the familiar debris, reflected Josh, of opencast mining.

He pulled the Mustang up at the side of the road. It was difficult to say where the town started or ended. The buildings broke down into splinters of wood and rubble, and whatever fences there might once have been had long since rotted away. Josh paused at the beginning of the street. At its edge was a sign, broken in two. '*Swan*—'it read. '*Popu*—'

'Whoever was the last man out of this place wasn't worrying about turning out the lights,' said Josh.

Kate smiled. 'It's the last man *in* that we need to worry about.'

Shafts of sunlight were shining right through the ruined structures as Josh started to walk down the main street. Twenty husks of buildings lined the eight-foot-wide track, but the walls were tumbling down, and weeds and cacti had started to take root in the mortar, turning it to dust. If you looked carefully, you could just make out what they might once have been – a bank, a hotel, an ironmonger's.

There had never been anything grand about Swansea, Josh decided as his eyes scanned the buildings. It had been built quickly and cheaply. The façades showed no signs of decoration: wood planks and steel girders flung together as fast as possible.

He picked his way carefully through the debris littering the street. This is just what I need, he thought. *A man with no past hides out in a town with no present.*

'Can you see anything?'

Josh noticed he was whispering, as if it was somehow wrong to raise your voice in this place. *As if you might wake the dead.*

Kate shook her head. 'But he's here somewhere,' she whispered back. 'I'm sure of it.'

Josh noticed the smell of the air. The accumulated dirt of decades had covered the place. Every broken wall and shattered slate seemed to be caked in a layer of filth. The wind had blown bricks, beams and plaster mouldings out into the streets where they had lain for years, breaking into fragments, embedding themselves in the surface of the ground. Nothing, he realised. Usually, you could smell a man. He left his scent imprinted on the air. Here there was nothing. Just the smell of decay.

'You sure you got the coordinates right?'

Kate nodded. 'Swansea,' she said. 'That's how the coordinates came out. You sure you got the *code* right?'

Josh nodded. 'We talked about it. That memory is quite clear. Luke's a rock kid – he knows all the classic albums off by heart. I think he must have learned them from his mum. We agreed on a whole bunch, and the tracks would be the clues. The Beatles and The Stones, of course. And Van Morrison. Some Dylan.'

'So where the hell is he, then?

'Water,' said Josh.

'We got some in the car.'

'No,' said Josh. 'I mean, there has to be a water source somewhere. Nobody can build a town unless there's fresh water. Luke's a smart kid. He'll be hiding out by the water.'

Kate looked at him, her eyes sparkling. 'So where is it?'

'Easy,' answered Josh. 'Look for the smelter. You can't run one of those without water.'

He started walking towards the smelter. Swansea's main street ran in a dead straight line with buildings on either side of it. Behind the buildings there were a few relics of what might have been residential houses. Straight ahead of them, Josh could see the mine. Its rusting hauling gear still rose high above the landscape. Next to it lay the disused conveyer belt that had taken the ore and started sorting it before depositing it in the smelter. The mine had been opencast. In this derelict country, no attempt had been made to cover up the damage after the mine had shut down. Huge pits were sunk into the sides of the mountains, and huge piles of rubble where explosives had been used to break up thousands of tons of rock lay in massive, crumbling piles.

A barbed-wire fence had been put up around the plant, but it had long since rusted. Josh pushed open the door and stepped inside. The machinery lay silent all around. He walked quickly towards the door of the smelter. Rust had settled into the hinges of the door, making it stiff. He leaned his shoulder into the door, giving it a hard shove. Once, then twice he heaved his weight against the door. The third time, the hinges cracked and the door swung open.

Josh stepped inside. The smelter still had a smell of charcoal and metal that had lingered through the decades since it had last been used.

'Luke,' shouted Josh. 'Luke.'

His voice echoed against the tin roof.

'Luke,' he shouted again, louder this time. 'Luke?'

The words coiled around the derelict building, bouncing off the walls. Each time it bounced back it lost a fraction of its strength, and Josh could hear the sound gradually dimming, like the fade at the end of a record. Where the hell are you? Josh asked himself. *Why aren't you answering?*

I just hope you haven't left already. You won't survive out there by yourself, not for a minute. *Too many people are looking for you.*

A flashlight came on, its beam trained on Josh. He jumped, instinctively recoiling from the harsh light. Raising his forearm to his eyes to shield them, he turned around. A thin pale figure was stepping out of the shadows.

'Is that you, man? Is that really you?' said the boy.

Josh looked closer. The figure was obscured by the light blazing out from the torch. Josh took a step forward. 'Luke?'

The light switched off. Josh could see clearly now. A thin boy, fifteen or sixteen, with straggly blond hair, thick lips, and a complexion that was pale and waxy. His eyes were sunken and there were dark shadows across his cheeks. His Limp Bizkit T-shirt had a couple of gashes in it. And he smelled strange: an acrid mixture of sweat, fear and dirt.

'Christ, you look terrible.'

Luke shrugged. 'You don't look so great yourself.'

Josh took another step forward. He reached out a hand, placing his palm against Luke's. The boy's hand was cold and sweaty, and his fingers were trembling. Scared, realised Josh. Scared the way an animal is scared. *Or a child.*

He pulled Luke closer, putting his arms around him and hugging him to his chest, the same way he might have greeted a long-lost brother. For a moment they remained silent.

'It's okay, man, it's okay,' said Josh. 'I'm here now. It's going to be okay.'

A tear was starting to trickle down the side of Luke's face. 'Hell, man, I've been so frightened. So fucking frightened, you wouldn't believe it.'

'We're here now,' said Josh. 'It's going to be okay.' He took the torch and started to look around. Luke had been living here alone for two weeks. Some dried leaves had been bundled into a pile to make a bed. A solar panel had been fixed up to provide enough electricity to run a laptop, and a tiny portable satellite dish had been set up to give the computer access to the Internet. Otherwise, Luke had been entirely by himself here, speaking to no one, frightened out of his skin. No surprise that he's starting to crack, realised Josh. There are many brave grown men who wouldn't be able to take that.

'Let's eat,' said Luke, nervously. 'We need to talk.'

Josh looked around. Luke's ideas, like those of many teenagers, of what he needed to survive while on the run were foolish. He had a dozen two-litre bottles of Coke, several boxes of crisps, and endless packets of biscuits. But little fresh water, no fruit, no bread, and no cereals. Another reason he looks in bad shape, thought Josh. He's just eating sugar and starch.

'Who's she?' said Luke, jabbing a finger towards Kate.

'Kate,' said Josh. 'She's a doctor. She's been helping me the last couple of weeks. I've been really lucky to have her along.'

'Are you okay, Luke?' said Kate. 'I can examine you if you want.'

Luke shook his head. 'I'm okay. Scared. But okay.'

He poured out three servings of Coke into some plastic cups, and took a hefty swig of his own, downing it in one gulp. Josh could see that his hand was still shaking nervously.

'What the fuck happened, man?' Luke said suddenly, looking accusingly towards Josh. 'You were meant to help me.'

'I don't know,' answered Josh.

'Hey, you were meant to get me out of here,' said Luke, sounding angrier. 'That was the deal.'

'I don't know about that, either,' said Josh.

Luke looked startled. Josh noticed how the fear in his eyes, which had started to abate in the last few minutes as he'd grown angry, had suddenly returned. 'You don't know much.'

'I lost my memory,' said Josh. 'After I got shot. What happened immediately before that is a blank.'

'Your memory? Shit!'

'You'll have to tell me everything that happened between us, Luke,' said Josh. 'So let's all sit down. And you start at the beginning.'

TWENTY-THREE

Tuesday, June 16th. Night.

'It started with me and Ben. Just a couple of kids, right? We hang out together at school because we're both into computers. We started out playing games, all the usual stuff. Then we did some programming, and started following some of the hacking websites. Nothing sinister. We were just testing ourselves, I reckon. Seeing what we might be able to do.'

Luke was sitting on the pile of leaves that he had swept together to make a bed for himself during the last two weeks. He had a cup of Coke in one hand, a biscuit in the other. Josh was sitting next to him, his legs crossed. Kate was sitting just behind him, her hands resting on Josh's shoulders. Above them some pale shafts of light were beaming down through the cracks in the ceiling of the smelter.

'We did some stuff like hacking into the computers at school, changing grades. We got into a bit of trouble for that. We were hacking into the phone company so that we could get our calls for free. We hacked into a few other company systems as well. Not to do any harm. We just wanted to have a look around, see what we might be able to do.'

'Like what?' said Josh. 'Why were you doing it?'

Luke looked up, a hint of a smile on his face. 'Why does anybody do anything? Money, right? You met my mom. Do we look rich? I mean, I love my mom, don't get me wrong, man, but she's a wacko. Right?'

Josh smiled. 'She takes her own path through life.'

'I never had a dad, at least not one that I knew. We never had a proper car or a proper house, or any of that stuff. So all the time I'm thinking, what if I could make some real money. A million dollars, two million dollars, something like that. Buy a place by the beach in Jamaica, where mom could just sit around smoking weed all day. Maybe go to London, visit some of the places The Clash used to play. Like that place on the cover of their first album.'

'The Westway?' said Josh. 'Forget it.'

'Well, whatever, man. I just wanted to get out of Hicksville. Me and Ben, both of us, that's what we wanted.' He paused, taking another hit on his Coke. 'You get onto the hacking websites, and go into the chat rooms, and you get all these stories from guys who hacked into corporate websites. You know, you get kids who hack into the Starbucks system and start messing with the prices of latte. Or whatever. And they're, like, the company pays them a million bucks or something just to tell them what the flaw in the system was and how they could fix it. All these stories going around of kids making millions just by sitting in front of their computers.'

'It's men, Luke,' interrupted Kate.

Luke looked up at her. Her red hair was tumbling down her neck, and her eyes were staring right into his. The perfume, noticed Josh. The perfume was drifting across the space between them, sweetening the fetid air of the smelter.

'What?' said Luke, his gaze darting up towards her the way a puppy's eyes flick up to its owner.

'When you're a bit older you'll realise that men talk a lot of rubbish. They sit around in bars, saying they've nailed this girl and that girl, done this deal and that deal. Usually, it's just bullshit.'

Josh laughed. 'Usually? It's *always* bullshit.'

'You think those kids didn't get money off Starbucks and the rest? Is that what you're saying?'

'I think it happens,' answered Kate. 'I just suspect it happens a lot less often than the people in the chat rooms say it does.'

Luke nodded. From his expression, Josh could tell that he was disappointed. Part of being a teenager, he reflected. One by one your illusions get chipped away, like the paint being stripped off a piece of wood. *Get used to it, pal. Life has a lot more disillusion in store for you.*

'Whatever, that's what Ben and I thought. I guess we were naive. We figured we could hack into some corporate system, maybe they'd pay us some money just to go away.'

'Porter-Bell, right,' said Josh. 'That's where you started.'

Luke nodded. 'There's kind of a buzz about it in the chat rooms. Hanging Bell, they call it, because they come down so heavy on hackers and because it's so tough to get into their systems. We figured we'd have a crack. After all, what did we have to lose? Nothing. It's not like we have girls calling us up for dates every night. We just hang out, playing with our computers.'

'The Three Cities Attack,' said Kate. 'That was you?'

Luke remained silent for a moment. A look of fear crossed his face, as if a nasty memory had just broken through. 'We got lucky, I guess. That's the thing about hacking. You just try different things, and see what works. They got firewalls, barriers, everything you can think of around this system. But Luke and I designed this worm. You know what a worm is?'

Josh shook his head.

'It's like a piece of software that tunnels into a system and comes out the other end. You wrap the instructions inside another bit of code, and that's what allows it to get through. The system doesn't recognise what's coming through.'

'Like hiding a gun inside a laptop or something when you're going through Customs?'

Luke grinned. 'Just like that. Usually they don't get

through. The firewalls are built to detect worms, along with everything else the hacker can throw at them.'

'But this did?' asked Kate.

'Well, we did a couple of dozen, and they kept getting thrown right back at us. Then we made it. A perfect worm. It sailed right into their system, undetected, and then, once it was inside, the thing unwrapped itself. And for a few minutes we had control of their system.'

'So you did The Three Cities Attack?' Josh asked.

Luke nodded. 'Ben and I planned it together. We figured we needed something pretty spectacular, something that was going to grab their attention. So we figured London, Paris and New York. They all use Porter-Bell software for their power grids, and they all use the latest version, which was all we had access to. So we switched it all off.' He flashed a smile at Kate, and Josh could tell that he was trying to impress her. 'It was a hell of a buzz, I can tell you. All that power, and all that chaos. All caused by Ben and me. We got a hell of a kick when we watched it all on TV.'

'Until people started saying it was terrorists,' said Josh.

'That frightened us a bit. I guess we hadn't really thought very much about what kind of reaction there might be.'

The light was fading from the ceiling. It was past eight, Josh noticed, and the burning heat of the day had already subsided, replaced by the chill that descended on the wilderness at night-time.

'We contacted Porter-Bell,' continued Luke. 'We didn't use our real names or anything. We're not that stupid. We just set up a dummy Internet address, told them we had access to their software, and told them to be in touch if they wanted to do some business.' He paused, as if trying to sort out all the memories lodged in his mind. 'They told us to get lost at first. Said they'd been contacted by hundreds of cranks from all over the world asking them for money. So we gave them a couple more demonstrations. We didn't turn the juice off for a whole hour. Just for a minute or two at a few places. Nothing to make the evening news.' Luke clicked his fingers together. 'But enough to let Porter-Bell know we had the power.'

'Then they wanted to play ball?' asked Josh.

'You bet. Once they knew we weren't just cranks, that we had a way into their system, they were all over us. Wanted to meet up right away. But again, Ben and I weren't that dumb. We knew we had to play it cool. I mean, what we were doing was illegal. And we wanted a lot of money. Five million dollars. Enough to set us both up for the rest of our lives. So we arranged to make a swap on a neutral piece of ground. They'd give us the money. We'd give them the worm.'

Luke looked up towards Josh, his eyes suddenly dark and intense. 'Then you showed up.'

Josh thought it was like watching a film you'd first seen as a kid: the outline of the story was dimly familiar, but you couldn't colour in any of the details. 'What the hell was I doing there?' he said.

Luke shrugged. 'Search me, man.'

'What did I say? I must have told you something.'

'I don't know how the hell you found us,' continued Luke, glancing between Josh and Kate. 'Ben reckoned it might have been because we were using a dummy Internet address we'd set up with one of the British Internet service providers. We didn't want to use an American one because we might have been traced. And we figured British was best, because that way we'd understand the language.'

Josh could feel something stirring within his mind. As Luke explained the sequence of events, more memories were flooding back. Fragments of meetings, orders and journeys were flashing through his brain, lighting up a path that had until now been shrouded in darkness. 'That's how we got you,' he said. 'British Intelligence were onto you as soon as the power got switched off in London. The British are bloody nervous about a terrorist attack on London, and we assumed it was our old pals at al-Qaeda. We were monitoring Internet traffic, and came across your e-mails to Porter-Bell. Then we used our search powers to get the ISP to tell us where you were.' Josh clenched his fists. Suddenly he knew what he had been doing in America. 'I was sent out here to find you.'

Luke grinned. 'You succeeded. And that's when things turned interesting.'

'What did I want?' asked Josh.

'You said that you were an SAS agent, sent over to the US because one of the cities attacked was London. Your task was to track us down and make sure it never happened again. You also had to find out who it was, because the British Government was convinced that al-Qaeda was planning to use our software to launch an attack against them. If there was any possibility of al-Qaeda getting hold of this software, that had to be stopped from happening. So that was your mission. To find us, and to get the software before anyone else did. You told us that every intelligence agency in the world was trying to track us down, and so was every terrorist group. Your intelligence was that al-Qaeda was trying to capture us, because they wanted the software to launch their own attacks. If we went to the meeting with Porter-Bell, you said, we'd be killed almost certainly.'

Josh shrugged. 'Makes sense.'

'Then you offered us a deal. You said that if we could help you track down the al-Qaeda man who was looking for us, you'd arrange for us to be smuggled out of the country, and we could keep whatever money we managed to squeeze out of Porter-Bell. You said that no one was really interested in us. So far as you were concerned, catching the al-Qaeda people on our trail, that was what you wanted to do.'

'Did I mention a name?'

'What name?' asked Luke.

'The name of the al-Qaeda operative who might be tracking us.'

Luke passed for just a fraction of a second. 'Azim. A guy called Khalid Azim.'

Azim, thought Josh. I was trying to capture him all along. And I still am. *Except this time I want him dead.*

'You took that deal?' asked Kate.

'Ben and I figured we were running out of choices. We'd already noticed strange things happening, around town, around our school. There were rumours of Federal agents checking through the state. We suddenly got a sense of what we'd unleashed. Everyone in the world was looking for us. If we were to get out alive, if we were to get our money, then we needed help. And you were the only guy making an offer.'

'So what did I want you to do?'

'This Azim guy, he was your main focus. It was him you wanted.'

More memories. The meetings with Ben and Luke. Josh could recall talking to them slowly, winning them over, earning their trust the hard way: by listening to them, understanding what they wanted, then doing his best to deliver. 'You and Ben took off for a few days, I remember that,' he said. 'We figured out a safe place in the mountains for you to lay up. Then we fixed the meeting with Porter-Bell. But we left a trail of clues on the Internet as to where and when the meeting would be. Enough clues that we could be certain that Azim would also be there on the day to try and get the software from us.'

There was a breath of excitement in Josh's voice as he recalled the events of those few days. He'd discovered that Azim was in the area, tracking down Luke to steal his software for al-Qaeda, and he'd realised that this was his one chance to catch him: the night he'd escaped his clutches on the Afghanistan border could be buried for ever. 'That's when I'd get him. Then I'd spirit you away. You'd get your money, and I'd catch one of the most wanted terrorists on our list.'

'We camped out the night before the meeting with Porter-Bell in the mountains,' said Luke, taking up the story. 'Sunday, May thirty-first. All three of us were sitting around a campfire, like a bunch of desperadoes. Man, it was fun. We swapped this code, just in case anything happened and the three of us got separated.'

Josh grinned. 'That was when we discovered we both liked The Clash.'

'And all the other 1970s rock greats,' said Luke. 'Proper music, as my mom likes to call it.' He fell silent. 'And then you fucked up, man. When the shit went down, you weren't there for us.'

Josh remained silent.

'What the fuck happened, man?' said Luke, his voice turning ragged. 'Why weren't you there for us? We trusted you, man. We fucking trusted you with our lives.'

TWENTY-FOUR

Tuesday, June 16th. Night.
Josh could see the pent-up anger in the boy's eyes. The story had been with him for days now, a noxious stew of betrayal and anger.

Believe me, thought Josh, if I could turn back the clock, I would.

He remembered that they had been standing at the side of the road. It was an empty stretch of track, deep in the heart of the Arizona wilderness. Josh knew the ground intimately by now. It was the same place where Kate had found him after he'd been shot. The same place he'd been back to with Marshall. The same place where Ben had been murdered.

Josh had scouted it out the day before. The ground next to the road was completely open but there was some cover in the boulders, where he was planning to lay up and provide covering fire when it was needed. He had equipped himself with an MP-5, issued to him by the British consulate in Los Angeles. And he had a stash of stun grenades in case the battle turned rough.

'You remember now, don't you?' said Luke accusingly.

Josh nodded, but remained silent. What had taken place in the next few minutes was now playing vividly across his mind. It was a scene, he suspected, that would remain etched on his soul until he sank into his grave. There are many terrible things that can happen on a battlefield, he reflected bitterly. A hundred different ways to die, and a thousand ways to get wounded. But there is nothing worse than betraying a comrade.

'It went like this,' said Josh. His voice was hushed, as if he were speaking in church. Outside, he could see the stars starting to brighten up the night sky. He could see both Kate and Luke tracking every word. 'Luke and Ben were sitting at the side of the road. You looked innocent, young. A couple of boys exploring the wilderness, maybe hitching a ride. I had the moves all worked out in my mind. The Porter-Bell people were going to come up, give you the money, and take the software. At some point, Azim was going to make his move. When that happened, I'd take him out. If there was any rough stuff from the Porter-Bell guys, I was going to take them out as well. Either way, I'd make sure you and Ben got out okay. If the plan went the way I wanted it to, Porter-Bell would have the software, so there'd be no more blackouts anywhere in the world. And I'd go home with Azim's scalp. A hero. *At least, that's what I thought.*

'Azim was there somewhere. I'd tracked the man for six months through the Afghanistan-Pakistan borderlands. I'd had him in the sights of my rifle once before. I could smell the bastard. I couldn't see him but I could sense him moving through the boulders and rocks like a breeze. He was out there somewhere. And when he showed himself, I was going to take him. The job would be finished. Properly, this time.

'Then, at the appointed time, a group of three bikers pulled up at the side of the road. The leader was a big, burly man, with a ponytail and beard, driving a big Honda bike. He had two other bikers flanking him. I recognise him now as Flatner, although I didn't know that at the time.

'Next there was a car. A Jaguar XJS, black. Not a car you see very often in Arizona. A man climbed out. In his late forties, maybe early fifties. He was dressed in blue jeans and a loose-fitting white linen shirt. He had black aviator shades covering his eyes. I recognised him, of course. Ed Porter.

'I was scanning the horizon. I had the rifle in my hand, and a set of binoculars. I'm a good shot, always have been. Show me a man's head at a range of up to five hundred yards, and I'll hit it ninety-nine times out of a hundred. Nobody knew I was there. Nobody *could* know. When Azim showed his hand, he was going to die.

'I was hooked up via a scrambled mobile phone link to The Firm back in Vauxhall. I had told my commanding officer, a Rupert called Mark Bruton, exactly what I was going to do. He'd approved the plan. He'd told me he didn't believe that Azim was still alive, but if he was they certainly wanted him dead. And so long as I made sure the software was safely back with Porter-Bell so there could be no more blackouts, then they were happy with the plan. All I had to do was execute it.

'Everything was set. I was certain that nothing could go wrong.'

'But it did, man,' said Luke. 'You fucked up.'

Josh nodded. He could feel the guilt passing across him like a dark cloud. 'Here's what happened,' he said softly. 'Luke and Ben were standing at the side of the road. Luke had his laptop in his hand. Porter approached both of you, with Flatner at his side. Porter was holding a black canvas bag in *his* hand. The money. Then everything started to move very quickly. Azim had hidden himself in the sand, just a few yards away. The bugger had literally buried himself, with just a straw sticking above the surface of the ground so that he could breathe. He rose up out of the ground like a zombie from its grave, clutching an AK-47 in his hand. In one swift movement, he strode up towards Ben, and jabbed the gun against his head. "There's dozens of us," he was shouting. "All over the area. Just give us the software, and drop your weapons, and you'll be okay."

'I had him. I had the bugger in my sights. In that moment, I knew that all I had to do was squeeze the trigger and he'd drop down dead. The shot was going to be a clean one, right through his skull. Nobody could survive a hit like that. Nobody.

'Then this voice comes through on my earpiece. It was Bruton.

'"You there, Harding?" he's shouting down my bloody ear. "You there?"

'"Here," I replied.

'My gun was still trained on Azim at this point. I could still drop him. I just had to squeeze the sodding trigger.

'"There's been a change of plan, Harding," says Bruton. "We reckon it's too dangerous to have a couple of teenage headbangers running around with the power to switch off the electricity in London or Paris or New York whenever they're feeling a bit bloody bored. HMG wants them dead."

'"I gave them my word," I snapped back at him.

'"Well, no one gives a bugger about your word," says Bruton. "Slot them. Now."

'"With respect, sir, fuck off."

'"You're heading for a fucking court martial, Harding," Bruton shouted back at me. "Now, sl—"'

Josh hesitated. He took a sip of Coke and chewed on one of the biscuits. Telling the story, reliving it exactly as it had been played out that day, had left him drained and exhausted. He glanced up at Luke: the boy's expression was turning from surprise to fascination. I'll make it up to you, Josh vowed silently to himself. *If I can . . .*

'I ripped the earpiece out,' continued Josh, his tone growing firmer all the time. 'I didn't want to listen to any more of that bollocks. Bruton was telling me to slot Ben and Luke — it was a direct order. But I wasn't about to do that. No way.

'I looked back down. I'd lost vital seconds arguing with

that idiot. It was chaos down there. Flatner and his two henchmen had pulled out their guns. Pistols. I recognised the make, Desert Eagles, the biggest automatic handgun in the world. One of them had grabbed Ben away from Azim. He was waving a gun at him. Two more Arabs had arrived as if from nowhere. Both of them were holding rifles. They were pointing them at you, Luke. They were trying to get the computer away from you but you were standing your ground.

'There wasn't any time to think. I couldn't get a clear shot at Azim. The moment had passed. I picked myself up, gripped the MP-5 tight in one hand, put a stun grenade in the other. And then I started my charge. There was only one thought in my mind. I had to save you and Ben. I'd given you my word, and I was bloody well going to live up to it no matter what the cost. You don't leave a mate in danger. That's the first rule of my Regiment. *And I was ready to live or die by that rule.*

'It was bloody chaos down there. For a few seconds there were bullets flying everywhere. It was bloody murderous. I fired once, then twice. I think I wounded one of Azim's men. Maybe two. I don't really know. There were so many people waving guns around, it was impossible to get a grip on anything. The whole mission was a complete fuck-up.

'I saw you, Luke. And I saw Ben. Flatner was about to fire at you. I just shouted, "Run Luke, run. Run for your fucking life." And then I saw you starting to head out across the open scrubland. You looked back at me, and said, "I'll be in touch, I'll be in touch."

'Then I could see the gun pointed at Ben. I could see Flatner's finger on the trigger, and he was starting to squeeze it. I hurled myself towards him, trying to knock him off balance and ruin his aim. And that was it. That must have been when the bullets hit me. One in the neck and one in the leg.

'Because that's the last thing I remember.'

'I trusted you,' said Luke. 'But I shouldn't have. And Ben died because of that.'

Josh shook his head. 'My Regiment let me down,' he answered. 'Azim is one of our most wanted terrorists. I could have taken him, then rescued you, but they changed the orders on me at the last moment.' He smashed his fists together, trying to deal with the anger that was building up inside him. 'The bastards. They turned on me. And now they want to arrest and court martial me for disobeying an order.'

'So you can't help me?'

'That's not what I meant,' said Josh. 'I said I'd help you and I will.'

'Like, how, man?' said Luke. 'You fucked up big last time.'

The words stung Josh. At school, he'd flunked a couple of his GCSEs. That was one reason why he'd joined the Army, to make something of himself. During his training for the Regiment, he'd failed a couple of courses and had had to retake them. His marriage to Paula, the way he'd remembered it, had failed, and had left Emily without two parents to raise her: talking to Luke had unlocked the flood-gates, and all his memories had come back to him now. And earlier this year, he'd failed to take out Azim when he'd had the man in his sights. Every time you failed, it diminished you as a man, until there was nothing left but a walking collection of disappointments, defeats and regrets.

I won't fail this time. I can't.

'In the Regiment, we have a saying and it's a good one,' said Josh. 'We bring our enemies out into the open, then we can take them. That's what we're going to do. We get Flatner and his boys, and Azim and *his* boys, out here. And we take them down. When all our enemies are dead, we've won.'

Luke smiled: some of the youthful vigour had started to return to his eyes. 'Where?'

Josh looked out through the door of the smelter, onto the dusty abandoned street. 'This looks like a good spot. We fight them right here.'

The meat was skewered on a piece of old wood. Kate was bathing the dead crane in its own fat, turning it gently over the campfire, making sure that it was evenly cooked on all sides. The smell was drifting across to where Josh was sitting: a beguiling mixture of poultry and steak that would tempt the most demanding gourmet.

'You ready to do this?' said Josh glancing across at Luke.

He nodded. They were sitting cross-legged on the dusty ground inside the old smelter. Outside, Josh could see that it was a clear night. The stars were beaming down on the mountains, and a half-moon was illuminating Swansea in a pale, silvery light. Looks better than the Welsh one, reflected Josh, smiling to himself. *It's quieter, and the food is better, too.*

The laptop computer was open on the ground between them: a Dell Inspiron with a blue cover, similar to the machine that had been analysed by Kessler. The solar panelling was generating enough power to recharge its batteries during the day, and so long as they didn't overuse it, it would be enough for their needs. A portable satellite link was hooking into the Internet, allowing them to send and receive e-mails: usually these services were very expensive, but Luke knew how to hack into the system of one of the operators, allowing him to access the web for free. If I'd had that kind of kit when I was a teenager, I wouldn't have had to join the Army, decided Josh ruefully. I'd be fighting electronic wars. A lot safer than the other kind.

'I'm ready,' answered Luke.

His fingers started tapping on the keyboard. Josh and Luke had discussed the plan, and had agreed exactly what they were going do. Luke would send through a message to Porter-Bell, using the same dummy e-mail address that he had been using earlier with Ben. He'd tell them that he was still willing to trade his software for five million dollars. All they had to do was agree, and he'd set up a time and place for the meeting.

'They've taken the bait,' said Luke, looking up towards Josh.

Josh was surprised by the speed of the response. It was less than five minutes since Luke had sent his message, and they had already got back to him. He keeps turning the juice off, realised Josh. *It's making them as nervous as a raghead in a Texas bar.*

'What's it say?'

'They agree to our terms, unconditionally,' said Luke. 'Five million. Whenever, wherever we want it.'

Josh looked across at the message.

'What shall I say?'

'Not tomorrow,' said Josh. 'We need a day to prepare. Thursday.'

'What time? Noon?'

'You've been watching too much TCM. Midday will be too hot. Make it dawn. And tell them we'll give them the place tomorrow.'

Luke started tapping on the laptop's keyboard.

'Why dawn?'

Because all the best soldiers die at dawn. With their boots on.

Josh laughed and smiled at Luke. 'Because there's no point wasting a whole day shooting these bastards.'

TWENTY-FIVE

Wednesday, June 17th. Dawn.
The sun was breaking across the horizon, its first bright beams flashing across Josh's skin. He could feel Kate sleeping in his arms. Her red hair was lying across his cheek, and her arm was stretched out over his chest. The warmth of her body felt reassuring next to his skin, and he could measure the beating of her heart as she breathed.

Perhaps we *will* have a shot together when this is over, he reflected. *Maybe, just maybe, I could make a relationship work this time.*

Her perfume was still lingering on her neck, but it was mixed with the sweat of the night so that only fragments of the smell still remained on her skin. *Clandestine* by Guy Laroche, realised Josh. The name had been somewhere inside his head for weeks. A nurse he'd spent the night with once had worn it, and when his wife had smelled it on his clothes she'd promptly chucked him out. *That's one memory I'd have been better off without.*

My memories, he realised. They're all back. My family, my school, my mum and dad, my ex-wife, my daughter. They're all there. All back in the right box.

I know who I am, and what I have to live for. *I know what I'm prepared to die for as well.*

Josh lifted himself from the ground. It was just after seven in the morning. Kate had curled up next to him, both of them resting on a pile of old leaves that had been swept up from the streets. Luke was a dozen yards away, his body covered by what looked like some ragged overalls he had found in one of the abandoned locker rooms. Let them sleep, thought Josh. I need to scout this place by myself.

He stretched, and walked out of the smelter, down into the main street. Swansea felt fresher in the morning: it was as if the ghosts had abandoned the place, and the buildings looked almost as if they could be occupied again one day. A flock of cranes were drifting overhead in close formation, and one of the grey birds had settled onto a slab of crumbling rock. It cast a wary glance at Josh, then decided to ignore him.

A mining town, Josh mused. The place must have been packed with explosives once.

He started rooting through the empty buildings. The hotel still had the remains of a check-in desk, but the staircase had collapsed, and all the furniture had long since been removed. The kitchen still had an old rusting stove in it, but no sign of any fuel. Next, he tried what looked as if it had once been a hardware store. The counter was still there, although the polish of the surface had long since faded. The shelves had collapsed leaving a dusty pile of debris. Josh picked up the first of a series of tin containers. The can crumbled in his hand, the brown metal flaking like a piece of pastry.

A bunch of heavy steel nails dropped to the floor. Josh gathered them up carefully. Put together into a home-made bomb, they might make useful shrapnel. He walked through to what must have been the stockroom. Looking at some piles of tea chests, he started levering them open one by one. Most were empty. Eventually he stumbled across one filled with hunting knives. He took them out one by one. They hadn't been used since they'd been left here eighty or more years ago, and their blades were still as sharp as razors.

Now we're getting somewhere, thought Josh. *Our own armoury.*

For the next hour, Josh kept searching. The sheriff's office, the houses, the blacksmith's – he inspected each building from top to bottom to see what he could scavenge. By the time he had finished, he was covered in a thin film of dust. His hands felt as if they had been dipped in history. But he had gathered a useful haul: several litres of heating oil from one of the old houses; a dozen cases of shotgun shells from the sheriff's office; some glass bottles from the saloon; and a collection of vicious-looking heavy steel hammers from what had once been the blacksmith's.

Enough kit to do a lot of damage. *If you have time to prepare and you know how to use it.*

Walking back towards the smelter, he kicked up the embers of the fire that they had built last night, tossing another broken floorboard onto the flames to rekindle it. Boiling some water, he brewed up some rough-tasting coffee, pouring it into a pair of the plastic cups that he and Kate had stashed in their kitbag.

'Okay, campers,' said Josh offering both Luke and Kate one cup each. 'No time to kip. We've got work to do. I want this place ready to blow up like it's the bloody fourth of July.'

Josh pointed to the entrance to the town. 'Here,' he said to Luke. 'We should plant them right here.'

A road snaked up the side of the mountain: when Swansea had been a working town, it had been a two-lane paved road, but in the years since then it had collapsed into a single dirt track.

'How deep?' asked Luke.

'An inch, no more,' said Josh. 'Cover them with a layer of dirt, and pat it down so it's not too obvious that the ground has been freshly dug.'

For the past hour, they had taken the shotgun shells and carefully opened up their caps. Using some old string, they had bound the shells together in clusters of four. Bury them beneath the surface, and anyone who trod on them was going to get their foot blown off. It was a simple, rough landmine. *But I've seen them used by men I've fought in Bosnia, and I know how lethal they can be.*

They worked for an hour, digging the pits and laying down the charges in neat formations at different spots around the town. *As soon as anyone attacks, we'll draw them onto the landmines.*

'Okay,' said Josh, as he inspected the last of the charges. 'On to the bottles.'

For the next hour, they filled several old glass bottles with nails, then poured heating oil into them and capped out each one with six inches of twisted rag. Josh crept carefully on top of the crumbling hotel, careful not to break any of the rotting beams that were still barely supporting what remained of its roof. Using some cord, he tied the bottles to the roof, spacing them a dozen feet apart.

A combined nail and petrol bomb, he reflected grimly. Anyone near one of these babies when they blow is going to be feeling very sorry for themselves in the morning. *If they ever wake up.*

'Just memorise where they are,' said Josh to Luke as he climbed back down into the dusty street. 'Look at each one a hundred times, and keep on telling yourself where it is until you can remember it backwards.'

'Shall I tell them where?' asked Luke, glancing across at Josh.

Josh had studied Kate's map of the area, and discussed it with her. He didn't want to let anyone at Porter-Bell know they were hiding up in Swansea. It would be too easy for their hired killers to infiltrate the area during the night, take them by surprise, and murder them all while they slept. Instead, they would give them a meeting place an hour's walk across the mountains and tell them to be there at eight a.m. tomorrow. When they arrived, they would find a note redirecting them towards Swansea. That way, they should arrive in the town around nine. *And we'll have dusted off the welcome mat.*

'Give them these GPS coordinates,' said Josh. 'And tell them not to even think about getting here early. Any tricks and the deal's dead. And so are they.'

Luke tapped the message into the keyboard, then pressed *send*.

'You really think Azim is going to get these e-mails?' asked Josh.

Luke nodded. 'I'm just using my regular old e-mail box. Anyone who knows anything can hack into that.'

Josh nodded. 'Then he'll know where we are, and he'll come and get us as well. He wants that software more than he wants anything on the planet.' He tried to smile, but it died on his lips. 'Get as much sleep as you can,' he said softly. 'Tomorrow is going to be a hell of a day.'

Josh cradled the pistol in his hand. It was a Wilder Survivor: a slim hunting handgun with an extended eight-inch barrel and a wood-sided grip. The Wilder was the one gun they had between them. Luke had brought it with him. He'd been carrying it ever since he'd left his house. Must be his mum's, Josh figured, and she'd probably picked it up from one of her old boyfriends.

But one gun is all you need. So long as it has the right finger on its trigger.

He toyed with the pistol, lining it up to his eye and making sure that its aim was true. He had twenty rounds of ammunition, and he didn't want to waste any of them on practice shots. The Wildey was a gun he knew almost nothing about: he'd seen Charles Bronson use one in *Death Wish 3* but that was the only time he'd encountered it. *Still, if it was good enough for Charlie, then it's good enough for me.*

Experience had taught Josh that every gun was like a woman: unique, temperamental, and to be handled with care. They fired a fraction to the left or to the right, they had to be held up or down, and their triggers liked to be squeezed hard or gently. If you didn't know their winsome little ways you didn't stand a chance.

I've got a few hours to get to know your character, thought Josh as he examined the Wildey. *And my life may depend on it.*

So for the next twenty minutes, Josh stripped the Wildey down, checking that every part of the gun was working just as it should be.

A quarter-moon was hanging in the sky. Josh was sitting just outside the smelter, on what might once have been a kerb but was now just a broken piece of rock. He glanced along the empty street, and for a moment he could see it as it must once have been, filled with people, horses, noise, dirt and life. *To watch it all winding down*, he reflected to himself. *That must have been hard. To have seen the families quit one by one, and then to be the last person left, alone.*

Time to go home, thought Josh. *Time to see my girl again. Time to hold her in my arms, take her to McDonald's, pick her up from school, take her to the cinema, build her a swing in the garden. Do all the things that a dad is meant to do. But it's a long and nasty twenty-four hours from here to there.*

Even if I survive tomorrow, the bloody system will still want to arrest me. No, Josh told himself firmly. *I'll bloody fight them, the only way I know how. So long as I get Azim, they can't court-martial me. They can throw the bloody book at me. They almost certainly will.* But the man who brings in the head of one of the most wanted al-Qaeda terrorists in the world — well, they can't throw *him* out of the Regiment. *They might want to, but they haven't got the guts.*

Josh kicked up a piece of dirt from the ground in front of him. He was struggling to control the anger inside him: it was surging through his chest, making his pulse race and his blood boil. Bruton had stopped him from taking down Azim twice already. *He's not going to stop me a third time.*

Josh squeezed the soil between his fists. Tomorrow his blood will be soaking this ground.

'What are you thinking about?' asked Kate.

She was holding a bottle of water in her hand. Sitting down next to him, she slipped an arm around his back and nestled her cheek into the side of his face. Her skin nuzzled against his, and he could feel the passion running beneath the surface.

'I'm thinking that you should get the hell out of here,' he said. His tone was flat and blunt.

Kate drew her face away and looked at him. Anger flashed in her eyes. 'I'm staying right here.'

'No,' said Josh sharply. 'It's too dangerous.'

Kate laughed: a hollow, shallow laugh that seemed to mock Josh. 'Like digging you out of a ditch wasn't too dangerous? Like taking you into my house wasn't too dangerous? Like hiding you from the cops? Like rescuing your butt when you were about to crack under torture?' She paused, the words choking her as her face reddened with anger. 'Like watching my father die as he tried to save you?'

A pang of guilt stabbed at Josh. Marshall took a bullet for me, he realised. But that's soldiering. You put yourself on the line, and you take a bullet for your unit. That was the way it worked. Marshall was an old soldier. *The rules of the trade were familiar to him.*

'That's the point,' he snapped. 'You've done enough for me. I can't let you take any more risks.'

'I can handle myself.'

Josh stood up. 'You've no idea how bloody dangerous this is going to be. I don't know how many men are coming to get us tomorrow. Five, six, maybe a dozen. How the hell can I tell? I've got one pistol, some home-made landmines, and a teenage boy who's never been closer to combat than a game on his Playstation. My chances? Pretty bloody miserable.'

'Then why are you doing it?'

'I've no choice.'

Kate tossed back her mane of red hair. 'Everyone has a choice.'

'I'm a soldier. We don't have choices. We have orders.'

'Your orders were to shoot Luke and Ben.'

'I have my own orders – those are the ones I follow,' said Josh. 'My orders are that I keep my word to Luke. And that I take out Azim, because he is an evil, dangerous man. And I don't care what the Ruperts say. I do it my way.'

'And my way is to stay right here,' said Kate. 'I don't care about the danger – I want to see it through.'

Josh shrugged. 'I've warned you. It's your decision.' He paused, looking straight into her eyes. 'But stay out of danger. I owe you my life. The least I can do is pay that back by keeping you safe.'

TWENTY-SIX

Thursday, June 18th. Dawn.

Josh took a swig from the water bottle, letting the liquid splash over his face. He glanced up at the sky. It was already a blazing, fierce blue, even though it was still only eight in the morning. He glanced anxiously along the main street of Swansea. Empty, as always. Yet in a few hours it would be as full of life as it had ever been. *And as full of death as well.*

In the past hour, he had walked down the side of the mountain, traversing rough, difficult terrain. Probably no man had walked across it for half a century or more. He surveyed the dirt-track crossroads where Porter-Bell had been told to leave the money if they wanted Luke's software. The place was empty, just as Porter-Bell had promised. The attacks of the past week, used by Luke to communicate with Josh, must have scared the company witless. Perhaps now they just wanted to hand over the money, get the software, and close the whole miserable chapter. After scouting the area to make sure that it was still empty, Josh pinned a note to a stick and stuck it down in the middle of the crossroads. We'll meet you in Swansea, it said. As soon as you can be there.

As he surveyed the empty town again, Josh ran the plan through his head for the hundredth time. It was eight now. In half an hour the Porter-Bell team would find the note. Assuming they had some all-terrain vehicles with them –

maybe Jeeps, maybe quad bikes, maybe sports bikes – they would be here half an hour later. We should expect them at nine.

Late last night, he'd told Luke to send a public e-mail confirming the time, then another one, encrypted, just to Porter-Bell, changing the meeting time from eight to eight-thirty. With any luck, Azim should only intercept the first message, telling them to meet at eight. That way he would be here first – at eight-thirty. *His neck delivered straight into my hands.*

Azim gets here in half an hour. We kill him, then the Porter-Bell mob show up. We get the money, give them the software. Job done. Then we get the hell out of here.

Bruton can burn on his own stake, decided Josh. *If they want robots for soldiers, they should bloody well build some. From now on, I make my own decisions on how this war should be fought.*

'You ready?' said Josh, glancing across at Kate.

She was standing in the shadows of the abandoned hotel, ten yards away, ready to let fall some of the petrol bombs on its roof. 'Ready,' she said firmly.

'When I say so, just get up on the roof, and toss the bombs into the street,' he said. 'Don't worry about aiming, that's not the point. They'll make a big enough explosion to take out anyone who gets in the way. Got that?'

'Got it.'

'You ready?' called Josh, glancing towards Luke. The boy was standing in the doorway of the old sheriff's office, fifteen yards away.

'Hell, man, can't wait,' said Luke.

Josh could hear the bravado in the boy's voice, but he could also see the fear in his eyes. Don't do anything stupid, Josh said silently to himself. Don't be too tough. Combat is bloody frightening, and you have to know when to hide as well as when to fight.

'Stay alert,' he snapped. 'We're not expecting anyone for at least another twenty minutes. But they may come at any time. The worst thing you can do in any battle is get taken by surprise.'

The stage is set, let the battle rage down, Josh told himself. *And if it consumes us all in its fire, then so be it.*

He fingered the trigger of the Wildey Survivor. If I could change anything, I'd have more guns, he mused. Some assault rifles, a machine gun, some grenades. Maybe a battalion or two as back-up. In the meantime, I'll have to make do with this pistol.

Soldiers don't choose their weapons or their battlefield. *If they did, there wouldn't be so many military cemeteries in the world.*

A noise. Josh's head spun around. The sound of a distant rumbling, as if thunder was rolling through the sky. He glanced up. The sky was clear. Holding the gun in his hand, he slipped behind the doorway of the hardware store. Some dust drifted down onto his head.

Another noise. Louder this time. A motorbike.

Eight-twenty. *There shouldn't be anyone here yet.*

Josh listened harder. The rumbling of the machines was maybe a mile away but getting closer all the time. It was a low roar, echoing out across the barren countryside. A minute away, maybe. Perhaps only thirty seconds.

Azim, decided Josh. It must be him. *And this time we meet on equal terms.*

The noise of the bikes was getting louder. Josh could almost smell the fumes of their exhausts. He could sense the wheels churning up the dusty ground, and the swirling plumes of black smoke trailing behind them.

Josh slipped out of the doorway and started to move down the main street. He kept close to the wall in case there were any snipers taking up position anywhere in the mountains.

He was planning to charge the attackers once they were in among the landmines. Kate and Luke would stay back, away from the danger. Maybe we can finish this without involving them at all, he decided. With luck.

'Take cover,' barked Josh towards Kate in the hotel. 'You see anyone you don't like, bomb the fuckers.' Then he glanced at Luke, still waiting in the doorway of the sheriff's office. 'Keep your head down.'

'I'm coming with you,' shouted Luke.

'No, you're bloody not,' snapped Josh.

Luke stepped forward. 'I'm coming,' he insisted.

'Stay where you bloody are,' yelled Josh. 'And that's a fucking order.'

He walked further forward, taking care to keep out of sight, each movement a careful step into the unknown. He could feel the sweat breaking out on his fist as he gripped the Wildey tight. He could also feel his ribcage vibrating as his heart thumped hard against his chest. As he reached the end of the street, he leaned hard against the last fissured stone wall and looked carefully out across into the wilderness that tumbled away from the edge of town.

I'll draw them into the minefield. And let the explosives send them back to whatever hell they crawled out of.

The three bikes arrived on the horizon. The machines were Honda XR650s: big, powerful off-road bikes, with raised handlebars, mud flaps, and huge spiked tyres, designed for cutting through mud and dust. A man weighing at least two-hundred and fifty pounds was sitting on each one. They were clad in leather from head to foot, and had shades pulled down over their eyes and helmets over their heads.

It was strange. They looked like Flatner's men, but whether they were his or Azim's, decided Josh, it didn't matter. Either way the choice was a simple one. *I kill them or they kill me.*

Fifty yards in front of him, he could hear the bikes halt, a man shouting, then the roar of throttles as the three bikes leaped into action again. The first bike was speeding out across the sand, the other two following closely in its wake. Great clouds of dust swirled around the accelerating machines. As he watched the lead biker, Josh could see him drawing a pistol, holding the gun in his right hand and the handlebars of his Honda in his left.

The minefield that Josh and Luke had prepared was twenty feet in front of them.

A shot. The bullet bounced off the stone wall, ricocheting harmlessly away. Josh knew that he'd been seen and kept his head down. The bikes must by now be tracking through the start of the minefield, gliding across it like stones skimming across the surface of a lake.

Nothing.

Christ, thought Josh. *If those mines don't work, I'm already dead.*

The explosion erupted against the morning sky as Josh looked over the wall. The mine had detonated, the blast shooting up into the innards of the Honda. The front wheel spun upwards, throwing the rider back. Already, the petrol tank was on fire. It would take just a moment for the fuel to react to the flame, blowing the tank and consuming the bike in a deadly fireball.

From every battlefield he'd ever been on, Josh knew that you saw your enemy die before you heard him. He had seen the rider spin into the air, his massive bulk now working against him. He fell heavily beside his machine, the petrol spilling from the tank and cascading over his denim trousers and his thick leather jacket. A hail of sparks was spitting out of the engine. Then Josh heard the second explosion. The wave of noise rocked him backwards. Somewhere from the middle of the inferno Josh could hear the pitiful screams of a man burning to death.

One down. Two to go.

Josh looked from behind the wall. The second bike had

veered sharply to the right, the third to the left. Josh had planned the minefield precisely, taking into his calculations all the lessons he'd learned in the Army. When you were putting down mines, you placed them to destroy your enemy, sure – but you also worked out that enemy's likely escape route and laid traps for them there as well. The second biker was already learning that lesson as he rode over another mine and triggered another deadly blast. Another fireball. Another scream.

Two down, one to go.

Thick clouds of heavy black smoke were now rising. The third bike was turning in a tight circle, its driver calculating that his best chance lay in riding back the way he'd come. Josh aimed his pistol. Forty yards now separated him from the biker. He fired one bullet, aiming at the biker's spine – an accurate shot there would paralyse the man instantly. It missed, the bullet hitting the dust harmlessly. Christ, thought Josh. I need practice with this bloody gun. *I'm not going to survive many missed shots.*

The driver swerved to the left, anxious to avoid the gunfire. Mistake, pal, decided Josh with a grim smile. *You're back on hostile ground.*

As the third mine blew, the bike skidded. The Honda's front wheel was blown clean off, spinning up into the air. The rider fell from his machine, his hands still gripping the handlebars. Petrol spilled out over his body, and a shower of sparks cascaded across him as the broken and twisted bike rolled over onto him. Flames leaped up all around him, engulfing his legs and torso before flicking across the skin of his face.

'Help me,' shouted the man desperately. 'Please, some-body – I'm fucking dying here.'

Before today, Josh had only witnessed it once on the battlefield, but there were few worse sights, sounds – and smells – than those of a man burning to death. You can smell the charred flesh, like meat roasting on a spit. You can feel the heat, as the flames curl around the body. And you can hear the terrifying screams, like those of a strangled cat, getting thinner and thinner as the vocal cords slowly get burned away.

'Help me,' the man shrieked desperately, his burning hands trying to push away the bike that was lying across his body.

No way, pal.

Josh started running back towards the town. Let's see what else you can throw at us he exulted inwardly.

Another noise. Racing down the main street, Josh cast his gaze up at the ramshackle roofs of the buildings. A scratching, like that of an animal. Or a man.

'Luke,' Josh hissed towards the sheriff's office. 'You there?'

A silence. Josh could feel his heart thumping. 'Luke?' he said, louder this time.

'He's gone.'

Josh spun around. Kate was still standing at the window of the old hotel. He could hear her, but only just see her: she was in the shadow of a pair of shutters hanging loose on their hinges.

'Why didn't you bloody stop him?' shouted Josh.

'With what?' Kate yelled back.

Her voice was raw and desperate. Nothing is going as I'd planned, Josh told himself. Porter-Bell have obviously decided to kill us all. At this rate, they'll succeed.

Josh heard a scratching noise. Then the sound of a slate being broken as someone stepped on it.

There was just a split second in which to react. A man was descending from the sky. Josh threw himself sideways onto the ground and narrowly managed to avoid being crushed by the man: a two-hundred-and-fifty-pound monster, clad in denim and leather. Josh realised that his spine would have snapped the instant the creature landed on top of him.

Both of them were lying flat in the dirt. The gun had fallen out of Josh's hand, leaving it out of reach. The man grabbed out, catching hold of Josh's wounded leg. He started pulling, wrenching the bones around Josh's feet. Josh could feel pain searing up through him as the wound reopened. Blood started to leak out into the cloth of his jeans. Now a fist started to pummel Josh's side. The blows were heavy and strong, delivered with pile driving force.

Reaching into his pocket, Josh grasped one of the heavy nails that he'd taken from the hardware store. The steel was rotten and rusty with age, but still sharp at the tip. Holding it in his right hand, Josh gripped hard and sat up sharply. Concentrating his strength into his fist, his slammed the nail hard into his attacker's hand. He could feel the point piercing the skin, then grating against the bone of the knuckle. Josh pushed harder, ignoring the way that the nail was digging into the skin of his own palm. The nail forced itself through the bone, its tip emerging on the other side of the man's hand.

The man screamed in pain, letting go of Josh's foot.

Josh kicked himself free. He ran inside the abandoned hotel. 'The bombs,' shouted Josh, looking up at Kate. 'Throw the bloody bombs at him.'

He could see the fear in her eyes. She started to move but her hands were shaking.

She's frozen. The fear has got to her.

'Throw the fucking bombs,' he shouted, his lungs straining to put as much force as he could into the words.

A tear was smudging her face. He could see that her hand was shaking. She can't do it, Josh told himself. She can't bloody do it.

Josh ran forward. His attacker had struggled to his feet. The man was holding on to his hand. The nail was still sticking through it, and his blood streaked the rust on the spike. His face was covered by a biking helmet and a scarf was wrapped around his neck, but Josh could see enough of his skin to tell that he was white, not Arab.

Where the hell is Azim? *If these are Flatner's men, where the hell is Azim?*

Josh was standing two yards from the man in the dusty street. Somewhere in the distance, he could hear shouting, more motorbikes. They were now coming into town from other the side. Christ, he told himself. *They just keep coming. I need to get rid of this one before his mates arrive.*

The man was edging towards him, growling like a bear. Then he lunged forward, putting his full weight behind the blow.

Mistake, pal, thought Josh. You're over-committed.

The punch narrowly missed Josh's jaw. He danced forwards so that now he was positioned behind the man. Reaching up, he snapped both his arms into a tight coil around the monster's neck. Josh pulled with all his strength. The muscles in his arms were screaming with pain as the man struggled to free himself. At two hundred and fifty pounds, he had the strength of a wild bull. A violent belch escaped from the man's gut as Josh pulled tighter, then tighter again. His hands were scrabbling at Josh's arms and his legs were kicking backwards as he tried to loosen Josh's grip. But Josh's lock on his neck was firm, slowly cutting the supply of oxygen to his brain.

It's a McDeath for you, you bastard. Quick, nasty and cheap.

Josh had only strangled a man once before – during a mission in Afghanistan – but he knew from his training that the most dangerous moment was just before an opponent died. The oxygen switched off in the brain, yet as the victim lost consciousness they knew that there was just one last chance of saving themselves, and they would throw all their remaining strength into it.

The man gave a horrific choked-off yell, then reared

back, trying to use the muscles in his massive shoulders to throw Josh off.

Josh was ready for him. He tightened his arms as hard as he could, squeezing the life out of the man. He could feel a last spasm of strength surge through his adversary, then start to ebb. The man's breathing slowed, then stopped. Finally his body slumped to the ground.

Josh started looking around desperately. There was still no sign of Luke. And the remaining bikes were only three hundred yards away.

He picked up his gun from the ground and ran towards the hotel. Kate was still standing mute behind the shutters like a statue, her face pale and drawn. 'I'm sorry,' she stuttered. 'I couldn't . . . I couldn't . . .'

'You bottled it,' Josh snapped.

Immediately, he regretted having spoken roughly to her. In the heat of battle, men spoke harshly: he'd been called a million different names in a firefight and shrugged them all off in the mess later. Kate wasn't to know that: this was his territory, not hers. 'It's not your fault,' he said, quickly. 'You're not a soldier. Just take cover and try not to cause any trouble.'

He started moving up the back staircase. The wooden slats were rotten and half the banister had crumbled away. Josh ignored the danger, flinging himself upwards. He could feel the boards flaking into pieces as he trod on them.

He climbed out and crawled across the flat roof. Ten home-made firebombs were laid out in a row. Glancing up, Josh could see the bikers advancing to the main street. The same big black Hondas, the same burly men clad in leather and helmets. The same pistols being brandished.

Serve them up a diet of death and mayhem, and they just keep coming back for more.

Josh waited, counting down the seconds. The bombs would work once and once only.

The bikes were advancing steadily, their engines roaring. The front biker was moving carefully, scrutinising the ground for stretched wires or freshly dug earth. They're checking for mines, realised Josh.

But this time the death will come down like rain from the sky.

After checking that the ground was undisturbed, the lead bike started to advance towards the corpse that was lying directly below Josh.

'Kate, take cover,' shouted Josh, aware that she was still down below.

He could see the bikers twenty feet below turning their heads up to look at him but before they could shoot Josh hurled down the first of the petrol bombs. It ignited as it hit the ground, sending a huge of ball of flame shooting out. He threw down more. The bottles splintered, at first sending tiny shards of glass spraying up into the air. Then the nails packed inside the bottle spun upwards, gathering velocity as they moved outwards, forming a lethal sphere of shrapnel.

One biker was already in flames, his arms flailing desperately as he tried to extinguish the fire enveloping his body. Another was lying face down on the ground. A pair of nails had shot straight through his head, piercing his skull and sending chunks of his brain splattering across the dusty ground.

Josh ran along the length of the roof, hurling down the bombs one by one. Suddenly the street was a bedlam of explosions. Burning petrol, steel nails and glass splinters were flying everywhere. Two of the bikes exploded, sending hot oil spewing out onto the burning ground. Swirling clouds of smoke were spiralling into the sky. The noise was deafening. Josh threw himself down and gripped the side of the roof, shutting his eyes and closing his mouth to stop the fumes from choking him. I just hope Kate has the sense to do the same, he thought.

When he opened his eyes again, the street was a chaos of burning rubber and petrol. The bikes were mangled heaps of metal. Corpses lay strewn across the ground, but the closer Josh looked the harder it became to count the dead. Too many severed limbs were scattered around.

One man was lying on the ground. His leg had been ripped off, and blood was pulsing from the open wound. His lips were trembling as he tried to cry out in pain, but his tongue had been burnt out and no sound could escape from his mouth.

Josh dropped down from the roof and landed on the ground. He approached the wounded biker and knelt down, putting the barrel of the Wildey to the man's head. *I'm saving my ammunition, but I'm still going to put you out of your misery, pal. One warrior should always be willing to spend a bullet on another.*

He squeezed the trigger. The bullet shattered the man's skull and pulverised his brain, killing him instantly.

'Hold it right there,' shouted a voice. Josh looked up. Twenty yards ahead, walking towards him, he could see Flatner who was holding Luke with his arm twisted behind his back. A pistol was pressed against the side of the boy's head. Luke's head was lowered and some blood was trickling down the side of his mouth where he had taken a blow to the face.

Flatner was walking along the main street with Edward Porter at his side. He was looking at Josh, a grin playing on his face.

'Stay where you are, Josh,' said Flatner. 'This time you're mine.'

TWENTY-SEVEN

Thursday, June 18th Morning

Josh stood perfectly still. The fires were still burning behind him and the flames continued to lick at the corpses of the fallen bikers. He could feel the heat on his back, but despite that the blood in his veins was starting to freeze.

Flatner was still walking towards him, a cruel smile on his lips. He was holding a Glock 18 in his hand, one of the simplest, most reliable and most accurate handguns in the world, and he was pushing Luke forwards roughly.

At his side, Edward Porter was standing with his own Glock 18 held almost casually in his right hand, as if he was not used to carrying a gun. Close up, he looked much older than he had looked in any of the pictures that Josh had seen. His hair was starting to thin, and his skin was greying and blotchy. The face of a man who is rapidly ageing, decided Josh. And of a man who doesn't waste time on negotiations or compromises but cuts straight to the deal. *Or the kill.*

'Where's the woman?' said Flatner.

Josh said nothing.

Flatner glanced left and right, his stare scouring both sides of the street. Whether he felt anything about the death of six of his men a few minutes ago, Josh couldn't tell.

'Come out now, or I shoot both of them.'

There was a pause. Behind him Josh could hear the continuing sounds of burning. Then he saw Kate. She stepped from the porch of the old hotel, walking carefully through the blazing wreckage. Her face was blackened and there was sweat running down her skin. Her eyes looked tired and frightened. 'Don't hurt the boy,' she said, glancing up at Flatner. She was choking back the tears in her voice. 'We'll do whatever you say. Just don't hurt him.'

'So,' said Porter. 'Are we ready to do some business?'

'You're a bloody idiot,' said Josh angrily, looking up at the man.

Porter nodded thoughtfully. 'According to the Forbes list, I'm the ninth richest man in the world,' he replied. 'That doesn't sound like an idiot to me.'

'We'd have given you the software all along,' said Josh. 'Luke wanted his money, that's all. If you'd just given him the five million we could have done this simply and without any bloodshed.'

Porter laughed. 'You don't get to be as rich as I am by going around giving five million dollars to every two-nickel hustler who wants to blackmail the company. I'm a straight-forward man. You treat me with respect, I'll treat you with respect. You try to fuck me, then I'll fuck you so hard back that you'll wish you were dead.' He glanced first at Luke, then at Josh. 'You've both tried to hustle me. Now it's payback time.'

Josh shook his head. 'It's no hustle. Luke found a flaw in your software. If he can find it so can someone else. He's performed a service for your business and he wants to be paid. Simple.'

'Then why the bombs and landmines?' said Porter.

'Why the bikers armed to the teeth?' snapped Josh.

Porter raised a hand. 'Enough of this,' he said. 'I'm a busy man. Now, I want the software − or the boy dies.'

Josh shook his head. 'Give us the money.'

'I said the boy dies.'

Josh glanced sideways. He could see Flatner jabbing the Glock harder against the side of Luke's head.

'I don't care,' said Luke fearfully. 'You already killed Ben. Kill me if you want to. I don't care.'

Flatner slapped him around the head. The blow rocked him but Luke stood his ground, and his lips stayed sealed.

'The kid's brave,' said Josh. 'You're not going to get anywhere by roughing him up.'

'Maybe we should just shoot him, then?' said Porter thoughtfully. 'No more Luke, no more problem.'

'You need him,' snapped Josh. 'Without him, the security flaw is still there. Someone else will find it.'

'I'll break them, boss,' said Flatner. 'Just give me a few minutes to knock them about. They'll break.'

Porter raised his hand. 'We haven't got time.' He looked across at Josh. 'What are you, the kid's agent or something? You collecting ten per cent on this deal?'

'I gave him my word to protect him,' answered Josh. 'I haven't managed to hang on to much in my life, but I keep my promises.'

Suddenly and inexplicably, Porter seemed to change his mind. 'Okay, you win. Give us the software, and we'll give you the money.' He placed a black briefcase that he'd been carrying in his left hand down on the ground between them. 'It's all here.'

Josh stepped forward. He opened the case. Inside, he could see a neat stack of freshly minted fifty-dollar notes. 'There's a million in notes,' said Porter. 'The rest is in bearer bonds. You can cash them at any bank, no questions asked.'

Josh nodded. 'You happy?' he said, looking towards Luke.

'Okay,' said Luke. 'Give them the computer.'

Josh glanced at Kate. 'Get it,' he said.

Kate started walking back towards the crumbling sheriff's office. Luke had left his laptop in there. A minute later she returned, carrying the machine in her hand. She handed it across to Luke.

He knelt down on the ground. Flatner stood over him,

his gun still to the boy's head. Josh knew there would be enough power in the laptop's battery to last for another hour, and its satellite connection was keeping it plugged into the internet. With a look of concentration on his face, Luke started tapping at the machine's keyboard.

'How do I know you're giving me the right computer?' said Porter. 'How do I know it's got the software in it?'

'Name a city,' said Luke, looking across to Porter.

'Any city?'

'Name me a city, and I'll switch off the power there,' said Luke. 'Then you'll see for yourself that this is the software.'

Porter's brow furrowed. 'Austin,' he replied. 'I've always hated Austin.' He chuckled grimly to himself. 'It'll be thirty degrees there already, even at this time of the morning. They'll all be sweating like pigs when the air-conditioning gets switched off.'

Josh remained still, watching while Luke tapped away at the keyboard. A single thought was now running through his mind. *Luke may get his money, but Azim hasn't shown up.*

I've miscalculated. I'm done for. Even if Porter and Flatner don't kill us, if I go back to Britain without taking out Azim I'll be court-martialled for sure. I disobeyed orders and I won't have a single argument to defend myself with.

'You got a PDA or something?' Luke said to Porter.

Porter pulled out a small, slim case from his breast pocket. 'A Blackberry.'

'Then check one of the news sites,' said Luke. 'The power in Austin is already down. The story should be running any minute.'

Porter was staring in fascination at the tiny screen embedded in the device resting on the palm of his hand. He might be a billionaire several times over, thought Josh. But he was still an engineer at heart: the thing that fascinated him most was machines, and how they worked.

Porter turned the Blackberry 7290 outwards so that everybody could see the tiny screen. It showed the CNN.com website. Across the bottom of the screen, under a flashing 'Breaking News' logo, the words were clearly spelled out: 'Blackout hits Austin . . . Blackout hits Austin. Details to follow . . .'

'Okay,' said Porter. 'I believe you. Now give those poor Texans their power back before you totally bankrupt this company.'

Josh stepped forward, putting his hand down on the briefcase.

'*You* might keep your promises,' said Porter. 'But to me, words are matchsticks.' He snapped his fingers. 'I break them just like that.'

As Josh looked up he saw that Porter's pistol was pointing straight at him.

'Get away from that case,' said Porter, pronouncing the words with the kind of force that comes easily to a man holding a gun in his hand. 'Then hand over the computer.'

Josh shook his head. 'I've been jerked around once too often.'

'Put down the gun,' shouted Porter. 'And get your hands in the air. *Now.*'

If I go this time, decided Josh, so be it. Without Azim, I've nothing. *I'd rather die here than go back to Hereford and get ripped to shreds by the Ruperts for disobeying an order.*

Josh sensed how his military training just might give him the edge in this fight. With one quick movement of his hand, he pulled the Wildey from the inside of his jacket where he had been hiding it for the last ten minutes. His mind was a blur but an adrenalin-fuelled mix of anxiety, anger and desperation was guiding his movements.

'You've got the safety catch on,' he barked at Porter. 'That gun's not going to kill anyone.'

Porter's gaze flicked towards his pistol. A split second of

delay. Josh jabbed his gun forward, squeezing the trigger hard. The bullet knocked the Glock clean out of Porter's hand. Swiftly, Josh cocked the Wildey and squeezed its trigger again. This time the bullet struck Flatner's right hand, smashing his knuckles. His Glock fell to the ground too. Unfired.

Luke leaped forwards, unscathed. He grabbed his computer and cowered behind Josh.

'You're worth billions,' said Josh to Porter. 'Yet you're about to throw your life away for the sake of a stupid five million.'

Josh stood rock-solid and nodded at Luke to pick up the briefcase. Stepping forward, Luke gripped its handle, cradling it to his chest. Many men have died for that money, thought Josh. *Don't let go of it now.*

'Now which of you wants the next bullet?'

'I . . . I . . .' stuttered Porter.

He can order the deaths of other men, thought Josh, but he can't face it himself. Josh held the gun up, so that Porter's forehead was neatly in its sights. 'I'll finish you nice and quick,' said Josh. 'As for Flatner, I'll make *that* slow and painful.' He glanced across at Flatner. 'I owe you that much.'

'N–no,' stammered Porter, his lips quivering. 'I can give you money . . . I can . . .'

'Stand still, and take it like a bloody man,' barked Josh.

'Put the gun down.'

Josh turned around. Kate was holding her own Glock. Its matt-black barrel was pointing straight at his chest.

'I said put the gun down,' she repeated.

TWENTY-EIGHT

Thursday, June 18th. Morning.
Josh looked into Kate's eyes. She was wearing the same expression he had seen nearly three weeks ago, when she had first pulled him bleeding out of the ditch. Spirit, fire and determination were the words that had flashed through his mind then, and now they seemed just as accurate.

Josh lowered the Wildey handgun to his side. His body had frozen, but his mind was calculating furiously. Of course, he told himself. You're a sodding moron, Josh. *She was working for Porter-Bell all along.*

Kate took two steps forward. She was holding the Glock straight out in front of her, her forearm steady yet relaxed, the way a trained marksman would hold himself just before an execution. 'Drop the gun, Josh,' she said, 'That's an order from your doctor.'

'Kill him, Kate,' snapped Porter.

'Who the hell *are* you?' growled Josh, looking at Kate.

'She works for me,' said Porter. 'Always has done. One of the advantages of being a billionaire. You can have a pretty big payroll.'

Josh looked at Kate again. The deception, he realised, had been perfect from start to finish. Every tender word, every moment of medical treatment, every kiss and caress – all of it had been a lie.

'Is this true?' he asked.

Kate shrugged aside the lock of red hair that had tumbled across her forehead.

'I don't know how things are on your planet, Josh,' she said. 'But on this one women don't usually start helping strange men who they find wounded in a ditch. Painful as it might be to your little soldier ego, you're not so irresistible that I took one look at you, fell in love, and decided to risk my life trying to look after you.' She chuckled. 'Only a man, and a pretty stupid one, would think that was possible.'

Kate placed the Glock closer to Josh's forehead: he could smell the grease and oil on the gun's firing mechanism.

'I took you in and took care of you because Mr Porter here paid me handsomely to do so,' she continued. 'Why? Because Luke escaped from us. Don't you remember his final words to you as he ran away? He said he'd be in touch. So we knew all along that if we were going to find him you were our best chance of doing so. So long as we had you, eventually you'd lead us to him. All I had to do was stick close, and sooner or later you'd take us to Luke. When you did so, Mr Porter would pay five million dollars. So thanks, Josh. You've made it a lucrative time. And you couldn't have played your part better if I'd scripted it myself.

'You took a nasty wound to the head,' Kate went on. 'That often causes short-term memory loss. Then I kept injecting you with mild barbiturates. You thought they were painkillers. But barbiturates cause and sustain amnesia. I didn't want your memory coming back until Luke sent you his signal.'

'And Marshall? Didn't he mind you prostituting yourself? His own daughter?'

Kate smiled. 'You're so gullible, it would almost be cute. If it wasn't about to cost you and Luke your lives.'

'He's not your father, is he?'

'Marshall? No,' answered Kate. 'My dad was in Florida

playing golf the last time I saw him. Marshall's a clever operator. He ruled these wastelands. After I was charged with keeping track of you until Luke got in touch, he was the obvious man to turn to.' She was watching him intently. 'So like I said, drop that gun.'

The Wildey was resting in his palm, but Josh felt as if all the fight had been punched out of him. He'd fought like a mad dog, and it had all been for nothing. Now the game was finally played out.

Porter stepped forward, a grin lighting up his face: the fear of a few moments ago had been banished, replaced by the easy, complacent composure of a man who now knew that he could buy his way out of anything. He picked up the briefcase, holding it firmly in his hands,

'First rule of business, son,' he said, glancing towards Josh. 'Know when you're beaten. And you two boys are beaten.' Bending over, he also picked up Luke's laptop from the ground. 'I don't think we need these two any more,' he said to Kate. 'Finish them off.'

At his side, Josh could sense Luke starting to tremble. It took a man of the strongest nerves to hear with calm his own execution being discussed, and Luke was just a boy: his lips were trembling, and his legs looked as if they were about to give way beneath him. I'm sorry, thought Josh. You put your trust in me again.

Kate kept the gun levelled at Josh's head. In her eyes he could see the cold, uncompromising stare of a natural-born killer.

'I'm sorry, Josh,' she said. 'In other circumstances, maybe we could have had a relationship.' She shrugged. 'But, you know, there's the money . . .'

Josh closed his eyes. The bullet was so close that he could almost feel it already, crashing through his skull, bursting through his brain, severing the membranes and nerves.

Of all the different deaths I thought fate might have planned

for me, I never expected to be shot by a woman.

A sound rang out through the empty town. A shot. Josh opened his eyes again. Kate's gun was lying on the floor, blasted out of her hands. A man was walking towards them, a pistol in his hand. He was wearing aviator shades, a cowboy hat on his head that shielded him from the sun, and a white scarf wrapped around his neck. The top two buttons on his blue linen shirt were undone, revealing some greying chest hair. And his walk had the steadiness of a man used to taking command.

Josh didn't need to give the man a second glance. He'd learned to recognise him the way he might recognise his own shadow.

Azim.

Azim walked forwards steadily, emerging from the swirling clouds of black smoke that were still rising from the burnt-out motorbikes behind them. Fifteen yards, then ten – he was drawing steadily closer to them.

'He's mine,' said Azim, indicating Josh with a brief nod.

'You take him, then,' said Kate.

Azim raised his revolver and aimed. He squeezed the trigger. As he did so, Kate made a strange, wordless sound. Then she seemed about to speak – but the blood was already foaming up through her mouth. It was spilling out across her cheeks, smearing her white skin. Her feet held steady for a second but then gave way, and her body collapsed onto the ground.

Josh saw that the bullet struck her heart. She had been killed in an instant. Good shot, he thought. *That woman's heart is a pretty small target.*

Azim raised his gun again. He fired once, then twice. The first bullet hit Flatner in the chest, the second pulped his right eye. Blood poured down the side of his face. The second bullet to hit him had blasted a hole clean through the centre of his skull. He tilted back on his heels, trying to steady himself, then fell backwards to lie twitching briefly on the ground.

Azim had fired four bullets, Josh realised. So there were two left in the chamber. *And one of them has my name on it.*

Azim raised his gun again in a smooth arc and held it steady in his right hand. Its muzzle swung past Josh and Azim hesitated briefly, then aimed it directly at Porter's head. 'Hold it right there,' said Azim coldly 'I'm taking that software on behalf of the British Government. If you try to resist me, you're a dead man.'

Josh had been tracking the movement of the gun. Now he was thinking, *What kind of stunt is the bastard pulling?*

Porter was frozen, paralysed with fear. Kate was dead. Flatner was dead. His protection had been stripped away from him.

Meekly, he picked up the laptop and handed it across to Azim. From his pocket, Azim took out a blank CD-ROM, slotted it into the machine, then looked back across to Josh.

'You and I are working for the same team, Josh,' said Azim. 'As I told you earlier, I am not by nature a cruel man. There's no need for us to fight any more.'

'The same team?' said Josh. 'What the bloody hell does that mean?'

'It means you've been wrong all along,' said Azim. 'I'm a double agent, the highest-ranking British Intelligence mole inside al-Qaeda. I have been feeding information to The Firm.'

Suddenly, Josh began to understand. 'That's why they didn't finish you off in Afghanistan,' he said. 'That's why Bruton told me not to shoot you when the handover was being made with Ben and Luke.'

'Exactly,' said Azim. 'They have to protect me. I'm the best source they have.'

'Why didn't they bloody tell me?' said Josh.

'Because you're just a cog in a big machine,' said Azim. 'They can't go around telling everyone I'm a double agent. I'd be dead within minutes. And they have to let the same monkeys who are chasing my colleagues chase me as well. After all, it would be suspicious if I was the only senior al-Qaeda man who wasn't being tracked by the British or the Americans.' He looked hard at Josh. 'You see, I'm one of the most important assets Western Intelligence has. Far more important than some ignorant squaddie.' He laughed. 'They can always get another solider. They can't find another agent like me.'

'But you tortured me. You were going to kill me,' snapped Josh. 'I don't call *that* being on the same bloody side.'

Azim smiled. 'But you'd left the team by then, Josh,' he said. 'You'd disobeyed Bruton's direct order. We had no idea who you were working for any more. And the priority was to get hold of this software. Luke turned all the lights off in London. We couldn't let that happen again. I was just doing what I had to do. Anyway . . .' Azim took the CD-ROM from the machine and slipped it into his pocket. 'Now that we have the software, our mission is closed.'

'So we destroy the computer?' said Josh.

Azim aimed his gun and blasted the laptop. At such close range, the bullet shattered the machine, leaving splinters of plastic on the ground.

'Luke's copy of the software is destroyed,' said Azim. 'It's finished. All we have to do now is execute Luke, then there will be no chance of him ever creating it again.'

The Wildey was still lying on the ground. Josh leaned down to pick it up.

'Not quite that simple,' he said and he raised the pistol, pointing it at Azim.

'I've just saved your life, Josh.'

Josh steadied his aim. His lips remained sealed, his expression focused.

'We're on the same team,' said Azim.

It was the first time that Josh had heard even a hint of nervousness in the man's voice.

'I'm on my own team.'

Josh tightened his finger on the trigger. The Wildey recoiled in his grip as the bullet exploded from its barrel. Josh cocked the gun, then squeezed the trigger again. Two bullets, he told himself. When you want to make sure you never hear from a man again, you need to put at least two bullets into him.

Azim crumpled to the floor.

It's over. At last it's over, thought Josh.

EPILOGUE

Monday, August 3rd. Afternoon.

Mark Bruton sat at the centre of the table. He was wearing uniform, but his jacket had been slipped over the back of his chair. He was flanked on either side by two sombre-faced men, both in their mid to late thirties, both with black hair. One had a blue suit and one a black suit. Both served The Firm as officers in the anti-terrorist unit, working the grey space between the Regiment and the intelligence services. Neither gave his name, nor would they at any point during the hearing. Ant and Dec, decided Josh. *It was hard to tell them apart.*

'I want you to understand something, Harding,' said Bruton. 'This isn't a court martial. Not yet. But it's a full-scale disciplinary hearing. Anything you say here may be used against you if this *does* go to a court martial. Understood?'

Josh glanced up at the officer. His expression, he reckoned, was one you only ever saw on the face of a Rupert: confident, self-righteous, and completely clueless. A 747 could land on his nose and he wouldn't bloody notice it.

'Understood,' replied Josh, deliberately inserting a pause before the next word. 'Sir.'

'And because this is a disciplinary hearing, you need to tell the truth,' continued Bruton. 'The complete truth, Harding. Otherwise things will get very nasty for you.'

'Understood.' Another pause. 'Sir.'

They were sitting in a concrete-walled room, sixteen

floors beneath The Firm's Vauxhall headquarters. Below the basement level, the building had a series of massively rein-forced bunkers designed to survive a full-scale nuclear attack: the intelligence agencies had no intention of stopping work after such a strike. There was a series of offices, each with their own oxygen supply, designed to keep working during a biological attack. And beneath those were a layer of cells and interrogation rooms. *Once you were thrown in there, even a nuclear strike wasn't going to get you out.*

Josh had been here for nine days already, kept in solitary confinement. After shooting Azim, he'd set Porter loose. The billionaire no longer interested him. Make your own way home, Josh had told him. He took the rented Mustang and drove back towards Los Angeles, stopping at a motel overnight to shower, shave, get a decent meal and have a good night's sleep.

The next morning, while Luke disappeared quietly back to Boisdale, Josh had reported back to the consulate in LA. He had been arrested immediately. Kept overnight, he had been flown back to London on a military jet. Twelve hours in his own plane, realised Josh. Just the fuel for that trip wasn't going to leave much change out of twenty grand. It was rare that an organisation as notoriously mean as the Army treated its guests so lavishly. I must be going up in the world, he'd thought.

As the plane touched down at RAF Northolt on Sunday morning, Josh was met by six military policemen and driven straight to Vauxhall. He was taken down to a cell, and apart from the twice-daily serving of food pushed under his door that was it as far as human contact went: he heard nothing more about where he was, or how long he might be there.

Maybe they've already thrown away the key, he decided bitterly as hours stretched into days.

Now Ant said: 'You disobeyed an order. Why?'

Josh glanced up at the man. 'The order didn't make any sense.'

Ant remained expressionless. Dec smiled, and looked at Josh. 'Now, now, Mr Harding. You're a soldier. A good one. You know very well that an order is an order. We can't start negotiating which we obey and which we don't.'

'I know the rules,' said Josh. 'But when the security of the country is at stake, they don't apply any more.'

'The security of the country?' said Ant. 'Azim was the best inside agent we've managed to get inside al-Qaeda yet. He helped us foil several planned atrocities in this country. And you shot him.'

'I did my job,' said Josh.

'Your job is to obey orders,' said Ant.

'My job is to serve my country,' said Josh. 'And protect it.'

There was a silence. Josh could see the anger in all six eyes glazing at him. If the rules allowed it, they'd probably shoot me on the spot, he mused.

'Tell us what happened,' said Dec.

Josh knew that there was no point. There had already been a full written debrief describing the mission. There was nothing else to add. 'You already know.'

'Then tell us why you shot him,' said Ant.

'It was revenge, wasn't it?' interrupted Bruton. 'You were just angry at him for beating you. He pissed you off. So you shot him.'

He looked savagely at Josh. 'Admit it, Harding. You're out of bloody control. You're not a soldier, just a bloody pub brawler. We don't need your kind.'

Both Ant and Dec glanced across at Bruton: they were silently telling him to keep his temper, but they were not disagreeing with anything that he'd said.

'If you can't explain yourself better than that, then it will be the duty of this hearing to recommend a full court martial,' said Dec stiffly. 'We'll have no other choice.'

Josh pulled a disk from his pocket: a single CD-ROM, green on one side, silver on the other. He stepped up from his chair, placing the disk on the desk. 'First take a look at this,' he said.

There was silence from all three men as they looked down at the disk. 'What is it?' asked Ant.

'Azim destroyed the computer that Luke had written the program on,' said Josh. He was standing up, looking down at all three men. 'He wanted us to believe that he'd destroyed the program that was causing all the blackouts. Before he did so, he took a copy on this disk. Now, why did he do that? So he could take it back to his al-Qaeda mates.'

'Meaning what?' said Bruton.

'Meaning that he was a *triple* agent,' snapped Josh. 'He fed you some information to make you think that you'd turned him but he was loyal to his movement. He had you guys protecting him every step of the way. That's why al-Qaeda sent him to get the software. They knew that you'd help Azim to get his hands on it.

'It was only because of me that we stopped him,' he continued, his tone turning intense. 'If it had been up to you lot, al-Qaeda would have had Luke's software by now. And the lights would be popping off all over the world every time the boys with towels on their heads felt like giving us a bit of a slapping.'

Josh paused, turning around. His face was reddening with anger as his blood pumped furiously through his veins. 'Like I said, I was just doing my job. Protecting my country.' He smiled. 'Now you do yours. If that means court-martialling me, so be it. If it means giving me a medal, so be it. I don't bloody care any more.'

He stopped, the last words left hanging in the air. He could see both Ant and Dec looking nervously at one another: this wasn't going to look good in their reports. Dec took the disk carefully in his hands. 'We'll examine this. If it's what you say it is, then I suppose that changes things.'

'And what do you want me to do?' said Josh. He paused again. 'Sir.'

'Go back to Hereford, Harding,' said Bruton. 'They can do what they like with you. I don't sodding care what happens to you.'

Josh could feel the breeze blowing off the Thames as he walked over Vauxhall Bridge. He paused to look down at the water streaming beneath him. It's all under the bridge, he told himself. Let it stay that way.

Darkness had already fallen. In the few days he'd been kept at The Firm, his sense of time had been shot to pieces. His nervous system was still recovering from the battering he'd taken over in America. When he got back to base, he'd need a full medical, but he already had some sense of the damage that he'd taken. The electric shocks had left him jittery, and there was still some swelling in his chest from where the snakes had chewed him. The wounds to his leg and his neck were still painful. But I can still walk, he told himself. For now, that's enough.

It was a clear night, and the rush-hour traffic was just starting to thin out. Off to the right he could see the lights of Big Ben playing across the waters of the Thames, on the other side of the river the lights on the London Eye slowly turning. Further out, a gentle electric haze stretched out to Canary Wharf and beyond.

In a couple of days, he'd be back with the Regiment. He'd see how he felt once he was back with his mates. Maybe it was time to move on. All he wanted to do now was to get back to Emily, check that she was okay, then start to get himself back in shape.

Josh looked down again at the water. Suddenly, the lights vanished.

It took a moment for him to react. He'd noticed the reflection of the Parliament building disappearing. Josh looked up. Everything had suddenly gone black. Christ, did something fuse? he wondered. Next he looked towards the London Eye. It had stopped moving, its capsules plunged into darkness.

A blackout, thought Josh. *Another blackout.*

He looked around. Yes, the whole city had been plunged into darkness. Across the bridge the lights were out. The cars were starting to back up across the bridge, and a few yards away he could hear the screeching of tyres and the honking of horns as the vehicles tried to get around the corner without any traffic lights. Nearby, he heard a woman screaming. A couple of hundred yards away, a police siren started to whine into life. All around, people were running.

Josh glanced back towards The Firm's building, the so-called Vauxhall Gaumont. Even there the power had shut down.

'That will teach them not to mess with my man,' said a voice.

Josh spun around.

'Luke,' he shouted. 'Luke? Where are you, you little bastard?'

His eyes scanned the crowd on the bridge. People were starting to run. He could hear a woman yelling that someone had stolen her handbag, then a father shouting for his little boy.

A pale figure suddenly stepped out of the shadows. Luke was dressed in jeans and sweatshirt, with a hood pulled down partly obscuring his face. His hands were stuffed into his pockets, and there was a black canvas rucksack slung over his shoulder.

He looked up at Josh. 'That's some blackout, man,' he said, grinning.

'Christ, what have you done?' snapped Josh. 'Turn the lights back on.'

'Are they treating you okay?' said Luke. 'Because if they're not, I'm going to make them pay.'

'No worse than usual,' said Josh. 'How the hell did you know where I was?'

'It took a bit of time,' Luke admitted. 'After I got back to my mum, we banked all that money we got from Porter-Bell, then I figured we had to make sure that you were okay. So we decided we'd both come to London. I always wanted to see that place on the cover of the first Clash album. And she wanted to see Abbey Road.'

'Your mum is here?'

'Well, she's in the hotel. Probably gone out to score some dope by now.' Luke grinned. 'Anyway, it took me a few hours to hack into your outfit's system. They've got some pretty good firewalls in place. But I got through. Found out they were keeping you there, then that you were being thrown out today. So I figured that if I just waited here for a bit, I'd see you soon enough. Even in the darkness.'

'You kept a copy of the software, didn't you?'

'Well, you never know when you might need it. I reckoned that if they started messing about I'd just get in touch and tell them that I'd keep shutting their country down until they let you out.'

'Well, I'm out,' said Josh firmly. 'So turn the bloody power back on. Before they send the Army out to get us.'

Luke sighed. 'I kind of like it in the dark,' he said. 'It doesn't matter who you are, what you look like or how much money you have. In a blackout we're all the same. Equal.'

Josh stepped forwards. 'Just turn it back on.'

From his pocket, Luke pulled out a PDA. He pressed a button, then fired a signal. Standing next to Josh, he leaned over the side of Vauxhall Bridge. Behind them he could hear the wail of sirens, and the sound of some police officers starting to order people to move along.

'Let there be light,' said Luke.

Up above, Josh could see the lights suddenly flooding across the city. Big Ben burst into life, and the London Eye started turning again. Cars screeched to a halt as traffic lights all across London turned red simultaneously.

'You know what?' said Josh. 'Maybe you're right. Perhaps it does look better with the lights out.'

Both of them laughed loudly.

'We make a pretty good team,' said Luke.

'What the hell makes you say that?' asked Josh.

Luke tapped his PDA. 'The wars of the future will be fought as much by boys like me equipped with gadgets like this as they will by men like you with your guns and knives.'

Josh stared down at the water. The lights were beaming out across the city, the sirens had stopped, and the traffic was returning to normal.

'Maybe you're right,' said Josh. 'A couple of kids like you could probably take out a battalion of men like me. No problem.'

The crowds were starting to pack the bridge as Luke stepped back. As Josh turned around, people were starting to press into the space between them, blocking Luke from view.

'You need me, man, you just get in touch.'

'How?' snapped Josh.

'Same record, man, that will show you the way,' said Luke, laughing. '*London Calling*. But this time it's a bonus question.'

Josh looked into the crowd. 'Luke,' he shouted. 'What the hell does that mean?'

But the crowd had already closed in. And Luke had slipped away.

Thermal Analysis and **Design**
of **Passive Solar Buildings**

Thermal Analysis and Design of Passive Solar Buildings

A K Athienitis and M Santamouris

Published by James & James (Science Publishers) Ltd
8–12 Camden High Street, London NW1 0JH, UK

A catalogue record for this book is available from the British Library.

ISBN 1 902916 02 6

Printed and bound in the UK by The Cromwell Press

Cover photograph: BedZED project by Bill Dunster architects.
Photo by Raf Makda / View Pictures.

Contents

Preface

The term 'passive solar buildings' was originally developed during the early days of solar energy research to distinguish thermal systems in which the primary driving force for solar-induced heat flow is buoyancy (natural convection) as opposed to heat transfer achieved primarily with the aid of fans and pumps.

Generally, if solar energy can be utilized immediately in a building or be directly stored in the thermal mass of the building, without expending a significant amount of energy in transferring heat by mechanical means, then the overall process will be more efficient. In terms of the second law of thermodynamics, it can be shown that the inherent irreversibilities introduced by adding mechanical devices are avoided or minimized.

The term 'passive solar buildings' is employed in this book to emphasize reliance on direct utilization of solar energy in buildings without the use of fans and pumps *as much as possible*. However, in many cases the utilization of fans or pumps is essential in order to transfer stored energy to the controlled space, or to prevent high room temperature swings. Shading devices also need to be effectively controlled to optimize utilization of solar energy, especially its visible component – daylight – while lowering cooling loads.

The 21st century building is rapidly evolving to accommodate three interrelated requirements:

- the achievement of a high quality, easily controllable indoor environment which will enhance comfort and productivity
- minimization of energy costs for processes such as heating, cooling and electric lighting
- sustainable development; one must strive to use environmentally friendly materials with low embodied energy and renewable energy sources such as daylight as much as possible. Furthermore, design solutions must ensure long-term durability of systems, which decrease the impact of waste on the environment.

The area of fenestration in buildings is continuously increasing, driven by two factors – first the higher demand for buildings with much daylight, and second the development of advanced windows with predictable or controlled solar transmittance characteristics (e.g. electrochromic coatings, motorized shading) and high thermal resistance. The increased fenestration areas often result in highly varying heating and cooling loads throughout the year, as well as overheating, especially when inadequate amounts of thermal mass are employed. The fragmented nature of the building process, in which no member of the design team considers the overall optimization of the indoor environment, further compounds the problem. For example, a building designer often implements advanced dynamic elements such as motorized shading devices in the building envelope or airflow windows which are usually not taken into account by the mechanical engineers responsible for heating/cooling system design.

It is the aim of this book to contribute towards the optimization of buildings as systems which act as natural filters between the indoor and outdoor environments, while maximizing the utilization of solar energy.

The book starts with an introduction of basic concepts for passive solar buildings, including a clear day steady-state model and notions of thermal comfort. Chapter 2 overviews essential concepts of heat transfer relevant to passive solar buildings and their dynamic behaviour. Chapter 3 considers analysis of different types of glazing systems, including transparent insulation, shading and daylighting concepts. Chapter 4 introduces several techniques for modelling and analysis of the thermal response of solar buildings, with emphasis on the admittance technique and the explicit finite difference approach; in both cases thermal networks are extensively employed to illustrate the basic modelling concepts. Chapter 5 focuses on the passive response of solar buildings and its analysis through a simple admittance model; this model may be employed to determine room temperature swings and to size thermal storage mass so as to prevent overheating.

Chapter 6 provides an introduction to natural ventilation for good indoor air quality. Chapter 7 presents models for thermal analysis of passive solar buildings intended to help the designer size small auxiliary heating/cooling systems; both convective and radiant systems are considered. Finally, a model of a building with utilization of underground channels for preheating/precooling fresh air for air-conditioning systems is introduced.

Chapter 8 considers in detail thermal comfort and dynamic control of passive solar buildings. Chapter 9 presents several integrative applications: thermal analysis of a building with transparent insulation is introduced in section 9.1, followed by analysis of a solar building with phase-change thermal storage in section 9.2; section 9.3 describes a simple solarium model, and section 9.4 covers photovoltaic systems for buildings, followed by a description of recent advanced fenestration system applications.

CHAPTER 1

Introduction and basic concepts

1.1 Passive solar design principles – an introduction

Solar radiation is the most abundant renewable energy source, without which life on earth would be impossible. It is the driving energy of our ecosystem and of the precipitation cycle. Passive solar design principles have been known to our ancestors since antiquity; for example ancient Romans oriented house openings towards the south so as to be warm in the winter and reduce solar gains in the summer. They also built massive dwellings that reduced room temperature fluctuations. In some countries of the Mediterranean the living room is known as the 'solar room', and in traditional architecture it connects into a south-facing courtyard.

The term 'passive solar building' is a qualitative term describing a building that significantly utilizes solar gains to reduce heating and possibly cooling energy consumption based on natural energy flows – radiation, conduction and natural convection; forced convection based on mechanical means such as pumps and fans is not expected to play a major role in the heat transfer processes. The term 'passive building' is often employed to emphasize utilization of passive energy flows both in heating and cooling.

Passive solar heating systems are generally separated into two broad categories, direct gain and indirect gain (see Section 1.7). When indirect passive systems are insulated from the heated space they are sometimes referred to as isolated.

Passive solar design techniques address the following basic requirements and principles:

- **Transmission and/or absorption of the maximum possible quantity of solar radiation** during winter so as to minimize or reduce to zero the heating energy consumption.
- **Utilization of received solar gains to cover instantaneous heating load and storage of the remainder in embodied thermal mass or specially built thermal storage devices**.
- **Reduction of heat losses** to the environment through use of the appropriate amount of **insulation** and windows with high solar heat gain factor.

- **Shading control devices** or strategically planted deciduous trees to exclude unwanted solar gains, which would create an additional cooling load.
- **Utilization of natural ventilation** to transfer heat from hot zones to cool zones in winter and for natural cooling in the summer; **ground cooling/heating** to transfer heat to/from the deep underground which is at a more or less constant temperature; **evaporative cooling.**
- **Development of integrated building envelope devices** such as windows which include photovoltaic panels as shading devices, or roofs with photovoltaic shingles; the dual role of these elements for electric power production and for exclusion of thermal gains increases their cost-effectiveness.
- Utilization of solar radiation for **daylighting; this requires measures for effective distribution of daylight onto the work plane.**
- **Integration of passive solar systems with the active heating/cooling air-conditioning systems both in the design and operation stages of the building**.

The last requirement is perhaps the most important for the successful design and operation of a building that utilizes passive solar design principles. However, it is usually overlooked because of the absence of collaboration for integration of building design between architects and mechanical engineers. Thus, the architect may often design the building envelope based on qualitative passive solar design principles and the engineer designs the HVAC (heating–ventilation–air conditioning) system based on extreme design conditions, ignoring the benefits due to solar gains and natural cooling. This results in an oversized system, which fights the building rather than using it. The absence of collaboration between the disciplines involved in building design is decreasing with the adoption of computer tools, but the fundamental institutional barriers remain owing to the basic training of architects and engineers which does not foster an integrated design approach.

The design approach proposed in this book is based on the principle that the building and its HVAC system are one thermal system and they must be designed together based on dynamic operation, taking into account thermal storage and control strategy. For example, a variable thermostat setpoint may result in different heating and cooling equipment sizes. Thus, passive solar gains and dynamic building behaviour must be estimated quantitatively under various control strategies to design both the building envelope and the HVAC system properly for harmonious operation.

Depending on climatic conditions and building function, certain heating/cooling systems are more appropriate than others and more compatible with passive systems. For example, the thermal mass in a floor may be used both to store passive solar gains and also for a floor heating system; however, this poses a control challenge which must be carefully considered to achieve acceptable thermal comfort.

A key aspect of passive solar design is choice of the following design parameters:

- **fenestration** area, orientation and type
- amount of **insulation**
- **shading** devices – type, locations and areas
- effective **thermal storage** (insulated from the exterior environment) amount and type (sensible – such as concrete in the building envelope with exterior insulation, or latent – such as phase-change materials).

The above basic design parameters are interlinked and dependent on each other.

The ultimate design objective is minimization of energy costs (heating, cooling, electricity) while maintaining good interior thermal comfort. The thermal mass of the building causes delays in its response to heat sources such as solar gains – the well-known thermal lag effect. This effect, if taken into account in the selection of thermal mass and appropriate control strategies, does not cause thermal comfort problems. It also needs to be taken into account in heating/cooling system sizing. Night ventilation may significantly reduce the need for mechanical cooling.

This book focuses on passive solar systems integrated in the building envelope.

1.1.1 Building enclosure design principles

In implementing passive solar design techniques one must consider all other aspects of building design. A building enclosure and its components should generally be designed to provide a protected and comfortable indoor environment. Building envelope components are built to protect from the weather elements – rain, sun, winds and variations of the environmental temperature. The external envelope acts like a 'filter' between the external environment and the indoor space. The filtering action is best illustrated with the effect of thermal mass on the fluctuations of outside temperature, which are modulated into a small room-temperature swing. Another filtering action is reduction of noise transmission.

In addition to protection from the weather elements there is a need for a structure to support the weight of the building envelope, building contents, snow and water on the roof, and to resist dynamic loads due to wind and earthquakes. In the great majority of buildings the structure is distinct from the enclosure. However, in many cases the structure and envelope functions are combined, such as in shear walls in traditional architecture and in flat roofs reinforced with steel.

This book focuses on thermal and solar performance of the building envelope. It is thus concerned with heat transfer through the building enclosure, including structural components; the thermal interaction between structural elements and building envelope components known as thermal bridge effects often leads to increased heat transfer as well as to differential expansion, which sometimes leads to formation of cracks.

Although the main function of the building external envelope is environmental it has only recently begun to attract the attention that it deserves. It is still relatively common for building designers to place primary emphasis on the visual function, that is, the appearance of a building. Architects, while being well equipped with building designs of traditional types that represent a number of basic models, find it difficult to deal with new concepts in building design such as passive solar techniques and components.

Even though a building envelope can be made of technologically simple components, because of its numerous functions it is still a very complex system. If its operation is not carefully considered throughout the year, a multitude of problems may occur; for example, a passive solar building with large south-facing windows may have a very low heating load, but unless proper shading measures are taken, it may be a 'sauna' in the summer. Furthermore, noise transmission may be another problem, and it should be considered simultaneously with natural ventilation.

Thus, the building envelope is both a barrier and a filter. Sometimes the barrier action is more important, as in shading, while at other times the filtering and modifying action is required. Apart from heat and noise, water must also be excluded from the interior. There are three well-known forms of keeping the interior dry:

- **Permeable barriers** thick enough to permit water that has penetrated the exterior surface to evaporate in dry periods before it reaches the interior surface; this has been the traditional solution for walls.
- **Air gaps**: continuous cavities in the building envelope which break the capillary paths along which water may travel from outside to the interior.
- **Impervious barriers** that prevent transmission of moisture; when they are used special attention to avoiding cracks must be given, otherwise if water penetrates through cracks and is not allowed to evaporate, interstitial condensation may occur.

Heat transmission, heat storage, solar heat gain and infiltration are the principal characteristics of exterior envelopes that influence room temperature and should be carefully considered when determining the effect of building enclosure on indoor climate.

The building shape and the ratio of surface area to volume are major determinants of thermal performance. Early decisions on shape limit future design options on passive solar features such as south-facing window area and natural ventilation strategies. A compact building with small surface area to volume ratio reduces both heat gains and heat losses. However, there are other constraints and factors which often dominate early decisions on form and shape, including:

- land plot shape and size
- building regulations on maximum area to be covered in the plot, maximum height and other urban planning requirements
- shading by adjacent buildings

- daylight needs
- visual and aesthetic factors, needs and preferences of owner
- function of the building and times of operation/occupancy.

The above factors largely constrain our choices on building form and shape. Nevertheless, the designer has several options available to optimize thermal performance, including advanced windows with effective shading mechanisms, natural ventilation strategies and sufficient amounts of thermal mass well distributed to reduce room temperature swings.

A discussion of fundamental considerations on the various building envelope components follows.

EXTERNAL WALLS

Basic decisions about external walls taken at a relatively early stage include the following:

- size, shapes, and position of openings including doors and windows
- treatment of openings, opening arrangement, and protection from heat and water penetration
- construction of solid portions of walls
- combination of passive solar components such as transparent insulation.

Once tentative choices have been made on sizes, positions and arrangements of windows and doors, the solid parts may be designed. A major decision is whether to use heavy or lightweight construction. Heavy construction is preferable for passive solar design and natural cooling in order to reduce room temperature swings. The choice is a function of:

- mass required for heat storage and sound reduction
- degree of fire-resistance required
- desired appearance
- maintenance
- structural, erection and assembly requirements
- availability of materials, cost and constraints.

When a window area is chosen the thermal conductance of the wall as a whole may then be selected. In choosing the different layers of the wall we need to consider the following:

- Water and moisture control. Rain exclusion may be achieved with a cavity in the wall or an impervious barrier. A simple ventilated cavity performs well and is easy to construct. An impervious barrier may be subject to interstitial condensation, and usually requires a vapour barrier and very good joints. Interstitial condensation risk is reduced with a ventilated and drained cavity.

- Thermal control. Methods for achieving the desired U-value include use of rigid thermal insulating sheet or slab materials, low-density insulating block wall materials, cavity wall construction, cavity with filling of insulating materials (plus impervious barrier) and low-emissivity surfaces in cavities.
- Fire control: fire resistance and limitations on combustibility of solid wall materials.
- Incorporation of services (electric, plumbing, heating/cooling, drainage, etc.).

Architects now have a variety of choices available in selecting materials for external walls including the following:

- Masonry: these walls rely on a process of absorption and subsequent evaporation of rainwater close to the surface. Exterior masonry is not useful in storing passive solar gains transmitted through windows.
- Cavity walls: these are designed so that rainwater may penetrate to the inner surface of the outer leaf; a ventilated cavity then allows its evaporation.
- Composite walls: masonry may be used as external skin or backing of external skin. In faced walls facing and backing are bonded so as to result in common action under load. In veneered walls there is no common action.
- Clad masonry walls: single-leaf and solid masonry walls may be used as backing to a cladding system.
- Concrete walls: different types of concrete are available with varying thermophysical properties; *in situ* or precast panels.
- Panels: external cladding panels are manufactured components that speed up construction time – they may be hung on the structure or form part of the structure. Infill panels are supported by the surrounding frames. Note that well-insulated panels exposed to strong sunlight may reach high temperatures (over 100°C), expanding and causing cracks.
- Curtain walls; these are non-load-bearing external walls. They usually consist of a rectangular grid filled with inserts of glass and panels of other materials such as insulation. They are usually suspended in front of a structural frame and their weight plus wind loads are transferred to the frame through point anchors. Curtain walls are increasingly used now in office buildings; special reflective absorptive glasses with shading should be used to reduce cooling loads.

ROOFS

Roofs are a very critical component of the building envelope. They must keep out water and sun, and provide thermal insulation. They must resist the destructive effects of heating and cooling cycles. They are typically of two types: flat and pitched. Flat roofs are protected with an impervious barrier, usually some type of mastic/tar, impregnated felt or metal sheet. Pitched roofs, however, do not have to be totally impervious; overlapping tiles should be backed by lining to prevent entry of wind, wind-driven rain or snow.

Flat roofs in hot climates should be painted with a reflective (e.g. aluminium) paint above waterproofing to reduce radiative gains in the summer, thereby reducing cooling loads. The surface temperature variations are also minimized, reducing the risk of crack formation due to expansion–contraction cycles and subsequent seepage of water.

A pitched roof with a ventilated attic avoids many of the problems of flat roofs. Water drains under gravitational force and heat absorbed by roof tiles (which are free to expand) is lost either to the environment or to the air in the attic space, which is ventilated.

In implementing passive solar systems such as photovoltaic shingles one should always design for proper water drainage and exclude moisture or water.

FLOORS
The lowest floor of a building may be at ground level, below ground level, or elevated on columns. A floor at ground level is the cheapest to build since it requires minimum excavation or fill, and for this reason is the most common in southern Europe. Use of a basement utilizes the stable temperature of the soil to provide a cool environment in the summer and to reduce heat losses in the winter, and for this reason it is popular in extreme climates. A raised floor is often used to provide covered space for parking or other functions, and in some cases for aesthetic reasons.

A floor in contact with the soil must be protected from rising moisture with an impervious barrier or ventilated cavity; the latter, most evident in suspended timber floors, is not as popular today.

Sound transmission through floors is usually not critical, especially for floor slabs, whether suspended or on the ground; the noise will usually be transmitted through windows and doors. A floor is often the best location for thermal mass for storing solar radiation transmitted through a window.

1.1.2 Fenestration and openings in the building envelope

The proper position and size of openings in the building envelope is typically based on experience, judgement, satisfaction of user needs, and building regulations. When passive solar design principles are followed south is the preferred orientation.

Doors are usually chosen based on access needs, security requirements and legislation (e.g. fire protection). One additional consideration in bioclimatic design should be natural ventilation. For example, a door located on the northern side of a house, when opened simultaneously with a south-facing window will induce high rates of airflow by natural ventilation.

Window shapes and sizes are often selected based on preliminary assessment of daylight and view needs; for example, a tall window may provide a view different to that of a wide window with the same area. Sound transmission into a building is usually through windows, especially when they are open. Excessive noise may be reduced with the following measures:

- re-orientation of window wall away from noise source
- use of fixed windows and mechanical ventilation
- use of openable double-glazed windows with 15–20 mm wide cavity
- openable windows with vinyl frame plus rubber lining at the edges, which is airtight when closed.

With the development of scientific techniques for estimating natural ventilation, solar gains and natural daylighting it is now possible to design fenestration systems for specific solar gains in winter, exclusion in summer, natural ventilation and daylighting.

Many modern buildings may be overglazed, sometimes for the sake of appearance, sometimes to achieve high levels of daylighting.

1.2 Solar energy availability

The earth rotates around the sun once a year and at the same time rotates about its polar axis once every 24 hours. During its rotation about the sun it follows an elliptical path with its axis tilted at 23.45° with respect to the plane of the earth's orbit about the sun. On 21 March (Spring Equinox) and 21 September (Autumn Equinox) the sun is directly over the Equator and the length of day and night are equal everywhere on the earth, except the poles. At other times the sun's rays form an angle with the equatorial plane known as the solar declination angle. This angle varies from 23.45° on 21 June to –23.45° on 21 December. All calculations involving solar radiation are based on solar time (ASHRAE 1989).

Solar time is based on the apparent angular motion of the sun across the sky, with solar noon the time that the sun crosses the meridian of the observer. Local standard time (LST) is converted to solar time as follows. First, there is a constant correction for the difference in longitude between the location and the meridian on which the local time is based. Note that 1° in longitude is equivalent to 4 minutes (since 360° is one day). Another correction is the equation of time, ET, which takes into account changes in the earth's rotation.

The apparent solar time (AST) is given by (ASHRAE 1989):

$$AST = LST + ET + 4(LSM - LON) \tag{1.1}$$

where
ET = Equation of Time, minutes
LST = Local Standard Time (positive east of Greenwich)
LSM = Local Standard Time Meridian, degrees
LON = Local Longitude, degrees
4 = minutes of time required for 1° rotation of the earth

A convenient correlation for the equation of time is the following:

$$ET = 9.87\sin[4\pi(n - 81)/364] - 7.53\cos[2\pi(n - 81)/364]$$
$$- 1.5\sin[2\pi(n - 81)/364] \tag{1.2}$$

where n = day of year (1–365)

The total solar radiation incident on an inclined surface (Figure 1.1) consists of a direct (beam) part, the sky diffuse solar radiation (e.g. reflected from clouds, and scattered radiation) and the ground-reflected radiation, also assumed to be diffuse.

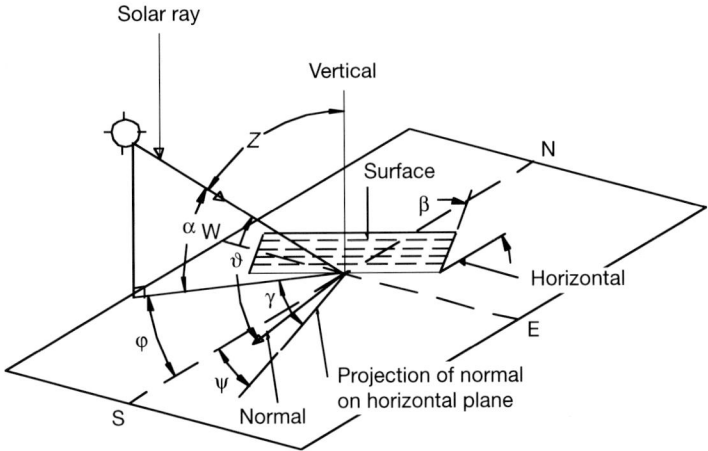

Figure 1.1 Solar radiation geometry for an inclined surface

The position of the sun and the geometric relationships between a plane and the beam solar radiation incident on it may be described in terms of the following angles:

- L latitude, equal to the angle of the location relative to the equator; north is positive
- δ declination, equal to the angular position of the sun at solar noon with respect to the equatorial plane (varies from −23.45 to 23.45°)
- α solar altitude, equal to the angle between the sun's rays and the horizontal (between 0 and 90°)
- z zenith angle, equal to the angle between the sun's rays and the vertical
- φ solar azimuth, equal to the angle between the horizontal projection of the sun's rays from due south (positive in the afternoon)

- γ surface solar azimuth, equal to the angle between the projections of the sun's rays and of the normal to the surface on the horizontal plane
- ψ surface azimuth, equal to the angle between the projection of the normal to the surface on a horizontal plane and due south (east is negative)
- β tilt (slope) angle between the surface and the horizontal (0–180°)
- θ the **angle of incidence** is the angle between the solar rays and a line normal to the surface.

The position of the sun may be expressed as a function of solar altitude and the solar azimuth as shown in Figure 1.1. These angles are a function of the local latitude L and the solar declination δ, which is a function of the date and the apparent solar time (AST) expressed as the hour angle h:

$$h = 0.25 \times \text{(number of minutes from local solar noon)}°$$

(h is positive in the afternoon). The declination angle is given by:

$$\delta = 23.45\sin[360(284 + n)/365]° \tag{1.3}$$

The solar altitude, solar azimuth and angle of incidence may be determined by:

$$\sin\alpha = \cos L \times \cos\delta \cos h + \sin L \sin\delta \tag{1.4}$$

and

$$z = 90 - \alpha°$$

$$\cos\varphi = (\sin\alpha \sin L - \sin\delta)/(\cos\alpha \cos L) \tag{1.5}$$

$$\cos\theta = \cos\alpha \cos|\gamma| \sin\beta + \sin\alpha \cos\beta \tag{1.6}$$

where $\gamma = \varphi - \psi$ (note that ψ is negative and φ positive).

Solar radiation is incident on a surface during daylight times (when the hour angle h is less than $|\tan L \tan\delta|$) if the incidence angle is between 0 and 90°.

The total solar radiation I_t incident on a surface is given by the sum of the direct (beam) component I_b, the diffuse sky component I_{ds} and the diffuse solar radiation reflected from the ground I_{dg}.

$$I_t = I_b + I_{ds} + I_{dg} \tag{1.7}$$

where

$$I_b = I_{on}\tau_b\cos\theta$$

with the extraterrestrial solar radiation given by

$$I_{on} = 1353[1 + 0.033\cos(360n/365)] \qquad (1.7a)$$

$$I_{ds} = I_{on}\sin\alpha(\tau_d F_{ws}) \qquad (1.7b)$$

where the view factor (see Chapter 2) from window to sky is

$$F_{ws} = (1 + \cos\beta)/2$$

$$I_{dg} = I_{on}\sin\alpha(\tau_b + \tau_d)\rho F_{wg} \qquad (1.7.c)$$

where the view factor from window to ground is

$$F_{wg} = (1 - \cos\beta)/2$$

where τ_b and τ_d are the beam and diffuse atmospheric transmittance respectively and ρ is ground reflectivity. Typical values of ground reflectivity are given in Table 1.1. There are more accurate anisotropic models for diffuse solar radiation (Klucher 1979) that may be employed.

Table 1.1 Solar reflectivity of various surfaces (Threlkeld 1970)

Surface	*Incidence angle (°)*					
	20	*30*	*40*	*50*	*60*	*70*
New concrete	0.31	0.31	0.32	0.32	0.33	0.34
Bright green grass	0.21	0.22	0.23	0.25	0.28	0.31
Bitumen and gravel roof	0.14	0.14	0.14	0.14	0.14	0.14
Bituminous parking lot	0.09	0.09	0.10	0.10	0.11	0.12
Crushed rock	0.20	0.20	0.20	0.20	0.20	0.20

For any transparent layer, part of the incident radiation (I) is transmitted (τI), another portion is reflected (ρI) and the remainder is absorbed (αI), that is

$$\alpha + \rho + \tau = 1 \qquad (1.8)$$

where
α = absorptance
ρ = reflectance
τ = transmittance

For grey bodies we assume that the radiation properties do not depend on wavelength. Usually the grey body model is applied over a specific wavelength range, and we determine averaged properties over this range. Details on computation of radiation properties are given in Chapter 2.

Example

Determine the local solar azimuth and altitude at 9.30 Central Time on 23 October at 35°N latitude and 95°W longitude. Also, determine the incidence angle for a vertical surface facing southeast.

First we determine ET, then AST and hour angle h:

$n = 273 + 23 = 296$

$ET(296) = 16.115$ min

$LON = 95°$

$L = 35°$

$AST = 9.5 + 16.115 + (90 - 95)/15 = 9.435$ h

$h = (AST - 12) \times 15 = -38.47°$

Knowing these basic quantities we can then determine the position of the sun and the angle of incidence.

$\delta = 23.45\sin[360(284 + n)/365] = -12.446°$

$\alpha = \arcsin[\cos(35)\cos(-12.446)\cos(-38.47)$
$+ \sin(35)\sin(-12.446)] = 30.175°$

$\varphi = \arccos\{[\sin(30.175)\sin(35) - \sin(-12.446)]/$
$[\cos(30.175)\cos(35)]\} = -44.646$

Note that the solar azimuth is negative because it is east of south. We now determine the incidence angle:

$\beta = 90°$

$\psi = -45°$ (negative – east of south)

$\gamma = \varphi - \psi = 0.354°$

$\theta = \arccos[\cos(30.175)\cos(0.354)\sin(90) + \sin(30.175)\cos(90)] = 30.117°$

The **sunrise and sunset times** may be determined by evaluating the times at which the incidence angle (or zenith angle) on a horizontal surface is equal to zero. The sunset hour angle h_s is given by:

$$h_s = \arccos[-\tan(L)\tan(\delta)] \tag{1.9}$$

Similarly, $-h_s$ is the sunrise angle. The corresponding times are determined by dividing by 15°/hour.

1.2.1 Hottel's clear sky model

A convenient method developed by Hottel (1976) is employed here to determine the beam radiation transmitted through a clear atmosphere. The atmospheric transmittance for beam radiation is given by:

$$\tau_b = a_0 + a_1 \exp[-k/\cos(z)] \tag{1.10}$$

where the constants a, k depend on climate and altitude A (km).

$$a_0 = r_0[0.4327 - 0.008\ 21(6 - A)^2]$$

$$a_1 = r_1(0.5055 - 0.005\ 95(6.5 - A)^2)$$

$$k = r_k(0.2711 + 0.018\ 58(2.5 - A)^2)$$

The correction constants for climate types are given in Table 1.2.

Table 1.2 Correction factors for Hottel's clear sky model (Hottel 1976)

Climate type	r_0	r_1	r_k
Tropical	0.95	0.98	1.02
Midlatitude summer	0.97	0.99	1.02
Subarctic summer	0.99	0.99	1.01
Midlatitude winter	1.03	1.01	1.00

After determining the beam transmittance (τ_b) of the atmosphere, we may determine also the diffuse transmittance (Liu and Jordan 1960):

$$\tau_d = 0.271 - 0.294\tau_b \tag{1.11}$$

The total daily extraterrestrial solar radiation H_{oh} on a horizontal surface may be determined by integration of the instantaneous radiation between sunset and sunrise times. For an inclined surface we also need to determine the sunset and sunrise hour angles on the surface, which may be different from the daily sunset and sunrise hour angles:

$$h_s' = \min\{\arccos[-\tan(L)\tan(\delta)], \arccos[-\tan(L - \beta)\tan(\delta)]\} \tag{1.12}$$

where min indicates the smaller of the two terms in the brackets.

Note that the solar radiation incident on a south-facing surface is symmetric about solar noon. Therefore, the total daily solar radiation incident on a south-facing surface is determined by integrating for a half day and multiplying by 2.

Example: Evaluation of solar radiation incident on an inclined surface

Determine the collector tilt angle for which the total daily solar radiation incident on a south-facing collector located at a latitude of 45°N is maximum on 21 January and for 21 March.

We need to numerically integrate the instantaneous solar radiation evaluated at several time intervals:

β = 0, 10, 20...90° ψ = 0 for south-facing surface

Assume ρ = 0.2 for ground reflectivity

δ = −20.14° for 21 January and 0 for 21 March

The sunrise time was found and divided into eight equal time intervals.

$t_s' = h_s'/15$
$\quad = \min\{\arccos[-\tan(L)\tan(\delta)], \arccos[-\tan(L - \beta)\tan(\delta)]/15\} = 4.56$ h

Time interval $\Delta t = t_s'/8$

For each value of tilt angle β and time t, the incidence angle was determined and then the beam and diffuse incident radiation were calculated. The atmospheric beam transmittance and beam radiation incident on a vertical surface (21 January) are shown in Figure 1.2. The total solar radiation as a function of tilt angle is given in Figure 1.3 for 21 January and 21 March.

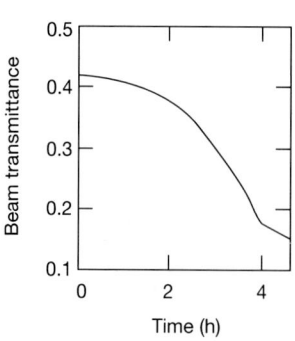
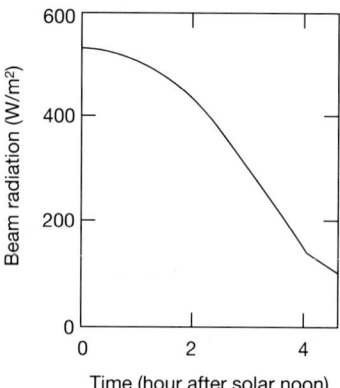

Figure 1.2 Beam transmittance of atmosphere and incident solar radiation on vertical surface for 21 January

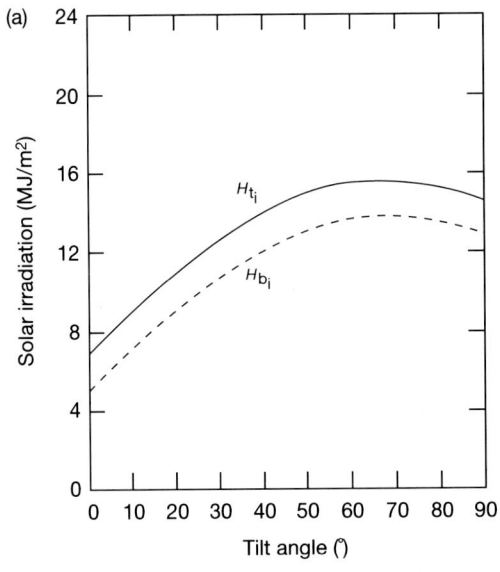

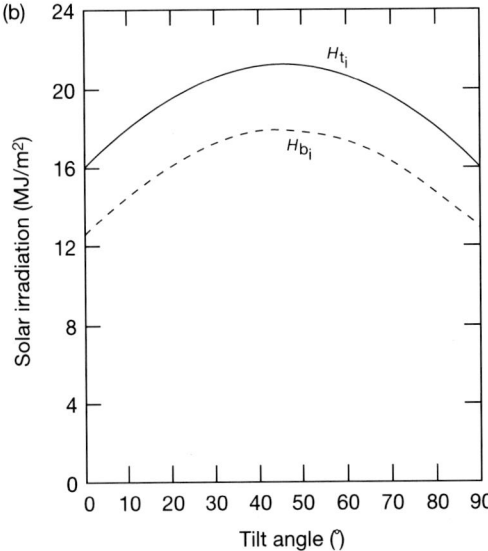

—— Total daily radiation
--- Beam daily radiation

Figure 1.3 Total solar radiation and beam radiation incident on south-facing surface as a function of tilt angle for (a) January and (b) March

As can be seen from Figure 1.3 the optimum tilt angle for this latitude for January is approximately 65° with a peak quantity of about 16 MJ, as opposed to 45° and 22 MJ for March. The difference between each pair of curves is the amount of diffuse solar radiation incident on the surface (from the sky plus ground-reflected). Note that the vertical surface is not significantly inferior to the optimally tilted surface for January (receives about 1.5 MJ less).

Figures 1.4 and 1.5 show the solar radiation incident on vertical surfaces of various orientations for latitudes 30°N, 40°N, 50°N and 60°N on typical clear summer days.

1.3 Microclimate and buildings

Climate is the average of the atmospheric conditions over an extended period of time over a large region. Small-scale patterns of climate, resulting from the influence of topography, soil structure, ground and urban forms, are known as **microclimates**.

The local environment around buildings may significantly alter the effective environment temperature 'felt' by the building (Honjo and Takakura 1990). For example, trees and lawns may lower the temperature in the summer by a few degrees compared with asphalt or concrete surfaces. A densely populated city centre such as Los Angeles (Akbari *et al.* 1992) may experience local outdoor temperatures as much as 8°C higher than green suburban areas.

The principal parameters characterizing climate are: air temperature, solar radiation, humidity, and precipitation and wind. The climate of cities differs from the climate of surrounding rural areas mainly due to the structure of cities and heat released by vehicles. In general, the climate in cities is characterized by high ambient temperatures, reduced relative humidity, reduced wind speed and reduced received direct solar radiation.

As a consequence of heat balance, air temperatures in densely built urban areas are higher than the temperatures of the surrounding rural country. The phenomenon, known as 'heat island', is due to many factors, the more important of which are summarized by Oke *et al.* (1991) and deal with: (a) the canyon radiative geometry that contributes to decrease the long-wave radiation loss from within street canyons due to the complex exchange between buildings and the screening of the skyline, (b) the thermal properties of materials that increase storage of sensible heat in the fabric of the city, (c) the anthropogenic heat released from combustion of fuels and animal metabolism, (d) the urban greenhouse, which contributes to increase the incoming long-wave radiation from the polluted and warmer urban atmosphere, (e) the canyon radiative geometry decreasing the effective albedo of the system because of the multiple reflection of short-wave radiation between the canyon surfaces, (f) the reduction of evaporating surfaces in the city putting more energy into sensible and less into latent heat, and (g) the reduced turbulent transfer of heat from within streets.

Urban heat island studies refer usually to the 'urban heat island intensity', which

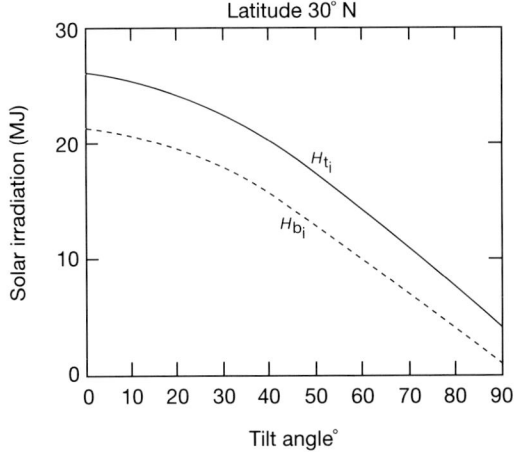

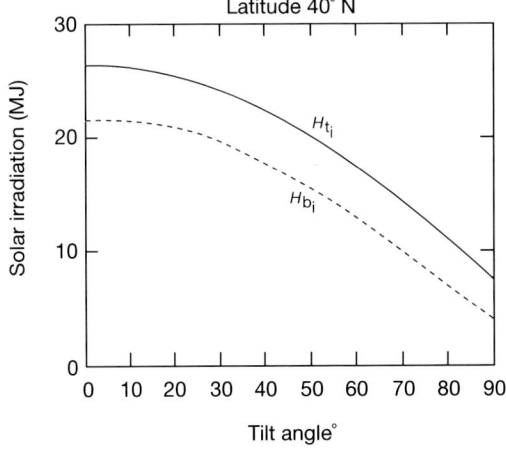

------ Total daily radiation
----- Beam daily radiation

Figure 1.4 Total solar radiation incident on south-facing inclined surface ($L = 30°N, 40°N$) for various tilt angles (30 June)

is the maximum temperature difference between the city and the surrounding area. Data compiled by various sources (Santamouris 2001a) show that heat island intensity can be as high as 15°C. Extensive studies on the heat island intensity in Athens involving more than 30 urban stations show that urban stations present temperatures higher than reference suburban stations by between 5 and 15°C.

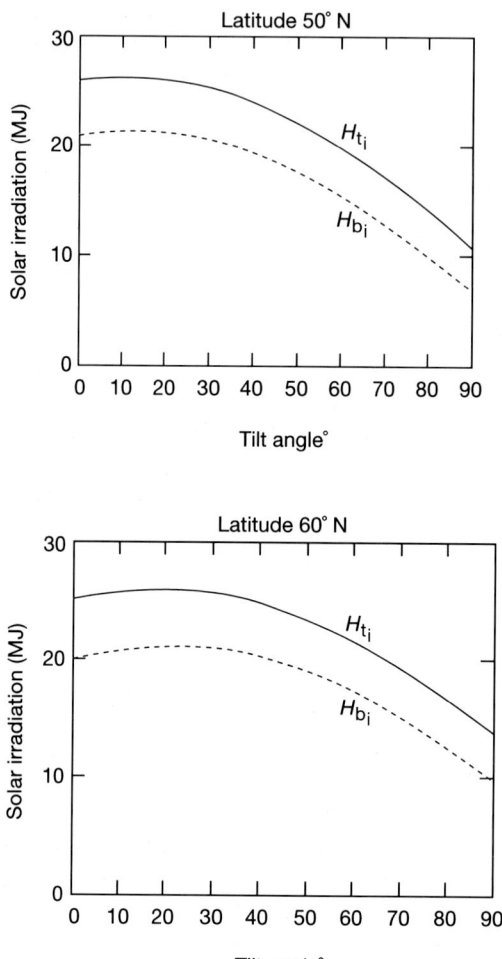

Figure 1.5 Total solar radiation incident on south-facing inclined surface ($L = 50°N, 60°N$) for various tilt angles (30 June)

In addition to the temperature increase, the urban environment affects many other climatological parameters. Global solar radiation is seriously reduced because of increased scattering and absorption. As mentioned by Landsberg (1991), the sunshine duration in industrial cities is reduced by 10–20% in comparison with the surrounding countryside, and similar losses are observed in received energy.

In a general way, wind speed and direction in the canopy layer are seriously decreased compared with the undisturbed wind speed. This is mainly due to the specific roughness of a city, channelling effects through canyons, and also because of the heat island effect.

In parallel, the urban environment affects precipitation and cloud cover. The exact effect of urbanization depends on the relative place of a specific city regarding the general atmospheric circulation. In Budapest, mainly because of industrialization, cloud cover has been increased by 3% during the winter period. As mentioned by Escourrou (1991), urbanization causes a proportional increase in precipitation in cities such as London, which because of its geographical location is more often in the zone of perturbations than in cities such as Paris. Studies in Bombay, India, have shown that the development of an industrial zone close to the city has increased precipitation by 15% (Rao and Murty 1973).

Addressing successful solutions to counterbalance the effects of temperature increase on the energy performance of urban buildings is an important priority. Successful solutions to counterbalance the effects of the urban microclimate involve the use of more appropriate materials, increased use of green areas, use of cool sinks for heat dissipation, appropriate layout of urban canopies, etc.

The optical characteristics of materials used in the outdoor facade of buildings or in streets and pavements and especially the albedo for solar radiation and long-wave emissivity have a very important impact on the urban energy balance and the performance of buildings. Increase of the surface albedo has a direct impact on the energy balance of a building. Large-scale changes on urban albedo may have important indirect effects on the city scale. Numerous studies have been performed to evaluate direct effects from albedo change and it has been concluded that important energy gains must be expected (Santamouris 2001a).

Vegetation modifies the microclimate and the energy use of buildings by providing solar protection, lowering air and surface temperatures and increasing the relative humidity of the air because of evapotranspiration. Trees also help mitigate the greenhouse effect, filter pollutants, mask noise, prevent erosion and calm their human observers. Water surfaces modify the microclimate of the surrounding area, reducing the ambient air temperature, either by evaporation or convection. Fountains, ponds, streams, waterfalls or mist sprays may be used as cooling sources, for lowering the temperature of the outdoor air and of the air entering the building.

Akbari *et al.* (1992) present the results of computer simulations aimed at studying the combined effect of shading and evapotranspiration of vegetation on the energy use of typical one-storey buildings in various US cities. They found that by adding one tree per house, the cooling energy savings range from 12% to 24%, while adding three trees per house can reduce the cooling load between 17% and 57%. According to this study, the direct effects of shading account for only 10–35% of the total cooling energy savings. The remaining savings result from temperatures lowered by evapotranspiration.

The presence of trees or buildings around a building may also significantly alter the wind environment around it. This should be taken into account in designing for enhancement of natural ventilation in the summer. It is important to orient certain openings (windows/doors) towards the prevailing wind direction and to design for some windows in the leeward direction so that the wind may easily flow through the building.

Shading of a building by surrounding buildings or trees should be taken into account when estimating solar gains for summer cooling calculations and in locating and designing passive solar components such as a solarium or an attached sunspace. A deciduous tree may be ideal in providing summer shading in front of a sunspace while letting the winter sun inside. In the case of office buildings daylighting considerations may be even more important.

Natural evaporative cooling may significantly reduce the temperature of outdoor air entering a building for natural ventilation in the summer. This may be achieved by air flowing over an outdoor pond and fountain. The saturation efficiency is an important factor in identifying the cooling potential for all evaporative cooling systems:

$$\text{Saturation (humidifying) efficiency} = (T_{db,in} - T_{db,out})/(T_{db,in} - T_{wb,in})$$

1.4 Steady-state thermal analysis of buildings

The basic steady-state heat flow (q) equation is based on Fourier's conduction law:

$$q = - Ak(dT/dx) \tag{1.13}$$

where
k = thermal conductivity
A = surface area through which heat flows
T = temperature
x = distance
L = thickness

Written in discrete (finite difference) form the above equation becomes:

$$q = -Ak(T_{x=L} - T_{x=0})/L \tag{1.14}$$
$$q = (T_{x=0} - T_{x=L})/R = \Delta/R$$

where thermal resistance of wall:

$$R = L/(kA)$$

The other basic steady-state equation describes heat flow based on a heat transfer coefficient h, which may represent convection (h_c), radiation (h_r) or an approximate combined coefficient, often called a film coefficient h (equal to $h_c + h_r$).

$$q = Ah(T_s - T_a) \tag{1.15}$$

Steady-state thermal analysis techniques are often employed to estimate peak heating loads for preliminary sizing of heating systems. For this purpose the following equation is used to estimate the maximum heating load q_{max}:

$$q_{max} = (U_{tot} + U_{inf})(T_{room} - T_{o\_min}) \tag{1.16}$$

where
T_{room} = room thermostat setpoint
T_{o_min} = minimum exterior design temperature
U_{tot} = sum of all building envelope element conductances (windows, walls, doors, etc.)
U_{inf} = conductance due to infiltration based on the following constitutive equation:

Infiltration heat loss $= q_{inf} = \dot{m}C_{p,air}(T_R - T_o) = U_{inf}(T_{room} - T_{o\_min})$
$U_{inf} = \dot{m}C_p = $ number of air changes per second $\times$ Vol$_{room} \times (\rho C_{p,air})$

where $\dot{m} = $ mass flow rate

The thermal resistance of a building envelope component is determined as the sum of the thermal resistance of each layer plus the resistance of the interior and exterior film coefficients (h_i and h_o respectively):

$$R = 1/h_i + 1/h_o + \Sigma_i(L_i/k_i) \tag{1.17}$$

where L_i and k_i are thickness and thermal conductivity of layer i. For an interior cavity, its thermal resistance is also added to the above equation. Typical heat transfer coefficients for various surfaces and cavities are computed in Chapter 2.

For a pitched roof with pitch angle b, a void and a horizontal ceiling, the total thermal resistance per unit area of ceiling is given by

$$R = R_r\cos(b) + R_v + R_c \tag{1.18}$$

where R_r, R_v and R_c are the thermal resistances of the roof, void and ceiling per unit area respectively.

In most building envelope components such as walls we have heat flow paths that cross structural support members such as wood studs in wood frame construction, concrete beams and columns in concrete structures, frames in windows and so on.

Computation of the effective thermal resistance of wall assemblies may be based on either of two simplifying assumptions:

- Parallel heat flow paths, one being through the wall area containing structural members and the other one through the remaining area without structural members. In this case we have two thermal resistances in parallel.
- Isothermal planes at different wall layer surfaces.

The actual value of the wall thermal resistance is expected to lie between the values given by the two models. The first model is usually closer to reality and is typically used. The actual wall thermal resistance may be determined using controlled tests, particularly the guarded hot box test (ASTM standard 1989), or *in situ* measurements (Norlen and Bloem 1994). It may also be determined with the two- or three-dimensional finite difference thermal bridge model (see Chapter 4).

In determining the thermal resistance of a wall with fraction of area containing structural members equal to A_s, the effective thermal resistance per unit area R_{eff} is determined by assuming parallel heat flow paths as follows:

$$R_{eff} = 1/[(A_s/R_s) + (1 - A_s)/R_i)] \qquad (1.19)$$

where:

A_s = wall surface area where heat flow crosses structural members
R_s = thermal resistance (per unit area) through path A_s
R_i = thermal resistance (per unit area) through path without structural members

Heat flow through solid ground floors is generally of a two- or three-dimensional nature and it may be accurately analysed with numerical models or approximate analytical solutions.

1.5 Principles of thermal comfort

The ultimate aim of the building thermal design process should be to ensure good thermal comfort under most operating conditions and weather patterns. There exist numeral comfort models for thermal comfort such as Fanger's predicted mean vote (PMV) model (ASHRAE 1989) and other models more appropriate for summer conditions (Athienitis *et al.* 1995). A person's feeling of thermal comfort is a function of air temperature T_{ai}, mean radiant T_{mr} at the location of interest, air movement and humidity, and also personal factors such as clothing and activity.

Various environmental indices are often used as a measure of thermal comfort, including equivalent temperature, effective temperature, humid operative temperature, globe temperature and (in the UK) the resultant temperature. Several environmental parameters that affect thermal comfort can be measured directly:

- air temperature T_{ai}
- wet-bulb temperature T_{wb}
- dew-point temperature T_{dp}
- water vapour pressure p_v
- total atmospheric pressure p
- relative humidity RH
- specific humidity W
- air velocity V
- mean radiant temperature T_{mr}; the temperatures of individual surfaces are usually combined into T_{mr}

The mean radiant temperature is a very important variable in all thermal comfort calculations. It is the uniform temperature of an imaginary black enclosure in which radiant heat transfer from a person equals the radiant heat transfer in the actual enclosure.

T_{mr} may be estimated from measurements of globe temperature, air temperature and air velocity. T_{mr} can also be calculated from measured temperatures of each room interior surface. Since building surfaces have a high long-wave emittance, the following blackbody approximation for T_{mr} is satisfactory:

$$T_{mr}^{\ 4} = \Sigma_i(T_i^4 \times F_{p-i}) \qquad (1.20)$$

where
$i = 1..N$ indicates room surface
T_i = temperature of surface i, k
F_{p-i} = view factor between a person and surface i
 If small temperature differences exist between the room surfaces, then the above equation can be expressed by its linear form:

$$T_{mr} = \Sigma_i T_i \times F_{p-i} \qquad (1.21)$$

In a rectangular room one possible approximation in calculating the view factors is to model a person as a sphere, for ease of calculation (this would be a reasonable approximation for a seated person). The mean radiant temperature may also be calculated from the plane radiant temperature in six directions (ASHRAE 1989).

The **operative temperature** is defined as the uniform temperature of an enclosure in which an occupant would exchange the same amount of heat by radiation plus convection as in the actual non-uniform environment (ASHRAE 1989); it is given by

$$T_e = (h_r T_{mr} + h_c T_{ai})/(h_r + h_c) \qquad (1.22)$$

where T_{ai} is the air temperature, T_{mr} is the mean radiant temperature, and h_r and h_c are radiative and convective coefficients, respectively, for a person or object (sensor). The operative temperature is a particularly important parameter for passive solar design because the mean radiant temperature is usually higher in well-insulated passive solar buildings. In a poorly insulated building with inefficient windows the mean radiant temperature in the winter will tend to be lower than that in an energy-efficient, well-insulated building for the same air temperature. Thus, to achieve the same thermal comfort in a poorly insulated building we need to achieve the same operative temperature by raising the air temperature to compensate for the lower mean radiant temperature.

One other factor that may be important in thermal comfort calculations for passive solar buildings is the effect of direct and diffuse solar radiation incident on people; it can raise the operative temperature felt by as much as 10°C (Athienitis and Haghighat 1992).

Example

Consider the room shown in Figure 1.6. For a wall R-value equal to 4 RSI (thermal resistance, m²°C/W), a window R-value equal to 0.3 RSI and an outside temperature of –10°C, determine the operative temperature for a room air temperature equal to 20°C. Assume room dimensions $3 \times 3 \times 3$ m³, window 2×2 m², infiltration one air change per hour, film coefficient on interior surfaces 10 W/m²°C.

$$R_w = 0.3 \text{ RSI}$$

$$R_{wall} = 4 \text{ RSI}$$

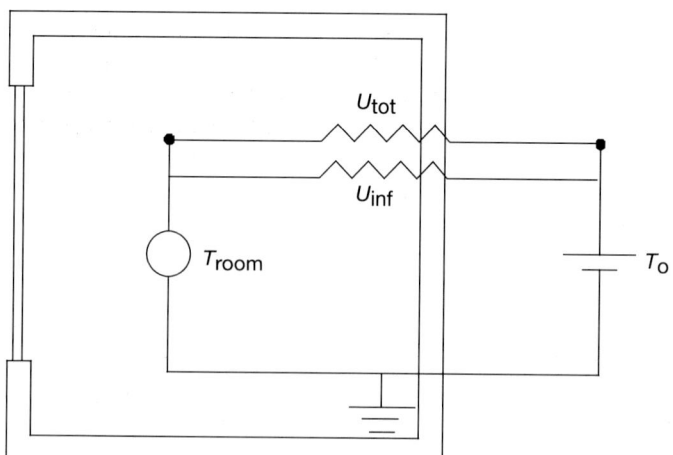

Figure 1.6 Simple steady-state model of heat transfer through building

$$T_o = -10°C$$

$$T_{ai} = 20°C$$

$$h = 10 \ W/m^2°C$$

Infiltration conductance:

$$U_{inf} = Vol \times (ach/3600) \times \rho c_{air} = 27(1/3600)1200 = 9 \ W/°C$$

Envelope conductance:

$$U_{tot} = (A_w/R_w) + (A_{wall}/R_{wall}) = 4/0.3 + (3 \times 3 \times 6 - 4)/4 = 25.8 \ W/°C$$

Temperatures:

$$T_w = T_{ai} - (T_{ai} - T_o)(A_w/R_w)/(A_w h) = 20 - (30/hR_w) = 10°C$$

$$T_{wall} = T_{air} - (T_{ai} - T_o)(A_{wall}/R_{wall})/(A_{wall}h) = 20 - (30/hR_{wall}) = 19.25°C$$

$$T_{mr} = (A_w T_w + A_{wall} T_{wall})/A_{total} = 18.56°C$$

$$T_e = T_{ai} + 2T_{mr} = 19.05°C$$

A more detailed discussion of thermal comfort is presented in Section 8.1.

1.6 Approximate estimation of solar savings

An approximate estimation of energy savings due to utilization of solar gains during the heating season can be made by means of a steady-state analysis using the techniques described above, including the mean monthly value of the transmitted solar radiation. Considering the simple zone model in Figure 1.6, and including now the mean transmitted solar radiation for the month G_0, we may perform an energy balance at the room interior node to obtain the resulting mean room temperature without heating as follows:

$$G_0 = (U_{tot} + U_{inf})(T_{room} - T_{o\_mean}) \tag{1.23}$$

Therefore we obtain

$$T_{room} = T_{o\_mean} + G_0/(U_{tot} + U_{inf}) \tag{1.24}$$

The solar savings as a fraction of the total auxiliary heating load (with no solar gains) are then given by the ratio:

$$Solar \ fraction = (T_{room} - T_{o\_mean})/(T_{setpoint} - T_{o\_mean}) \tag{1.25}$$

The above technique gives a very preliminary approximate estimation of solar savings, without taking into account overheating and the effect of thermal mass. However, despite its shortcomings, this estimate can provide the designer with a good estimate of the potential building thermal performance as a function of window type, area, orientation and amount of insulation.

More detailed dynamic thermal analysis is necessary to size the heating and cooling systems properly as well as for more accurate analysis of building energetic performance under different control strategies such as a lower thermostat setpoint at night.

Example

Consider the room shown in Figure 1.6. Determine the percentage solar savings for the room, assuming that the outside temperature is 0°C and the mean daily solar gains for December are 12MJ/m^2 of window.

$T_{room} = 0°C + (A_w \times 12000000 \text{ J})/[86400 \text{ s } (25.8 + 9)] = 12°C$

Solar fraction $= (12 - 0)/(20 - 0) = 0.6 = 60\%$

1.7 Conceptual design of passive solar buildings

One of the basic decisions in building design concerns form and shape. Generally basic passive solar principles dictate a rectangular form with the longest side facing south or near-south. Another basic decision is the type of passive solar system to be selected for each zone of the building, type of fenestration, thermal storage and insulation. The main types of passive solar systems are shown in Figure 1.7 and discussed below.

Direct gain systems rely primarily on south-facing windows (north-facing in the southern hemisphere) and thermal mass distributed on room interior surfaces. The room acts essentially as both thermal collector and thermal storage. The key decisions to be made are choice of window area and type and quantity of thermal mass. A dynamic thermal analysis is necessary to ensure that the ratio of peak solar gains to thermal mass does not exceed the maximum room temperature swing set by thermal comfort considerations.

The major advantage of direct gain systems is their simplicity: that solar energy is directly absorbed by the thermal storage or released by convection into the room air. Thus, no heat transfer devices are required, with their inherent inefficiencies, and temperatures remain relatively low, resulting in reduced heat losses. Well-designed shading systems are required to reduce unwanted solar gains in the summer, but to allow maximum gains in winter. Because they are the simplest to design and build, direct gain systems are also the most popular.

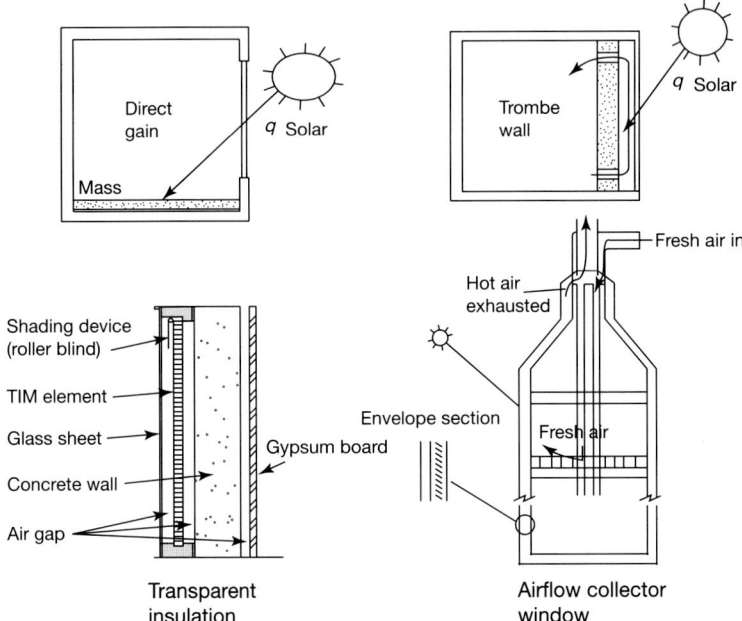

Figure 1.7 Main types of passive solar systems integrated in the building envelope

Systems in which the thermal storage mass is separate from the main building envelope systems are known as **indirect gain systems**. Of these, the most common is the collector-storage wall, also known as the mass or Trombe wall.

- **Collector-storage wall (Trombe wall) systems:** part of the south-facing wall is glazed and inside the glazing there is a thick layer of thermal mass such as concrete, brick or water tanks with a black surface to absorb and store the trans-mitted solar radiation. It may have vents at the top and bottom to permit transfer of some of the stored heat by convection from the face across the glazing, which may reach a high temperature (e.g. 70°C). Most of the stored heat is transferred by convection and radiation from the interior surface to the room interior, but a portion is lost through the glazing or glazings to the exterior. Night insulation and high thermal resistance fenestration systems reduce this loss.
- **Transparent insulation systems:** the same principle as for the storage walls is employed but in this case the solar energy collection and storage is achieved in an exterior wall. Instead of having glazings in front of the thermal mass, in this case we have transparent or translucent insulation such as a plastic honeycomb with relatively high thermal resistance.
- **Air heating systems such as air-flow windows and air collectors:** in air-flow windows, a dark surface such as dark blinds between two glazings is employed

to absorb the solar heat, which then rises by natural convection, and assisted by the fan to flow through hollow floors/ceiling mass or an isolated thermal storage device such as a rock bed. The principle is very similar to **air flow solar collectors**, installed in the past on the roof of a building. By integrating air flow collectors into the building envelope, the overall building cost is reduced.

- **Solar chimneys** are often employed for natural cooling. In these systems, one wall of the chimney is heated by solar radiation, warming up the air, which rises by buoyancy to the outside, creating a negative pressure and drawing cooler outside air into the building. Use of thermal mass keeps the solar chimney warm at night so that this beneficial natural cooling process continues during night-time when the outside air is even cooler. If the air is passed over water we may also enhance this process through evaporative cooling. The thermosyphon effect may also be employed with water-heating solar collectors for domestic hot water. In this case, the collector is usually a separate mechanical device not integrated in the building envelope.

1.8 Bibliography

Akbari H., Davis S., Dorsano S., Huang J. and Winett S. (1992) *Cooling our Communities – A Guidebook on Tree Planting and Light Colored Surfacing*, US Environmental Protection Agency, Office of Policy Analysis, Climate Change Division.

ASHRAE (1989) *ASHRAE Handbook – Fundamentals*, Atlanta, Georgia, USA.

ASTM (1989) Guarded Hot Box Test (C236), *ASTM Book of Standards*, ASTM, USA.

Athienitis A.K. (1990) 'A method and algorithm for estimation of transmitted solar radiation and its long-term averages using Fourier series', *Solar Energy*, **45**:5, 257–263.

Athienitis A.K. (1994) *Building Thermal Analysis*, Electronic Mathcad Book, MathSoft Inc., Boston, USA.

Athienitis A.K. and Haghighat F. (1992) 'A study of the effects of solar radiation on the indoor environment', *ASHRAE Transactions*, **98**:1, 257–261.

Athienitis A.K., Berger X. and Santamouris M. (1995) *Thermal Analysis of Buildings for Summer Comfort*, European Commission Directorate General for Energy DG XVII Publication.

CIBSE (1986) *CIBSE Guide*, Volume A, CIBSE, London.

Escourrou G. (1991) *Le Climat et La Ville*, Nathan Université, Paris.

Fanger P.O. (1970) *Thermal Comfort*, McGraw Hill, New York.

Gianccone A. and Gianfranco R. (1986) 'The influence of solar radiation distribution in a room on thermal comfort evaluation', *Proc. CIB*, 3185–3192.

Honjo T. and Takakura T. (1990) 'Simulation of thermal effects of urban green areas on their surrounding areas', *Energy and Buildings*, **15**:3–4, 443–446.

Hottel H.C. (1976) 'A simple model of transmittance of direct solar radiation through clear atmospheres', *Solar Energy*, **18**.

Klucher T.M. (1979) 'Evaluation of models to predict insolation on tilted surfaces', *Solar Energy*, **23**, 111–114.

Landsberg H.E. (1981) *The Urban Climate*, Academic Press.

Liu B. and Jordan R. (1960) 'The interrelationship and characteristic distribution of direct, diffuse and total solar radiation', *Solar Energy*, **4**, 1–19.

Norlen U. and Bloem J.J. (1994) 'Comparison of methods for thermal resistance estimation', European Conf. on Energy Performance and Indoor Climate in Buildings, Lyon, France, Nov., pp. 804–809.

Oke T.R, Johnson G.T., Steyn D.G. and Watson I.D. (1991) 'Simulation of surface urban heat islands under "ideal" conditions at night – Part 2: diagnosis and causation', *Boundary Layer Meteorology*, **56**, 339–358.

Rao T.R. and Murty Bh. V.R. (1973) 'Effect of steel mills on rainfall at distantly located stations', *Indian Journal of Meteorology and Geophysics*, **24**:1, 15–26.

Santamouris M. (2001a) *Energy and Climate in the Urban Built Environment*, James and James (Science Publishers) Ltd, London.

Santamouris M. (2001b) 'Solar and natural resources for a better built environment', *Solar Energy, the State of the Art*, James and James (Science Publishers) Ltd, London.

Threlkeld J.L. (1970) *Thermal Environmental Engineering*, 2nd edn, Prentice Hall, Englewood Cliffs, NJ.

CHAPTER 2

Transient heat transfer and thermal storage

2.1 Transient heat conduction

Conduction is the process of heat transfer in which heat is transferred due to the presence of a temperature gradient in a body without macroscopic movement of the molecules. Molecules within a high-temperature region have a higher internal energy, and through microscopic agitation transfer some of their energy to adjacent 'cooler' molecules. At a macroscopic (not molecular) level, the heat flow was first described by Fourier's conduction law.

In the x, y, z directions, we have the following heat flows:

$$q_x = -k_x \partial T/\partial x \tag{2.1}$$
$$q_y = -k_y \partial T/\partial y$$
$$q_z = -k_z \partial T/\partial z$$

where k_x, k_y and k_z are the thermal conductivities (W/mK) in the three directions. For most materials, which are isotropic, the thermal conductivity is equal in all directions.

Now considering a control volume of dimensions dx dy dz, and applying an energy balance over a time interval dt we obtain the three-dimensional heat flow equation:

$$\rho c \partial T/\partial t = k_x \partial^2 T/\partial x^2 + k_y \partial^2 T/\partial y^2 + k_z \partial^2 T/\partial z^2 + S \tag{2.2}$$

where S is an internal heat source (W/m^3), c is specific heat capacity and ρ density.

The thermal capacity of a building, most of it due to thermally massive materials – so-called thermal mass – stores heat during the day and modulates room temperature swings. Solar radiation incident on the exterior building envelope as well as high outside temperature cause heat flow into the building interior. Solar radiation absorbed by a wall and outdoor temperature may be combined into an equivalent temperature known as sol-air temperature T_{eo} (ASHRAE 1989).

Part of the solar radiation incident on the wall outer surface is absorbed while the remainder is reflected. If the wall is covered with transparent insulation, then part of the incident solar radiation is also transmitted. A portion of the absorbed solar radiation plus heat gain from outside air is conducted into the wall; part of this conduction heat is stored in the solid wall layers, raising their temperature while the remainder reaches the room interior surfaces. Hotter surfaces exhibit a net loss of radiant heat (long wave) to colder room interior surfaces, as well as heat loss by convection to the room air, raising its temperature.

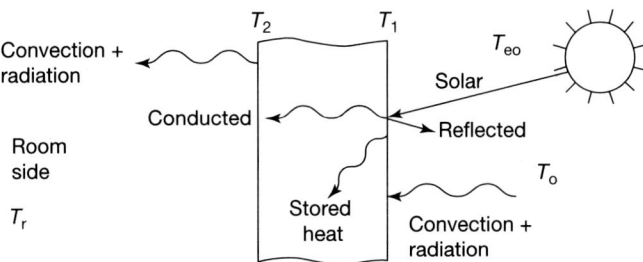

Figure 2.1 Heat exchange mechanisms for a layer of thermal mass

The heat transfer process for the wall in Figure 2.1 is governed by the following parabolic, diffusion-type partial differential equation:

$$\partial T/\partial t = \alpha \partial^2 T/\partial x^2 \tag{2.3}$$

with boundary conditions ($x = 0$ corresponds to exterior surface)
(i) at $x = 0$

$$q = -k\partial T/\partial x = G + h_o(T_o - T_1) = h_o(T_{eo} - T_1) \tag{2.3a}$$

where the sol-air temperature, $T_{eo} = T_o + \alpha_s G/h_o$
(ii) at $x = L$

$$q = h_i(T_2 - T_r) \tag{2.3b}$$

where α is thermal diffusivity, k thermal conductivity, α_s solar absorptance, q heat flux and h heat transfer coefficient.

One-dimensional conduction through the walls is generally assumed, as well as uniform irradiation of their surfaces by solar radiation. However, when thermal bridges are present, such as at corners in rooms and for heat loss through the floor, two-dimensional or three-dimensional analysis is required.

2.1.1 Special cases of one-dimensional heat transfer with analytical solution

HEAT CONDUCTION IN SEMI-INFINITE SLAB

Heat conduction in a semi-infinite slab is the closest one-dimensional model for heat transfer to the ground. Although not an exact representation of real situations, it can provide preliminary estimates which may be used to validate more detailed numerical models.

A semi-infinite slab is a model for a body with a single plane surface ($x = 0$) and its other surfaces distant enough to ignore for time periods of interest in transient analysis. If a uniform boundary condition is applied at $x = 0$, it is reasonable to assume that this case can be analysed as transient one-dimensional conduction. One case that closely fits this model is the ground, with a uniform surface or air temperature; if we measure the soil temperature deep into the ground away from the surface, one would expect that the temperature is not significantly affected by what is happening at the surface. We have three main boundary conditions:

Case 1: Specified temperature T_s at $x = 0$ imposed at time $t = 0$ with initial uniform body temperature T_i. The solution is given by:

$$T(x,t) = T_s + (T_i - T_s) \times \text{erf}[x/2(\alpha t)^{1/2}] \tag{2.4}$$

Case 2: Specified heat flux q_s at $x = 0$ with initial temperature T_i:

$$T(x) = \frac{2q_s}{k} \sqrt{\frac{\alpha t}{\pi}} \exp\left(\frac{-x^2}{4\alpha t}\right) - \frac{q_s x}{k}\left(1 - \text{erf}\left(\frac{x}{2\sqrt{\alpha t}}\right)\right) + T_i \tag{2.5}$$

The relation between surface temperature T_s, initial temperature and heat flux is given by

$$q_s = (T_s - T_i)/2(\alpha t/\pi)^{\frac{1}{2}}$$

Case 3: Convective boundary condition h at $x = 0$, environment temperature T_e and initial temperature T_i:

$$T(x,t) = (T_e - T_i)\left[1 - \text{erf}\left(\frac{x}{2\sqrt{\alpha t}}\right) - \exp\left(\frac{hx}{k} + \frac{h^2 \alpha t}{k^2}\right)\left(1 - \text{erf}\left(\frac{x}{2\sqrt{\alpha t}} + \frac{h\sqrt{\alpha t}}{k}\right)\right)\right] + T_i \tag{2.6}$$

The heat flow at the surface at time t is given by

$$q_s = h(T_e - T_i) \times \exp(h^2 \alpha t/k^2) \times \{1 - \text{erf}[h(\alpha t)^{1/2}/k]\} \tag{2.7}$$

Example

The ground is initially at uniform temperature 20°C. If it is then subjected to a temperature of –10°C, determine the depth at which a pipe should be laid to prevent freezing.

This is case 1 of the semi-infinite model. Of course, the ground is never at a uniform initial temperature; however, for design purposes, this is an adequate model to locate the safe depth for placing the pipe to avoid freezing.

Assume soil properties:

ρ = 2000 kg/m³
c = 840 J/kg K
k = 0.9 W/m K
α = $k/\rho c$ = 5.37 × 10⁻⁷ m²/s
t = 60 days × 86 400 s/day

$$T(x,t) = -10 + (20 - -10) \times \text{erf}[x/2(\alpha t)^{\frac{1}{2}}] \tag{2.4}$$

Figure 2.2 shows the temperature variation with depth. As can be seen, the depth at which the temperature is 0°C after 60 days is about 1 m.

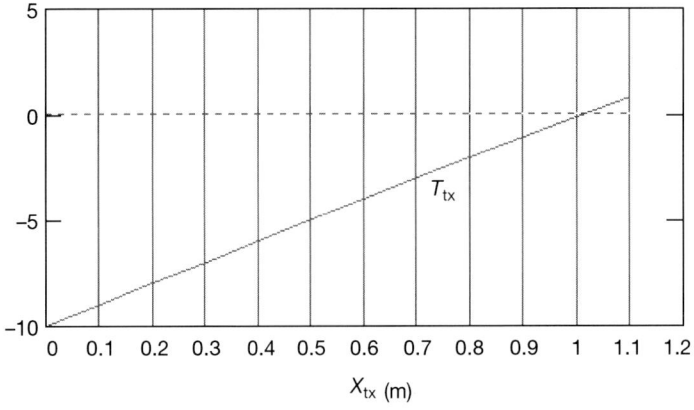

Figure 2.2 Temperature variation with depth for example (case 1)

Example

A high-intensity infrared ceiling heating system is employed to keep a factory floor warm. If the heating system is switched on with the floor initially at temperature 10°C, determine the radiant heat flux intensity on the floor required to warm the floor surface to a temperature of 20°C after time t. What is the floor temperature at the bottom surface of the concrete slab?

Assume that the concrete floor slab is 20cm thick and that the semi-infinite model case 2 applies.

Concrete properties:

$\rho = 2200 \ \text{kg/m}^3$

$c = 840 \ \text{J/kg K}$

$k = 1.7 \ \text{W/m K}$

$\alpha = k/\rho c = 9.66 \times 10^{-7} \ \text{m}^2\text{/s}$

$q_s = (20 - 10)k/2(\alpha t/\pi)^{\frac{1}{2}} = 147.5 \text{W/m}^2$

Now, we will determine the temperature as a function of depth using equation 2.5 with $t = 3$ hours.

Examination of the temperature variation (Figure 2.3) with depth at $t = 3$ hours shows that the heat flux on the surface has no significant effect below a depth of 0.2m. Therefore, the present model is satisfactory. Note that if there was a significant heating of the lower boundary of the slab then heat loss through this boundary would have to be included in the analysis.

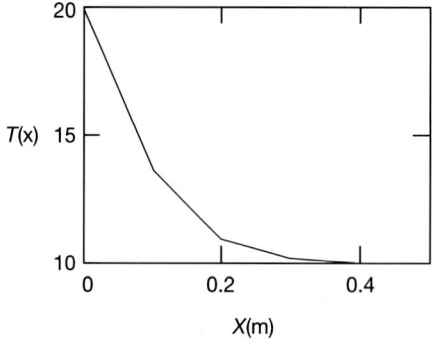

Figure 2.3 Temperature variation with depth for example (case 2)

Example

A floor slab made of concrete 30cm thick is initially at a uniform temperature 20°C. Suddenly, one of its surfaces is subjected to convective cooling with a heat transfer coefficient of 14W/m²K into an environment at 30°C. Calculate the temperature at various depths from the surface at time t after the change.

Concrete properties:

$\rho = 2200 \ \text{kg/m}^3$

$c = 840 \ \text{J/kg K}$

$k = 1.7 \ \text{W/m K}$

$\alpha = k/\rho c = 9.66 \times 10^{-7}$ m^2/s
$h = 14$ W/m^2 K
$T_e = 30°C$
$T_i = 20°C$

Substituting in equation 2.6 and calculating the temperature at two depths (surface and bottom) we obtain the results in Figure 2.4.

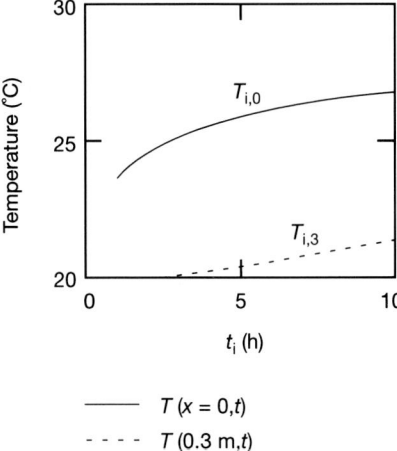

$T (x = 0,t)$
$T (0.3 \text{ m},t)$

Figure 2.4 Temperature variation with time for two depths ($x = 0$ m, $x = 0.3$ m) for example (case 3 of semi-infinite solid–convective boundary condition)

WALL WITH INTERNAL HEAT GENERATION

Heat may be generated within a wall. For example, electric radiant panels, which often form the interior layer of a ceiling or a wall to provide radiant heat, contain electric resistance elements that generate heat. This heat can be approximated as internal heat generation.

We often may assume one-dimensional heat conduction. If a steady-state analysis is performed then the relevant energy balance is given by the following ordinary differential equation:

$$kd^2T/dx^2 + Q = 0 \tag{2.8}$$

where k is the thermal conductivity of the wall layer and Q is the rate of internal heat generation. Consider, for example, a radiant panel of area 1m^2 and thickness 13mm made of gypsum board with electric resistance elements built into it with a total power output of 100W assumed to be uniformly generated within the panel (Figure 2.5).

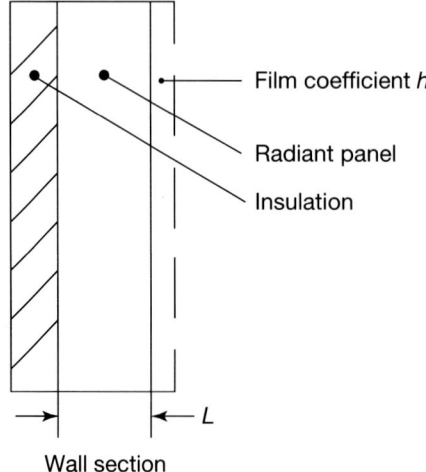

Wall section

Figure 2.5 Radiant panel built into wall

Boundary conditions:
1. At $x = 0$ – adiabatic: $dT/dx = 0$
2. At $x = L$ – convective: $-kdT/dx = h(T - T_{room})$

Solution:
$$T(x) = T_{room} + Q(L/h - (L^2 - x^2)/2k)$$
For the particular case of gypsum board (Figure 2.6) assume
$L = 13$ mm, $k = 0.16$ W/m K, $T_{room} = 20°C$, $h = 12$ W/m²°C

CONDUCTION SHAPE FACTORS

Conduction shape factors are convenient parameters for expressing the effect of geometry in two-dimensional heat transfer problems, usually involving a source and a sink. The conduction shape factor S is defined based on the relationship:

$$q = kSD_T \qquad (2.9)$$

where q is heat flow, k the thermal conductivity and D_T the temperature difference between source and sink. The factors S have been determined for various situations with analytical techniques. One useful case is that of a pipe buried in soil.

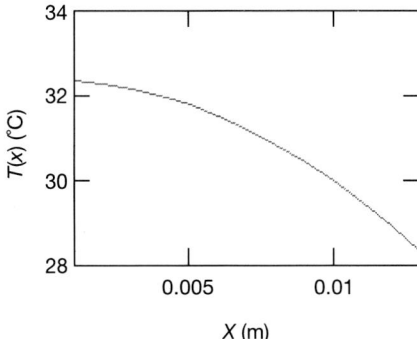

Figure 2.6 Temperature variation with distance from room surface for gypsum panel

Example

Consider a long pipe of diameter D, length L and temperature T_p buried horizontally at a depth z in soil with constant surface temperature T_s.

$L = 20$ m, $D = 0.2$ m, $T_s = 0°C$, $T_p = 70°C$, $k = 0.7$ W/m K

The variation of heat loss from the pipe with depth at which it is buried is given in Figure 2.7.

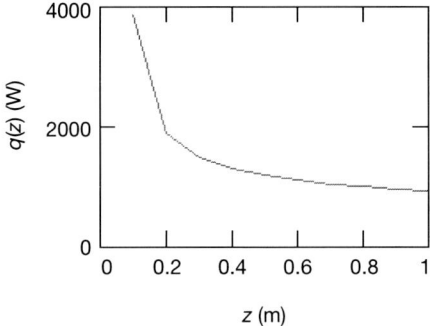

Figure 2.7 Variation of heat loss from isothermal pipe buried at depth z horizontally

2.2 Natural and forced convection

When a fluid is locally heated or cooled its density changes relative to that of the surrounding fluid and a buoyancy force is created which causes the warmer and lighter fluid to rise; cooler parts of the surrounding fluid descend and a natural circulation pattern is created. This process is observed in a direct gain passive solar zone as shown in Figure 2.8.

The floor, which is heated by incoming solar radiation, warms the air, which rises along the back wall and the ceiling and then descends along the cooler window surface – getting cooled until it reaches the floor. This process is known as **natural convection**. It is the basic process for transfer of heat by fluids in passive solar buildings.

Usually heat transfer by convection is described by a linearized heat transfer coefficient h_c:

$$q = Ah_c(T_w - T_{ai}) \qquad (2.10)$$

where T_w and T_{ai} are wall and air temperatures respectively. Before considering simplified relationships for h_c for air, which can be linearized to obtain constant h_c values, we will consider a simple form of the general (Navier–Stokes) fluid flow equations for two-dimensional natural and forced convection.

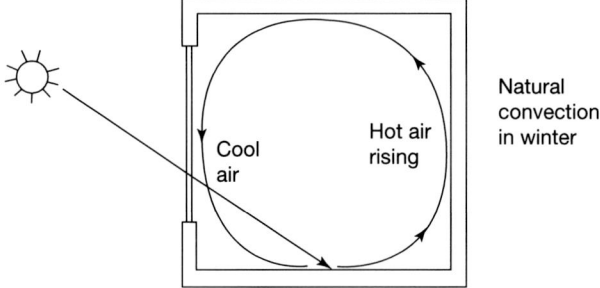

Figure 2.8 Natural convection in a direct gain room in winter

Forced convection is the fluid flow caused by an external force or device, which imposes a free stream velocity U_o. The basic differential equations that describe fluid flow are the continuity (conservation of mass), momentum and energy equations.

These are given below in dimensionless form as follows for two dimensions for a boundary layer over a plate of length L (in the x direction and free-stream flow U_o in the same direction).

Continuity, which expresses the conservation of mass:

$$\frac{\partial U}{\partial X} + \frac{\partial V}{\partial Y} = 0 \qquad (2.11)$$

where $U = u/U_o$, $X = x/L$, $Y = y/L$, $V = v/U_o$ with u and v being the velocity components in x and y directions, U_o the free stream velocity.

Momentum:

$$U\frac{\partial U}{\partial X} + V\frac{\partial V}{\partial Y} = -\frac{dP}{dX} + \frac{1}{Re}\frac{\partial^2 U}{\partial Y^2} \qquad (2.12a)$$

where $P = p/(\rho/U_o^2)$.

Energy conservation:

$$U\frac{\partial T}{\partial X} + V\frac{\partial T}{\partial Y} = \frac{1}{Re \cdot Pr}\frac{\partial^2 T}{\partial Y^2} \qquad (2.12b)$$

where T is dimensionless temperature $T = (T' - T_o)/(T_s - T_o)$; T' = fluid temperature at (x,y), T_s = plate temperature and T_o is free stream temperature.

In the case of combined natural and forced convection over a plate the momentum equation becomes (with the addition of a buoyancy term):

$$U\frac{\partial U}{\partial X} + V\frac{\partial V}{\partial Y} = -\frac{dP}{dX} + \frac{1}{Re}\frac{\partial^2 U}{\partial Y^2} + \frac{Gr}{Re^2}T \qquad (2.12c)$$

The dimensionless numbers employed in the above equations are:

$Re =$ Reynolds number $= U_o L/v$ (ratio of inertia and viscous forces)
$Pr =$ Prandtl number $= v/\alpha =$ kinematic viscosity/thermal diffusivity
$Gr =$ Grashof number $= g\beta\Delta T L^3/(v^2) =$ ratio of buoyancy to viscous forces
  where $\beta = 1/T$, expansion coefficient for air (approximated as ideal gas) at temperature T, K
$Ra =$ Rayleigh number $= g\beta\Delta T L^3/(v\alpha) = Gr\,Pr$
$Nu =$ Nusselt number $= hL/k =$ dimensionless heat transfer coefficient (for $Nu = 1$ we have pure conduction across an air layer with $h = L/k$).

Heat flow relationships that apply to different fluids are often obtained experimentally and then expressed as correlations of the dimensionless numbers discussed above. Based on these general correlations we develop specific equations that apply to airflow in buildings, air heating devices, etc. These equations are often linearized and approximate representative values of heat transfer coefficients are obtained for use in linear thermal system analysis.

When a detailed analysis of heat and fluid flow in 3D is desired the usual approach is discretization in space and time using the control volume method. Numerical techniques are extensively applied to passive solar analysis in Chapter 3; numerical and spatial discretization is usually applied to conduction heat transfer because of its dominant role in energy storage, thermal lag effect and room temperature fluctuation. Detailed numerical analysis of convection heat transfer is not usually necessary for building design purposes.

2.2.1 Natural convection in wall cavities and windows

Cavities (air spaces) exist in walls, windows, etc. The unit cavity conductance is given for different surface emissivities in several design handbooks (ASHRAE 1989). This conductance is the sum of the radiative and convective heat transfer coefficients. Here, we consider primarily the convective coefficient. Combined radiation and convection are considered in Section 2.4.

There are a number of relationships for heat transfer by convection across a rectangular cavity. These are usually correlations of experimental data in terms of three dimensionless parameters: the Nusselt number Nu, the Rayleigh number Ra, and the Prandtl number Pr.

The convective heat transfer coefficient (h_c) for vertical cavities (Figure 2.9) is conveniently determined as follows (see ElSherbiny et al. 1982):

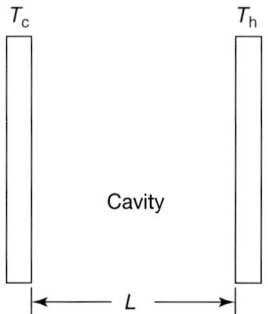

T_c = cold glazing temperature, T_h = hot glazing temperature

Figure 2.9 Cavity (window or in wall)

T_c = cold glazing temperature, T_h = hot glazing temperature
Thermal conductivity of air:

$$k_{air} = 0.002528T_m^{1.5}/(T_m + 200) \tag{2.13a}$$

$$Ra = 2.737(1 + 2a)^2a^4(T_h - T_c)L^3p^2 \tag{2.13b}$$

$$Nu_1 = 0.0605Ra^{1/3} \tag{2.13c}$$

$$Nu_2 = [1 + 0.104Ra^{0.293}/(1 + (6310/Ra)^{1.36})^3]^{1/3} \tag{2.13d}$$

$$h_c = \max(Nu_1, Nu_2)k_{air}/L \tag{2.13e}$$

The variation of heat transfer coefficient with gap thickness is shown in Figure 2.10. Note that the convective heat transfer coefficient h_c reaches its minimum value for a cavity width equal to 13mm.

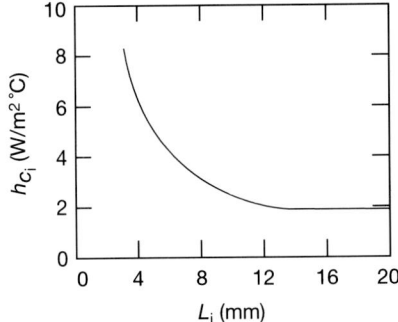

Figure 2.10 Variation of convective coefficient for a vertical cavity with width L_i

2.2.2 Convective heat transfer coefficients in rooms

For heat flow downward, that is conduction across the air-film, the following correlation is recommended (McAdams 1959). We apply it here to a cold floor. Laminar flow is assumed with Rayleigh number in the range 3×10^5 to 3×10^{10}.

$$h_c = 0.59[(T_s - T_{ai})/L]^{1/4} \tag{2.14}$$

where T_s = surface temperature, T_{ai} = air temperature and L = characteristic dimension (m).

Figure 2.11 shows the variation of h_c with T_s. Typically, an h_c in the range 0.6–0.7°C would be expected for cold floors in the winter.

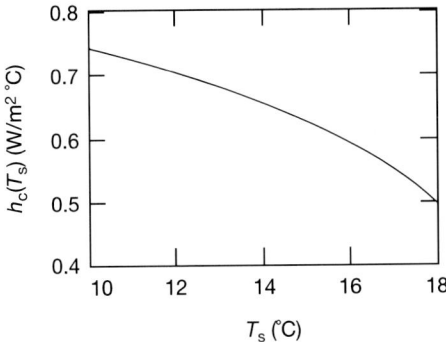

Figure 2.11 Variation of convective coefficient for heat flow downward – horizontal surface, $T_{ai} = 20°C$, $L = 1$ m

For **heat flow upward**, such as on a heated floor, the following turbulent flow relationship for air is recommended:

$$h_c = 1.52(T_s - T_{ai})^{1/3} \qquad (2.15)$$

Figure 2.12 depicts the variation of h_c with surface temperature. Thus, for a floor heating system, if the average surface temperature is 26°C and the room temperature 20°C, then h_c is about 3.1 W/m²°C.

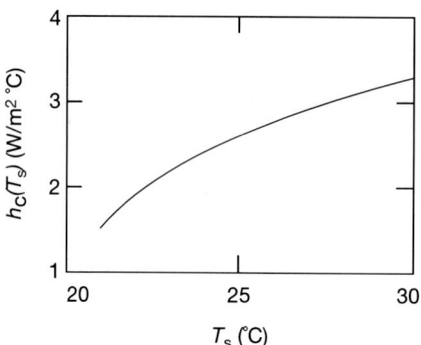

Figure 2.12 Variation of convective coefficient for heat flow upward – horizontal surface, $T_{ai} = 20°C$

For **vertical surfaces** we have horizontal heat flow, which is independent of direction. Because flow is well developed after a short distance from the bottom or top of a wall, it is generally turbulent, and the following correlation is often used for h_c (MacAdams 1959):

$$h_c = 1.31(T_s - T_{ai})^{1/3} \qquad (2.16)$$

The Rayleigh number is assumed to be over 10^9.

The detailed variation of h_c with temperature difference is plotted in Figure 2.13. Generally, h_c would be expected to vary in the range 2–3 W/m²°C, most of the time being near the low end.

Note that the above relationships give values of h_c averaged over a wall – there could be considerable variation of the local h_c depending on flow development and local geometry. There is also considerable disagreement among different researchers and organizations on recommended values for h_c to be used in building energy analysis. Table 2.1 gives different values of h_c recommended by various organizations.

In residential buildings the air in each room is usually assumed to be at a uniform temperature. General equations, derived by various workers from correlations of

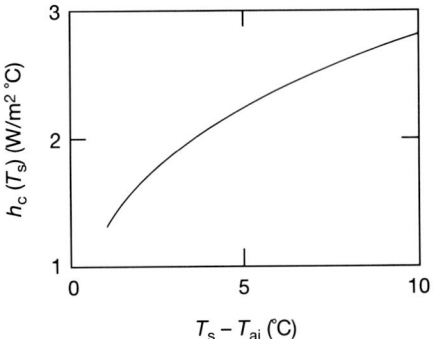

Figure 2.13 Variation of convective coefficient for heat flow at a vertical surface as a function of temperature difference

experimental results for convective heat transfer from plane surfaces, are described by Raithby and Hollands (1984). The heat flow depends on the surface inclination and whether the flow is laminar or turbulent. Equations for convection in buildings are given by ASHRAE (1989).

Convective heat transfer coefficients are typically linearized by calculating constant values based on assumed temperature differences between air and a surface. For routine analysis, detailed hourly simulation programs usually employ constant convective coefficients. The convective heat transfer coefficients suggested by ASHRAE, the corresponding British organization CIBSE, and by Kimura (1977), are given in Table 2.1

Table 2.1 Convective heat transfer coefficients ($W/K/m^2$) for winter conditions and still air

Surface	Reference		
	ASHRAE (1981)	*CIBSE (1976)*	*Kimura (1977)*
Vertical	3.08	3.0	3.5
Horizontal – heat flow down	1.0	1.5	1.0
Horizontal	4.0	4.3	4.0

2.2.3 Natural convection between rooms

In passive solar buildings, where a significant temperature swing is permitted in a direct-gain room connected through a doorway to a north-facing room, temperature differences of 1–7°C may exist between the air in the two rooms, leading to a significant amount of heat being transferred by natural convection.

Bauman *et al.* (1983) developed a correlation based on the temperature difference between a hot driving surface in a room and a cold heated surface in the other room.

The interzone convective coefficient is given by

$$h_{iz} = 73C_{iz}(H_d T_{ab})^{\frac{1}{2}} \tag{2.17}$$

where H_d is the door height, and C_{iz} is a constant depending on room geometry (between 0.65 and 1.0). The temperature difference T_{ab} is equal to $(T(1a) - T(1b))$ for the case of two zones with temperatures $T(1a)$ and $T(1b)$; a constant value must be assumed for linearization (this is the standard procedure also used for surface convective coefficients).

2.3 Radiation heat transfer

Thermal radiation is electromagnetic radiation emitted by a body as a function of its temperature. All types of radiation are propagated at the speed of light, 3×10^8 m/s. The speed c is equal to

$$c = \lambda v \tag{2.18}$$

where λ = wavelength and v = frequency.

Thermal radiation is in the range from about 0.1 to 100μm. The visible portion lies in the range of about 0.35–0.75μm. In building thermal analysis we generally separate thermal radiation into two regions – the short-wave region with wavelength less than or equal to 3μm and the long-wave region with wavelength greater than 3μm. More than 99% of the radiation emitted by the sun is short wave, while more than 99% of the radiation emitted by bodies at earth temperatures (–40°C to 45°C) is long wave.

Radiation may be also described with quantum mechanics, which stipulates that it is propagated as discrete quanta, each quantum having energy

$$E = hv \tag{2.19a}$$

where h = Planck's constant = 6.625×10^{-34} J s.

Based on the principle of relativity we also have

$$E = mc^2 \tag{2.19b}$$

Applying quantum-statistical thermodynamics, an expression for the radiation density may then be obtained per unit volume and unit wavelength as:

$$u_\lambda = \frac{8\pi h_c \lambda^{-5}}{\rho^{hc/(\lambda kT)} - 1} \tag{2.19c}$$

where k = 1.38066×10^{-23} J/(molecule K) (Boltzmann constant).

When the above expression is integrated over all wavelengths, we obtain the total thermal radiation emitted by a blackbody. Its emissive power is given by the Stephan–Boltzmann law:

$$E_b = \sigma T^4 \tag{2.20}$$

where $\sigma = 5.669 \times 10^{-8}$ W/m^2 K^4 and temperature is in kelvin.

The spectral emissive power of a blackbody is given by

$$E_{b\lambda} = C_1 \lambda^{-5}/[\exp(C_2/\lambda T) - 1] \tag{2.21}$$

where λ = wavelength (μm), T = temperature (K), $C_1 = 3.743 \times 10^8$ W μm^4/m^2 and $C_2 = 1.4387 \times 10^4$ W μm/K.

The spectral emissive power is related to u_λ by

$$E_{b\lambda} = u_\lambda c/4 \tag{2.22}$$

A blackbody is a body that emits the maximum possible amount of radiation and absorbs all radiation incident on it – hence the term blackbody as it appears black to the eye.

Figure 2.14 shows the spectral emissive power of the sun, approximated as a black body at 6000K. The peak of all spectral emissive power curves may be shown (by differentiating equation 2.21 and setting it equal to 0) to satisfy Wien's displacement law:

$$\lambda_{max} T = 2897.6 \text{ μm K} \tag{2.23}$$

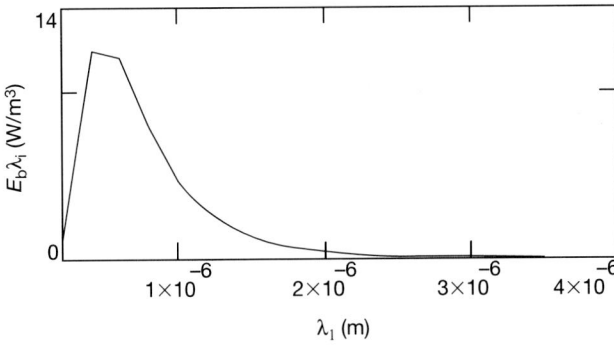

Figure 14 Spectral emissive power of the sun

Note that the peak emissive power of the sun lies in the visible region. The area under the curve is equal to the emissive power E_b given by equation 2.20.

We often need to determine the fraction of emitted radiation f_{12} in a given wavelength range $\lambda_1 - \lambda_2$.

$$f_{12} = \frac{\displaystyle\int_{\lambda_1}^{\lambda_2} \frac{C_1}{\lambda^5 \left(\exp\left(\dfrac{C_2}{\lambda T}\right) - 1 \right)} \, d\lambda}{\sigma T^4} \tag{2.24}$$

Example

A tungsten filament is heated to 2400 K. What fraction of the radiation is in the visible range?

Equation 2.24 is applied and evaluated numerically with $\lambda_1 = 0.38\ \mu m$, $\lambda_2 = 0.78\ \mu m$ and $T = 2400$ K.

$$f_{12} = 0.048$$

Therefore only 5% of emitted radiation is in the visible range.

RADIATION PROPERTIES

The absorptance of a surface is the fraction of total irradiation (incident radiation) absorbed by the body. The reflectance of the surface is equal to the fraction of the irradiation reflected from the surface. The transmittance of surface is the fraction of the irradiation transmitted by the surface (equal to 0 for opaque surfaces). An energy balance at the surfaces shows that

$$\rho + \tau + \alpha = 1$$

where ρ = reflectivity, τ = transmittance and α = absorptance.

Emissivity, absorptance, transmittance and reflectance generally vary with wavelength. It can be shown that the monochromatic emissivity and absorptance of a surface are equal.

$$\varepsilon_\lambda = E_\lambda / E_{b\lambda} \tag{2.25}$$

The total hemispherical emissivity of a surface is equal to the ratio of the total hemispherical emitted radiation to the total blackbody emissive power:

$$\varepsilon = \frac{\displaystyle\int_0^\infty \varepsilon_\lambda E_{b\lambda} \, d\lambda}{\sigma T^4} \tag{2.26}$$

Example

The total hemispherical emissivity of aluminium paint is 0.30 at wavelengths below 3 mm and 0.7 at longer wavelengths. Determine the total emissivity at a room temperature of 20°C:

$$\varepsilon = \frac{\int_{0.1\mu m}^{3\mu m} \varepsilon_s \dfrac{c_1}{\lambda^5 \left[\exp\left(\dfrac{c_2}{\lambda T_1}\right) - 1\right]} d\lambda + \int_{3\mu m}^{100\mu m} \varepsilon_1 \dfrac{c_1}{\lambda^5 \left[\exp\left(\dfrac{c_2}{\lambda T_1}\right) - 1\right]} d\lambda}{\sigma T_1^4}$$

$$\varepsilon = 0.697$$

As can be seen, at low temperatures the emissivity is equal to the long-wave emissivity.

Grey bodies are surfaces with radiation properties whose values can be approximated as independent of wavelength. An acceptable approximation in building thermal analysis is selective grey surfaces; a surface may be assumed to be grey over specific wavelength ranges and associated temperature ranges.

For example, using the integration technique of the previous example, a long-wave emissivity of approximately 0.85–0.90 is determined for most building materials and paints (not metals) at ordinary temperatures. However, the solar (short-wave) absorptance of a glossy white surface, for example, can be as low as 0.2.

2.3.1 Calculation of view factors between room surfaces

The view factor, or shape factor F_{ij} from surface i to surface j, is equal to the fraction of diffuse radiation leaving surface i which is directly incident on surface j. The view factor between two surfaces at distance r is given by

$$A_1 F_{1,2} = \int_{A_1}\int_{A_2} (\cos \varphi_1 \cos \varphi_2 / \pi r^2) dA_1 dA_2 \tag{2.27}$$

where r is the distance between the two areas and φ_1 and φ_2 are the angles between the local normals to the surfaces and the ray r connecting the two surfaces (Figure 2.15). The above equation may integrated analytically in some cases. When this is not possible, numerical integration techniques may be applied, replacing the integrals with summations over the discretized surfaces.

There are three main types of view factors between room surfaces:

- between surfaces at right angle,
- between parallel surfaces, and
- between the window and another surface.

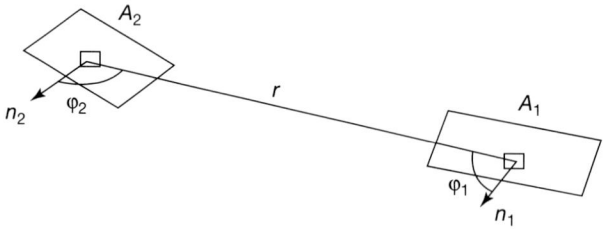

Figure 2.15 View factor F_{12} geometry

The view factors for the room below are determined after first calculating the view factor between two rectangular finite surfaces inclined at 90° to each other with one common surface as follows:

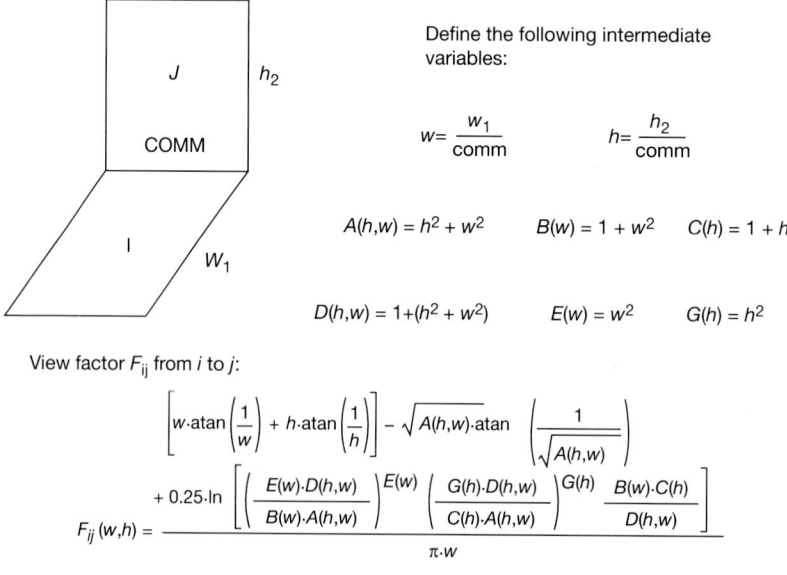

Define the following intermediate variables:

$$w= \frac{w_1}{comm} \qquad h= \frac{h_2}{comm}$$

$$A(h,w) = h^2 + w^2 \qquad B(w) = 1 + w^2 \qquad C(h) = 1 + h^2$$

$$D(h,w) = 1+(h^2 + w^2) \qquad E(w) = w^2 \qquad G(h) = h^2$$

View factor F_{ij} from i to j:

$$F_{ij}(w,h) = \frac{\left[w\cdot atan\left(\frac{1}{w}\right) + h\cdot atan\left(\frac{1}{h}\right) \right] - \sqrt{A(h,w)}\cdot atan\left(\frac{1}{\sqrt{A(h,w)}}\right) + 0.25\cdot ln\left[\left(\frac{E(w)\cdot D(h,w)}{B(w)\cdot A(h,w)}\right)^{E(w)} \left(\frac{G(h)\cdot D(h,w)}{C(h)\cdot A(h,w)}\right)^{G(h)} \frac{B(w)\cdot C(h)}{D(h,w)}\right]}{\pi\cdot w}$$

Figure 2.16 Calculation of view factor between two perpendicular surfaces

The other view factors between the room surfaces are calculated by applying the following principles:

- Reciprocity

$$A_i F_{i,j} = A_j F_{j,i} \qquad\qquad\qquad (2.28a)$$

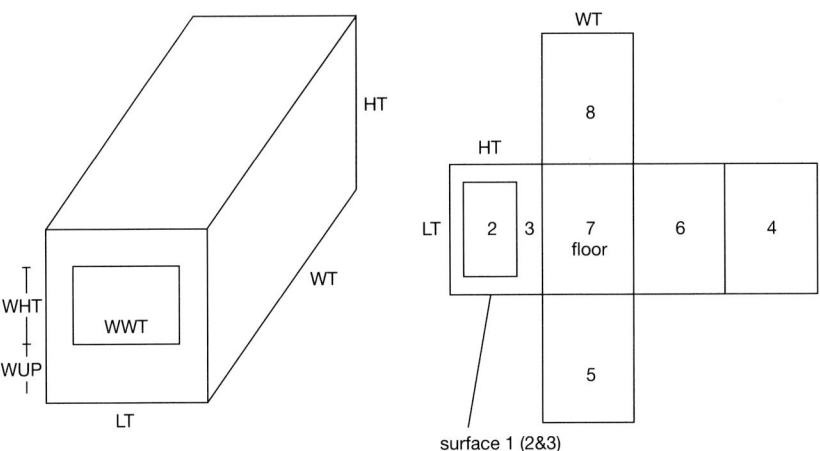

Figure 2.17 Room geometry for view factor calculation

- Symmetry:

   e.g. $F_{7,8} = F_{7,5}$

- Energy conservation:

   $\Sigma_j F_{i,j} = 1$ for any surface i (2.28b)

Example

Calculate the view factors for a room with dimensions HT = 2.8 m, LT = 4.0 m, WT = 6.0 m, WWT = 3.0 m, WUP = 0.4 m, WHT = 1.6 m. We set COMM = LT in the function of Figure 2.16, W1 = HT and H2 = WT and we compute:

$$F_{6,7} = F_{ij}(HT/LT, WT/LT) = 0.268$$

Applying reciprocity:

$$F_{7,6} = A_6 F_{6,7}/A_7 = 0.125$$

From symmetry $F_{6,4} = F_{6,7}$ and $F_{4,6} = F_{7,6}$. Then for $F_{6,5}$ we set w1 = LT, h2 =WT and COMM = HT.

$$F_{6,5} = F_{ij}(LT/HT, WT/HT) = 0.191$$

Applying reciprocity we find $F_{6,5} = 0.127$.
From symmetry: $F_{8,5} = F_{5,6}, F_{1,5} = F_{6,8}, F_{5,1} = F_{8,6}, F_{1,8} = F_{6,8}, F_{8,1} = F_{8,6}.$

Using the function F_{ij} with w1 = HT, H2 = LT and COMM = WT we find:

$$F_{8,4} = 0.276$$
$$F_{4,8} = 0.193$$

From symmetry:

$$F_{5,7} = F_{8,4}$$
$$F_{7,5} = F_{4,8}$$
$$F_{4,5} = F_{4,8}$$
$$F_{5,4} = F_{8,4}$$
$$F_{7,8} = F_{7,5}$$
$$F_{8,7} = F_{5,7}$$
$$F_{4,8} = F_{7,8}$$
$$F_{8,4} = F_{8,7}$$

Now, we may apply equation 2.28b to determine the view factors between opposite parallel surfaces:

$$F_{1,6} = 1 - 2 \times F_{6,8} - 2 \times F_{6,4} = 0.082$$

and $F_{1,6} = F_{6,1}$ (equal areas)

$$F_{5,8} = 1 - 2 \times F_{5,4} - 2 \times F_{5,6} = 0.194$$

and $F_{8,5} = F_{5,8}$

$$F_{4,7} = 1 - 2 \times F_{4,8} - 2 \times F_{4,6} = 0.364$$

and $F_{7,4} = F_{4,7}$

Now, using the same techniques and Figure 2.18 one may determine the view factors between the window and the other surfaces. Note that surface 1 is subdivided into nine surfaces and so are the adjacent surfaces (we do not need to repeat the calculation for the other surfaces as the window is located in the centre of surface 1).

After similar calculations for Fab_c1c2d2 and Fa_c1c2, Fab_c2d, Fa_c2, Fb_d we may calculate the view factor between the window and the floor.

$$\text{Fa\_2d: } = \frac{(Aab \cdot Fab\_c1c2d2 - Aa \cdot Fa\_c1c2 - Ab \cdot Fb\_2d)}{2 \cdot Aa}$$

$$\text{Fa\_d: } = \frac{Aab \cdot Fab\_c2d - Aa \cdot Fa\_c2 - Ab \cdot Fb\_d}{2 \cdot Aa} \qquad \text{F2\_a } := (Fa\_2d - Fa\_d) \cdot \frac{Aa}{A2}$$

$$F_{2,7} := 2 \cdot F2\_a + F2\_b \qquad F_{2,7} = 0.27 \qquad F_{7,2} := A2 \cdot \frac{F_{2,7}}{A7} \qquad F_{7,2} := 0.054$$

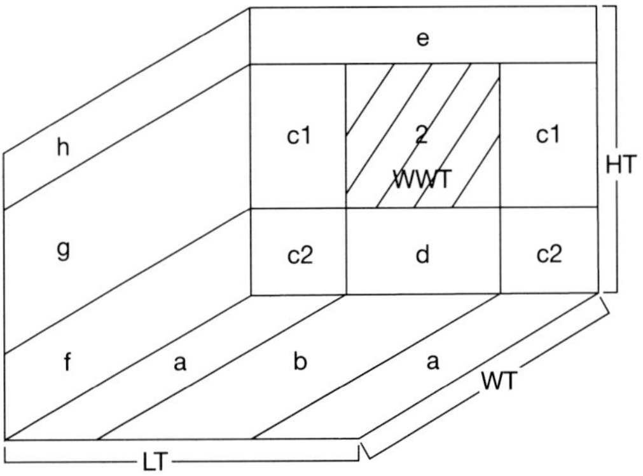

$$Ab := WWT \cdot WT$$

$$Ad := WWT \cdot WUP$$

$$A2 := WWT \cdot WHT$$

$$DIS := \frac{LT - WWT}{2}$$

$$Ac1 := WHT \cdot DIS \qquad Ac2 := WUP \cdot DIS \qquad Aa := DIS \cdot WT \qquad Aab := WT \cdot (DIS + WWT)$$

$$w1 := WT \qquad h2 := WHT + WUP \qquad comm := WWT \qquad w := \frac{w1}{comm} \qquad h := \frac{h2}{comm}$$

$$Fb\_2d := Fij(w, h) \qquad\qquad ..F \text{ from Ab to A2 + Ad}$$

Figure 2.18 Schematic used in calculation of view factors between window and walls

2.3.2 Radiative exchange between two surfaces

The net radiative heat exchange between black surfaces 1 and 2 emitting radiation E_{b1} and E_{b2} is given by

$$q_{r1-2} = A_1 F_{1,2}(E_{b1} - E_{b2}) = A_1 F_{1,2} \sigma(T_1^4 - T_2^4) \qquad (2.29)$$

When grey surfaces exchange radiation we have a more complex relationship because part of the radiation incident on a surface is reflected, and in an enclosure we have an infinite number of reflections. In this case we may define a radiation exchange factor F' which is a function of view factors and surface emissivities.

$$q_{r1-2} = A_1 F'_{1,2}(E_{b1} - E_{b2}) = A_1 F'_{1,2} \sigma(T_1^4 - T_2^4) \qquad (2.29a)$$

where $F'_{1,2} = f(F_{i,j}, \varepsilon_i)$.

The exchange factor between two parallel planes is given in the next section which calculates total thermal resistance in a cavity.

2.4 Convective and radiative heat transfer coefficients

2.4.1 Thermal resistance of cavities

The great majority of thermal insulation materials owe their resistance to heat flow to a cellular structure with isolated air cavities. Thus, cavities are also employed in walls, windows and other building components to reduce heat transfer, while simultaneously they retard transmission of water vapour due to capillary action; in windows they also transmit solar radiation.

Cavities usually contain air. However, in newer, high-technology windows, they may also contain a vacuum or rare gases such as argon in order to reduce convection heat transfer. The unit conductance is given for different emissivities of the two cavity surfaces in several design handbooks (ASHRAE 1989). The total heat transfer coefficient of a cavity is equal to the sum of the radiative (h_r) and convective (h_c) heat transfer coefficients.

Convective heat transfer through a cavity may be calculated by a number of correlations reviewed by Daskalaki *et al.* (1994). The variation of convective coefficient based on a correlation (ElSherbiny *et al.*) (Figs 2.10 and 2.11) for a vertical cavity as a function of width is given in Table 2.2. Values given are based on an outside temperature of 35°C and an inside temperature of 25°C.

Table 2.2 Convective heat transfer coefficient for sealed vertical cavities (summer conditions)

Cavity width (mm)	h_c (W/m²°C)
6	4.4
8	3.1
10	2.6
12	2.2
14	1.9

The cavity convective heat transfer coefficient does not change significantly for widths larger than about 13 mm. The change is even smaller for winter conditions. The radiative heat transfer coefficient between two parallel surfaces in a cavity is given by

$$h_r = \sigma F'_{12}(4T_m^3) \tag{2.30}$$

where

$\sigma = 5.67 \times 10^{-8}$ W/m^2 K^4 (Stefan–Boltzmann constant)

$T_m = (T_1 + T_2)/2$ (mean temperature, K)

$F'_{12} = 1/[(1/\varepsilon_1) + (1/\varepsilon_2) - 1]$ (radiation exchange factor)

The term $(4T_m^3)$ is a linearization factor for radiation heat transfer (approximately equal to $[T_1^4 - T_2^4]/[T_1 - T_2]$).

Most building materials have a high emissivity, about 0.85–0.95, and radiation usually accounts for about two-thirds of the heat transfer in a cavity. The radiative coefficient is about 5.0 W/m^2 K for regular glass surfaces with emissivities of about 0.9. When a low-emissivity coating is applied on one of the two surfaces facing the cavity h_r is reduced to 0.6 W/m^2 K, i.e. a dramatic reduction of about 90%. Therefore, low-emissivity coating (emissivity 0.05–0.1) is one of the most cost-effective techniques to reduce radiation heat transfer through a double-glazed window.

For a wall with an aluminium foil on one side and a width of 12 mm, the total heat transfer coefficient is therefore given by

$$h = h_c + h_r = 2.2 + 0.6 = 2.8 \text{ W/m}^2 \text{ K}$$

For a window, the value would be 7.4 without a low-e coating and 2.8 with a low-e coating. Note that this value is accurate near the centre of the window. Near the frame we have edge effects.

2.5 Bibliography

ASHRAE (1989) *ASHRAE Handbook – Fundamentals*, Atlanta, Georgia, USA.

ASTM (1989) Guarded Hot Box Test (C236) *ASTM Book of Standards*, ASTM USA.

ASTM (1989) Calibrated Hot Box Test (C976) *ASTM Book of Standards*, ASTM USA.

Athienitis A.K. (1998) *Building Thermal Analysis*, Electronic Mathcad Book, 2nd edn MathSoft, Boston, USA.

Bauman F., Anderson B. and Carroll W.L. (1981) 'Verification of BLAST by comparison with measurements of a solar-dominated test cell and a thermally massive building', *Proc. of ASME Solar Ener. Div. 3rd Annual Conf.*, Reno, Nevada, pp. 299–307.

Bauman F., Gadgil A., Kammerud R., Altmayer E. and Nansteel M. (1983) 'Convective heat transfer in buildings: recent research results', *ASHRAE Transactions,* **89** Pt.1, paper no. 2750.

Daskalaki E., Santamouris M., Balaras C.A. and Asimakopoulos D. (1994) 'Natural convection heat transfer coefficients from vertical and horizontal surfaces for building applications', *Energy and Buildings,* **20**, 243–249.

Dick H.V. and Linden G.P. (1994) 'PASSYS test method for thermal and solar characteristics of building components', European Conf. on Energy Performance and Indoor Climate in Buildings, Lyon, France, Nov., pp. 1092–1097.

Dijk H.A.L. and Linden G.P. (1994) 'The PASSYS test method for thermal and solar characterization of building components', European Conf. on Energy Performance and Indoor Climate in Buildings, Lyon, France, Nov., pp. 1092–1097.

ElSherbiny S.M., Raithby G.D. and Hollands K.G.T. (1982) 'Heat transfer by natural convection across vertical and inclined air layers', *Journal of Heat Transfer*, **104**:1, 96–102.

Energy in Architecture – The European Passive Solar Handbook (1992) EC Publication No. 13446, Batsford, London.

Goulding J.R., Lewis O.J., Steemers T.C. *Energy Conscious Design*, Batsford for CEC, London.

Harazono Y., Shigeaki T., Nakase I. and Ikeda H. (1990) 'Effects of rooftop vegetation using artificial substrates on the urban climate and the thermal load of buildings', *Energy and Buildings*, **15**:3–4, 435–442.

LBL (1988) Window 3.1 Program, LBL25-686, USA.

McAdams W.H. (1954) *Heat Transmission*, 3rd edn McGraw-Hill, New York.

Norlen U. and Bloem J.J. (1994) 'Comparison of methods for thermal resistance estimation', European Conf. on Energy Performance and Indoor Climate in Buildings, Lyon, France, Nov., pp. 804–880.

PASSYS II (1994) Final Report, CEC.

Raithby G. and Hollands K.G.T. (1984) 'Natural convection', in *Heat Transfer Handbook*, McGraw-Hill Inc., New York.

Santamouris M. (1994) PASSPORT Manual, CEC.

Sullivan H.F. (1987) VISION computer program, Univ. of Waterloo, Canada.

CHAPTER 3

Fenestration components and systems

3.1 Window thermal and solar properties

Fenestration is an essential component of any building enclosure, in the form of windows, glass doors, skylights, sunspaces or atria. It provides the path for visual and psychological communication with the external environment. Sunlight is an essential requirement for our everyday life.

Design of fenestration systems should consider all factors that affect performance and indoor environment:

- **Net heat transfer** across the fenestration system by conduction, convection and long-wave radiation; this is usually assessed as proportional to the window effective thermal conductance (U), measured with techniques such as the guarded hot box method (ASTM 1989).
- **Net transmitted solar radiation**, some of which enters the living space directly (as diffuse or beam solar radiation). A smaller portion of the incident solar radiation is absorbed by the fenestration and part of it is transferred to the interior of the zone as infrared radiation or by convection; ASHRAE (1989) uses the concept of solar heat gain factor (SHGF) to assess this. The PASSYS (1994) test procedures in Europe denote this as the total solar heat gain factor (g); g is defined as equal to the heat flux through the component under steady conditions for zero temperature difference between indoor and outdoor environment, divided by intensity of solar radiation incident on the component.
- **Daylighting effectiveness**: assessed as a function of the illumination of the working or living space at the desired locations, and a glare index. The total amount of solar radiation incident on each room surface also depends on the solar reflectance of the room interior surfaces. The daylight factor (DF) is a commonly used parameter to assess daylighting effectiveness; it is the ratio of illumination at the point of interest (e.g. work plane) to illumination outside the fenestration due to unobstructed sky.
- **Influence of fenestration interior temperature on thermal comfort**: if this temperature is too high or too low and the window area is large, it raises or

reduces the mean radiant temperature significantly, particularly near the window.
- **Acoustic performance**, noise transmission.

Aesthetic factors such as **external view** also depend on fenestration shape, landscape and surrounding vegetation, but are difficult to assess objectively based on scientific methods.

3.1.1 Transmission of solar radiation

The solar transmittance, reflectance and absorptance of windows or other transparent building components such as solar collectors need to be determined in order to calculate how much solar radiation they transmit.

First we determine the solar properties of a layer of glass with thickness L, refractive index n and extinction coefficient k. Consider Figure 3.1.

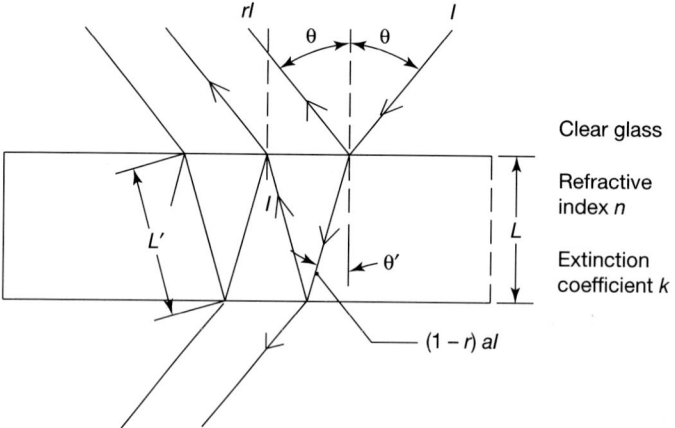

Figure 3.1 Transmission of solar radiation through glazing

Snell's law: $\sin \theta' = (\sin \theta)/n$ (3.1)

Component reflectivity (r) is the fraction of each ray component reflected. It is determined from the Fresnel relations of electromagnetic theory:

$$r = \frac{1}{2}\left[\left(\frac{\sin(\theta-\theta')}{\sin(\theta+\theta')}\right)^2 + \left(\frac{\tan(\theta-\theta')}{\tan(\theta+\theta')}\right)^2\right] \qquad L' = \frac{L}{\sqrt{1-\left(\frac{\sin(\theta)}{n}\right)^2}} \qquad (3.2)$$

The transmittance of transparent glazing decays exponentially with its extinction coefficient × thickness product. Some extinction coefficients are given in Table 3.1.

Table 3.1 Extinction coefficients

Type of glass	Extinction coefficient k (per metre)
Double strength, A quality	7.76
Clear plate glass	6.96
Heat-absorbing glass	132

The intensity $I(x)$ of radiation after it has travelled a distance x in a material is an exponential decay function of its intensity at $x = 0$, I_0 and the extinction coefficient k:

$$I(x) = I_0 e^{-kx} \tag{3.3}$$

Therefore, after travelling a distance L' as shown in Figure 3.1, the intensity is equal to

$$I(L') = I_0 a \text{ where } a = e^{-kL'}$$

The quantity $a = e^{-kL'}$ is the fraction of radiation available after each reflection in the glazing. Through simple ray-tracing techniques, one may show that

$$\tau = (1 - r)^2 a + r^2(1 - r)^2 a^3 + r^4(1 - r)^2 a^5 + \dots$$

This is a convergent geometric series. Therefore, the effective transmittance of the glazing is determined from the limit of a geometric series as:

$$\tau = (1 - r)^2 a/(1 - r^2 a^2) \tag{3.4}$$

Similarly, the effective reflectance of the glazing is

$$\rho = r + [r(1 - r)^2 a^2/(1 - r^2 a^2)] \tag{3.5}$$

The absorptance is then determined from the energy conservation relationship which states that the incident energy is equal to the amount transmitted plus the amount reflected plus the portion absorbed:

$$\alpha = 1 - \rho - \tau \tag{3.5a}$$

Note that the above properties are a function of incidence angle and wavelength.

Typically properties are averaged over two wavelength ranges:

- solar: 0.3–3 μm
- long wave: 3–30 μm.

The averaged properties are determined as a weighted average of spectral values. For example, the solar absorptance is given by:

$$\alpha_s = \frac{\int_{0.3\mu m}^{3\mu m} \alpha_\lambda I_\lambda d\lambda}{\int_{0.3\mu m}^{3\mu m} I_\lambda d\lambda} \tag{3.6}$$

For efficient conversion of solar energy to heat, a high solar absorptance and a low long-wave emissivity are required. Selective surface coatings may be used to achieve such properties.

3.1.2 Double-glazed windows

For a double-glazed window, the effective transmittance t_e is usually required given τ_i, τ_o, ρ_2 and ρ_3 for the two glazings. The effective transmittance is given by:

$$\tau_e = \tau_i \tau_o / (1 - \rho_2 \rho_3) \tag{3.7}$$

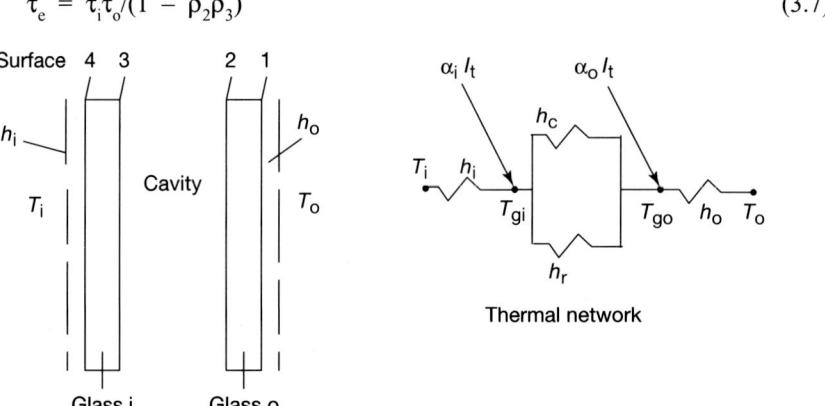

Figure 3.2 Double glazing and thermal network

In heat transmission calculations, the effective absorptance of each glazing is also required:

$$\alpha_o = \alpha_1 + \alpha_2 \tau_o \rho_3 (1 - \rho_2 \rho_3) \tag{3.8}$$

$$\alpha_i = \alpha_3 \tau_o (1 - \rho_2 \rho_3) \tag{3.9}$$

where
α_o = absorptance of outer glass
α_i = absorptance of inner glass
α_2 = absorptance of outer glass for solar radiation incident on indoor surface (2)
α_3 = absorptance of glass i for solar radiation incident on surface (3)
ρ_j = reflectance of surface j

Total solar radiation aborbed in the outer glass is $I_{ao} = \alpha_o I_t$.
Total solar radiation aborbed in the inner glass is $I_{ai} = \alpha_i I_t$.

Note that for uncoated surfaces the directional reflectance (and absorptance) of the glazing surfaces are equal. (Note: the diffuse component of I should be multiplied by the diffuse absorptance for a more accurate calculation.)

Part of the solar radiation absorbed in the glazings is transmitted by convection or as long-wave radiation heat into the room. An energy balance at the two glazings will show that the total amount of solar radiation that flows as heat into the room (after absorption in the glazings) is:

$$q_{sa} = \frac{U}{h_o}\left(\alpha_o I_t\right) + U\left(\frac{1}{h_o} + \frac{1}{h_g}\right)\left(\alpha_i I_t\right) \tag{3.10}$$

where

$$U = \frac{1}{\left(\dfrac{1}{h_o} + \dfrac{1}{h_g} + \dfrac{1}{h_i}\right)} \qquad \text{(window U – value)} \tag{3.10a}$$

h_o = outside film coefficient
h_g = cavity heat transfer coefficient = $h_c + h_r$
h_i = inside film coefficient

The variation of normal transmittance and absorptance (for incidence angle 0) is given in Figure 3.3 for various kL (extinction coefficient $\times$ thickness value) values. As can be seen, for clear glass 5 mm thick (kL is equal approximately to 0.04) the transmittance is 0.86 while for $kL = 0.65$, which is heat-absorbing glass, the transmittance is 0.47. In the latter case, the solar absorptance is also about 0.47.

As can be seen from Figure 3.4, the transmittance of glazing for direct radiation remains relatively steady until about 50° and drops fast after 60°. It is often assumed that the transmittance for diffuse radiation is equal to the beam transmittance at 60°.

Glazings may be specially treated to control their optical properties, e.g.:

- body-tinted glass with high absorptance
- surface-coated glasses with high directional reflectivity
- variable-transmission glasses

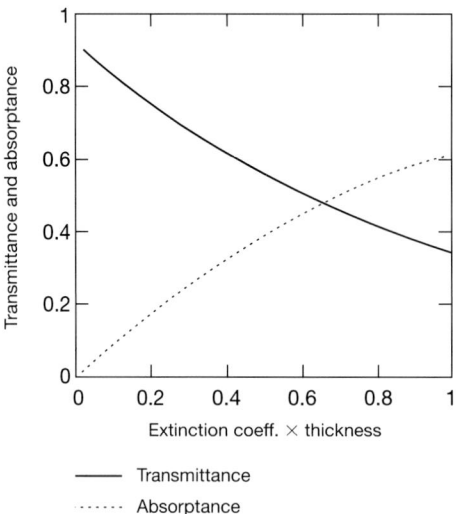

Figure 3.3 Transmittance and absorptance for various *kL* values

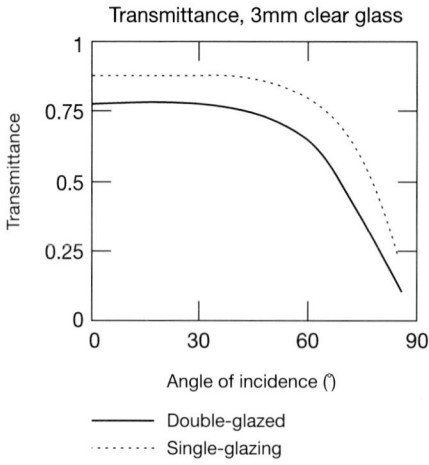

Figure 3.4 Transmittance of single and double glazing

- translucent glazings which diffuse beam solar radiation
- special sun-control membranes
- electrochromic coatings whose properties may be electrically controlled.

Body-tinted (absorptive) glasses have high extinction coefficient, low transmittance and high absorptance. The low transmittance also reduces the amount of daylight transmitted. The body-tint is produced by adding small quantities of metal oxides (iron, cobalt, selenium) which usually also give an apparent colour to the glass – green, blue, bronze or grey.

Surface coatings applied on one or both surfaces may modify its long-wave or short-wave radiation properties. They are usually reflective or low-e coatings.

Reflective glasses are used for solar control by increasing the reflection of solar radiation with special coatings of silver, gold, copper, etc.; these glasses usually have high absorptance.

Low-emissivity (low-e) glass has a special coating on one surface which reduces its long-wave (for wavelengths greater than 3 µm) emissivity from about 0.9 for regular glass to about 0.1. The radiative heat transfer coefficient for the cavity in a double-glazed window is then dramatically reduced as described above. Special coatings that allow high solar gains into a room while minimizing conduction heat losses through the glazing are very effective in passive solar heating. They are also useful for cooling in that they reduce the window U-value and summer heat gains, provided they are properly shaded. Typical coatings consist of three layers – a thin metal layer (usually gold, silver or copper) sandwiched between dielectric layers of tin oxide.

Variable-transmission glasses are a new development that permit the building envelope to be used dynamically, responding to outdoor climate and interior thermal needs. The transmittance may be varied by photochromic, thermochromic and electrochromic films.

The principle of operation of **electrochromic glazing** (Cogan *et al.* 1986) is based on the change of the optical properties of certain laminated materials when subjected to an external electric field. This type of glazing has an electrochromic coating. The coating is activated by a small electric voltage, generated by the building automation system or manually by the occupants. This voltage changes the tint of the coating and therefore its transmittance. The original transmittance is restored by reversing the voltage. Currently there are only small-scale applications, such as rear-view mirrors in cars. These products vary their transmittance between 15% and 70%. Their life expectancy is presently rather short. This is a major drawback for their generalized use in buildings.

Thermochromic glazing (Lee *et al.* 1986) is made from tungsten trioxide or vanadium dioxide and can be applied on windows as a thin film. It passively switches between a heat-transmitting and heat-reflecting state. Therefore it can reduce the cooling loads and provide solar protection.

Translucent glazings have low solar transmittance and they diffuse daylight; they are suitable for atria and skylights where one does not need visual communication with the exterior environment.

3.2 Transmitted solar radiation and its distribution

3.2.1 Performance evaluation

Two important parameters commonly employed in comparing fenestration systems are the solar heat gain factor (SHGF) and the shading coefficient (SC) (ASHRAE 1989). These parameters are based on an energy balance of the system.

The total instantaneous rate of heat transfer through a glazing element may be determined from an energy balance for unit area of the fenestration and its thermal environment:

Total energy transfer through window = heat transfer due to temperature difference between inside (T_i) and outside (T_o) + solar radiation transmitted through glazing + inward flow of solar radiation absorbed in glazing

For single glazing, the above energy balance may be written as follows:

$$q = U(T_o - T_i) + \tau_b I_b + \tau_d I_d + (U/h_o)(\alpha I) \tag{3.11}$$

where the conductance U for single glazing is given by:

$$U = 1/[(1/h_i) + (1/h_o)]$$

Total incident solar radiation $= I = I_b + I_d$

The above equation may be written in the form

$$q = U(T_o - T_i) + (\tau_{eff} + U\alpha/h_o)I \tag{3.12}$$

where τ_{eff} is the effect transmittance for total solar radiation.

The solar heat gain (SHG) is the second term of equation 3.12, and may be expressed as

$$SHG = FI = (\tau_{eff} + U\alpha/h_o)I \tag{3.13}$$

where the dimensionless ratio of solar heat gain to incident solar radiation is given by

$$F = (\tau_{eff} + U\alpha/h_o)$$

The solar heat gains through sunlit double-strength (3 mm) sheet glass (DSA) are defined as the SHGF. Clear day SHGF are tabulated for various latitudes and dates by ASHRAE (1989). However, in polluted city centres SHGF may be up to

20% lower, for humid locations up to 30% lower, and for high elevations up to 15% higher than tabulated values.

The solar heat gain of any fenestration system, including curtains, etc. is related to the standard SHGF using a **shading coefficient** (SC). The SC is given by the ratio of solar heat gain of the fenestration to the solar heat gain of DSA glass:

$$SC = SHG \text{ of fenestration/SHGF for DSA glass} \tag{3.14}$$

Therefore, SC may be written as

$$SC = F \text{ of fenestration}/F \text{ of DSA}$$
$$SC = F/0.87 \tag{3.15}$$

Thus

$$SC \times SHGF = (\tau_{eff} + U\alpha/h_o)I \tag{3.16}$$

and equation (3.11) for total heat transfer through the glazing may be written as

$$q = (SC)(SHGF) + U(T_o - T_i) \tag{3.17}$$

or as

$$q = FI + U(T_o - T_i)$$

The most general parameters that are universally applicable are the thermal conductance (U-value) and the dimensionless F-factor of the fenestration. For double glazing (Figure 3.5) these parameters are given by

$$U = 1/[(1/h_i) + (1/h_g) + (1/h_o)] \tag{3.18a}$$

where h_i and h_o are the interior and exterior film coefficients respectively and h_g the cavity heat transfer coefficient.

$$F = \tau_{eff} + U(\alpha_o/h_o) + [(U/h_o)+(U/h_g)]\alpha_i \tag{3.18b}$$

where the first term is the effective transmittance, the second term is the factor for inward flow of solar radiation absorbed in the outer glazing (absorptance α_o) and the third term is the factor for inward flow of solar radiation absorbed in the inner glazing (absorptance α_i).

The overall thermal conductance U_o of a fenestration system depends on the

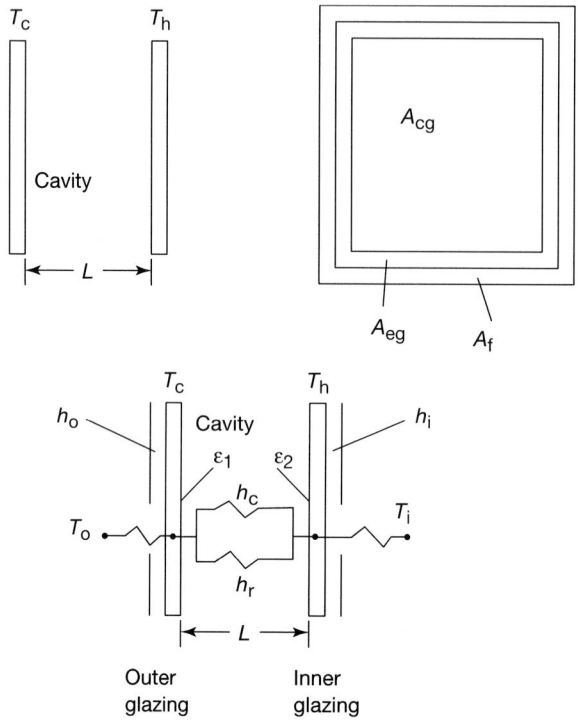

Figure 3.5 Double-glazing, area definitions and thermal network indicating heat flows

type of framing employed and the heat transfer regime at the edge of the glass. ASHRAE (1989) recommends subdivision of a window into three regions (see Figure 3.5) in calculating U_o: centre of glass region with area A_{cg} and conductance U_{cg}, edge of glass region with parameters A_{eg} and U_{eg}, and frame with parameters A_f and U_f. Since we have three heat flow paths in parallel U_o is given by:

$$U_o = (U_{cg}A_{cg} + U_{eg}A_{eg} + U_fA_f)/(A_{cg} + A_{eg} + A_f)$$

Centre-of-glass U-values are calculated based on one-dimensional heat flow correlations (Elsherbiny *et al.* 1982). Insulating glass units have continuous members around the perimeters to separate glazings and to provide an edge seal. Aluminium spacers are highly conductive and act as thermal bridges, greatly increasing heat transfer. The edge region is typically about 6 cm wide, adjacent to the frame. Aluminium frames sometimes have thermal breaks (wood or plastic inserts) that reduce U_f and U_{eg}. Vinyl frames have a much lower U-value. ASHRAE (1989) recommends the following values for frames:

Aluminium without thermal break: $U_f = 10.8$ W/m^2 K

Aluminium with thermal break: $U_f = 5.68$ W/m^2 K

Vinyl: $U_f = 2.27$ W/m^2 K

Note that the above values are approximate and may vary significantly for different company products owing to the three-dimensional character of the flow around window edges. The *ASHRAE Handbook* presents U-values for various windows including 1–3 glazings (glass, acrylic or polyester film), spacings of 6, 10 and 13 mm, emittances of 0.84, 0.4 and 0.15, and gas fills of air and argon.

Public domain programs such as WINDOW (LBL 1987) and VISION (Sullivan 1987) may also be used in computing U_o.

The transmission properties and shading coefficients for various types of window are shown in Table 3.2. It may be seen that thickness is not important for reflective glasses, although it is for body-tinted glasses.

Table 3.2 Transmission properties and shading coefficients for various types of glazing and window (Button and Rte 1992)

Glass type Thickness	Light/heat ratio	Light τ	ρ	Solar radiation α (direct)	τ (total)	Shading coefficient (SC)
Clear float						
4 mm		0.89	0.08	0.11	0.86	0.98
6 mm		0.87	0.08	0.15	0.83	0.95
10 mm		0.84	0.07	0.23	0.78	0.89
Reflective						
Silver						
6 mm	10/23	0.10	0.38	0.60	0.23	0.26
10 mm	10/23	0.10	0.37	0.60	0.23	0.27
6 mm	20/34	0.20	0.23	0.66	0.34	0.39
Bronze						
6 mm	10/24	0.10	0.19	0.73	0.24	0.27
10 mm	10/24	0.10	0.18	0.76	0.24	0.27
Blue						
6 mm	10/24	0.20	0.20	0.64	0.33	0.38
10 mm	10/24	0.20	0.20	0.66	0.33	0.38
Body-tinted						
Green						
6 mm	76/62	0.72	0.06	0.49	0.62	0.72
Blue						
6 mm	54/62	0.54	0.05	0.49	0.62	0.72
Bronze						
6 mm	50/62	0.50	0.05	0.36	0.70	0.72
10 mm	33/51	0.33	0.04	0.49	0.62	0.59

Example: Solar radiation transmitted through double glazing

We have seen how solar radiation incident on an inclined surface is calculated and how window transmittance is determined as a function of time. Now these methods are used together to calculate the instantaneous and daily total solar radiation transmitted through single-glazed and double-glazed windows. Consider a south-facing vertical window located in Montreal (latitude 45°N).

Determine the solar radiation transmitted for January 1 and June 30 for a double-glazed clear window.

Geometry: $L = 45°N$, $\beta = 90°$, $\psi = 90°$

For January 1

$n = 1$

For June 30

$n = 31 + 28 + 31 + 30 + 31 + 30 = 181$

Assume ground reflectance is 0.2. First perform calculations for 1 January:

$\delta = 23.45\sin[360(284 + n)/365)] = -23°$

The sunrise time is found and divided into eight equal time intervals.

$t_s = h_s/15 = \min\{\arccos[-\tan(L)\tan(\delta)], \arccos[-\tan(L - \beta)\tan(\delta)]\}/15$
$= 4.324\ \text{h}$

Time interval

$\Delta t = t_s/8 = 0.541\ \text{h}$

The position of the sun is then computed at the different times from noon to sunset (we only need to perform the analysis for half a day as the movement of the sun is symmetric about solar noon relative to a south-facing surface).

$h_j = t_j 15°/\text{h}$

where $t_j = j \times \Delta t$ with $j = 0, 1, 2, 3, 4$ ($j = 4$ corresponds to sunset).

$\sin \alpha_j = \cos L + \cos \delta \cos h_j + \sin L \sin \delta$ (solar altitude)

$\cos \varphi_j = (\sin \alpha_j \sin L - \sin \delta)/(\cos \alpha_j \cos L)$ (solar azimuth)

The incidence angle is then calculated:

$$\cos \theta_j = \cos \alpha_j \cos \gamma_j \sin \beta + \sin \alpha_j \cos \beta$$

where $\gamma = \varphi - \psi$.

The beam atmospheric transmitted is calculated (using Mathcad (MathSoft 2000)) based on Hottel's clear sky model:

$$A = 0.5 \text{ km}$$

The atmospheric transmittance for beam radiation is given by:

$$\tau_b = a_0 + a_1 \exp[-k/\cos(z)] \tag{3.19}$$

where the constants a and k depend on climate and altitude A (km).

$$a_0 = 1.03[0.4327 - 0.008\ 21(6 - A)^2]$$
$$a_1 = 1.01[0.5055 - 0.005\ 95(6.5 - A)^2]$$
$$k = 1.0[0.2711 + 0.018\ 58(2.5 - A)^2]$$

After determining the beam transmittance of the atmosphere, we may also determine the diffuse transmittance (Liu and Jordan 1960):

$$\tau_d = 0.271 - 0.294\tau_b$$

The solar properties of a single glazing are then computed using the equations given in Section 3.1 (assuming $kL = 0.03$), and these are used in the calculation of the double-glazed window properties. The results are shown in Figure 3.6.

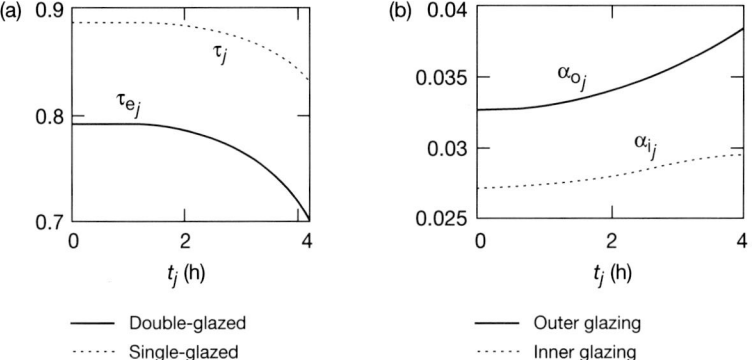

Figure 3.6 (a) Effective transmittance for double and single glazing; (b) absorptance of inner and outer panes

In calculating how much diffuse solar radiation is transmitted, it is assumed that the window diffuse transmittance is equal to the beam transmittance at an angle of incidence equal to 60°.

The total solar radiation I_t incident on the surface is given by the sum of the direct (beam) component I_b, the diffuse sky component I_{ds} and the diffuse solar radiation reflected from the ground I_{dg}.

$$I_t = I_b + I_{ds} + I_{dg}$$

where

$$I_b = I_{on}\tau_b\cos\theta$$

with the extraterrestrial solar radiation given by

$$I_{on} = 1353[1 + 0.033 \cos(360n/365)]$$

$$I_{ds} = I_{on} \sin\alpha\ \tau_d(1 + \cos\beta)/2$$

$$I_{dg} = I_{on} \sin\alpha(\tau_b + \tau_d)\rho(1 - \cos\beta)/2$$

The transmitted solar radiation is then determined by multiplying the diffuse $(I_{ds} + I_{dg})$ radiation by the window diffuse transmittance and I_b by the window transmittance at the corresponding time:

$$G_t = \tau_e I_b + \tau_{ed}(I_{ds} + I_{dg})$$

Figure 3.7 shows the beam (G_{2b}) and diffuse (G_{2d}) parts of the transmitted radiation.

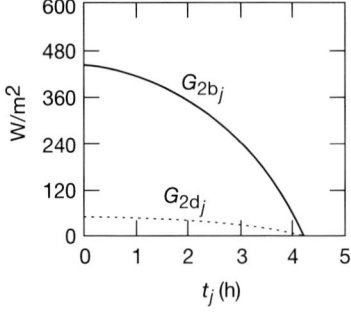

Figure 3.7 Transmitted beam and diffuse solar radiation for double-glazed clear window in January

The total transmitted daily solar radiation per square metre is twice the area under the curves in Figure 3.7, 10.54 MJ/m².

The solar radiation absorbed in each of the two glazings is given in Figure 3.8. The glazings absorb a small amount of radiation as they are clear (low extinction coefficient). Thicker glazing with body tint would absorb a significantly higher amount of solar radiation. In this case, the total solar radiation absorbed in the outer and inner glazings is 0.46 MJ/m² and 0.38 MJ/m² respectively. The portion transmitted inwards may be estimated by means of equation 3.10. The corresponding results for 30 June are given in Figure 3.9.

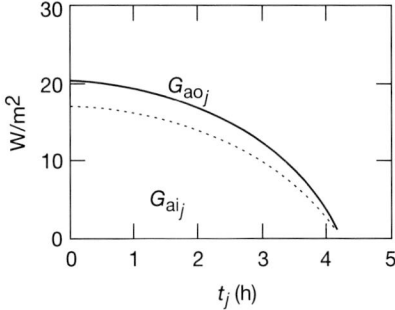

Figure 3.8 Solar radiation absorbed in inner (G_{ai}) and outer (G_{ao}) glazings

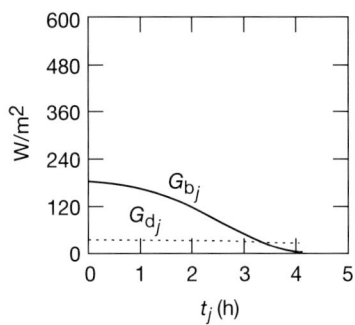

Figure 3.9 Transmitted beam and diffuse solar radiation for double-glazed clear window in June

Comparison of the results in Figures 3.7 and 3.9 reveals a very important result and useful principle for passive solar design: a south-facing window transmits a high amount of solar radiation in the winter and a low amount in the summer. This is due to the low incidence angles of the sun on the window in the winter, and the high incidence angle in the summer; at incidence angles in excess of 60° the window transmittance falls rapidly. In this case all incidence angles on 30 June are over 60°, whereas on 1 January they vary from a low of 22° at solar noon to 55° at sunset.

3.3 Transparent insulation

Transparent insulation materials (TIM) combine the properties of good optical transmission (described by the total solar transmittance) and good thermal insulation (described by the heat loss coefficient or U-value). One of the widely known applications of transparent insulation materials is in the cladding of building walls, replacing conventional opaque insulation.

Utilization of a TIM in a solar collector wall has been proved to have a significant potential to reduce heating load in passive solar buildings (Twidell *et al.* 1994). Transparent insulation converts one or more walls of the building into solar collectors. Initially, a single glazing was used as the transparent cover of a wall. This was known as a Trombe wall system (Trombe *et al.* 1977). Cellular transparent materials were introduced to improve the solar transmittance and thermal resistance of the wall system (Olsen 1982, Goetzberger *et al.* 1984) after being applied to solar collectors (Francia 1961, Hollands 1965). These materials enhance thermal resistance, in addition to having high solar transmittance. Other types of TIM are in use in the industry such as capillary glasses and aerogels. TIM classes have been reviewed by Platzer (1994) and they fall broadly into four categories:

- Type A: with material structures parallel to the surface plane (multiple glazing, plastic films, IR-reflective glass).
- Type B: with material structures perpendicular to the absorber (parallel slats, honeycombs, capillaries).
- Type C: scattering structures (duct plates, foams, and bubbles).
- Type D: quasi-homogeneous materials (glass fibres, aerogels).

The most popular type used today is type B, the honeycomb-structured materials made from plastics such as acrylic or polycarbonate (Platzer 1997). These materials have very high solar transmission with good insulation properties.

In a passive solar system, the thermal radiative heat losses from the absorber can be reduced by application of selective coatings. Once radiation losses have been restricted, natural convection dominates heat losses. Minimizing this convective heat loss requires the determination of some parameters such as (Hollands *et al.* 1978)

- the temperature difference between the absorber and the cover
- the distance between the absorber and the cover
- the angle of inclination of the air layer

- the air properties
- the geometry of the enclosure.

One of the methods for reducing the convective heat transfer is to divide the enclosure into a large number of cells (Figure 3.10). Owing to the reduced dimension of each cell, in comparison with the enclosure, the viscous forces acting on the air in each cell are increased and the movement of air in the cell is restricted. If the cell were sized correctly to maintain stagnant air (motionless air), the natural convection between the absorber and the cover would be suppressed. This gives an opportunity to increase the distance between the absorber and the cover and therefore to augment the insulating value of the air layer. Thus, honeycombing the air space will improve the thermal resistance of the wall system by means of convection suppression.

The honeycomb cell size must be chosen so as just to suppress the free convective heat transfer at the value of the design temperature difference. Use of smaller cell sizes will result in more of the expensive honeycomb being used than is actually necessary and will also cause unnecessary loss in solar transmission of the honeycomb. However, using a cell size larger than needed to suppress convection will result in greater heat loss. These factors underline the importance of properly choosing the cell size.

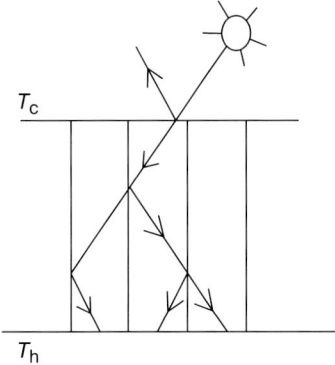

Figure 3.10 Trajectory of solar rays through honeycomb transparent insulation

The advantage of the honeycomb structure is that the solar radiation striking the insulation panel is reflected and re-reflected by the walls in the forward direction and thus reaches the absorber (Figure 3.10). Thus, if reflections are perfectly specular and there is no scattering or absorption in the walls, the solar transmission will be 100% (Hollands 1988). However, the transmittance of the honeycomb insulation is dependent upon the angle of incidence of solar radiation, i.e. it will be affected by the sun's position throughout the year.

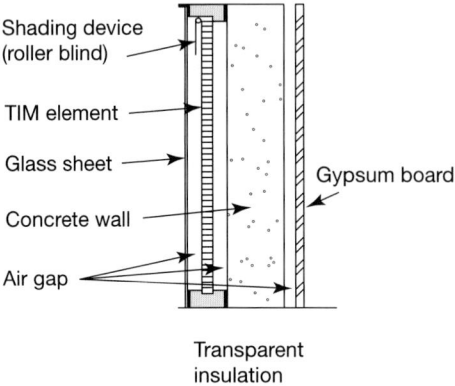

Figure 3.11 Transparently insulated wall (Athienitis and Ramadan 1999)

The high solar transmittance of the transparent honeycomb is matched with a good thermal insulation property. The conditions for having good insulation with low U-value (total heat transfer coefficient) may be described as follows:

- The structure must be thick enough to prevent heat conduction by air.
- The thickness of honeycomb walls must be low to minimize heat conduction through the transparent material.
- For reduction of radiative heat transfer, one practical solution is the use of a selective coating on the absorber. However, this should be paired with the introduction of an air gap between the TI unit and the absorber to minimize the coupled radiative and conductive heat transfer induced by the physical contact between TI and the absorber (Hollands *et al.* 1984).

A typical transparently insulated wall is shown in Figure 3.11. The transparently insulated wall system consists of an exterior single glazing protector, an air cavity, a transparent honeycomb material, a second air cavity, a concrete layer, a third air cavity and an interior gypsum board layer. The first air cavity permits the use of a shading device (roller blind) to enhance the thermal performance of the TI wall. The second cavity reduces the heat transfer between the absorber and the TI unit, especially when low-emissivity coatings cover the thermal mass (Hollands and Iyankaran 1985). The third air cavity increases the thermal resistance of the TI wall system and provides space for electrical wiring and other services. Heat transfer through air cavities is calculated based on the model of ElSherbiny *et al.* (1982) (see Chapter 2).

The plastic transparent honeycomb material is modelled as a square cell. The cross-sectional area of the cell is determined to suppress convective heat transfer which may occur between the protector and the absorber prior to the introduction of the TIM (Hollands *et al.* 1976). The aspect ratio of the cell, which is defined as the thickness of TIM over the hydraulic diameter of the cell, must be high to reduce the conductive (air conduction) and radiative heat transfer of the TIM layer (Tabor 1969). In addition, the thickness of the honeycomb wall material should be low to reduce the conductivity of the TIM material (about 50 μm).

Blinds have been introduced in the wall collector system to prevent overheating during days with excessive solar radiation (Twidell *et al.* 1994). The operation of the blind must satisfy the thermal comfort conditions. Thus, the blind is opened during winter days to allow the transmission of solar radiation to the thermal mass, and closed in winter nights to reduce heat losses from the heating space. In addition, closing the blind during cloudy winter days will contribute to the reduction of heating load.

Several researchers have examined the radiation heat transfer reduction and convection suppression properties of the transparent honeycomb materials. They focused first on the idea that, for large aspect ratio, the cell structure acts as a thermal radiation shield (Perrot 1967). However, as the reduction of thermal radiation heat transfer can be achieved by the selection of the absorber's material and coating, the convective heat transfer will dominate.

Honeycomb structures were used to reduce the convective heat losses between the cover and the absorber (Hollands 1965, Edwards 1976, Charters and Peterson 1972, Guthrie and Charters 1982). Generally, reduction of cell size reduces convection heat transfer. Hollands (1965) demonstrated that a cell size range between 0.4 and 0.6 inch (10–15 mm) suppresses convection for aspect ratios equal to 1 and 5 respectively. The use of glass has the advantage of better ultraviolet thermal stability than plastics. But the honeycomb wall thickness can be reduced with the use of plastics, resulting in less conduction heat loss and material conservation.

Using plastic honeycombs as an alternative to expensive glass partially solves the cost problem but creates other difficulties. If the wall covers a big area with a honeycomb cell, the cost of the wall material and manufacturing may become high. Furthermore, a thick wall of honeycomb cell may induce conduction. Therefore, the trend is towards very thin transparent materials (about 50 μm). However, care must be taken during transportation of these very thin materials. Also, their long-wave transmittance increases the thinner they become.

Rectangular-celled extruded polycarbonate honeycombs from various plastics have been developed, but only some of them are on the market. Commercial products of small-celled honeycomb with improved optical and thermal properties were developed in the early 1980s by companies such as Diveno and Okalux Kapillargles GmbH in Germany. These products use PMMA (polymethylmeth-acrylate) and PC (polycarbonate) materials, which also provide ultraviolet stability behind a cover glass.

The heat transfer in large-celled honeycombs has been investigated by a number of researchers (Symon and Peck 1983, Hoogendoorn 1985 and Hollands *et al.*

1984, 1992). This structure guarantees low transmission losses in the solar spectrum and permits easy combination with selective coatings. Meanwhile, different shapes of honeycomb structures have been investigated for heat losses and solar transmission such as sinusoidal (McMurrin and Buchberg 1981), hexagonal (Marshall *et al.* 1976) and cylindrical shape honeycomb (Buchberg *et al.* 1976). For applications dealing with daylighting and light-guiding, the material is used also in modified forms. The honeycomb cells need not be perpendicular to the glazing surface, but may also be inclined, usually 45°. Also, honeycombs parallel to the glass sheets are used.

The activities in testing and monitoring TI applications have increased significantly since the late 1980s. Braun *et al.* (1992) reported 20 projects of transparently insulated walls, most of them honeycomb type, granted by the German Ministry for Research and Technology. In 1986 the European Commission Directorate General XII for Science, Research and Development launched the PASSYS project to develop reliable and affordable procedures for the testing of thermal and solar characteristics of passive solar components in a building system. The TIM component, honeycomb structured, was tested in five countries – Belgium, Germany, Italy, the United Kingdom and the Netherlands (Vandaele and Wouters 1994). The largest demonstration project was the students' residence at Strathclyde University in England (Twidell *et al.*1994), where 1040 m² of TIM were applied.

3.3.1 Design of honeycomb cell

The main purpose of the honeycomb is to reduce the free convection currents that would otherwise occur in the air layer. Once the value of honeycomb thickness has been decided, the cell size must be chosen so as to just suppress the free convective currents at the value of design ΔT (the temperature difference between the hot and cold faces of the honeycomb). The use of smaller cell sizes will result in more expensive honeycomb being used than is actually necessary and will also cause unnecessary loss in solar transmission of the honeycomb. However, as Cane *et al.* (1977) observed, the use of cell sizes larger than needed may induce a convective heat exchange greater than that which would take place without the honeycomb. If the aspect ratio is less than 2, very little convection suppression is possible and it is difficult to avoid the region of free convection augmentation by honeycomb. Consequently, a honeycomb with aspect ratio less than 2 should be avoided. The free convection heat transfer across a honeycomb can be characterized by the Nusselt number, *Nu*, which represents the ratio of the combined conductive and free convective heat transfer through the air to the corresponding heat transfer when the air is stagnant (Holman 1986). Hence, a Nusselt number of unity indicates purely conductive heat transfer and complete suppression of convective motion.

On the other hand, as observed by Charters and Peterson (1972) through flow visualization tests, there is never a complete suppression of convection motion for an inclined cell. Thus, the Nusselt number is never exactly unity even at very small Rayleigh numbers (Ra). However, the Nusselt number increases rather slowly with Ra until it reaches approximately 1.2 after which it rises rather steeply with Ra (Cane *et al.* 1977). Consequently, when $Nu = 1.2$ is reached, the effective suppression will be assumed to have taken place where purely conductive heat transfer of still air is augmented by 20%.

Cane *et al.* (1977) reported an extensive experimental study on free convection across inclined square and hexagonal celled plastic honeycomb. They recommend the following for Nusselt number:

$$Nu = 1 + 0.89\cos(\beta - 60)\left(\frac{Ra}{2420\,A_{hc}^4}\right)^{2.88 - 1.64\sin\beta} \qquad (3.20)$$

where β is the tilt angle (angle of inclination for honeycomb panel in degrees) and A_{hc} is the aspect ratio of the cell.

This relation is valid when $30° \le \beta \le 90°$ and $Ra/A_{hc}^4 \le 6000$.

Although based on data for $A_{hc} \ge 4$, this relation is approximately valid for $A_{hc} = 3$ as well (Cane *et al.* 1977).

Substituting $Nu = 1.2$ in equation 3.20:

$$A_{hc} = f(\beta)(Ra/2420)^{1/4} \qquad (3.21)$$

where $\qquad f(\beta) = \left[4.45\cos(\beta - 60)\right]^{\frac{1}{11.52 - 6.56\sin\beta}}$

for $30° \le \beta \le 90°$.

For air at atmospheric pressure and moderate temperatures equation 3.21 can be expressed dimensionally as:

$$A_{hc} = C(\beta)(1 + 2x)^{1/2} \times \Delta T^{1/4}L^{3/4} \qquad (3.22)$$

where $C(\beta) = 1.03f(\beta)$ and $x = 100/T_m$. T_m is the mean air temperature expressed in kelvin, ΔT is the temperature difference across the honeycomb and L is the depth of the honeycomb expressed in cm.

It can be seen that the cell dimensions depend on mean temperature and temperature difference. However, as shown by Hollands (1978), with a good factor of safety, a cell size of the order of 12 mm in hydraulic diameter is appropriate for a cell length of 100 mm.

In choosing the cell size, the honeycomb designer must first make a decision choice concerning the chief function of the honeycomb, and this differentiation on the basis of function leads to a calculation of honeycomb into what may be called 'large-celled' and 'small-celled' honeycombs. Another classification may be governed by the cell geometry and shape. However, when met with the concept of honeycomb, a host of questions arise concerning the best geometry, dimensions and shape of the cell. In fact, the amount of the material that must go into making the transparent insulation is the key factor in answering these questions. Two factors demonstrate the importance of the material content:

- the amount of absorption and scattering of solar radiation inside the honeycomb wall is proportional to the material content, as is the heat transfer by conduction through the cell
- the material cost.

Reducing the amount of material may be achieved by reducing the thickness of the walls and increasing the cell dimensions. However, a decision should be made whether the cell is designed to suppress radiative or convection heat transfer. Long-wave radiation suppression needs a small cell and a minimum thickness of wall to establish the required degree of opaqueness. On the other hand, for convection suppression, a minimum cell size is required below which no added advantage is gained. As designing to suppress radiant heat transfer is more exacting, another method may be applied. It is the use of a selective surface on the absorber to help the radiant suppression. However, the cost of the coating has to be considered and an air gap should be added between the absorber and the TI element to decouple the conductive and radiative heat transfer mode.

3.3.2 Solar transmittance of transparent honeycomb insulation

The successful use of honeycomb transparent insulation for solar energy application depends on not only cost, convection suppression and thermal radiation reduction considerations but also on its transmittance to incoming solar radiation over different angles of incidence (Symons 1982). The solar collection effectiveness of a solar device can be judged by an accurate determination of its solar transmittance. Theoretical studies for such determinations have been made using methods such as Monte Carlo ray-tracing techniques (Morris 1976, Feland 1978). The complexities of this technique have hindered its use. Hollands *et al.* (1978) derived an approximate equation for honeycomb transmittance. However, as shown by Jesch *et al.* (1987), the values calculated by this method deviate from experimental data after 60° angle of incidence. Symons (1982) suggested empirical solar transmittance correlation equations based on a simple convection suppression solar transmittance model. The results match the measured data to within 2%. Later, Chattha and Jesch (1989) used and validated this method.

3.3.3 Beam transmittance of honeycomb transparent insulation

Symons (1982) reported a simple set of formulations for calculating the solar transmittance of transparent honeycombs. Chattha and Jesch (1989) have used these formulations for investigating the variation of solar transmittance with incidence angle and included the effect of scattering and absorption of radiation by vertical walls.

Solar radiation falling on the top surface of a honeycomb propagates through the cell as well as through the cell walls. The portion propagating through the cells undergoes reflection (specular as well as diffuse), refraction and absorption by the vertical walls.

The radiation of the cell walls is propagated downwards through the walls because of total internal reflection and, in the process, is absorbed and scattered inside the material of the walls. Following Symons (1982) and Chattha and Jesch (1989), the beam radiation transmittance $T(\theta)$ can be approximated as:

$$T(\theta) = (\tau_s + \rho_s)^{nw} \tag{3.23}$$

where nw is the number of walls intercepting incoming rays at angle of incidence θ and azimuth ϕ and is equal to $A_{hc} \tan(\theta)$ for square celled honeycomb.

For smooth wall materials, the sum of specularly reflected and transmitted radiation is essentially independent of angle of incidence. For example, Symons (1982) evaluated the value of $\tau_s + \rho_s$ for FEP Teflon honeycomb as approximately equal to 0.983. He measured the variation of this value with the angle of incidence and concluded a reduction of less than 1% when the angle of incidence increases from 0 to 75°. On the other hand, equation 3.23 is only applicable for very thin honeycomb wall materials. It can shown from equation 3.24 that for θ equal 0, $T(\theta)$ is equal to 1.

Therefore, equation 3.23 should be modified to accommodate thicker and wavy honeycomb wall. It may be expressed as:

$$T(\theta) = F_e F_r^{A_{hc} \tan(\theta)} \tag{3.24}$$

where F_e is the fraction of effective cross-sectional area of honeycomb not occupied by wall material. That is (Kaushika and Padma Priya 1991)

$$F_e = 1 - \frac{\delta_{hc}(\delta_{hc} + 2D_{hc})}{D_{hc}^2} \tag{3.25}$$

F_r is the fraction of radiation that is reflected and transmitted specularly at each wall intercept, and it is measured experimentally taking into account the absorption and scattering of solar radiation. Hollands *et al.* (1978a), Kaushika and Padma

Priya (1991) and Chattha and Jesch (1989) reported measured values for different types of honeycomb. These values are summarized in Table 3.3.

Table 3.3 F_r and δ_{hc} for different honeycomb materials

	Acrylic	Polycarbonate	Glass	Lexan	FEP Teflon
F_r	0.963	0.988	0.955	0.999	0.999
δ_{hc}	1 mm	0.03 mm	1 mm	0.076 mm	0.013 mm

3.3.4 Solar diffuse radiation transmittance of transparent honeycomb

Solar diffuse radiation transmittance for the plane glass cover of a flat plate collector has been investigated by Brandemuehl and Beckman (1980). Their approach involves the consideration of solar diffuse radiation made up of two components (sky and ground reflected) to be hemispherical isotropic in nature. For the derivation of transmittance of diffuse radiation the results of beam radiation transmittance are integrated over the appropriate range of the solid angle of incident diffuse radiation. The effective beam incidence angle θ_e is defined for a given range and transparent system such that

$$T_d = T(\theta_e)$$

The same approach may be applied to cellular array (honeycomb structured) materials. The transmittance for solar diffuse radiation is expressed as:

$$T_d = \frac{\int_{\omega 1}^{\omega 2} T(\theta)\cos(\theta)\sin(\theta)d\phi d\theta}{\int_{\omega 1}^{\omega 2} \cos(\theta)\sin(\theta)d\phi d\theta} \tag{3.26}$$

where $\omega 1$ and $\omega 2$ represent the angular range of incident diffuse radiation, and θ and ϕ are the angle of incidence and azimuth respectively. The angular range has been determined earlier by Brandemuehl and Beckman (1980) and the results are adopted in the present work.

For honeycomb transparent material tilted at an angle β, the diffuse radiation from the ground will have an angle of incidence ranging from $\theta = \pi/2 - \beta$ to $\theta = \pi/2$. For a given value of θ the azimuth angle will range from $\phi = $ asin $[\cot(\beta)/\tan(\theta)]$ to $\phi = \pi - $ asin$[\cot(\beta)/\tan(\theta)]$.

Using these integration limits and due to axial symmetry, the transmittance for diffuse ground radiation is:

$$T_{dground} = \frac{\int_{\frac{\pi}{2}-\beta}^{\frac{\pi}{2}} \int_{a \sin\left[\frac{\cot(\beta)}{\tan(\theta)}\right]}^{\frac{\pi}{2}} T(\theta)\cos\theta \sin\theta \, d\phi \, d\theta}{\int_{\frac{\pi}{2}-\beta}^{\frac{\pi}{2}} \int_{a \sin\left[\frac{\cot(\beta)}{\tan(\theta)}\right]}^{\frac{\pi}{2}} \cos\theta \sin\theta \, d\phi \, d\theta} \tag{3.27}$$

Diffuse radiation from the sky will have angle of incidence ranging from $\phi = 0$ to $\phi = \pi/2$. For the incidence angle $\phi < \pi/2 - \beta$, the angle ϕ will vary from 0 to 2π and for the incidence angle $\phi > \pi/2 - \beta$ the angle ϕ will range from $\phi = \pi - a\sin(\cot(\beta)/\tan(\theta))$ to $\phi = 2\pi + a\sin(\cot(\beta)/\tan(\theta))$. By applying these integration limits and due to axial symmetry the sky diffuse transmittance for a transparent honeycomb is expressed as:

$$T_{dsky} = \frac{\int_{0}^{\frac{\pi}{2}} \int_{\frac{\pi}{2}}^{\frac{\pi}{2}} T_b(\theta)\cos(\theta)\sin\theta \, d\phi \, d\theta + \int_{\frac{\pi}{2}-\beta}^{\frac{\pi}{2}} \int_{\frac{\pi}{2}}^{a \sin\left[\frac{\cot(\beta)}{\tan(\theta)}\right]} T_b(\theta)\cos\theta \sin\theta \, d\phi \, d\theta}{\int_{0}^{\frac{\pi}{2}} \int_{\frac{\pi}{2}}^{\frac{\pi}{2}} \cos(\theta)\sin\theta \, d\phi \, d\theta + \int_{\frac{\pi}{2}-\beta}^{\frac{\pi}{2}} \int_{\frac{\pi}{2}}^{a \sin\left[\frac{\cot(\beta)}{\tan(\theta)}\right]} \cos\theta \sin\theta \, d\phi \, d\theta} \tag{3.28}$$

Arulanantham and Kaushika (1994) used numerical integration techniques to solve the above equations. The results were reduced in terms of equivalent beam angle of incidence and its variation as a function of tilt angle and aspect ratio of the transparent device. The variations are represented as polynomial expressions. The polynomial representation is based on the theoretical calculation covering the aspect ratio range from 2 to 40.

Example

Determine the thermal and solar properties of a square-celled Lexan honeycomb with the properties given below. First let us consider the appropriate properties of the transparent material used (Lexan square-cell honeycomb). The calculations are performed in Mathcad (MathSoft 2000).

$L_{hc} = 47.6$ mm — Honeycomb depth (height)

$\delta_{hc} = 0.076$ mm — Honeycomb wall thickness

$D_{hc} = 9.5$ mm — Honeycomb wall spacing

$E = [\delta_{hc}(\delta_{hc} + 2D_{hc})]/D_{hc}^2$ — Fraction of cellular cross-section area occupied by wall material (for a square cell)

$\rho_{se} = 0.97\ (\Phi = 0)$ — Equivalent specular reflectivity of honeycomb wall

$\rho_{de} = 0.02\ (\Phi = 0)$ — Equivalent diffuse reflectivity of honeycomb wall

$\alpha_e = 1 - \rho_{se} - \rho_{de}$ — Equivalent absorptivity of honeycomb wall $(\alpha_e = 0.01)$

$\alpha_s = \alpha_e$ — Absorptivity of single-sheet honeycomb

$F_{sq} = \frac{1}{2}$ — Hottel's shape factor for radiative exchange

$N_{hc_i} = \dfrac{L_{hc}}{D_{hc}}\tan\left(\theta_{i,0}\right)$ — The number of walls intercepted by the solar ray in its propagation through the honeycomb array (for square cell)

$nt_i = \text{floor}\left(N_{hc_i}\right)$ — Truncated value of N_{hc}

$T_{d_i} = \rho_{se}{}^{nt_i}\left(nt_i + 1 - N_{hc_i}\right)$
$\quad + \rho_{se}{}^{nt_i + 1}\left(N_{hc_i} - nt_1\right)$ — Fraction of irradiation on the top of the cell which arrives at the bottom of the cell via specular reflections only

$T_{c_i} = T_d + \left[\dfrac{\rho_{de}}{\rho_{de} + \alpha_s}\right] F_{sq}\left(1 - T_{d_i}\right)$ — Honeycomb cell transmittance

$\mu = 1.5$ — Index of refraction of honeycomb wall

$R_{sv} = (1 - \mu)^2/(1 + \mu)^2$ — Single surface reflectivity at vertical incidence

$$a_{\Phi 0} = \frac{\rho_{se} - R_{sv}}{1 - 2R_{sv} + R_{sv}\rho_{se}}$$

$$a(\Phi) = \exp\{-\mu(K_a + K_s)\delta/\mu^2 - [\sin^2(\Phi)]^{1/2}\}$$

Let $K_a + K_s = K_b$, where K_s and K_a are the scattering and absorption coefficient of honeycomb and wall, respectively. This will lead to the following formula:

$$K_b = \frac{\log\left(a_{\Phi 0}\right)\left(\mu^2 - \sin(0)^2\right)^{\frac{1}{2}}}{-\mu \cdot \delta_{hc}} = \log(a)/\delta_{hc}$$

$$b_{\theta_i} = \frac{K_b \mu L_{hc}}{\left(\mu^2 - \sin\left(\theta_{i,0,0}\right)^2\right)^{\frac{1}{2}}} \quad \text{where i refers to time interval}$$

The transmittance through the walls of the honeycomb is then calculated, followed by the calculation of the effective transmittance, taking into account repeated reflections and transmission in the honeycomb.

The calculations are shown below and the transmittance (using Mathcad) is shown in Figure 3.12.

$$\phi w_I = (\pi/2) - \phi_{i,0} \qquad \text{Angle of incidence of solar radiation on honeycomb wall}$$

$$rs_i = a\sin[\sin(\phi_{i,0})/\mu] \quad \sin(rs) = \sin\theta/\mu$$

$$R_{\theta_i} = \frac{1}{2}\left[\frac{\tan\left(\theta_{i,0} - rs_i\right)^2}{\tan\left(\theta_{i,0} + rs_i\right)^2} + \frac{\sin\left(\theta_{i,0} - rs_i\right)^2}{\sin\left(\theta_{i,0} + rs_i\right)^2}\right] \qquad \begin{array}{l}\text{Single surface reflectivity as a} \\ \text{function of solar angles incidence} \\ \text{on honeycomb top surface}\end{array}$$

$$\theta_{\text{esradiant}} = 1.007$$

$$\text{let } K_u = k_s / (k_s + k_a) \qquad rsd = a\sin\left[\frac{\sin(\theta_{\text{esradiant}})}{\mu}\right]$$

$$K_u = \frac{\rho_{de}}{\rho_{de} + \alpha_e} \qquad R_{\theta sd} = \frac{1}{2}\left[\frac{\tan\left(\theta_{\text{esradiant}} - rsd\right)^2}{\tan\left(\theta_{\text{esradiant}} + rsd\right)^2} + \frac{\sin\left(\theta_{\text{esradiant}} - rsd\right)^2}{\sin\left(\theta_{\text{esradiant}} + rsd\right)^2}\right]$$

$$T_{e_i} = \left(1 - R_{\theta_i}\right)^2 \exp\left(-b_{\theta_i}\right) + F_{sq}K_u\left[1 - \exp\left(-b_{\theta_i}\right)\right]\left(1 - R_{\theta_i}\right) \qquad \begin{array}{l}\text{Transmittance through} \\ \text{cell walls}\end{array}$$

$$T_{\text{beam}_i} = \frac{T_{c_i} + T_{e_i}E}{1 + E}$$

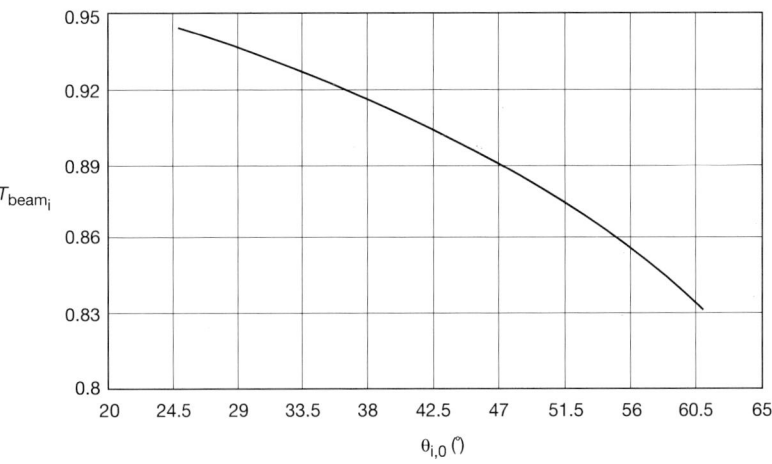

Figure 3.12 Calculation of beam transmittance of TIM (for south-facing surface in January)

3.3.5 Diffuse transmittance

Given that the aspect ratio of the honeycomb is $A_{hc} = L_{hc}/D_{hc}$ Arulanantham and Kaushika (1994) propose the following correlation and calculation technique to determine the honeycomb transmittance for ground-reflected and sky diffuse radiation.

$$\theta_{e1} = 90 - 0.608\,4518\beta + 3.709\,793 \times 10^{-4}\beta\,A_{hc} + 3.0577183 \times 10^{-5}\beta\,A_{hc}^{2}$$
$$\qquad + \left[3.30328929 \times 10^{-3}(\beta)^{2}\right]$$
$$\theta_{e2} = -5.0287694 \times 10^{-5}(\beta)^{2}\,A_{hc} + 4.1570456 \times 10^{-7}(\beta)^{2}\,A_{hc}^{2}$$
$$\theta_{e3} = 59.69678 - (0.380\,2643\,A_{hc}) + \left(4.2715073 \times 10^{-3}\,A_{hc}^{2}\right) - 0.142\,9023\beta$$
$$\theta_{e4} = -8.0555677 \times 10^{-3}\,A_{hc}\beta + 2.122\,9684 \times 10^{-4}\,A_{hc}^{2}\beta + 1.527757 \times 10^{-3}(\beta)^{2}$$
$$\theta_{e5} = 7.0696505 \times 10^{-3}\,A_{hc}\beta - 2.149\,6235 \times 10^{-6}\,A_{hc}^{2}(\beta)^{2}$$

The equivalent beam angle of diffuse ground radiation is:

$$\theta_{eg} = \theta_{e1} + \theta_{e2} \qquad \theta_{eg} = 89.056 \qquad \theta_{egradiant} = \frac{\theta_{eg}\pi}{180} \qquad \theta_{egradiant} = 1.554\,\mathrm{rad}$$

The equivalent beam angle of diffuse sky radiation is:

$$\theta_{es} = \theta_{e3} + \theta_{e4} + \theta_{e5} \qquad \theta_{es} = 57.678 \qquad \theta_{esradiant} = \frac{\theta_{es}\pi}{180} \qquad k = 1..2$$

$$b_{\theta e_{k}} = \frac{K_{b}\mu L_{hc}}{\left[\mu^{2} - \sin(\theta_{k,0})^{2}\right]^{\frac{1}{2}}} \qquad \theta_{ek} = \theta_{egradiant} / \theta_{esradiant}$$

$$T_{e_{k}} = (1 - R_{sv})^{2}\exp(-b_{\theta_{k}}) + F_{sq}K_{u}\left[1 - \exp(-b_{\theta e_{k}})\right](1 - R_{sv})$$

$$N_{hc_{k}} = \frac{L_{hc}}{D_{hc}}\tan(\theta_{k,0}) \qquad nc_{k} = \mathrm{ceil}(N_{hc_{k}})$$

$$T_{d_{k}} = \rho_{se}^{nc_{k}}\left(nc_{k} + 1 - N_{hc_{k}}\right) + \rho_{se}^{nc_{k}+1}\left(N_{hc_{k}} - nc_{k}\right)$$

$$T_{c_{k}} = T_{d_{k}} + \left[\frac{\rho_{de}}{(\rho_{de} + \alpha_{s})}\right]F_{sq}(1 - T_{d_{k}}) \qquad T_{equ_{k}} = \frac{T_{c_{k}} + T_{e_{k}}E}{1 + E}$$

$$T_{eqground} = T_{equ_{1}} \qquad T_{equ_{1}} = 0.836 \qquad \text{Transmittance of ground diffuse radiation}$$
$$T_{eqsky} = T_{equ_{2}} \qquad T_{equ_{2}} = 0.841 \qquad \text{Transmittance of sky diffuse radiation}$$

The beam solar absorptance of the TIM is equal to 1 minus the reflectivity and the transmittance (Figure 3.13).

Next we compute the diffuse solar absorptance of the TIM.

1 For sky radiation   For $\theta = \theta_{esradiant}$

$$rsds = asin\left(\frac{sin(\theta_{esradiant})}{\mu}\right) \qquad R_{\theta sd} = \frac{1}{2}\left[\frac{tan(\theta_{esradiant} - rsds)^2}{tan(\theta_{esradiant} + rsds)^2} + \frac{sin(\theta_{esradiant} - rsds)^2}{sin(\theta_{esradiant} + rsds)^2}\right]$$

$R_{\theta sd} = 0.079 \qquad \alpha_{skydiffuse} = 1 - \left(R_{\theta sd} + T_{eqsky}\right)$ Sky diffuse absorptance

2 For ground radiation

$$rsdg = asin\left(\frac{sin(\theta_{egradiant})}{\mu}\right) \qquad R_{\theta gd} = \frac{1}{2}\left[\frac{tan(\theta_{egradiant} - rsdg)^2}{tan(\theta_{egradiant} + rsdg)^2} + \frac{sin(\theta_{egradiant} - rsdg)^2}{sin(\theta_{egradiant} + rsdg)^2}\right]$$

$R_{\theta gd} = 0.909 \qquad \alpha_{grounddiffuse} = 1 - \left(R_{\theta gd} + T_{eqground}\right)$ Sky diffuse absorptance

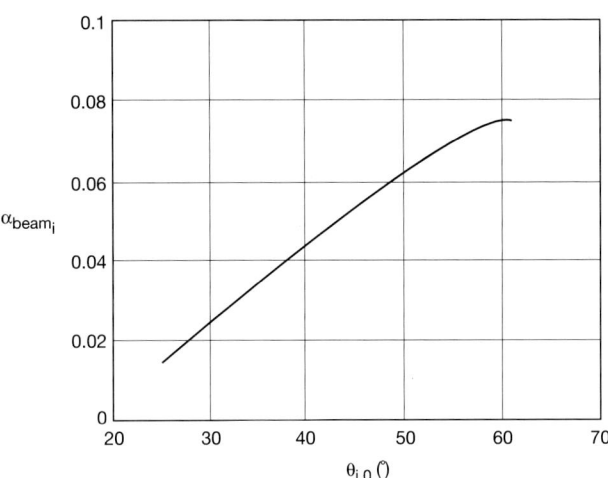

Figure 3.13 Calculation of absorptance of TIM (in Mathcad)

3.4 Shading

Shading provision should be considered as an integral part of fenestration system design. Blocking the sun before it reaches the building interior is the most effective method of reducing cooling loads.

The design of a fixed shading system depends on the opening area and the orientation of the aperture with respect to the position of the sun. In general, horizontal shading is used in south facades, while vertical is more efficient on the east or west facade.

The majority of fixed shading systems are installed in the exterior of a building in order to dissipate the heat that they absorb from the sun to the outside air. The same device used as internal shading will result in an average 30% reduced efficiency. This is because the shading devices dissipate heat by convection and long-wave radiation. Therefore, internal devices dissipate this heat inside the building space, since convection is due to the indoor air and glazing is opaque to long-wave radiation, which is also blocked indoors.

In designing shading systems for windows there are several conflicting design requirements that must be considered before an optimal solution is reached:

- blocking of direct solar gains during the cooling season
- allowing the maximum possible amount of solar radiation into the building interior during the heating season
- control of the intense daylight during clear days by diffusing it into the space or reflecting part of it towards the ceiling for example
- to allow the possibility of simultaneous shading and natural ventilation.

Shading of fenestration components may be achieved using fixed or movable devices (Figure 3.14). Fixed shading devices include:

- continuous overhangs, or horizontal louvres above the window
- side fins, or vertical louvres on the sides
- awnings (fixed in summer, retractable in winter).

Louvres, when strategically placed, allow winter sun to pass between their gaps, while blocking it in summer.

The window is also usually recessed into the wall (with the exception of curtain walls) resulting in the same shading effect as side fins and overhang of the same dimension.

Movable shading devices for fenestration systems may be external or internal. They include:

- roller shades (retractable)
- venetian blinds
- curtains (usually internal).

Adjustable devices may be lifted or rolled or drawn back from the window either automatically or manually. Venetian blinds are also sometimes built into double-glazing between the two glazings, and are operated by an indoor mechanism.

Architectural projections, known as **overhangs** when they are horizontal or **side fins** when vertical, are commonly employed in the building envelope to control the amount of solar radiation reaching a surface. The shading device is typically designed to exclude solar radiation in summer when it contributes to a reduction in cooling loads, and to admit it in winter when it contributes to a pleasant indoor environment and a reduction of heating requirements.

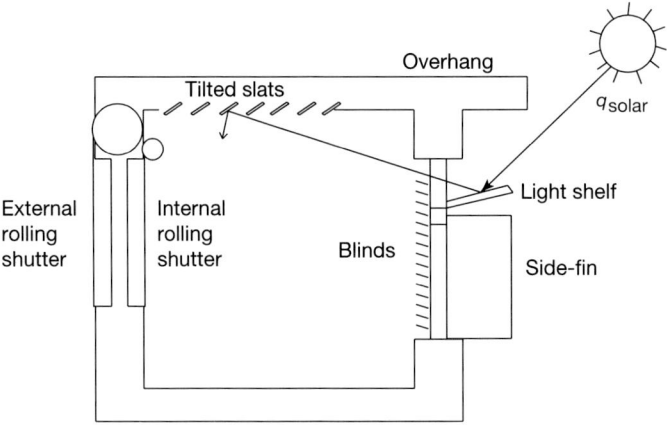

Figure 3.14 Shading devices

Shading of windows by exterior or adjacent components may be computed using basic solar geometry and projection equations, computer graphics techniques or graphical techniques.

A geometric technique for finding the shaded area of a recessed window with an overhang is based on Figure 3.15. A window of dimensions $c \times a$ recessed at a distance b from the wall outside surface is shown. The objective is to design an overhang with length equal to $c + 2g$ and width f, at a distance e above the window. The ray projection diagram shows the minimum dimensions for complete shading of the window for the given solar altitude α, surface solar azimuth angle γ and surface azimuth angle ψ. Point E at the outer edge of the overhang is projected to point O on the window plane.

The profile angle d is given by

$$\tan d = \tan \alpha/\cos \gamma \qquad (3.29)$$

It can be shown that the geometric dimensions of the overhang that satisfy our constraints are given by:

$$f = [(a + e)/\tan d] - b$$
$$g = f \tan \gamma \qquad (3.30)$$

Example

Consider a south-facing window located in Athens. The design objective is to shade the window from 9 a.m. to 3 p.m. solar time on 15 May. Because it is south-facing, 9 a.m. and 3 p.m. are symmetrical times and only 9 a.m. needs to be considered.

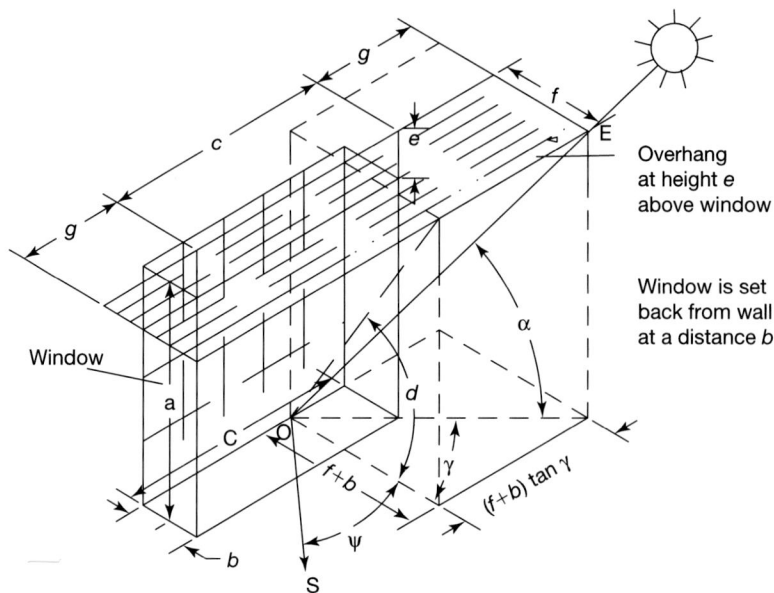

Figure 3.15 Recessed window with an overhang

Window geometry:

$a = 1.5$ m $c = 2.0$ m $b = 0.2$ m $e = 0.2$ m

$L = 38°$ $\varphi = 0$ $\beta = 90°$

$\delta = 18.8°$ (declination)

$\alpha = 46.6°$ (solar altitude)

$\varphi = \gamma = -76.7$ (solar azimuth and surface solar azimuth)

Profile angle $d = 77.7°$

Overhang dimensions:

width $f = 0.17$ m, $g = 0.72$ m, i.e. length $c + 2g = 3.44$ m

If these dimensions are chosen, the window will be completely shaded from 15 May to 28 July (symmetrical dates about 21 June).

It is interesting to check how much of the window is shaded at solar noon on 21 December. In this case the solar altitude is 24.5° and it is also equal to the profile angle d. The projection of the overhang edge on the window plane lies at a distance a' from the window upper edge:

$$a' = (f + b) \tan d - e$$

$$a' = 0.002 \text{ m}$$

Therefore only 0.2% of the window is shaded.

Overhangs are appropriate for near-south-facing surfaces while side fins shade better east- and west-facing surfaces. For a side fin (Figure 3.16) of width D the shaded part of the window h can be estimated as follows:

$$h = D \times \tan(\text{solar azimuth} - \text{window azimuth})$$

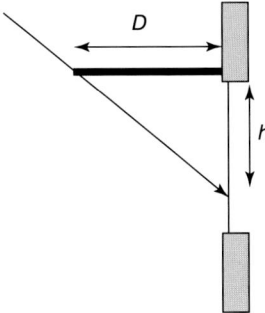

Figure 3.16 Shading of a window with a tall side fin of width D

Graphical techniques may also be employed for determination of the position of the sun and shading estimation.

A simplified method to determine the mean monthly shading coefficient has been developed under the PASSYS (1994) programme and is implemented in the PASSPORT computer program developed for the EC in 1994. The method considers three types of shading device:

- recessed window
- side fins
- overhangs.

All the geometric dimensions are input to PASSPORT, which computes the mean monthly incident solar radiation based on the following expression:

$$H_{b,g} = (1 - H_d/H)R_b H \, SB_1 \, SB_2 + H_d(1 + \cos b)/2SD$$
$$+ rH(1 - \cos b)/2SR \qquad (3.31)$$

where:
SB_1 = direct radiation shading factor for remote obstacles

SB_2 = direct radiation shape factor for facade obstacles
SD = diffuse radiation shading factor
SR = reflected radiation shading factor

$$SB_1 = (h_{ss} - h_{sr})/(2h_s)$$

h_{ss}, h_{sr} = sunset and sunrise times corresponding to the average angle of the remote obstacle

$$2h_s = 2(\text{sunset hour angle}) = \text{daylength}$$

For a recessed window SB_2 is determined by

$$SB_2 = \exp[(A_1 + B_1(L - \delta))R/H + (A_2 + B_2(L - \delta))R/W] \qquad (3.32)$$

where W is the window width and R the depth of the opening. The constants A_1, B_1, A_2 and B_2 were calculated from detailed simulations and are given in Table 3.4. Similarly, SB_2 for side fins is given by

$$SB_2 = 1 + [A_1 + B_1(L - \delta)]l/W + [A_2 + B_2(L - \delta)](l/W)(D/W) \qquad (3.33)$$

where:
l = length of side fin
D = distance between window and side fin

Table 3.4 Constants for monthly shading calculation [Santamouris 1994]

Shading component	Direction	A_1	B_1	A_2	B_2
Recessed window	S	−5.695	0.081	−1.342	0.009
	SE, SW	−2.418	0.032	−1.479	0.017
	E, W	−0.868	0.009	0.232	−0.022
	NE–NW	0.336	−0.013	−0.320	−0.074
	N	−1.193	0.036	−1.825	−0.163
Side-fins	S	−1.175	0.012	0.860	−0.008
	SE, SW	−0.799	0.009	0.684	−0.006
	E, W	0.118	−0.014	0.005	0.010
	NE, NW	0.155	−0.041	0.680	0.009
	N	0.275	−0.133	0.641	0.039
Overhang	S	−3.023	0.045	1.285	−0.006
	SE, SW	−1.255	0.015	0.905	−0.008
	E–W	−0.684	0.005	0.610	−0.004
	NE, NW	−0.654	0.006	0.616	−0.006

For overhangs the parameter SB_2 is calculated with the following expression:

$$SB_2 = 1 + [A_1 + B_1(L - \delta)]l/W + [A_2 + B_2(L - \delta)](l/W)(D/W)$$

where
l = length of overhang
D = distance between window and overhang

Graphical methods may also be employed in shading analysis using sunpath diagrams and shadow charts. A simple graphical technique to visualize solar access and shading is to obtain a shadow pattern plot by finding the shadow of one shading object on the component under consideration.

3.4.1 Light shelves

The light shelf is a horizontal baffle placed at a certain height of the window opening, intended to provide shade below it and at the same time to reflect the light to the ceiling. In most cases the light shelf is fitted some distance up the window, dividing the window opening in two parts (Figure 3.17).

The benefit resulting from the use of light shelves is to increase daylight penetration deeper into the building core. Furthermore, light shelves can reduce cooling loads due to a reduction of solar gains. There are two types of light shelves, internal and external. Internal light shelves provide less daylight penetration than the external ones, under all types of sky, except when direct sunlight impinges on them. In this case they shade a portion of the space close to the aperture. However, since this type of shelf does not shade the glazing surface, cooling load reduction is negligible.

External light shelves improve daylight penetration under all sky types. The performance of light shelves varies with the reflectance of the upper and lower surface. A highly reflective material can cause glare.

Recent studies on the performance of light shelves lead to the following conclusions (Littlefair 1995):

- Light shelves do not result in a large increase of core daylight illuminances. The highest relative increases (12–20%) occur when there are large external obstructions. In most cases, small light shelves made little difference to illuminances at the back of the room. Larger light shelves tended to reduce this illumination.
- Light shelves do improve uniformity of illuminance by reducing light levels near the window.
- Light shelves provide good shading from sunlight especially in summer.
- Light shelves perform better in high ceiling spaces (>3 m).
- The reflectance of the upper light shelf surface must be as high as possible.

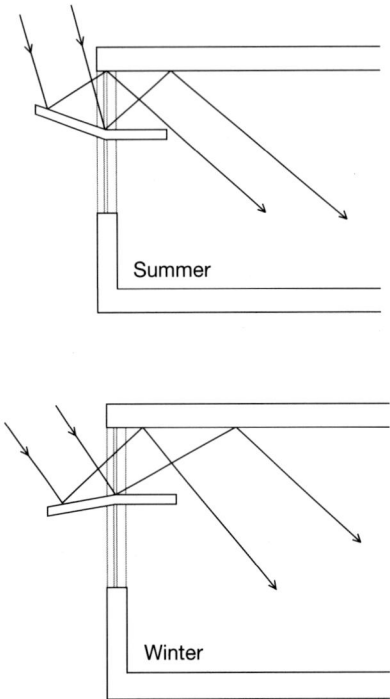

Summer

Winter

Figure 3.17 Light shelves

3.4.2 Adjustable shading devices

EXTERNALLY INSTALLED BLADES

The use of externally installed blades changes the entire appearance of the building. The lower part of the blades can be closed to avoid direct solar penetration. The upper part can be adjusted horizontally to reflect daylight deeper into the room. Daylighting levels are increased by up to 30% at 4 m distance away from the external wall. This device can be used in conjunction with inclined reflected ceiling in order to increase daylight levels on the working surface.

HORIZONTAL MOVABLE EXTERIOR LIGHT SHELF

This element can be used for shading areas near the opening and to increase daylight levels away from it. The tilt of the light shelf depends on the position, orientation and sky luminance distribution. The main disadvantage is that its efficiency is rather reduced when used under overcast sky conditions. This type of shading device is used on south facades in predominately sunny conditions.

MOVABLE AWNING

Awnings can reduce heat gains in summer by up to 65% on south facades and by up to 80% on west- or east-oriented facades. Their geometry is similar to that of horizontal overhangs, but their efficiency depends on the direct and diffuse transmittance of the material used. An additional feature of the awning is that it allows air circulation and hence natural ventilation. The transmittance of the fabric deteriorates with age. This system can be applied to almost all windows.

VENETIAN BLINDS

These are mainly internal devices, consisting of semi-transparent polyester or metal blinds. These blinds can be fixed or operable. Operable blinds can be automatic and designed in such a way as to track the sun or to track the shade. For sun tracking, they continuously change their tilt angle with respect to solar altitude to control sunlight to enter the room. For shade tracking, they change their tilt in order to reflect sunlight toward the ceiling or the exterior.

Glare adjustment can be performed by a proper choice of material. A factor for the determination of the effectiveness of a particular blind system is the ratio D/h. The parameters D and h are identified in Figure 3.18. Varying the ratio D/h from 1/1 (overhang) to 0.03/1 (thin blade) reveals three distinct phases in the penetration of daylight through the blades:

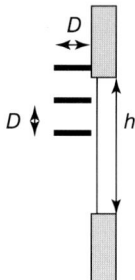

Figure 3.18 Venetian blinds

- The first phase ($1/1 > D/h > 0.5/1$) is characterized by a daylight distribution similar to that of an overhang. As the ratio of D/h approaches 0.5/1, a rapid reduction of illuminance near the window is observed, followed by a gradual improvement before the illuminance starts to drop again.
- The second phase ($0.5/1 > D/h > 0.08/1$) is characterized by a considerable variation in performance. Illuminance near the window is decreased as the ratio D/h decreases.
- During the third phase ($0.08/1 > D/h$) as the ratio D/h decreases, the performance close to the aperture increases. Performance levels drop fast at 0.01/1.

PERFORATED BLADES

These blades can be installed in the exterior or in the interior of a building as well. Depending on the perforation ratio, daylight levels can be adjusted. In general, these are not efficient for working spaces and their use is restricted to corridors, staircases and places without requirements for increased daylight.

VARIABLE-AREA LIGHT-REFLECTING ASSEMBLY

A reflective plastic film is rolled along a tilted surface so that a small steeply tilted mirror is created in summer and a larger, nearly horizontal mirror in winter. Hence sunrays are reflected to the rear of the room, both in winter and summer.

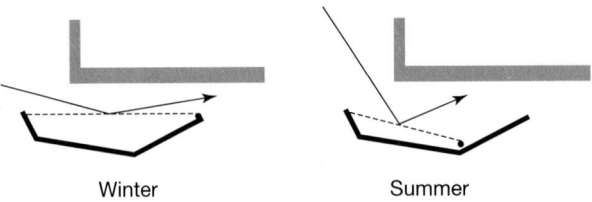

Winter   Summer

Figure 3.19 Variable-area light-reflecting assembly

Shading devices such as venetian blinds were evaluated experimentally (Aleo *et al.* 1994) for optical and thermal characteristics, and with the LAMAS software (Coronel *et al.* 1994). LAMAS is based on a detailed method for evaluation of the solar-optical performance of louvre-type shading devices. This detailed model has the following features:

- three-dimensional characterization of louvre-type devices, including different tilt angles, overlapping shades, etc.
- accurate model for direct and diffuse solar radiation
- reflection from shading elements
- semi-transparent behaviour
- coupled solar-optical performance of shading device and glazing
- coupled thermal performance of shading element and fenestration
- actual film coefficients for natural and forced convection.

Some major results of Aleo *et al.* (1994) were obtained with CFD analysis. It was found that unless the slats are horizontal the flow regime on both faces is laminar and the thickness of the boundary layer is negligible compared with the slat spacing. The correlation by Fuji and Kimura (1972) was found to be accurate for this purpose:

$$Nu = 0.56(Gr\ Pr\ \cos\ \theta)^{1/4} \qquad \text{for } 10^5 < Gr\ Pr < 10^{11} \qquad (3.34)$$

where Pr = Prandtl number = 0.7 for air, and θ is the angle of the slat with the vertical. Nu is the Nusselt number (hL/k) and Gr the Grashof number.

Coronel *et al.* (1994) also report a wind convective heat transfer coefficient for outdoor louvre-type devices which varies from about 6 W/m² K for a wind speed of 0.2 m/s to about 8 W/m² K for a wind speed of 3 m/s. This is reduced by about 33% compared with a flat surface. To calculate the total film coefficient for outdoors, a radiative component of about 5 W/m² K must be added.

CURTAINS (DRAPERIES) AND FABRIC SHADES

These are another common means of internal shading. Draperies are commonly used in houses to exclude unwanted solar gain, to control glare, for thermal insulation and to provide privacy. Shading coefficients as a function of fabric reflectance, yarn reflectance and average openness are given in ASHRAE (1989) for various types of curtain weave; values are given for single and double glass types. Experiments by Pennigton (1964) gave an SC (at normal incidence) of about 0.6 for non-planar light-coloured draperies with double glazing (clear glass) and SC = 0.4 when heat-absorbing double glazing was substituted. The SC values decreased to about 0.5 and 0.33 respectively for incidence angles of 60°. Shading factors (F-factors) for double glazing with internal draperies or venetian blinds have been reported (Blanchet and Girard 1993) (Table 3.5).

Table 3.5 Shading factor F for curtains and blinds (Blanchet and Girard 1993)

Shading device	Period of year	F
Double-glazed clear (4 mm sheets and 8 mm gap)	August	0.70
	April	0.68
Internal drapery		
light	July	0.44
dark	August	0.65
External drapery		
light	September	0.15
dark	September	0.22
Internal venetian blind		
angle 0°	November–December	0.38
angle 45°	February	0.41
angle 90°	January	0.57

The experimental data in Table 3.5 are based on the PASSYS test procedure.

PRISMATIC SYSTEMS

Prismatic panels control transmitted light by refraction. The direction of the incoming daylight is altered by passing through a prism or a triangular wedge of glass or plastic (Figure 3.20). Further investigation of these systems has led to the development of two forms of prismatic glazing:

- sunlight-directing prisms
- sunlight-excluding prisms

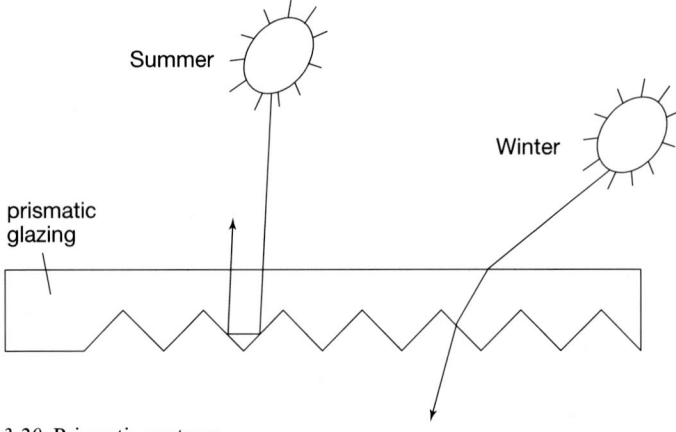

Figure 3.20 Prismatic systems

These systems when used for shading offer some advantages:

- Even though the sky cannot be seen through the systems it remains perceptible. Thus the system does not disturb the overall appearance of a window seen from the inside.
- Glare due to the sky brightness seen through a conventional window is reduced to a high degree.

3.4.3 Use of vegetation as shading device

The position and density of trees around a building contribute significantly to the reduction of solar gains. Factors that should be taken into account during the design stage of a building are the rate of growth, the size of the trees when they are mature and root development.

Basically, the luminance of one tree is a function of the illuminance on the foliage, the reflectance of the foliage, the amount of sky visible within the envelope of the crown and the sky luminance. The effective luminance of the tree crown is given by the following expression (Wilkinson 1992):

$$L_f/L_s = L_s p_s + (E_f \rho_f/\pi)(1 - p_s) \tag{3.35}$$

where L_f is the effective luminance of tree crown, L_s is the luminance of the sky behind the crown, ρ_f is the crown reflectance and p_s is the fraction of sky visible through the crown.

The crown reflectance varies with the angle of view and is less than the reflectance of individual leaves. For most purposes, the crown reflectance may be taken as 0.1 and the illuminance is taken as equal to the value on a vertical surface.

The following equation gives the luminance of a tree crown, as a function of the luminance of the overcast sky obscured:

$$\frac{L_f}{L_s} = p_s + \frac{\pi\left(3 + 7\rho_g\right) + 8}{6\pi\left(1 + 2\sin\gamma\right)}\rho_f\left(1 - p_s\right) \tag{3.36}$$

where ρ_f is the mean reflectance of the crown, ρ_g is the reflectance of the ground, p_s is the fraction of sky visible through the crown, and γ is the mean altitude of the sky patch hidden behind the crown. This angle can be visualized as follows: imagine the solid angle that is formed from viewpoint to the projected area of the tree crown. Draw a line that is located at the centre of the formed cone. The elevation of this line is the angle γ.

For an angle of view just above the horizon, when $\rho_g = 0.2$ and $\rho_f = 0.1$ the above equation becomes:

$$L_f/L_s = p_s + 0.1(1 - p_s) \tag{3.37}$$

This is an adequate approximation for most purposes where the reflectance and sky fraction parameters of the trees are not known in detail. Table 3.6 presents typical values of the sky cover fraction for individual mature tree crowns during summer and winter.

Table 3.6 Sky cover fraction for mature trees

Type of tree	Fraction of sky visible through crown (p_s)	
	Summer	Winter
Oak	0.17	0.5
Sycamore	0.18	0.54
Birch	0.24	0.54
Lime	0.11	0.54
Alder	0.24	0.49
Scots pine	0.27	0.3
Horse chestnut	0.19	0.52

3.5 Design of fenestration systems for daylighting

Daylighting is another important consideration and several measures may be taken to improve its quality and reduce glare. Daylighting considerations were introduced in the previous section on shading systems. Until the beginning of the 20th century, buildings were designed to exploit daylight. Then, owing to inexpensive electricity, old daylighting principles were forgotten. Now, new techniques are being developed (Kristensen 1994) and old ones are being rediscovered; see Figure 3.21. Internal reflective light shelves placed at about two-thirds height of the window reflect part of the incoming light towards the ceiling, while external overhangs situated below the top window edge may provide some shading while reflecting some of the light towards the ceiling. Skylights with shutters or electrically operated blinds may also achieve a similar effect.

Zenithal openings (Couret *et al.* 1994) are also attracting interest because they provide a high illuminance level; an anidolic toplighting consists of a compound parabolic concentrator which concentrates light in its top mirror and then diffuses it with its bottom one (Figure 3.21). It protects against direct sunlight, something difficult with atria.

Computer simulations of toplighting systems were performed with the ADELINE package, which combines heating–cooling–lighting analysis, and RADIANCE (Ward *et al.* 1988), a backward stochastic adaptive ray-tracing program. They considered diffusive glazing, a shed system (sawtooth apertures facing north) and the anidolic zenithal opening. The latter system collects skylight and guides it inside the building, always rejecting direct light. Ward *et al.* found that the zenithal anidolic lighting concept guarantees total protection against beam radiation, and without any movable parts lets diffuse skylight penetrate a large part of the building, with reduced glare.

Recent innovative solutions to diffusion of solar radiation into interior space include light-directing holographic optical elements (HOE) (Dietrich 1993). An HOE is made with a special film (laser technique); it may concentrate direct light, do a spectral division of light (like a prism), and diffuse direct light to avoid glaring effects.

Another notable technological innovation in window systems is the reversible window (Feuermann and Novoplansky 1998) in which a double-glazed window comprising a clear and a tinted glazing is rotated so that the tinted glazing is exterior in summer and interior in winter, resulting in the desirable SHGF for each season (Figure 3.21).

Another reason for avoiding direct solar radiation in office buildings is its strong effect on the effective temperature felt by persons in its path. Athienitis and Haghighat (1992) report that the effect of transmitted solar radiation on 'effective globe temperature' for double-glazed windows can be about 10°C (see Section 8.1).

Windows are unique from the occupant's perspective because they provide light and view, functions not provided by other elements. From the designer's point of view they are unique because they represent a significant element in the

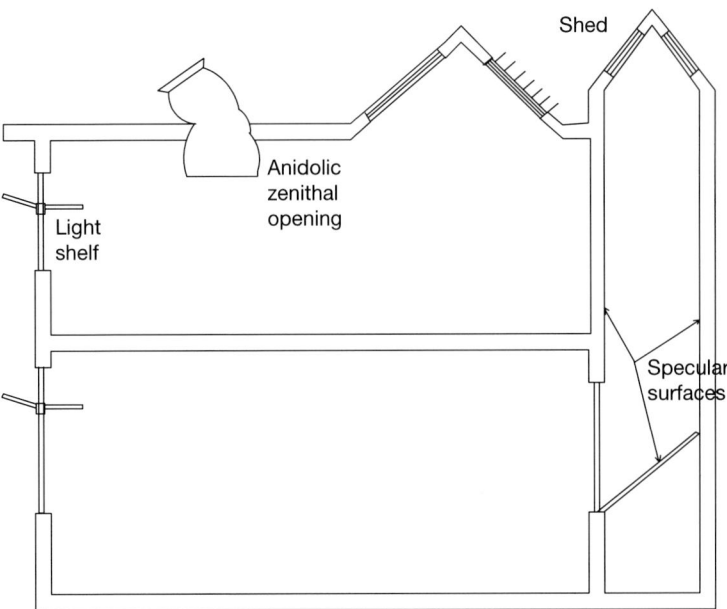

Figure 3.21 Daylighting techniques

vocabulary of architectural design. As such they are often used as formal elements of architectural expression in addition to the energy and non-energy performance requirements discussed previously.

The window is a dynamic element in the building envelope and must respond to continuously changing occupant needs as well as continuously changing environmental conditions.

A large portion of the energy consumed by buildings is due to lighting. There are many ways of saving lighting energy, but once again these solutions must be consistent with maintaining or improving productivity. Despite the high cost of energy, the value of human productivity is many times greater. In North America, the annual cost of providing lighting energy for a small office occupied by a single occupant is approximately equal to that worker's salary for a single hour. Thus, if a poor lighting design costs the employer even one hour's worth of productivity in return for large annual lighting savings, the employer has lost money overall.

A complete discussion of daylighting in buildings would consider its impacts on the following issues: electric lighting integration, energy savings, peak load impacts, HVAC systems impacts, lighting quality, view and glare. As an architectural design element, daylighting influences the built environment at many different scales: urban planning, building form, envelope design, fenestration design and interior design.

There are significant differences between using sun and sky as a source of light and using electric light sources. A primary difference is the inherent variability in daylight and its unpredictability. Standard clear and overcast skies have been defined and used for some time by the international lighting community:

- **Uniform luminance sky distribution**. This model represents a sky with constant value of luminance (in this case the resulting horizontal illuminance is πL).
- **CIE overcast sky distribution**. In this model the luminance is varied with elevation and corresponds to a situation where the sky is covered with light clouds and the sun is not visible (Figure 3.22). The luminance in a point (L) of the sky with elevation θ is given by:

$$L = L_z(1 + 2\sin\,\theta)/3 \tag{3.38}$$

where L_z is the zenith luminance. The transfer process of the radiation through clouds, in the absence of severe pollution, produces white light by colour mixing. If the atmosphere is heavily polluted, the overcast sky colour appearance is yellow.

- **Clear-sky luminance distribution**. This type of sky has a strongly non-uniform luminance distribution. The CIE has recommended standard luminance distributions of the clear sky which are simplifications of a complex process of atmospheric scattering in the presence of different pollutants. Most clear-sky luminance models are variants of the same basic form. The formula presented below relates the luminance L in one point of the sky vault with the zenith luminance L_z:

(a)   (b)

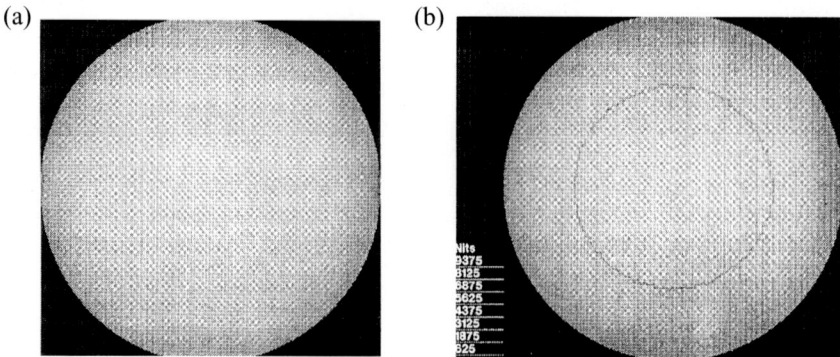

Figure 3.22 (a) Hemispherical view and (b) luminance distribution of an overcast sky (simulation with RADIANCE)

$$\frac{L}{L_z} = \frac{\left(a + b_e^{-3\theta} + c\cos^2\theta\left(1 - e^{-d\sec z}\right)\right)}{\left(a + b_e^{-3z_s} + c\cos^2 z_s\right)\left(1 - e^{-d}\right)}$$

(3.39)

where a, b, c, d are adjustable coefficients, θ is the angle (in radians) between the point with luminance L and the sun, z is the zenith angle of the point and z_s is the zenith angle of the sun.

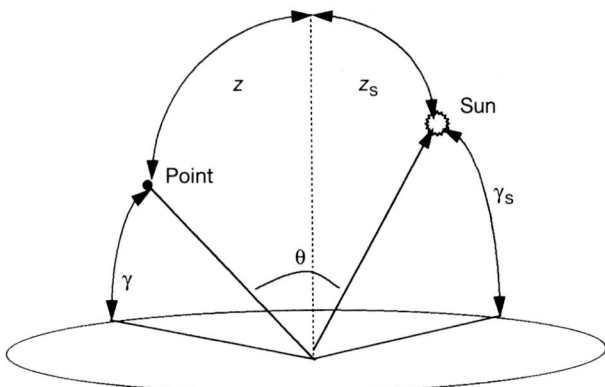

Figure 3.23 Definition of parameters used in sky luminance distribution functions.

The CIE clear sky model has $a = 0.91$, $b = 10$, $c = 0.45$, $d = 0.32$. Additionally CIE has also standardized a clear sky for polluted atmospheres, using the following coefficients: $a = 0.856$, $b = 16$, $c = 0.3$, $d = 0.32$ (Figure 3.23).

The blue colour of the clear sky is strongly dependent on the height of the site above sea level and by the amount of atmospheric pollution. Nitrogen dioxide makes the colour of the atmosphere brown and this can be seen when looking towards an urban area from the surrounding countryside. High water vapour levels, in the absence of pollution, tend to give the sky a white appearance (Figure 3.24).

However, these standards were often created with minimum conditions in mind, in order to verify a minimum design standard. For the purposes of either estimating occupant satisfaction or calculating energy effects, these sky models must be expanded to include partly cloudy and direct sun effects and to account for the variability in daylight levels and sky luminance distribution over the entire year. Research is under way in many locations worldwide to fill these gaps.

To characterize the way in which daylight penetrates a building, it is useful to examine the distribution of indoor illuminance as a function of the external luminous conditions. Owing to the simplicity of the luminous distribution function of the overcast sky, the interior illuminance in a point of a building is proportional to the external horizontal illuminance. This ratio of the daylight illuminance at an

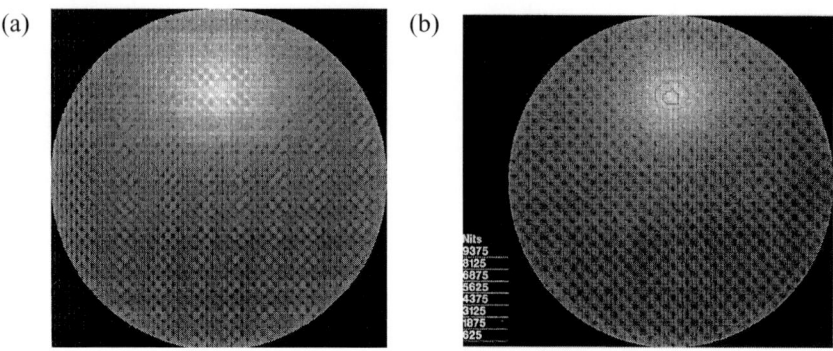

Figure 3.24 (a) Hemispherical view and (b) luminance distribution of a clear sky (simulation with RADIANCE)

interior point to the instantaneous illuminance outside the building on a horizontal surface from a complete hemisphere of sky is called the **daylight factor** and can be expressed as a percentage:

$$DF = E_{in}/E_{ext} \times 100 \tag{3.40}$$

Thus the distribution of the indoor illuminance can be carried out by the use of daylight factors (i.e. having as reference the overcast sky). Under clear sky conditions the above-mentioned concept of daylight factor cannot be used as a design criterion since it varies significantly throughout the day.

A convenient way to evaluate the total amount of daylight in a room and hence the room brightness in relation to the view outside is the average daylight factor. The working surface is considered to be a horizontal surface at 0.7 m above the floor for offices. The estimation of average DF is based on the calculation of total luminous flux entering the window, the ratio of window opening to internal surface and the overall interreflections.

The calculation of the average daylight factor with simple external obstruction can be done as follows.

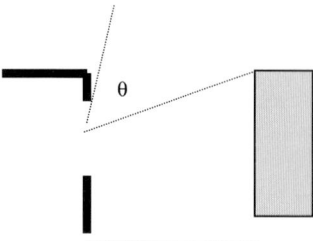

Figure 3.25 Definition of obstruction angle

$$DF = \tau\{A_w\theta/[A(1 - \rho_{mean})]\} \tag{3.41}$$

where τ is the diffuse light transmittance of the glazing, A_w is the area of the window in m^2, A is the total area of ceiling, floor and walls including windows in m^2, θ is the angle subtended by the visible sky (Figure 3.25), measured from a point in the plane of the internal wall at the centre of the window, in degrees and ρ_{mean} is the area-weighted reflectance of ceiling, floor and walls including the windows. However, during the design process it is useful to investigate how daylight arrives at a point inside a room. This can be done by splitting the available indoor illuminance into three components:

- Sky component (DF_{SC}), which is the illuminance received at a point in the interior of a building, directly from the sky.
- External reflected component (DF_{EXT}), which is the illuminance in the interior due to light reflected from external obstructions.
- Internal reflected component (DF_{INT}), which is the illuminance received at a point and is composed of light received indirectly from daylight that is interreflected around the internal surfaces of the space.

Therefore, for any point indoors:

$$DF = DF_{SC} + DF_{EXT} + DF_{INT} \tag{3.42}$$

It follows therefore that if no sky is visible from the point, $DF_{SC} = 0$. Further, if no window can be seen from the point, $DF_{SC} = DF_{EXT} = 0$.

For over 80% of the floor area in most buildings daylight factors fall in the range of 0–5%. Close to the windows, however, they can reach 10–15%. The values of the daylight factors, therefore, provide a guide to the brightness achieved in a room from daylight. A classification of the brightness of building zones based on the values of daylight factors is given in Table 3.7.

Table 3.7 Average daylight factors and the associated daylight contribution

Zone	DF (%)	Daylight contribution
Bright	>6	Very large
Average	3–6	Good
Dark	1–3	Fair
Very dark	0–1	Poor

To take into account the impact of the deterioration of room surfaces, the presence of window bars on the reduction of solar radiation and the transmission of window glass, a number of correction factors should be introduced to the above equation. Thus the equation becomes:

$$DF = (DF_{SC} + DF_{EXT} + DF_{INT} \times MF) \times FR \times GL \times MG \qquad (3.43)$$

where MF is the maintenance factor for room surfaces, FR is a factor related to the light loss due to window bars, GL is a correction factor due to glass transmission losses and MG is related to window maintenance. Typical values of the above-mentioned correction factors are presented in Tables 3.8–3.11.

Table 3.8 Typical values of the factor MF

	Non-industrial type of activity	Industrial type of activity
Non-industrial	0.9	0.7
Dirty industrial	0.9	0.6

Table 3.9 Typical values of the factor FR

Large paned windows	FR
All metal windows	0.8
Metal windows in wooden frames	0.75
All wood windows	0.7

Table 3.10 Typical values of the factor GL

Material	Diffuse transmittance	GL
6 mm clear glass	0.85	1
6 mm rough cast	0.8–0.85	0.95
Plastic moderately diffusing	0.75–0.8	0.9

Table 3.11 Typical values of the factor MG

Location of the building	MG for non-industrial work	MG for industrial work
Non-industrial area, vertical glazing	0.9	0.8
Industrial area, vertical glazing	0.8	0.7

The sky component DF_{SC} can be estimated using graphical tools such as the following:

- **The BRE overcast sky protractors** (Figure 3.26). These protractors consist of a set of 10. Five are for overcast sky conditions and five for uniform. There are protractors for vertical, 30°, 60°, horizontal and one protractor for windows without glazing. Each BRE protractor is composed of two parts. One part is used only with section drawings while the other is used only for plan drawings to establish the correction factor for the width of the aperture.

- **The Waldram diagram method** (Figure 3.27). In this method a series of droop lines are used to establish the view of the sky through the aperture and to estimate the DF due to sky. Its basic principle is the use of the equal area method whereby the view factor of the sky plotted on the diagram describes an area proportional to the daylight represented by the view.
- **The Pilkington sky dot method** (Figure 3.28). This method is also called the pepper dot method and is an orthographic projection technique in which the user constructs an interior perspective using the point where the calculation of illuminance is to be performed as the perspective reference point. An elevation view of the aperture is overlaid on the sky dot chart. The horizontal line of the diagram is placed on the true horizon. The sky component of DF (%) is simply the number of dots in the area of the aperture divided by 10.
- **The Bryan sky component protractors.** This set of protractors was developed for clear and overcast conditions. The protractors are used similarly to the BRE protractors but are based, in the case of clear sky, on the diffuse illuminance falling on a horizontal level from the clear sky.

The estimation of DF_{SC} in geometrically complicated scenes needs the use of a computer model. The external reflected component could be estimated by calculating the obstructed area of the sky, estimating the DF_{SC} for the obstructed part and then converting this value to DF_{EXT} by multiplying it by the ratio of the luminance of the obstructed area to the sky luminance. A simpler approach is to multiply the DF_{SC} by the average reflectance of the obstruction:

$$DF_{EXT} = DF_{SC} \times \rho$$

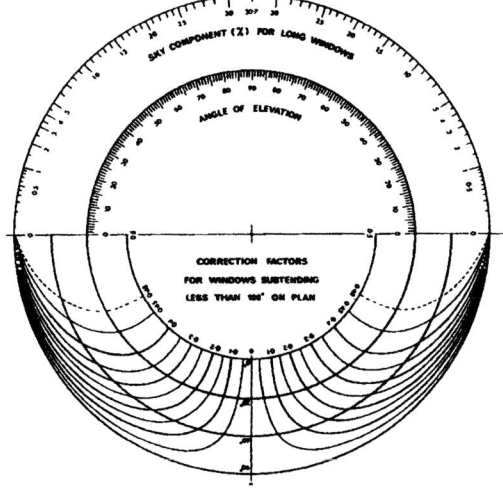

Figure 3.26 BRE protractor for vertical aperture

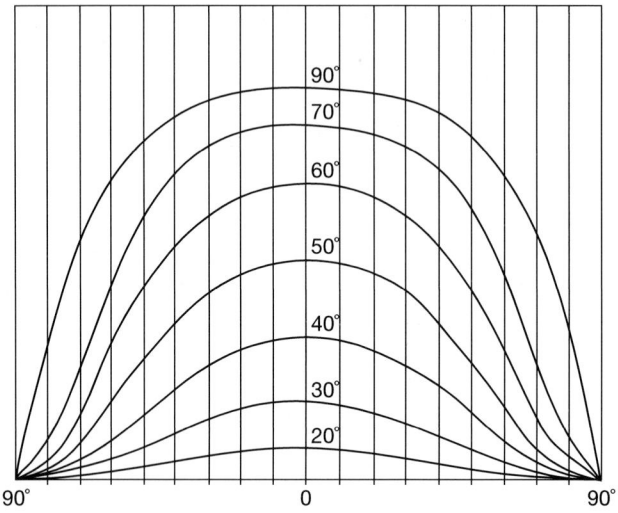

Figure 3.27 Waldram diagram

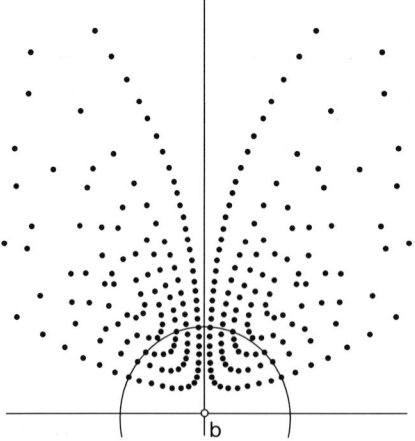

Figure 3.28 Pilkington sky dot diagram.

Under overcast conditions DF_{EXT} is much lower than DF_{SC}.

The most common approach to estimate DF_{INT} is to establish an average internal reflected component value for the entire room. This can be performed by using the split-flux method developed by BRE:

$$DF_{INT} = \frac{\tau A}{A_t (1-\rho)} \left(C_1 \rho_u + C_2 \rho_1 \right)$$

(3.44)

where A_t is the sum of all the room surfaces, glazed and opaque, A is the area of the opening, and τ is the transmittance of the glazing. ρ_u and ρ_l are the average reflectance of the room, the reflectance of the upper and lower parts respectively (split along the middle of the window). The coefficients C_1 and C_2 represent the impact of external obstructions and ground. Typical values are listed in Tables 3.12 and 3.13.

Table 3.12 Values for coefficient C_1

Angle of obstruction (°)	C_1
No obstruction	39
10	35
20	31
30	25
40	20
50	14
60	10
70	7
80	5

Table 3.13 Values for coefficient C_2

Ground reflectance	C_2
0.10	5
0.20	10
0.30	15
0.40	20
0.50	25
0.60	30
0.70	35
0.80	40

The basic daylighting component is the vertical window. This permits luminous, thermal and acoustic interchange as well as natural ventilation and view. A window is characterized by its type, size, shape, position and orientation. The absolute surface of the window influences only the possibilities of ventilation and vision. Fenestration, which is expressed as the ratio between the window surface and the room area, affects the amount and distribution of light.

The performance of the window depends on the properties of the transparent element. Recently the glazing industry has made great research efforts to improve the physical and optical properties of glazing systems. Hence today there are glasses on the market with overall heat loss coefficients (U-values) from 0.4 to 5 W/m² K and light transmittances from 5% to 90%. There are three fundamental approaches to improving the energy performance of glazing products (two or more of these approaches may be combined):

- Alter the glazing material itself by changing its chemical composition or physical characteristics. An example of this is tinted glazing.
- Apply a coating to the glazing material surface. Reflective coatings and films were developed to reduce heat gain and glare, and more recently, low emittance and spectrally selective coatings have been developed to improve both heating and cooling season performance.
- Assemble various layers of glazing and control the properties of the spaces between the layer. These strategies include the use of two or more panes or films, low-conductance gas fills between the layers, and thermally improved edge spacers.

A new class of materials is that of translucent insulation materials (TIM). These are characterized by good optical transmission and good thermal performance. They can also replace conventional insulation. TIMs are classified into four categories:

- Multiple glazing or plastic films, with their surfaces parallel to the surface of the facade.
- Parallel slats of different materials, honeycombs and capillaries with their surface perpendicular to the surface of the facade.
- Synthetic foams, bubbles.
- Glass fibres, aerogels.

Recently, glazings with control capabilities have appeared on the market, for example electrochromic glazings, thermochromic glazings and photochromic glazings.

To evaluate the **performance of a specific glazing material**, in addition to the previously mentioned parameters such as SHGC and SC there are some other parameters:

- **Coolness factor** is the ratio of the visible transmittance to the shading coefficient. For example if the value is greater than 1, the glass is considered selective and will offer better performance in a hot climate than a similar glazing with a lower coolness factor.
- **Energy rating**. A more simplistic approach was adopted by the Canadian Window and Door Manufacturers Association. According to this approach, window energy performance is dependent on three factors: heat loss (U-value), SHGC and air infiltration. Having these essential window performance numbers, the net heat flow through a glazing can be calculated. The energy rating (ER) is a net heat flow calculation procedure and is designed to compare window products for their heating season efficiency under average winter conditions for the northern USA and Canada. This index permits a convenient standard of comparison for all glass products. ER is currently utilized by the Canadian Window and Door Manufacturers Association and is a part of Canadian

Standard CSA A440. The ER employs average weather data for winter temperatures and sunlight intensity representing several North American cities having a heating-dominated energy use pattern. The sunlight level used to calculate solar gain is an average of four building elevations. The ER is calculated using the following energy balance equation:

$$ER = (72.2SHGC) \times (21.9U_w) \times (0.54L/A_w)$$

where ER is the effective energy rating (W/m²), SHGC is the solar heat gain coefficient of total window, U_w is the U-value of total window (W/m²/°C), L is the average air leakage of the window (m³/hour) and A_w is the area of the window (m²). Slightly different procedures are energy rating specific (ERS) and energy rating index (ERI). The ERS procedure determines a specific ER value for a window used in any of 13 cities throughout Canada. In addition to material options and window size, ERS is dependent on the climate of the particular location, the window to floor area ratio and the window orientation on the house. The ERI is designed to compare window products for their heating season efficiency under average winter conditions for the northern USA and Canada. The ERI employs average weather data for winter temperatures and sunlight intensity representing several North American cities having a heating-dominated energy use pattern. The sunlight level is an average of four building elevations. Air infiltration is assumed to be zero, which is a valid assumption if glass-only comparisons are being made or when comparing windows having equal air infiltration values:

$$ERI = 100(0.87SCI) \times U \times (T_i - T_o)$$

where the units for ERI are BTU/hour/ft².
SC = shading coefficient (unit-less)
I = 22.9 BTUs/hour/ft² (constant for average solar intensity)
T_i = 70°F (constant for average inside temperature)
T_o = 31°F (constant for average outside temperature)
U = U-value (BTU/hour/ft²/°F)

As the window height increases, the DF generally increases, as a greater portion of the brighter part of the sky (brightness increases towards the zenith) will be visible. Therefore the height and proportion of glazing above the working plane are more important than the actual shape or total area of a window. For this reason, tall Georgian windows provide better illumination than modern ribbon or strip windows, which are horizontally oriented and generally at a lower elevation, even for the same overall glazing area.

Decisions as to whether to increase the window height, or overall size, must consider the nature of the external view, and the proportions of the interior space, relative to the positioning of work stations. Windows that are too high may restrict the sight lines of occupants positioned close by, whereas windows which are too large may cause an unacceptable contrast between light levels next to, and far from, the external walls.

Minimum total areas of glazing for side-lit rooms are recommended as given in Table 3.14.

Table 3.14 Suggested window areas for daylighting

Depth of room from external wall (max., m)	% of window on external wall as seen from interior (min.)
>8	20
8–11	25
11–14	30
>14	35

Source: BS 8206: Part 2 1992 'Code of Practice for Daylighting'

The distribution of this area should ensure all parts of the room enjoy some external view and provide occupants with opportunities to focus on objects at varying distances from the working plane.

A window is one of the most fundamental components in a building. As an opening in the external enclosure, it provides a solar, thermal, acoustic and climatic relationship between the interior and exterior. When considered three dimensionally, it can manipulate light, views, sound and air to define and enhance the character and experience of any space. Variations in type, size, shape, location and orientation offer a number of design possibilities when characterising fenestration.

3.5.1 Type

A window 'type' is defined functionally by the primary purpose of the aperture, which will determine design decisions on size, shape, position, orientation and any control systems required (Table 3.15).

Table 3.15 Window design requirements

Purpose	Design requirements
1. Daylighting	Optimum height and size for required daylight factor
2. Natural ventilation	Positioned in the wall with respect to local wind directions and internal air currents
3. Daylighting and view	Size and sill height above floor level and exterior suited to occupant positions and external features
4. Daylighting and natural ventilation	Sizing and location must be suited to all parameters

Generally, windows will be required for light, views and ventilation so type should be distinguished by considerations of specific climatic characteristics of the building location.

3.5.2 Size

In terms of vision and ventilation, the absolute surface area (m^2) of a window is important. Size classifications are made with consideration of human scale (Table 3.16).

Table 3.16 Size classification of windows

Classification	Surface area (m^2)
Small	<0.5
Medium	0.5–2
Large	>2

The amount, and distribution, of light internally are affected by the ratio of total window surface to the area of the room. This is termed the **fenestration**, expressed as a percentage (Table 3.17).

Table 3.17 Classification of fenestration as % of room surface area

Classification	%	
Very low	<1	Risks low illumination, especially if low overcast skies, atmospheric pollution or external obstructions occur
	1–4	
Medium	4–10	
High	10–25	Problems with thermal control and glare unless controls used
Very high	>25	

Design decisions regarding the provision of one large window, or several smaller ones of the same total surface area, must recognize that while the amount of light admitted will be comparable, views, natural ventilation patterns and internal distribution of the light will be markedly different, particularly if the smaller windows are located in different walls. The nature of the activities within the space, external views and orientation of the building are important factors.

3.5.3 Shape

Window shapes are classified according to the ratio of height to width, which influences light distribution, depth of penetration, proportions of the view and natural ventilation strategies (Table 3.18).

Table 3.18 Effect of height/width ratio

Window shape	Height/width ratio	Characteristics
Horizontal	½	Illumination primarily parallel to the window wall; distribution is fairly unchanging throughout the day with little glare.
Intermediate	½–2	Enables a panoramic-type view.
Vertical	2	Illumination primarily perpendicular to the window wall; light distribution greatly varies throughout the day. Depth of daylighting increased but glare may be a problem.

As the window proportions become more vertical, exterior views may be laterally restricted but depth of field increases. Vertical configurations offer greater potential for natural ventilation strategies.

3.5.4 Location

The vertical location of a window relative to the height of the wall in which it is contained determines whether it is high, intermediate or low. Higher windows enable greater depth of penetration and distribution of daylight but sill levels must consider the human scale. Depending on the climate and strategy, natural ventilation may benefit from high opening lights.

The horizontal location relative to wall width is classed as central, lateral or corner. Light distribution from a central window may be greater, but glare is less of a problem in corner locations. The choice of location must consider occupant sight lines when seated and standing, relevant external view features, and layout of working planes/tasks requiring daylight.

3.5.5 Orientation

Windows should be oriented with respect to the sun path so that comfortable internal daylight levels are obtained, without excessive solar heat gain, glare or contrast.

The climatic, geographical and legislative (planning, fire) conditions specific to each site will determine the optimum window configurations, but the following effects generally apply:

- **South facing**: high luminous levels. High solar heat gain in winter, medium in summer. Illumination is variable throughout the day. Preferable for cold/temperate climates in the northern hemisphere (solar gain)

- **North facing**: low luminous level. Low solar heat gain, illumination is fairly constant throughout the day. Preferable for hot climates in the northern hemisphere and cold/temperate climates in the south (solar gain).
- **East and west facing**: medium luminous levels. High energy gain in summer, low in winter. East orientation has high illumination in the morning, west is high in the afternoon.

East- and west-facing windows can be considered comparable, although their maximum light levels occur at different times of the day, so any control systems (in terms of solar shading or heat gain) should be movable.

Fixed systems are more suitable for south- and north-facing windows, next to which activities requiring higher light levels should preferably be located.

3.5.6 Roof lights

When properly designed and located, **horizontal** roof lights admit up to three times more daylight per square metre of glazing than vertical windows, as the brightness of the sky increases towards the zenith. This light will be distributed more uniformly throughout the space over a day, and glare can be controlled by translucent glazing, shading devices and/or redirection of the light. Roof/ceiling apertures limit views to a portion of the sky, so visual contact with the landscape may be lost. Site-specific conditions will determine whether this is acceptable or not.

Vertical roof lights are sometimes preferred in single-storey deep plans, as horizontal glazing experiences greater solar heat gain in summer than winter, so may require integration with a natural ventilation system. Various configurations of horizontal or vertical lights are available.

Clerestory, lanterns, north lights and monitor roof windows are openings in the vertical plane which increase internal illuminance with predominantly zenithal light, usually diffused. Typically incorporated into the roof construction, natural ventilation can be provided if the apertures can be opened.

Skylights are openings in a horizontal or tilted roof that admit zenithal light into the space under the skylight, and can be opened for ventilation. Generally in standard units of up to 1 m width and length, they can be larger and with a variety of shapes. Hemispherical roofs may be partially or fully constructed with translucent materials, such as glass, polycarbonate, acrylic or fibreglass.

Some key ideas about the design of windows are the following:

- Feasibility factor should be above 0.25 in order for daylight to have the potential for significant energy savings. The feasibility factor is defined as:

$$\text{WWR} \times T \times \text{OF}$$

where WWR is the window to wall ratio, T is the visible transmittance and OF is the obstruction factor

- Incorporation of envelope features such as rounded edges and splayed reveals, which usually soften light contrasts.
- Spaces with windows on two sides often have better daylighting distribution and glare is reduced.
- The depth of the room should be within 1–2.5 times the window head height for balanced daylight distribution.
- The higher the window the deeper the daylighting zone.
- Strip windows provide more uniform daylight.
- Effective aperture should be around 0.3. The effective aperture is the product of visible transmittance with WWR.

3.5.7 Design and control recommendations for windows

- The best way of avoiding overheating in hot climates is to minimize the transmission of solar gains into the building interior.
- Exterior shading is always more effective than interior shading.
- Sizing of south- or near-south-facing windows in relation to thermal mass is usually best based on passive solar heating design principles.
- East- and west-facing windows should not be too large (not more than 10% of the zone floor area) because they allow high solar gains in the morning and the afternoon during summer.
- The building should be insulated from the external gains during the day and its interior from the glare from direct sunlight without diminishing the level of diffuse daylight and view.
- A good inexpensive means of reducing heat gains in the summer and heat losses in the winter is double-glazing with a low-emissivity coating on the inner pane; this keeps the exterior glazing warm, reducing the risk of condensation; the risk of winter condensation is similarly reduced for the inner pane (room-side) in winter.
- Some shading devices offer a lot of flexibility, e.g. an external blind with insulated louvres can offer shade while allowing natural ventilation when the louvres or slats are rotated to the correct angle.
- Size-fixed shading devices only as large as required based on computational or graphical techniques.
- The following glass types are suitable for the corresponding orientations (northern hemisphere):
    SW to SE: clear glass with shading (preferably external)
    SE to NW and SE to NE: reflective or absorptive glass
    NW to NE: clear glass, not much shading (e.g. a tree).

Active control of shading devices such as shutters is beginning to attract a lot of interest in passive solar building design. It is already used in some buildings such as museums and in high locations to achieve continuous remote control of motor-operated venetian blinds and shutters (Lee and Selkowitz 1995). The motor controlling the shutter/blind may be connected to a photosensor and/or thermostat. Van Paassen describes computerized control of such a system for a passive solar test-cell (Chapter 8).

Lee and Selkowitz (1995) investigate the use of control strategies for coordinating the solar-optical properties of a dynamic building envelope system with a daylight-controlled lighting system to reduce electricity consumption and enhance perimeter zone comfort in commercial buildings. Their computer simulation results (with DOE-2) showed that (1) predictive control algorithms may significantly increase energy efficiency of systems with non-optimal solar-optical properties such as the automated venetian blinds, and (2) simpler on/off control strategies may suffice for more advanced envelope systems that have spectrally selective narrow-band electrochromic coatings.

Another recent development in dynamic building envelope systems is solar-acoustical-ventilated (SAV) windows (Bonhevi *et al.* 1994), which attempt to balance the need for passive solar gain utilization with the need for ventilation, good indoor air quality and sound insulation. SAV windows consist of a window with controlled ventilation inlets and outlets, built-in controlled venetian blinds, all connected to an expert controller which is also connected to the auxiliary heating/cooling system. Finally, a European advanced window information system (WIS) is available for determining the thermal and solar characteristics of advanced windows (Dijk and Bakker 1994).

3.6 Bibliography

Aleo F., Sciuto S. and Viedera R., (1994), 'Solar transmission measurements in outdoor conditions of non-homogeneous shading devices', *European Conference On Energy Performance and Indoor Climate in Buildings*, Lyon, France, Nov, 1074–1079.

Arulanantham M. and Kauskika N.D. (1994) 'Global radiation transmittance of transparent insulation material', *Solar Energy*, **53**: 4, 323–328.

ASHRAE (1989) *ASHRAE Handbook – Fundamentals*, Atlanta, GA, USA.

ASTM (1989) Calibrated Hot Box Test (C976), *ASTM Book of Standards*, ASTM.

Athienitis A.K. (1994), *Building Thermal Analysis*, Electronic Mathcad Book, Mathsoft, Boston, MA.

Athienitis A.K. and Haghighat F. (1992), 'A study of the effects of solar radiation on the indoor environment', *ASHRAE Transactions*, **98**, Part 1, 257–261.

Athienitis A.K. and Ramadan H. (1999) 'Numerical model for a building with transparent insulation', *Solar Energy* **67**: 1, 101–109.

Balaras C. (1996) 'Thermal comfort' in *Passive Cooling of Buildings*, James & James (Science Publishers) Ltd, London, Chapter 6.

Blanchet Y. and Girard M. (1993) 'Thermal and visual effectiveness of shading devices', *3rd European Conference on Architecture*, Florence, Italy, May, 153–156.

Bonhevi F., Trias A. and Traver X. (1994) 'Ventilation techniques integrated in the building envelope', *European Conference On Energy Performance and Indoor Climate in Buildings*, Lyon, France, Nov., 860–865

Brandemuehl M.J. and Beckman W.A. (1980) 'Transmission of diffuse radiation through CPC and flat plate collectors glazing', *Solar Energy* **24**, 511-513.

Braun P.O., Goetzberger A., Schmid J. and Stahl W. (1992) 'Transparent insulation of building facades – steps from research to commercial applications', *Solar Energy*, **49**: 5, 413–427.

BRE (1986) *Estimating daylight in buildings*, Digest 310, BRE.

Brunello Z. (1987) *Solar Properties of Fenestration, Solar and Thermal Properties of Windows: Expert Guide*, Annex XII, IEA.

Buchberg H. (1969) 'Sensitivity of room thermal response of buildings to perturbations in the climate', *Building Science*, **4**, 43–61.

Button D. and Rte B. (1992) *Glass in Building*, Pilkington Ltd., Butterworth, London.

Cane R.L.D., Hollands K.G.T., Raithy G.D. and Unny T.E., (1977) 'Free convection heat transfer across inclined honeycombs panels', *ASME Transactions*, Feb, 86-91.

CEC (1993) *Daylight in Architecture, a European reference book*, CEC, DGXII, James & James (Science Publishers) Ltd, London.

Charters W.W.S. and Peterson L.F. (1972) 'Free convection suppressing using honeycomb cellular materials', *Solar Energy*, **13**, 353–361.

Chattha J.A. and Jesch L.F. (1989) 'Solar transmission potential of transparent honeycomb insulation', *Proceedings of the ISES World Congress*, Japan.

Cogan et al. (1986) 'Optical switching in complementary electrochromic windows', *Pro. SPIE Conference*, V. 692, San Diego, CA.

Coronel J.F., Alvarez S. and Molina J.L. (1994) 'Solar-optical and thermal performance of Louver's type shading devices', *European Conference On Energy Performance and Indoor Climate in Buildings*, Lyon, France, Nov, 691–696.

Couret, G., Paule B., Scartezzini, (1994), 'Anidolic Zenithal Openings', *European Conference On Energy Performance and Indoor Climate in Buildings*, Lyon, France, Nov, 569–574

Dietrich U. (1993) 'A partly transparent shading system based on holographic optical elements', *3rd European Conference on Architecture*, Florence, Italy, May.

Dijk H. and Bakker L.G. (1994) 'Development of a European advanced windows information system', *European Conference On Energy Performance and Indoor Climate in Buildings*, Lyon, France, Nov., 920–935.

Dijk H.A.L. and Linden G.P. (1994), 'The PASSYS test method for thermal and solar characterization of building components', *European Conference On Energy Performance and Indoor Climate in Buildings*, Lyon, France, Nov., 1092–1097.

Edwards D.J., Arnold J.R. and Catton I. (1976) 'End clearance effects on rectangular-honeycomb solar collectors', *Solar Energy*, **18**, 253–257.

Elsherbiny S.M., Raithby G.D. and Hollands K.G.T. (1982), 'Heat transfer by natural convection across vertical and inclined air layers', *Journal of Heat Transfer*, **104**:1, 96–102.

Energy in Architecture – The European Passive Solar Handbook, 1992, EC Publication No. 13446, Batsford, London.

Fellands J.R. and Edwards D.K. (1978) 'Solar and infrared radiation properties of parallel plate glass honeycomb", *Journal of Energy*, **2**:5, 253–257.

Feuermann D. and Novoplansky A., 'Reversible low solar heat gain windows for energy savings', *Solar Energy* (special issue: advanced glazings), **62**:3, 169–175.

Francia G. (1961) 'Un nouveau collecteur de l'energie rayonnante solaire – theorie et verifications experimentales', *Conference des Nation Unies sur les sources nouvelles d'energie*, E/conf.35/S/71, 554–558.

Fuji T. and Imura H. (1972) 'Natural convection heat transfer from a plate with arbitrary inclination, *International Journal of Mass Transfer*, **15**, 755.

Guthrie K.I. and Charters W.W.S. (1982) 'An evaluation of a transverse slatted flat plate collectors', *Solar Energy*, **28**:2, 89–97.

Goetzbeger A., Schmid J., Wittwer V (1984), 'Transparent insulation system for passive solar energy utilization in buildings', *International Journal of Solar Energy*, **2**, 289–308.

Griffiths J. (1990) 'Thermal comfort in buildings with passive solar features: field study', *Final Report to CEC*, University of Surrey, Guildford, UK.

Hollands K.G.T. (1965), 'Honeycomb devices in flat-plate collectors', *Solar Energy*, **9**, 159.

Hollands K.G.T. and Iyankaran K. (1985) 'Proposal for a compound honeycomb collector', *Solar Energy*, **34**:4, 309–316.

Hollands K.G.T., Marshall K.N. and Wedel R.K. (1978), 'An approximate equation for predicting the solar transmittance of transparent honeycomb', *Solar Energy*, **21**, 231–236.

Hollands K.G.T., Raithby G.D. and Unny T.E. (1976*), Studies on methods of reducing heat losses from flat plate solar collectors, Phase I report*, University of Waterloo.

Holman J.P. (1986) *Heat Transfer*, McGraw-Hill Inc. New York.

Hoogendoorn C.J. (1985) *Natural Convection*, Hemisphere Publ. Corp.

Hottel H.C. (1976) 'A simple model of transmittance of direct solar radiation through clear atmospheres', *Solar Energy*, **18**.

IHVE (1971) *IHVE Guide Book 1970, Book A*, Institution of Heating and Ventilating Engineers, London.

Jesch L.F. (1993) 'Introduction', *Proceedings of the Sixth International Meeting on Transparent Insulation Technology*, Birmingham, UK, p5.

Jesch L.F., Chattha J.A. and Jankovic L. (1987), 'Transparent insulation for retrofit applications', *Proceedings of ISES World Solar Congress*, Hamburg, FRG.

Kaushika N.D. and Padma Priya R. (1991) 'Solar transmittance of honeycomb and parallel slat arrays', *Energy Conversion Management*, **32**:4, 345–351.

Kenny P. (1999) 'Design with daylight' in *FOS ToolBook*, CEC, DGXVII.

Kimura K. (1977) *Scientific Basis for Air-Conditioning*, Applied Science Publishers Ltd.

Knudsen H.N., deDear R.J., Li T.L., Puntner T.W. and Fanger P.O (1989) 'Thermal comfort in passive solar buildings', *Final Report*, CEC Research Project EN3S-0035-DK(B), Laboratory of Heating and Air Conditioning, Technical University of Denmark, May.

Kristensen P.E. (1994) 'Daylighting design of European buildings', *European Conference On Energy Performance and Indoor Climate in Buildings*, Lyon, France, Nov., 587–595.

LBL (1988), Window 3.1 Program, LBL25-686, USA.

Lee E. and Selkowitz S. (1995) 'The design and evaluation of integrated envelope and lighting control strategies for commercial buildings', *ASHRAE Transactions*, **101**, Part 1.

Lee J. *et al* (1986) 'Thermochromic materials research for optical switching', *Proc. SPIE Conference* V.692, San Diego,CA.

Littlefair P. (1995) 'Light shelves: computer assessment of daylight performance', *Lighting Research and Technology*, **27**:2, 79–91.

Liu B. and Jordan R. (1960) 'The interrelationship and characteristic distribution of direct, diffuse, and total solar radiation' *Solar Energy*, **4**,1–19.

Marshall K.N., Wedel R.K. and Damann R.E. (1976) 'Development of plastic honeycomb flat-plate solar collectors', *Report*, Lockheed Missiles and Space Company Inc, Palo Alto, California, USA, Contract No. SAN/1081-76/1.

MathSoft (2000), *Mathcad 2000*, Matsoft Inc., Boston, MA.

McMurrin J.C. and Buchberg H.B. (1971) 'Design optimization of sinusoidal glass honeycomb for flat plate solar collectors', *Journal of Solar Engineering*, **103**, 268–274.

Morris P.A. (1976) 'Radiative transfer through thin walled glass honeycomb', *ASME* paper No. 76-HT-48.

Narenda Basal, Hauser G. and Minke G. *Passive Building Design*, Elsevier Science.

Olsen L. (1982) 'Transparent insulation for thermal storage walls', *Solar Energy R & D in the European Community Series A*, D. Reidel Publishing Company, Dordrecht, **2**, 127.

PASSYS II (1994) Final Report, CEC.

Pennington, C.W. (1964) 'Experimental analysis of solar heat gain through insulating glass with indoor shading', ASHRAE Transactions, **70**, 54–68

Perrot M. (1967) 'Les structures cellulaires antirayonament et leurs applications industrielles', *Solar Energy*, **101**, 34–40.

Platzer W.J. (1992) 'Total heat transport data for plastic honeycomb-type structures', *Solar Energy*, **49**:5, 351–358.

Platzer,W. J. (1994) 'Transparent insulation materials: A review', *SPIE Conference Proceedings* 2255, Optical Materials Technologies for Energy Efficiency and Solar Energy XIII, 616–627.

Ramadan H. (1998) 'Numerical simulation model of a test-room with transparent insulation', M.A.Sc. Thesis, Concordia University, Montreal, Canada.

Santamouris M. (1994) *PASSPORT Manual*, CEC.

Santamouris M. *et al.* (1994) *Passive Cooling of Buildings*, CIENE, University of Athens.

Sullivan H.F. (1987), VISION computer program, University of Waterloo, Canada.

Symons J.G. (1982) 'The solar transmittance of some convection suppression devices for solar energy applications: an experimental study', *Journal of Solar Energy Engineering*, **104**, 251–256.

Symons, J.G and Peck M.K. (1983) 'An overview of the CSIRO project on advanced flat solar collectors', *Proceedings of the ISES Solar World Congress*, Perth, August, 748–752.

Tabor H. (1969) 'Cellular insulation (honeycombs)', *Solar Energy*, **12**, 549–552.

Tips for daylighting, The integrated approach, LBNL-39945.

Trombe F., Robert J.F, Cabonot M. and Sesolis B, (1977) 'Concrete walls to collect and hold heat', *Solar Age* **2**, 13.

Tsangrassoulis A. (1997) *Daylight techniques in buildings, Reference Manual*, Chapter 8.

Twidell J.W, Johnstone C., Zuhdy B., Scott A. (1994), 'Strathclyde university's passive solar, low energy residences with transparent insulation', *Solar Energy*, **52**:1, 85–109.

Vandaele L. and Wouters P. (1994) *The PASSYS Services*, Summary report, European Commission, Directorate General XII for Science, Research and Development, Belgium.

Ward G.J., Rubinstein F.M. and Clear R.D. (1988) 'Ray tracing solution for diffuse interreflection', *Computer Graphics*, **22**:August.

Warres M., Selkovitz S., Morse O., Benton C. and Jewell J. (1986) 'Lighting system performance in an innovative daylight structure: an instrumental study', *Proceedings of the 2nd International Daylighting Conference*, Long Beach, CA.

Wilkinson D. (1992) 'Modelling attenuation by urban trees', PhD thesis, Manchester Metropolitan University.

CHAPTER 4

Dynamic models of heat transfer in solar buildings

4.1 Introduction

During the thermal analysis and design of a passive solar building it is necessary to evaluate heating or cooling loads and room temperature fluctuations with given weather data, such as solar radiation and ambient temperature. Moreover, it is desirable to evaluate the building response under extreme weather conditions for many design options, each time changing only a few of the building parameters, until an optimum response is obtained. Thus, it is desirable to have efficient simulation and design tools that can be used for routine passive solar analysis.

In developing methods for building thermal simulation and analysis two basic steps are involved. The first step is to develop a mathematical model describing the heat transfer processes; the thermal exchanges are usually modelled as accurately as possible, while at the same time the model complexity is kept within reasonable limits so that it can be used for practical analysis and design. The second step is to develop an appropriate method of solution for the variables of interest (usually room temperature and auxiliary energy loads) and possibly a method of analysis of the system without necessarily performing actual simulation.

The desirable degree of detail in the analysis of a building depends on the design stage. For conceptual design or the very early stages of design, a steady-state model is often satisfactory. For preliminary design more detail is required, taking into account all objectives of thermal design and the specific characteristics of the system considered.

The primary objective in the design of a passive solar building is to prevent overheating while at the same time achieving high savings in energy consumption. In direct gain systems the solar energy transmitted through south-facing windows is stored directly in the space where it is to be used, that is, in storage mass distributed in the room interior. In indirect systems the energy is stored in specially built storage elements such as a rockbed or a Trombe wall (a collector–storage wall).

In passive solar buildings the natural energy flows are the most important, and controlled auxiliary heating becomes less significant than in thin-walled conventional residential buildings in which intermittent heating is required to respond to sudden changes in the weather. The passive solar building is essentially a low-pass thermal filter that highly attenuates the high-frequency fluctuations of the weather inputs.

There exist numerous simulation and design methods for buildings. These methods are described in handbooks (ASHRAE, etc.). The work done in building energy analysis before the surge of interest in passive solar cannot in itself be considered passive solar because solar gains in the rooms were usually considered as a nuisance rather than as a benefit and heat storage in building elements was not treated accurately. Further, no emphasis was placed on the natural energy flows in the building – the most important objective was equipment sizing.

Modelling of the room interior radiant heat exchanges is more important with direct gain than with indirect gain systems and generally requires more modelling detail. In designing direct gain buildings (that is, a building with at least one direct gain room) the basic aim is to store energy in the walls during the daytime for release at night without having uncomfortable temperature swings.

A basic characteristic of passive solar building is the strong convective and conductive coupling between adjacent rooms which constitute thermal zones. This coupling is very important between south-facing direct-gain rooms receiving a significant amount of solar radiation transmitted through large windows and adjacent north-facing rooms which receive very little solar radiation. For example, heat transfer by natural convection through a doorway connecting a warm direct-gain room and a cool north-facing room can be an effective way of heating the cool room.

The design of direct-gain buildings can be separated into two phases. First, we have determination of room temperature swings on relatively clear days during the heating season (assuming no energy dumping) in order to decide how much storage mass to include so as to ensure that overheating does not occur frequently. Second, to determine the optimum amount of insulation and window area and type, the net increase of the room mean (daily or monthly) temperature above ambient temperature due to the solar gains is calculated, or auxiliary heating loads are computed until the desired energy savings are achieved.

Periodic conditions are usually assumed (explicitly or implicitly) in dynamic building thermal analysis and load calculations. Heating or cooling load, that is the auxiliary heat energy input/removal required to maintain comfort conditions, is usually calculated for a design day. The peak heating load is used to size heating equipment and the peak cooling load to size cooling equipment.

The approximations commonly introduced in mathematical models describing the building thermal behaviour can be separated into three categories:

- **Linearization of heat transfer coefficients**. Convective and radiative heat transfer are non-linear processes and the respective heat transfer coefficients are usually linearized so that the system energy balance equations can be solved by direct linear algebra techniques such as Gaussian elimination. The appropriate linear system matrix is time-invariant and its inverse can be obtained once and for all for a certain set of system parameters.

- **Spatial and/or time discretization**. The equation describing conduction is a parabolic, diffusion-type partial differential equation. Thus in using finite difference methods, a conducting medium with significant thermal capacity must be discretized into a number of regions which are modelled by lumped elements. Also, time domain discretization is required in which an appropriate time step is employed. In response factor methods only time discretization is necessary. For frequency domain analysis none of these approximations is required; in periodic models, however, the number of harmonics employed must be kept within reasonable limits.

- **Approximations for reduction in model complexity**. These approximations are usually employed in order to reduce the number of simultaneous equations to be solved or to enable the derivation of closed-form analytical solutions. They are by far the most serious and error-prone approximations and are usually done by combining radiative and convective heat transfer coefficients, assuming that many surfaces are at the same temperature, or completely ignoring certain heat exchanges.

A major aspect of the modelling process considers heat conduction in the building envelope. In most cases relating to heating or cooling load estimations, energy savings calculations and thermal comfort analysis, it is generally accepted that one-dimensional heat conduction may be assumed. Thermal bridges such as those present around corners and at the structure are generally accounted for in calculating the thermal resistance of building envelope elements. However, the thermal storage process may be adequately modelled as one dimensional.

Consider again the one-dimensional heat diffusion equation given in Chapter 2:

$$\partial T/\partial t = \alpha \partial^2 T/\partial x^2 \tag{4.1}$$

with boundary conditions
(i) at $x = 0$, $q = -k\partial T/\partial x = h_o(T_{eo} - T_1)$
(ii) at $x = L$, $q = h_i(T_2 - T_r)$
where α is thermal diffusivity, k thermal conductivity, q heat flux and h heat transfer coefficient.

One-dimensional conduction through the walls is generally assumed, as well as uniform irradiation of their surfaces by solar radiation. The above equation is usually solved with finite-difference techniques, response factor methods and frequency domain techniques (Carter 1980). The main advantage of finite difference methods is that they can accurately model the system non-linearities, but they are more cumbersome and less efficient than the other two approaches; response factor and frequency domain techniques do not require spatial discretization of wall, but they are linear techniques which utilize the superposition theorem.

In using finite difference methods, a conducting medium with significant thermal capacity must be discretized into a number of regions which are modelled by lumped elements. Also, time domain discretization is required in which an appropriate time step is employed. An energy balance at all nodes (i) may be expressed in the form:

$$C_i(\mathrm{d}T_i/\mathrm{d}t) = Q_i - B_i T_i + \Sigma_j U_{ij}(T_j - T_i) \tag{4.2}$$

where U_{ij} is the internode heat transfer conductance, C_i is the capacity of node i, and $Q_i - B_i T_i$ is the source term (due to specified temperatures Q_i and heat inputs T_i). Finite difference models may employ explicit, implicit or mixed discretization schemes.

In response factor methods only time discretization is necessary. For frequency domain analysis none of these approximations is required; in periodic models, however, the number of harmonics employed must be kept within reasonable limits.

Response factor models form the basis of large building energy simulation programs such as DOE. They usually assume that the system is linear and time-invariant and use the superposition principle. Wall response factors relate the heat flow at the surface of a wall to the history of heat flows into the building. The heat flow $q^{in}(t)$ at the inside surface of a wall may be described by the following discrete convolution equation (Kimura 1977):

$$q^{in}(t) = \sum_{n=1}^{\infty} W_n T^{in}(t - n\Delta) + M_n T^{out}(t - n\Delta) \tag{4.3}$$

where W_n and M_n are response factors for inside and outside temperature respectively and n is the number of time lags. The response factors must be calculated for the time step Δ (usually one hour) and this reduces the flexibility of the method (i.e. precalculated response factors can only be used for the same time step as used in determining the factors).

Calculation of response factors can be done using Laplace transforms, and no discretization is required. A more efficient method, the z-transform, can also be used (Stephenson and Mitalas 1971).

4.1.1 Thermal mass characteristics and implications

The modulating-filtering action of thermal mass has two effects:

- Heat gain into the room is reduced and the cooling load drops; in winter, passive solar gains are effectively stored.
- The reduction in surface temperature results in a drop of the room mean radiant temperature and the operative temperature (ASHRAE 1989), enhancing thermal

comfort in the cooling season; in the heating season solar gains are stored with a small temperature swing.

The thermal properties of major thermal storage materials and a few other materials (for comparison) are given in Table 4.1. Generally, thermal mass has high thermal capacitance but low thermal resistance. For example in 1 m^2 of concrete 10 cm thick we can store (for 1°C temperature rise)

$$Q = c\rho \text{ vol} = 840 \text{ (J/kg°C)} \times 2200 \text{ (kg/m}^3) \times 0.10 \text{ m} \times 1 \text{ m}^2$$

$$= 184\ 800 \text{ J}$$

By contrast, its thermal resistance is only 0.1/1.7 K/W, i.e. negligible.

The equation describing conduction is a parabolic, diffusion-type partial differential equation. Thus, in using finite difference methods, a conducting medium with significant thermal capacity must be discretized into a number of regions that are modelled by lumped elements. Also, time domain discretization is required in which an appropriate time step is employed. In response factor methods only time discretization is necessary. For frequency domain analysis none of these approximations are required; in periodic models, however, the number of harmonics employed must be kept within reasonable limits.

Table 4.1 Properties of thermal mass and other building materials (ASHRAE 1989, CIBSE 1988)

Material	Mass density (kg/m^3)	Thermal conductivity (W/m K)	Specific heat (J/kg K)
Heavyweight concrete	2243	1.73	840
Clay tile	1121	0.57	840
Gypsum	1602	0.73	840
Gas-entrained concrete	400	0.14	1000
Water	1000	0.58	4200
plasterboard	840	0.16	950
expanded polystyrene	25	0.035	1400
Timber			
softwood	630	0.13	1360
hardwood	630	0.15	1250
plywood	530	0.14	1214
chipboard	800	0.15	1286
Common brick (full)	1922	0.727	840
Stone			
granite	2600	2.50	900
limestone	2180	1.59	720
sandstone	2000	1.30	712
marble	2500	2.00	802
Screed finish (lightweight)	1200	0.41	840

Frequency domain analysis techniques with complex variables are usually employed for steady periodic analysis of multilayered walls. They provide a convenient means for periodic analysis, in which the main parameters of interest are the magnitude and phase angle of room temperatures and heat flows.

4.2 Admittance transfer functions for walls

This section demonstrates techniques for steady-periodic thermal analysis of wall heat flow based on frequency domain techniques and the use of simple Fourier series models for outside temperature and solar radiation. Frequency domain transfer functions such as wall admittance are studied in terms of magnitude and phase lag and are then used together with Fourier series models for the weather variables to determine steady-periodic thermal response of walls. The technique is applied for passive solar analysis and design.

Significant insight into wall dynamic thermal behaviour may be obtained by studying the wall's admittance transfer functions (magnitude and phase angle) as a function of frequency, thermal properties, and geometry.

Figure 4.1 shows conceptually how wall response to weather inputs (e.g. $T\sin(\omega t)$) may be obtained for one harmonic, and the time lag between the input and output waves. For inputs with more than one harmonic, the total response may be obtained by superposition of the response harmonics.

The thermal admittance of a wall is a transfer function parameter useful for analysis of the effects on room temperature of cyclic variations in weather variables such as solar radiation, outside temperature and dynamic heat flows under steady periodic conditions.

There are two transfer functions of primary interest, namely the self-admittance Y_s relating the effect of a heat source at one surface to the temperature of that surface, and the transfer admittance Y_t relating the effect of an outside temperature variation to the resulting heat flow at the inside surface.

These two transfer functions are determined as demonstrated in the following model (Athienitis *et al.* 1986). The wall in Figure 4.2 consists of insulation and thermally non-massive layers (low thermal capacity) with conductance value U per unit area, and a thermally massive layer of thickness L.

The Norton equivalent network for a wall with a specified temperature on one side (such as basement temperature or sol-air temperature) is obtained from the cascade form of the wall equations which relates temperature and heat flow at one surface to those at the other surface. The cascade form of the equations is derived by first taking the Laplace transformation of the one-dimensional heat diffusion equation to obtain an ordinary differential equation, which can then be solved to relate heat flux and temperature at one surface of a one-dimensional medium to those at the other surface, without discretizing. The cascade equations relating temperature T_1 and heat flux q'_1 at one surface of a slab to those (q_2 and T_2) at its other surface are given by (Kimura 1977):

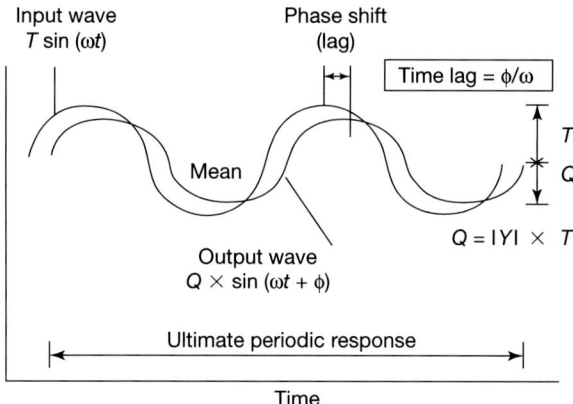

Figure 4.1 Schematic of temperature and heat flow waves (Y = admittance transfer function with magnitude $|Y|$ and phase angle φ)

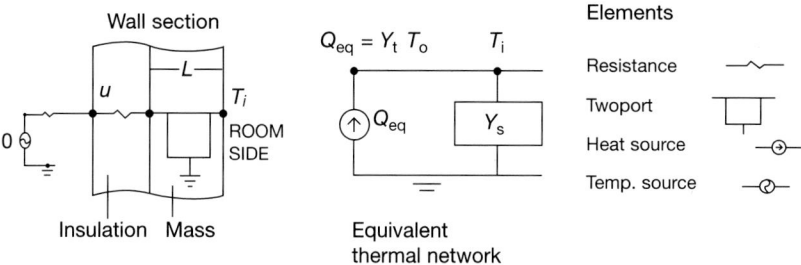

Figure 4.2 Exterior wall with massive interior layer, and equivalent thermal network

$$\begin{bmatrix} T_1 \\ q'_1 \end{bmatrix} = \begin{bmatrix} D & B \\ C & D \end{bmatrix} \cdot \begin{bmatrix} T_2 \\ -q'_2 \end{bmatrix} \tag{4.4}$$

where $D = \cosh(\gamma x)$, $B = \sinh(\gamma x)/(k\gamma)$ and $C = (k\gamma)\sinh(\gamma x)$, and q' is positive into the slab.

The quantity k is the thermal conductivity, x is thickness, and γ is equal to $(s/\alpha)^{1/2}$, s being the Laplace transform variable and α being the thermal diffusivity. For admittance calculations s is set equal to $s = j\omega$ where $j = \sqrt{-1}$ and $\omega = 2\pi/P$. For diurnal analysis, period $P = 86\,400$ s.

The cascade matrix for a multilayered wall is obtained by multiplying the cascade matrices for consecutive layers. Usually the temperatures of interest are either the inside or the outside temperature. In this way, wall interior temperatures of no interest are easily eliminated. A linear subnetwork connected to a network at only two terminals (a port) can be represented by its Norton equivalent, consisting of a heat source and an admittance connected in parallel between the terminals (Athienitis *et al.* 1986).

The admittance is the subnetwork equivalent admittance as seen from the connection port (the two terminals), and the heat source is the short-circuited heat flow at the port. Consider for example the wall in Figure 4.2, assumed to be made up of an inner layer of storage mass of uniform thermal properties and a massless insulation layer, also of uniform thermal properties. The region behind the thermal mass may be represented by equivalent conductance U in series with the outside temperature T_o (for exterior walls the sol-air temperature T_{eo}). The conductance U combines the insulation resistance and a film coefficient.

The determination of Y_s (called the wall self-admittance), and the equivalent source Q_{sc} produced by the transformation, will now be explained. A first step obtains the total cascade matrix by multiplying the cascade matrix for the storage mass by that for u (note: $u = U/A$):

$$\begin{bmatrix} T_s \\ q_s \end{bmatrix} = \begin{bmatrix} D & B \\ C & D \end{bmatrix} \cdot \begin{bmatrix} 1 & 1/u \\ 0 & 1 \end{bmatrix} \cdot \begin{bmatrix} T_o \\ -q_o \end{bmatrix} \tag{4.5}$$

After multiplying, we temporarily set $T_s = 0$, to get the Norton equivalent source as

$$Q_{eq} = -Y_t T_o$$

where the transfer admittance Y_t is given by

$$Y_t = -A/[(A \cosh(\gamma x)/U) + \sinh(\gamma x)/(k\gamma)] \tag{4.6}$$

The transfer admittance has been multiplied by the area A to obtain its total value. To obtain Y_s, we temporarily set $T_o = 0$ and obtain the admittance as seen from the interior surface, yielding (after multiplying by A):

$$Y_s = A[(U_o/A) + k\gamma \tanh(\gamma x)]/[(U_o/k\gamma A)\tanh(\gamma x) + 1] \tag{4.7}$$

If there is no mass then we obtain the simple equality $Y_s = -Y_t = U$. A similar result is obtained for windows in eliminating all nodes exterior to the inner glazing. An important result is obtained for an infinitely thick wall or a wall with no heat loss at the back (adiabatic surface, or high amount of insulation); in this case Y_s is given by

$$Y_s = Ak\gamma \tanh(\gamma x) \tag{4.8}$$

Thick walls have admittance that is close to that given by the above equation. When the penetration depth, given by

$$d = \sqrt{[2k/(c\rho\omega)]} = \sqrt{(2\alpha/\omega)} \qquad (4.9)$$

is significantly less than the wall thickness then the wall behaves like a semi-infinite solid.

The magnitude, phase angle (and time lag/lead) of a transfer function such as Y_s and Y_t are computed by means of complex variables.

Analysis: substantial insight into wall and building thermal behaviour may be gained by studying the magnitude and phase angle of the important transfer functions such as Y_s and Y_t (Athienitis 1994). The time lead d_s of Y_s is the time difference between the peak of a sinusoidal input function, such as solar radiation in the case of the room interior surface, and the resulting peak of the interior surface temperature T_i. Now, we consider the variation of wall thermal admittance with thermal mass thickness L for the fundamental frequency (one cycle per day, $n = 1$) for unit wall area. Note that the diurnal ($n = 1$) frequency is important in the analysis of variables with a dominant diurnal harmonic such as solar radiation. High frequencies are important in analysing the effect of varying heat inputs such as those due to on/off cycling of a furnace.

A wall with an interior massive layer of concrete is considered and exterior insulating layers with insignificant thermal capacity and thermal resistance equal to 4 RSI. The concrete has a specific heat capacity of 800 J/kg°C, a density of 2200 kg/m³ and a thermal conductivity of 1.7 W/m K. The results presented below are specific to this concrete, but they generally indicate the expected trends for concrete/brick/masonry type materials. Note that the thermal conductivity of these materials increases with moisture content and density.

Figure 4.3 shows an extremely important result in steady-periodic analysis of building thermal response – the fact that there is a wall thermal mass thickness that will most reduce room temperature fluctuations – in this case for $L = 0.2$ m, corresponding to the maximum admittance. Therefore, this is the optimum thermal mass thickness for passive solar design.

As indicated in Figure 4.4, the magnitude of wall admittance (for mass thickness of 20 cm) increases with frequency (decreases with period). Thus, the inside room temperature fluctuations are smaller for high-frequency fluctuations in internal heat gains. For harmonic numbers higher than about 8, that is periods less than 3 h, the wall behaves like an infinitely thick wall; in this case the phase angle is 45°.

The variation of transfer admittance Y_t with mass thickness is depicted in Figure 4.5. In this case, the magnitude of Y_t decreases with thickness and therefore the fluctuations of the sol-air temperature are significantly modulated as they are transmitted to the room interior. This is a well-known phenomenon, efficiently employed in traditional architecture in adobe buildings. The time lag of the heat gains transmitted ($q = Y_t \times T_{eo}$) into the interior is the time lag of Y_t. This time lag increases to about 7.5 h for a mass thickness of 30 cm.

The time delay in the transmission of a heat wave through a wall is another positive effect of thermal mass in addition to the attenuation of the temperature

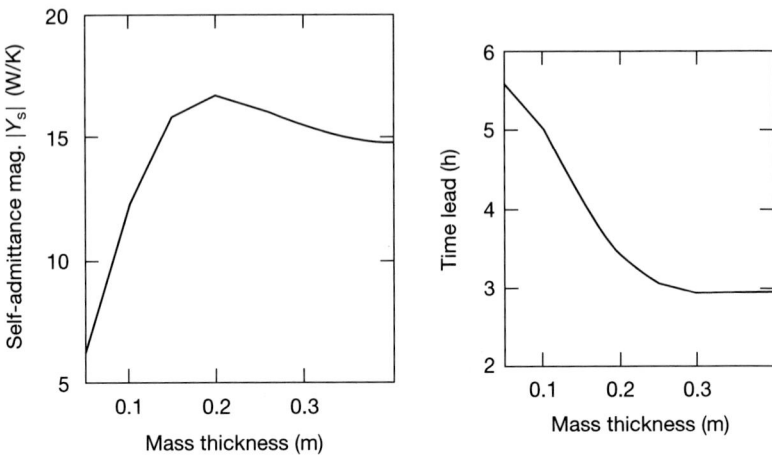

Figure 4.3 Variation of the self-admittance and its time lead with mass thickness

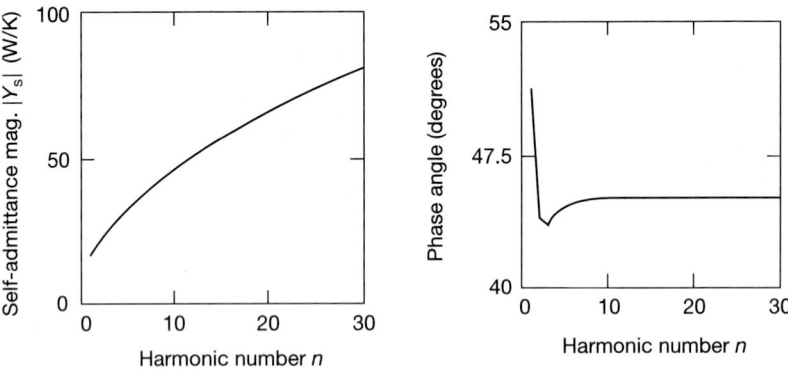

Figure 4.4 Variation of the self-admittance and its phase angle with harmonic number n

swings. Thus, the peak heat gains through the structure coincide with cooler outside conditions when natural ventilation may be employed to reduce total instantaneous cooling loads.

Figure 4.6 shows that the magnitude of the transfer admittance decreases relatively quickly with increasing harmonic number n and decreasing period. Thus, the heat gain fluctuations transmitted into the room as a result of sol-air temperature fluctuations are significantly reduced at high frequencies. For example, a temperature swing of 2°C in sol-air temperature over a period of about 2 h will result in a heat gain swing of about

$$0.1 \text{ W/°C} \times 2\text{°C} = 0.02 \text{ W (per m}^2 \text{ of wall)}$$

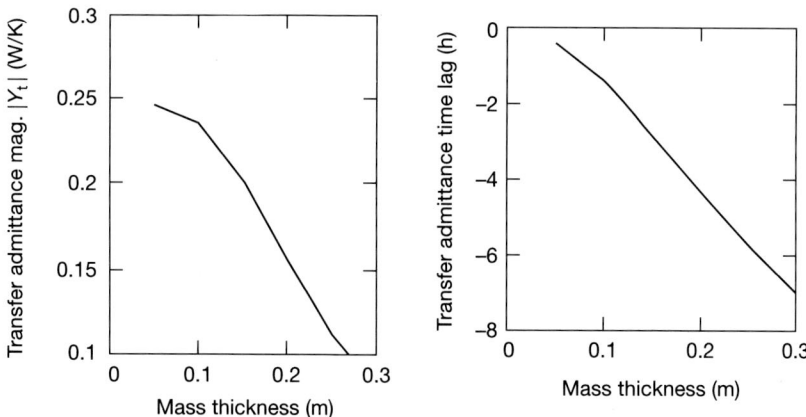

Figure 4.5 Variation of the transfer admittance and its time lag with mass thickness

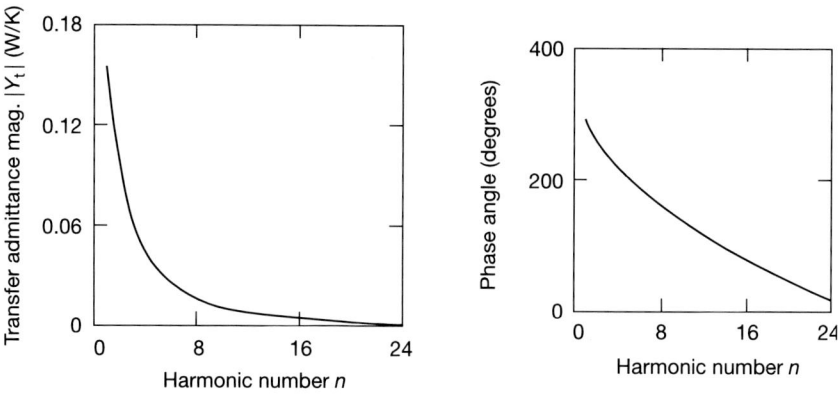

Figure 4.6 Variation of the transfer admittance magnitude with harmonic number n

4.3 Building transient response analysis

Transient thermal analysis of walls or rooms may be performed with the following objectives:

- Peak heating/cooling load calculations
- Calculation of dynamic temperature variation within walls, including solar effects, room temperature swings and condensation on wall interior surfaces; two-dimensional steady-state temperature profiles in walls (e.g. for investigation of thermal bridge effects).

For a multilayered wall, an energy balance is applied at each node at regular time intervals to obtain the temperature of the nodes as a function of time. These equations may be solved with the implicit method as a set of simultaneous equations or with the explicit method in which we march forward in time from a set of initial conditions.

We will consider the **finite difference thermal network approach**. In this approach, each wall layer is discretized (divided) into a number of sublayers (regions). Each region is represented by a **node** and is assumed to be isothermal. Each node (i) has a thermal capacitance (C_i) associated with it and resistances connecting it to adjacent nodes.

Wall transient thermal response analysis with finite difference techniques may generally provide a more accurate estimation of temperatures and heat flows owing to the capability to model non-linear effects such as convection and radiation. One disadvantage is that the initial conditions are usually unknown. Thus, the simulation is repeated until a steady periodic response is obtained.

The explicit finite difference method is particularly suitable for modelling of non-linear heat diffusion problems such as the present case of heat transfer through a wall. It can easily accommodate non-linear heat transfer coefficients and control actions. Figure 4.7 shows the thermal network for a wall with transparent insulation. The wall consists of an exterior layer of transparent insulation, an air cavity, and a thermal storage layer of concrete.

In the transient one-dimensional finite difference method we represent each wall layer by one or more sublayers (regions). Each region is represented by a node

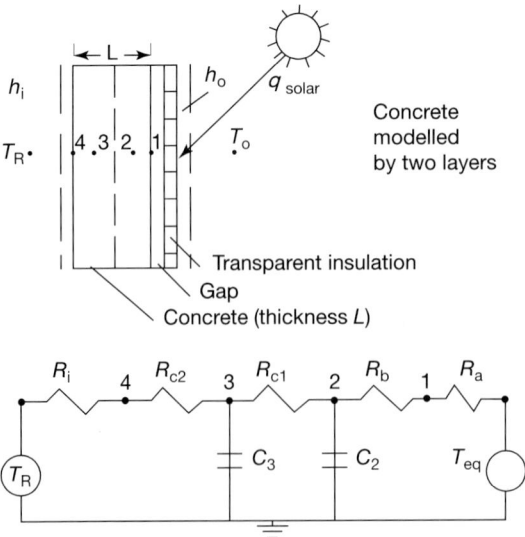

Figure 4.7 Wall with transparent insulation, and its thermal network

with a thermal capacitance C connected to two thermal resistances, each equal to half the R-value of the layer, forming a T-section as shown in Figure 4.7 for the concrete layer. Thus, the finite difference thermal network model for the wall consists of two capacitances for the concrete thermal capacity and interconnecting thermal resistances. The energy balance for the thermal network is:

$$T_{i,p+1} = \frac{\Delta t}{C_i} \times \left(q_i + \sum \frac{T_{j,p} - T_{i,p}}{R_{i,j}} \right) + T_{i,p} \tag{4.10}$$

Subscript i indicates the node for which the energy balance is written and j all nodes connected to node i, while p is the time interval; q_i represents a heat source at node i such as solar radiation.

The time step was selected based on the following condition for numerical stability:

$$\Delta t \leq \min \left(C_i \sum_j \frac{1}{R_{i,j}} \right) \qquad \text{for all nodes } i \tag{4.11}$$

We show below the specific calculations for the above model in Mathcad (Athienitis 1994) and the resulting temperature variation of a south-facing wall for two winter days with high solar gains. For summer simulations a shutter is assumed to be closed in the cavity reflecting outwards 90% of transmitted solar gains. (See also Figure 4.8.)

$L = 0.20\text{m}$ $\qquad A = 1 \text{ m}^2$ concrete thickness and face area (perpendicular to heat flow)

Concrete
properties:

$C = 800 \text{ J} / \text{kg}^\circ\text{C}$ $\qquad k = 1.7 \text{ W} / \text{m}^\circ\text{C}$ $\qquad p = 2200 \text{ kg} / \text{m}^3$

specific heat $\qquad\qquad$ conductivity $\qquad\qquad$ density

Film coefficients: $\qquad\qquad\qquad\qquad h_i = 10 \text{ W} / \text{m}^2 {}^\circ\text{C}$ $\qquad h_o = 20 \text{ W} / \text{m}^2 {}^\circ\text{C}$

$\tau\alpha = 0.7$ $\qquad$ effective transmittance – absorptance of transparent insulation system and concrete face

$R_{\text{ins}} = 0.5 \text{ m}^2 {}^\circ\text{C} / \text{W}$ $\quad R_{\text{gap}} = 0.3 \text{ m}^2 {}^\circ\text{C} / \text{W}$ $\qquad$ transparent insulation and gap resistances

$$R_{\text{a}} = \frac{R_{\text{ins}} + R_{\text{gap}} + \dfrac{1}{h_o}}{A} \qquad R_{\text{a}} = 0.85 {}^\circ\text{C} / \text{W} \quad \text{resistance from outside to concrete face}$$

$R_{\text{c}} = \dfrac{L}{k\,A}$ $\qquad$ total concrete resistance $\qquad R_{\text{b}} = \dfrac{R_{\text{c}}}{4}$ $\qquad R_{\text{b}} = 0.029 {}^\circ\text{C} / \text{W}$

$R_{\text{c1}} = \dfrac{R_{\text{c}}}{2}$ $\qquad R_{\text{c1}} = 0.059 {}^\circ\text{C} / \text{W}$ $\qquad R_{\text{c2}} = \dfrac{R_{\text{c}}}{4}$ $\qquad R_i - \dfrac{1}{A\,h_i}$ $\qquad R_i = 0.1 {}^\circ\text{C} / \text{W}$

$C2 = \rho c \dfrac{L}{2} A$ $\qquad C2 = 1.76 \times 10^5 \text{ J} / {}^\circ\text{C}$ $\quad C3 = C2$ $\quad$ thermal capacitance for each layer

Stability test

$$TS = \left[\frac{C2}{\frac{1}{R_a + R_b} + \frac{1}{R_{c1}}} \quad \frac{C3}{\frac{1}{R_{c1}} + \frac{1}{R_{c2} + R_i}} \right]$$

The time step Δt should be lower than the minimum of the two values in the vector TS

$\Delta t_{\text{critical}} = \min(TS)$ $\Delta t_{\text{critical}} = 7.118 \times 10^3$ s $\Delta t = 1800$ s

$i = 0.,1..96$ number of time steps

Assume $w = 2 \cdot \dfrac{\pi}{86400} \cdot \text{rad} / \text{s}$ frequency based on period of one day

$T_o(t) = \left[5\cos\left(wt + 3\dfrac{\pi}{4} \right) - 10 \right]$°C   outside temperature   incident solar radiation modelled as half-sinusoid

$f(t) = 500\cos[w(t - 43200\text{s})]$W $q_{\text{solar}}(t) = \text{if}(f(t) > 0\text{W}, f(t), 0\text{W})$

$T_{\text{eq}}(t) = T_o(t) + q_{\text{solar}}(t)\tau\alpha \, R_a$ equivalent 'sol - air' temperature at node 1 (concrete surface)

$T_R = 22$°C   room temperature

Initial estimates of temperatures: $\begin{bmatrix} T2_0 \\ T3_0 \end{bmatrix} = \begin{bmatrix} 10 \\ 10 \end{bmatrix}$°C

Simulation for nodes with capacitances

$$\begin{bmatrix} T2_i + 1 \\ T3_i + 1 \end{bmatrix} = \begin{bmatrix} \dfrac{\Delta t}{C2}\left(\dfrac{T_{\text{eq}}(i\,\Delta t) - T2_i}{R_a + R_b} + \dfrac{T3_i - T2_i}{R_{c1}} \right) + T2_i \\ \dfrac{\Delta t}{C3}\left(\dfrac{T2_i - T3_i}{R_{c1}} + \dfrac{T_R - T3_i}{R_i + R_{c2}} \right) + T3_i \end{bmatrix}$$

Finite difference simulation (i is present time and $i+1$ next time step)

Now we can also calculate intermediate temperatures

$T4_i = T_R + R_i \dfrac{T3_i - T_R}{R_{c2} + R_i}$ $T1_i = T2_i + R_b \dfrac{T_{\text{eq}}(i\Delta t) - T2_i}{R_b + R_a}$

4.4 Ground coupling, basement heat transfer

A building is usually in direct contact with the ground either through a ground-level floor or through the floor and walls of a basement. The ground temperature does not vary as much as the ambient temperature because the ground acts as a heat sink, modulating the daily and seasonal temperature variations. Thus, the ground may be a source of heat (or reduced heat losses) in the winter while being a source of coolness in the summer.

The ground may be modelled as a semi-infinite medium and the ambient temperature may be modelled as sinusoidal (Mihalakakou *et al.* 1994, Tzaferis *et al.* 1992). The heat transfer problem is therefore:

$$\partial T/\partial t = \alpha\partial^2 T/\partial z^2 \tag{4.12}$$

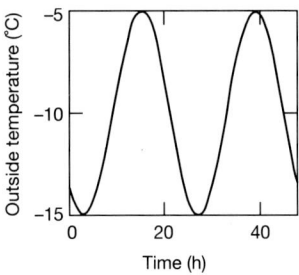

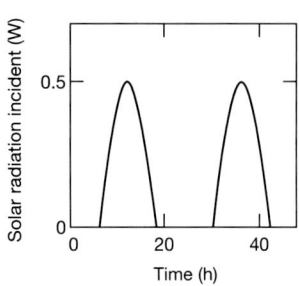

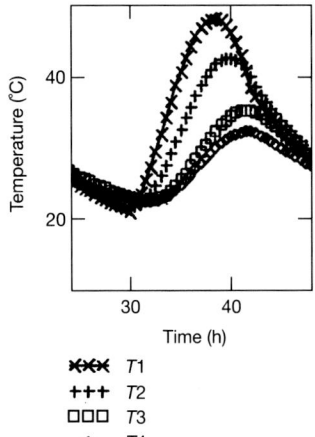

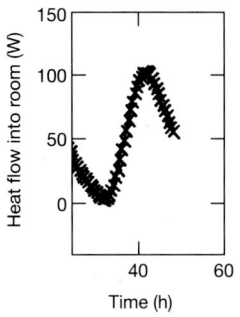

Figure 4.8 Weather conditions and temperature variation under winter conditions for wall with transparent insulation

with boundary conditions
(i) at depth $z = 0$ the ambient temperature is

$$T(t) = T_m + \Delta T \cos (\omega t)$$

with frequency $\omega = 2\pi/P$ where P is period, T_m is the mean ambient temperature and ΔT the amplitude.
(ii) at infinite depth, temperature is constant
The solution to the above equation is

$$T(t,z) = T_m + \Delta T e^{-z/d} \cos(\omega t - z/d)$$

where $d = \sqrt{(2\alpha/\omega)}$ is the penetration depth.

At a depth of d the temperature swing is about one-third of ΔT while at depths of about $5d$ the temperature variations are almost completely damped out. Figure

4.9 shows the penetration depth as a function of thermal diffusivity for the diurnal frequency ($P = 86\ 400$ s) and for the yearly frequency. The thermal diffusivity of limestone soil is about 0.58×10^{-6} m²/s, for sandstone 1.06–1.26×10^{-6} m²/s and for marble 1.39×10^{-6} m²/s.

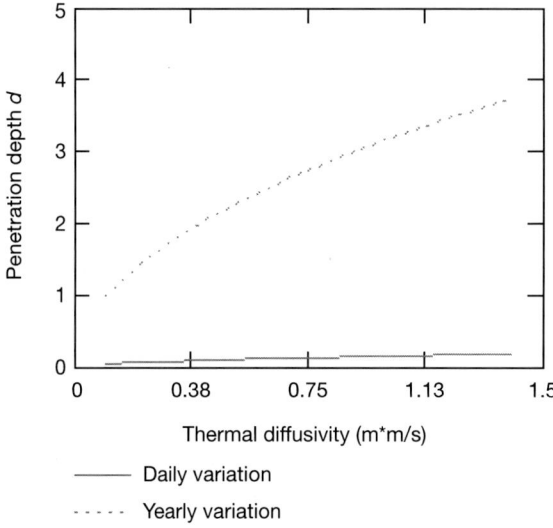

Figure 4.9 Penetration depth *d* as a function of thermal diffusivity

Therefore, it may be concluded that at a depth of about 1 m the diurnal temperature variation of the soil is insignificant. This is the principle on which ground cooling is based. Earth-to-air heat exchangers are employed in either open-loop or closed-loop circuits (Tzaferis *et al.* 1992). In an open-loop system air is drawn by fan from the ambient through a buried pipe into the building. During summer the air is cooled since the ground is colder than the air; a temperature differential of at least 5–6 K between ambient and the ground around the pipe is required for effective operation (Santamouris 1994). In a closed-loop system both inlet and outlet are inside the building.

For homogeneous soils with constant thermal diffusivity, the daily temperature of the ground at depth *z* may be represented by (Santamouris 1994):

$$T(z,t) = T_{m} - A_{s}\exp(-z\sqrt{(\pi/365\alpha)})\cos\{(2\pi/365)[t - t_{o} - z\sqrt{(3/4\pi)}]\} \qquad (4.13)$$

where
T_{m} = average annual temperature
A_{s} = amplitude of surface temperature variation
t = time, days, t_{o} = phase constant (days)

Floors in contact with the ground lose or gain heat through cyclic paths going from the floor to the surface of the ground. CIBSE (1988) recommends the following relationship for the U-value of uninsulated concrete floors (for heat transfer from/to outside air) with four edges exposed:

$$U = \frac{4ke^{b/2L}}{b\pi} \tanh^{-1}\left(\frac{b}{b+w}\right) \tag{4.14}$$

where
k = soil thermal conductivity, W/m K (about 0.7–2.1)
b = breadth (smaller dimension) of floor, m
w = thickness of surrounding wall, m (about 0.3 m)
L = length of floor, m
For example, for a room with dimensions 4×6 m: let $k = 0.7$ W/m K , $L = 6$ m, $b = 4$ m. This gives $U = 0.516$ W/K m^2.

For floors with two parallel edges exposed use equation 4.14 for the appropriate breadth but set L equal to infinity (i.e. $\exp(b/2L) = 1$). For floors with two edges exposed the U-value is the same as for floors of twice the length and breadth with four edges exposed. For a single edge exposed U is the same as for two parallel edges but of twice the breadth. If insulation is used, add the thermal resistance of insulation to that of the floor. The U-value must be reduced when edge insulation is employed (see Table 4.2).

Table 4.2 Percentage reduction in floor U-value for insulation up to indicated depth (m) (CIBSE 1988)

Floor dimensions (m)	% reduction for insulation up to 0.5 m	% reduction for insulation up to 1.0 m
10 × 10	14	22
6 × 6	15	25
4 × 4	18	28

Basement heat transfer may be evaluated in detail numerically using finite difference techniques and in particular two-dimensional models (three-dimensional at corners).

4.5 Bibliography

ASHRAE (1989) *ASHRAE Handbook – Fundamentals*, Atlanta, GA, USA.
Athienitis A.K. (1994) *Building Thermal Analysis*, Electronic Book Mathcad, MathSoft, Boston, USA.
Athienitis A.K., Sullivan H.F. and Hollands K.G.T. (1986) 'Analytical model, sensitivity analysis, and temperature swings in direct gain rooms', *Solar Energy*, **36**, 303–312.

Carslaw H.S. and Jaeger J.C. (1959) *Conduction of Heat in Solids*, 2nd edn, Oxford University Press, London.

Carter C. (1980) 'Solving the heat transfer network equations in passive solar simulations', Proc. ASES 5th Passive Solar Conf., Amherst, MA, October, pp. 238–242.

CIBSE (1988) *CIBSE Guide*, Volume A, CIBSE, London.

Cook J. (ed.) (1989) *Passive Cooling*, MIT Press, Cambridge, MA.

Kimura K. (1977) *Scientific Basis for Air-conditioning*, Applied Science Publishers, Ltd.

Mihalakakou G., Santamouris M. and Asimakopoulos D. (1994) 'Modelling the thermal performance of earth-to-air heat exchangers', *Solar Energy*, **53**:3, 301–305.

Santamouris M. *et al.* (1994) *Passive Cooling of Buildings*, CIENE, University of Athens.

Stephenson G.D. and Mitalas G.P. (1971) 'Calculations of heat conduction transfer functions for multi-layer slabs', *ASHRAE Transactions*, **77**:2, 117–126.

Tzaferis A., Liparakis D., Santamouris M. and Argyriou A. (1992) 'Analysis and accuracy of eight models to predict performance of earth-to-air heat exchangers', *Energy and Buildings*, **18**, 35–43.

CHAPTER 5

The passive response of buildings and its use in design

5.1 Introduction

The passive response of a building is primarily reflected in its temperature variation without operation of the heating or cooling system. This response helps us assess the effectiveness of the building passive systems. In the case of heating analysis, it is useful to compare the response on a cold sunny day with that on a cold cloudy day. In both cases, the outdoor temperature profile should be the same in order to assess the solar savings by comparing the mean room temperatures in the two cases. This simple approach was introduced in Section 1.4.

However, such a simple approach does not consider the significant issue of thermal comfort in passive solar buildings. In fact, unless adequate thermal storage mass is present, the possibility of room overheating is very high for well-insulated buildings even during winter months when the exterior temperature may fall below 0°C. In this chapter a simple analytical model is presented for determining the temperature swings in direct-gain rooms for relatively clear days. It is primarily intended for study of the relative effects of fundamental design variables such as storage mass thickness and area on room temperature fluctuations.

It is useful to develop such a special-purpose simple model for studying temperature swings in a direct-gain room for the following reasons:

- The relative effects on room temperature swings of the storage mass thickness and area, the amount of insulation and the daylength may be studied by modelling the room interior as consisting of a few isothermal surfaces. Thus, an analytical solution may be obtained including only a few fundamental variables, which permits an efficient and basic sensitivity analysis.
- An analytical solution with only a few inputs permits efficient application of the superposition principle for the study of the relative importance of various weather inputs and their harmonic components.

There are several simple periodic models for determining temperature swings. However, they often employ simple heat transfer modelling assumptions, such as an isothermal (single-node) storage mass (e.g. Kirkpatrick and Winn 1984) which may introduce substantial errors. One well-known simplified design method is the diurnal heat capacity (DHC) method (Balcomb *et al.* 1980). Based on a distributed (non-isothermal) model for the storage mass, it determines the swings in room air temperature for typical clear days. Like other simplified methods, the DHC method does not incorporate the effect of change in daylength, an important parameter, as this chapter will show. Also, it only finds the room air temperature swings; however, thermal comfort is also affected by the room surface temperatures, so a weighted average of air temperature and surface temperatures is to be preferred. This chapter presents a model and a method which are an attempt to eliminate the above shortcomings.

5.2 Simple direct-gain room model and solution

5.2.1 The model

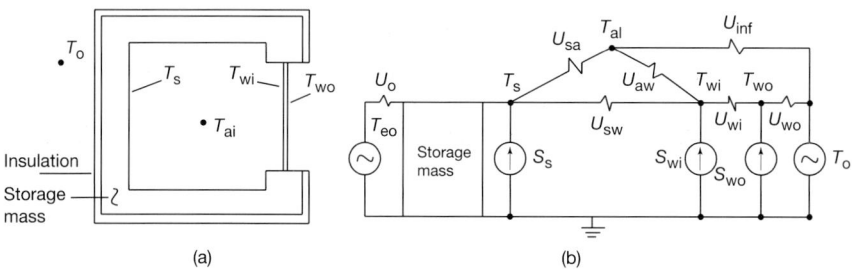

(a)   (b)

Figure 5.1 (a) Direct-gain room with uniformly distributed thermal storage mass; (b) thermal network for room with wall model by distributed RC element

The model is shown schematically in Figure 5.1(a). The walls (all of which are external) are assumed to be made up of an inner lining of storage mass material of uniform thermal transport properties, and an outer massless insulation, also of uniform thermal transport properties. Walls with storage mass are assumed to be at the same surface temperature and they are thus treated as one exterior wall, which is modelled as a two-port distributed element (Carslaw and Jaeger 1959) as described in Section 4.2; its internal surface is thus assumed to be uniformly irradiated by solar radiation. The thermal mass of the window glazings is assumed to be negligible. The important temperatures are shown in Figure 5.1(a): the storage mass internal surface temperature T_s, the (double-glazed) window internal glazing temperature T_{wi}, the room air temperature T_{ai}, and the outdoor air temperature T_o.

The assumed thermal network, shown in Figure 5.1(b), contains several conductances. The equivalent conductance U_{inf} due to infiltration heat loss links T_{ai} and T_o. Convective conductances U_{sa} and U_{aw} link T_{ai} with T_s and T_{ai} with T_{wi}

respectively, while radiative conductances U_{sw} links T_s and T_{wi}. Combined radiative and convective conductances U_{wi} and U_{wo} thermally link T_{wi} with T_{wo} and T_o respectively. The components outside the thermal mass have been replaced in Figure 5.1(b) by an equivalent conductance U_o in series with the sol-air temperature T_{eo} associated with the external wall surface. The conductance U_o combines the insulation resistance R_{ins} and the external surface radiative-convective conductance (equal to $A_o h_o$). The equations for the conductances (time-invariant) are given in equation 5.1. While the model as just described assumes a uniformly distributed storage mass, by a small extension it can model a situation where some of the walls (normally the ceiling) are non-massive, by modelling them as conductances in parallel with U_{inf}. Therefore, U_{inf} is replaced by $U_{inf} + U_{non-massive}$.

The network also contains several sources. The major source S_s is the solar radiation transmitted through the window and absorbed by the storage mass. Sources S_{wi} and S_{wo} are the rates at which solar radiation is absorbed (uniformly) by the inner and outer glazings respectively.

5.2.2 Transformation and frequency domain solution

A delta to star transformation (a three-terminal transformation; see Roe 1966) permits the network of Figure 5.1(b) to be reduced to that of Figure 5.2(a). This transformation has permitted a 'natural' representative room temperature T_{ei} to be obtained at an important node; T_{ei} is a weighted average of T_a, T_{wi} and T_s:

$$T_{ei} = (U_{ew}T_{wi} + U_{ea}T_{ai} + U_{es}T_s)/(U_{ew} + U_{ea} + U_{es}) \tag{5.1}$$

where

$$U_{ew} = U_{sw}(1 + U_{aw}/U_{sa}) + U_{aw} \tag{5.2a}$$

$$U_{ea} = U_{aw}(1 + U_{sa}/U_{sw}) + U_{sa} \tag{5.2b}$$

$$U_{es} = U_{sw}(1 + U_{sa}/U_{aw}) + U_{sa} \tag{5.2c}$$

The temperature T_{ei} can serve as a representative 'sensed' temperature because it should closely follow the effective temperature that would be felt by an occupant who senses, through radiant exchange, the temperature of the room surfaces, and through convective exchange the room air temperature.

More simplifications are applied to obtain the simplified network in Figure 5.2(b). The first transforms the minor sources S_{wi} and S_{wo} to the equivalent source S_{ei} given by

$$S_{ei} = U_{ew}[S_{wi}(h_i + h_o) + S_{wo}h_i]/[h_i h_o A_w + (h_i + h_o)U_{ew}] \tag{5.3}$$

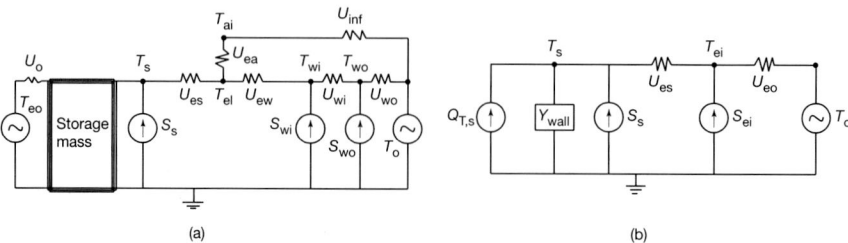

Figure 5.2 (a) Thermal network after delta-star transformation and (b) simplified network

Source S_{ei} represents the portion of solar radiation that is absorbed in the glazings and then transferred to the room interior by thermal radiation or convection. After obtaining S_{ei}, we can determine the equivalent conductance U_{eo} coupling T_{ei} and T_o as

$$U_{eo} = 1[(1/U_{ew} + 1/U_{wi} + 1/U_{wo}) + 1/(1/U_{ea} + 1/U_{inf})] \qquad (5.4)$$

(If there is no mass on the ceiling, the ceiling is modelled as a pure conductance in parallel with U_{inf} and its conductance is added to U_{inf} in eqn 5.4.) Both S_{ei} and S_s are proportional to the solar irradiance of the window, so that S_{ei} is expected to be proportional to S_s. It was found that S_{ei} is typically about 4% of the magnitude of S_s (for standard double glazing and mid-latitudes in winter). As can be seen from Figure 5.2(b), S_{ei} can be transformed to node s and added to S_s. Thus, we multiply S_s by the appropriate transformation factor so as to include the effect of S_{ei}; this factor is equal to $[1+(S_{ei}/S_s)U_{es}/(U_{es} + U_{eo})]$ (an average value of the ratio S_{ei}/S_s can be determined from equation 5.3 in the middle of the design period).

The final simplification is replacement of the wall by its Norton equivalent, which is determined as explained in Section 4.2. Since we are only interested in the interior surface temperature T_s, unimportant nodes are eliminated by this transformation and the resulting network consists of only two-terminal components. These two simplifications yield the network in Figure 5.2(b).

As shown in Figure 5.2(b), the Norton equivalent consists of Y_{wall} (called the wall self-admittance) and the equivalent source $Q_{T,s}$. The Norton equivalent source is given by

$$Q_{T,s} = -Y_{seo}T_{eo} \qquad (5.5)$$

where the transfer admittance Y_{seo} is given by

$$Y_{seo} = -A_s/[A_s\cosh(\gamma x)/U_o + \sinh(\gamma x)/(k\gamma)] \qquad (5.6)$$

The wall self-admittance is given by

$$Y_{\text{wall}} = A_s[(U_o/A_s) + k\gamma E]/[(U_o/k\gamma A_s)E + 1] \qquad (5.7)$$

where $E = \tanh(\gamma x)$.

Important design approximation: For rooms with well-insulated walls and a high amount of mass (more than 10 cm of concrete or equivalent) we can approximate the wall self-admittance with the following equation:

$$Y_{\text{wall}} \approx A k\gamma\tanh(\gamma x) \qquad (5.7a)$$

For very thick mass (more than 25 cm of concrete or equivalent) we may approximate the wall as a semi-infinite solid with admittance equal to:

$$Y_{\text{wallsemi-inf}} \approx A k\gamma \qquad (5.7b)$$

In both of the above cases the transfer admittance (for all frequencies apart from the mean) is negligible.

The solutions for T_s and T_{ei} are easily obtained from a heat balance at the two nodes (note that S_{ei}, a small source, is not explicitly included in the heat balance as it has been transformed to node s and added to S_s). The storage mass surface temperature is found to be given by

$$T_s(\omega) = (S_s + Q_{T,s} + U_L T_o)/Y_s \qquad (5.8)$$

where Y_s is the room total admittance as seen from the port formed by the reference and the T_s node, given by

$$Y_s = Y_{\text{wall}} + U_L \qquad (5.9)$$

where

$$U_L = (1/U_{es} + 1/U_{eo})^{-1}$$

The conductance U_L represents the total loss conductance between the storage mass interior surface and the ambient temperature T_o.

The representative temperature is found to be given by

$$T_{ei}(\omega) = (\text{TF})_{eis}(S_s + Q_{T,s}) + (U_{eo}T_o)/Y_{ei} \qquad (5.10)$$

where

$$(\text{TF})_{eis} = 1/((Y_{\text{wall}}/U_L + 1)U_{eo}) \qquad (5.11)$$

and

$$Y_{ei} = U_{eo} + Y_{wall}U_{es}/(Y_{wall} + U_{es}) \tag{5.12}$$

The transfer function $(TF)_{eis}$ determines the effect of the primary source S_s, while Y_{ei} is the total room admittance as seen from the port formed by the T_{ei} node and reference node.

5.2.3 Source models

Steady-state periodic conditions are assumed in computing the swing (difference between maximum and minimum) in T_{ei} or T_s over a particular day. The period is assumed to be one day, implying that the day in question has been preceded by identical days. Although deviations from the one-day periodic assumption (e.g. previous day overcast and current day clear) would cause errors in the *mean* value of T_{ei} for the day considered, the variation of the waveform of T_{ei} about its mean should not be affected and therefore the difference between its maximum and minimum points should be close to the actual swing. Another option would have been to include the effect of the previous day, i.e. to assume a two-day periodicity; the present method can be readily generalized to include such a model. Note that because of the one-day periodic assumption, weather input is needed only for the particular day in question.

Fourier series models are required for the sources S_s, T_{eo} and T_o, in order to obtain the time domain solution for T_s and T_{ei} under periodic conditions. For equatorial facing windows (e.g. south facing in the northern hemisphere) the primary source S_s can be closely modelled over the daytime as a half sinusoid. The constraints on the half sinusoid are chosen to satisfy two conditions: first that it has an integrated energy equal to the actual solar radiation H_a absorbed in the room over the day, and second that it must start at sunrise and terminate at sunset. Thus, S_s for a single day is defined by

$$S_s = 0, |t| > t_s \text{ and}$$
$$S_s = (\pi H_a/4t_s) \cos(\pi t/2t_s), |t| < t_s \tag{5.13}$$

where t is the time measured from the solar noon (t is negative in the morning, positive in the afternoon) and t_s is the value of t at sunset. This expression for S_s can be approximated by the following truncated Fourier series:

$$S_s = q_0 + \sum_{n=1}^{N} q_n \cos(\omega_n t) \tag{5.14}$$

where $\omega_n = 2\pi n/t_d$, $q_0 = H_a/t_d$ and $q_n = H_a f_n$, f_n being given by

$$f_n = \sin[\pi(t_d + 4t_s n)/(2t_d)]/(t_d + 4t_s n)$$
$$+ \sin[\pi(t_d - 4t_s n)/(2t_d)]/(t_d - 4t_s n) \tag{5.14a}$$

As can be seen, the *relative* magnitude of the harmonics is determined completely by the daylength $2t_s$. The number of harmonics necessary to model S_s was found to increase with decrease of the daylength because of the more abrupt increase of the absorbed radiation at sunrise, and its more rapid decrease at sunset. For windows that are not equatorial facing, the Fourier coefficients can be determined by direct numerical integration of the instantaneous absorbed irradiation. Various methods can be used for determining the total daily irradiation absorbed H_a. Either real weather may be employed, which is cumbersome, or instead the daily clearness index may be used to generate values of the hourly clearness index (Athienitis *et al.* 1986).

The variation of the ambient temperature T_o was modelled by a single sinusoid, with maximum at 3 p.m. and minimum at 3 a.m. (solar times). Thus, if T_{om} is the daily average of T_o, and ΔT_o the daily range of T_o then

$$T_o = T_{om} + (\Delta T_o/2)\cos(\omega_1 t - \pi/4) \tag{5.15}$$

The model does not distinguish between the differing orientations of the exterior wall surfaces and hence it is not possible to accurately model the effect of fluctuations in the solar radiation absorbed by the wall exterior surfaces. A sensitivity analysis given in a later section showed that the effect of this absorbed solar radiation on the temperature swing is small, provided there is at least a medium amount of insulation (about 5 RSI) behind the mass. Thus, the sol-air temperature T_{eo} can be modelled as equivalent to T_o.

5.2.4 Periodic solution

The time domain solution for the representative temperature T_{ei} is obtained after substituting the source models in equation 5.10 and evaluating magnitudes and phase angles for the complex transfer functions. Since we are only interested in fluctuations, the mean source terms can be ignored. The following solution is obtained for the variation of T_{ei} about its mean T_{eim}:

$$
\begin{aligned}
T_{ei}(t) - T_{eim} = {}& [\Delta T_o U_{eo}/(2|Y_{eil}|)]\cos(\omega_1 t - \varphi_{eil} - \pi/4) \\
& + (\Delta T_o |Y_{seol}||(TF)_{eis1}|/2)\cos(\omega_1 t + \varphi_{eis1} + \varphi_{seol} - \pi/4) \\
& + \sum_{n=1}^{N} |(TF)_{eisn}|q_n \cos(\omega_n t + \varphi_{eisn})
\end{aligned} \tag{5.16}
$$

where $|(TF)_{eisn}|$ and φ_{eisn} are respectively the magnitude and phase of $(TF)_{eis}$ for $\omega = \omega_n$. Similar definitions apply for $|Y_{eil}|$ and φ_{eil}, and $|Y_{seol}|$ and φ_{seol}. For the variation of T_s we obtain:

$$T_s(t) - T_{sm} = [\Delta T_o U_L/(2|Y_{s1}|)]\cos(\omega_1 - \varphi_{s1} - \pi/4)$$
$$+ (\Delta T_{eo}|Y_{seo1}|/(2|Y_{s1}|))\cos(\omega_1 - \varphi_{s1} + \varphi_{seo1} - \pi/4)$$
$$+ \sum_{n=1}^{N} (q_n /|Y_{sn}|)\cos(\omega_n t - \varphi_{sn}) \tag{5.17}$$

The swings in T_s and T_{ei} can be determined by differentiating the appropriate equation, finding the two zeros corresponding to the times at which the maximum and minimum temperatures occur, and then substituting these times back into the original equation.

Approximate design method for temperature swings: for a well-insulated room with massive walls, with equation 5.7a or 5.7b applicable, we can quickly estimate maximum temperature swings with the following approximation:

$$\text{Temperature swing} = 2F_h|q_1|/|Y_{wall}|$$

where q_1 is estimated from equation 5.14, $F_h = 1.12$ is a factor to approximate for the effect of higher harmonics, and $|Y_{wall}|$ may be estimated by

$$|Y_{wall}| = Ak|\gamma| \times |\tanh(\gamma x)|$$
$$= Ak(2\pi/(P\alpha))^{1/2}[(\cosh X - \cos X)/(\cosh X + \cos X)]^{1/2} \tag{5.17a}$$

with $X = 2L[\pi/(P\alpha)]^{1/2}$.

The phase angle of Y_{wall} is given by

$$\text{Phase } (Y_{wall}) = 45° + \text{atan}(\sin X/ \sinh X) \tag{5.17b}$$

Note that the first term (45°) in equation 5.17b corresponds to the phase angle for $k\gamma$ and is equivalent to a time lead of 3 h (15° is equivalent to 1 h for a period of 24 h).

5.2.5 Sensitivity analysis

The objectives of the sensitivity analysis are to study the relative significance of fundamental design variables and to document the effects of various modelling assumptions. It consists of two parts. The first analyses the transfer function's dependence on the resistance R_{ins}, the mass thickness x and the main heat loss conductance U_L. The second analyses the temperature swing's dependence on the above variables, plus the half-daylength t_s.

The assumed room data are: the dimensions of the south wall were 6.10 m wide by 2.44 m high, the north–south depth was 4.57 m, and the (south-facing, double-glazed) window area was 8.36 m². The infiltration value used was 0.5 air changes per hour. The heat transfer coefficients were as follows: $h_{cs} = h_{cw} = 3$ W/K/m²,

h_i = 7.4 W/K/m^2 and h_{rw} = 5 W/K/m^2. The uniformly distributed storage mass was concrete with k = 1.73 W/K/m, ρ = 2242 kg/m^3 and c = 840 J/kg/K.

Three values were used for each of the four sensitivity variables: low (L), medium (M) and high (H); all are given in Table 5.1. The basis for choosing the thickness values shown relates to the non-dimensional thickness of the slab (Davies 1973) for the fundamental harmonic (X_1), which is equal to $(\omega_1/2\alpha)^{1/2}x$ (also shown in Table 5.1). For concrete, X_1 becomes equal to 6.3x and it is the most important quantity in determining Y_{wall} (equation 5.7) whose maximum magnitude is for approximately medium thickness.

Table 5.1 Variables for sensitivity analysis ($X_1 = (\omega_1/2\alpha)^{1/2}x$)

	x (m)	X_1	U_L (W/K)	R_{ins} (m^2 K/W)	t_s (s)
Low	0.08	0.50	27	1	14 000
Medium	0.14	0.88	37	5	20 000
High	0.20	1.26	47	10	26 000

SENSITIVITY OF TRANSFER FUNCTIONS

The most important transfer functions are Y_s and $(TF)_{eis}$ because they determine the effect of the primary source S_s on T_s and T_{ei} respectively. A sensitivity analysis is reported for Y_s but not $(TF)_{eis}$; because the latter is mainly a function of the same admittances as Y_s, similar results were found.

Room admittance Y_s. The room total admittance Y_s (equation 5.9) is the most important transfer function since it determines the effect of the absorbed solar radiation on the storage mass surface temperature. The variation of $|Y_{sn}|$ as a function of U_L, R_{ins} and x for six harmonics is shown in Table 5.2. Examination of Table 5.2 shows a low sensitivity to U_L: 27% increase in U_L causes a less than 1% increase in $|Y_{sn}|$. The effect of R_{ins} on $|Y_{sn}|$ is also small, the change being an increase

Table 5.2 Variation of room admittance magnitude $|Y_{sn}|$(W/K)

R_{ins}	U_L	x	Harmonic no. n					
			1	2	3	4	5	6
L	M	L	985	1863	2595	3176	3631	3990
		M	1494	2300	2735	3045	3314	3570
		H	1624	2154	2529	2878	3209	3513
	H	L	988	1867	2599	3181	3636	3997
		M	1498	2306	2742	3052	3322	3577
		H	1630	2162	2536	2886	3216	3524
M	M	L	1000	1895	2633	3213	3663	4017
		M	1530	2325	2746	3048	3314	3566
		H	1648	2158	2527	2877	3208	3517
H	M	L	1003	1900	2638	3218	3667	4020
		M	1536	2328	2748	3049	3314	3568
		H	1651	2158	2527	2877	3208	3517

of about 2% when R_{ins} changes from low to high. Not unexpectedly, the mass thickness x is the most important parameter. The magnitude $|Y_{sn}|$ increases with the harmonic number n due primarily to the increase of γ, corresponding to a decrease of the penetration depth $(\alpha/\omega)^{1/2}$.

Wall transfer admittance Y_{seo1}. The magnitude of the wall transfer admittance Y_{seo1} (first harmonic) determines the magnitude of the (single harmonic) transformed source $Q_{T,s}$ (equation 5.5) and thus the effect of the sol-air temperature. The variation of $|Y_{seo1}|$ is shown in Table 5.3 as a function of both R_{ins} and x. As expected, $|Y_{seo1}|$ is highest for low R_{ins} and low for x.

Both R_{ins} and x are important in determining $|Y_{seo1}|$. Comparing these values of $|Y_{seo1}|$ with the values of $|Y_{sn}|$ given in Table 5.2 shows that Y_{seo} is small compared to Y_s. Thus the effect of fluctuations in the sol-air temperature on swings of T_s or T_{ei} is expected to be small.

Room admittance Y_{ei}. A sensitivity analysis was also performed for Y_{ei} (equation (5.12)), whose magnitude $|Y_{ei1}|$ for the first harmonic determines the effect of the swing of the ambient temperature on T_e (see equation 5.16). As shown later, it is a relatively unimportant transfer function since the contribution which ΔT_o (range of T_o) makes to the variation in T_s is small. It was found that Y_{ei1} is more sensitive to changes in U_L than is Y_s; a change of U_L from low to high causes a maximum increase in $|Y_{ei1}|$ of approximately 5% (in changing U_L it was assumed that U_{eo} changes but not U_{es}; this is equivalent to assuming that the main causes of changes in U_L are changes in the infiltration loss and in h_i and h_o).

Table 5.3 Variation of $|Y_{seo1}|$(W/K)

x	R_{ins}		
	L	M	H
L	83	18	9.0
M	71	15	7.8
H	51	11	5.6

SENSITIVITY OF MASS SURFACE TEMPERATURE SWINGS

The variation of the mass surface temperature T_s results from the highly important heat storage and release process. Since superposition applies, the temperature swings in T_s caused by each source may be studied separately.

Swings caused by absorbed solar radiation. An important objective of this analysis was to study how many harmonics are needed to model the effect of S_s. Using equation 5.17 the magnitude of each harmonic of T_s is given by $q_n|Y_{sn}|$. Thus, in order to study the importance of higher harmonics of S_s, a non-dimensional sensitivity function Sens(ω) was defined as the ratio of higher T_s harmonics to the fundamental:

$$\text{Sens}(\omega) \ = \ (q_n/|Y_{sn}|)/(q_1/|Y_{s1}|) \tag{5.18}$$

The two variables essentially determining the sensitivity function are the daylength $2t_s$ and the storage mass thickness. Table 5.4 shows the results for low (L), medium (M) and high (H) value combinations of the two variables. As can be seen, the higher harmonics become more important for low mass and low daylength. This observation is further illustrated in Table 5.5, which shows how accurately the temperature swing would be determined using only a few harmonics.

For the other extreme case of high mass and high t_s, the fundamental harmonic would be enough for determining the temperature swings. The study indicates that between three to five harmonics should be sufficient to ensure accuracy of the swings of about 0.1 K.

Table 5.4 Sens(ω_n) (equation (5.18))

| x | t_s | Harmonic no. n | | | | |
		2	3	4	5	6
L	L	0.385	0.150	0.036	−0.012	−0.019
	M	0.260	0.024	−0.027	−0.009	0.008
	H	0.126	−0.037	−0.006	0.011	−0.002
M	L	0.480	0.221	0.058	−0.020	−0.033
	M	0.324	0.035	−0.043	−0.015	0.014
	H	0.157	−0.054	−0.009	0.019	−0.004
H	L	0.557	0.258	0.066	−0.022	−0.036
	M	0.376	0.041	−0.049	−0.017	0.015
	H	0.182	−0.063	-0.011	0.021	−0.004

Table 5.5 Swings of T_s (K) due to S_s (H_a = 83.6 MJ)

| x | t_s | Number of harmonics used | | | | | |
		1	2	3	4	5	6
L	L	3.50	4.21	4.23	4.23	4.26	4.32
M	L	2.29	2.92	3.07	3.05	3.07	3.11
M	M	2.06	2.37	2.36	2.42	2.43	2.43
M	H	1.77	1.85	1.91	1.92	1.93	1.93
H	H	1.65	1.72	1.77	1.77	1.77	1.77

Swings due to ambient and sol-air temperatures. The ambient temperature T_0 causes swings of the room temperature by virtue of its variation ΔT_0. Its effect will be compared to that of the fundamental harmonic q_1 of the absorbed radiation, the latter accounting for about 70% of the swing of T_s caused by S_s. The ratio of the two effects is $U_L \Delta T_0 / 2q_1$. Assuming an extreme value for ΔT_0 equal to 20 K, a value for U_L of 40 W/K and for q_1 of 2000 W, the maximum value of this ratio is 0.2. This means that the maximum effect of T_0 on the total swing of T_s is at most 14% of the contribution of S_s.

The effect of T_{eo} on T_s can be studied by a similar order of magnitude analysis. The ratio of the effect of T_{eo} on T_s to the effect of T_0 on T_s can be shown to be equal to the ratio $|Y_{seo1}|/U_L$, which, for the typical case of medium insulation and medium wall thickness, is less than 0.5. The difference between the maximum and minimum values of T_{eo} on a clear day is shown by Threlkeld (1970) to be a maximum of about 40 K for a horizontal surface (latitude = 42°N and surface absorptance = 0.9). Since only the roof is horizontal, the fluctuation of T_{eo} about its mean would be at most between 25 and 30 K, of which 20 K would be contributed by T_0 thus, roughly speaking, on a clear day, the swings in T_{eo} will be roughly twice the swings in T_0. After correcting by the factor $|Y_{seo1}|/U_L$, we conclude that the contribution of T_{eo} to the swing in T_s will be about the same as that of T_0, or about 14% of the contribution of S_s. Since the externally absorbed solar radiation contributes only one half of the variation in T_{eo}, we conclude that the externally absorbed solar radiation provides a contribution to the swings in T_s equal to at most about 7% of the contribution of S_s. The contribution of the externally absorbed radiation can be shown to be even smaller if the effect of the phase shift introduced by Y_{seo} is considered. Thus, it is sufficient for this simplified model to assume T_{eo} equivalent to T_0 and hence ignore the effect of the externally absorbed solar radiation.

5.3 Bibliography

Athienitis A.K., Sullivan H.F. and Hollands K.G.T. (1986) 'Analytical model, sensitivity analysis and algorithm for temperature swings in direct gain rooms', *Solar Energy*, **36**:4, 303–312.

Balcomb J.D. *et al.* (1980) *Passive Solar Handbook*, Vol. 2, Los Alamos Scientific Laboratory, USA.

Carslaw H.S. and Jaeger J.C. (1959) *Conduction of Heat in Solids*, 2nd Edn, Oxford University Press, London.

Davies M.G. (1973) 'The thermal admittance of layered walls', *Building Science*, **8**, 207–220.

Kirkpatrick A.T. and Winn C.B. (1984) 'Spectral analysis of the effective temperature in passive solar buildings', *Journal of Solar Energy Engineering*, **106**, 112–119.

Roe P.H. (1966) *Networks and Systems*, Addison Wesley Co.

Threlkeld J.L. (1970) *Thermal Environmental Engineering*, 2nd Edn, Prentice Hall, Englewood Cliffs, NJ.

Winn C.B. (1987) 'Control in solar energy systems', *Advances in Solar Energy*, ASES, pp. 209–240.

CHAPTER 6

Ventilation and indoor air quality

6.1 Airflow processes in buildings

Ventilation of buildings may be achieved by natural or mechanical means, in order to provide thermal comfort, humidity control and acceptable indoor air quality. In particular, ventilation is used to dilute indoor concentration of pollutants and renew building air. In parallel, thermal comfort depends to a certain degree on indoor air velocity and appropriate indoor air movement can provide thermal comfort, even when the temperature and humidity are not the most appropriate. If temperatures are high, too little air movement can cause discomfort, and higher air movement may be welcome. The sizing and the design of the ventilation system should consider the effect that the air movement in the room will have on comfort if the occupants are not to subvert the ventilation strategy. Existing standards for indoor air movement assume that high air velocities and turbulence may cause discomfort through draughts. Appropriate ventilation for humidity control may prevent microbiological growth on walls, floors and ceilings as well as protect the building construction from damage.

Mechanical ventilation can be used when a constant or controlled airflow is necessary or when outdoor conditions are not favourable to provide a healthy and comfortable indoor environment for building occupants. The provision of ventilation air to a mechanically ventilated building requires that outdoor air is 'cleaned' and conditioned before it enters the building, which may be an important cost in building operation. Cleaning of the circulating air through filters is well used in everyday practice; however, it removes only the coarse particles, which may not be so hazardous to health as fine particles, which are difficult to remove.

Recently, energy conservation measures have promoted the application of heat recovery from exhaust air and a higher recirculation of the return air. In some cases, they have led to the reduction of the quantities of outside air, which may have serious impact on indoor air quality. Recent ventilation standards consider both energy conservation and indoor air quality and propose methodologies to optimize the ventilation strategy; however, the level of requirements between the various proposed standards varies considerably. In parallel there is an uncertainty regarding the IAQ requirements. For example in the CEN approach, the uncertainty in the real indoor air quality needs varies by 250%: from 4 to 10 l/s per person in relation to occupants' related pollution. If one takes into consideration smoking, the variation is even larger (see Table 6.1).

Table 6.1 Ventilation requirements for the various building categories

Category	Required ventilation rate (l/s per occupant)			
	No smoking	*20%*	*40%*	*100%*
A	10	20	30	30
B	7	14	21	21
C	4	8	12	12

It is certain that in practice the ventilation performances do not satisfy the specifications found in the standards and regulations. To achieve ventilation systems with good performances with respect to indoor air quality and energy efficiency, it is important that the system is designed appropriately, while the performance of the different components as well as the quality of execution is of a correct level. Therefore, it is important to consider appropriate mechanisms for achieving a better compliance.

When the local climate and the concentration of the outdoor pollutants are not restrictive factors, the use of natural ventilation techniques may be an efficient and energy-saving procedure to maintain an appropriate indoor air quality, achieve thermal comfort and provide free cooling. Driving forces of natural ventilation are wind and the thermal difference between indoor and outdoor air. Possible problems related to the use of natural ventilation techniques involve the lack of particle filtration; possible poor indoor temperature control; exposure to outdoor noise; and probably low ventilation rates under adverse weather conditions.

6.2 Natural ventilation

6.2.1 Airflow in urban areas

Airflow around isolated buildings is well known and is characterized by a bolster eddy vortex due to flow down the windward façade. Behind there is a lee eddy drawn into the cavity of low pressure due to flow separation from the sharp edges of the building top and sides, and further downstream is the building wake characterized by increased turbulence but lower horizontal speeds than the undisturbed flow.

The airflow patterns in urban canyons have received important attention over the past years (Table 6.2). Natural ventilation of buildings located in urban canyons is seriously reduced because of important decrease of the wind velocity inside the canyons.

Table 6.2 Airflow in urban canyons

Flow along the canyon	Perpendicular flow	Oblique flow

Wind speed above the canyon < 4 m/s

Type of flow: chaotic. There is no coupling between the undisturbed and the wind speed inside the canyon. The maximum expected wind speed should not exceed 0.5 m/s. This value may be used in ventilation models especially when the ambient speed exceeds 3 m/s and the H/W ratio is low (<1). For lower speeds a value close to 0.2–0.3 m/s may be used. There is no predominant wind direction inside the canyon. When the ambient wind speed exceeds 3 m/s, it may be considered that the flow is almost parallel to the axis of the canyon with a very small uplift component parallel to the walls of the canyon.	**For $H/W > 0.7$** **Type of flow: Chaotic.** There is no coupling between the undisturbed and the wind speed inside the canyon. Thermal as well as mechanical influences play an important role in the canyon circulation. The maximum expected wind speed should not exceed 0.4 m/s. This value (0.4 m/s) may be used in ventilation models especially when the ambient speed exceeds 3 m/s. For lower speeds a value close to 0.2 m/s may be used. There is no predominant wind direction inside the canyon.	Similar to the perpendicular flow.

Wind speed above the canyon > 4 m/s

Type of flow: Mean wind along the canyon axis with possible uplift along the canyon walls. **Prediction of the along-canyon wind speed $v(z)$** Use: $v(z) = U_0 e^{z/Z_0}$ where z is the height, U_0 is a constant reference speed (see Figure 6.1) and Z_0 is the roughness length of the obstructed sublayer calculated by the expression: $$Z_0 = h_b D^*/z_0$$ where D^* is an effective diameter of air space between obstacles and can	**For canyons with $H/W < 2$ and $L/W > 20$** **Type of flow:** A stable circulatory vortex is established in the canyon. **Prediction of the cross-canyon u and vertical, w, air speeds:** $$u = u_0(1 - \beta)^{-1}[\gamma(1 + k\gamma) - \beta(1 - k\gamma)/\gamma]\sin(kx)$$ and $$w = -u_0(1 - \beta)^{-1}ky[\gamma - \beta/\gamma]\cos(kx)$$ where $k = \pi/W$, $\beta = \exp(-2kH)$,	**For canyons with $L/W > 20$** **Type of flow:** A spiral vortex is induced along the length of the canyon, a corkscrew type of action. **Prediction of the cross-canyon u and vertical, w, air speeds:** $$u = u_0(1 - \beta)^{-1}[\gamma(1 + k\gamma) - \beta(1 - k\gamma)/\gamma]\sin(kx)$$ and $$w = -u_0(1 - \beta)^{-1}ky[\gamma - \beta/\gamma]\cos(kx)$$ where $k = \pi/W$,

Table 6.2 (continued)

be tentatively approximated for the city by:

$$D^* = 0.1 h_b$$

The parameter h_b is equal to the height of buildings.

Typical values of z_o are given by Oke (1987); see Table 6.3.

Alternatively $v(z)$ may be calculated by the following expression proposed by Yamartino and Wiegard (1986):

$$v(z) = v_r \, \log \, [(z + z_o)/z_o]/ \log[(z_r + z_o)/z_o]$$

where v_r is the value at reference height z_r and z_o is the surface roughness.

For canyons with $L/W < 20$

Type of flow: Intermittent vortices are shed on the building corners. These vortices are responsible for the mechanism of advection from the building corners to mid-block creating a convergence zone in the mid-block region of the canyon.

Prediction of the wind speed: Use mean wind speed close to 0.4 m/s. Prevailing direction: Parallel to the axis of the axis with a downward direction.

$\gamma = \exp(ky)$, $y = z - H$, and u_o is the wind speed above the canyon and at the point $x = W/2$, $z = H$.

For canyons with $H/W > 2$ and $L/W > 20$

Type of flow: Two vortices are developed, an upper one driven by ambient airflow and a lower one driven in the opposite direction by the circulation above.

Prediction of the cross-canyon u and vertical, w, air speeds:

For the lower part of the canyon use a mean wind speed close to 0.3 m/s.

For the upper parts use the following expressions:

$$u = u_o(1 - \beta)^{-1} \, [\gamma(1 + k\gamma) - \beta(1 - k\gamma)/\gamma] \sin(kx)$$

and

$$w = -u_o(1 - \beta)^{-1} ky \, [\gamma - \beta/\gamma] \cos(kx)$$

where $k = \pi/W$, $\beta = \exp(-2kH)$, $\gamma = \exp(ky)$, $y = z - H$ and u_o is the wind speed above the canyon and at the point $x = W/2$, $z = H$.

For canyons with $L/W < 20$

Type of flow: Intermittent vortices are shed on the building corners. These vortices are responsible for the mechanism of advection from the building corners to mid-block creating a convergence zone in the mid-block region of the canyon.

Prediction of the wind speed: Use mean wind speed close to 0.4 m/s. Prevailing direction: Parallel to the axis of the axis with a downward direction.

$\beta = \exp(-2kH)$, $\gamma = \exp(ky)$, $= z - H$ and u_o is the wind speed above the canyon and at the point $x = W/2$, $z = H$.

For canyons with $L/W < 20$

Type of flow: Intermittent vortices are shed on the building corners. These vortices are responsible for the mechanism of advection from the building corners to mid-block creating a convergence zone in the mid-block region of the canyon.

Prediction of the wind speed: Use mean wind speed close to 0.4 m/s. Prevailing direction: Parallel to the axis of the axis with a downward direction.

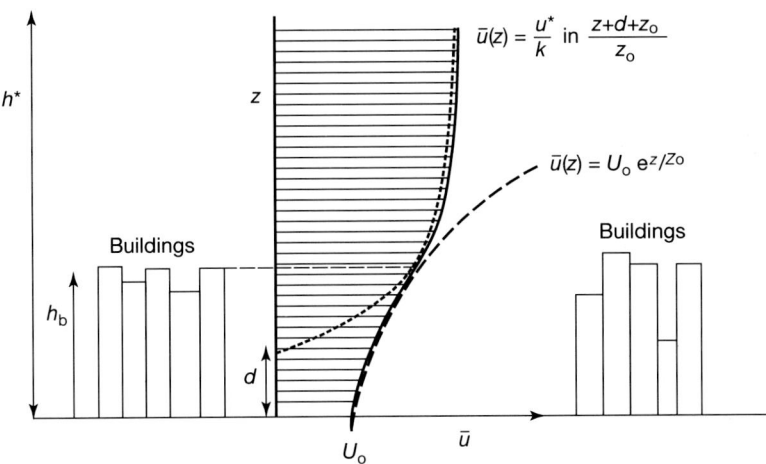

Figure 6.1 Logarithmic and exponential wind profiles in the surface layer, above and below building height (after Nicholson 1975)

Table 6.3 Typical roughness length z_0 of urbanized terrain

Terrain	z_0 (m)
Scattered settlement	0.2–0.6
Suburban	
Low-density residences and gardens	0.4–1.2
High-density residences and gardens	0.8–1.8
Urban	
High density, more than five-storey row and block buildings	1.5–2.5
High density plus multistorey blocks	2.5–10

From Oke (1987)

Natural ventilation of buildings is due either to the wind forces or to the temperature difference between the indoor and outdoor environment or to a combination of both. Design of urban buildings to improve natural ventilation potential should consider the appropriate wind data and not routine meteorological observations collected in open fields. Also, the specific temperature regime in a canyon should be considered.

Knowledge of the air speed inside urban canyons is of great importance for passive cooling applications and especially for naturally ventilated buildings. Various methods, simplified or detailed, have been proposed to calculate the wind speed inside a canyon. A detailed presentation of the existing methods to calculate the wind speed in urban canyons has been presented in Santamouris (2000).

Urban canyons are characterized by three main parameters: H, the mean height of the buildings in the canyon, W, the canyon width and L, the canyon length. Given these parameters, the geometrical descriptors are limited to three simple measures.

These are the ratio H/W, the aspect ratio L/H and the building density $j = A_r/A_1$ where A_r is the plan of roof area of the average building and A_1 is the 'lot' area or unit ground area occupied by each building.

When the predominant direction of the airflow is approximately normal (say 30°) to the long axis of the street canyon, three types of airflow regime are observed as a function of the building (L/H), and canyon (H/W) geometry. When the buildings are well apart ($H/W > 0.05$), their flow fields do not interact. At closer spacing, the wakes are disturbed and the flow regime is known as **isolated roughness flow**. When the height and spacing of the array combine to disturb the bolster and cavity eddies, the regime changes to one referred to as **wake interference flow**. This is characterized by secondary flows in the canyon space where the downward flow of the cavity eddy is reinforced by deflection down the windward face of the next building downstream. At even greater H/W and density, a stable circulatory vortex is established in the canyon because of the transfer of momentum across a shear layer of roof height, and transition to a 'skimming' flow regime occurs where the bulk of the flow does not enter the canyon.

Skimming regime is the most common in urban areas. Under these conditions the airflow in the canyon can been seen as a secondary circulation feature driven by the above roof-imposed flow. If the wind speed out of the canyon is below some threshold value the coupling between the upper and secondary flow is lost, and the relation between wind speeds above the roof and within the canyon is characterized by a considerable scatter. According to many studies carried out in almost symmetrical canyons where $1 < H/W < 1.4$, the threshold value is between 1.5 and 2 m/s. In all these studies higher wind speeds have been found to produce a stable vortex circulation within the canyon. For lower wind speeds thermal as well as mechanical influences may play an important role in the canyon circulation.

Parallel ambient flow generates a mean wind along the canyon axis, with possible uplift along the canyon walls as airflow is retarded by friction by the building walls and street surface. Regarding the relation between the free stream wind speed, U, and the along-canyon velocity, v, it is reported that the along-canyon wind component, v, in the canyon is directly proportional to the above-roof along-canyon component, through the constant of proportionality that is a function of approach flow azimuth.

The more common case in the urban environment is that where airflows at a certain angle are relative to the long axis of the canyon. Unfortunately, the existing research on this topic is considerably less than the scientific information for perpendicular and along-canyon flows. However, it is known that when the flow above the roof is at some angle of attack to the canyon axis, a spiral vortex is induced along the length of the canyon, similar to a corkscrew type of action. For intermediate angles of incidence to the canyon long axis, the canyon airflow is the product of both the transverse and parallel components of the ambient wind, where the former drives the canyon vortex and the latter determines the along-canyon stretching of the vortex.

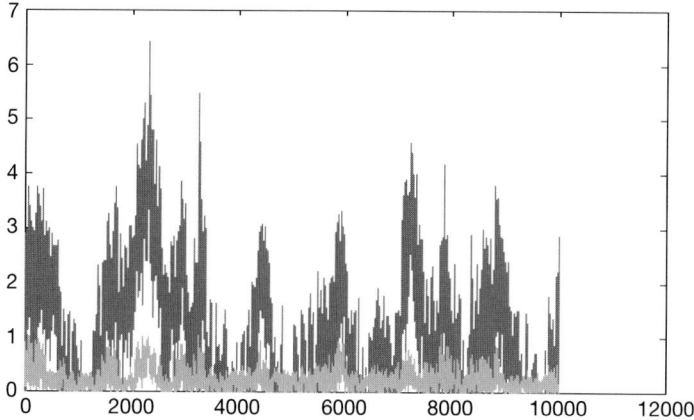

Figure 6.2 Wind velocity inside the canyon (grey) and above the canyon (black)

As a result of the above mechanisms, wind speed inside the canyons in an urban environment is seriously decreased and as a mean value is close to 10–30% of the undisturbed wind speed over the buildings. Figure 6.2 shows the values of the wind speed measured over and inside the canyon in an urban canyon in Athens. As shown, although ambient wind speeds easily exceed 4 m/s, the speed inside the canyon increases up to 1 m/s, and rarely exceeds it.

Decrease of wind speed seriously affects the potential for natural ventilation of buildings in the urban environment. For better design of natural ventilation in urban buildings, different methods have been proposed to consider realistic wind speeds. In fact, various methods, simplified and detailed, have been proposed to calculate the effects of the building location on the natural ventilation effectiveness. The methods in general propose techniques to reduce either the wind speed or the airflow rate due to the relative location of the building and the characteristics of the neighbourhood buildings.

A detailed method to calculate or select the appropriate wind speed in the urban environment is presented below. The methodology classifies the undisturbed wind flow in three main classes: flow (a) parallel to the canyon axis, (b) perpendicular and (c) oblique to the axis of the road. It classifies canyons as a function of their height (H) to width (W) ratio, as well as of the ratio of the canyon length (L) to the canyon width (W). The methodology considers that when the ambient wind speed above the canyon is lower than 3–4 m/s, there is no clear coupling between the flow above and inside the canyon, while it takes into account advection phenomena and end effects from the canyon corners. For these cases empirical wind speeds are proposed.

For higher wind speeds, and when the coupling between the ambient and the canyon wind speeds is established, the model proposes using the Hotchkiss and Harlow (1973) methodology to calculate the canyon transverse air speed $(w^2 + u^2)^{0.5}$, for perpendicular or oblique to the canyon axis winds, where u and w are the cross-canyon and vertical air speeds respectively. This model considers incompressible flow, absence of sources or sinks of vorticity within the canyon, and appropriate boundary conditions for the simple $2 - d$ rectangular notch of depth H and width W. For wind speeds parallel to the canyon axis and when coupling between the ambient and canyon wind speeds is established, the proposed methodology is based on the algorithms proposed by Yamartino and Wiegnard (1986).

6.2.2 Natural ventilation calculation methodologies

Transfer of air between the building and the surrounding environment as well as among the various zones of the buildings plays a very important role in the overall thermal balance of buildings, which also affects the levels of thermal comfort and indoor air quality. Exchange of air can be achieved either by mechanical means (mechanical ventilation) or through large openings of the building's envelope (natural ventilation). Air is also exchanged in an uncontrolled manner through cracks and other small size openings (infiltration).

Knowledge of the exact air supply to a building is necessary to determine its thermal performance and the concentration of the indoor pollutants. Classical fluid dynamics provides the theoretical framework to calculate the airflow when mechanical ventilation systems are used. This can be achieved by using either computerized fluid dynamic techniques (CFDs), or more simplified network models. Calculation of airflow through large openings, natural ventilation, is a more complicated task. The random nature of the wind makes estimation of airflow characteristics much more complicated than in the case of mechanical ventilation. Computerized flow dynamic and network tools have been proposed to treat natural ventilation problems. These tools are more efficient when airflow is due to temperature differences and not to wind. However, the use of complicated CFD techniques is not the more suitable solution, especially for small and medium projects. The basic principles as well as details of simplified, network and CFD calculation models are discussed in Allard (1998).

Computerized fluid dynamics tools are based on the solution of the Navier–Stokes equations combined with turbulence models. These tools determine the field of air velocity in a zone, the flow rate through various components, and the concentration of indoor pollutants in zones. Also, they combine efficient heat transfer models to calculate the thermal balance of various building elements. Although these tools are very powerful, only experts are able to use them while their cost is high.

Network calculation models are based just on the equation of mass conservation combined with some empirical knowledge. These tools can efficiently simulate the airflow rate in a building, when natural ventilation techniques are used, as well as the concentration of indoor pollutants, but they do not provide any information on the velocity field in a space. Network models are easy in their use, and their cost is minimal. Some of the models, such as the AIOLOS software (Allard 1998), are free to the public.

In network models, the flow rate (Q) through an opening of relatively large free area is calculated using the common orifice flow equation:

$$Q = C_d A \sqrt{(2\Delta P / \rho)} \tag{6.1}$$

where
C_d = the discharge coefficient of the opening
A = the opening area in m²
ΔP = the pressure difference across the opening in Pa
ρ = the air density in kg/m³

For the calculation of the total pressure difference across the opening, the terms of the dynamic pressure due to the wind must be added to those representing the stack effect. Thus:

$$\Delta P = P_{1,0} - P_{2,0} + \rho_1 C_p V_1^2 / 2 - \rho_2 C_p V_2^2 / 2 + (\rho_1 - \rho_2)gz \tag{6.2}$$

where V_1, V_2 are air velocities at the two sides of the opening and at height z, C_p = pressure coefficient (wind) and g = acceleration due to gravity.

The zonal method is based on the concept that each zone of a building can be represented by a pressure node. Boundary nodes are also used to represent the environment outside the building. Nodes are interconnected by flow paths, such as cracks, windows or doors, to form a network.

Pressure at boundary nodes is known but has to be determined for internal nodes. Application of mass balance equation on a zone i with j flow paths gives:

$$\sum_{i=1}^{j} \rho Q_i = 0 \tag{6.3}$$

A multi-zone problem involving N zones is therefore described by a set of N equations with an equal number of unknown pressures. The application of mass balance on each internal node of the network leads to a set of simultaneous non-linear equations, the solution of which gives the internal node pressures. The flow rates through the building openings can then be determined as discussed previously.

Empirical manual methods have been also proposed to calculate airflow through large openings (natural ventilation). Some of them are the British Standard method (1980) and the manual algorithms of NORMA (Santamouris 1996). These tools provide an estimate of the airflow but should always be used within the limits of their validity.

6.2.3 Sizing of windows for natural ventilation purposes

Sizing of windows in a building is a compromise between various parameters defining mainly the thermal, visual and energy performance of the building. To determine the optimum size of the openings in a building to achieve a specific ventilation performance, any of the above methodologies, and in particular any network model, may be used.

Various simplified methods to size windows have been proposed. A summary of the main characteristics and limitations of six simplified empirical opening sizing methodologies is presented in Table 6.4.

Table 6.4 Characteristics of six simplified empirical methodologies to design openings for natural cross ventilation of buildings

Method	Openings characteristics	Flow forces
The Florida Solar Energy Center Method – I	Considers equal inlets and outlets. Calculates the gross opening area. Considers a screen with a porosity factor of 0.6.	Considers only the wind forces. Proposes correction factors for the orientation of the wind, terrain type, neighbouring buildings and height of openings.
The Florida Solar Energy Center Method – II	Considers non-equal inlets and outlets. It calculates an effective window area. Proposes a method-ology to account for screens and window porosity.	Considers only the wind forces. Takes into account the pressure coefficients due to wind. Proposes correction factors for the neighbouring buildings and the height of openings.
The ASHRAE Method	Considers non-equal inlets and outlets. Proposes a coefficient to account the effectiveness of the opening as a function of the incidence angle of the wind.	Considers wind or temperature difference effects. Does not consider combined effects of wind and temperature difference.
Simplified Method of the University of Athens	Considers non-equal inlets and outlets. Valid for ratio inlets/outlets lower than 2.	Considers only the wind forces. Takes into account the pressure coefficients due to wind.
Aynsley Method	Considers non-equal inlets and outlets.	Considers only the wind forces. Takes into account the pressure coefficients due to wind.
British Standards Institution Method	Considers non-equal inlets and outlets.	Considers both the effect of the wind and temperature difference. It proposes criteria for combined effects.

A simplified but efficient methodology for windows sizing is proposed by the Florida Solar Energy Center (Chandra *et al.* 1986). The method assumes that the inlet and outlet areas are equal. The method can be used for slight differences; e.g. inlet = 40% of the total area. It does not account for airflows due to temperature difference. For a two-storey building the calculations should be done for each floor.

According to the method, the required gross total opening area, TOA, inlets plus outlets, in order to achieve a certain number of air changes per hour, ach, can be calculated by the following expression:

$$\text{TOA} = 0.00079V(\text{ach})(Wf_1f_2f_3f_4) \tag{6.4}$$

where
TOA = total opening area in ft^2
V = volume of the building in ft^3
ach = design air change rate per hour
W = wind speed (mph), as measured by the nearest meteorological station
f_1 is the inlet to site 10 m windspeed ratio. This coefficient is a function of the wind incidence angle and is given in Table 6.5. Data are mainly obtained from Vickery and Baddour (1983), wind tunnel data. Incidence angle is zero when winds are perpendicular to a building face.

Table 6.5 f_1 inlet to site 10 m windspeed ratios

Wind incidence angle (°)	f_1
0–40	0.35
50	0.30
60	0.25
70	0.20
80	0.14
90	0.08

f_2 is the terrain correction factor. It is a function of the building location and the ventilation strategy. It can be obtained from Table 6.6.

Table 6.6 f_2: terrain correction factor

Terrain type	f_2: 24 h ventilation	f_2: night only ventilation
Oceanfront or >3 miles (2 km) water in front	1.30	0.98
Airports, or flatlands with isolated-wall separated buildings	1.00	0.75
Rural	0.85	0.64
Suburban or industrial	0.67	0.50
Centre of large city	0.47	0.35

f_3 is the neighbourhood correction factor. This coefficient is a function of the wall height of the upwind building, h, as well as of the gap between the building and the adjacent upwind building, g. Values of f_3 are given in Table 6.7 as a function of the ratio g/h, and are extrapolated data from wind tunnel results by Lee *et al.* (1980).

Table 6.7 f_4: neighbourhood correction factor

Ratio g/h	f_3
0	0.00
1	0.41
2	0.63
3	0.77
4	0.85
5	0.93
6	1.00

f_4 is a height multiplication factor. If sizing windows for the second floor or for house on stilts, f_4 is equal to 1.15. Otherwise, use $f_4 = 1$.

Example

For a given location $W = 8.8$ mph. Also, $V = 10672$ ft^3, ach $= 30$, while the incidence angle is 10°. The building is located in a suburban area and is ventilated on a 24 h basis. The wall height of the upwind building, $h = 8$ ft, while $g = 24$ ft. Use $f_4 = 1$. Determine the total opening area.

From Tables 6.5–6.7 we get: $f_1 = 0.35, f_2 = 0.67, f_3 = 0.77$. Then from the previous equation we get:

$$TOA = 0.00079V(\text{ach})/(Wf_1f_2f_3f_4)$$

$$TOA = (0.00079 \times 10\ 672 \times 30)/(8.8 \times 0.35 \times 0.67 \times 0.77 \times 1)$$

$$TOA = 159.1\ \text{ft}^2$$

For widely different inlet and outlet areas, use of the method developed by the same authors (Chandra *et al.* 1983) is proposed. This method is a simple procedure for sizing inlet and outlet window areas in cross-ventilated rooms. The method is based on the pressure difference coefficient across the inlet and outlet and permits the calculation of an effective window area, A, which is a combination of the open inlet and outlet areas. The method does not account for the airflow due to temperature difference between indoors and outdoors. The proposed procedure is for rooms with one effective inlet and one effective outlet; all the inlet windows are assumed to experience identical positive pressures and all outlet windows to experience identical negative pressures.

A is defined by the following expression:

$$A = A_o A_i / (A_o + A_i^2)^{0.5} \qquad (6.5)$$

where A_o and A_i are the open outlet and inlet respectively in ft^2.

To calculate A, the method proposes the following expression:

$$A = 0.000296V(\text{ach})/[Wf_1(f_3 f_4 \text{PD})^{0.5}]$$

where the parameter PD is the pressure difference coefficient acting across the inlet and outlet given by:

$$\text{PD} = \text{WPC} - \text{LPC} \qquad (6.6)$$

where WPC is the windward pressure coefficient and LPC the leeward pressure coefficient. The method proposes to use pressure coefficients given by Vickery and Baddour (1983) and Cermak et al. (1981) for the four facades of a residential building (see Table 6.8). Recommended pressure coefficient, PC, values for other apertures are:

- inlet with wingwall assist, PC = 0.40
- outlet with wingwall assist, PC = −0.25
- roof outlets, e.g. Venturi type, PC = −0.30.

Table 6.8 Pressure coefficients as a function of the wind incidence angle

Wind incidence angle, φ (°)	PC at surface a	PC at surface b	PC at surface c	PC at surface d
0.0	0.40	−0.40	−0.25	−0.40
22.5	0.40	−0.06	−0.40	−0.60
45.0	0.25	0.25	−0.45	−0.45
67.5	−0.06	0.30	−0.55	−0.40
90.0	−0.4	0.40	−0.40	−0.25

Source: Chandra et al. (1983)

To account the effect of blockage due to insect screens, partially open windows, etc., a porosity factor, PF, defined as the product of an insect screening porosity factor, IPF, with a window porosity factor, WPF, is proposed:

$$\text{PF} = \text{IPF} \times \text{WPF}$$

Values of IPF and WPF for various type of screens and windows are given in Tables 6.9 and 6.10. Then, the total, not open, inlet and outlet areas, TA_i, TA_o, are given by the expressions:

$$TA_i = A_i/PF$$

$$TA_o = A_o/PF$$

Table 6.9 Insect screening porosity factors, IPF

Screen type	Typical IPF
No screen	1.00
Bronze, 14 wires/inch	0.80
Fibreglass, 18 wires/inch	0.60

Source: Chandra *et al.* (1983)

Table 6.10 Window porosity factors, WPF

Window type	Typical WPF
Single or double hung	0.40
Awning, hopper, jalousi or projection that swivels open on a horizontal joint	0.60
Casement depending on fixed sash amount. Need to measure porosity	Varies

Source: Chandra *et al.* (1983)

Example

The volume of a building is 1536 ft^3, the required air changes per hour are 30, the wind speed is 8.8 mph, and the incidence angle on windward face, a, is 45°, while there is a wing wall assisted outlet at surface d. The building is in an urban area. The ratio g/h is equal to 3 (see previous example). Calculate: (a) the required open effective area A, (b) the inlet and outlet surface, if equal inlet and outlets are desired, and (c) the total, not open, inlet and outlet window areas if fibreglass screen and awning windows are considered.

(a) From Tables 6.5 and 6.6 we get: $f_1 = 0.67, f_3 = 0.59, f_4 = 1$. Also, from Tables 6.8–6.10 WPC = 0.25 and LPC = –0.25, then PD = 0.5. Then, using the previously given expressions, we get:

$$A = 0.000296V(\text{ach})/[Wf_1(f_3f_4\text{PD})^{0.5}]$$

$$= (0.000296 \times 1536 \times 30)/[(8.8 \times 0.67 \times 0.59^{0.5} \times 0.5)^{0.5}]$$

$$= 4.26 \text{ ft}^2$$

(b) If $A_o = A_i$ then $A_i = 1.41A$. Therefore, $A_i = A_o = 6.00$ ft^2.

(c) From Tables 6.8–6.10 we get: IPF = 0.8 and WPF = 0.60, then PF = 0.48. Therefore, $TA_i = TA_o = 6.00/0.48 = 12.5$ ft^2.

6.2.4 Ventilation for indoor air quality

Indoor environmental quality can be seen as a combination of acceptable indoor air quality together with satisfactory thermal, visual and acoustic comfort conditions. Outdoor pollution is one of the sources of the so-called 'sick building syndrome'; others are related to indoor sources. Numerous studies have shown the serious impact of the outdoor environment on indoor air quality (Godish 1989). Solutions to indoor air pollution problems are source control, avoiding or attenuating the emission of contaminants, air cleaning and appropriate use of ventilation.

Inadequate ventilation may be the primary cause of poor indoor air quality in buildings. Monitoring of 356 public access buildings has shown that in approximately 50% of the buildings improper ventilation rates were the primary cause of illness complaints and poor air quality (Wallingford and Carpenter 1986). Ventilation problems have been exacerbated during the past years by certain energy-conserving measures. The reduction or elimination of fresh air, the reduction of infiltration and exfiltration, the lowering of thermostats in winter and the raising in summer, the elimination of the humidification or dehumidification systems and the early shut-down and late start-up of ventilation systems are some of the measures contributing to poor indoor air quality (Godish 1989).

The main objective of any ventilation system should be to provide good indoor air quality and satisfaction for the occupants (European Common Research Centre 1996). In addition, indoor air quality should protect the health of the occupants, promote productivity and protect the building, installations and furnishings.

As already mentioned, the more appropriate ventilation strategies are those that save energy and improve indoor air quality in parallel. Seppänen (1999) has summarized the more appropriate ventilation technologies and strategies for indoor air quality (see Table 6.11).

Inappropriate ventilation and indoor air quality may have a serious impact on the occupants' health, human well-being, employee performance and productivity at work. Improving indoor air quality in buildings is probably one of the most profitable investments. Seppänen and Palonen (1998) have estimated the total effects of poor indoor climate on national economy in Finland to be approximately 18 billion FIM.

Table 6.11 Summary of ventilation strategies for better indoor air quality and energy efficiency

Strategy or technology	Phase of the technology	Indoor air quality	Estimated energy savings in ventilation
Target values for indoor climate	Available	Improved	Up to 60% depending on climate
Particulate filtration of intake air	Available	Improved	No effect
Chemical air cleaning	Developing	Improved	Up to 100%
Balancing of airflows	Available	Improved	10–20%
Better ventilation efficiency	Available/ developing	Improved	Up to 50 %
Location of air intakes	Available	Improved	No effect
Heat recovery for large buildings	Available	No effect	Up to 70%
houses	Available	No effect	Up to 50%
Demand controlled ventilation	Available/ developing	No effect	Up to 30–40%, up to 50% in large spaces
Control of specific pollution sources	Available	Improved	Depends on application
Control of material emissions	Developing	Improved	Up to 50%
Task ventilation	Available/ developing	Improved	10–30%
Local exhausts	Available	Improved	Depends on application
Natural ventilation and free cooling	Available/ developing	Improved	Up to 60%
Operation and maintenance	Available/ developing	Improved	High (depends on initial level)

6.3 Bibliography

Allard F. (ed.) (1998) *Natural Ventilation in Buildings*, James and James (Science Publishers) Ltd, London.
BSI (1980) BS5925, 'Code of practice for design of buildings: Ventilation principles and designing for natural ventilation', British Standards Institution, London.
Cermak J.E. *et al.* (1981) 'Passive and hybrid cooling developments: natural ventilation – a wind tunnel study', Colorado State University, Fluid Mechanics and Wind Engineering Program Report No. CER81-82JEC-JAP-55A-MP24.
Chandra S., Fairey P.W. and Houston M.M. (1983) 'A handbook for designing ventilated buildings', Florida Solar Energy Center, Final Report, FSEC-CR-93-83, Cape Canaveral, FL.
Chandra S., Fairey P.W. and Houston M.M. (1986) 'Cooling with ventilation', SERI/SP-273-2966, DE86010701, Solar Energy Research Institute, Golden, CO.

European Common Research Centre (1996) 'European concerted action on indoor air quality and its impact on man', Report on ventilation and indoor air quality, European Common Research Centre, Ispra, Italy.

Godish T. (1989) *Indoor Air Pollution Control*, Lewis Publishers.

Hotchkiss R.S. and Harlow F.H. (1973) *Air Pollution Transport in Street Canyons*, Report by Los Alamos Scientific Laboratory for US Environmental Protection Agency, EPA-R4-73-029, NTIS PB-233 252.

Lee B.E., Hussain M. and Soliman B. (1980) 'Predicting natural ventilation forces upon low-rise buildings', *ASHRAE Journal*, February.

Nicholson S.E. (1975) 'A pollution model for street-level air', *Atmospheric Environments*, **9**, 19–31.

Oke T.R. (1987) *Boundary Layer Climates*, Cambridge University Press, Cambridge.

Santamouris M. (ed.) (2000) *Energy and Climate in the Urban Built Environment*, James and James (Science Publishers), London.

Santamouris M. (1996) 'NORMA – A method to calculate the thermal performance of passively cooled buildings', Vol. 5: Cooling Load of Buildings. Version 1.1.

Seppänen, O. (1999) 'Ventilation strategies for good indoor air quality and energy efficiency', *Proc. IAQ & Energy Conference*, Louisiana, ASHRAE, 1998.

Seppänen O. and Palonen J. (1998) 'The effects of indoor climate on national economy in Finland in billion FIM', FISIAQ, SIY Rapportti 10.

Vickery B.J. and Baddour R.E. (1983) 'A study of the external pressure distributions and induced internal ventilation flows in low rise industrial and domestic structures', University of Western Ontario, Boundary Layer Wind Tunnel Laboratory Report No BLWT-SS2-1983.

Wallingford K.M. and Carpenter J. (1986) 'Field experience overview: investigating sources of indoor air quality problems in office buildings', *Proc. IAQ 86*, ASHRAE, Atlanta.

Yamartino R.J. and Wiegnard G. (1986) 'Development and evaluation of simple models for the flow, turbulence and pollution concentration fields within an urban street canyon', *Atmospheric Environment*, **20**, 2137–2156.

CHAPTER 7

Sizing of small auxiliary heating/cooling systems

A major objective of solar building design is the reduction or, if possible, elimination of the need for auxiliary heating or cooling. By utilizing the thermal storage capacity of the building, the designer may reduce the size of auxiliary heating/cooling systems. Heating systems may generally be separated into two main categories: convective heating systems that heat primarily the room air, and radiant or panel heating systems in which the source of heat is integrated into the building envelope or interior surfaces. Radiant heating systems operate in a mode similar to direct gain systems, that is, they rely on a high surface temperature (up to 29°C for floor heating) in a room, and lower air temperature.

Section 7.1 considers a convective system while Section 7.2 focuses on a floor heating system. Section 7.3 describes the analysis of a ground cooling/heating system integrated with central air-conditioning.

7.1 Heating and cooling load calculations

7.1.1 Mathematical model

Calculation of peak heating and cooling loads should take into account building thermal storage capacity and dynamic variation of solar radiation and outdoor temperature in order to avoid oversizing of auxiliary heating and cooling systems. For most mild temperate climates, a heat pump will provide an efficient auxiliary heating and cooling system. Well-insulated buildings with effective shading systems and natural ventilation will minimize the need for auxiliary cooling. Similarly, appropriate sizing of the fenestration systems facing towards the equator (south or near-south in the northern hemisphere) will satisfy most heating requirements on sufficiently clear days.

The design of a building auxiliary heating/cooling system based on passive solar principles should therefore be based on the following principles:

- The heating system should be sized based on a sequence of cloudy cold days, but with the thermal mass utilized to minimize peak loads.

- The cooling system capacity should be estimated based on a sunny hot day but with the use of natural ventilation and effective shading devices.
- A variable room thermostat setpoint should be employed when necessary to reduce peak loads.
- If a convective heating/cooling system such as a heat pump is utilized, the air distribution system should be designed for acceptable thermal comfort.

Analysis is performed for a design day with major objective to determine peak heating or cooling load.

The principle of mass utilization to reduce peak heating or cooling loads is simple. In the case of heating, the peak demand is expected to occur just before sunrise at about 6 a.m. If the thermal storage mass of the building is kept relatively warm at night, then the peak load will be reduced. Similarly, on a hot day, the peak load will typically occur in the afternoon; if the building mass is precooled in the morning or at night by natural ventilation, then the peak cooling demand will be reduced.

Traditionally, heating systems for traditional buildings were oversized by using a steady state peak heat loss calculation technique. For peak cooling load calculations, a steady periodic method is often employed such as the CLTD (cooling load temperature difference) recommended by ASHRAE (1997). Here, it is proposed to employ a steady-periodic admittance method, similar to the one employed for calculation of temperature swings.

A simple analytical solution for the heating/cooling source may be obtained by specifying the zone temperature and assuming combined radiative-convective surface conductances between the heat conductive elements (e.g. walls) and the room air. We thus have a star thermal network and parallel heat transfer paths between inside and outside similar to the calculation of the house/zone steady state total conductance as shown in Figure 7.1. For steady periodic calculations, a frequency domain technique may be employed to calculate the zone admittance for about three frequencies plus the mean (steady state). By utilizing complex number algebra and Fourier series, we may then compute design day profiles for auxiliary heating (positive) and cooling (negative) loads.

The main advantage of the admittance method is that it is convenient for steady-periodic analysis (with about three harmonics). However, it cannot accommodate non-linearities. The explicit finite difference method may accommodate non-linear heat transfer coefficients, and control strategies. Here, we will consider a detailed model based on the **admittance method**. Each wall is modelled by a self-admittance and a transfer admittance as described in Chapter 5. The following inputs are required.

The **energy balance** may be written in a similar form to that for the simple model of equation (5.1) used for the passive analysis. All walls are represented by their self-admittances, together with the equivalent heat source Q_{sc} at their inside surface, equal to the transfer admittance times the outside or other equivalent

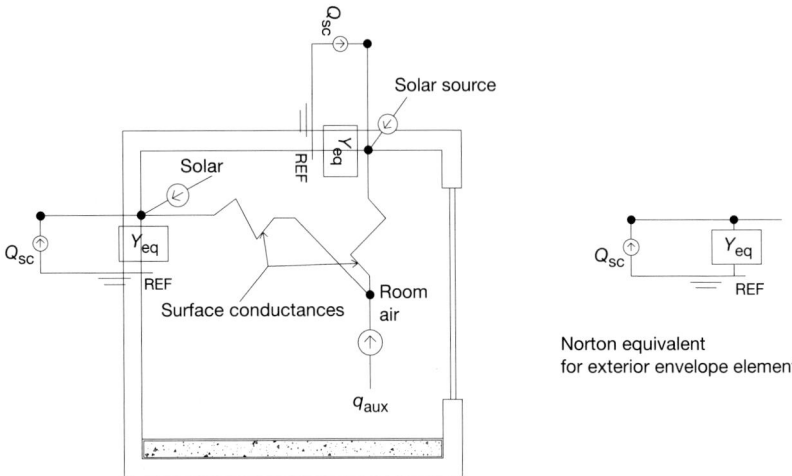

Figure 7.1 Schematic of zone thermal network showing Norton equivalent for typical walls; Y_{eq} is admittance and Q_{sc} is equivalent heat source

known temperature as shown in Figure 7.1. Radiation and convection in the room are represented by combined film coefficients. Thus, an analytical solution for room temperature or auxiliary heating may be obtained. A more detailed model with separate radiation exchanges requires an energy balance at the interior surfaces (Athienitis *et al.* 1990).

Energy balance at room air node (in admittance form):

$$[Y]\{T\} = \{Q\} \tag{7.1a}$$

where $[Y]$ is the admittance matrix and $\{T\}$ and $\{Q\}$ the temperature and source vectors respectively.

Since we have a star network at the room air node (1), all heat sources at surfaces may be transformed to equivalent heat sources at the air node by multiplying by the factor $U_i/(U_i + Y_s)$ where U_i is the surface conductance ($A \times h_i$) and Y_s the self-admittance of each wall. Thus, surface nodes may be eliminated and we obtain the following energy balance at the room air node:

$$Y_z T_R = \Sigma Q_{eq} + q_{aux} \tag{7.1b}$$

where q_{aux} = auxiliary heating (or cooling if negative), Y_z is room admittance and T_R is room air temperature.

All heat gains/losses are expressed as equivalent heat sources (negative if losses) Q_{eq} (the short-circuit source Q_{sc} in Figure 7.1 is similar to Q_{eq}) at the room temperature node based on a reference temperature of 0°C as follows:

1. Internal gains plus heat source due to infiltration

$$= Q_{\text{intc}_n} + \left(U_{\text{inf}} + \sum_{iw} U_{\text{w}_{iw}} \right) T_{\text{o}_n} \tag{7.2}$$

2. Equivalent heat sources at wall interior surfaces due to sol-air temperatures or specified temperatures in adjacent zones. These can be added to internal radiant gains Q_{intr} at the interior surfaces:

$$\left(Y_{\text{t}_{n,i}} \cdot T_{\text{eq}_{n,i}} + Q_{\text{intr}_{n,i}} \right) \tag{7.3}$$

The source in equation 7.3 must be converted to a heat gain at the room air point so that we can perform an energy balance at this node. The equivalent heat source at the air node is given by:

$$\left(Y_{\text{t}_{n,i}} \cdot T_{\text{eq}_{n,i}} + Q_{\text{intr}_{n,i}} \right) \cdot \frac{U_{\text{i}_i}}{Y_{\text{s}_{n,i}} + U_{\text{i}_i}} \tag{7.4}$$

The energy balance to determine auxiliary heating or cooling q_{aux} yields:

$$q_{\text{aux}_n} = \left[\text{TR}_n - \frac{\left[Q_{\text{int}_n} + \left(U_{\text{inf}} + \sum_{iw} U_{\text{w}_{iw}} \right) \cdot T_{\text{o}_n} \right] + \sum_{i} \left[\left(Y_{\text{t}_{n,i}} \cdot T_{\text{eq}_{n,i}} + Q_{\text{intr}_{n,i}} \right) \cdot \frac{U_{\text{i}_i}}{Y_{\text{s}_{n,i}} + U_{\text{i}_i}} \right]}{Y_{\text{z}_n}} \right] \cdot Y_{\text{z}_n} \tag{7.5}$$

Equation (7.5) is valid for the steady state (mean) as well as for all harmonics n, a consequence of the superposition principle for linear systems. It is equally valid for heating and cooling analysis. In all cases, the auxiliary heating/cooling convective source is assumed to act at the air node (representing the air in the zone), which is kept at a specified temperature $T_R(t)$ which could be constant, square-wave, sinusoidal or any other desired function.

For heating load calculations we will consider a minimal level of solar radiation equivalent to a cloudy day. The outside temperature will be modelled by a three-harmonic Fourier series based on its value at eight different times.

The model employed for cooling load calculations is the same as the model used for heating load calculations. The main difference here is that solar radiation transmitted through windows or absorbed by outside surfaces is calculated in detail. Also, latent cooling load is calculated. A passive analysis may be performed by setting the source q_{aux} to 0 in equation 7.5 and solving for the room temperature.

The following weather inputs and building data are required for the calculation.

WEATHER INPUTS
- Outside temperature (daily mean and range).
- Solar radiation transmitted by each window and solar radiation absorbed by each exterior surface. For a clear day (cooling load analysis or passive solar analysis) this can be readily estimated from Hottel's clear sky model. For heating loads, a conservative low estimate of solar radiation may be used.

BUILDING DATA
NS = number of surfaces contributing to the zone energy balance.
NS_e = number of exterior surfaces (walls and roof).
A_i = area of exterior surface i.
N_w = number of windows; A_{wi} = area of window i.
ψ_{se} with se = $0,1..N_{se}$ exterior surface azimuth angle.
α_{se} with se = $0,1..N_{se}$ solar absorptance of exterior surfaces.
Window type: U-value or thermal resistance, single or double glazing and kL value (extinction coefficient × thickness) – for cooling load.
A_{door} = external door area; R_{door} = external door R-value.
Wall construction: Wall layer properties. Interior layer properties for transient analysis are also required.
ach: infiltration – air changes per hour.
h_i: inside surface heat transfer coefficient for surface i (typical combined radiative convective coefficients are assumed).
Internal gains: Q_{intr} = radiative internal gains; Q_{intc} = convective internal gains

Example

Consider a house that consists of a basement and a ground-level floor, with a pitched roof (Figure 7.2). Here we consider the ground-level zone.

H_h = 2.7 m, L_h = 14 m, W_h = 12 m
Surfaces contributing to energy balance:
NS = 6 (= 1,2..NS)
1–4 walls, 5-ceiling, 6-floor
se = 1..5 exterior surfaces
N_w = 4 (number of windows), i = $1,2..N_w$
(assume four windows – sum the window areas on each house side)
ψ_1 = –45°, ψ_2 = –135°, ψ_3 = 135°, ψ_4 = 45°
αs_{iw} = 0.9 wall absorptances
Window and door areas: A_{w1} = 12 m², A_{w2} = 3 m², A_{w3} = 2 m², A_{w4} = 3 m²
A_{d1} = 2 m², A_{d2} = 2 m², A_{d3} = 2 m², A_{d4} = 2 m²

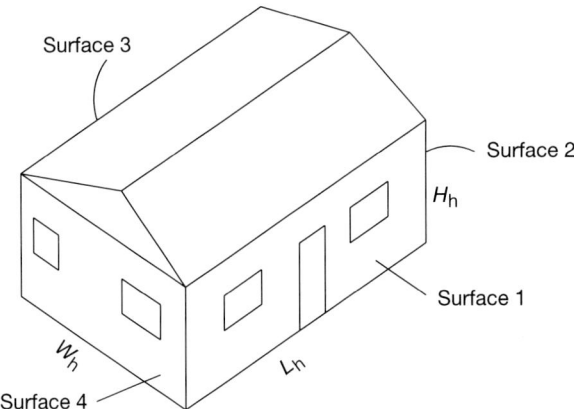

Figure 7.2 Schematic of one-zone house considered in Example

Wall net areas:

$$A_1 = L_h H_h - A_{w1} - A_{d1}$$

$$A_2 = W_h H_h - A_{w2} - A_{d2}$$

$$A_3 = L_h H_h - A_{w3} - A_{d3}$$

$$A_4 = W_h H_h - A_{w4} - A_{d4}$$

$$A_5 = W_h L_h - A_{w5} - A_{d5}$$

Internal height, $H_1 = 2.4$ m
Volume $= A_5 H_i$
Door thermal resistance, $R_d = 1$ m²°C/W
Window resistance (double glazed), $R_w = 0.34$ m²°C/W
Film coefficients, $h_1 = 8.3$ W/m²°C, $h_2 = h_1, h_3 = h_1, h_4 = h_1$
$h_5 = 9.3$ W/m²°C, $h_6 = 6.1$ W/m²°C (cold floor)
air changes/hour, ach $= 0.5$
Calculation of infiltration conductance (infiltration heat transfer):
Specific heat, $c_{pair} = 1000$ J/kg°C
Density of air, $\rho_{air} = 1.2$ kg/m³
$U_{inf} = $ (ach $\times$ Vol)/(3600. s) $\times \rho_{air} \times c_{pair}$
$U_{inf} = 67.2$ W/°C

THERMAL RESISTANCE OF WALLS (INCLUDING AIR FILMS)

To calculate the effective resistance of a building envelope element, we typically assume parallel heat flow paths through each area with a different composition (e.g. through wood structure versus through insulation).

Vertical walls (compute resistance assuming parallel heat flow paths)
Gypsum board

Thickness, L_1 = 0.013 m
Density, p_1 = 800 kg/m³
Conductivity, k_1 = 0.16 W/m°C
Specific heat, c_1 = 750 J/kg°C

Insulation

R_{ins} = 2.2 m²°C/W

Siding + sheathing

R_{sid} = 0.37 m²°C/W

Exterior film

h_o = 22 W/m²°C (assume)

Assume 15% of wall area is structural framing. The fraction of area that is framing:

f_f = 0.15

2 by 4 wood stud with *R*-value (with framing resistance)

R_f = 0.77 m²°C/W

$$R_1 = \cfrac{1}{\cfrac{1-f_f}{\left(\dfrac{L_1}{k_1} + R_{ins} + R_{sid} + \dfrac{1}{h_o} + \dfrac{1}{h_1}\right)} + \cfrac{f_f}{\left(\dfrac{L_1}{k_1} + R_f + R_{sid} + \dfrac{1}{h_o} + \dfrac{1}{h_1}\right)}}$$

$$= 2.44°Cm^2 / W$$

Calculation of wall conductance excluding interior layer and film (to be used for admittance calculations):

$$u_1 = \cfrac{1}{R_1 - \dfrac{L_1}{k_1} - \dfrac{1}{h_1}}$$

Assume that all exterior walls (ii) are of the same construction:

$ii = 1,2..4, L_{ii} = L_1, R_{ii} = R_1$

$u_{ii} = u_1, k_{ii} = k_1, \rho_{ii} = \rho_1, c_{ii} = c_1$

Calculation of roof-ceiling thermal resistance

Ceiling

Gypsum board

$L_5 = L_1, k_5 = k_1, c_5 = c_1, \rho_5 = \rho_1$

Insulation

$R_{insc} = 2.8 \ \text{m}^2{}^\circ\text{C/W}$

Air-film (attic)

$h_a = 12 \ \text{W/m}^2{}^\circ\text{C}$

$$R_c = \cfrac{1}{\cfrac{1-f_f}{\left(\dfrac{L_5}{k_5} + R_{insc} + \dfrac{1}{h_a} + \dfrac{1}{h_5}\right)} + \cfrac{f_f}{\left(\dfrac{L_5}{k_5} + R_f + \dfrac{1}{h_a} + \dfrac{1}{h_5}\right)}}$$

$$= 2.377 {}^\circ\text{C}\,\text{m}^2\,/\,\text{W}$$

$R_c = 2.377 \ {}^\circ\text{C} \ \text{m}^2/\text{W}$

Roof

Exterior air film

$h_o = 20 \ \text{W/m}^2{}^\circ\text{C}$

Shingle backer board

$R_b = 0.19 \ \text{m}^2{}^\circ\text{C/W}$

Wood shingles

$R_{sh} = 0.17 \ \text{m}^2{}^\circ\text{C/W}$

$$R_r = \cfrac{1}{\cfrac{1-f_f}{\left(R_b + R_{sh} + \dfrac{1}{h_o} + \dfrac{1}{h_a}\right)} + \cfrac{f_f}{\left(R_f + R_b + R_{sh} + \dfrac{1}{h_o} + \dfrac{1}{h_a}\right)}}$$

$$= 0.53 {}^\circ\text{C}\,\text{m}^2\,/\,\text{W}$$

Assuming a 30° slope for the roof, we calculate the ceiling-roof combined resistance per unit ceiling area as follows:

$$A_r = A_s/\cos 30°$$

$$R_S = (R_c/A_s) + (R_r/A_r) \times A_s$$

For admittance calculation:

$$u_S = 1/[R_S - (L_S/k_S) - (1/h_S)]$$

$$R_S = 2.848 \ m^2°C/W$$

Floor

Carpet and underpad

$$L_6 = 0.02 \ m, k_6 = 0.06 \ W/m°C, \rho_6 = 800 \ kg/m^3$$

Insulation and plywood

$$R_{ins} = 1.0 \ m^2°C/W, c_6 = 1400 \ J/kg°C$$

Air film (horizontal heat flow downward)

$$h_o = 6.13 \ W/m^2°C, R_6 = R_{ins} + (L_6/k_6) + (1/h_o) + (1/h_6),$$
$$R_6 = 1.66 \ m^2°C/W, u_6 = 1/[R_6 - (L_6/k_6) - (1/h_6)] \ .$$

CALCULATION OF WALL ADMITTANCES

The self-admittance and the transfer admittance will be calculated for each wall, considering the thermal capacity of the room interior layer. Note that the steady-state value of the admittance is equal to the wall conductance. We will calculate admittances from outside to the interior surface and to the room air point. The analysis will be performed for the mean term and three harmonics of the weather inputs.

Admittances

Steady-state admittance is equal to wall U-value (excluding interior film); first subscript indicates frequency, second subscript indicates surface number.

$$Y_{s_{0,i}} = \frac{A_i}{R_i - \dfrac{1}{h_i}}$$

Admittances from outside to room air (steady state):

$$Y_{t_{0,i}} = Y_{s_{0,i}}$$

$$Y_{o,i} = \frac{A_i}{R_i} \qquad Y_{ta_{0,i}} = Y_{o,i}$$

$$N_h = 5, n = 1,2 ... N_h$$

Let $j = \sqrt{-1}$

$$\gamma_{n,i} = \sqrt{j\frac{2\pi n}{\frac{k_i}{\rho_i c_i}} \times 86\,400\,\mathrm{s}}$$

Interior and exterior surface conductances:

$$U_{i_i} = A_i h_i \quad U_{o_i} = h_o A_i$$

$$I_w = 1,2..4$$

Total conductance of double-glazed windows and doors:

$$U_{w_{iw}} = \frac{A_{w_{iw}}}{R_w} + \frac{A_{d_{iw}}}{R_d}$$

Self-admittance Y_s and transfer admittance Y_t for each wall:

$$Y_{s_{n,i}} = A_i \frac{u_i + k_i \gamma_{n,i} \tanh\left(\gamma_{n,i} L_i\right)}{\left(\dfrac{u_i}{k_i \gamma_{n,i}} \tanh\left(\gamma_{n,i} L_i\right)\right) + 1}$$

$$Y_{t_{n,i}} = \frac{A_i}{\dfrac{\cosh\left(\gamma_{n,i} L_i\right)}{u_i} + \dfrac{\sinh\left(\gamma_{n,i} L_i\right)}{k_i \gamma_{n,i}}}$$

Wall admittances from outside to inside air:

$$Y_{n,i} = \frac{Y_{s_{n,i}} U_{i_i}}{Y_{s_{n,i}} + U_{i_i}}$$

$$Y_{ta_{n,i}} = Y_{t_{n,i}} \frac{U_{i_i}}{Y_{s_{n,i}} + U_{i_i}}$$

Zone admittance Y_z (from air point):

$$Y_{z_n} = U_{\mathrm{inf}} + \sum_{iw} U_{w_{iw}} + \sum_i Y_{n,i}$$

Note that Y_{z0} is simply the total U-value of the house. The value of Y_z for the steady state and first three harmonics is given by:

$$Y_z = \begin{bmatrix} 340.267 \\ 403 + 298.766j \\ 539.342 + 519.654j \\ 683.104 + 670.462j \end{bmatrix} W / {}^\circ C$$

Outside temperature (T_o)
The outside temperature is modelled by a Fourier series based on $N_{To} + 1$ values. If more detail is required, N_{To} may be increased. In this example assume 3 hour intervals.
Time index (it):

$$N_{To} = 7, it = 0, 1..N_{To}$$

Time:

$$t_{it} = it\, 3\ h$$

Harmonics:

$$n = 0,1..N_h$$
$$w_n = 2\pi n/24\ h$$

The harmonics of T_o are calculated from the NT_o values with the following discrete Fourier transform (DFT):

$$T_{on_n} = \left(\sum_{it} T_{o_{it}} \frac{\exp(-j w_n \cdot t_{it})}{N_{To} + 1} \right) {}^\circ C$$

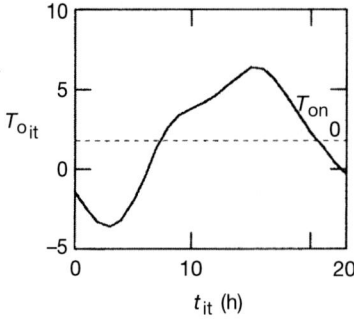

$T_{o_{it}}$

t_{it} (h)

Figure 7.3 Outdoor temperature (from hourly or 3-hour interval values)

Harmonics of T_o:

$$T_{on} = \begin{bmatrix} 1.875 \\ -1.811+1.332j \\ -0.125+0.25j \\ 0.311+0.082j \end{bmatrix}$$

Mean daily temperature:

$$T_{on,0} = 1.875°C$$

The T_o curve in Figure 7.3 was calculated from the following inverse discrete Fourier transform:

$$T_{o_{it}} = T_{on_0} + 2\sum_{n1} \mathrm{Re}\left[\left(T_{on_{n1}}\right)\exp\left(jw_{n1}\cdot t_{it}\right)\right]$$

where $n1 = 1,2,3$

SOLAR RADIATION
Solar radiation will be modelled by a half-sinusoid from sunrise $(-t_s)$ to sunset time t_s.

Redefine time array:

$it = 0,1..23$, $t_{it} = it$ h

Let $t_s = 5$ h (time from solar noon to sunset). The peak solar radiation at noon (assuming minimal level for a cloudy day) will be:

$$S_{max} = 100 \ W/m^2$$

$$f_{it} = S_{max} \cos\left(\pi \cdot \frac{t_{it} - 12h}{2t_s}\right)$$

(positive function, otherwise set to 0 – at night)

$S(t)$ may be modelled with a discrete Fourier series as follows. We multiply by total window area to determine total solar radiation:

$$S_{n_n} = \left(\sum_{it} S_{it} \frac{\exp\left(-jw_n t_{it}\right)}{24}\right)\sum_{iw} A_{w_{iw}}$$

We will assume that the fraction of this radiation absorbed by each interior surface is proportional to its area:

$$A_{tot} = \Sigma_i A_i$$

$$Q_{r_{n,i}} = S_{n_n} \frac{A_i}{A_{tot}}$$

We may similarly model internal gains with Fourier series. In this example, we will ignore internal gains. Also, we will ignore solar radiation absorbed on wall exterior surfaces since our **objective is to determine the peak heating load**.
Room-air temperature T_R (assume specified):

$$T_{R_0} = 20°C \qquad nl = 1,2..3 \qquad T_{R_{nl}} = 0°C$$

A variable room temperature may be employed, e.g. with a night setback/setup. In such a case T_R should be modelled by a Fourier series like T_o.
Equivalent temperatures for exterior surfaces (ignoring solar effects):

$$T_{eq_{n,se}} = T_{on_n}$$

For basement:

$$T_b = 20°C \qquad T_{eq_{0,6}} = T_b \qquad T_{eq_{nl,6}} = 0°C$$

First determine the mean auxiliary load:

$$q_{aux_0} = \left[T_{R_0} - \frac{\left(U_{inf} + \sum_{iw} U_{w_{iw}}\right) T_{on_0} + \sum_i \left(Y_{t_{0,i}} \cdot T_{eq_{0,i}} + Q_{r_{0,i}}\right) \cdot \dfrac{U_{i_i}}{Y_{s_{0,i}} + U_{i_i}}}{Y_{z_0}} \right] \cdot Y_{z_0}$$

$$= 3.841 \times 10^3 \, W$$

$$q_{aux_{nl}} = \left[T_{R_{nl}} - \frac{\left(U_{inf} + \sum_{iw} U_{w_{iw}}\right) T_{on_{nl}} + \sum_i \left(Y_{t_{nl,i}} \cdot T_{eq_{nl,i}} + Q_{r_{nl,i}}\right) \cdot \dfrac{U_{i_i}}{Y_{s_{nl,i}} + U_{i_i}}}{Y_{z_{nl}}} \right] \cdot Y_{z_{nl}}$$

Auxiliary heating power. This is calculated using an inverse discrete Fourier series:

$$q_{auxt_{it}} = q_{aux_0} + 2 \sum_{nl} Re\left[q_{aux_{nl}} \exp(j w_{nl} t_{it})\right]$$

Peak heating load (used to size heating system):

$$\max(q_{auxt}) = 5.641 \times 10^3 \, W$$

Heating energy consumption Q_h obtained by numerical integration of the positive part of the auxiliary power curve:

$$Qh = \sum_{it} \frac{q_{\text{aux}_{it}} + |q_{\text{auxt}_{it}}| + q_{\text{auxt}_{it+1}} + |q_{\text{auxt}_{it+1}}|}{4} (t_{it+1} - t_{it})$$

$$= 331.838 \text{ MJ}$$

which is equal to

$$q_{\text{aux}_0} 24\,\text{h} = 331.838 \text{ MJ}$$

Note that in this case, because there is no cooling, Q_h may be obtained from the mean power.

A variable room temperature may be employed, e.g. with a night setback. In such a case, T_R should be modelled as a Fourier series.

Note that combined radiative-convective coefficients were employed in the above model in order to permit a simple analytical solution. A more detailed model is described by Athienitis *et al.* (1990) and utilized in Chapter 8. The method is similar in concept to the CLTD and transfer functions methods of ASHRAE (1997). However, all building transfer functions (admittances) are directly calculated.

Next, we will consider the same analysis but with a night setback in the thermostat setpoint (Figure 7.4).

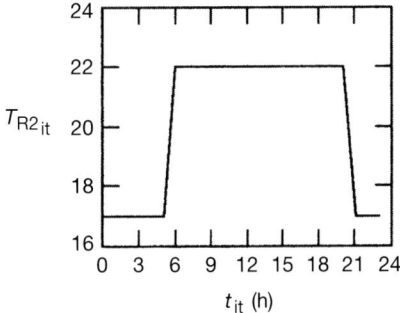

Figure 7.4 Thermostat night setback setpoint profile

First represent the thermostat setpoint with a discrete Fourier series whose coefficients are:

$$T_{R2n_n} = \left(\sum_{it} T_{R2_{it}} \frac{\exp(-jw_n t_{it})}{24} \right) {}^\circ\text{C}$$

Then determine the mean auxiliary load:

$$q^2{}_{\text{aux}_0} = \left[T_{\text{R2n}_0} - \frac{\left(U_{\text{inf}} + \sum_{iw} U_{\text{w}_{iw}}\right)T_{\text{on}_0} + \sum_{i}\left(Y_{t_{0,i}} \cdot T_{\text{eq}_{0,i}} + Q_{\text{r}_{0,i}}\right) \cdot \dfrac{U_{i_i}}{Y_{s_{0,i}} + U_{i_i}}}{Y_{z_0}} \right] \cdot Y_{z_0}$$

$$= 3.883 \times 10^3 \, \text{W}$$

(close to that without the night setback since the average setpoint is approximately the same).

$$q^2{}_{\text{aux}_{nl}} = \left[T_{\text{R2n}_{nl}} - \frac{\left(U_{\text{inf}} + \sum_{iw} U_{\text{w}_{iw}}\right)T_{\text{on}_{nl}} + \sum_{i}\left(Y_{t_{nl,i}} \cdot T_{\text{eq}_{nl,i}} + Q_{\text{r}_{nl,i}}\right) \cdot \dfrac{U_{i_i}}{Y_{s_{nl,i}} + U_{i_i}}}{Y_{z_{nl}}} \right] \cdot Y_{z_{nl}}$$

Auxiliary power with night setback is given by:

$$q^2{}_{\text{auxt}_{it}} = q^2{}_{\text{aux}_0} + 2\sum_{nl} \text{Re}\left[q^2{}_{\text{aux}_{nl}} \exp(j w_{nl} t_{it})\right]$$

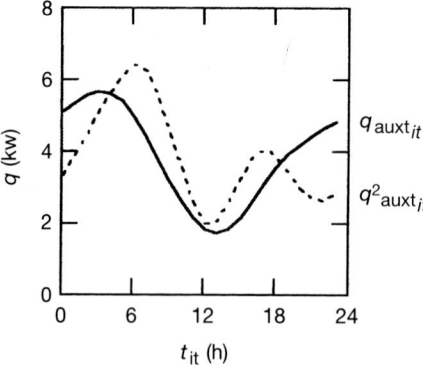

$q_{\text{auxt}_{it}}$

$q^2_{\text{auxt}_{it}}$

Figure 7.5 Auxiliary heating load with constant setpoint (q_{auxt}) and with setback (q^2_{auxt})

Peak heating load (used to size heating system):

$$\max (q2_{\text{auxt}}) = 6.3252 \times 10^3 \, \text{W}$$

We therefore conclude that the peak heating load increases owing to the sudden increase in setpoint (from 17°C to 22°C) even though the mean load is approximately the same (Figure 7.5).

An effective strategy to reduce energy consumption at night while avoiding high peak loads is to have a slowly changing setpoint in the early morning such as a sinusoidal or ramp change.

7.1.2 Special considerations for cooling

For peak cooling load estimates to size cooling systems the following principles should be kept in mind:

- The best method to lower sensible cooling loads is to prevent solar radiation from being transmitted into the building interior through effective, preferably exterior, shading devices. All building envelope elements should also have effective insulation and windows should be at least double-glazed.
- The solar radiation may be modelled in more detail as indicated in Chapter 3.
- Sensible cooling loads may be lowered through night-time natural ventilation, and evaporative cooling.
- The same basic thermal model as for heating loads may be employed, with the inclusion of internal gains, transmitted solar radiation and for the exterior walls, sol-air temperatures.

For the previous example we obtain the solar radiation curves given in Figures 7.6 and 7.7 (latitude 45°N). Without shading, a peak load of about 11 kW is obtained. When shading is employed, the peak sensible load is reduced by about 50%.

The **latent cooling load** is due to exchange of inside air and outside air with different moisture contents and due to generation of moisture by occupants, equipment, etc. If moisture must be removed from the outdoor air to reduce the humidity level to the comfort range, the energy required (assume indoor relative humidity 50% and outdoor humidity 80%) is determined as follows.

Latent heat of water:

$$h_{fg} = 2465 \text{ kJ/kg}$$

Interior and exterior humidity ratios:

$$W_i = 0.0073$$
$$W_o = 0.0117$$
$$q_{lat} = (\text{ach}/3600)\rho_{air}\text{Vol}(W_o - W_i)h_{fg} = 728 \text{ W}$$

Note that there is also a small, usually negligible, additional load (sensible) due to the difference in temperature between the room air moisture and the outside air moisture.

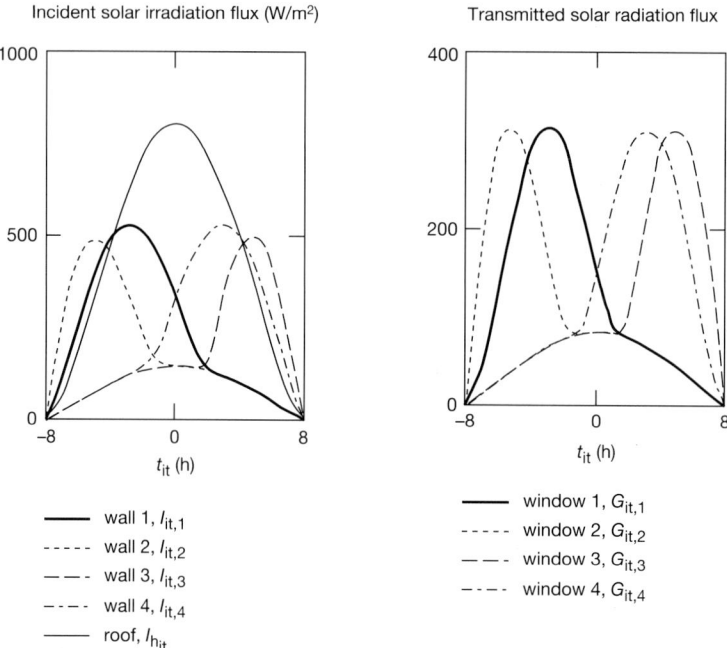

Figure 7.6 Solar irradiance on exterior surfaces *I* and transmitted irradiation *G* (assuming no shading) based on Hottel's clear sky model (see Chapter 3)

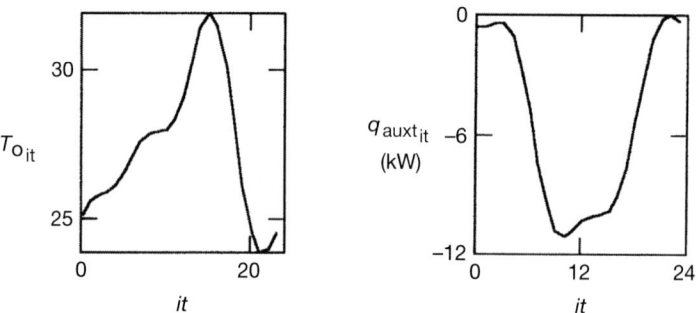

Figure 7.7 Outside temperature profile employed for cooling load calculation

An internal heat gain of approximately 67 W per person (for residences) may also be included, as well as a heat gain of 470 W from appliances. These heat gains may be assumed to be approximately 50% convective and 50% radiative (absorbed by each wall proportionally to its area).

7.2 Analysis and design of solar-assisted radiant heating systems

7.2.1 Introduction

This section presents a model of an integrated radiant floor heating–direct gain passive solar system. Thermal mass is utilized for both storage of auxiliary heating energy and direct solar gains incident on the floor. An explicit finite difference model is employed to study the performance of a passive solar building.

A direct-gain passive solar building usually combines efficient south-facing fenestration systems which transmit high amounts of solar radiation, while reducing heat losses to the outdoors, with an optimal amount of thermal storage mass. The thermal storage mass should be distributed on an interior building surface directly illuminated with transmitted solar radiation. Also, sufficient quantities of thermal mass must be employed to store passive solar gains while reducing temperature swings. Optimal quantities of thermal mass for storage of passive solar gains so as to reduce room temperature swings may be determined with frequency domain techniques (see Chapter 5); however, this analysis does not consider the effect of heating system type.

A floor heating system is potentially highly compatible in operation with a direct gain passive solar system which would also store solar gains within the floor mass. However, there is a significant difference between the solar gains and the auxiliary heat applied; the solar gains are absorbed at the top surface of the floor slab, while the auxiliary heat is supplied at the bottom of the slab. The slab introduces a different thermal lag effect in each case.

Design of floor heating systems requires several important decisions on a number of design or control variables as follows:

- Maximum heating device output (maximum auxiliary heating).
- Type and thickness of thermal mass integrated in the floor heating system.
- Appropriate control strategies for the system to maintain desired thermal conditions in the heated space and to prevent the floor surface temperature from exceeding 29°C as required by current standards (ASHRAE 1987).

All three design decisions are interrelated and should be considered simultaneously in order to achieve energy-efficient operation of the system and satisfactory thermal comfort. There are various design approaches that may be followed. Traditionally, high amounts of thermal mass were used (10 cm thick concrete or equivalent) with continuous heating and a fairly constant indoor temperature as well as a relatively low floor surface temperature (24–26°C). Recently, with the increased use of floor heating systems in timber frame houses, lower amounts of thermal mass are encountered – often as little as a 3 cm thick concrete slab or equivalent.

Peak loads may also be reduced and shifted to night-time when electricity costs may be lower. The key problem with the performance of a passive solar building with a floor heating system is overheating. This is because when a significant amount of solar radiation is incident on the floor, its thermal storage mass is already warm from continuous auxiliary heating input during the night and in the early morning. Also, the floor surface temperature may in some cases exceed the comfort limit. These problems may be addressed by lowering the setpoint at night and slowly increasing it during the daytime, or alternatively increasing the amount of thermal storage mass. Here, we focus on the first option, which essentially involves antici-patory or predictive control. Therefore, such systems may present comfort control problems and lead to overheating. These problems may be reduced by employing various forms of anticipatory control such as ambient temperature reset of setpoints, with which the indoor setpoint or the instantaneous auxiliary heat energy output is linked to the outdoor temperature. Usually, the reset ratio relating outside temperature to supply water temperature in hydronic systems must be adjusted after installation to take into account the as-built system characteristics. However, this frequently used technology for control of radiant heating systems does not solve the current problem because the outside temperature usually increases significantly in the afternoon after most of the solar gains have been absorbed.

Proportional control of room temperature with a constant setpoint is effective. However, when energy-saving strategies are implemented, such as storage of passive solar gains in the floor and a lower setpoint at night, effective control becomes difficult. For example, when a simple thermostat setpoint night setback is employed, it contributes to energy conservation but leads to a very high increase in the peak heating load on cold days. If this demand is not satisfied by using a large-capacity heating system, the room temperature will rise too slowly to the desired temperature. Thus, the setpoint should be gradually changed, starting a few hours before the desired effect. If storage of solar gains is to be effectively achieved, then a lower night-time setpoint is required to keep the floor mass cool in antici-pation of the upcoming solar gains, followed by a gradual increase in the morning to the desired comfort range.

7.2.2 Mathematical model

The explicit finite difference method is particularly suitable for modelling of non-linear heat diffusion problems such as the present case of heat transfer through the floor heating system and its control. It can easily accommodate non-linear heat transfer coefficients and temperature-dependent heat sources, such as auxiliary heating; non-linear simulations were performed in the present study.

Figure 7.8 shows the thermal network for the zone and floor heating system. The finite difference thermal network model for the room consists of two capacitances for the floor thermal capacity, interconnecting thermal resistances, and another thermal capacitance for the rest of the room. Node 1 represents room air. Node 2 is the floor surface and node 6 the unheated surfaces; both surfaces are coupled by convection with room air (resistances R_{12} and R_{16}) and together by radiation (R_{26}). The energy balance for the thermal network is:

$$T_{i,p+1} = \frac{\Delta t}{C_i}\left(q_i + \sum \frac{T_{j,p} - T_{i,p}}{R_{i,j}}\right) + T_{i,p} \qquad (7.6)$$

Subscript i indicates the node for which the energy balance is written and j all nodes connected to node i, while p is the time interval; q_i represents a heat source at node i such as auxiliary heating (node 4) or solar radiation (nodes 2 and 6).

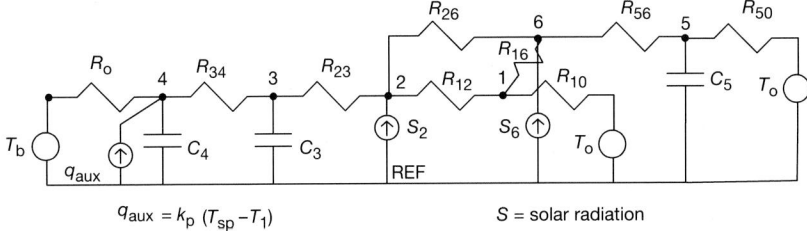

$$q_{aux} = k_p (T_{sp} - T_1) \qquad\qquad S = \text{solar radiation}$$

Nodes: 1, Room air, 2, Floor surface, 6, Unheated surfaces

R_{10} = resistance between inside and outside due to windows, doors and infiltration

T_b = basement temperature C = thermal capacitance

Figure 7.8 Thermal network of zone with floor heating system (corresponding to house of Figure 7.2)

The time step is selected based on the following condition for numerical stability (Holman 1986):

$$\Delta t \leq C_i \sum_j (1/R_{i,j}) \qquad (7.7)$$

for all nodes i.

For the room under consideration, the time step selected was 400 seconds. The solar radiation transmitted by the windows is assumed to be absorbed 70% by the floor and 30% by the remaining surfaces.

This section presents a model for a space (one zone) heated with a floor heating system. It is assumed that the heat delivered by the system is q_{aux}.

The auxiliary heating q_{aux} is proportional to the error between the setpoint T_{sp} and the actual room air temperature T_1:

$$q_{aux} = K_p(T_{sp} - T_1) \qquad\qquad (7.8)$$

where K_p = proportional control constant

Note that the source of the heat could be electric panels or hot water pipes covered by a layer of thermal storage mass such as light concrete plus ceramic tiles. If we have a hydronic hot water system, then the heating power delivered is also equal to the mass flow rate times the difference in temperature between supply and return.

Example

Consider a house as in the previous section, which consists of a basement and a ground-level floor, in Montreal, Canada. Here we consider the ground-level zone, heated with floor heating.

$$H_h = 3 \text{ m}, L_h = 15 \text{ m}, W_h = 10 \text{ m}, N_w = 4, iw = 1,2..N_w$$

(assume four windows – sum the window areas on each house side)

Window and door areas:

$$A_{w1} = 8 \text{ m}^2, A_{w2} = 4 \text{ m}^2, A_{w3} = 4 \text{ m}^2, A_{w4} = 4 \text{ m}^2$$
$$A_{d1} = 1.8 \text{ m}^2, A_{d2} = 1.8 \text{ m}^2, A_{d3} = 1.8 \text{ m}^2, A_{d4} = 1.8 \text{ m}^2$$

Door thermal resistance:

$$R_d = 2 \text{ m}^2{}^\circ\text{C/W}$$

Window resistance (double glazed):

$$R_w = 0.43 \text{ m}^2{}^\circ\text{C/W}$$

Vertical film coefficients:

$$h_1 = 8.3 \text{ W/m}^2{}^\circ\text{C}$$
$$h_5 = 9.0 \text{ W/m}^2{}^\circ\text{C}$$
$$h_6 = 9.3 \text{ W/m}^2{}^\circ\text{C}$$

(cold ceiling, hot floor).

$$\text{ach} = 0.5$$

Calculation of infiltration conductance:

$$c_{pair} \equiv 1000 \text{ J/kg}^\circ\text{C}$$
$$\rho_{air} \equiv 1.2 \text{ kg/m}^3$$
$$U_{inf} = [(\text{ach} \times \text{Vol})/3600 \text{ s}] \times \rho_{air} \times c_{pair} = 60 \text{ W/}^\circ\text{C}$$

We then calculate all resistances as in the previous section.

Outside temperature
The outside temperature for a day is modelled by a Fourier series based on $N_{\text{To}} + 1$ values that are an input to the array. If more detail is required, N_{To} may be increased. Then, the Fourier series may be used to generate intermediate values as required by the time step of a finite difference model.

Solar radiation (approximate model – for detailed model see Chapter 3)
Solar radiation transmitted through the windows may be modelled by a half-sinusoid from sunrise to sunset time t_s. For initial analysis of radiant heating, the solar radiation may be set to a low value (50 W/m² of window).

$$S_{\text{max}} = 50 \text{ W/m}^2$$

$$S_{it} = S_{\text{max}}\cos[p(t_{it} - 12 \text{ h})/2t_s]^+ \text{ (only positive part)}$$

S_{it} may be modelled with a discrete Fourier series as follows: we multiply by total window area to determine total solar radiation.

$$S_{n_n} = \left(\sum_{it} S_{it} \frac{\exp(-jw_n t_{it})}{24}\right) \sum_{iw} A_{w_{iw}}$$

FINITE DIFFERENCE MODEL (ATHIENITIS 1994)

The general form of the explicit finite difference formulation corresponding to node i and time interval p is:

$$T(i,p+1) = \left(\frac{\Delta t}{C_i}\right)\left(q_i + \sum_j \frac{T(j,p) - T(i,p)}{R(i,j)}\right) + T(i,p) \tag{7.9}$$

where C is capacitance, j represents all nodes connected to node i, and q is a heat source such as auxiliary heating or solar radiation.

Critical time step (for all nodes i):

$$\Delta t_{\text{critical}} = \min\left(\frac{C_i}{\sum_j \frac{1}{R_{i,j}}}\right) \tag{7.10}$$

(the selected time step should be lower to ensure numerical stability).

The thermal network is shown below. The floor is discretized into two layers (one thermal capacitance and two resistances for each layer). The unheated surfaces are represented by node 6. S represents solar radiation transmitted into the room and absorbed by the surfaces (a low value is assumed). Resistance R_{10} represents heat loss by infiltration and through the windows and doors.

Thermal capacitances and resistances:

$$C_{floor} = c_6 \rho_6 A_6 L_6$$

$$C_4 = C_{floor}/2$$

$$C_3 = C_4$$

Thermal capacitance of the interior layer of unheated surfaces:

$$C_5 = \Sigma_{se} A_{se} L_{se} c_{se} \rho_{se}$$

$$R_o = (1/u_6 A_6) + (L_6/4k_6 A_6)$$

$$R_{34} = L_6/2k_6 A_6$$

$$R_{23} = R_{34}/2$$

$$R_{12} \ 1/A_6 h_6$$

Radiation heat transfer coefficient between floor and unheated surfaces:

$$h_{6r} = 4 \ \text{W/m}^2\text{°C}$$

$$R_{56} = \cfrac{1}{\displaystyle\sum_{se} \cfrac{k_{se} A_{se}\,2}{L_{se}}}$$ This represents the thermal resistance of half of the innermost layer of the unheated surfaces

$$R_{26} = \cfrac{1}{h_{6r} A_6}$$

$$R_{16} = \cfrac{1}{\displaystyle\sum_{se} A_{se} h_{se}}$$

$$R_{50} = R_{56} + \cfrac{1}{\displaystyle\sum_{se} \cfrac{A_{se}}{R_{se}}}$$

$$R_{10} = \cfrac{1}{U_{inf} + \displaystyle\sum_{ii} \left(\cfrac{A_{w_{ii}}}{R_w} + \cfrac{A_{d_{ii}}}{R_d} \right)}$$

STABILITY TEST TO SELECT TIME STEP

The time step Δt should be lower than the minimum of the three values in the vector TS:

$$TS = \frac{C_3}{\left(\dfrac{1}{R_{23}} + \dfrac{1}{R_{34}}\right)} \quad \frac{C_4}{\dfrac{1}{R_0} + \dfrac{1}{R_{34}}} \quad \frac{C_5}{\left(\dfrac{1}{R_{56}} + \dfrac{1}{R_{50}}\right)}$$

$$\Delta t_{critical} = \min(TS) = 215.686 \text{ s}$$

Select smaller time step than critical: $\Delta t = 200$ s.

The simulation will be performed for two days (periodic). Thus, weather data have to be generated for NT times as follows:

$$NT = 86400 \text{ s}/\Delta t \times 2 = 864$$

(number of time steps for two days).

$$p = 0,1..NT$$

Times at which simulation is to be performed:

$$t_p = p\Delta t$$

Assume basement temperature, $T_{bp} = 16°C$.

Initial conditions must first be assumed. Also, the size of the heating system q_{max} has to be decided together with the proportional control constant K_p. A good estimate for q_{aux} can be determined by multiplying the zone conductance Y_{z0} with the maximum indoor–outdoor temperature differential and increasing the result by

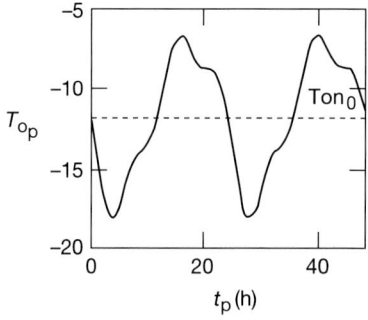

Figure 7.9 Ambient temperature (typical cold day profile (2% probability) for Montreal)

Figures 7.9 and 7.10 show the ambient temperature and solar radiation profiles employed in simulations.

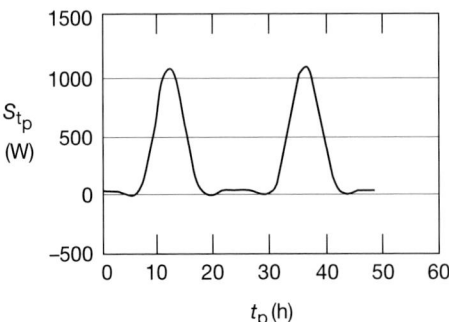

Figure 7.10 Solar radiation (total in zone)

50%. The transient room temperature response will then show whether this assumption was correct. For example:

$$q_{max} = |Y_{z0}|30°C \times 1.5 = 1.054 \times 10^4 \text{ W}$$

Initial estimates of temperatures:

$$\begin{pmatrix} T_{1,0} \\ T_{2,0} \\ T_{3,0} \\ T_{4,0} \\ T_{5,0} \\ T_{6,0} \end{pmatrix} = \begin{pmatrix} 21 \\ 24 \\ 26 \\ 29 \\ 17 \\ 18 \end{pmatrix} °C$$

$$q_{aux} = 0 \text{ W}$$

Setpoint can vary with time of day if desired:

$$T_{sp} = 22°C$$

Proportional control constant (a good value is $q_{max}/2$):

$$K_p = 5000 \text{ W/°C}$$

The equations below were employed in Mathcad (Athienitis 1998) to determine the response of the system. The first equation describes the heating source (no heating is provided if the difference $(T_{sp} - T_1) < 0°C$).

$$\begin{pmatrix} q_{\text{aux}_{p+1}} \\ T_{1,p+1} \\ T_{2,p+1} \\ T_{3,p+1} \\ T_{4,p+1} \\ T_{5,p+1} \\ T_{6,p+1} \end{pmatrix} = \begin{bmatrix} \left(\text{if}\left[K_p\left(T_{\text{sp}} - T_{1,p}\right) > q_{\max}, q_{\max}, K_p\left(T_{\text{sp}} - T_{1,p}\right)\right]\left[\left(T_{\text{sp}} - T_{1,p}\right) > 1.0\right]\right) \\ \dfrac{\dfrac{T_{2,p}}{R_{12}} + \dfrac{To_p}{R_{10}} + \dfrac{T_{6,p}}{R_{16}} + 0.7St_p}{\left(\dfrac{1}{R_{12}} + \dfrac{1}{R_{10}} + \dfrac{1}{R_{16}}\right)} \\ \dfrac{\dfrac{T_{3,p}}{R_{23}} + \dfrac{T_{6,p}}{R_{26}} + \dfrac{T_{1,p}}{R_{12}}}{\left(\dfrac{1}{R_{23}} + \dfrac{1}{R_{26}} + \dfrac{1}{R_{12}}\right)} \\ \dfrac{\Delta t}{C_3}\left(\dfrac{T_{4,p} - T_{3,p}}{R_{34}} + \dfrac{T_{2,p} - T_{3,p}}{R_{23}}\right) + T_{3,p} \\ \dfrac{\Delta t}{C_4}\left(\dfrac{T_{b_p} - T_{4,p}}{R_0} + \dfrac{T_{3,p} - T_{4,p}}{R_{34}}\right) + T_{4,p} \\ \dfrac{\Delta t}{C_5}\left(\dfrac{T_{6,p} - T_{5,p}}{R_{56}} + \dfrac{To_p - T_{5,p}}{R_{50}}\right) + T_{5,p} \\ \dfrac{\dfrac{T_{2,p}}{R_{26}} + \dfrac{T_{5,p}}{R_{56}} + \dfrac{T_{1,p}}{R_{16}} + 0.3St_p}{\left(\dfrac{1}{R_{56}} + \dfrac{1}{R_{26}} + \dfrac{1}{R_{16}}\right)} \end{bmatrix}$$

The results for second day (first day is affected by assumed initial conditions) are given in Figures 7.11 and 7.12.

Heating energy consumption by numerical integration for second day:

$$Qh = \sum_v \frac{q_{\text{aux}_v} + \left|q_{\text{aux}_v}\right| + q_{\text{auxt}_{v+1}} + \left|q_{\text{aux}_{v+1}}\right|}{4}\left(t_{v+1} - t_v\right)$$

$$= 5.785 \times 10^8 \text{ J}$$

Peak heating load $= 8.7$ kW

The above load may be employed as a basis for sizing the system based on the extreme weather conditions assumed. Strategies for reduction of peak load include increasing the mass and preheating to a higher setpoint during the daytime when loads are lower than night-time on very cold days.

However, on sunny days this will reduce the amount of solar radiation that can be stored in the mass; on these days it is preferable to use a lower setpoint during the day and allow the floor mass to be heated by solar radiation transmitted through a south-facing window.

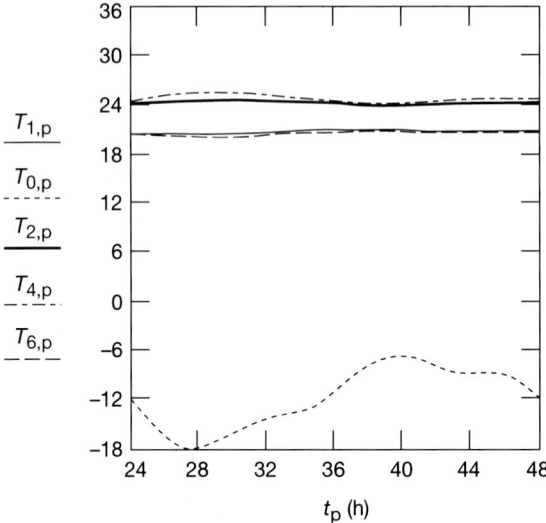

$T_{1,p}$

$T_{0,p}$

$T_{2,p}$

$T_{4,p}$

$T_{6,p}$

Figure 7.11 Temperatures (T_1 is room air temperature)

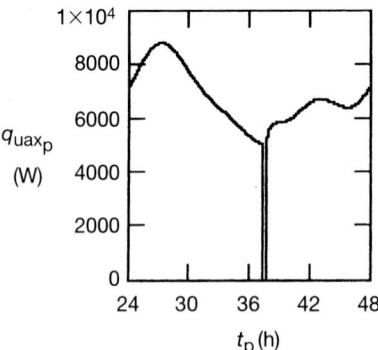

q_{uax_p}

(W)

Figure 7.12 Heating profile

7.3 Analysis of integrated passive–active systems: a ground cooling/heating application

In most locations the temperature of the soil at depths of 2 m or more varies with small amplitude throughout the year. This provides an opportunity for passing air through long underground ducts to condition it in winter by warming it up and cooling it down in summer. This process can be particularly effective when the air is relatively dry.

Several researchers have studied the use of the ground for heat dissipation, for example Mihalakakou *et al.* (1994), who developed a transient numerical model of coupled heat and mass transfer for buried pipes and validated it with experimental data. This section considers combination of ground cooling/heating of air with a variable air volume (VAV) system. The basic idea is to preheat or precool the fresh air intake of the VAV system in order to reduce energy costs.

This study describes application of this principle to the design of three buildings (nos 11, 12, 13) of the new University of Cyprus campus, located at latitude 35°N with a mild temperate dry climate. The winter and summer design temperatures are typically about 0°C and 40°C respectively. However, the temperature of the soil at a depth of 2 m varies from a maximum of approximately 22°C in September to a minimum of 16°C at the end of February. Thus, given the dry climate, this provides an opportunity to cool room air in summer and heat it in winter by passing through underground channels.

7.3.1 Mathematical model for ground heat transfer

The basic objective of the model developed for the underground channels was to determine optimum dimensions so as to achieve maximum heat transfer between the air and the ground. At the same time, pressure drops needed to be reduced to a reasonable value so as not to require very large fans and waste much of the thermal energy potentially saved in fan energy requirements.

Fresh air will be drawn through wind towers (which will function as simple fresh air intakes); after passing it through the underground channels (at a depth of about 2 m) it will be fed into the fresh air intake of a variable air volume HVAC system. In designing the air channels under the buildings, the objective is to achieve maximum heat transfer and minimum pressure drop, while limiting the maximum velocity of air in the vertical ducts leading to the air-handling units to about 10 m/s. The design concept for the systems is shown in Figure 7.13.

Since the university will typically not operate late at night, fresh air requirements at that time will be minimal and the ground will be expected to recover its normal average temperature during the night. Thus, it is reasonable to assume approximately constant ground temperature for periods of operation of 10–15 hours, as also indicated by the results of Mihalakakou *et al.* (1994) (the temperature of the ground rises by only about 2°C after continuous operation in summer).

By performing an energy balance on a strip of width dx of the soil all around the underground channel, and air flowing over it, assuming that the soil (at depth D) in contact with the channel is at a constant surface temperature, the following ordinary differential equation is obtained:

$$V H W c \rho \, \mathrm{d}T = 2 f (H + W) \, \mathrm{d}x \, h \, (T_w - T) \qquad (7.11)$$

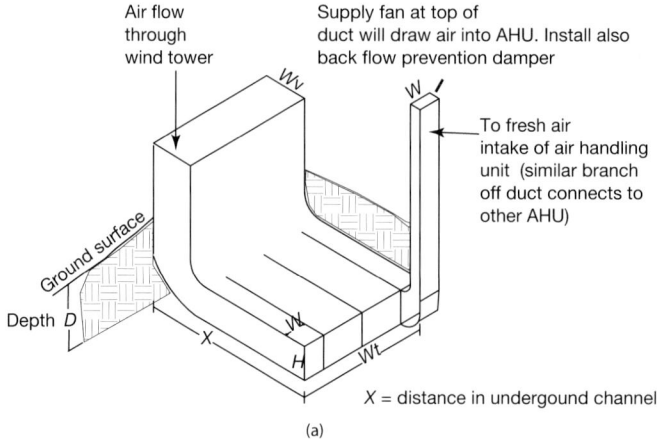

(a)

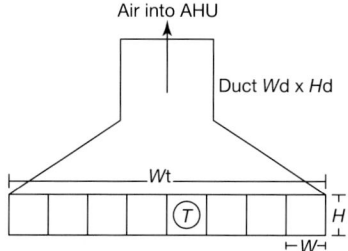

0.4 m x 0.4 m partitions with grooved surface
to enhance heat transfer

$W = 0.4$ m

T = temperature sensor connected to economizer

(b)

Figure 7.13 (a) Schematic of wind tower and underground tunnel concept for buildings (only one duct connecting to a typical air-handling unit (AHU) is shown); (b) section showing one underground channel connected to only one AHU (building 11)

where
V = air velocity
H = channel height
W = channel width
f = area increase factor if a corrugated surface is used
h = heat transfer coefficient
T_w = channel soil surface temperature (assumed constant)
T = air temperature as a function of distance travelled x

Thus, the differential equation can be written as

$$a\, d(T - T_w)/dx + (T - T_w) = 0 \tag{7.12}$$

where

$$a = VHWc\rho/[2f(H + W)h]$$

The solution for the above ordinary differential equation gives an exponential relationship for the air temperature:

$$T(x) = T_w + (T_o - T_w)e^{-x/a} \tag{7.13}$$

The heat transfer coefficient h was determined using the Dittus–Boelter correlation (Holman 1986):

$$Nu = 0.023Re^{0.8}Pr^n \tag{7.14}$$

where Nu is Nusselt number, Re is Reynolds number and Pr the Prandtl number for air (Holman 1986); $n = 0.4$ for heating and 0.3 for cooling.

The temperature of the air rises as it flows through the tower in winter and drops in summer following an exponential curve. If the channel is long enough, the air temperature will approach the ground temperature, especially if the heat transfer area is high. However, if the flow diameters (hydraulic) are too small and the duct too long, the friction losses and pressure drops will be too high, requiring too large a supply fan to draw the air into the air handling unit.

Figure 7.14 shows typical air temperature rise with distance travelled in winter and Figure 7.15 the air temperature drop in summer. Figure 7.16 depicts typical pressure losses for the air as it flows through the underground channel. Correlations suggested by ASHRAE (1997) were utilized for the pressure drop calculations. These correlations may be employed for pressure drop in air duct systems.

The optimum air speed range when the size of the AHUs, pressure drops and ground heat transfer were considered was found to be 2–3 m/s.

For building 11, which will consist primarily of classrooms with high fresh air requirements (served by one AHU), the optimum height (H) of the channel (see Figure 7.13) was 0.4 m; the width (W_t) was fixed at 3.6 m and the length was set at about 40 m based on architectural constraints. The AHU was at the opposite end from the wind tower, thus creating an optimum arrangement for heat transfer from the soil. The channel will be subdivided into eight sections to enhance heat transfer (Figure 7.13b). The vertical duct connecting to the AHU will have a section of about $1.00 \text{ m} \times 0.60 \text{ m}$, delivering fresh air at a maximum speed of about 9 m/s.

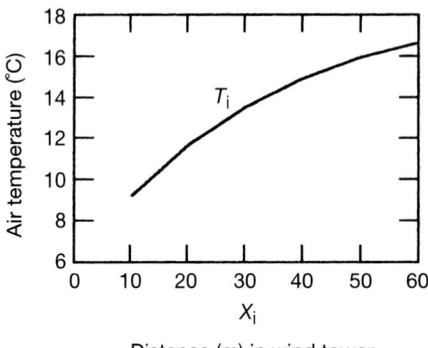

Distance (m) in wind tower

Figure 7.14 Temperature rise of the air as it flows through the underground channel in winter (outside temperature = 6°C, ground temperature = 19°C, air speed 3 m/s)

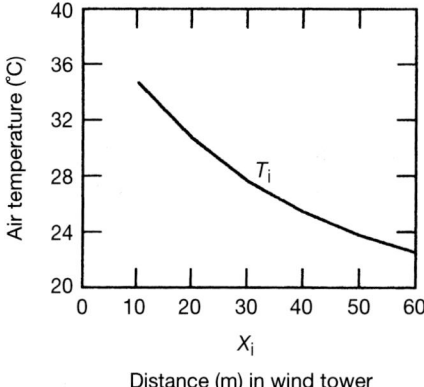

Distance (m) in wind tower

Figure 7.15 Temperature drop of the air as it flows through the channel in summer (outside temperature = 40°C, ground temperature = 19°C, air speed 3 m/s)

In the case of buildings 12 and 13 the length of the underground channel is 60–70 m but several AHUs were to be situated in the centre of the buildings. Thus, with air intake from both sides of the channel, the path travelled underground will be 30–40 m. As can be seen from Figure 7.15, with a distance travelled of 40 m we have a substantial cooling of air from 40°C to about 25°C (ground temperature 19°C). Thus, this length is adequate (for building 11) to achieve a temperature that is close to what would be obtained with a channel of infinite length (limiting case, in which the air comes out at ground temperature).

Figure 7.17 shows the temperature and pressure profiles for building 11.

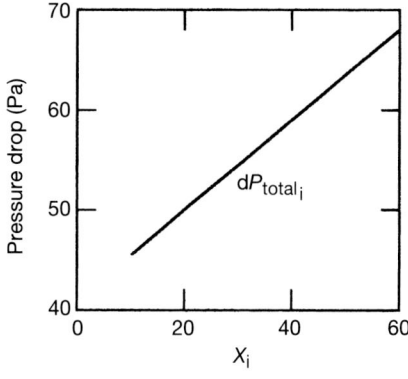

Distance along wind tower X (m)

Figure 7.16 Pressure losses (Pa) of the air as it flows through the channel in summer (air speed 3 m/s)

7.3.2 Simulation results

Detailed simulation results are described for building 11. This building has a floor area of about 1200 m^2. It consists primarily of classrooms and generally has a lower fraction of window area than buildings 12 and 13. Thus, the solar gains are lower but it has high internal gains owing to the large number of occupants (maximum about 800) and high fresh air requirements (minimum 6000 l/s). The internal gains were assumed to be about 63 kW between 8 a.m. and 5 p.m.

Peak refrigeration loads and heating loads were calculated by selecting extreme design days in July and January respectively. For the refrigeration load calculation, a design day with maximum temperature of 40.5°C and minimum 25.5°C was chosen. For the heating calculations, the outdoor temperature varied from a minimum of 0°C to a maximum of 10°C. The peak load is dictated primarily by the maximum temperature for cooling and the minimum temperature for heating. In both cases a sinusoidal temperature profile was employed. For cooling, high solar gains and internal gains were used, while for heating medium gains were assumed. The calculation was dynamic, taking into account heat storage in the building envelope. A dynamic thermal analysis simulation program based on the model described in Section 7.1 was employed (Athienitis 1994b) modified to represent ventilation and solar radiation in detail. A supply air temperature of about 13°C was assumed for cooling and 24–27°C for heating. Indoor temperature was set to 24°C for cooling and 20°C for heating (18°C at night).

Detailed dynamic thermal simulations were performed for an average day of each month of the academic year to evaluate the potential energy savings due to the underground channels as well as the thermal mass of the building. The thermal mass

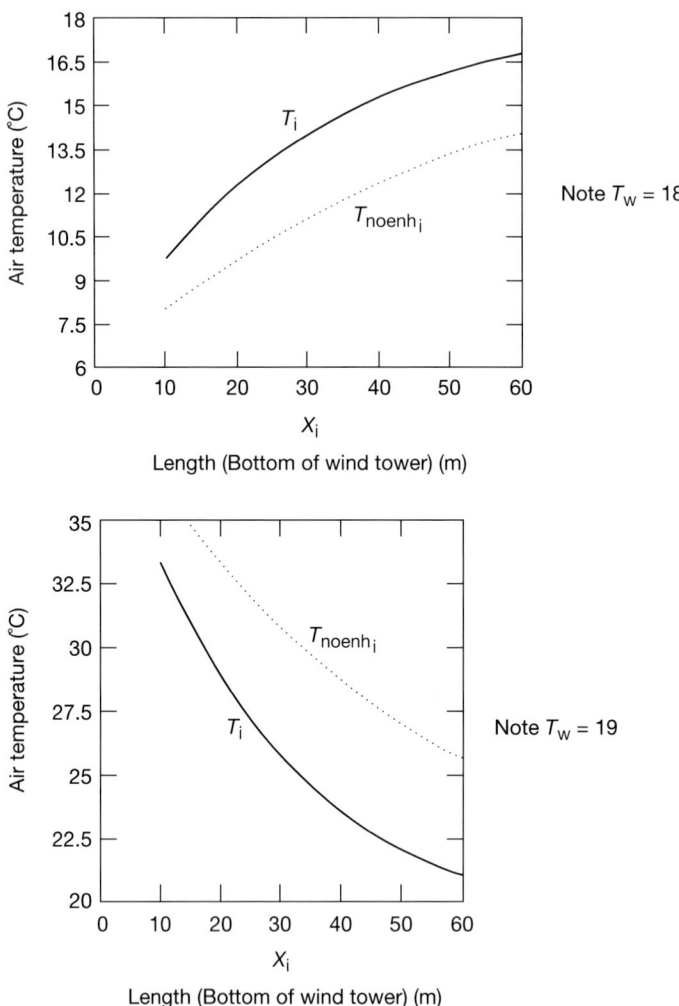

Figure 7.17 Windtower-channel temperature profiles for air preheating and air precooling

generally reduces peak loads. Table 7.1 presents summary results for building 11.

The peak refrigeration load (see Figure 7.18) is about 142 kW. The maximum quantity of supplied air required is about 10–12 m³/s. Without fresh air precooled by the underground channels, the peak load rises by about 90–100 kW. When internal reflective rolling shutters are used the peak load is reduced by 10 kW. The energy consumption is reduced by about 500 MJ (per day).

In Figure 7.18 the air circulation rate at night is set to a minimum of two air changes per hour. During the period 8 a.m. to 5 p.m. the minimum circulation rate,

Table 7.1 Energy analysis for building 11 (for average day in each month; note: thermal energy consumption only, negative denotes cooling, soil temperature is at 2 m depth)

Month	Mean outdoor temp. (°C)	Soil temp. (°C)	Energy (MJ) With ground channel	Energy (MJ) Without ground channel	Typical peak load (kW)
September	25.9	23	–4602	–5975	–124
October	20.8	22.5	–2829	–3310	–92
November	15.9	21	635	1004	47
December	11.9	19	1969	2683	82
January	10.1	16	3155	3550	105
February	10.4	15.5	2884	3367	94
March	12.4	16	1990	2205	77
April	17.3	16.5	–1144	–1934	–36
May	22.0	18	–2460	–4000	–73
June	25.6	19	–3523	–5603	–98

Total heating energy with channel = 10630 MJ
Total heating energy without channel = 12810 MJ
Total cooling energy with channel = 14560 MJ
Total cooling energy without channel = 20820 MJ
Assumptions in energy simulations:
- Internal gains are 70% of the maximum on an average day during the cooling season.
- Internal gains are 50% of maximum on an average day during the heating season.
- Reflective roller shades are not used very much i.e. solar gains are about 60–70% of those on a clear day.
- Thermostat setpoint for heating 20°C (16°C at night).
- Thermostat setpoint for cooling 24°C.
- Fresh air is obtained either from the wind tower or from outside by comparing the two temperatures in the economizer of the HVAC system. For example, in October it is often preferable to use outdoor air directly.

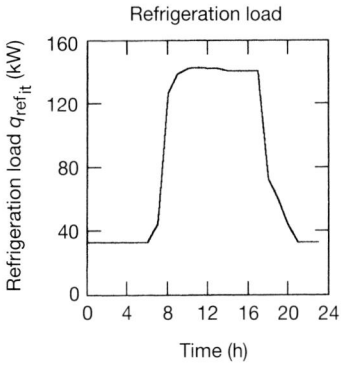
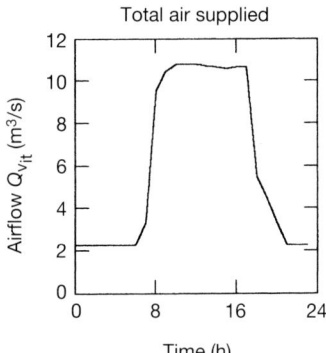

Figure 7.18 Refrigeration load (maximum) and supplied air for building 11. Outside temperature: maximum = 40.5°C, minimum = 25.5°C.

which is 100% fresh air from the wind tower, is about 6000 l/s. The fresh air is normally all supplied from the wind tower precooled to 24–27°C, i.e. close to the temperature of the return air from the zone, with which it is mixed in the AHU. Thus, if the temperature of the air supplied from the wind tower is less than 24°C then it may be beneficial to draw even higher amounts.

As can be seen from Table 7.1, the cooling energy consumption is about 60% higher than the heating energy consumption (without counting July and August). The energy consumption without the channel is about 40% higher for cooling and 20% higher for heating.

The highest refrigeration load with ground cooling is in September and not in June. The reason for this difference is the lower soil temperature in June, which increases the effectiveness of the ground channels by precooling the fresh air to a lower temperature than in September. Similarly, the highest heating savings are observed for December when the soil temperature is still high. The temperature of the soil at a depth of 2 m varies a few degrees about an annual average of 19°C. Because of the large thermal lag, the highest soil temperature is in September.

In calculating the energy consumption in Table 7.1, the temperature of the outside air is compared with that which would be obtained from the underground channel and the preferred source of fresh air is chosen. This strategy will also be implemented in the economizer controls of the variable air volume systems.

Generally the air-conditioning system sizes are dictated by cooling loads for this climate. However, heating loads are also important, particularly in the early mornings in January and February. The peak heating loads were determined as follows for building 11: a peak heating load of 125 kW in January and an energy consumption of 5720 MJ (see Figure 7.19). Without preheated air from the wind tower, the peak load is 171 kW and the energy consumption 7223 MJ.

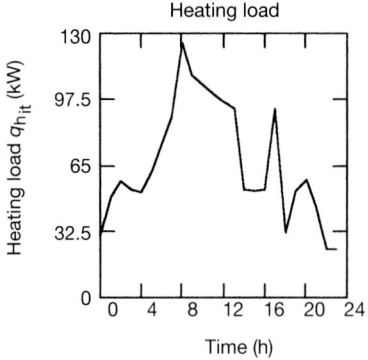 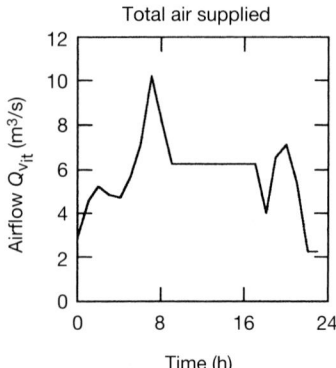

Figure 7.19 Heating load (maximum) and supplied air for building 11. Outside temperature: maximum = 10°C, minimum = 0°C

In all simulations a conservative approach was employed in evaluating the potential benefits due to the wind tower; for heating it was assumed that the air from the towers reaches a temperature equal to the average of the outdoor and deep ground temperatures (see Table 7.1). For cooling it was assumed to reach a temperature equal to $2/3 \times T_{soil} + 1/3 \times T_{exterior}$. As can be seen from Figures 7.14 and 7.15, these assumptions are justified. Note that the peak of the heating curves occurs in the early morning and is of short duration. The flat part of the air supply curves indicates the minimum amount of air required to satisfy the fresh air requirements.

The dynamic variation of the load and airflow for average days in June and January are shown in Figures 7.20 and 7.21 respectively. Comparison of Figure 7.18 (peak summer day) with Figure 7.20 (average summer day) indicates a substantially lower load on an average summer day, and hence less demand for

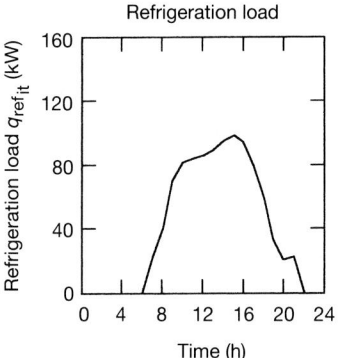
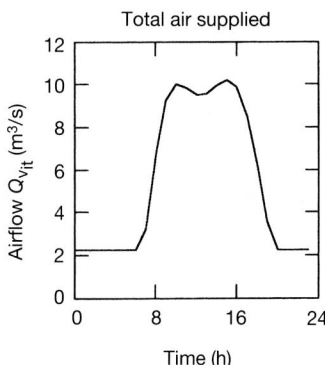

Figure 7.20 Refrigeration load and airflow for an average day in June for building 11 (at night there are a minimum of two air changes per hour)

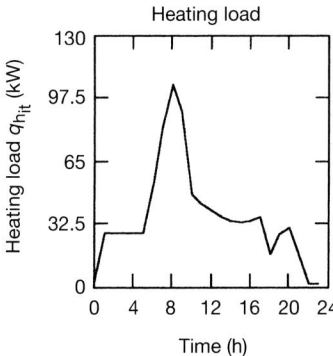
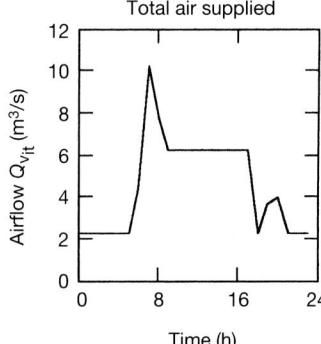

Figure 7.21 Heating load and airflow for an average day in January for building 11 (at night we have minimum two air changes per hour)

ground cooling. An analogous observation is made by comparing Figures 7.19 (peak winter day) and 7.21 (average winter day); the peak heating demand has a very short duration (a couple of hours) in the early morning, and the ground preheating of the fresh air will be very effective for this short period.

7.4 Bibliography

ASHRAE (1997) *ASHRAE Handbook 1997 Fundamentals*, American Society of Heating, Refrigerating, and Air-Conditioning Engineers, Inc., Atlanta, GA.

Athienitis A.K. (1994a) *Building Thermal Analysis*, Electronic Mathcad Book, MathSoft Inc., Boston, MA.

Athienitis A.K. (1994b) 'Numerical model for a floor heating system', *ASHRAE Transactions*, **100**:1, 1024–1030.

Athienitis A.K. (1997) 'Theoretical investigation of thermal performance of a passive solar building with floor radiant heating', *Solar Energy*, **61**:5, 337–345.

Athienitis A.K. (1998) *Building Thermal Analysis*, Electronic Mathcad Book, 2nd edn, Mathsoft Inc., Boston, USA.

Athienitis A.K., Stylianou M. and Shou J. (1990) 'A methodology for building thermal dynamics studies and control applications', *ASHRAE Transactions*, **96**, Part 2, 839–848.

Holman J.P. (1986) *Heat Transfer*, McGraw-Hill Inc., New York.

Mihalakakou G., Santamouris M. and Asimakopoulos D. (1994) 'Modelling the thermal performance of earth-to-air heat exchangers', *Solar Energy*, **53**:3, 301–305.

CHAPTER 8

Control of passive solar buildings

Before considering the dynamic thermal control of passive solar buildings, it is necessary to establish the desired thermal comfort parameters and their acceptable ranges. Thermal comfort is discussed in Section 8.1, while a detail dynamic model for control is discussed in Section 8.2.

8.1 Thermal comfort

Comfort is affected by several factors: physical health, mental health, social factors, environmental factors, etc. Considering only the environmental factors, one must analyse the thermal environment, the visual factors, the acoustical factors and indoor air quality to be able to assess human comfort. Thermal comfort is basically a condition of mind that expresses satisfaction with the thermal environment. In order to achieve good thermal comfort, many personal and environmental conditions must be fulfilled, ranging from physical to physiological and psychological (see Figure 8.1).

The main factor affecting thermal comfort is the temperature. However, the temperature is not the only environmental factor affecting thermal comfort. The thermal environment is a combination of air temperature, radiant temperature, air velocity and air humidity. These thermal factors and two personal factors (clothing insulation and activity level) are the main parameters influencing thermal comfort. In a solar building, we may also have diffuse and possibly beam solar radiation incident on a person.

The human body produces heat by metabolism (i.e. oxidation of food), and exchanges heat with the environment through the skin and by respiration. Under neutral conditions, for sedentary activities the heat exchange results in an internal body temperature of about 37°C, a skin temperature between 33°C and 34°C, and negligible skin moisture content (ASHRAE 1997). If there is any thermal disturbance to this neutral condition, the body's temperature control system makes an effort to maintain the neutral temperature (37°C) for the vital organs. The body heat balance at any moment results in an internal body temperature, a skin temperature and skin moisture content that are felt (sensed) by the brain. The mind

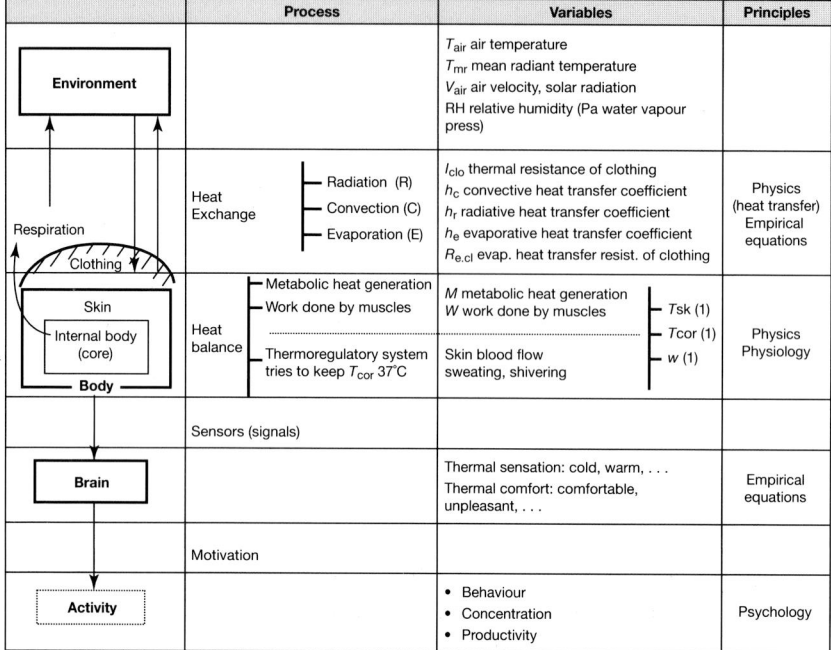

		Process	Variables	Principles
Environment			T_{air} air temperature T_{mr} mean radiant temperature V_{air} air velocity, solar radiation RH relative humidity (Pa water vapour press)	
Respiration Clothing	Heat Exchange	Radiation (R) Convection (C) Evaporation (E)	I_{clo} thermal resistance of clothing h_c convective heat transfer coefficient h_r radiative heat transfer coefficient h_e evaporative heat transfer coefficient $R_{e,cl}$ evap. heat transfer resist. of clothing	Physics (heat transfer) Empirical equations
Skin Internal body (core) **Body**	Heat balance	Metabolic heat generation Work done by muscles Thermoregulatory system tries to keep T_{cor} 37°C	M metabolic heat generation W work done by muscles — Tsk (1) — Tcor (1) Skin blood flow — w (1) sweating, shivering	Physics Physiology
	Sensors (signals)			
Brain			Thermal sensation: cold, warm, . . . Thermal comfort: comfortable, unpleasant, . . .	Empirical equations
	Motivation			
Activity			• Behaviour • Concentration • Productivity	Psychology

(1) Skin temperature (T_{sk}), core temperature (T_{cor}) and skin wettedness (w).

Figure 8.1 Schematic showing mechanisms affecting thermal comfort

perceives the thermal sensation (cold, warm, etc.) and draws conclusions about the comfort level (pleasant, unpleasant, etc.).

Simultaneously, the body's temperature control system (thermoregulatory system) tries to maintain the normal temperature of vital organs by different means depending on the magnitude of the thermal disturbance. When low-magnitude disturbances occur, the vasomotor control system supplies more blood to the extremities to lose heat (when warm), or less blood to maintain the heat in the vital organs (when cold). If the magnitude of the disturbance increases, the thermal sensation forces a behavioural response from the body (e.g. take off sweater, move to the shade when warm). If the disturbance increases even more, the body tries to lose more heat by evaporative sweating (when warm) or increase the heat generation by shivering (when cold).

Metabolic heat generation varies directly with the activity level: higher activity levels generate more heat, and lower activity levels less heat. Researchers (Gagge *et al.* 1973) have found that, for sedentary activities, under cold conditions the mean skin temperature is a good indicator of cold discomfort and usually ranges between 28°C and 33°C. Under warm conditions the mean skin temperature becomes a poor indicator of warm discomfort; it varies between 34°C and 36°C (only two degrees).

The 2 deg C difference limit of change in mean skin temperature is caused by evaporation from sweating and, therefore, the skin wetness becomes the best indicator of warm discomfort.

8.1.1 Body heat balance

The metabolic energy (M) produced by the body is expended in part as work (W) done by the muscles, and the difference is stored (S) as heat in the body. The stored heat (S) is dissipated to the environment through the skin surface and the respiratory tract. Because the heat exchange between the body and the environment occurs mostly through the skin, all heat balance variables are expressed per unit area of skin. Therefore, the heat balance equation is as follows.

$$M - W = Q_{sk} + Q_{res} + S \qquad (8.1)$$

$$= (C + R + E_{sk}) + (C_{res} + E_{res}) + S \qquad (8.2)$$

where
M = rate of metabolic heat rate production, W/m^2
W = rate of mechanical work accomplished, W/m^2
Q_{sk} = total rate of heat loss from skin, W/m^2
Q_{res} = total rate of heat loss through respiration, W/m^2
$C + R$ = sensible heat loss from skin by convection and radiation
E_{sk} = rate of total evaporative heat loss from skin, W/m^2
C_{res} = rate of convective heat loss from respiration, W/m^2
E_{res} = rate of evaporative heat loss from respiration, W/m^2
S = rate of heat storage in the body, W/m^2

8.1.2 Thermal exchange with the environment

Thermal exchange with the environment occurs in the form of sensible and latent heat through the skin and by respiration.

THERMAL EXCHANGE THROUGH THE SKIN
This takes the form of sensible heat by convection (C) and radiation (R), latent heat flow from evaporation of sweat (E_{rsw}), and from evaporation of moisture diffused through the skin (E_{dif}). For the sensible heat exchange by convection and radiation the heat exchange can be expressed in terms of the convective and radiative heat transfer coefficients, as follows:

$$C = f_{cl}h_c(T_{cl} - T_a)$$
$$R = f_{cl}h_r(T_{cl} - T_{mr}) \qquad (8.3)$$

where:

h_c = convective heat transfer coefficient, W/m² K
h_r = radiative heat transfer coefficient, W/m² K
f_{cl} = body area correction factor area clothed body/area nude body (A_{cl}/A_D)
T_{cl} = mean temperature of the outer surface of the clothed body
T_a = air temperature
T_{mr} = mean radiant temperature from the surrounding surfaces
The total sensible heat exchange is obtained by adding C and R as follows:

$$C + R = f_{cl}h(T_{cl} - T_o) \qquad (8.4)$$

where:

$$T_e = \frac{h_r T_{mr} + h_c T_a}{h_r + h_c} \qquad (8.5)$$

$$h = h_r + h_c \qquad (8.6)$$

T_e is defined as the operative temperature. It is the average of the air temperature and the mean radiant temperature, weighted by their respective heat transfer coefficients, and it is the closest approximation to the actual temperature as felt by a person.

h is combined convective (h_c) and radiative (h_r) heat transfer coefficient, W/m² K.

The above equations relate the heat exchange to the clothing surface temperature. It is more convenient to relate them to the mean skin temperature. The sensible heat through the clothing can be written as a function of the thermal resistance of clothing:

$$C + R = (T_{sk} - T_{cl})/R_{cl} \qquad (8.7)$$

Therefore, combining equations 8.4 and 8.7 to eliminate T_{cl} the following steady-state sensible heat-exchange equation is obtained:

$$q / A_{sens} = h_{sens}\Delta T \quad (C + R) = \frac{1}{R_{cl} + \dfrac{1}{(f_{cl}\, h)}}(T_{sk} - T_e) \qquad (8.8)$$

where
R_{cl} = thermal resistance of clothing, m² K/W
T_{sk} = mean skin temperature, °C
Similarly for the latent heat exchange the following equation is obtained:

$$Q/A_{latent} = h_{latent}\Delta p \qquad (8.9)$$

$$E_{sk} = \frac{w}{R_{e,cl} + \dfrac{1}{(f_{cl}\, h_e)}}(P_{sk} - P_a) \tag{8.10}$$

where:
$E_{sk} = E_{rsw} + E_{dif}$
E_{sk} = rate of total evaporative heat loss from skin, W/m^2
w = wet skin fraction, dimensionless (skin wettedness)
$R_{e,cl}$ = evaporative heat transfer resistance of clothing (analogous to R_{cl}), m^2 kPa/W
h_e = evaporative heat transfer coefficient (analogous to h_c), W/m^2 kPa
P_{sk} = water vapour pressure at skin, normally assumed to be that of saturated water vapour at T_{sk}, kPa
P_a = water vapour pressure in ambient air, kPa
E_{rsw} = rate of evaporative heat loss of regulatory sweat, W/m^2
E_{dif} = rate of evaporative heat loss of natural diffusion water through skin, W/m^2

Empirical expressions are used to determine the values of the heat and moisture heat transfer coefficients for different personal and environmental situations. According to ASHRAE (1997) 'h_r is nearly constant for typical indoor temperatures, and a value of 4.7 W/m^2 K suffices for most calculations'. This value is affected by the parameter $f_D = 0.73$ for a standing person (Dubois effective body area factor (ASHRAE 1997)).

THERMAL EXCHANGE BY RESPIRATION

Thermal exchange by respiration is the sensible heat flow during respiration (C_{res}) and latent heat flow due to evaporation of moisture during respiration (E_{res}). Respiratory heat losses are expressed in terms of pulmonary ventilation rate, humidity ratio of exhaled and inhaled air, specific heat of air and other variables. After some approximations the following equation is obtained (ASHRAE 1997):

$$C_{res} + E_{res} = 0.014M(34 - t_a) + 0.0175M(5.87 - P_a) \tag{8.11}$$

The convective and evaporative heat losses are then given in terms of the metabolic heat production (W/m^2), the air temperature (T_a, °C), and the water vapour pressure in the ambient air (P_a, KPa).

8.1.3 Thermal comfort models

Among the various types of thermal comfort model two have been utilized most widely: Fanger's steady-state energy balance model, and Gagge's two-node transient model. These models apply the energy balance equation, and estimate thermal comfort by empirical equations, under different assumptions. The thermal comfort predicted by these two models is general thermal comfort. Therefore, a neutral thermal sensation means that a person feels thermally neutral for the body as a whole, not knowing whether they would prefer a higher or lower ambient temperature level.

Fanger's model utilizes the PMV index (predicted mean vote) as the parameter to evaluate thermal sensation. The PMV index predicts the mean response of a large group of people according to the following thermal sensation scale: ±3 (hot/cold), ±2 (warm/cool), ±1 (slightly warm/cool), 0 (neutral). Gagge's model predicts thermal sensation by TSENS index, and discomfort by DISC index. TSENS is based on the PMV scale, but with extra terms for ±4 (very hot/cold) and ±5 (intolerably hot/cold). DISC recognizes the same positive/negative convention for warm/cold discomfort with the following scale: ±5 intolerable, ±4 limited tolerance, ±3 very uncomfortable, ±2 uncomfortable and unpleasant, ±1 slightly uncomfortable but acceptable, 0 neutral.

For most purposes these two models are sufficient to predict thermal comfort. In fact ISO comfort standard 7730 (1984) is based on thermal comfort results calculated by the Fanger model; and ASHRAE standard 55 (1992) is based on the results obtained from Gagge's model. However, these models have some limitations. Fanger's steady-state model is applicable for mainly sedentary people and assumes that the body is in steady-state thermal equilibrium. Therefore, vasoregulation, shivering and sweating are not considered. The model represents the body as a point, therefore the same skin temperature is assumed for the whole body. Internal body temperature (core temperature) is not considered. Gagge's two-node model is applicable for mainly sedentary people and assumes the body is divided by two concentric cylinders: the internal one is the core and the external one is the skin or shell. The temperature in each cylinder is assumed to be uniform, so that the only temperature gradients occur between cylinders.

8.1.4 Thermal non-uniform conditions

The above thermal comfort models calculate thermal comfort for the body as a whole. However, the body may be thermally neutral but at the same time any part of it may be too cold or too warm. Therefore, it is a further requirement for thermal comfort that no local warm or cold discomfort exists at any part of the body. Such a local discomfort may be caused by:

- asymmetric radiation
- draught: undesired local cooling of the body caused by air movement
- vertical air temperature gradients
- hot or cold floors.

To account for these non-uniformities of the environment the standards (ASHRAE 55-92, ISO 7730) specify limits for them. The effect of solar radiation is not considered in these standards.

THERMAL COMFORT STANDARDS

ASHRAE standard 55 (1992) and ISO standard 7730 (1984) are the basis for the design and operation of buildings' HVAC systems. Both standards specify the thermal environmental conditions for thermal comfort in buildings.

An acceptable thermal environment is defined in both ASHRAE standard 55-92 and ISO standard 7730 as an environment that at least 80% of the occupants would find thermally acceptable. Therefore, it is assumed that less than 20% will be dissatisfied when the recommendations of the standard are followed. The 20% dissatisfaction criterion includes dissatisfaction due to local and general thermal discomfort. In ISO standard 7730 the recommended limits for an acceptable thermal environment are:

$$-0.5 < PMV < 0.5$$

$$PPD < 10\% \text{ (percent dissatisfied)}$$

The standard recommends **operative temperature** intervals for different combinations of clothing insulation and activity level. The recommended relative humidity ranges from 30% to 70%. ASHRAE standard 55-92 recommends also the required **operative temperature** and relative humidity combinations for primarily sedentary activity ((1 met = 58.2 W/m^2), during winter and summer seasons with typical indoor clothing for each season as shown in Table 8.1.

Table 8.1 ASHRAE standard 55. Optimum acceptable ranges of operative temperature for people during light, primarily sedentary activity ($\leq$1.2 met) at 50% relative humidity and mean air speed (0.15 m/s)

Season	Typical clothing I_{cl} (clo)	Optimum operative temp. (°C)	Operative temp. range (10% dissatisfaction criterion) (°C)
Winter	0.9	22	20–23.5
Summer	0.5	24.5	23–26
	minimal 0.05	27	26–29

In Table 8.1 the difference between summer and winter recommended operative temperatures is due to the lighter indoor clothing worn during the summer. ASHRAE also recommends a maximum relative humidity of 60% and a minimum humidity given by a dew point temperature of 2°C.

8.1.5 Local thermal discomfort

In ISO standard 7730 and ASHRAE standard 55-92 the recommended limits for local discomfort for people occupied with light, mainly sedentary activity (1.2 met) are as follows:

- The radiant temperature asymmetry from windows or other cold vertical surfaces shall be less than 10°C.
- The radiant temperature asymmetry from a heated ceiling must be less than 5°C.
- Vertical air temperature difference between head and ankle level shall be less than 3 deg C. In ASHRAE standard 55-92 it is specified as the difference between the air temperature at the 0.1 m and 1.7 m levels.
- Surface temperature of the floor shall normally be between 19°C and 26°C, but floor heating systems can be designed for 29°C. In ASHRAE 55-92 a general range of 18–29°C is specified.
- Draught can be the most critical variable because it is more difficult to control. It depends on many factors such as: air distribution system, air turbulence, position of furniture, air temperature, position of the person within the space, area of skin exposed, etc.

Both standards present in charts the allowable mean air velocity as a function of air temperature, and turbulence intensity that result in less than 15% dissatisfaction. Both standards also present in a graphic way the required air velocities to offset elevated temperatures above 26°C. However, the maximum allowable mean air velocities specified by ISO 7730 and ASHRAE 55-92 are 1 m/s and 0.8 m/s respectively, for sedentary activities. According to ASHRAE 55-92 'higher air speeds may be acceptable if the person has individual control of the local air speed'.

Finally ASHRAE 55-92 states that 'more active people are less sensitive, and they will be able to accept higher degrees of non-uniformity than people with light, primarily sedentary activity'. Some laboratory-based studies (Knudsen *et al.* 1989) recommend an optimal operative temperature in winter for a person undergoing sedentary activities (1.2 met) and who has a clothing level of 1 clo (typical indoor winter ensemble) as 22 ± 2°C. During summer warm condition with light clothing (0.5 clo) they recommend an operative temperature equal to 24.5 ± 1.5°C. However, in a field-based research, Griffiths (1990) shows that, generally, the temperatures required for thermal comfort are significantly lower in all building types than those predicted from models established through laboratory-based researches. He gave, for instance, the following operative temperature for optimal conditions: 21°C for office workers in Germany and France; 19°C for schoolteachers in France; 19°C for hospital occupants in the UK; and still lower temperatures for houses in the UK and France.

8.1.6 Effect of solar radiation

Solar radiation transmitted through fenestration has two effects on the indoor thermal environment: (1) immediate effects due to the incidence of direct and diffuse transmitted solar radiation on people, and (2) indirect effects due to absorption of part of the solar radiation by the room interior surfaces and furnishings and subsequent re-radiation (long wave) or convection from these surfaces.

The amount of direct solar radiation absorbed by a person depends on the position of the sun, the window properties and the person's average solar absorptance. Gianccone and Gianfranco (1986) developed a computer program to calculate thermal comfort maps that show the influence of the internal distribution of hourly radiation on thermal comfort taking into account the presence of direct, diffuse and reflected radiation falling on the occupant. Solar radiation was modelled with two different methods: (1) as uniformly distributed on all room surfaces, and (2) its internal distribution was accurately calculated taking into account the hourly path of solar radiation and external as well as internal shadowing effects. The two methods showed great differences in their estimation of thermal comfort. The PMV model was applied to estimate the thermal comfort level (Fanger 1970).

The *CIBSE Guide* (1987) states that the only significant component of transmitted solar radiation (for thermal comfort calculations) is the direct component. It gives the effect of varying levels of direct solar radiation on effective mean radiant temperatures. For example, for a clothing/skin absorptance of 0.8 and incident solar radiation equal to 500 W/m^2, a rise of 14.4°C in the effective mean radiant temperature is reported (equivalent to 7.7°C in the dry resultant temperature – which is what would be approximately measured with a globe thermometer having the same absorptance). Similar results have been reported by Olesen *et al.* (1989).

A study by Athienitis and Haghighat (1992) used experiments and simulation to further quantify both the direct and indirect effects of solar radiation on thermal comfort. An approximate form of the equation recommended for the effect of solar radiation is to increase the effective operative temperature as follows:

$$T_e = [h_r T_{mrt} + h_c T_{ai} + \alpha_s(q_d + q_b/4)]/(h_r + h_c)$$

where α_s is the skin/clothing average solar absorbtance. Note that the beam radiation q_b is divided by 4 because the projected area of a sphere (approximating a person) is a quarter of its surface area; it is assumed that the diffuse radiation q_d is received uniformly from all sides (acceptable for a lightly coloured room). The approximate effect of uniform diffuse radiation is thus $q_d/10$°C and for beam $q_b/40$°C. For example, 400 W of beam radiation transmitted through a window and incident on a person would cause an apparent increase of approximately 10°C in the operative temperature.

In the case of daylighting, we must also consider glare discomfort and control shading and light distribution devices to reduce the non-uniformity in daylight distribution (see also Sections 3.4 and 3.5).

8.2 Control analysis of passive solar buildings

8.2.1 Introduction

This section presents an integrated methodology for dynamic thermal analysis of passive solar buildings and their auxiliary HVAC systems. The methodology is based on the use of Laplace transfer functions for the building, its heating–cooling system and control components. These transfer functions can be used for building thermal control studies, frequency domain analysis and energy analysis. Laplace transfer functions for the building are obtained by means of thermal network models that include both distributed parameter elements such as thermal mass and lumped elements such as the room lightweight contents. The radiant exchanges are represented accurately. The methodology is applied to obtain both air temperature and operative temperature transfer functions. Laplace transfer functions are also used for HVAC system and control components. Transient thermal control studies are performed by means of an efficient numerical Laplace transform inversion technique. Building heating/cooling load calculations may be performed by means of discrete Fourier series techniques.

Building thermal dynamics and control studies are usually performed separately from HVAC system design and building energy analysis without sufficient consideration of the system loads, their variability and the interactions between the building shell, the HVAC system and the control system. These interactions and load variability are even higher in today's buildings because of the trend towards larger window areas and other passive solar design features in both commercial and residential buildings, the implementation of novel heating/cooling systems coupled with energy conservation measures and increased ventilation for improved indoor air quality. The interaction between the three building thermal subsystems (envelope, HVAC system, control system) is a complex process, which leads to delays in the building response. The order of magnitude of the thermal time lags introduced by the building envelope is of the order of hours, and sometimes a day or more for passive solar buildings. In general, high radiant gains have delayed effects that influence both load and room temperature significantly as the amount of building interior thermal mass increases. Time delays and thermal lags are also introduced by the HVAC system and the sensor–control system. The order of magnitude of these time delays is typically minutes, since time constants of heating/cooling coils (Bhargava *et al.* 1975) are usually smaller than a minute (Shavit *et al.* 1982), transportation times within ducts and pipes usually take less than 10 seconds, and sensor time constants are rarely greater than 1 min (Omega Engineering 1987). The time lags introduced by the building, its HVAC system, and the sensor–control system are one of the major causes of complexity in controlling indoor environments.

Neglect of the interaction between a building and its HVAC system and of the combined effect of the various time delays in building design may lead to comfort problems during building operation. Building operation may be made more energy efficient and comfortable by fully utilizing the capabilities of the new digital controllers that permit continuous modification of operating parameters, such as setpoints, as a result of predicted and sensed performance. To achieve this, one must address the interaction between the long-term building dynamics associated with the building thermal capacity – measured in hours – and short-term dynamics associated with the HVAC system and the control system – measured in minutes. Thus we can then investigate all aspects of dynamic control strategies (Hartman 1988, Athienitis 1988) that seek to improve whole building performance by exploiting the interaction between the building thermal mass and the HVAC system.

Park *et al.* (1989) concluded that their choice of initial conditions for the simulations affected the results significantly, and that the most difficult task was the preparation of input data for a simulation.

An alternative approach to complete simulation of whole building systems is to focus on specific interactions between the building, its HVAC system and the control system through frequency response studies, and with transient analysis (Athienitis *et al.* 1990). This can be achieved by means of frequency domain techniques in conjunction with Laplace transforms. Building Laplace transfer functions, which typically represent the effect of heat sources or temperature changes on room temperatures, may be employed for three types of studies:

- **Frequency domain analysis:** the building significant thermal characteristics can be identified, and various design options may be compared on a relative basis though frequency domain studies of the magnitude and phase variation of the building transfer functions; this technique is particularly suitable for passive solar analysis (Mathews and Richard 1989).
- **Thermal control studies:** these studies are performed by first combining the building s-domain transfer functions with the HVAC system and control Laplace transfer functions. After determining the overall transfer functions through standard block diagram algebra techniques we may perform two types of analysis: (a) transient control studies such as the system response to setpoint and load changes (these are performed through numerical inversion of Laplace transforms); and (b) frequency response analysis of the open-loop and closed-loop transfer functions for stability studies (Athienitis *et al.* 1987).
- **Building heating/cooling load and temperature calculations:** these are performed by means of discrete Fourier series. The building transfer functions are calculated at discrete frequencies ($s = j\omega$). A discrete Fourier transform (DFT) of the weather data is performed and the time domain load or room temperature variation is obtained through complex algebra techniques and an inverse discrete Fourier transform (IDFT). Moreover, z-transfer functions, readily obtainable from the s-transfer functions, may be used for energy analysis.

Design of thermal control systems and operation strategies for buildings has often been based on frequency response techniques which employ simple building thermal models (Fisk 1981), and thus simplified transient analysis (Zhang and Warren 1988) As reported by Borresen (1981), the use of oversimplified models for rooms in selecting control parameters results in throttle temperature ranges and integral times in proportional integral control that are larger than necessary.

The method described uses detailed building thermal network models to determine the Laplace transfer functions that are employed for both energy calculations and thermal control analysis. A unified approach to building energy analysis and building thermal dynamics/control studies is proposed. By using such an approach, the thermal processes in a building and the dynamic interactions with an HVAC system can be modelled in detail, and with high accuracy. The building, its HVAC system and the control system are considered as one thermal dynamic system with all components represented by Laplace transfer functions.

8.2.2 Methodology

A building is represented by a thermal network, and transfer functions are obtained by performing an energy balance at all nodes in the Laplace domain. Both lumped and distributed elements can be considered with this approach. Simple models that do not represent in detail infrared radiation heat exchanges between room interior surfaces can usually be solved analytically (e.g. Section 5.1). For such cases the building transfer functions are determined in symbolic form as a continuous function of the Laplace domain variable s; s is equal to $j\omega$ in the frequency domain. For detailed thermal network models an analytical solution is usually not feasible. The admittance matrix that arises from the energy balances of the network is then inverted at discrete frequencies and the transfer functions are thus obtained only at these frequencies. The analytical function is obtained by fitting a polynomial $N(s)/D(s)$ through a modified least squares technique. Analytical transfer functions (Athienitis *et al.* 1987, Fisk 1981) may be used for parametric analysis in order to examine for effects of variables such as thermal mass on the thermal lag time (related to phase angle of the relevant transfer function) associated with radiant gains. Analytical s-transfer functions are also required for transient control studies in which a numerical inversion technique for Laplace transforms is employed.

BUILDING TRANSFER FUNCTIONS
Building transfer functions generally provide the response of interest – heat flow or temperature for unit heat input or unit temperature change at a node in the thermal network. The most important transfer function required in the present method is the impedance transfer function

$$Z(i,j) = T(i)/Q(j) \tag{8.12}$$

which represents the temperature change for node i due to unit heat input at node j for a given frequency. Thus, for heat input $Q(j)$ the room temperature change $T(1)$ (1 = room air node) is equal to

$$T(1) = Z(1,j) \times Q(j)$$

It is often useful to determine a transfer function not only for individual room temperatures, but also for an effective room temperature such as the operative temperature (ASHRAE 1997). The operative temperature is defined as the uniform temperature of an enclosure in which an occupant would exchange the same amount of heat by radiation plus convection as in the actual non-uniform environment; it is given by

$$T_e = (h_r T_{mr} + h_c T_{ai})/(h_r + h_c) \tag{8.13}$$

where T_{ai} is the air temperature, T_{mr} is the mean radiant temperature, and h_r and h_c are radiative and convective coefficients, respectively, for a person or object (sensor). The operative temperature transfer functions $X(i)$ are given by

$$X(i) = T_e/Q(i) \tag{8.14}$$

and represent the effect of a source $Q(i)$ acting at node i on the operative temperature.

The thermal network model for a typical room over a basement, with one window and convective auxiliary heating, is depicted in Figure 8.2. The thermally massive walls are modelled by a two-port distributed element, while the room air and lightweight room contents are modelled by a lumped thermal capacitance. Although this capacitance has no effect on load calculations because of the relatively low frequencies involved, it is important to include it for short-term (high-frequency) control studies. Each two-port element in Figure 8.2 represents the equivalent two-port for each wall, obtained after multiplying the cascade matrices for each massive and non-massive layer. The resistances connecting node 1 (room air) to the interior surfaces represent convective conductances given by

$$U_{1j} = A(j)h_c(j) \tag{8.15a}$$

The radiation conductances interconnecting room interior surface nodes 2–8 are given by

$$U_{ij} = A(i)\sigma 4 T_m^3 F^*_{ij} \tag{8.15b}$$

where σ is the Stefan–Boltzman constant and $4T_m^3$ is a linearization factor which is based on an estimated mean temperature, T_m. The radiation exchange factors

(a)

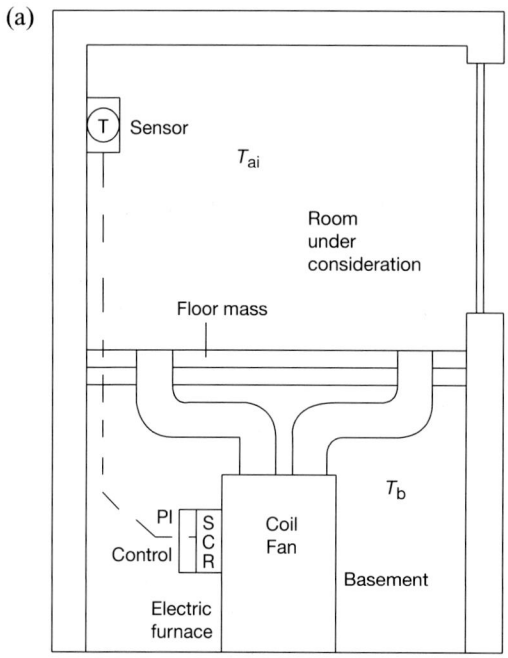

(b)

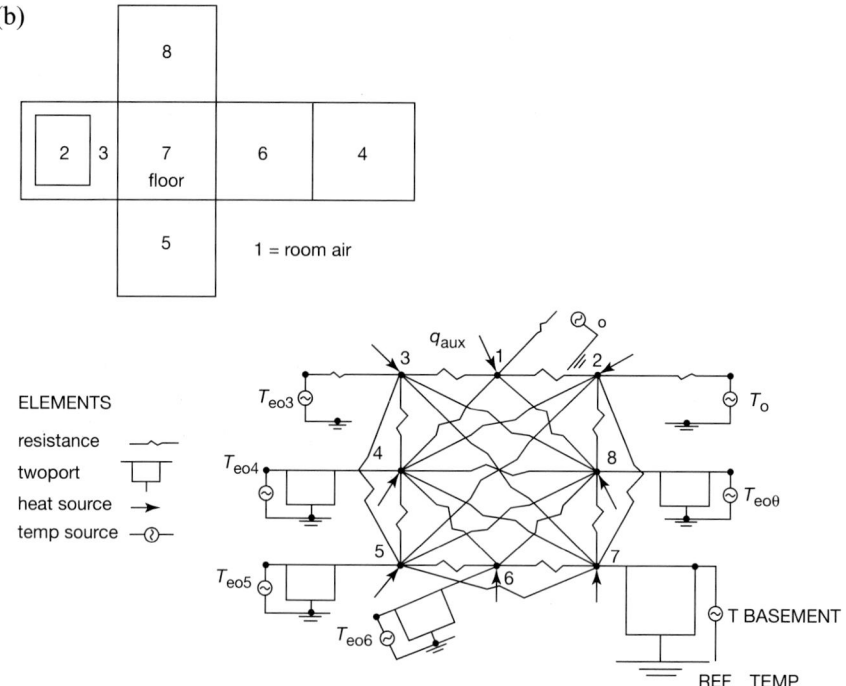

Figure 8.2 (a) Room with convective heating; (b) thermal network for top zone. Nodes: 1 = room air, 2–8 are room interior surfaces – 2 = window, 3 = front wall, 4 = ceiling, 5 = right wall, 6 = back wall, 7 = floor, 8 = left wall

(F^*_{ij}) between the pair of surfaces under consideration (i and j) are determined from the radiation view factors, F_{ij} (also denoted by $F(i,j)$), and the radiative properties of the room surfaces as follows:

$$F^*(i,j) = m(i,j)\varepsilon_i\varepsilon_j/\rho_i \qquad (8.15c)$$

where $[m] = [M]^{-1}$; the elements of matrix $[M]$ are: $M(i,j) = I(i,j) - \rho_i F(i,j)$, with $I(i,j) = 1$ if $i = j$; otherwise, $I(i,j) = 0$ (identity matrix).

The energy balances at the room interior nodes for both models are readily obtained after replacing each wall by its Norton equivalent subnetwork (see Chapter 5) which consists of an equivalent heat source Q_{sc} and a self-admittance Y_{eq}, thereby eliminating all exterior nodes without discretizing the massive elements. The equivalent source Q_{sc} is equal to the wall transfer admittance times at external specified temperature. For the floor with self admittance Y_{fs} and transfer admittance Y_{ft} we have $Q_{sc} = -T_b Y_{ft}$ (the negative sign is because of the sign convention used).

The energy balance for the model (with summations ΣU_{ij} over $j = 1–8$) is as follows:

$$\begin{bmatrix} sC_a + \Sigma U1J + U_{inf} & -U12 & -U13 & -U14 & -U15 & -U16 & -U17 & -U18 \\ -U12 & Y_{2s} + \Sigma U2J & -U23 & -U24 & -U25 & -U26 & -U27 & -U28 \\ -U13 & -U23 & Y_{3s} + \Sigma U3J & -U34 & -U35 & -U36 & -U37 & -U38 \\ -U14 & -U24 & -U34 & Y_{4s} + \Sigma U4J & -U45 & -U46 & -U47 & -U48 \\ -U15 & -U25 & -U35 & -U45 & Y_{5s} + \Sigma U5J & -U56 & -U57 & -U58 \\ -U16 & -U26 & -U36 & -U46 & -U56 & Y_{6s} + \Sigma U6J & -U67 & -U68 \\ -U17 & -U27 & -U37 & -U47 & -U57 & -U67 & Y_{7s} + \Sigma U7J & -U78 \\ -U18 & -U28 & -U38 & -U48 & -U58 & -U68 & -U78 & Y_{8s} + \Sigma U8J \end{bmatrix} \begin{bmatrix} T1 \\ T2 \\ T3 \\ T4 \\ T5 \\ T6 \\ T7 \\ T8 \end{bmatrix} = \begin{bmatrix} Q1 \\ Q2 \\ Q3 \\ Q4 \\ Q5 \\ Q6 \\ Q7 \\ Q8 \end{bmatrix}$$

$$[Y]_{N \times N}\{T\}_N = \{Q\}_N \qquad (8.16)$$

The elements of the admittance matrix may be obtained by inspection from the topology of the network. The diagonal entry $Y(i,i)$ is equal to the sum of the component admittances connected to node i. Off-diagonal entry $Y(i,j)$ is the sum of component admittances/conductances connected between nodes i and j, multiplied by -1. The heat source vector element $Q(i)$ is the sum of the heat sources connected to node i (positive if directed to the node). As can be seen, for thermal networks the admittance matrix has certain important characteristics: (1) it is symmetric, with all off-diagonal elements $Y(i,j)$ being real, and equal to $-$(conductance U_{ij}); (2) all capacitances and all self-admittances appear in the diagonal entries which are consequently complex. Note that the diagonal element $Y(i,i)$ also contains the lumped capacitance for air C_a. The transfer functions of interest are the elements of the inverse of $[Y]$, that is the impedance transfer functions $Z(i,j)$. The temperature of node i for each frequency is given by:

$$T(I) = \sum_{j=1}^{8} Z(i,j)Q(j) \qquad (8.17)$$

The functions $Z(i,j)$ are determined at specific frequencies ($s = j\omega_n$) by inverting the admittance matrix $[Y]$. The operative temperature, T_e, is a scalar function of nodal temperatures $\{T(1)...T(8)\}$.

Operative temperature transfer functions, $X(i)$: the key to accurately determining the weighting factors for the individual surface temperatures in T_e is to utilize a detailed model for radiant exchanges and for T_{mr}, which is obtained through the appropriate radiative energy balances. In the derivation below, the sensor is assumed to sense the same operative temperature as a person. The long-wave radiant heat gain, q_s, sensed at a location in the room is given by

$$q_s = A_s\varepsilon_s \{[q^+_i F(s,i) +...+ q^+_I F(s,I)] - \sigma T_s^4\} \qquad (8.18)$$

where A_s is the effective sensing area, q^+ represents radiosity, $i = 1,...,I$ (surface number), and T_s is the temperature of the sensor (or object/person). The mean radiant temperature, T_{mr}, is defined by the equivalent energy balance:

$$q_s = A_s\varepsilon_s\sigma(T_{mr}^4 - T_s^4) \qquad (8.19)$$

For simplicity the sensor or person is assumed to be located in the centre of the room, and the view factors $F(s,i)$ between the sensor and surface i are approximated as equal to A_i/A_t (A_t = room area). If the effect of location within the room is to be studied the factors $F(s,i)$ must be calculated accurately. The surface radiosities, q^+_i, are given by the matrix equation (Edwards 1981):

$$\{q^+\} = [M]^{-1}\{q_e\} \qquad (8.20)$$

where $q_e(j) = \varepsilon_j T_j^4$.

Note that the inverse $[M]^{-1}$ is already obtained in evaluating the exchange factors F^*_{ij} (equation (8.15b)), so no new matrix inversion is required. The long-wave emissivities, ε_j, of the surfaces can usually be approximated as $\varepsilon = 0.9$. After substituting in equation (8.18) for q^+, then for $F(s,i)$ equal to A_i/A_t and linearizing the T^4 terms, q_s may be expressed with the following matrix equation:

$$q_s = A_s h_r[(\varepsilon/A_t)\{A\}'[M]^{-1}\{T\} - T_s] \qquad (8.21)$$

where $h_r = \varepsilon_s 4\sigma T_m^3$, and $\{A\}' = [A_1,...,A_i,.A_I]$ (transpose of the area vector).

After linearizing equation (8.19) and comparing it with equation (8.21) we may deduce that T_{mr} is given by

$$T_{mr} = \{D_{mr}\}'\{T\}$$

with row vector $\{D_{mr}\}'$ given by

$$\{D_{mr}\}' = (\varepsilon/A_t)\{A\}'[M]^{-1} \tag{8.22}$$

($' =$ transpose).

The transfer functions $X(i)$, which denote the effect of source elements $Q(i)$ on the operative temperature, will now be derived. First, rewrite equation (8.13) as a function of room interior temperatures in matrix form,

$$T_e = \{D\}'\{T\} \tag{8.23}$$

where $\{D\}' = [D(1),D(2),...D(8)]$, while $\{T\}$ is the room interior temperature vector. The weighting factors, $D(i)$, are given as follows. The weight, $D(1)$, for the room air temperature is equal to $h_c/(h_r + h_c)$, as can be seen from equations (8.13) and (8.23). The entries $D(2)...D(8)$ are equal to the relative weighting factors of the surface temperatures in the mean radiant temperature times the ratio $h_r/(h_r + h_c)$; they are therefore determined by multiplying vector $\{D_{mr}\}$ of equation (8.22) by $h_r/(h_r + h_c)$. Substituting for $\{T\}$ from equation (8.23) we may deduce that

$$T_e = \{D\}'[Y]^{-1}\{Q\} \tag{8.24}$$

Now define an adjoint vector $\{X\}$ by

$$\{X\}' = \{D\}'[Y]^{-1} \tag{8.25a}$$

Multiplying both sides of equation (8.25a) by $[Y]$, we obtain

$$\{X\}'[Y] = \{D\}' \tag{8.25b}$$

Now, taking the transpose of both sides of equation (8.25a),

$$[Y]'\{X\} = \{D\}$$

but $[Y]' = [Y]$, therefore,

$$[Y]\{X\} = \{D\} \tag{8.25c}$$

and

$$\{X\} = [Y]^{-1}\{D\} \tag{8.25d}$$

Since $\{D\}$ is a function of room geometry and surface properties only, it must be evaluated only once for a particular room. Further, since $[Y]$ is a function of room construction and frequency only, it has to be determined only once for each frequency. Thus, equation (8.25d) needs to be solved only once for each frequency to obtain the operative temperature transfer functions $\{X\}$.

8.2.2 Analysis of building transfer functions

Substantial insight into building thermal behaviour may be obtained by studying the magnitude and phase angle of the important transfer functions. Consider for example the transfer functions Z11 and Z17 in the detailed model which represent the effects of heat sources at node 1 (room air) and 7 (floor) respectively on the temperature of node 1:

$$Z11(s) = \frac{T1(s)}{Q1(s)}\bigg|_{\text{all other sources set to zero}} \tag{8.26a}$$

$$Z17(s) = \frac{T1(s)}{Q7(s)}\bigg|_{\text{all other sources set to zero}} \tag{8.26b}$$

where s is the Laplace domain variable.

The magnitude of $Z17(j\omega)$ may be used to determine the approximate room temperature swings due to solar radiation absorbed at the floor surface as follows.

If S_7 represents solar radiation absorbed at the floor interior surface and $|S_7(j\omega_1)|$ represents the magnitude of its fundamental harmonic, the approximate temperature swing amplitude is given by $|Z17(j\omega_1)| \times |S_7(j\omega_1)|$. Perhaps a more significant result is the time delay between the peak of $S(t)$ (noon for south-facing windows) and the resulting peak of the room temperature; this is approximately equal to φ_{17}/ω_1 (seconds) where φ_{17} is the phase angle of Z17 ($\varphi_{17} = \tan^{-1} \text{Im}(Z17)/\text{Re}(Z17)$).

Results. The room considered in the example is 7.3 m wide by 2.4 m high and the north–south depth is 6.7 m. The south-facing double-glazed window area is 11.1 m^2. The thermal mass is 4 cm thick concrete on the floor with thermal conductivity equal to 1.8 W/m^2 K, density 2242 kg/m^3 and specific heat capacity 840 J/kg K. The interior lining on vertical walls and on the ceiling is a 13 mm thick gypsum board. The insulation is 3.5 RSI on vertical walls, 7.4 RSI on the ceiling and 1 RSI on the floor, which connects to a basement.

Figure 8.3 depicts the magnitude and phase variation (Bode plots) for Z11 with a carpeted floor versus a concrete floor (4 cm thick). The magnitudes are non-dimensionalized by dividing by the steady-state ($\omega = 0$) values of the transfer functions. Examination of Figure 8.3 indicates that the room response can be approximately separated into a short-term dynamics high-frequency range and a low-frequency range. The separation between short-term and long-term building thermal dynamics begins at frequencies of approximately 35 cycles per day (cpd) or periods of 40 minutes. In the high-frequency, short-term dynamics region, the room's air thermal capacitance is significant and the difference between Z11 for the concrete floor and the carpeted one is small in both phase and magnitude: that is, the effect of thermal mass is minimal in this region. More extensive studies (Stylianou 1989) for different constructions have produced similar results for Z11 which represent the effects of convective heat gains or losses. Short-term dynamics are particularly important for feedback control studies. For lower frequencies such as one cycle per day the magnitude and phase of Z11 is a strong function of room construction.

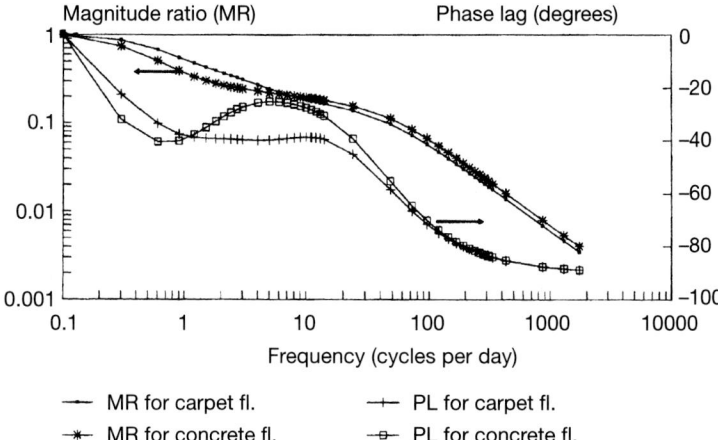

Figure 8.3 Magnitude and phase (Bode) plot of transfer function Z11 for a room with two different floor inner linings: 4-cm thick concrete; carpet. (Magnitudes are divided by Z11(*C*=0)

Examination of Figure 8.4 shows that for Z17, which represents the effect of radiant gains at the floor on room air temperature, there is no clear separation between short- and long-term dynamics. There is a significant difference between the response of the room with the carpeted floor and that with the concrete floor for all frequencies. The thermal lag time is significantly larger for the concrete floor. As expected, this indicates that feedback control of systems with high radiant loads or radiant heating systems is more complex due to the larger thermal lag times involved. Therefore, transfer functions such as Z17 need to be determined accurately for such applications.

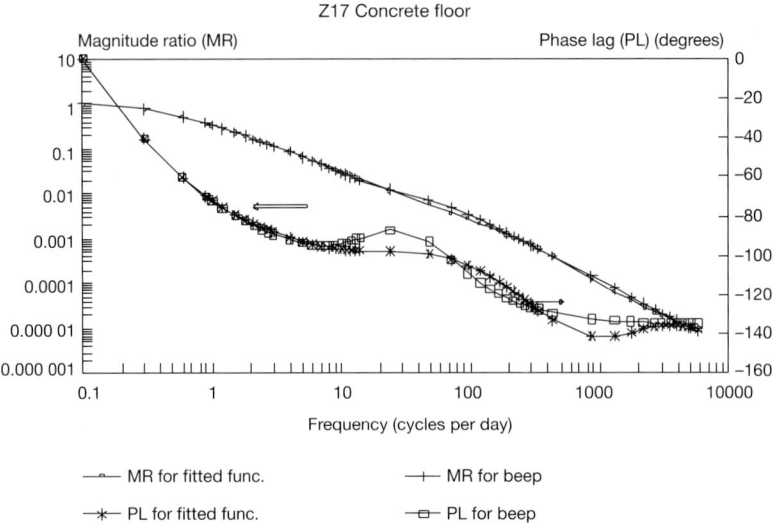

Figure 8.4 Exact discrete frequency responses and fitted third-order transfer function for Z17

8.2.3 Determination of s-transfer functions from discrete responses

The transfer functions in Figure 8.3 were obtained at the discrete frequencies shown through inversion of the admittance matrix [Y] defined by equation (8.16). The objective now is to synthesize transfer functions $Z_f(s)$ as ratios of complex polynomials $N(s)/D(s)$ from the discrete frequency response data. They are determined as a continuous function of s by performing a least-squares complex interpolation on the discrete values by means of a technique developed by Levy (1959), appropriately modified for the present application. The method is briefly described next. Let $Z(j\omega)$ be the actual discrete frequency responses (generated by BEEP, Building Energy and Enviroment Program) which may be represented by the sum of its real and imaginary parts:

$$Z(j\omega) = R(\omega) + jI(\omega) \tag{8.27a}$$

The fitted polynomial function $Z_f(s) = N(s)/D(s)$ may be expressed at the given frequencies as:

$$Z_f(j\omega) = \frac{A_0 + A_1(j\omega) + A_2(j\omega)^2 + \cdots + A_m(j\omega)^m}{B_0 + B_1(j\omega) + \cdots + B_n(j\omega)^n} \tag{8.27b}$$

Examination of equation (8.27a) reveals that $A_0 = Z(\omega = 0)$ and $B_0 = 1$. Because the steady-state value of Z, that is $Z(\omega = 0)$, is known, A_0 does not need to be evaluated. Separating the numerator and denominator into real and imaginary parts and using a least-squares technique (Athienitis *et al.* 1990), we may obtain a satisfactory third-order transfer function for Z11 and Z17.

Typical results obtained with the technique are given in Figure 8.4 for Z17 which shows both magnitude and phase variation of the fitted and exact transfer functions over the frequencies of interest, and the magnitudes are non-dimensionalized by dividing by the steady-state ($\omega = 0$) values of the transfer functions. The resulting magnitude ratio was determined with an accuracy of 1%.

8.2.4 Thermal control studies

The building, HVAC system and control transfer functions are combined through block diagram algebra to obtain the overall system s-transfer functions. These transfer functions are then studied in the frequency domain ($s = j\omega$) for stability and other analyses or are used for transient analysis of overall system response to setpoint and load variations using numerical inversion of Laplace transforms. This technique is described and illustrated through examples in the next section.

Consider a room with convective heating, simple feedback control and N input-loads $Q(J)$ influencing room temperature $T(1)$ (also denoted T_{ai}) through transfer functions $Z(I,J)$ (see Figure 8.5) or $X(J)$ if we employ a sensor which detects operative temperature – the ideal variable to control. The resulting room air temperature variation as a function of setpoint and load changes is then obtained through block diagram algebra as

$$T_{ai}(s) = T_{sp}\frac{G_f G_c G_p Z11}{1 + G_f G_c G_p Z11\, G_s} + \sum_{J=1}^{N}\left\{Q(J)\frac{Z(I,J)}{1 + G_f G_c G_p Z11\, G_s}\right\} \qquad (8.28)$$

where T_{sp} is the setpoint and G_f, G_c, G_p (equal to $G_{p1} \times G_{p2}$) and G_s are the transfer functions of the final control element, controller, heating system, and sensor respectively. All variables are a function of s. $G_f G_c G_p Z11 G_s$ is the loop transfer function that may be used for stability analysis using the Nyquist criterion or the Bode criterion (Stephanopoulos 1984). For example, the Bode criterion may be used to determine the period and gain at the stability limit, known as the ultimate period and ultimate gain K_u respectively, at which the phase angle of the loop transfer function (for proportional control) is equal to 180°. The selection of the actual gain is then based on various tuning techniques such as the Ziegler–Nichols method (1942). Normally tuning is performed on site for HVAC systems because the system parameters are usually not accurately known; self-tuning adaptive algorithms may also be used. However, the analysis is useful for comparison of

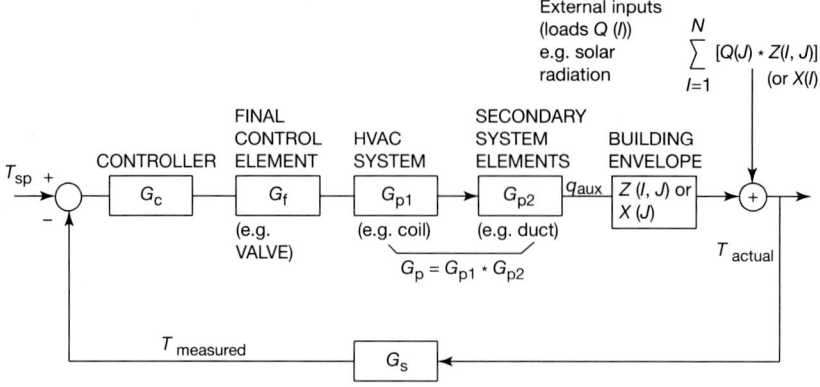

NOTE: 1. External load $Q(J)$ acts at node J and affects room
air temperature through transfer function $Z(1,l)$, or
operative temperature T_e through transfer function $X(J)$.
2. In some systems (e.g. electric home heating systems) the
transfer functions G_{p1} and G_{p2} may be expressed as one
combined heating system transfer function Gp for convenient
analysis.
3. The auxiliary heating/cooling q_{aux} is equivalent to a source
$Q(J)$ applied at node J ($J=1$ for convective systems:– $T(1)$ =
room air temperature; $J=4$ for ceiling heating; – $T(4)$=
ceiling temp.; $J=7$ for floor heating; – $T(7)$ = floor temp.)

Figure 8.5 Block diagram for thermal control analysis

alternative control algorithms, the effects of sensors with different time constants, and of system parameters such as coil time constant and amount of thermal mass. After the control parameters are determined for the cases of interest, the system transient response to setpoint and load changes can be investigated using numerical inversion of Laplace transforms. Such studies also greatly assist the on-site tuning process.

For radiant heating analysis the transfer function Z11 in the first term of equation (8.28) is replaced by Z1j, where j is equal to the node number corresponding to the heated surface (in the model shown in Figure 8.2(b), j = 4 for ceiling heating). Moreover, the controlled temperature may not be the air temperature, but another temperature such as the operative temperature. In such a case the operative temperature transfer functions $X(I)$ are used instead of $Z(I,J)$ in equation (8.28).

8.2.5 Transient simulation with numerical inverse Laplace transforms

Different numerical methods for Laplace transform inversion are available, but in general, they require the determination of poles and residues which might be computationally prohibitive if multiple poles occur. The method employed for numerical inversion of Laplace transforms such as $T_{ai}(s)$ given by equation (8.28) has been developed and applied to circuits by Vlach (1969) and Vlach and Singal (1983). This method provides an efficient way to calculate the time response of systems without determining poles or residues; that is, transfer functions that are transcendental and time delays may be included in the system. This permits the use of transfer functions for the building envelope which model the thermal mass as distributed elements. For numerical inversion, s is set equal to z_i/t, where t is the time and z_i are constants determined once and for all by Vlach and Singhal (1983) (Table 8.2). Thus, the overall closed-loop transfer functions, such as those defined by equation (8.24), do not need to be evaluated analytically but only at the selected time steps; for example, $s = z_i/t$ for one time step and $s = z_i/(t + dt)$ for the next. Thus the method can be easily incorporated in programs dealing with frequency response analysis of systems. Note that also for frequency domain studies loop transfer functions need only be evaluated at specific frequencies using complex algebra. Table 8.2 summarizes the numerical inversion of the Laplace domain response of T_{ai}.

Representative studies of room temperature response to step increases in heat gains will now be described (Figures 8.6 and 8.7) for the two different constructions in Figure 8.3, which represent different amounts of thermal mass. Figure 8.6 illustrates the effect of a radiative step heat input (1 kW) for the carpeted floor and for the concrete floor. It is determined by the inverse Laplace transform (ILT) of a step input times the relevant transfer function, i.e.

$$\text{Change of } T_{ai}(t) = \text{ILT}\{T_{ai}(s)\}$$

where

$$T_{ai}(s) = 1000/(sZ17_f(s))$$

Figure 8.6 also shows the analytical result (denoted ANL), and excellent agreement is indicated. Figures 8.5–8.7 also show the equivalent first-order time constants obtained from the transient response as the time by which the temperature reaches 63% of its steady state value. As expected, because of its higher thermal mass, a concrete floor takes longer to reach steady state than a carpeted floor (10.75 versus 5.5 hours) and results in a lower temperature rise due to its larger thermal resistance. Thus, for radiative loads the effect of thermal mass on room temperature response is higher than for convective loads, and longer times are

Table 8.2 Numerical inversion of Laplace domain response (z are poles and K' residues)

$z_1 \equiv 11.830\ 093\ 739\ 168\ 19 + 1.593\ 753\ 005\ 885\ 813\text{j}$	$z_2 \equiv 11.220\ 853\ 779\ 395\ 19 + 4.792\ 964\ 167\ 565\ 670\text{j}$
$z_3 \equiv 9.933\ 383\ 722\ 175\ 002 + 8.033\ 106\ 334\ 266\ 296\text{j}$	$z_4 \equiv 7.781\ 146\ 264\ 464\ 616 + 11.368\ 891\ 649\ 049\ 93\text{j}$
$z_5 \equiv 4.234\ 522\ 494\ 797\ 000 + 14.957\ 043\ 781\ 281\ 56\text{j}$	$K'_1 \equiv 16\ 286.623\ 680\ 504\ 79 - 139\ 074.711\ 551\ 605\ 1\text{j}$
$K'_2 \equiv -28\ 178.111\ 713\ 051\ 63 + 74\ 357.582\ 372\ 741\ 76\text{j}$	$K'_3 \equiv 14\ 629.740\ 252\ 331\ 42 - 19\ 181.808\ 185\ 018\ 36\text{j}$
$K'_4 \equiv -2870.418\ 161\ 032\ 078 + 1674.109\ 484\ 084\ 304\text{j}$	$K'_5 \equiv 132.165\ 941\ 247\ 487\ 6 + 17.476\ 747\ 988\ 771\ 64\text{j}$

$$p = 1, 2..80 \qquad \Delta t = 30\ \text{s} \qquad t_p = p\Delta t \qquad \text{time array} \qquad s_{i,p} = \frac{z_i}{t_p}$$

The Laplace transfer function to be inverted is $\qquad V_{i,p} = T_{ai}\left(s_{i,p}\right)$

with initial condition: $\qquad T_{ai_0} = 0°C$

The time domain response is given by: $\qquad T_{ai_p} = \frac{1}{-t_p}\left[\sum_i \text{Re}\left(K'_i V_{i,p}\right)\right]$

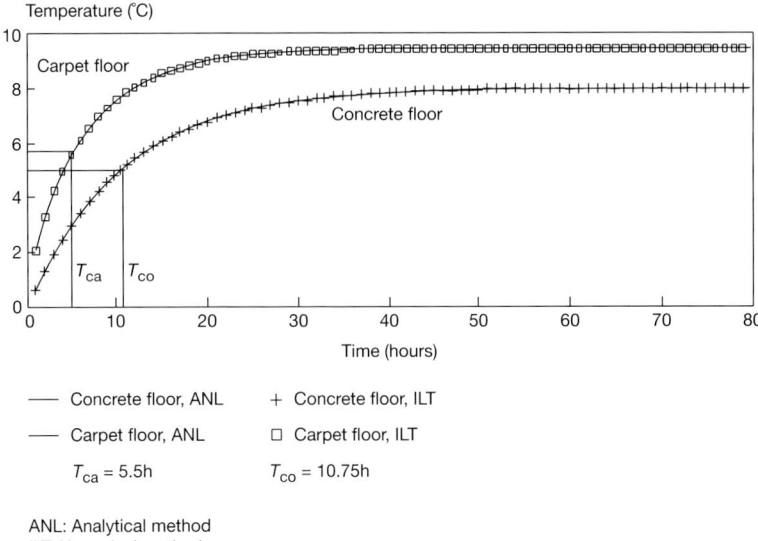

Temperature (°C)

Carpet floor

Concrete floor

T_{ca} T_{co}

Time (hours)

—— Concrete floor, ANL   + Concrete floor, ILT

—— Carpet floor, ANL   □ Carpet floor, ILT

T_{ca} = 5.5h T_{co} = 10.75h

ANL: Analytical method
ILT: Numerical method

Figure 8.6 Room temperature response (change) to step input of convective heat gains (1 kW) for carpet floor and for concrete floor (4 cm) (ANL analytical, ILT numerical inverse Laplace transform)

required to achieve steady state. The effect of thermal mass thickness on room temperature response to radiative loads is shown in Figure 8.7; for 4 cm thick concrete floor lining the time constant is 10.8 hours, while for 6 cm thick concrete it is 14.5 hours.

The transfer functions describing the HVAC system components as well as the transfer functions describing the room model can easily be used to study their frequency responses by simply substituting s with $j\omega$ and can be combined to produce the system's overall transfer function if needed, or can be studied individually or in subsystems in both the frequency and time domain.

This method does not require discretization of distributed elements such as a massive floor slab and also allows the use of dead times (time lags) without any artificial manipulation of the constants present, as is required if other numerical methods are used (Clark 1985). Further, it can be readily incorporated within a program for frequency response analysis because the transfer functions are already determined as functions of s (= $j\omega$).

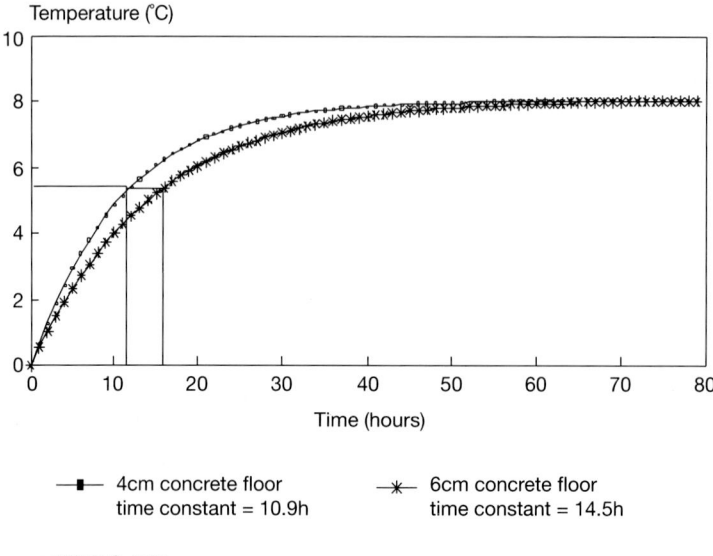

Figure 8.7 Effect of floor thermal mass (concrete) thickness on room temperature response to input of radiative gains (1 kW) at the floor surface (node 7)

8.2.6 Heating/cooling load and room temperature calculation

Heating/cooling load and associated room temperature calculations are performed with the same building transfer functions employed in frequency response and thermal control studies. These computations are performed by means of discrete Fourier series. The building transfer functions are calculated at discrete frequencies ($s = j\omega_n$) and a discrete Fourier transform (DFT) of the weather data is performed. The frequency domain response is then evaluated through complex algebra and the time domain load or room temperature variation is subsequently obtained through an inverse DFT as follows.

In frequency domain simulation periodic conditions are usually assumed; for example, if the simulation is to be performed for a week, it is assumed that all previous weeks have been the same. The steps needed for a periodic steady-state solution are as follows:

- Decide the number N of harmonics to be analysed for. If n represents a harmonic number and P is the time length of the simulation or analysis (e.g. a day or a week), then a harmonic's frequency ω_n is equal to $2\pi n/P$.
- Obtain the appropriate discrete Fourier series representations for the sources. An arbitrary source $M(t)$ is represented by a Fourier series (IDFT) of the form

$$M(t) = \sum_{n=-N}^{N} m_n(j\omega)\exp(j\omega_n t) \tag{8.29a}$$

the complex coefficients $m_n(j\omega_n)$ being determined numerically by a DFT

$$m_n = \left[\sum_{k=1}^{K} M(t_k)\exp(-j\omega_n t_k)\right] / P \tag{8.29b}$$

where $M(t_k)$ is the value of M at time t_k corresponding to point k (for a total of K values over the time length P).

- Determine the discrete frequency response $Z(j\omega_n)$ of the output of interest to unit input at each node. The periodic response to each source is obtained by superposition of the output harmonics using complex (phasor) multiplication. For example, for an output temperature $T(t)$, we have

$$T(t) = \sum_{n=-N}^{N} Z(j\omega_n)m_n(j\omega_n)\exp(j\omega_n t) \tag{8.29c}$$

The total response to more than one input is determined by a double summation for all inputs $Q(i)$ and all frequencies of interest ω_n.
For example, for convective auxiliary heating we have

$$Q(1) = q_{aux} + q_{int} + q_{eq} \tag{8.29d}$$

where q_{int} represents the convective portion of internal gains and q_{eq} is an equivalent source representing heat flow due to infiltration and is given by $U_{inf}T_o$. Therefore, by substituting equation (8.29d) in (8.16) and assuming that the room air temperature $T(1)$ is specified, we may determine the auxiliary heating/cooling power q_{aux} at each frequency of interest as:

$$q_{aux}(j\omega) = \left\{ T(1) - Z(1,1)[q_{int} + U_{inf}T_o] - \sum_{j=2}^{N} Z(I,J)Q(J) \right\} / Z(1,1) \tag{8.30}$$

where all quantities are evaluated as complex numbers for $s = j\omega$ (N = number of nodes). Each source or specified temperature is represented by a discrete Fourier series (DFT) and the time domain variation of q_{aux} is obtained through an IDFT. For design day analysis 5–9 harmonics are usually adequate. These are the harmonics necessary for adequate representation of the inputs, that is, heat sources such as absorbed solar radiation, internal gains and ambient temperature T_o. One advantage of this approach over more commonly used methods is that the superposition principle is applied directly. Therefore, effects of various inputs may be studied separately, or a passive analysis ($q_{aux} = 0$) can be easily performed – in this case equation (8.29d) is directly applied. Note that the air temperature $T(1)$ in equation (8.30) can be a profile, that is, it may vary with time. Thus, optimum setpoint profile variations may be determined. The discrete Fourier series approach is described in more detail by Athienitis *et al.* (1987), including a model for a proportional control source in the thermal network and a technique for modelling time-varying parameters, such as a conductance representing infiltration based on the substitution network theorem.

8.3 Bibliography

ASHRAE (1989) *Ventilation for Acceptable Indoor Air Quality*. Standard 62-1989. ASHRAE, Atlanta, Georgia.

ASHRAE (1992) *Thermal Environmental Conditions for Human Occupancy*. Standard 55-1992, ASHRAE, Atlanta, Georgia.

ASHRAE (1995) *ASHRAE Handbook – Systems*, Atlanta, Georgia.

ASHRAE (1997) *ASHRAE Handbook – Fundamentals*, ASHRAE, Atlanta, Georgia.

Athienitis A.K. (1988) 'A predictive control algorithm for massive buildings', *ASHRAE Transactions*, **94**:2, 1050–1068.

Athienitis A.K. and Haghighat F. (1992) 'A study of the effects of solar radiation on the indoor environment', *ASHRAE Transactions*, **98**:1, 257–261.

Athienitis A.K., Sullivan H.F. and Hollands K.G.T. (1986) 'Analytical model, sensitivity analysis and algorithm for temperature swings in direct gain rooms', *Solar Energy*, **36**:4, 303–312.

Athienitis A.K., Sullivan H.F. and Hollands K.G.T. (1987) 'Discrete Fourier series models for building auxiliary energy loads based on network formulation techniques', *Solar Energy*, **39**:3, 203–210.

Athienitis A.K., Stylianou M. and Shou J. (1990) 'A methodology for building thermal dynamics studies and control applications', *ASHRAE Transactions*, **96**:2, 839–848.

Bhargava S.C., McQuiston F.C. and Zirkle L.D. (1975) 'Transfer functions for crossflow multirow heat exchangers', *ASHRAE Transactions*, **81**:2, 294–314.

Borresen B.A. (1981) 'Thermal room models for control analysis,' *ASHRAE Transactions*, **87**:2, 251–261.

Brandt S.G. (1986) 'Adaptive control implentation issues', *ASHRAE Transactions*, **92**:2, 211–219.

CIBSE (1986) *CIBSE Guide*, Volume A, CIBSE, London.

Clapp M.D. (1985) 'Cost savings using building management and control systems', *Proc. CLIMA 2000*, Vol. 3, Copenhagen, Denmark, pp. 33–36.

Clark D.R. (1985) *HVACSIM+ Building Systems and Equipment Simulation Program Reference Manual*, National Information Service, NBSIR 84-2996.

Edwards D.K. (1981) *Radiation Heat Transfer Notes*, Hemisphere Pub. Corp.

Fanger P.O. (1970) *Thermal Comfort*, McGraw-Hill, New York.

Fisk D.J. (1981) *Thermal Control of Buildings*, Applied Science Publishers, London.

Gagge A.P., Nishi Y. and Gonzalez R.R. (1973) 'Standard effective temperature – a single index of temperature sensation and thermal discomfort', Thermal comfort and moderate heat stress, Proceedings of the CIB Commission W45 (human requirements) Symposium held at the Building Research Station, London.

Gianccone A. and Gianfranco R. (1986) 'The influence of solar radiation distribution in a room on thermal comfort evaluation', *Proc. CIB*, 3185–3192.

Hartman T.B. (1988) 'Dynamic control: fundamentals and considerations', *ASHRAE Transactions*, **94**:1 599–609.

Hirsch J. (1985) 'Plan for the development of the next generation of building energy analysis computer software', *Proceedings of the Building Energy Simulation Conference*, Seattle, Washington, August, pp. 396–404.

ISO 7730 (1984) *Moderate Thermal Environments. Determination of the PMV and PPD Indices and Specifications of the Conditions for Thermal Comfort*. Geneva.

Kimura K. (1977) *Scientific Basis for Air-conditioning*, Applied Science Publishers, London.

Kelly G.E. (1988) 'Control system simulation in North America', *Energy and Buildings*, **10**, 193–202.

Levy E.C. (1959) 'Complex curve fitting', *IRE Transactions on Automatic Control*, May, 37–43.

Mathews E.H. and Richards P.G. (1989) 'A tool for predicting hourly air temperature and sensible energy loads in buildings at sketch design stage', *Energy and Buildings*, **14**, 61–80.

Olesen B.W., Rosendahl J., Kalisperis L.N., Summers L.H. and Steinman M. (1989) 'Methods for measuring and evaluating the thermal radiation in a room', *ASHRAE Transactions*, **95**:1, Paper no. CH-89-17-4.

Omega Engineering (1987) *Temperature Measurement Handbook*, Omega Engineering, Stanford, Connecticut.

Park C., Bushby S.T. and Kelly G.E. (1989) 'Simulation of a large office building system using the HVACSIM$^+$ program', *ASHRAE Transactions*, **95**:1, 642–651.

Park C., Clark D.R. and Kelly G.E. (1985) 'An overview of HVACSIM$^+$, a dynamic building/HVAC/control systems simulation program', *Proceedings of the Building Energy Simulation Conference*, pp. 175–185.

Shavit, G. and Brandt S.G. (1982) 'The dynamic performance of a discharge air-temperature system with a P-I controller', *ASHRAE Transactions*, **88**, 826–838.

Singhal K. and Vlach J. (1975) 'Computation of time domain response by numerical inversion of the Laplace transform', *Journal of the Franklin Institute*, **299**, 109–126.

Stephanopoulos G. (1984) *Chemical Process Control, An Introduction to Theory and Practice*, Prentice-Hall, Englewood Cliffs, New Jersey.

Stoecker W.F. *et al.* (1981) 'Reducing the peaks of internal air-conditioning loads by use of temperature swings', *ASHRAE Transactions*, **87**:2, 599–608.

Stylianou M. (1989) 'A computer method for building–HVAC system interaction and control applications', M.Eng. thesis, Centre for Building Studies, Concordia University, Montreal, Canada.

Thompson J.G. (1981) 'The effect of room and control systems dynamics on energy consumption', *ASHRAE Transactions*, **87**:2, 883–896.

Tobias J.R. (1973) 'Simplified transfer function for temperature response of fluids flowing through coils, pipes or ducts', *ASHRAE Transactions*, **79**:2, 19–22.

Vlach J. (1969) 'Numerical method for transient responses of linear networks with lumped, distributed or mixed parameters', *Journal of the Franklin Institute*, **288**, 99–113.

Vlach J. and Singhal K. (1983) *Computer Methods for Circuit Analysis and Design*, Van Nostrand Reinhold Co., New York.

Zhang, X. and Warren, M.L. (1988) 'Use of a general control simulation program' *ASHRAE Transactions*, **94**, Part 1, 1776–1791.

Ziegler J.G. and Nichols N.B. (1942) 'Optimal settings for automatic controllers', *ASME Transactions*, **64**, 759–765.

CHAPTER 9

Solar energy utilization techniques and systems

Several key modelling issues have been discussed in previous chapters concerning thermal analysis of solar buildings. This final chapter considers several integrative applications. Thermal analysis of a building with transparent insulation is presented in Section 9.1, followed by analysis of a solar building with phase-change thermal storage in Section 9.2. Section 9.3 describes a simple solarium model, Section 9.4 covers photovoltaic systems for buildings and Section 9.5 gives a description of recent advanced fenestration system applications.

9.1 Numerical model of a building with transparent insulation

9.1.1 Introduction

Transparent insulation (TI) used to replace conventional insulation in a solar collector wall has been proven to have a significant potential to reduce heating load in passive solar buildings (Twidell *et al.* 1994). Transparent insulation converts one or more walls of the building into solar collectors. Initially, a single glazing was used as the transparent cover of a wall. This was known as a Trombe wall system (Trombe *et al.* 1977). Cellular transparent materials were introduced to improve the solar transmittance and thermal resistance of the wall system (Olsen 1982, Goetzberger *et al.* 1983) after being applied to solar collectors (Francia 1961, Hollands 1965). These materials enhance thermal resistance, in addition to having high solar transmittance. Other types of TI are in use in the industry such as capillary glasses and aerogels. TI classes have been reviewed by Platzer (1994).

Use of TI with an appropriate amount of thermal storage achieves high solar energy utilization, especially for south-facing surfaces in winter. However, if too much solar radiation is absorbed, or if the thermal storage is inadequate, over-heating problems will be experienced. There also several issues that need to be addressed during the design of a building with transparent insulation:

- The transparent insulation system should ideally be designed to satisfy the heating requirements on cold winter sunny days with solar energy, requiring practically no auxiliary heating.
- When more solar radiation is available than necessary it should be excluded through active means such as integrated motor-controlled blinds, or passive means such as thermotropic layers which change transmittance based on temperature (Georg *et al.* 1998).
- Appropriate design and control criteria need to be developed for the shading device to prevent overheating.
- While room air may not overheat, the room surface of the TI wall may exceed 30°C; this should be prevented by including an adequate amount of thermal storage mass and/or transporting some of the stored energy through forced or natural convection into the room.

The thermal lag effect in a building with a transparently insulated wall is more pronounced than in an ordinary building (Athienitis 1994, Ramadan and Athienitis 1998). The transfer admittance of a layer of concrete 20 cm thick, as considered in the TI wall of this section, introduces a time lag of about 5 hours in the room temperature rise; a further 3–5 hours is introduced by the rest of the room. Therefore, the maximum room temperature occurs between 8 p.m. and 11 p.m. Thus, it is necessary to determine the thermal response of a building with TI as a system. The fourth issue, while particularly important for practical implementation of TI into building systems, has not received much attention until now. It is considered in detail in this section. A thermal analysis simulation model of a building with one transparently insulated wall is described. It is employed to provide insight into issues of thermal comfort and energy conservation for a transparently insulated building during the design phase and to determine the effectiveness of various control strategies.

9.1.2 Transparent insulation system

A single zone building with a south-facing transparently insulated wall is modelled. The transparently insulated wall system, shown in Figure 9.1 (also considered in detail in Chapter 3), consists of an exterior single glazing protector, an air cavity, a transparent lexan honeycomb, a second air cavity, a concrete thermal storage layer, a third air cavity and an interior gypsum board layer.

The plastic transparent honeycomb material is assumed to be square cell. The cross-sectional area of the cell is determined to suppress convective heat transfer which may occur between the protector and the absorber prior to the introduction of the TI (Hollands *et al.* 1976). The aspect ratio of the cell, which is defined as the thickness of TI divided by the hydraulic diameter of the cell, must be high to reduce the conductive (air conduction) and radiative heat transfer of the TI layer (Tabor 1969). In addition, the thickness of the honeycomb wall material should be low to reduce the conductivity of the TI material (about 50 µm). However, with these thin materials, the aspect ratio is restricted to a value of around 5.

The *U*-value of the TI is assumed to be constant. For an inclined honeycomb layer, the dimensions of the cell may be calculated using the following equation (Hollands 1976):

$$A = f(\beta)(\text{Ra}/2420)^{1/4} \tag{9.1}$$

with

$$f(\beta) = [4.45\cos(\beta - 60)]^{1/(11.52 - 6.56\sin\beta)}$$

for inclination angles 30–90° where A is the area of the honeycomb cell, β is the angle of inclination and Ra is the Rayleigh number (Holman 1986).

The thickness of the TI is chosen to preserve the high aspect ratio for the honeycomb cell to reduce radiative and conductive heat transfer. However, the material cost and transmission capability for thin honeycomb sheets restrict the value of the aspect ratio to about 5.

The air gap between the protector and the TI unit permits the use of a roller blind with low-emissivity reflective coatings; the blind enhances the thermal performance of the TI wall and excludes solar gains that would cause room overheating and discomfort. This is used to prevent overheating during days with excessive solar radiation. On winter nights the blind covers the facade to reduce

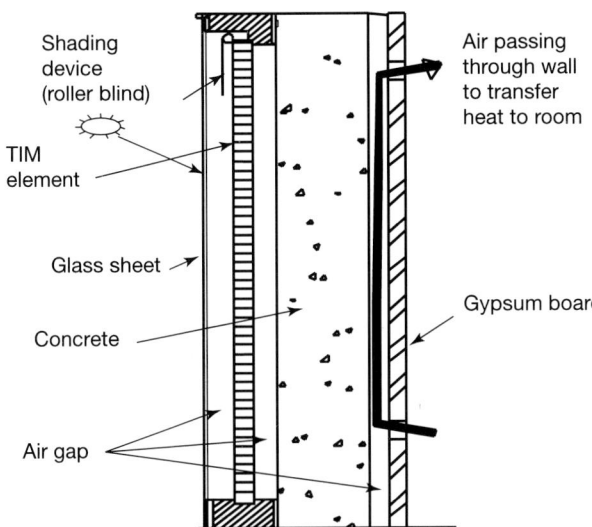

Figure 9.1 Cross-section of transparent insulation system and wall also showing how circulation can enhance heat transfer to room

long-wave radiation losses. However, the shading device is opened during summer nights to contribute to the reduction of the cooling load. The second air gap between the TI unit and the thermal mass decouples the radiative and conductive heat transfer of the transparent material. This air gap reduces the thermal conductance of the TI wall, especially when selective coatings cover the concrete layer (Hollands and Iyankaran 1985).

A third air gap is employed between the concrete thermal mass and the interior gypsum board layer. In addition to increasing the overall thermal resistance of the TI wall system, it prevents the inside surface temperature of the wall from rising too much and provides space for electrical wiring and other services. Thus, during clear winter days, the third air gap will aid in maintaining the inside wall temperature around comfort level. This space may also be coupled with room air and forced or natural ventilation may be employed to transfer some of the stored energy into the room air, thus preventing local overheating of the TI wall room surface, and improving utilization of solar gains. Forced convective heat transfer from the third air gap into the room is considered here.

The heat transfer through the air gaps is calculated as the combination of convective and radiative heat transfer based on relationships given by Elsherbiny *et al.* (1982).

The lexan transparent insulation used in the numerical simulations is square-celled honeycomb 48 mm wide with cell size 9.5 mm and wall thickness 0.076 mm. Various theoretical studies on the computation of solar transmittance of honeycomb transparent insulation used the Monte Carlo ray tracing technique. However, the complexity of this method has reduced its use. Hollands *et al.* (1978) has developed a simple approximate method to predict the incidence angle-dependent beam transmittance of honeycombs. This method considers refraction, scattering and absorption of radiation by the honeycomb walls. The sky and ground

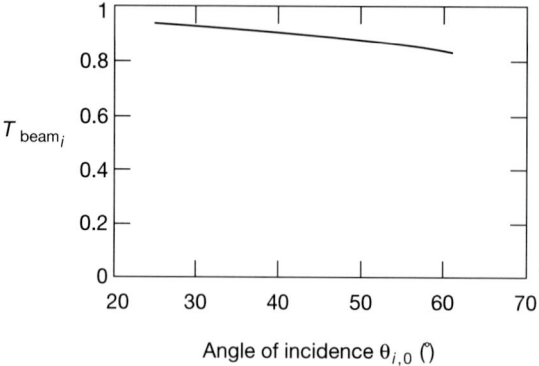

Figure 9.2 Beam transmittance of lexan honeycomb TI as a function of angle of incidence

diffuse solar transmittance of the TI is calculated as the transmittance for beam radiation at an equivalent incidence angle (Arulanantham and Kauskika 1994).

The solar diffuse radiation is assumed to be isotropic. Hence, the diffuse transmittance can be approximated as the transmittance of the same transparent material for beam radiation at an equivalent incidence angle. The diffuse transmittance is expressed in terms of sky and ground diffuse radiation (Brandemuehl and Beckman 1980). The incidence angle-dependent solar transmittance of the transparent honeycomb material is considered here based on these techniques. As can be seen from Figure 9.2, the beam transmittance is relatively high for most important incidence angles during the heating season. Figure 9.3 shows the total solar radiation transmitted through the TI system on a clear January day in Montreal. Hottel's clear sky model was employed (Hottel 1976).

The free convection heat transfer across a honeycomb can be characterized by a Nusselt number, Nu, which represents the ratio of the combined conductive and free convective heat transfer through the air to the corresponding heat transfer when the air is stagnant (Holman 1986). Hence, a Nusselt number of unity indicates conductive heat transfer and complete suppression of convective motion. On the other hand, as observed by Charters and Peterson (1972) through flow visualization tests, there is never a complete suppression of convection motion for an inclined cell. Thus, the Nusselt number is never exactly unity even at very small Raleigh number (Ra). However, the Nusselt number increases rather slowly with Ra until it reaches approximately 1.2, after which it rises rather steeply with Ra (Cane et al. 1977). Consequently, when $Nu = 1.2$ is reached, effective suppression is assumed to have taken place with purely conductive heat transfer of still air augmented by 20%.

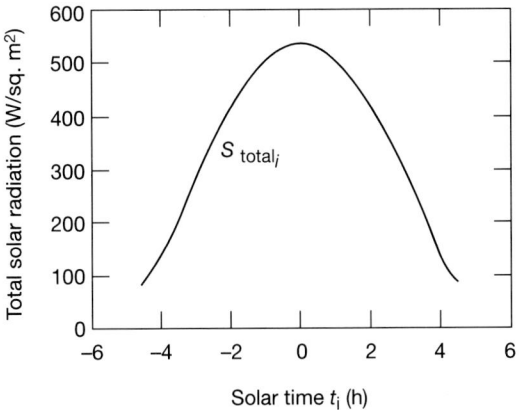

Figure 9.3 Total solar radiation transmitted through the transparent insulation system

Cane *et al.* (1977) reported an extensive experimental study on free convection across inclined square and hexagonal celled plastic honeycomb. They recommend the following relationship for Nusselt number:

$$Nu = 1 + 0.89\cos(\beta - 60)(Ra/2420A_{hc}{}^4)^{2.88 - 1.64\sin\beta} \qquad (9.2)$$

where β is the tilt angle (angle of inclination for honeycomb panel in degrees) and A_{hc} is the aspect ratio of the cell. This relation is valid when $30° \leq \beta \leq 90°$ and $Ra/A_{hc}{}^4 \leq 6000$.

Although based on data for $A_{hc} \geq 4$, this relation is approximately valid for $A_{hc} = 3$ as well (Cane *et al.* 1977).

9.1.3 Simulation model

A numerical simulation model is presented in this section. The thermal performance of a test-room (dimensions $3 \times 3 \times 3$ m³) with a south-facing transparently insulated wall is examined under different control strategies. The total thermal resistance of the walls is assumed to be 3.2 m²/W K. The thermal mass in the TI wall is 20 cm of concrete. There is also 5 cm of concrete on the floor (top layer) and gypsum board on all vertical walls. The east wall has a double-glazed window with area equal to 2 m². The thermal behaviour of the room is simulated to evaluate whether any auxiliary heating is required for cold sunny days under different control strategies based on thermal comfort considerations. A cloudy day is also considered to evaluate the potential solar savings by comparison with a sunny day having the same mean temperature.

The explicit finite difference method is employed to solve the differential equation of heat transfer through the TI wall and between the other room components (walls, ceiling, floor and window). The thermal network of the TI wall and room is shown in Figure 9.4. The thermal mass (concrete layer) is discretized into five sublayers (control volumes); more layers did not significantly improve accuracy.

One thermal capacitance represents the thermal storage capacity of each wall interior layer. Using the explicit form of the finite difference approximation, an energy balance equation is applied for each node i as follows:

$$T(i,p+1) = \left(\frac{\Delta t}{C_i}\right)\left(q_i + \sum_j \frac{T(j,p) - T(i,p)}{R(i,j)}\right) + T(i,p) \qquad (9.3)$$

where j represents all nodes connected to node i, q_i represents all heat sources at node i, p is the time interval and Δt is the time step, C_i is the thermal capacitance for node i and $R(i,j)$ is the conductive, radiative or convective thermal resistance between nodes i and j. An auxiliary heating system with proportional control is utilized and the room air temperature is permitted to fluctuate between 18°C and 24°C (up to 25°C is allowed).

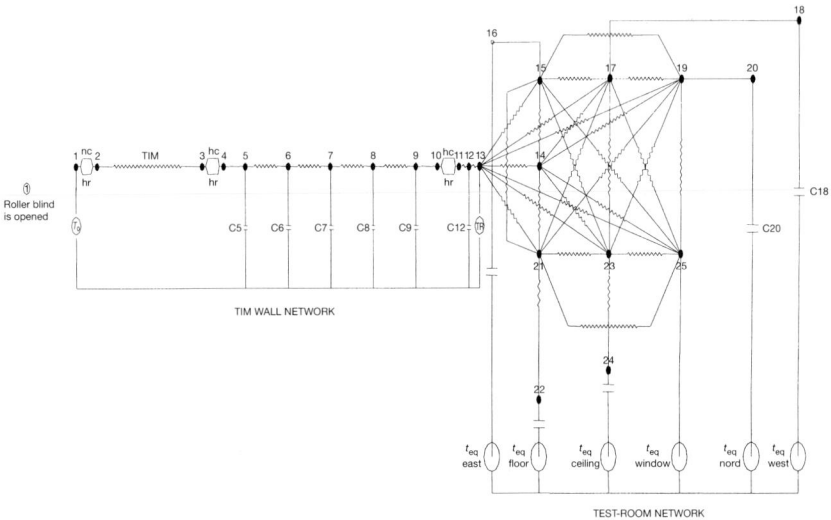

Figure 9.4 Thermal network of TI wall and room (node 14 is room air)

The TI wall is connected between nodes 1 (outside temperature) and 13 (inside surface of gypsum board). Node 14 represents room air, while nodes 15, 17, 19, 21, 23 and 25 represent the other room interior surfaces. Walls are connected to each other by surface nodes through a thermal radiative resistance and to the zone air node by a convective resistance. Both types of resistance are accurately calculated for each time step. Convective coefficients are calculated at each time step based on the following correlations recommended by ASHRAE (1989).

For horizontal air layer and upward flow (T_s = surface temperature):

$$h = 1.52(T_s - T_{air})^{1/3}$$

For horizontal air layer and upward flow (X = characteristic length):

$$h = 0.59[(T_s - T_{air})/X]^{1/4}$$

$$h = 1.31(T_s - T_{air})^{1/3} \tag{9.4}$$

The radiant exchange between the interior surfaces (assumed to be grey) may be calculated as follows (Holman 1986):

$$q_{i,j} = A_i F_{i,j} \sigma(T_i^4 - T_j^4) \tag{9.5}$$

where $F_{i,j}$ is the radiation exchange factor. (This factor includes the view factor and surface resistance of thermal radiation flow.)

The program developed accurately models the solar radiation on each face of the building. However, it does not model the actual distribution of the incoming solar radiation through the window to the interior surface of the zone. Instead, this distribution is approximated to be 70% for the floor and 30% for the other room surfaces.

Discretization or stability error results from the replacement of the differential equation by the explicit finite difference expression. This can be avoided by reducing the time step based on the following criterion (Holman 1986):

$$\Delta t \le \min\left(\frac{C_i}{\sum_j \frac{1}{R(i,j)}}\right) \tag{9.6}$$

where the above summation is performed for any node with capacitance C_i connected to it; the summation considers all resistances connecting node i with neighbour nodes j. A time step of about 200 seconds was employed in most simulations.

To reduce the possibility of room overheating the blind is closed based on the following criteria:

- If $S < 100$ W/m^2 or $T_o > 14°C$ where S is the total incident radiation and T_o is the ambient temperature (cloudy or warm weather).
- When $T_{13} > 29°C$ or $T_{14} > 25°C$ (where T_{13} is the the temperature of the surface of the TI wall facing the room and T_{14} is room air temperature (T_{ai})) to maintain good thermal comfort.

The last set of conditions is necessary and complementary as in certain cases the room temperature may be lower than 25°C but the TI wall surface temperature may exceed 29°C. Note that, owing to the thermal lag effect, T_{13} and T_{14} may continue to rise above 29°C and 25°C respectively even after the blind is shut. After several simulations, it was determined that if the second control measure above is applied, we would be excluding useful solar energy on several occasions; for example on several occasions $T_{14} < 20°C$ (the setpoint) while $T_{13} > 29°C$ and the blind shuts, excluding solar radiation while auxiliary heating is supplied. The best way to prevent this, and to reduce losses from the TI wall to the exterior environment while maintaining good thermal comfort, is to move air by natural or forced convection into the room. In this study, forced convection was assumed, with air flowing at 1 m/s through the cavity between the gypsum board and the concrete layer of the TI wall when $T_{13} > 24°C$ if $T_{14} < 24°C$. Note that no air flow is necessary if the room temperature rises to 24°C. A heat transfer coefficient of about 10 W/m^2°C from the wall to the flowing air was estimated; this heat transfer is modelled with a negative heat source at node 12 and a positive source at node 14. The two heat sources are therefore given by

$$q_{12} = -A_{12}10(T_{12} - T_{14})$$

and

$$q_{14} = -q_{12} = A_{12}10(T_{12} - T_{14})$$

A useful temperature for evaluating thermal comfort is the operative temperature. This is defined as the uniform temperature of an enclosure in which an occupant would exchange the same amount of heat by radiation plus convection as in the actual non-uniform environment (see Section 8.1); it is given by:

$$T_{op} = (h_r T_{mr} + h_c T_{ai})/(h_r + h_c) \qquad (9.7)$$

where T_{ai} is the air temperature, T_{mr} is the mean radiant temperature, and h_r and h_c are radiative and convective coefficients, respectively, for a person or object (sensor).

The model has been verified by comparison with experimental data (Ramadan 1998).

9.1.4 Simulations and results

An extreme cold day was initially considered for Montreal, Canada, latitude 45°N in January with the following sinusoidal outdoor temperature variation:

$$T_o = T_{om} + \Delta T_o \cos(wt - 5\pi/4) \qquad (9.8)$$

where
T_{om} = mean (average) outside temperature = −15°C
ΔT_o = amplitude of T_o = 5°C
$w = 2\pi/(86\ 400\ s)$

The auxiliary heating system is assumed to have a capacity of 2000 W. It is operated under proportional control; the room air is permitted to fluctuate between 18°C and 24°C ($q_{aux} = K_p(T_{14} - 20)$). Simulations were performed first to evaluate the potential energy savings due to the TI wall by comparing the energy consumption on a sunny cold January day with that on a cloudy cold day.

Figure 9.5 shows the room air temperature variation on two consecutive days after steady periodic conditions are achieved (5–8 days). For this sunny cold period (minimum outside temperature −20°C) the auxiliary heating required was 7.8 MJ per day without air flow through the TI wall and without blind control based on

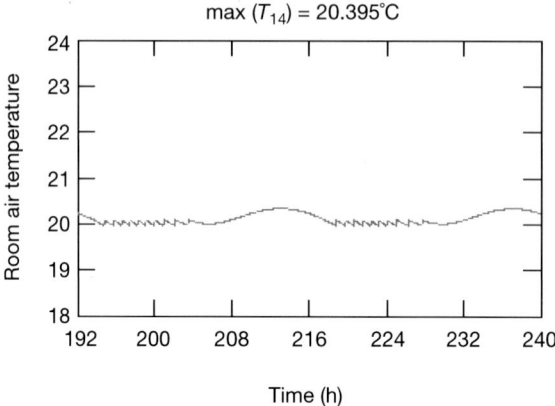

Figure 9.5 Variation of room air temperature on two consecutive sunny days (mean ambient temperature –15°C, setpoint 20°C). Q_h = 7.8 MJ (without control of T_{13} and no air flow through TI wall)

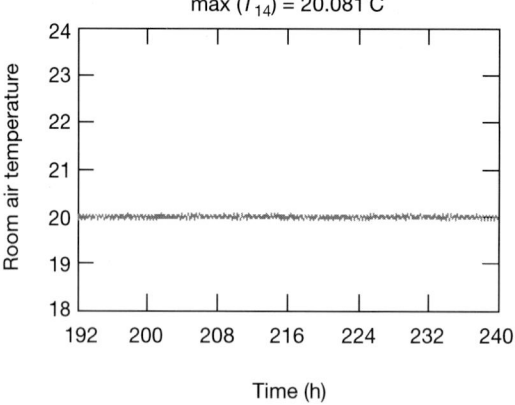

Figure 9.6 Variation of room air temperature on two consecutive cloudy cold days (mean ambient temperature –15°C, setpoint 20°C). Q_h = 72.5 MJ

T_{13} (blind control based on the other criteria), but T_{13} approached 32°C. Figure 9.6 shows the air temperature profile for the same outside temperature but cloudy conditions; in this case the energy consumption was 72.5 MJ, that is, the TI wall reduced energy consumption by almost 90% without forced airflow through the third cavity into the room. Further examination of Figure 9.5 reveals that the maximum air temperature occurs at approximately 9 p.m. due to the thermal lag effect of the TI wall (about 5 hours) and the rest of the room (between 3 and 4 hours) (Athienitis 1994).

The room air temperature fluctuates very little in the two cases because of the low outside temperature. The simulation shown in Fig. 9.6 was repeated with shut-off of the blinds when $T_{13} > 29°C$. The resulting energy consumption rose to 37 MJ. The resulting temperature profiles for the TI wall are given in Figure 9.7 for several days. The increase in energy consumption is due to the fact that the blind is shut when $T_{13} > 29°C$, excluding useful solar energy to maintain thermal comfort. The simulation was repeated with airflow through the third cavity of the TI wall when $T_{13} > 24°C$ (and $T_{14} < 24°C$). The resulting air temperature, operative temperature (ASHRAE 1989) and T_{13} are given in Figure 9.7 for several days. The resulting energy consumption was zero, i.e. no auxiliary heating was required on this extreme cold day when warm air is transferred through the TI wall to the room interior. Thus, one may conclude that the TI wall is adequate for this room. The resulting passive (no heating, since it is not required) response in Figure 9.8 shows that the maximum air temperature is 22.45°C, while the maximum T_{13} is about 27°C. The operative temperature is lower than the air temperature owing to the lower mean radiant temperature resulting from the low exterior temperature.

Simulations were also performed for mild cold days with mean temperature of 0°C and amplitude 5°C. In this case the risk of overheating is high. Figure 9.9 shows the resulting room air and operative temperature profiles for several days when all

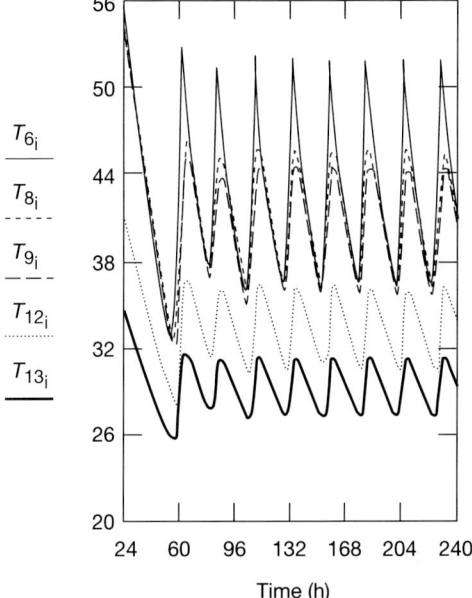

Figure 9.7 Temperatures in TI wall when outside temperature is −15°C (mean) for sunny conditions with blinds shut when $T_{13} > 29$ °C. $Q_h = 37$ MJ

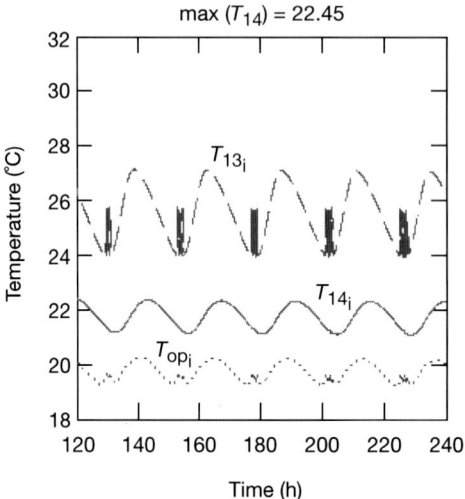

Figure 9.8 Room air temperature (T_{14}), operative temperature (T_{op}) and T_{13} (room facing temp. of TI wall) variation with blind shut when $T_{13} > 29$ °C or $T_{14} > 25$°C and air flow from TI wall to room when $T_{13} > 24$°C (and $T_{14} < 24$°C). Mean outdoor temp. -15°C, clear days (no heating required)

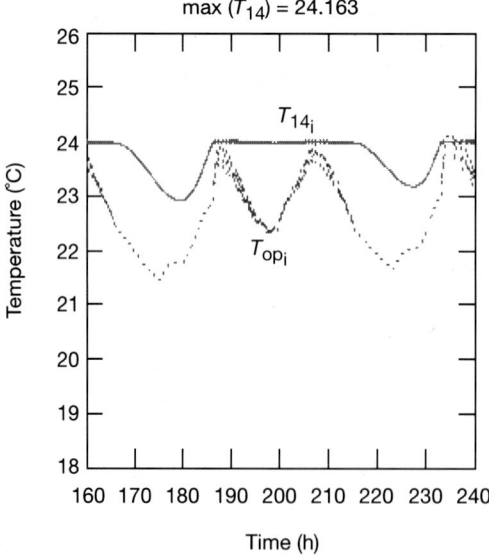

Figure 9.9 Room air temperature (T_{14}) and operative temperature (T_{op}) variation with blind shut when $T_{13} > 29$°C or $T_{14} > 25$°C and air flow from TI wall to room when $T_{13} > 24$°C. Mean outdoor temperature 0°C, clear days (no heating required)

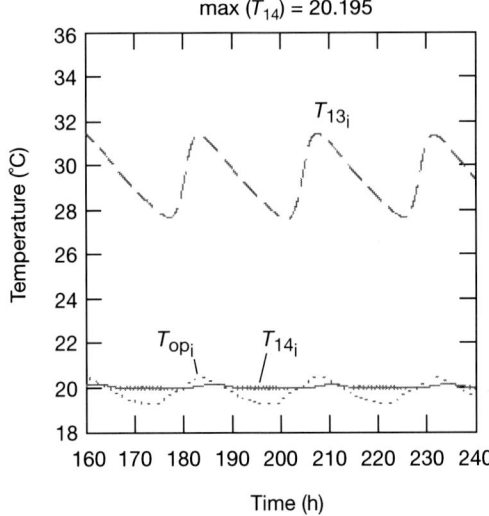

Figure 9.10 Temperature variations for same conditions as in Figure 9.9 but no air flow through TI wall into room ($Q_h = 10$ MJ)

control options are applied. No heating is required on a clear day and the maximum air temperature is about 24°C; however, the operative temperature, which is a more important comfort indicator, is for 90% of the time below 23°C. T_{13} reaches briefly a maximum of 31°C, i.e. higher than 29°C owing to the thermal lag effect. The simulation was repeated but with no air flow and Figure 9.10 shows the resulting temperature profiles. In this case, the room temperature remains around 20°C, but the daily heating energy consumption is 10 MJ and T_{13} reaches 31.5°C.

After comparing all the results shown above one may conclude that a south-facing transparently insulated wall may meet the heating energy requirements of an adjacent room on very cold sunny days. Appropriate control strategies for thermal comfort while maintaining the potential energy savings include shading (blind) control based on room temperature and TI wall temperature, as well as airflow through the TI wall into the room. Simultaneous implementation of these measures achieves the best energy performance and thermal comfort.

9.2 Thermal energy storage in solar buildings with phase-change materials

9.2.1 Introduction

Effective use of thermal storage in buildings will result in significant energy savings, but more importantly it will lower the peak demand for electrical power, thus reducing the need for construction of more power plants and contributing to a cleaner, less polluted, outdoor environment.

Energy demand from a system may be too high at times, and it may not coincide with availability. Thus, storage of energy is an effective way of reducing peak heating or cooling demand. Examples of possible use of thermal storage include the following:

- Storage of solar energy in the building envelope, or in an insulated enclosure such as a packed rockbed. Solar energy stored during the daytime is then used at night to reduce peak heating loads.
- Storage of heat or coolness generated electrically during off-peak hours for use during peak hours. Note that use of thermal storage, such as chilled water tanks, or ice storage, permits the installation of smaller chillers in large air-conditioning systems. The building envelope such as hollow-core floors may be utilized to store coolness (Zmeureanu and Fazio 1988).

HEAT STORAGE

Heat storage can be divided into two major areas, which reflect the time during which the heat is stored: short and long term (seasonal). These two categories reflect several periodicity patterns: diurnal (ambient air temperature, solar radiation, consumer habits), several days (typical weather period) and weekly (commercial electricity demand during weekends) for short-term storage. Long-term storage is mainly seasonal, such that heat produced during the summer can provide for heating demand during winter months. These categories can be subdivided according to the type of storage used. Although there are numerous ways to store heat, those that apply to space heating, that is, sensible, latent or chemical, are of the greatest interest.

BUILDING ENVELOPE MASS STORAGE

Thermal mass is used in the interior of buildings in order to reduce the room temperature swings caused by fast changes in the ambient temperature, by high solar gains, and by on/off cycling of a heater. Buildings with large glazed areas, such as office buildings or passive solar residential buildings, may present the most frequent discomfort problems during the heating season, when the solar radiation is utilized both for reducing the heating load and for natural daylighting. Maximum room temperatures as high as $32°C$ when the outside temperature is $-15°C$ have been reported (Athienitis 1988). Of course, the problem can be eliminated, as in the summer, by preventing the solar radiation from entering the building through the use of shading devices or by opening the windows; this approach, however, defeats the use of windows as a means of reducing energy consumption. Another approach (Athienitis 1988) is to anticipate the room temperature rise and devise a control strategy for its prevention that makes more effective use of the storage capability of the thermal mass. A simple example of such a strategy is the use of a night setback in the thermostat setpoint. In a building with high interior solar gains, this leads to a faster cooldown of its thermal mass; thus, in the early morning, the mass, by being a couple of degrees lower in temperature than usual, may store more solar gains during the following daytime and reduce the room temperature swing.

Building envelope thermal mass reduces the room temperature swings caused by fast changes in the ambient temperature, by high solar gains, and by on/off cycling of heating/cooling systems. Buildings with large glazed areas, such as office buildings or passive solar residential buildings, may present the most frequent discomfort problems during the heating season, when the solar radiation is utilized both for reducing the heating load and for natural daylighting. Overheating is often observed in passive solar buildings during spring and autumn when some heating is required – usually in houses with large window areas with near-south (SE to SW) orientation and ineffective or inadequate thermal mass. During these shoulder periods, the solar gains are significant and usually exceed the instantaneous heating loads. Thus, significant amounts of thermal mass are required to store the excess solar gains without causing large room temperature swings. The use of phase-change materials (PCMs) in building products has rendered it feasible to store significant amounts of thermal energy in the building envelope without the uncomfortable temperature swings and large structural mass associated with sensible heat storage.

Storage as latent heat is caused by a phase change in the PCM. Energy storage may be achieved by melting the PCM and energy recovery by freezing it. This process involves the absorption or release of heat, even though little or no change in temperature occurs. PCMs may be incorporated in the building envelope to achieve latent heat storage. Feldman *et al.* (1989a, 1991) carried out extensive research on the use and stability of organic compounds for latent heat storage, including fatty acids (capric, lauric, palmitic and stearic), butyl stearate, dodecanol and polyethylene glycol 600. In addition to the studies of their properties, research was also carried out on materials that act as PCM absorbers. Various materials were considered, including different types of concrete and gypsum. The utilization of latent heat storage over a comfortable indoor temperature range in buildings can result in an increase in the thermal storage capacity in the range of 100–130% (Feldman *et al.* 1989b, Hawes 1991].

In the application described, PCM gypsum board was made by soaking conventional gypsum board in liquid butyl stearate (BS) (Feldman *et al.* 1989b), a PCM with phase change range of 16.0–20.3°C. The PCM gypsum board used contained about 25% by weight proportion of BS. Its thermal properties were measured with a differential scanning calorimeter (DSC).The objectives of this study were the following:

- Investigation of the thermal performance of PCM gypsum board used in a passive solar building.

- Estimation of the benefits from the application of PCM gypsum board in passive solar buildings in terms of the reduction of room overheating and energy savings.

Experiments in an outdoor test-room were performed and a mathematical model was developed to simulate the transient heat transfer process in the walls of the test-room which contain PCM gypsum board as inside lining.

9.2.2 Application

An outdoor test-room was used for this study (Athienitis and Shou 1991). The test-room, shown in Figure 9.11, is located in Montreal (45°N latitude). It has a double-glazed window facing 10° east of south. The room has three heating systems – baseboard, ceiling panels and floor heating – all electric and controlled by a computer that also controls the data acquisition system. The floor heating system was used. PCM gypsum board was attached over the existing drywall on the vertical walls of the test-room. Proportional control with a programmable setpoint was employed. The auxiliary heating power supplied is given by:

$$q_{aux} = K_p[T_{ai}(t) - T_{sp}(t)] \tag{9.9}$$

where $T_{ai}(t)$ = measured room air temperature, °C
$T_{sp}(t)$ = setpoint temperature at time t.
    The experiments were conducted under winter weather conditions with outside temperature as low as –25°C. During the test, the room air temperature (or the globe temperature in some cases) was set to a high setpoint of 23°C during

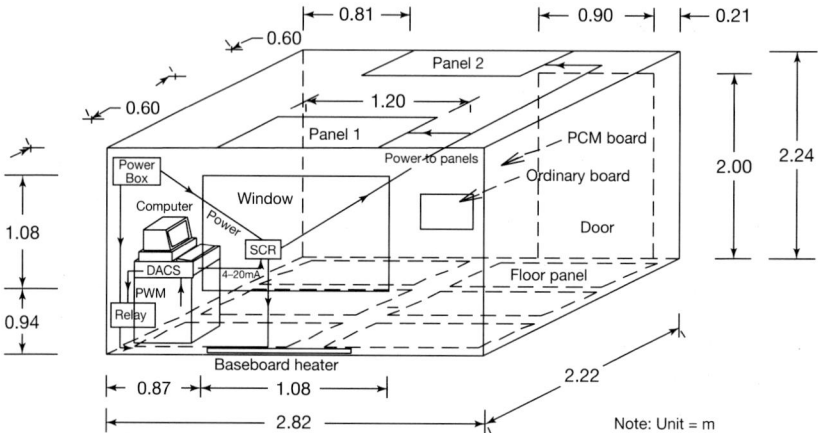

Figure 9.11 Schematic of outdoor test-room

the daytime (6 a.m. to 5 p.m) and 16°C during the rest of the time. When the room air temperature changes, the PCM in the gypsum board undergoes solid–liquid transition in the phase change range of BS (16–20.8°C). If the temperature rises through this range, the PCM wallboard acts as a thermal storage device. Conversely, if the temperature drops through this range, energy will be released.

Temperatures at approximately 30 different locations in the test-room were measured and recorded against real time. These included the front and back surface temperatures of the PCM gypsum board on each wall, the air temperature, the temperature of heating panels, etc. A 30 cm × 30 cm piece was cut out from the PCM gypsum board and replaced with ordinary gypsum board in order to compare the thermal behaviour of the two drywall specimens (with and without PCM) under similar thermal conditions. The front and back surface temperatures of the small piece of ordinary board were measured and recorded. The same measurements were taken on the PCM gypsum board immediately adjacent to this piece of ordinary gypsum board.

9.2.3 Mathematical model

The heat transfer mechanism in the PCM gypsum board is complex, especially when the butyl stearate is in the phase transition stage. During the freezing process, the PCM in the gypsum board could exist in three states (solid, liquid and two-phase). In addition, the physical and thermal properties of the gypsum matrix and the PCM in the gypsum pores are also different. To simplify the mathematical model, the following assumptions are made:

- The PCM and the gypsum matrix are considered as a body of uniform equivalent physical and thermal properties, such as specific heat, density, thermal conductivity and latent heat.
- The heat transfer process across the PCM gypsum board and the original wall is treated as a one-dimensional problem.

Based on the above assumptions, the wall heat transfer is treated as a one-dimensional, transient heat diffusion problem with uniform physical and thermal properties. The model takes into account the transient boundary conditions, absorbed solar radiation, the melting/freezing of the PCM and employs a non-linear film coefficient. The simulation of rate of latent heat release or absorbtion by the PCM is based on the test results from a DSC. The equivalent measured uniform properties of the PCM gypsum board were: a density of 900 kg/m^3, a specific heat capacity of 1260 J/kg°C, a thermal conductivity of 0.21 W/m°C and a latent heat equal to 30 700 J/kg.

The heat diffusion through the wall (Figure 9.12) is described by the following one-dimensional heat diffusion equation:

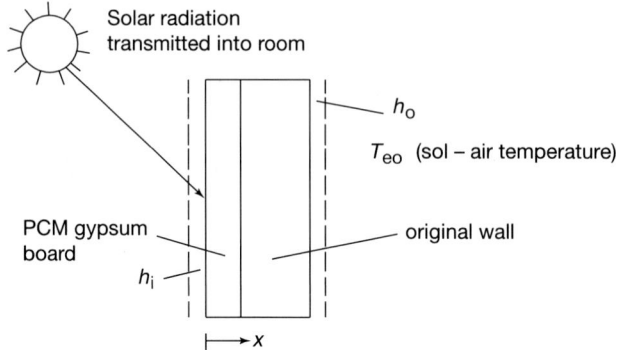

Figure 9.12 Wall section schematic for heat transfer model

$$\rho c \frac{\partial T(x,t)}{\partial t} = k \frac{\partial^2 T(x,t)}{\partial x^2} + q_1 \qquad (9.10)$$

with boundary conditions

$$-k \frac{\partial T(x,t)}{\partial x} = h_i(t) \left[T_{ai} - T(0,t) \right] + q_s(t) \qquad \text{at } x = 0 \qquad (9.10a)$$

$$-k \frac{\partial T(x,t)}{\partial x} = h_o \left[T(x,t) - T_{eo} \right] \qquad \text{at outside surface} \qquad (9.10b)$$

where
ρ = density, kg/m³
c = specific heat, J/(kg°C)
k = thermal conductivity, W/m°C
$h_i(t)$ = inside film coefficient, W/m²°C
h_o = outside film coefficient, W/m²°C
q_1 = latent heat flux when phase change occurs, Wq_s
(t) = absorbed solar radiation, W/m²°C
t = time, s
$T(x,t)$ = temperature, °C
T_{eo} = temperature, °C
x = distance, m

The latent heat flux, which represents equivalent internal heat generation due to freezing of PCM at a specific temperature, was modelled by the enthalpy method. The enthalpy method (Özisik and Uzzell 1979) simulates the heat released from solidification as a volumetric heat-generation term:

$$q_1 = \rho L (df_s/dt) \qquad (9.11)$$

where f_s is the solid fraction in the two-phase region at the solidus front and L is the latent heat for complete phase transition.

The value of latent heat L and the rate of solidification df_s/dt in equation (9.11) were obtained from a DSC test. The DSC curve was modelled in the temperature range of interest as shown in Figure 9.13. In the figure, T_1 and T_2 indicate the temperatures at which freezing process starts and ends respectively; q_{max} indicates the maximum latent heat flow. The area of triangle $T_1 T_2 q_{max}$ is the value of latent heat for the phase transition range T_1 to T_2. With known heating or cooling rate, R, we have:

$$L_p = \tfrac{1}{2} q_{max}(T_2 - T_1)(1/R) \tag{9.12}$$

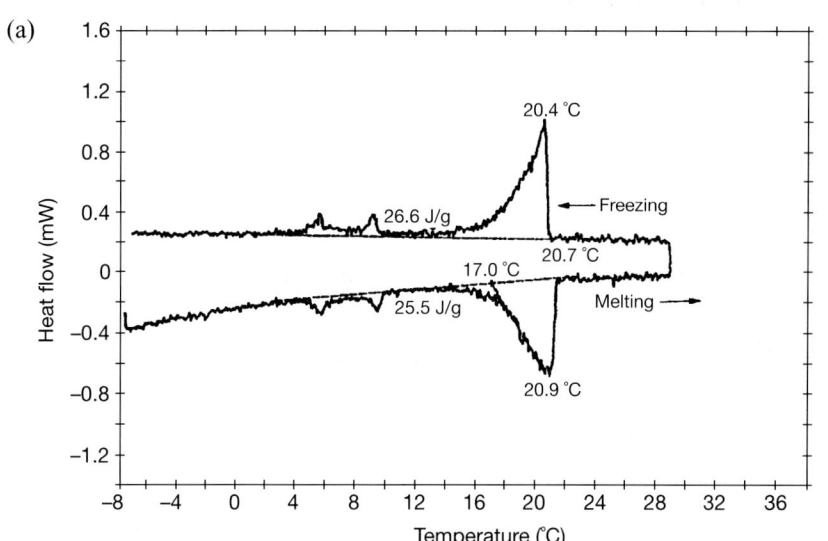

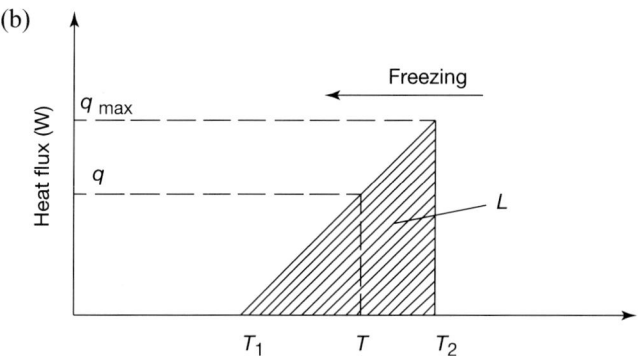

Figure 9.13 (a) Actual phase transition curve for PCM gypsum board from DSC; (b) approximation of DSC curve

where L_p is the latent heat for the temperature range T_1 to T_2, J/kg, R is the heating or cooling rate, °C/s, and T_1 and T_2 are the temperatures at which the freezing process starts and ends, respectively.

From trigonometry and interpolation, the latent heat flow, q_1, is thus determined at a temperature T as:

$$q_1 = 2 L_p R \frac{T - T_1}{(T_2 - T_1)^2} \tag{9.13}$$

Comparing the actual DSC curves with the approximation, it was found that the relationship between L_p and L is:

$$L_p = 0.62L \tag{9.14}$$

Numerical solutions have been successfully applied to modelling of building components with PCMs (Kedl 1991). The explicit finite difference method is particularly suitable for modelling non-linear heat diffusion problems such as the present case of heat transfer through the PCM gypsum board. It can easily accommodate non-linear heat transfer coefficients and temperature-dependent heat sources, such as those due to release of latent heat.

The finite difference thermal network model for the wall consisted of 14 nodes for the PCM board and 3 more nodes for the original wall behind it, as shown in Figure 9.14. The energy balance equation for the thermal network is:

$$T_{i,p+1} = \frac{\Delta t}{C_i} \left(q_i + \sum \frac{T_{j,p} - T_{i,p}}{R_{i,j}} \right) + T_{i,p} \tag{9.15}$$

The subscript i indicates the node for which the energy balance is written and j all nodes connected to node i, while p is the time interval; $R_{i,j}$ is the thermal resistance between nodes i and j, C_i is the thermal capacitance associated with node i, and q_i represents a heat source at node i such as absorbed solar radiation or internal heat generation (latent heat flow). The time interval Δt was selected based on stability considerations (see Chapter 4).

9.2.4 Results

Figure 9.15 shows representative experimental results for a sunny day. Temperatures of the front and back surfaces of the PCM drywall and the ordinary drywall cut-out are shown. As can be seen, the maximum front surface temperature of the PCM board is significantly lower (by 6°C) than the maximum temperature of the piece of ordinary drywall adjacent to it. This is due to the storage of solar gains as latent heat in the PCM board, while in the ordinary board the solar radiation is

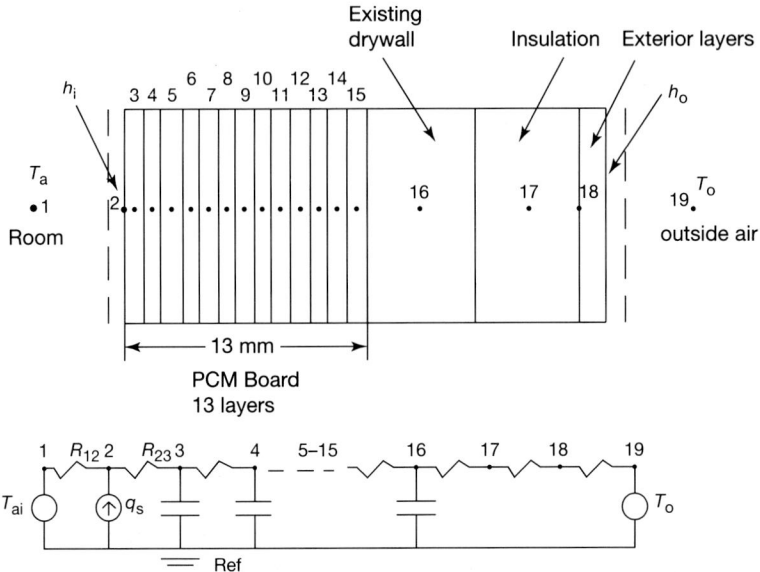

Figure 9.14 Wall section, nodal discretization and finite difference thermal network model

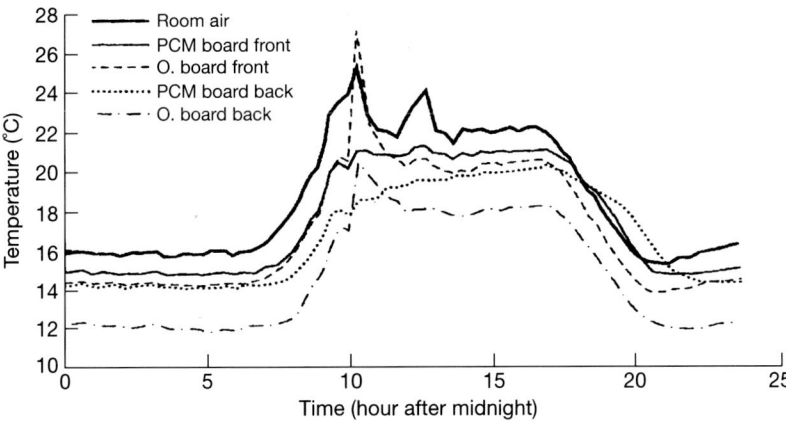

Figure 9.15 Experimental results from a typical winter sunny day

stored as sensible heat, resulting in an increase of surface temperature. The reduction of mean radiant temperature resulting from PCM use improves thermal comfort significantly, while permitting effective storage of solar gains.

In a previous study with the same test-room (Athienitis and Chen 1993) before PCM wallboard was employed, room air temperature was often as high as 30°C at noon on sunny days. Under similar circumstances such as Figure 9.15, the room air temperature was only 25–26°C when PCM wallboard was used. This decrease in maximum room temperature of about 4°C represents a significant improvement in thermal comfort. Therefore, a major conclusion is that the application of PCM gypsum board can significantly reduce overheating in a passive solar building.

Figure 9.16 compares experimental and simulation results for freezing of the PCM board in terms of front surface temperatures. The corresponding results for ordinary board (o. board) are also given. Generally, there is good agreement, with maximum error during the freezing process. This difference is primarily due to non-uniform phase change of the PCM in the drywall.

The above results show that during the freezing process which could last 7–11 hours, the surface temperature of PCM gypsum board is approximately 1–1.5°C higher than the surface temperature of ordinary board. With a total of about 20 m^2 PCM gypsum board used in the test-room, the increase in heat transferred from the wall to the room as compared to ordinary board (if it were used over the same area) is approximately 10 MJ. This is approximately equal to 15% of the total heating load, which indicates a significant potential for the reduction of energy consumption and peak loads.

The simulation results are generally in reasonably close agreement with the experimental results, indicating that the explicit one-dimensional non-linear finite difference model is satisfactory for simulating PCM gypsum board. The mathematical model may be used in conjunction with other building thermal analysis software to evaluate the design parameters and operational characteristics of

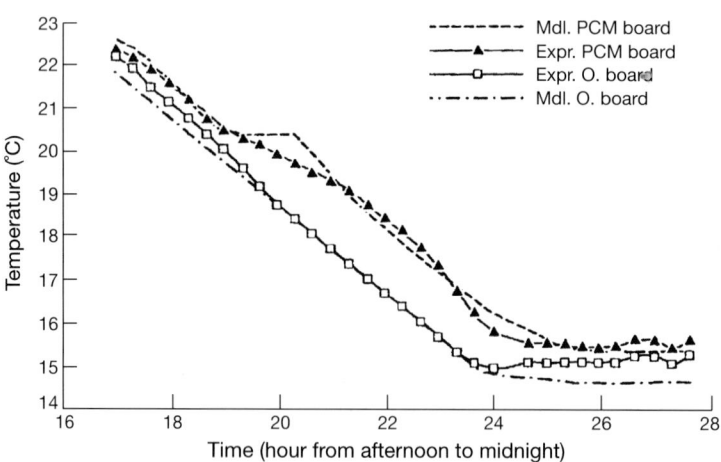

Figure 9.16 Comparison of experimental and theoretical results for freezing of the PCM (o. board = ordinary board)

buildings with PCM gypsum board or other phase change materials as inside wall lining.

9.3 Solarium design

This section discusses the thermal behaviour of a solarium and its optimum design and control. Recent developments in energy-efficient windows permit construction of solariums that can capture high amounts of solar gain while reducing transmission losses. Design guidelines for optimizing the design of a solarium in terms of shape, glazing type, orientation, thermal mass and integration of photovoltaic systems are discussed.

A solarium may be considered as a particular case of the direct gain passive solar system, but with most surfaces transparent, that is, made up of fenestration. Traditionally, a solarium, also often called a sunspace, is a space that the user will usually occupy during the daytime, enjoying the sunshine and doing mainly leisure activities. Thus, a small rise or decrease in temperature outside the comfort zone is acceptable because of the psychological benefits of the pleasant environment, which may also include plants; in some cases part of a solarium may act as a small greenhouse.

Solariums are becoming increasingly attractive both as a retrofit option for existing houses and as an integral part of new buildings. The major driving force for this growth is the development of new advanced energy-efficient glazing systems coupled with their drop in price. Low-emissivity double glazing with a thermal resistance close to 0.5 RSI is not significantly more expensive (10–15%) than ordinary double glazing (0.3 RSI) when the potential energy savings are considered. Reliable framing systems with thermal breaks that eliminate the thermal bridge effect are also readily available at relatively affordable prices. It is thus increasingly cost-effective to add a solarium to an existing house as a major renovation option to enhance the quality of the built environment and the value of the house. For example, consider a typical two-storey cottage built in Montreal with the rear of the house facing south or south-east. An appropriate location for a solarium would be the corner shown in Figure 9.17 because the exterior brick layer of the two walls may also function as thermal storage. Additional thermal storage will be added on the floor to reduce temperature swings, and provide better thermal comfort.

The design of a solarium requires several important decisions:

- The shape (dimensions L, W); it is best to make L/W as large as possible if L is the length of the surface facing south or near-south.
- The tilt of surface At is an important variable; in order to maximize net energy gains (solar gains minus transmission heat losses) a simulation for average days in each month must be performed determining this quantity.
- One design option is to integrate a photovoltaic system into one surface to

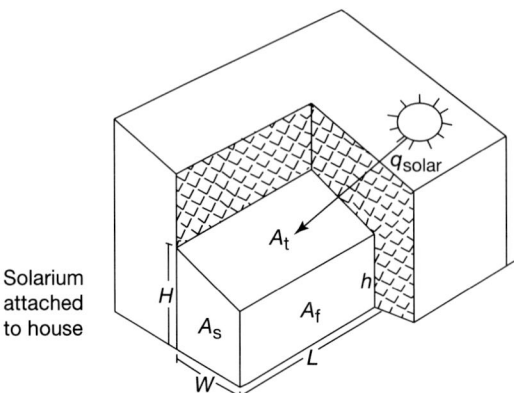

Figure 9.17 Schematic of solarium built as retrofit to existing house

generate also some electric energy while providing shading (Eicker and Fux 1999).
- Determination of the quantity of thermal storage required to prevent overheating of the solarium and to prolong the possible period of stay during the daytime.

Shading control measures are necessary to reduce the risk of overheating when only some or little solar radiation is needed, such as in September or in May. Retractable, motor-controlled reflective shades may be utilized between the glazings to allow the desired quantity of solar radiation based on the signal from a photosensor and a programmable controller. Because a solarium will most likely not be used on cold nights, even if its temperature is controlled to a low value such as 10°C, it can still act as a buffer zone for the adjacent rooms of the house, reducing their nocturnal heat losses.

9.3.1 Simple thermal network model of solarium

Consider the solarium shown in Figure 9.17. A simplified thermal network that models thermal storage in the walls and floor of the solarium with one lumped capacitance is shown in Figure 9.18. The main house temperature T_r will be assumed to be constant. The outdoor temperature T_o will be assumed to vary in a sinusoidal manner, as is very common in building thermal analysis.

Ur3 represents the conductance between the mid-point of the thermal mass and the interior of the house; U31 is the conductance of half of the thermal mass; U12 is the film conductance (convective – radiative) between the mass surface in the solarium and the solarium air (or solarium 'effective temperature node'); U2o is the sum of the conductance of the exterior (glazed) surfaces of the solarium U_g and U_{inf} (the infiltration conductance).

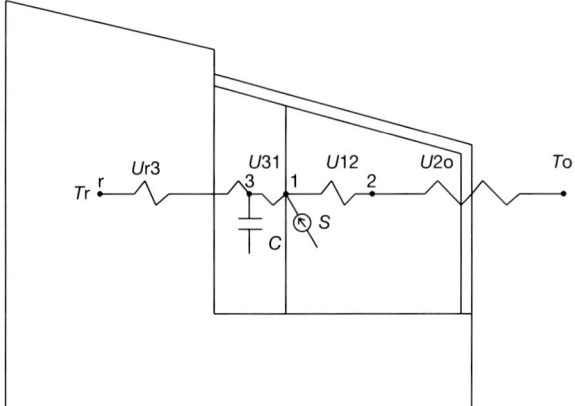

Figure 9.18 Simple thermal network model of solarium

We perform discretization in space and time; we represent the thermal mass with one capacitance and two resistances (T section); for more accuracy we may subdivide the mass into more layers (about one layer per inch) and an equal number of T sections. The thermal storage equation for a capacitance is

$$Q_{stored} = CdT/dt \tag{9.16}$$

The temporal derivative dT/dt is approximated using explicit (forward) differencing as

$$dT/dt = (T_{p+1} - T_p)/Dt$$

where Dt = time step, selected to prevent numerical errors.

9.3.2 Finite difference equations

Energy balance at node 3:

$$U3r(Tr_p - T3_p) + U31(T1_p - T3_p) = C(T3_{p+1} - T3_p)/Dt$$

Energy balance at node 2:

$$U12(T1_p - T2_p) + U2o(To_p - T2_p) = 0$$

Energy balance at node 1:

$$U31(T3_p - T1_p) + U12(T2_p - T1_p) + S_p = 0$$

Rearranging:

$$T3_{p+1} = T3_p + [U3r(Tr_p - T3_p) + U31(T1_p - T3_p)]Dt/C \qquad (9.17)$$

$$T2_p = (U12\,T1_p + U2o\,To_p)/(U12 + U2o)$$

$$T1_p = (U31\,T3_p + U12\,T2_p + S_p)/(U31 + U12)$$

After selecting initial conditions, the above equations may be solved for the temperatures at the next time step $p + 1$. Note that only the equation for node 3 involves a capacitance. The last two equations may be solved simultaneously, or a small time step Dt may be chosen and the left-hand side approximated by the values at $p + 1$. Therefore we can then solve all three equations marching forward in time from p to $p + 1$. The approximate solutions are given therefore by

$$T3_{p+1} = T3_p + [U3r\,(Tr_p - T3_p) + U31(T1_p - T3_p)]Dt/C$$

$$T2_{p+1} = (U12\,T1_p + U2o\,To_p)/(U12 + U2o)$$

$$T1_{p+1} = (U31\,T3_p + U12\,T2_p + S_p)/(U31 + U12)$$

Example

Assuming a clear day (1 February, latitude 45°N) and T_o

$$T_o = T_{om} + \Delta T_o \cos(\omega t - 5\pi/4)$$

where
T_{om} = mean (average) outside temperature = $-10°C$
ΔT_o = amplitude of T_o = $10°C$,
$\omega = 2\pi/(86\ 400\ s)$
Mass: 10 cm thick bricks on walls ($k = 1.0$ W/m K, $p = 1500$ kg/m³, $c = 800$ J/kg°C). Determine the daily temperature variation with the finite difference method.

The result is shown in Figure 9.19.

For this case, no heating would be required during the daytime. Use of night insulation will also reduce nocturnal heat losses. Optimization of solarium dimensions may be achieved through performance analysis over typical days of each month in the heating season for several design options and selection of the optimum.

9.4 Photovoltaic systems for buildings

Photovoltaic (PV) systems found their first cost-effective applications to power remote buildings and devices located far from the existing electrical grid. They are

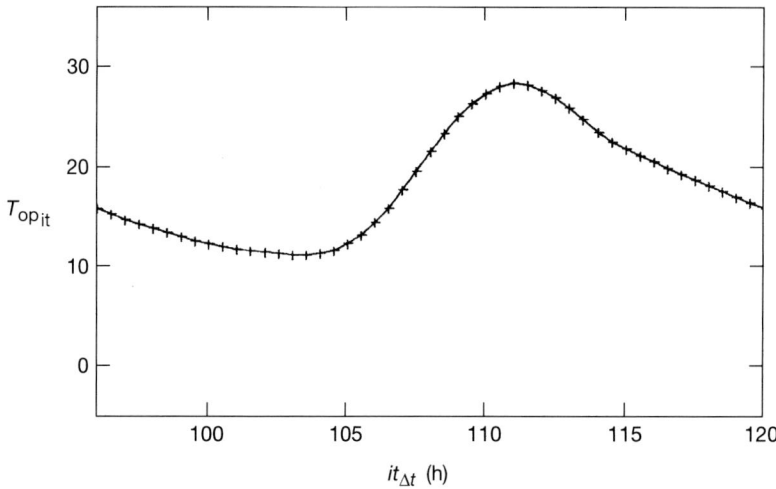

Figure 9.19 Operative temperature (T_{op}) on a clear winter (February) day

still a more expensive means of producing electricity than other energy sources. However, this is changing with their integration into the building envelope. When integrated into the building shell, such as the roof to replace ordinary shingles with photovoltaic shingles, or between two glazings in a semitransparent window, they perform a thermal function as well. Thus, their cost-effectiveness increases. Here we will consider first principles of PV systems design and typical building applications.

The central component of a photovoltaic system are the **photovoltaic (PV) modules** which generate electricity (direct current, DC) from sunlight. Other components are:

- **batteries (e.g. lead–acid)** which store the electric power generated and not immediately utilized
- **power conditioning circuitry such as battery charge regulators, DC–DC converters (to change DC output level), or DC–AC inverters which convert DC power to AC power**; they are essential in order to modify the power from the PV array and make it compatible with the current and voltage requirements of the load.

9.4.1 PV modules and solar cells

A PV module consists of solar (PV) cells permanently wired in series and/or parallel to form a single power unit, which is packaged for protection from the environment while permitting sunlight to reach the active surfaces of the cells. When solar radiation is incident on a semiconductor, the photons may transmit their energy to the valence electrons. Each time a photon breaks a bond an electron becomes free to move through the lattice. The absent electron leaves behind a vacancy (hole) that can also 'move' through the lattice as the electrons move around it. These holes can be considered like particles (positive). The movement of electrons and holes, if passed through an external circuit, can be just like any other current source.

A solar cell is made from a semiconductor material such as silicon or gallium arsenide which sometimes acts as conductor, other times as insulator. When solar radiation is absorbed it causes electrons to break loose from atoms, leaving atoms with a positive charge (hole). Under certain conditions the electrons and holes move in opposite directions, creating a current. In a solar cell the free electrons and hole move randomly and they eventually may recombine, or reach regions of the semiconductor containing different types of impurity, called **p-n junctions** (p indicates conduction by holes and n by electrons). When they reach the junction, they will move through an external circuit connected at the p-n junction, creating a current (see Figure 9.20a).

When a load is connected to an illuminated solar cell the current that flows is equal to the photogenerated current I_L due to generation of carriers by the sunlight minus the diode or dark current I_D due to recombination of carriers driven by the external voltage:

$$I = I_L - I_D$$

Thus, a PV cell is a **current source.** The main types of PV cells are **crystalline silicon, polycrystalline silicon cells** and **amorphous silicon** as well as **gallium arsenide, cadmium telluride**, etc. Crystalline cells are made from a single crystal (most expensive), polycrystalline cells from many small crystals (less expensive), while amorphous cells have no orderly atomic structure.

Crystalline silicon solar cells may be manufactured in single crystal wafers sown from boron-doped ingots grown from a melt, or in crystalline wafers cut from cast ingots. Wafers are usually sown to 10 cm × 10 cm size and 250–500 μm thick. Cells are produced by diffusing phosphorus into the p-type silicon wafer to make an n-type surface region. An electrical contact grid is deposited on the top face of the wafer exposed to sunlight and a solid contact on the other side (see Fig. 9.20a).

Amorphous silicon cells absorb incident solar radiation in a thin layer and they can thus be made thin; cells are made from layers of silicon about 1 μm thick deposited automatically on a substrate. The efficiency of conversion of sunlight to electricity is lower for amorphous cells (typically about 5–8%) than for crystalline cells (12–16%). (Note: laboratory efficiencies much higher have been obtained in 2001.) Amorphous silicon cells are typically used in applications such as calculators, but also increasingly in buildings such as for PV-shingles (cells integrated into roof shingles). For all cells, efficiency typically drops with rising operating temperature.

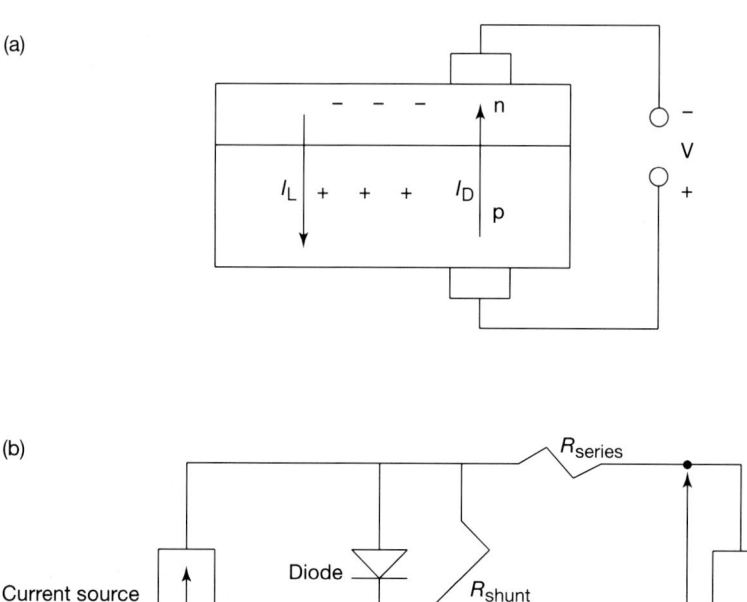

Figure 9.20 (a) Schematic of solar cell (+ represents holes and – electrons). (b) Equivalent circuit for PV cell and associated components

Gallium arsenide, which is much more expensive than silicon, also absorbs sunlight in a thin surface layer. Because its optimum operating temperature is higher than that of silicon, it is suitable for concentrating PV arrays where reflectors concentrate radiation onto the cells. It has a high potential efficiency of over 22%, with a theoretical maximum exceeding 30%. Another promising thin film is cadmium telluride with a record efficiency of about 14%.

Commercial modules usually consist of 30–40 cells in series to produce a voltage of about 12 V as required to charge batteries. Interconnections between cells in a module are usually made with flexible tinted copper strips soldered to the cells. The cells are usually encapsulated with a material such as ethylene vinyl acetate and covered with low-iron (high-transmittance) glass for weather protection. A frame is also included for mechanical strength and for easy mounting. An electrical junction box is usually attached to the back of the module, including the positive and negative leads; the junction box may also contain ground points, bypass diodes, etc. Crystalline modules are usually more reliable, with an expected minimum lifetime of 20 years.

SOLAR CELL EFFICIENCY

Part of the incident solar radiation is converted to electricity while the rest is reflected or converted to heat. An untreated surface reflects up to 35% of the incident solar radiation; surface coatings can reduce this to about 5%. Losses in the conversion of light to electricity occur because some of the sunlight (long wave) does not have enough energy to release electrons and passes through the semi-conductor to be absorbed or reflected by the base of the electrode. Ultraviolet and very short wavelength light has more energy than required to release electrons and generates heat. These two opposing effects limit the maximum theoretical efficiency of single p-n junction cells to about 30%.

Other effects such as recombination of electrons and holes at defects reduces actual efficiency further. In addition, we have **resistance losses** due to the cell base material, the surface layers and connections; this is modelled by a **series resistance** R_s in the cell circuit (see Figure 9.20). Generally the efficiency also decreases with rise in temperature (about 0.5% per °C). We also have **shunt losses** because imperfect cell fabrication allows current shunt paths through the junction or around the edges. These losses reduce cell efficiency to between 5 and 30% (theoretical maximum).

The current I produced by the cell is approximately proportional to the solar irradiance. It also varies exponentially with voltage V (a function of load). At a fixed temperature and solar radiation, the voltage characteristic of the equivalent circuit in Figure 9.20b is given by

$$I = I_L - I_D - I_{shunt}$$
$$= I_L - I_0\{\exp[e(V + IR_{series})/(mkT)] - 1\} - (V + IR_{series})/R_{shunt} \quad (9.18)$$

where I_D is diode current, e is the charge of an electron (1.602×10^{-19} C), k is the Boltzman constant (1.381×10^{-23} J/K), m is ideality factor (between 1 and 2) and T the cell temperature (K).

In a modern cell, the shunt resistance is usually high and I_{shunt} can be ignored. In addition, the term $\exp[e(V + IR_{series})/(mkT)]$ is much greater than 1. Finally, I_L is equal to the short-circuit current I_{sc}.

Setting $V_t = mkT/e$ (equal to about 25 mV at 300 K), equation 9.18 becomes:

$$I = I_{sc} - I_0\exp[(V + IR_{series})/V_t] \quad (9.18a)$$

This equation can be expressed in terms of open circuit voltage V_{oc} as

$$I = I_{sc}(1 - \exp[(V - V_{oc} + IR_{series})/V_t] \quad (9.18b)$$

For a PV module with N_s cells in series and N_p in parallel ($N_s \times N_p$ array) the above equation is modified as:

$$I = I_{scm}(1 - \exp[(V - V_{ocm} + I_m R_{sm})/(N_s V_t)] \tag{9.18c}$$

where the module parameters are:

$$I_{scm} = I_{sc} N_p$$
$$V_{ocm} = V_{oc} N_s$$
$$R_{sm} = R_{series} N_s / N_p$$

A cell/module is characterized by its maximum power (peak watt rating of cell) given by:

$$P_{max} = V_{mp} \times I_{mp} \tag{9.19a}$$

under standard conditions of: $G = 1000$ W/m^2, $T = 25$°C (cell operating temperature).

The power output curve (Figure 9.21) is given by the power law:

$$P = V \times I \tag{9.19b}$$

where $V = I \times R$ (Ohm's law).

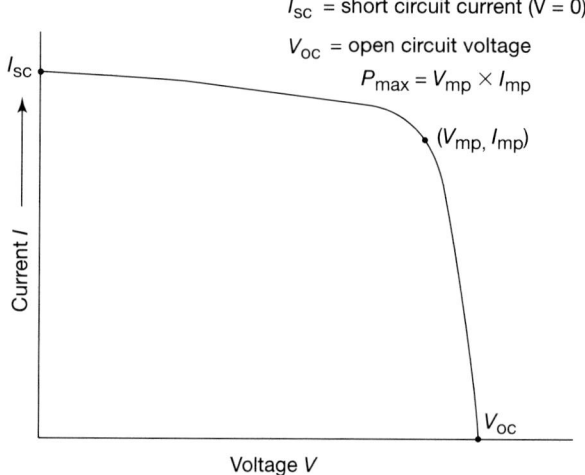

I_{SC} = short circuit current (V = 0)

V_{OC} = open circuit voltage

$P_{max} = V_{mp} \times I_{mp}$

(V_{mp}, I_{mp})

Figure 9.21 Variation of output for PV cell

When $V = 0$ we obtain the short-circuit current I_{sc}. As resistance increases, the voltage increases up to the open-circuit voltage V_{oc} (with $I = 0$).

A useful parameter for characterizing solar cells/modules is the **fill factor** FF defined by

$$FF = P_{max}/(V_{oc}I_{sc}) \tag{9.20}$$

Because V_{oc} and I_{sc} are the maximum possible voltage and current respectively, FF is always less than 1, and typically in the range 0.7–0.8 for most crystalline cells (Si, GaAs, etc.). The **energy conversion efficiency of a cell,** which is equal to electric power output divided by incident solar radiation (G_t), may be written as:

$$\eta_c = FFV_{oc}I_{sc}/(G_t) \tag{9.21}$$

Temperature effect

Usually, at high incident solar radiation the cell may operate at about 25°C higher than the ambient temperature due to the solar radiation absorbed and converted to heat. This rise in temperature reduces the cell efficiency by about 0.002 V/°C for each silicon cell. Thus, if a module operates at an ambient temperature of 25°C, its own temperature will be 50°C, and given that the PV module consists of 40 cells, we have a reduction in output voltage equal to:

$$DV = 0.002 \text{ V/°C/cell} \times 40 \text{ cells} \times (50°C - 25°C) = 2 \text{ V}$$

Therefore, if the operating temperature of the cell is reduced, its efficiency increases. Thus, it may often be advantageous to combine a thermal application with a PV application to remove some heat from the modules, cooling them and enhancing their efficiency. A typical application would be integration of PV modules into an airflow window (between two glazings). Air flows over the warm modules, absorbing useful heat and transporting it to a heated space.

The operating temperature T_c of the cell may be determined by performing an energy balance on the cell:

Absorbed solar radiation $=$ electric power ouput $+$ heat loss to environment

$$\tau\alpha G_t = \eta_c G_t + U(T_c - T_e) \tag{9.22}$$

where τ is cover solar transmittance, α is cell solar absorptance, U is the heat transfer coefficient to the environment and T_e is environment effective temperature; normally the product $\tau\alpha$ is about 0.9.

The nominal cell operating temperature (NCOT) is based on a solar radiation level of 800 W/m² (at normal incidence), T_e equal to 20°C and a wind speed of 1 m/s with no load (no output). From equation 9.22 we can see that:

$$\tau\alpha/U = (\text{NCOT} - T_e)/800 \tag{9.23a}$$

Since $\tau\alpha/U$ remains approximately constant, we can find the cell temperature at other than nominal conditions by rearranging equation (9.23a):

$$T_c = T_e + (G_t \tau\alpha/U)(1 - \eta_c/\tau\alpha) \tag{9.23b}$$

9.4.2 PV systems

A PV array consists of connected PV modules which deliver power to an external device such as a power conditioner. It contains interconnect cabling, a support structure and components such as blocking diodes, bypass diodes, test points, switches, junction boxes, fuses, reflectors, lightning protection systems and a grounding system. Some suppliers offer about four to ten modules assembled into a panel to reduce installation labour.

A bypass diode prevents a poorly performing (e.g. shaded or damaged) module from affecting other modules connected in series, by acting as a low-impedance bypass path. It maintains the current from the other modules and simply reduces the total output voltage by that of the poorly performing module. Bypass diodes may be integrated into modules. Blocking diodes prevent a reverse current from flowing from a source such as a battery into the PV modules.

SERIES AND PARALLEL CONNECTIONS
To charge a 36 V battery we need, for example, three standard 12 V modules connected in series. The number of modules in parallel is decided by the required total peak power output; the voltage is the same across each module as well as the current giving:

$$P_{\text{total}} = N \times V \times I$$

where N = number of modules in parallel.

If certain modules are shaded they should be bypassed. In an array with parallel groups of modules connected in series, shading of one module causes the bypass diode to activate, bypassing the affected group and taking it out of operation. Thus, arrays using series strings of PV modules connected in parallel are more common than parallel strings of modules connected in series (see Figure 9.22), as only a faulty module needs to be bypassed and not a whole group.

Grounding equipment protects from lightning, static charges, leakage currents from faulty components, etc. System grounding is also necessary; one of the conductors carrying current is ground at one point.

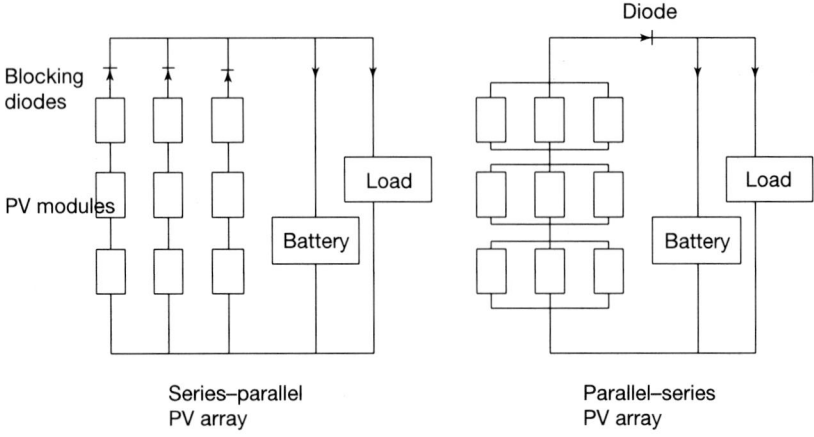

Figure 9.22 Typical PV array circuits

ENERGY STORAGE AND BATTERIES

There are various types of **lead–acid** batteries that store electricity as chemical energy such as:

- **simple lead–acid** with lead, lead oxide electrodes and sulphuric acid electrolyte
- **lead–antimony** batteries, in which antimony is added to the lead grid to provide extra strength; they can be discharged by 50–80% of capacity, but produce gas sometimes during recharge and lose water near full-charge; water must be added periodically
- **maintenance-free lead–calcium batteries** contain **calcium** on the lead grid which reduces gas formation and water loss; enough liquid is added to compensate for water loss during its estimated five-year life; its life is reduced if discharged to more than 25% of capacity.

Lead–acid battery cells have a nominal voltage of 2 V, which may vary from 1.75 V to 2.45 V. Six cells in series give a 12 V battery.

The **capacity** of a battery is given in **ampere-hours** under a temperature of 25°C and a charge rate of 8, 24 or 100 hours. The discharge rate is given in amperes or discharge time. The discharge time is the time required to discharge a battery completely at the discharge current.

Discharge rate (amps) = capacity (amp-hours)/discharge time (hours)

A C/10 rate means 10 hour discharge time and is the fastest possible without bubble formation (gassing). A C/20 rate is more acceptable, while for PV a C/100 rate is often assumed in design.

The **depth of discharge (DOD)** is the fraction of battery discharge before recharging; 20% is considered shallow discharge while 50–85% is deep. Battery voltage varies with DOD and specific gravity of electrolyte, as well as temperature. Battery capacity is often given at C/100.

Lead–antimony and nickel–cadmium batteries perform better at higher temperatures while lead–acid batteries have a decreasing charging voltage with rising temperature. If a battery is discharged deeply (e.g. more than 50%), its life is reduced; deep discharge also reduces the recharge voltage level and causes degradation of electrode separator material.

PV systems require batteries that can be charged during daytime and discharged at night, and to withstand many cycles of charge–discharge. Batteries' charge–discharge cycles can vary from 200 to 10 000 over their lifetime.

Days of autonomy (DOA) are the number of days for which the battery can supply electricity without recharge (and no damage).

The battery capacity C (amp-hours) required can be chosen based on the following equation:

$$C = L \times \text{DOA/DOD}$$

where
L = daily load in ampere-hours (A h)
DOD = depth of discharge per daily cycle

Systems designed to use 15–25% battery capacity each night are called **shallow cycle systems.** If we design for shallow discharge, battery lifetime is increased and lead–calcium batteries may be used. Remote telecommunication systems are designed for 30 days of autonomy (30 cloudy days) and a shallow discharge. In **deep cycle systems** the batteries are selected based on 50% or more DOD; in this case DOA is low.

Nickel–cadmium (NiCd) batteries are suitable for applications that require reliability, high DOA and low maintenance. They may last 20 years.

POWER CONDITIONING

Battery charge regulators switch off current from the PV array to the batteries when they are fully charged. Two-stage controllers allow regular charging during the first stage and trickle charge rate at the second stage permitting the voltage to increase to 18 V on a 12 V system; this trickle charging is good for most batteries. Battery charge regulators may also have a built-in blocking diode.

D.C.–D.C. converters change the voltage which varies as a function of insolation to a level required by the load. They are not very common in stand-alone systems with battery storage.

Inverters, which convert D.C. to A.C., are necessary when powering A.C. loads. In a system with a battery the inverter is connected to the battery. An inverter must have adequate surge capacity because inductive loads (such as motors) require a current surge for several seconds to start. The output voltage should also be regulated, so that as battery capacity drops, the output A.C. voltage does not vary by more than 5%. The inverter should not consume much energy, i.e. it should have an efficiency of at least 90%, so as not to significantly reduce overall system efficiency. **Square-wave** inverters switch the D.C. input into a square-wave A.C. output; they are suitable only for small resistive heating devices and lights, but not for motors. **Modified sine-wave inverters** use transistors or silicon-controlled rectifiers (SCR) to produce an approximate sine wave with low harmonic distortion.

A **maximum power point tracker** maintains the maximum possible power voltage independent of variations in insolation and load impedance; it is essentially an impedance matching device. An **array switcher** may be used to change the series/parallel configurations of modules in the array to achieve desired current level even though insolation level drops.

Load management controllers typically switch off loads from the battery in a sequential order as the battery voltage drops.

9.4.3 Load analysis in stand-alone systems

The electrical load is the sum of the individual power demands from each device connected to the system. Whenever possible, D.C. devices should be used because some power is lost in converting from D.C. to A.C. Fluorescent lighting fixtures with D.C. ballasts are suitable for PV systems. PV power is not very efficient for heating applications (except possibly small heat pumps). D.C. refrigerators are available.

SIZING METHOD
All-year systems should be sized based on the period with minimum insolation – December or January. Summer-only systems may be sized based on September or early October data. Typically, about 3–15 days of autonomy are desirable for a stand-alone systems.

- Identify weather and insolation conditions; find mean monthly insolation per day at the tilt angle of interest (three tilt angles may be considered – latitude, latitude plus 15° and latitude minus 15°) for each month; tabulate also mean ambient temperature.
- Estimate electrical load.
- Estimate required batteries to satisfy load for the required period of autonomy.
- Size array to charge batteries in one average day during the period with low insolation.

9.4.4 Building-integrated photovoltaic systems

One of the most promising applications of PV today is supplemental utility generation. A major benefit of PV is that it tends to generate more electricity at times of the year when more is needed. In most of North America, for example, utility companies struggle to keep millions of power-hungry air conditioners running in the summer months, when photovoltaic cells are most productive. Many utilities are using PV to help cover peak loads, rather than building entirely new plants. Because PV is so modular in design, these supplemental stations can easily grow from year to year, covering higher and higher loads. Several applications are described below.

BUILDING WITH PHOTOVOLTAICS (SCHOEN 1997)
Photovoltaics permit the on-site production of electricity without concern for fuel supplies or environmental adverse effects. Power is produced without noise and no depletion of resources. It is expected that in the 21st century building-integrated grid-connected PV systems will contribute significantly to power production. However, costs must still be lowered further. Cost reductions are achieved not only by increasing solar cell efficiency, but also by integrating the cells with the building envelope. In cases where PV facades replace expensive components such as granite or marble they can be cost-effective already, especially in the Mediterranean areas.

THE ARCHITECTURAL POTENTIAL OF THE GRATZEL CELL (FITZMAURICE 1997)
This is a transparent regenerative photoelectrochemical cell utilizing low to medium purity materials and simple construction processes, with a conversion 7–12%. While in conventional cells the semiconductor assumes the functions of both absorption and carrier transport, in the Gratzel cell light is harvested by dye molecules at the surface of the semiconductor film while charge transport is achieved by the nanostructured semiconductor film. The advantage of this cell is simplicity of production and low investment; the cost per kW is five times lower than that of opaque cells. Gratzel cells may be combined with conventional glazing by choosing a dye concentration such that the solar radiation transmitted is appropriate for interior daylighting.

In another approach, conventional and solar (with Gratzel cells) glazing may be combined.

THE INTEGRATION OF NEW TECHNOLOGIES IN BUILDINGS
PV cells have been integrated through various techniques into building envelopes:

- amorphous photovoltaic modules as a roofing material (Finland, Canada)
- insulated roof panels with amorphous PV modules on the top face (Japan)

- crystalline PV modules as atrium glazing – a skylighting system
- crystalline PV modules as a fixed shading device
- crystalline PV modules as wall cladding
- semitransparent amorphous PV cells as window panes (Germany).

PV systems need to be considered early in the building design process for their successful integration. Four successful applications are shown in Figures 9.23 and 9.24.

THE POMPEU FABRA LIBRARY MATARO BARCELONA (LLORET AND ACEVES 1997)

This is a 53 kW_p grid-connected building with integrated PV-thermal multi-functional modules (Figure 9.24, top). The building is the first of its kind in the European Union. Large-scale prefabricated multifunctional architectural modules producing both electrical and thermal solar energy were designed for industrial production. Various shapes and degrees of transparency were developed for curtain walls, roofs and blinds; solar thermal energy generated by solar absorption in the modules may be used for heating or evacuated via a ventilation chamber. The building is rectangular in shape with the largest facade facing south. The PV-thermal modules are the major innovation of the building, as they provide versatile and aesthetic possibilities for the building envelope while generating electricity and warm air which is fed into the gas heating system for further heating if necessary. The prefabricated PV-thermal modules include the complete electric connection system and are installed in the structure of the building using curtain wall construction methods. The building can produce about 125% of the calculated electricity needs.

9.5 Advanced fenestration system applications and integration issues

The building envelope may be designed as an energy-generating and storage system. Integration of photovoltaic systems is one possible option in this direction. However, there are also several other alternatives that integrate the concept of window–solar air collector with storage. Several examples are discussed below.

9.5.1 The new parliamentary building in London (23 000 m² floor area; six storeys)

Ventilated floor voids heat/cool structural slabs and enable displacement venti-lation. The facade light shelves, which are also overhangs, reflect daylight to the back of the room. The floor bottom layer is high thermal capacity concrete which is the ceiling facing layer of the floor below; it was painted white to act as daylight reflector of the room below (Figure 9.25).

Figure 9.23 Use of PV panels on roof/solarium and as overhangs

Facade: the cladding system provides an integrated solution to the provision of view, daylight control, passive and active solar energy collection, shading, minimization of heat loss in winter, ventilation exhaust and supply and heat recovery. The fenestration consists of triple glazing with internal ventilated blinds; the outer part is double-glazed, argon-filled with low-emissivity coating. The inner cavity

Figure 9.24(a) Pompeu Fabra Library, Barcelona: utilization of semitransparent window systems with PV cells.

Figure 9.24(b) National Assoc. of Home Builders 21st century townhouse, Maryland, USA: effective roof integration of PV panels. © Bekaert ECD Solar Systems LLC., UNI-SOLAR® 2 kW of Solar Metal Roofing.

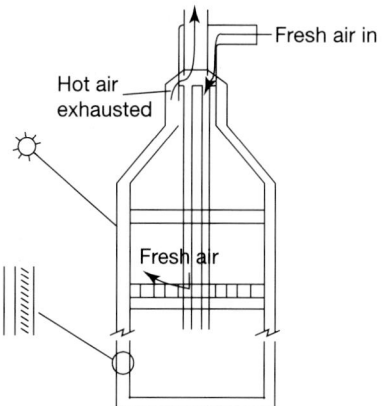

Figure 9.25 Schematic of new parliamentary building in London

contains retractable dark louvre blinds to maximize the absorbed solar heat. This cavity is ventilated with a proportion of room exhaust air and acts as solar collector. The window arrangement uses a light shelf to maintain room daylight when blinds are closed, thus avoiding the commonly observed case of blinds closed and lights on, with its consequent heat gain due to luminaires and extra cooling load. The facade is a passive system – only the blinds move.

Cooling: solar heat collected during daytime is stored for possible night use. When the outside air is above 19°C, groundwater at 14°C is drawn from two on-site boreholes to cool the outside supply air to room temperature. Night ventilation is used for mass precooling.

Ventilation: the mechanical ventilation system serves a network of floor plena linked via a ductwork in the facade to provide 100% outside air ventilation to each room. High-efficiency heat recovery is the key benefit of mechanical ventilation over natural ventilation (rotary heat exhangers at 85% effectiveness; can also be hygroscopic to recover winter moisture). Low-pressure-loss air-handling equipment is employed – energy use of 1 W per litre/s of air supplied; total fan pressure 640 Pa with fan efficiencies 65%; typical air handling unit face velocities 1.2 m/s with filters at 0.8 m/s.

Heating: condensing natural gas boilers, variable-water-volume system with thermostatic valves on room heat emitters; water at 70°C supply and 50°C return; mass of water flow is halved compared with practice and using piping at 50 Pa/m pressure loss results in significant pump power reduction (90 kWh/m² annual energy consumption – possibly 65 in optimized design).

9.5.2 New tax office (Enschede, Netherlands)

The project was part of the THERMIE project 'Energy Comfort 2000', a group of eight innovative projects in Europe. It is 4300 m^2 and five storeys. Natural ventilation was employed – a central atrium was used for extraction of air. Fresh air enters by means of ventilation grills independent of wind pressure and situated near the workstations on the facades.

Daylighting: two strips of window separated by a light shelf are used for each storey; the lower part provides a view and the higher part admits extra daylight. The light shelf reduces glare and reflects some daylight onto the ceiling and then deep into the room. Venetian blinds are used on the outside of the lower window strip; a central control system closes the blinds in the morning when necessary, while during the day they are operated manually by the user.

High-frequency lamps are used with automatic dimmers capable of lowering emission to 30% when daylight is plentiful.

9.5.3 Thermotropic materials and systems for overheating protection

Thermotropic materials that change from transparent to white and vice versa as a function of temperature may contribute to the reduction of room overheating by preventing unwanted solar radiation from entering the room when the temperature is high. Thermotropic systems consist of at least two components with different refractive indices. At low temperatures these are mixed at the molecular level so that the material is transparent. If the material temperature rises to a certain level (depends on the mixture ratios) the two components separate into microscopic domains and incident radiation is scattered, most being diffusely reflected, and the material appears white.

Two types of materials are investigated at the Fraunhofer ISE – hydrogels and polymer blends. Hydrogel layers have good optical properties and low switching temperatures (20–50°C), which makes them suitable for glazings (see Figure 9.26). Polymer blends have switching temperatures of 30–120°C and they are thus suitable for transparent insulation systems. Thermotropic hydrogels and polymer blends have been produced in areas of more than a square metre with industrial technology; they switch solar energy transmittance by 55%. More research is being carried out on their further improvement and durability, and to achieve a steeper switching gradient.

9.5.4 Intelligent control of window shading systems

Software is available that can evaluate energy benefits from the use of various shading systems and daylight control devices. However, it is important to utilize the potential of today's smart digital controllers and building automation systems

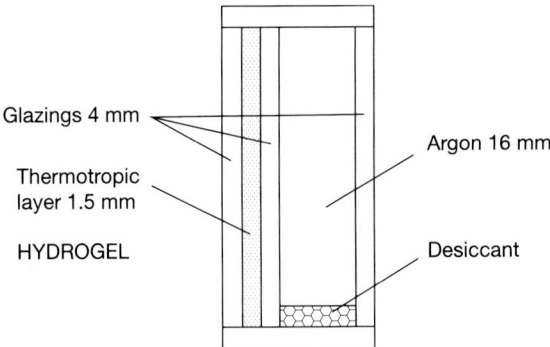

Glazings 4 mm

Thermotropic layer 1.5 mm

HYDROGEL

Argon 16 mm

Desiccant

Triple-glazed window with thermotropic layer

Figure 9.26 Use of thermotropic material in a window

(BAS) to optimally control the level of daylight and its quality (reduction of glare), while reducing cooling loads and heating loads. For example, they may be employed to dim electrical lights as a function of available daylight, while choosing an optimal position for motorized shading devices to reduce heating and cooling energy consumption.

Effective utilization of fenestration with motorized shading devices, preferably operated through a building automation system, requires two major design objectives which address the daylighting and energy aspects as follows:

- First, there is a need to **control the quantity and direction of the daylight transmitted**, especially in an office area, so as to minimize the need for electric lighting while avoiding glare problems.
- **Overall energy costs for electric lighting, heating and cooling need to be minimized**. If the first objective above is achieved, then the electric lighting costs are reduced and cooling loads are lowered because of avoidance of heat emission from light fixtures. Ideally, if the available daylight does not meet the required illuminance levels in the work area, the intensity of electric lights should be variable (dimmable) to provide the additional required illuminance. However, if more than enough daylight is available during the cooling season, then the excess should be excluded in order to prevent increase of cooling loads. Finally, there is one more case to be considered: if passive solar heating is desirable, then the amount of total solar radiation transmitted into a zone should be maximized.

Figure 9.27 shows the schematic of an outdoor test-room (at Concordia University in Montreal) with a window having motor-operated reflective blinds between two glazings. These blinds are operated by a computer, which also controls the heating/cooling system and electrical lights.

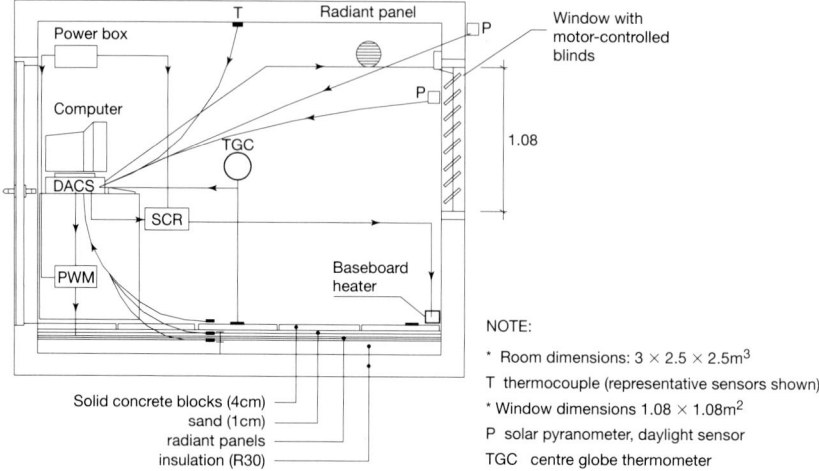

Figure 9.27 Schematic of outdoor test-room with computer controlling venetian blinds integrated in glazing, and heating system; DACS, data acquisition system; PWM, pulse-width modulation; SCR, silicon-controlled rectifier

The focus of the project is on development of control techniques and software for operation of shading devices, in conjunction with dimming of electrical lights and heating/cooling control so as to optimize building energy efficiency and occupant comfort. Its specific objectives are the following:

- Development of control procedures and algorithms for operation of motorized window shading devices, so as to transmit an **optimum amount of daylight** while reducing glare problems. Input variables include exterior incident daylight, and the control variable is the blind tilt angle or roller shade position.
- Development of control procedures and algorithms for operation of motorized shading devices in conjunction with control of electrical lights and heating/cooling control in order to **enhance overall energy efficiency** (minimize heating and cooling energy consumption, as well as electricity consumption for lighting).
- Implementation of the above control algorithms in a BAS (computerized energy management and control system).
- Evaluation of the potential improvement in energy efficiency and luminous environment due to implementation of the above algorithms.

The digital control algorithms developed (Athienitis and Tzempelikos 2001) may be implemented in local smart controllers operating the window shading systems or in a central automation system (BAS). Figure 9.28 shows typical results from implementation of the algorithm for a typical office with windows having motorized blinds. A blind tilt angle is selected to prevent beam solar radiation from directly entering the workspace thus preventing glare.

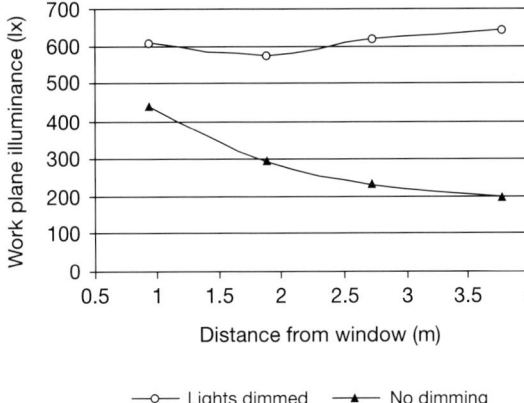

Figure 9.28 Work plane illuminance as a function of distance from window for typical 5 m × 5 m office with daylight only (no dimming) and with dimmed lights plus daylight (Montreal latitude 45°N, clear day at 9 a.m. in December)

Morel *et al.* (1996) developed a fuzzy logic controller to decide roller blind position. The objective of this project at LESO was the development of an optimal blind controller, taking into account optimization of thermal comfort, daylighting, minimization of energy consumption (thermal and lighting) and user wishes. Fuzzy logic was employed. Control algorithms were tested with simulation. The controller was installed in an office with high passive solar gains.

Optimization of blind position takes into account both daylighting and artificial lighting as well as passive solar gains. The control algorithm takes into account passive solar gains, internal gains etc. using solar sensor, electric power sensor and infrared occupancy sensor.

9.5.5 Integrated facade concept

Figure 9.29 illustrates a perimeter office in a commercial building which integrates several 'green' renewable energy technologies:

- photovoltaic panels integrated on the opaque (spandrel) section of the curtain wall
- a vent for natural ventilation
- top window with motorized integrated reflective blinds for reflecting daylight into adjacent corridor and interior zone of the building
- middle window with roller blind.

An important characteristic of the design is the requirement for a high ceiling, and two thirds of the facade glass (vision area) to maximize usable daylight. The

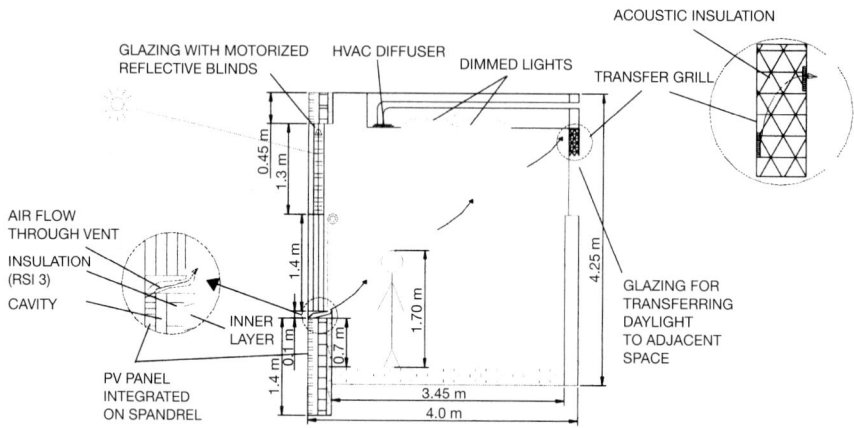

Figure 9.29 Perimeter office with facade-integrated photovoltaic panels, vent and motorized reflective blinds

transfer grill serves to transfer air coming through the vent and may or may not be necessary, depending on the natural/hybrid ventilation concept for the building.

The ideal type of glazing for maximization of daylight penetration in the building is clear glass. This requires careful selection of shading devices with optimal transmittance and low absorptance. High solar gains and natural ventilation through the integrated vent make the presence of exposed thermal mass essential in minimizing room temperature fluctuations. Therefore, in such a perimeter office with an acoustic ceiling, it is essential to avoid the use of carpets which insulate floor thermal mass. Instead, it is preferable to have a concrete or tile floor, which is also better than a carpet for good indoor air quality. Using the techniques introduced in previous chapters it may be shown that the room admittance is much lower with a carpeted floor than without the carpet.

9.5.6 Conclusion

Development of new technologies such as small-scale fuel cells, combined heat and power (CHP) cogeneration devices, lowering of the costs of photovoltaic systems integrated in buildings, and the adoption of advanced fenestration systems, will revolutionize building design in the twenty-first century. In certain climates, a building may eventually become a net energy producer as opposed to an energy consumer.

The focus on a high-quality indoor environment, both at home and in the workplace, will be the primary objective of building design, with energy efficiency being the essential constraint.

These changes will radically affect the way we live and the way we transport ourselves. Electric or hybrid cars will inevitably get a boost from an electric power producing building. Environmental concerns, which correctly call for urgent measures to reduce carbon dioxide emissions, coupled with rising oil prices, have created a renewed interest in electric and hybrid cars, as well as in solar buildings. The coming revolution or evolution in building design and operation will inevitably cause significant changes in the way cities and transportation systems are designed and built.

There is one essential requirement in the development of better buildings: building design and operation planning will have to be carried out in an integrated manner, with architects and engineers working together towards the creation of an energy efficient high-quality indoor environment.

9.6 Bibliography

Arulanantham M. and Kauskika N.D. (1994) 'Global radiation transmittance of transparent insulation material', *Solar Energy*, **53**:4, 323–328.

ASHRAE (1989) *ASHRAE Handbook – Fundamentals*, Atlanta, GA.

Athienitis A.K. (1988) 'A predictive control algorithm for massive buildings', *ASHRAE Transactions*, **94**:2, 1050–1068.

Athienitis A.K. (1994) *Building Thermal Analysis*, Electronic Mathcad Book, MathSoft Inc., Boston, MA.

Athienitis A.K. (1997) 'Theoretical investigation of thermal performance of a passive solar building with floor radiant heating', *Solar Energy*, **61**:5, 337–345.

Athienitis A.K. (1998) *Building Thermal Analysis*, 2nd edn, Electronic Mathcad Book, MathSoft Inc., Boston, MA.

Athienitis A.K. and Chen T. (1993) 'Experimental and theoretical investigation of floor heating with thermal storage', *ASHRAE Transactions*, **99**:1, 1049–1057.

Athienitis A.K. and Shou J. (1991) 'Control of radiant heating based on the operative temperature', *ASHRAE Transactions*, **97**:2, 787–784.

Athienitis A.K. and Tzempelikos A. (2001) 'A methodology for detailed calculation of room illuminance levels and light dimming in a room with motorized blinds integrated in an advanced window', eSim2001 Building Simulation Conference, Ottawa, Canada, June.

Boonstra C. and Vollebregt R. (1997) 'Space for architecture in passive office buildings', *European Directory of Sustainable & Energy Efficient Building*, James and James Ltd, Hong Kong, 25–28.

Brandemuehl M.J. and Beckman W.A. (1980) 'Transmission of diffuse radiation through CPC and flat plate collectors glazing', *Solar Energy*, **24**, 511–513.

Cane R.L.D., Hollands K.G.T., Raithy G.D and Unny T.E. (1977) 'Free convection heat transfer across inclined honeycombs panels', *ASME Transactions*, **Feb.**, 86–91.

Charters W.W.S. and Peterson L.F. (1972) 'Free convection suppressing using honeycomb cellular materials', *Solar Energy*, **13**, 353–361.

Dunster B. and Pringle J. (1997) 'Sustainable architecture and the low energy urban office', *European Directory of Sustainable & Energy Efficient Building*, James and James Ltd, Hong Kong, 16–24.

Eicker U. and Fux V. (1999) 'Thermal performance of building-integrated ventilated PV facades', Proc. ISES99 World Solar Congress, Jerusalem.

Elsherbiny S.M., Raithby G.D. and Hollands K.G.T. (1982) 'Heat transfer by natural convection across vertical and inclined air layers', *ASME Transactions*, **104**:1, 96–102.

Feldman D., Banu D., Hawes D. and Ghanbari E. (1991) 'Obtaining an energy storing building material by direct incorporation of an organic phase change material in gypsum wallboard', *Solar Energy Materials*, **22**, 231–242.

Feldman D., Khan M.A. and Banu D. (1989a) 'Energy storage composite with an organic phase change material', *Solar Energy Materials Journal*, **18**, 333–341.

Feldman D., Shapiro M., Banu D. and Fuks C.J. (1989b) 'Fatty acids and their mixtures as phase change materials for thermal energy storage', *Solar Energy Materials Journal*, **18**, 201–216.

Fitzmaurice D. (1997) 'The architectural potential of the Gratzel cell', *European Directory of Sustainable & Energy Efficient Building*, James and James Ltd, Hong Kong, 84–85.

Francia G. (1961) 'Un nouveau collecteur de l'energie rayonnante solaire – theorie et verifications experimentales', *Conference des Nation Unies sur les sources nouvelles d'energie*, E/conf.35/S/71, 554–558.

Georg A., Graf W., Schweiner D., Wittwer V., Nitz P. and Wilson H. (1998) 'Switchable glazing with a large dynamic range in total solar energy transmittance (TSET)', *Solar Energy,* **62**:3, 215–228.

Goetzbeger A., Schmid J. and Wittwer V. (1984) 'Transparent insulation system for passive solar energy utilization in buildings', *International Journal of Solar Energy*, **2**, 289–308.

Hawes D.W. (1991) 'Latent heat storage in concrete', Ph.D. Thesis, Concordia University, Montreal, Canada.

Hollands K.G.T. (1965) 'Honeycomb devices in flat-plate collectors', *Solar Energy*, **9**, 159.

Hollands K.G.T and Iyankaran K. (1985) 'Proposal for a compound honeycomb collector', *Solar Energy*, **34**:4, 309–316.

Hollands K.G.T., Marshall K.N. and Wedel R.K. (1978) 'An approximate equation for predicting the solar transmittance of transparent honeycomb', *Solar Energy*, **21**, 231–236.

Hollands K.G.T., Raithby G.D. and Unny T.E. (1976) *Studies on Methods of Reducing Heat Losses from Flat Plate Solar Collectors, Phase I Report*, University of Waterloo.

Holman J.P. (1986) *Heat Transfer*, McGraw-Hill Inc., New York.

Hottel H.C. (1976) 'A simple model of transmittance of direct solar radiation through clear atmospheres', *Solar Energy*, **18**.

Kaushika N.D. and Padma Priya R. (1991) 'Solar transmittance of honeycomb and parallel slat arrays', *Energy Conversion Management*, **32**:4, 345–351.

Kedl R. (1991) 'Wallboard with latent heat storage for passive solar application', ORNL/TM-11541 Distribution Category UC-202.

Lloret A. and Aceves O. (1997) 'The Pompeu Fabra Library Mataro Barcelona', *European Directory of Sustainable & Energy Efficient Building*, James and James Ltd, Hong Kong, 92–95.

Lorenzo E. (1994) *Solar Electricity*, Progensa, Sevilla, Spain.

Morel N. *et al.* (1996) *Delta: A Blind Controller Using Fuzzy Logic*, Final Report, LESO, Switzerland.

Olsen L. (1982) 'Transparent insulation for thermal storage walls', *Solar Energy R & D in the European Community Series A*, **2**, 127.

Özisik M.N. and Uzzell J.C. (1979) 'Exact solution for freezing in cylindrical symmetry with extended freezing temperature range', *Journal of Heat Transfer*, **101**, 331–334.

Platzer W.J. (1992) 'Total heat transport data for plastic honeycomb-type structures', *Solar Energy*, **49**:5, 351–358.

Platzer,W.J. (1994) 'Transparent insulation materials: a review', *SPIE Conf. Proc.* 2255, Optical Materials Technologies for Energy Efficiency and Solar Energy XIII, 616–627.

Ramadan H. (1998) 'Numerical simulation model of a test-room with transparent insulation', MASc. thesis Building Engineering, Concordia University, Montreal, Canada.

Ramadan H. and Athienitis A.K. (1998) 'Numerical simulation of a building with transparent insulation', *Proceedings of the Solar Energy Society of Canada*, 24th Annual Conference, Montreal, May.

Santamouris M. *et al.* (1994) *Passive Cooling of Buildings*, CIENE, University of Athens.

Schoen T. (1997) 'Building with photovoltaics', *European Directory of Sustainable & Energy Efficient Building*, James and James Ltd, Hong Kong, 78–83.

Tabor H. (1969) 'Cellular insulation (honeycombs)', *Solar Energy*, **12**, 549–552.

Trombe F., Robert J.F., Cabonot M. and Sesolis B. (1977) 'Concrete walls to collect and hold heat', *Solar Age*, **2**, 13.

Twidell J.W., Johnstone C., Zuhdy B. and Scott A. (1994) 'Strathclyde University's passive solar, low energy, residences with transparent insulation', *Solar Energy*, **52**:1, 85–109.

Wilson H.R., Raicu A. and Nitz P. (1997) 'Thermotropic materials and systems for overheating protection', *European Directory of Sustainable & Energy Efficient Building*, James and James Ltd, Hong Kong, 63–66.

Zmeureanu R. and Fazio P. (1988) 'Thermal performance of a hollow core concrete floor system for passive cooling', *Building and Environment*, **23**:3, 243–252.

Index